JollyJupiter
an Adventure Brewing

aethonbooks.com

BEERS AND BEARDS: AN ADVENTURE BREWING

©2023 Jolly Jupiter

This book is protected under the copyright laws of the United States of America. No part of this publication may be reproduced, stored in a retrieval system, or transmitted, in any form or by any means, without the prior permission in writing of the publisher, nor be otherwise circulated in any form of binding or cover other than that in which it is published and without a similar condition including this condition being imposed on the subsequent purchaser. Any reproduction or unauthorized use of the material or artwork contained herein is prohibited without the express written permission of the authors.

Aethon Books supports the right to free expression and the value of copyright. The purpose of copyright is to encourage writers and artists to produce the creative works that enrich our culture.

The scanning, uploading, and distribution of this book without permission is a theft of the author's intellectual property. If you would like to use material from the book (other than for review purposes), please contact editor@aethonbooks.com. Thank you for your support of the author's rights.

Aethon Books
www.aethonbooks.com

Print and eBook formatting by Josh Hayes.

Published by Aethon Books LLC.

Aethon Books is not responsible for websites (or their content) that are not owned by the publisher.

This book is a work of fiction. Names, characters, places, and incidents are the product of the author's imagination or are used fictitiously. Any resemblance to actual events, locales, or persons, living or dead is coincidental.

All rights reserved.

ALSO IN SERIES

An Adventure Brewing

A Brewtiful Life

Check out the entire series here!

This book is dedicated to my dearest wife Jessica, who gave me the impetus and the support necessary to write a whole book and then some.
And
For Karl!

ACKNOWLEDGMENTS

My first acknowledgement goes to my readers at Royal Road. Every dutiful reader is another reason to keep writing, and all the great review helped!!

The good people at Ghost Ship Games, whose boisterous joyful dwarves in Deep Rock Galactic gave me the inspiration to write Beers and Beards. Rock and stone brothers!

The team at Yogscast, who gave me my first look into the world of dwarves, and who gave me permission to use their song 'Diggy Diggy Hole' in my book!

To JRR Tolkien, who started it all. May his road go ever on and on.

I want to thank my daughter who 'willingly' went to bed at 8pm every day so I could write in the late hours of the night.

Cheers to Bay 12 Games, who generously donated a million cats to the city of MInnova. I've never been able to 'finish' a game of Dwarf Fortress, but it still left its mark on this book!

My loving family, mom, dad, and little bro, who put up with my awful puns for years and years. See? I always knew they would eventually make me money!

I'd like to thank my beta readers, who took time on their own to read over my work and let me know what to fix before it hit Patreon.

I'd like to acknowledge the work of what I consider to be one of the greatest cartoons of all time, Avatar, and the hard work of the people at Team Avatar. I consider their world one of the greatest living worlds in all of fiction, and you should go watch it again!

My first readers were from the LITRPG Books Facebook group, and I want to shout them out for allowing me to share my work.

Hey Actus, look, I got published! And it's all your fault!

Thanks to my editors, publisher, cover artist, and my extra fine narrator - Christian Gilliland. If you haven't bought the audiobook yet, why not??

My very first shout-out came from Matador, a fellow author on Royal Road, and I'd like to give him a shout-out here. He unfortunately passed in 2022, but his book: Monster Menu can be found on Amazon. I hope the reading is good wherever you are now buddy.

Michael Jackson, Queen, Prince, The Spice Girls, ACDC, Guns N Roses, and all the other Rock and Roll bands within these pages that have rocked harder than any dwarf could ever imagine.

And finally, I'd like to thank my Patrons. Beers and Beards started out as something just for fun, but ended up saving my financial situation more than once in the past year. May the Gods Bless you all!

PROLOGUE

"Pete, dish ta' table four!"

"Got it!" I took the plate, heaped tall with steaming goat meat and roasted root vegetables, and walked into the pub. I tucked my beard into my belt to keep it from dipping into the food and looked for table four. My destination was a single customer in a well-lit corner, but first I had to navigate the zoo. It was time for the dinner rush, and the pub was full to the brim with excited dwarves of every shape and size and even a few adventurous gnomes. I dodged some tables as they exploded with laughter and merriment and waved down a few invitations to join in.

"Here's your food! Beer-braised goat with roasted vegetables and mashed erdroot!" I presented the meal with a flourish to the dwarf seated at the table before me. He wore a set of rather conservative chainmail barding, with the barest hint of silver ornamentation. His beard was long and scruffy, a dark brown mixed with black, and his hair was cut short to fit beneath an armoured cap. It was a sight I'd grown used to over the past year.

"Thank ye! Barck's Beard, this looks amazin'! An adventurin' buddy wouldn't stop talkin' about this place, so I had to try it meself!" He rubbed his palms together with glee and stuffed a napkin down his gorget. His stained and calloused hands spoke of a labourer, likely fresh from the mines and hankering to try some food from the city's most notorious and popular new establishment.

"Glad you could make it! Can I get you anythin' else?"

He took a big bite of tender two-day braised goat and grunted with pleasure. Juice dribbled into his beard and he wiped it away with a leather vambrace. "This is amazin'! I can't believe it's made with *beer*!"

I chuckled. "Aye, we have a few dishes that use beer in the recipe. It's one of our specialties."

"Not fer long! With food this good everyone'll start copyin' ya soon enough." He took another enormous bite and sighed with pleasure.

"Imitation is the sincerest form of flattery. Everyone in town will know who made it first, and that's what matters."

He was silent for a moment, then began in a hoarse whisper. "I heard—" he licked his lips, "I heard from an Adventurer that came by the mine that you lot have a *New Brew*."

This was another sight I'd grown accustomed to. I leaned in conspiratorially. "Aye, we do. A few actually, would ya like to try one?"

"Aye! But in a plain mug! Don't want to call attention to meself!" He looked around nervously.

"Don't ya worry, everyone in this pub loves our ales. In fact, they can *beerly* live without them!" I waggled my enormously shaggy eyebrows.

"What?"

"Never mind. One ale coming right up."

He stopped me as I turned to go. "Do folk ever get upset about all this? Tha' new beers I mean?"

"Sometimes, but I'm not concerned. This isn't just a game – we're serious about improving the brew. Besides, not even *death* could stop me from brewing."

We laughed together, but the laughter didn't quite reach my eyes.

After all, it wasn't a lie – even if I *was* a human on earth when I died.

PART ONE
THE MINE

CHAPTER ONE
A BREWING STORY

I lived in grapes and I'll die in grapes.

"Dad," a tender voice called from my bedside. "You can't be buried in grapes, that's just weird."

I looked over to where my little daughter Samantha, now a young woman freshly graduated from college, held my hand. Her brown eyes peered at me with laughter, but I could see the tears welling up behind them. She leaned over and adjusted my pillow, her hair brushing up against my cheek. She always smelled like the wildflowers of our home in the Okanagan, but all I could smell now was the acrid scent of the hospital.

"If people want to *wine* about it, let them." I deadpanned, and then coughed as the act of speaking irritated the tubes in my throat. "Where's your mother?"

"Ugh, that was *awful*. Mom is talking to the head nurse. Should I tell her you're awake?" She turned to the door.

I shook my head and looked out the window beside my bed. It was a beautiful sunny day outside, and I could hear some geese honking on the lawn. I always hated the vicious buggers when they crapped all over my vineyard, but their warbling was a nostalgic sound. A few clouds dotted the sky, and a slight breeze ruffled the reddening maple trees outside the window.

Indeed, it was a good day to die. Well, it was a terrible day to *die*, but it was a good *day* to die. Terminal brain cancer in your late forties sucked. I barely got to watch my kid graduate and now the metaphorical rug got pulled out from under me. It happened so fast – I was out picking grapes under the hot sun when I had a dizzy spell and collapsed. The last few weeks were a blur of doctors, tests, tears, and making final plans. The company would be going to my vice-president for a tidy sum, Samantha got the car and my darling redheaded wife got everything else. Including the crushing pain of suddenly losing her husband after twenty years of marriage.

Sorry dear. Looks like we won't be spending our fifties going on cruises together.

I laid my head down and closed my eyes, reminiscing.

First was mead. A fun thing to pass the time in business school that rapidly turned into a side hustle. A girl I met at a frosh party, sprawled on a blanket in a cherry sundress with a slight flush from an Earl Grey Mead. Caroline, her lips pulled back in a honeyed smile.

Then came beer. Playing percentages with hops while experimenting with bitters, sours, and ales. I chose a name, and Caroline drew the logo, a goofy buck-toothed moose for *Beavermoose Brewery*. The originals were stashed in the attic at home. Caroline quit art school and started working for me full time. We were married in the spring.

\\\ I wish that beeping would stop... I'm so tired...\\\

Then came whiskey. The shrieking from the still as it exploded was nothing compared to the screech of a very pregnant Caroline when she found out. I had to promise to stop; our future child would need a father. Samantha was born in November; three kilos and a full head of hair. She was the light of our lives, and the end of our sleep.

Then came champagne. The moment we made it big, when our *Beavermoose IPA* got lauded on live TV by a hockey star. Some influencers started reviewing it, and suddenly – we were big. I bought a ten acre apiary from a retiree, and we converted a barn on the property into a microbrewery. Soon I had staff and bills, God so many bills. I'm dying, why am I sitting here thinking about bills? Must be the geese... The whole company celebrated the night we shipped our first full flat to the liquor stores. Caroline and I popped some bubbly and then we had a crazy thought.

\\\ It's getting hard to breathe. Where's Caroline with the nurse? Why is Sammy yelling? \\\

From that thought came wine. I tilled the field alongside the apiary and planted some grapes. Our little slice of paradise in the Okanagan Valley was perfect for growing them, and I visited a few neighbouring vineyards to get some ideas. Our first few bottles weren't going to win any awards, but the beer and the mead kept the money flowing. Soon, fifteen years had passed, and I had one of the biggest wineries in the valley. The *Beavermoose* logo still sat over the old barn, but the new storage shed filled with casks of fine wine proudly proclaimed *Veritas Vinum Vineyard*.

\\\ I wasn't... joking about the bury me in grapes bit. Sammy? Are you there? \\\

\\\ It was our veritas... our truth.... I hope....\\\

\\\ Carol are.... \\\

\\\ Sammy? \\\

\\\ ... \\\

"Doc!" A gruff voice called next to my ear. "He's wakin' up!"

My eyes peeled open, and a splitting headache immediately snapped them back shut. Gawd! I knew brain cancer hurt, but that felt more like my sinuses being ripped out! The acrid scent of the hospital had... changed. It smelled quite strongly of sulphur. The sound of the geese was replaced with the sound of... hammers? What was going on?

"Gods damned fool! What was he thinkin', stickin' his head into a freschie?" another voice on the other side of the bed grumbled in a gruff ... Scottish accent? No, that wasn't quite right.

I groaned as a wide calloused hand was placed on my head and a soothing feeling spread from it.

"It was touch and go there for a while, but it looks like the aether-stone did the trick," said a slightly higher-pitched and more cultured voice. "He should be fine after a bit of rest."

"Thank ye, Doctor." Said the second voice. "We'll add yer bill to his indenture and see that yer paid from the mine's accounts."

"Of course, Grim. Send a runner to Healer Bastion if he gets worse. I've done all I can and a [Healer] would be the next step."

There was a weird inflection on the word 'Healer.' Heaaaler? *HEAler*? [Healer]?

"That bad?"

"I lost him for a moment there. If he's awake, then the worst of it should be gone. He's either got the Blessing of Barck or the luck of fools." The sound of a door opening and closing was followed by footsteps, before a wide hand pulled roughly at my beard.

I don't have a beard. Sammy made me shave it when she was four because she hated it. How long had I been unconscious?

"Wake up sleepy 'ead! You won't want me to call Healer Bastion. It'll add years to your indenture. Doc Opal was bad enough! Oy, Pete!"

Well, Pete was my name, so rise and shine. I squinted my eyes to peer at the two men sitting beside me. What struck me first was the beards. Each of them had a *massive* beard; real lumberjack and then some. They each had a wide nose peeking out above equally big moustaches. The one named Grim had a bristly straight-edge moustache, but the other guy had a handlebar that practically reached his eyebrows.

Seriously, this was some epic facial hair, and I don't use the word epic lightly. Then it struck me, both of them were wearing what looked like padded leather armour. Handlebar even had an iron helmet on. What the heck?

I sat bolt upright and looked around, the motion giving me a new stab of pain in the sinuses. We were in what looked like a carved stone room. The walls were slate and the floor was made of worked blue stone with patterns carved into it. The ceiling overhead was the same slate as the wall and a metal lantern hanging over my bed gave off a soft yellow light. Where was the window? Where was Sammy?

"You okay, Pete?" Asked handlebar, leaning closer. "You should know better than ta stick your head in a freschie. There's a bonus for findin' a vein, but ya really shoulda let tha [Whisperer] check the air first! Yer lucky the sulphur didn't kill ya! The whole cave was full of it!"

Wow, those were certainly words. At least my head was starting to hurt a bit less. There was something about these guys that was stirring something in the back of my mind. Something about the beards, and the accent... Oh my God! These guys looked JUST like dwarves! They were short and squat, with whiskers nearly half their height! Was this a cosplay convention or something?!

That was when I glanced at the mirror and a short, squat, reddish-brown-bearded dwarf peered back at me from the bed with bleary black eyes.

I may have passed out again.

Grim sighed as labourer Balin Roughtuff, No. 30865 helped labourer Peter Samson, No. 30895 spoon some porridge into his mouth. He'd almost run to fetch the Healer before Balin stopped him. Pete's breathing had been fine and he seemed to have fainted from exhaustion. He eventually woke up again, but seemed listless and confused, muttering about 'Sammy' and 'Karul.' Nobody in the camp had those names. Perhaps some people from his past?

Not even a week into the new year, and already a major accident. Barck's Beard, that didn't bode well for the rest of the year.

As the foreman for the *Dwarven City of Minnova Reform Mine*, Grim's job was not the most glamorous. At least it paid well, and he'd even received his first Blessing! Most of the indentured not-quite-prisoners were paying off bills from fights in the city or were vagrants without a copper to their name. A few months to years in the reform mine would see them leave with a small purse, some skills, and if they were lucky, a Blessing of their own. Some were back the next day, but most found work in the local mines.

He could certainly understand Pete's desire to stick his head into a freshly made tunnel. When Pete's pickaxe had caused a small crack to widen into a fresh cavern, Pete had joyously called the whole crew over. An indentured miner who found a new vein or – Gods forbid – a gem cache, could become rich overnight. The Ordinances were quite strict about fair compensation! Chapter 32, Section 4, Subsection 12c in fact!

Which meant there was no reason for the damn fool to stick his head into the tunnel to check! Grim had gone to ask the [Whisperer] to check the local aether for toxins, and returned to find the small crew clamouring around the unconscious form of Pete. He had called for Doc Opal, who declared it to be sulphur poisoning, and the rest of the day was a nightmare of paperwork. Pete was a simple vagrant, and Grim didn't really know him well, but his death would have meant a review by City Hall.

Grim went to the cupboards. They had propped Pete up in Grim's own chambers, and he wanted a stiff drink after today's debacle. Both the [Whisperer] and the [Speaker] had checked the tunnel and found nothing but a large sulphur deposit. Sulphur had some uses, but it wasn't as though the populace of Minnova were falling all over themselves for soap! Daily baths were an elvish perversion, like that grape juice they called 'wine.'

Grim poured himself a fine amber ale. It was a fresh batch of True Brew from *Browning Brewery*, and it had quite a kick! After a moment's thought he poured some for Pete and Balin too. They'd *all* had a rough day, and Pete would be all the worse after Doc Opal's bill got added to his indenture. Grim filled a trio of large iron tankards studded with fine oak wood and passed them off to Pete and Balin.

"To Minnova, the Firmament, and the luck of fools!" He and Balin bellowed, though Pete simply raised his mug. Grim downed his drink and revelled in the fresh nutty flavour. Balin's eyes twinkled beneath his bushy brows as the alcohol hit him.

Pete spat his beer in a spray across the both of them, soaking their beards, and yelled in a deep baritone, "WHAT THE HELL!?"

I could barely follow what was happening. I was a dwarf? I was an indentured labourer? In Minnova? Where the hell is that?

At least my name was still Pete. I could barely process it as handlebar, I mean Balin, fed me some basic gruel. Don't fantasy dwarves eat rats? Is this rat porridge? Am I being racist right now? Or is that speciest?

The dwarf named Grim passed us each a massive tankard of what looked like an amber ale. He and Balin made some kind of toast to dirt and then pulled. That's right, dwarves were supposed to be big drinkers, and master crafters of beers and ales, right? At least I could drown my sorrows in fine alcohol.

I shot the drink back myself, before spitting it out in an atomized arc.

"WHAT THE HELL!?"

Dwarves drank *WATERY BEER*!?

CHAPTER TWO
I WAS REINCARNATED AS A DWARF BUT ALL THE BEER IS BAD!

Dwarf's Log, Deathdate 003

These are the voyages of the starsoul Peter Phillips. I appear to have died and been transported from my loving family and home to an underground prison hellscape of bad BO and worse beer. I am trapped in the body of a dwarf named Pete Samson. Samson arrived in the city of Minnova about three months ago, where he was picked up by the local guards after he was caught begging for beer in the streets. I took over Pete's body after my untimely demise on Earth. I am working in the City of Minnova Reform Mine, where I will remain until such a time as I have paid off Pete`s indenture. I appear to be in deep shit.

I scooped some shit up and plunked it into the cart beside me, then avoided brushing the sweat out of my eyes. The unigoat in the stall beside me chuffed and added to my work. Yep, a real deep *canyon* of shit. After the sulphur and spit debacle I got put on punishment duty by Grim. Goods from the mine were carted down to the city by unigoats, and nobody had cleaned the manure pit in ages because... dwarves. Seriously, some of this stuff was crusting over.

I admit to being a bit disillusioned here. I don't know what I was expecting after I died. I wasn't religious, so heaven was out. I grew up Catholic, but that wore off around the fourth time I got blackout drunk in college. Hell? Purgatory? I certainly wasn't expecting a small mining camp filled with boisterous and outgoing, if slightly surly, hairy alcoholics.

And my God, the alcohol! It was sour with a bitter aftertaste, had almost no alcohol content, and left my mouth feeling filmy. It's SO BAD, and they're drinking it ALL THE TIME! They even call it the *Sacred Brew*.

Wake up? Take a drink.
Break? Take a drink.
Lunch? Take a drink.
Go mining? Take a drink.
Almost die? You guessed it! Take a drink!

They all love the stuff and seem to have zero actual tolerance for alcohol. I'd put their beers at around 1 percent actual alcohol content, and I haven't seen anything that appears to be a harder drink. As far as I can tell, some dwarf invented beer ages ago, and they all fell so in love with the stuff that they never bothered improving it. It's a cultural institution, and the idea that it could be better is completely foreign to them.

"How ya' doin, Pete?" A voice interrupted my reverie from the other side of the stables.

"Hi, Balin. I'm doing a bit better," I replied, taking the opportunity to get out of the pit.

"'Ave yer memories come back?" Balin asked, as he took a step back. His handlebar moustache quivered at the stench wafting from the manure pit. We both looked to the side as the sound of rumbling drew our attention.

Another pair of dwarves, Annie and Wreck, pushed a massive cart filled with ore past us. A total of twenty dwarves lived in the camp: sixteen miners, the warden Grim, Doc Opal, Speaker John, and Whisperer Gemma. Doc Opal was the one who saved me from sulphur poisoning, and she's also the one helping take care of my 'amnesia,' or as she calls it, "damage to the spirit." I was pretty sure "spirit" referred to my mind and soul, so wasn't that a comforting thought?

"Not yet," I replied to Balin as I washed my hands in a trough.

"Nothin' in yer Status Sheet?" Balin kept his distance as I washed up, his eyes tracking Annie. Last night he confided to me in a drunken stupor that Annie had "the finest beard this side of Crack," whatever that means. It *is* a really nice beard though, long and silky with finely woven tresses and a Dali moustache. She was one of the few blonde dwarves as well; the rest of the miners were mostly brunettes with only Doc Opal and Speaker John having white hair.

Yes, female dwarves *did* have beards and moustaches. Contrary to certain pop-culture, it was still possible to tell them apart. Their beard hair was usually softer and downier than the males, and they had softer, more feminine facial features. Some discrete questioning revealed they also had breasts, but traditional dwarven clothing favoured chest-flattening armour.

I replied as I opened my ... Status Sheet ... by intoning 'status' in my head. A slightly translucent blue box appeared in my vision with a cheerful *Bing!*

Status: Provided by the Firmament

Name: Peter ~~Phillips~~ Samson
Age: *48*
Conditions: *None*
Race: *Dwarf*
Blessings: *None*
Title: *None*
Milestones: *[Otherworlder]*
Strength: *12*
Vitality: *12*
Agility: *10*
Dexterity: *11*
Wisdom: *12*
Intelligence: *10*
Perception: *13*
Charisma: *8*

I focused on [Otherworlder] and another little blue box popped up.

[**Otherworlder**] – *Your spirit has found a new spark! Your mental statistics have been replaced with their previous values, and you are more likely to gain Blessings and Milestones!*

If [Otherworlder] meant what I thought it did, my current intelligence, wisdom, perception, and charisma were based off their values from Earth. As a college grad, I felt my intelligence should have been higher, but I *was* essentially a child when it came to local knowledge. At least my 'amnesia' made it easy to ask questions that everybody should already know.

"Nope, no Conditions. Run it by me, Balin. What do these numbers *actually* mean? Practically speaking?"

"Midna's Mullet, Pete, how much did ya ferget? A youngster's about an eight in each stat, and an adult has around ten. Every additional point is just a bit stronger than the last." Balin was always willing to give a hand and was only a slightly sappy drunk. "Strength is how much you can lift and how hard ya can hit. Vitality is how well ya can hold yer beer! Agility is fer runnin' and movin', while dexterity is about fine coordination. Wisdom is tricky, since you can always ignore tha voice that says 'don't stick yer head in a freschie!' Ha! Intelligence is book smarts, perception is spottin' things, and charisma keeps ya from spittin' beer all over yer mates!"

"Hardy, har. So, if I got my strength up to one hundred, could I smash solid stone apart with my bare fist?" That sounded pretty cool!

"Nah, yer limit's 'bout a thirty-two in any stat. You'd need Abilities or Conditions ta go higher, and even then, it won't be by much. Every four stat points is around one and a half times as strong, so a person with sixteen strength would be half again stronger than someone with twelve."

That put me at mostly average, with good wisdom and perception, and shit charisma. I wouldn't have called myself uncharismatic back on Earth, so maybe it had to do with how I compared to everyone else in this new world? I admit that I've made a *ton* of social faux pas since I got here. Or maybe it's just the dad jokes.

Balin and I continued to chat about my status as we walked towards the mess hall. He was still wearing the same leather armour that all the miners wore, including me. It was comfy and helped protect against the sharp edges of stone in the mining tunnels. Oh, and it helped against monster attacks, because of course those were a thing.

A couple more dwarves walked past in the other direction, likely headed to the mining tunnels. They nodded to us as they passed, the manacles on their arms twinkling in the light. I looked down at my own metal shackles. While we were technically not 'prisoners,' it was functionally the same. Outside of a few rare vacation days, we were not allowed to leave the mine until we completed our indenture. The manacles were magical and would notify Grim if we tried to leave the mine. *I* felt like a prisoner, but the dwarven legal codes were very clear that I was *not*. It was just another thing about this place that was alien to my sensibilities. In my eyes we were all members of the chain-gang; I should really start teaching everyone the blues.

Speaking of alien, I looked up to the 'night sky' above us. While we were technically underground, a ceiling was actually a couple hundred metres above us. A luminescent moss on the roof gave the impression of an ethereal starry night that lasted the whole day. Rivers of blue-white light flowed every which way through the cavern like a multitude of milky ways. The effect was pretty amazing, and I often spent the evening looking at the 'stars' after everyone else had passed out from drinking.

The space was massive, and several other mining outposts could be spotted in the distance – lights in the dark. Each mining outpost was a small collection of buildings with the actual mining tunnels snaking beneath them. A few mountains dotted the landscape, monoliths that loomed out of the dim twilight. Our camp was actually on top of one of them, and the city of Minnova could be seen far below us to the south, in the centre of the cavern. An enormous purple crystal hanging above the city filled the entire cavern with a soft glow. It was too far to make out any details, but Minnova seemed fairly mediaeval, with tall walls and a large palace at its centre.

We reached the mess hall in short order, which was a large, nondescript stone building with lights of some kind festooned around it. They didn't have electricity around here, so the lights were a mystery for another time.

Balin took a deep sniff as we went through the door. "Ach, smells great!"

The interior of the mess hall was laid out almost exactly like a school cafeteria back home, with a door to the kitchen, a food service counter, and a lot of wooden picnic-style tables with benches. A stage was set up against one side for Grim to make announcements, and one table at the back was reserved for the permanent staff, like Doc Opal or Speaker John.

It was lunch time, which meant sandwiches with a slice of lettuce, goat cheese, and chicken breast. It was pretty tasty, and I was continually surprised by the quality of our 'cafeteria fare.'

Balin grabbed a plate from the short-bearded dwarf handing out food. "Thankee, Bran. Looks delicious as always."

Bran gave an acknowledging nod, his black bristle moustache quivering. "I added my special sauce today. It's a treat for the Blessin' party. Annie got Blessed!"

"Ach, good for her!" Balin's eyes sparkled. "She deserves it!"

We sat down next to a trio of dwarves who ignored us to continue their argument about the superiority of axes over swords. The sandwich was a perfect ratio of filling to bread and crunched between my teeth. I closed my eyes and appreciated the flavour of roasted chicken mixed with slightly melted cheese. Bran's special sauce was a tangy white cream sauce that reminded me of a standard bechamel sauce. A hard day of work shovelling poop would make *anything* taste good, but Bran really spoiled us.

Most dwarves were messy eaters, and I snickered as I glanced down the line of tables. Twenty dwarves were joyfully devouring their sandwiches, each with a near identical dribble of white sauce flowing down their beard. Balin made joyful munching sounds beside me and gave an *mmm* of happiness.

"Bran's secret sauce is sooo good! I wonder how he makes it!"

"It's a pretty standard white sauce. I could probably figure it out."

Balin gave me a wide-eyed look. "How would ya know that!?"

I turned the topic of our conversation towards the news instead. "Annie got Blessed, eh? You said that Grim and Opal are Blessed too?"

"Aye, Grim's Blessed by Lunara for all his 'ard work as Mine

Manager, and Doc Opal's twice Blessed by Archis and Lunara. That makes 'er a Titled [Doctor]!"

Apparently, Gods were real here, and they each embodied a pair of the fundamentals of reality and civilization, or the *Firmament*. I couldn't keep them all straight yet, but I did know Barck was the God of Spark and Innovation and Tiara was the Goddess of Matter and Possessions. Barck got called on a lot because his Blessing was [Good Luck], and Tiara because she was the Goddess of Gems and everyone wanted to strike it rich.

I wondered what Blessing Annie got. It looked like we were about to find out, as Grim walked up onto the stage.

"Cheers, you rascals!" Grim shouted. "We managed to exceed our quota today! Great work Annie and Wreck, for bringing in an entire extra cart of ore!" Grim pointed to Annie and another dwarf with a long stringy reddish-brown beard that reached her feet. "And a special congratulations to Annie for receivin' a Blessing from Barck!" The crowd erupted into cheers and splashes as dwarves clinked glasses. Annie stood up to the applause, her ruddy cheeks blushing as she took the iron helmet off her head.

"Thank you everyone!" She shouted in a surprisingly sweet alto as the applause died down. "I noticed that the minecart wheels kept seizing up from dust when we spent a lot of time in the tunnels, so I designed a new grease using sap from dungeon vines. It worked, and Barck gave me his Blessing!" There was a fresh round of cheering and clinking of glasses. I tapped on Balin's shoulder as people went up to congratulate Annie. He was staring wistfully at her and turned a distracted eye back towards me.

"Dungeon?" I asked.

"Oh, it's tha main reason that Minnova is built 'ere. There's a plant dungeon down below the city. It's the main source of our veggies. Killer Cabbages an' Peashooters, an' others. There's an 'ole lotta gold to be made down there."

"Killer, what-now?" I asked, looking at the leafy greens on my sandwich. Had I been eating monstrous vegetables?

"Killer cabbages, they're full o' vitamins and good fer the body! Tasty too!" Balin grinned as he took a big bite from his sandwich before chugging down some of his beer. I started on my beer as well.

I'd almost prefer water to this swill, but apparently nobody down here drank water. It was all beer and sometimes goat milk, though that's apparently for kids. Of both kinds.

They've only got two kinds of beer. The ale – True Brew, and a lager – Light Brew. There're no stouts, no IPAs, no sours, nothing that could be considered a craft beer at all. My tankard was currently full of slightly flat Light Brew. It was completely the wrong glass for this kind of beer. A lager should at the very least be served in a shaker – or pint – glass, which is wide at the mouth and narrow at the base. This tankard was simply the giant deuce on top of the shit sandwich that was this beer. At least the *actual* sandwich was good.

I took another bite and tried not to reminisce about Caroline's signature BLT. Would I ever taste it again? Could I go home, or was this my new life now? A bearded life filled with awful ale...

You know what, *no*. This entire situation was a crime against beer, and as a lifelong brewer I was going to take it personally. I've been wondering why I reincarnated here, and I think I finally figured it out. It was my job, nay, my *duty* as a proud Canadian Craft Brewer to SAVE BEER! I would see a Hefeweizen behind every dwarven bar within the next decade. A Saison in the hand of every dwarven child, or my name wasn't Peter Phillips – er, Samson! If they didn't like it, *fine* – lots of people don't like beer – but at least dwarven craft beer would no longer be stuck in boozy limbo.

First though, I had to get out of this stupid mine. I mulled it over for a while, until I was broken out of my reverie by Doc Opal's voice at my side. I looked up and gave her a wide smile. I would come back to this later; I had a whole new life to work on it after all. At least, unless I stumbled on a way to go back to my old one.

Somewhere else.

On the side of a cliff stood a white stone gazebo. Mist fell from a great waterfall that stretched beneath it, vanishing into the clouds below. A black mountain rose up behind it, seeming to touch the sky.

A circular marble table covered by a complex game-board sat in the centre of the gazebo. The edges of the board seemed to stretch into the distance while still somehow filling a defined space. Eight ornate figurines sat upon the board – a dragon, an elf, two humans, two dwarves, a gnome, and a beastfolk. One of them, a white porcelain dwarf holding a tankard, tentatively slid across the board.

CHAPTER THREE
A CREAMPUFF A DAY

Doctor Opal Sifsdotter made her way through the mess hall, her plate heaped high with meat and vegetables along with a large hunk of bread and a cream puff she couldn't wait to bite into. Her white [Doctor] uniform could be a liability when the beer flew, like tonight. While she was paid a retainer to stay here at the city's camp, she actually served a large number of mines in the area.

There were ten other camps within a short unigoat ride, and not a single day went by without her getting called in for some kind of illness, injury, or mishap. She wasn't quite as good as a [Healer] for injuries, but her Milestones made it easier to diagnose problems with the body. Those were plentiful up here in the mines, and she blamed the non-stop stress for her prematurely white beard.

Speaking of injuries, Opal looked around the room for Peter Samson and spotted him sitting dejectedly next to Balin. A simple case of sulphur poisoning, and all it took was an aetherstone and some knowhow to get him back on his feet. Sure, a [Healer] could have fixed it with mana straight out, but that required at least two decades of study in magic even *before* studying the dwarven body. [Doctors] were just so much more *efficient*.

She made her way over and sat down next to Pete, who was nursing his beer.

"How's the memory doing Peter?" She asked, nodding at Balin and smiling at Peter.

"No better, I'm afraid," Peter smiled back. He really was very handsome, with a well-groomed Garibaldi beard and an Asterix moustache. Quite her type, but she wasn't interested in bad boys or vagrants. "I can't seem to remember much of anything, but I'm learning again really quick. Balin's been a great help." Balin heard his name and glanced at them before turning back to watch Annie get hoisted into the air by Wreck to a chant of *Chug!* *Chug!* *Chug!*

"It's a rather fascinating case. Your heart stopped for about five seconds, but that shouldn't have been enough to damage your spirit. You're sure you have no conditions?"

"My Sheet says, 'none.'" Peter shrugged.

"Amnesia is a fully recognized Condition, so I'm afraid I'm stumped. I'm not an expert in spirit, so you'll probably need a Titled [Hypnotist] to see if they can jog your memory." Peter looked like he was about to ask something and then stopped, his attention arrested.

"Is... is that a cream puff?" he stammered. "With cream and everything? Is it sweet?"

"Yes? I'm afraid I can't share. The staff gets slightly different meals. If you want some dessert, you'll need to do something extra like Annie over there, or work hard and end your indenture. By the way, I'm sorry about my fees, they're set by City Hall." Opal shrugged apologetically.

"No, I mean, do dwarves..." Peter paused and pulled his moustache, "I mean, does the mine have sugar? Can I have some?"

"Some of the vines in the dungeon contain sugar sap. Do you have a sweet tooth?" Opal wouldn't have pegged Peter for a lover of ladylike treats, but she couldn't deny any dwarf the love of sweets. She was going to need to watch her own figure, given how much the cook pampered her. "I'm afraid that you'll need to do something special before Bran allows you any of his confections."

"If I have sugar, I can try and fix this awful beer!" Peter jumped up and shouted, drawing glares from the people sitting around them. Balin growled.

"Pete, I told ya not to be insultin' tha most Sacred Brew o' the dwarves!" Balin hissed. Peter sat back down, his face reddening, and Opal shook her head. While amnesia was one thing, a sudden dislike for the perfection that was beer was another thing altogether. Opal made more small talk with Balin and Pete, but secretly wanted nothing more than to get back to her cabin. She planned to finish her cream puff in peace, along with the second one that Bran had given her to hide in her hood. She really needed to watch her figure...

Sugar! They had sugar! How was their beer such shit?! Even a complete novice could make a half decent *Kit and Kilo* beer if they had a malt base and some sugar...

Moreover, if I had sugar, I could make syrup! If I had syrup, I could fix the flavour of this damp disaster of a draught! There were several things I could do using a sweetener to adjust flavour, and I was willing to try them all at this point.

Things were looking up for Peter Phillips!

I continued chatting with Opal while Balin made moon-eyes at Annie. Opal was chatty, and the most well-spoken dwarf in the mine. She could wax on and on about nearly any subject you could think of. I got her started on dwarven skeletons earlier this week and she talked about it for *hours*. Apparently dwarves had weak toe bones, which explained why some of the miners were so protective of their padded socks.

After dinner there was a Blessing party thrown for Annie, and Bran brought out an actual cake! A triple layer sponge cake with goat-butter cream! It had nuts and some kind of vanilla glaze, but no chocolate unfortunately. It was an incredibly impressive bit of baking for a 'not-a-prison' cafeteria chef! Annie gave a really long, boring speech thanking everyone for coming and for the opportunity to improve Minnova's industry. Then Wreck mushed her face into the cake while everyone else grabbed handfuls to munch on. That seemed to be the kick-off for the actual party, which started in earnest.

A dwarven party mostly involved a lot of drinking, cheering, merrymaking and tossing dwarves around. Dwarven architecture had windows to let in light, but didn't bother with glass. That's a plus when screaming, bearded projectiles are getting chucked through them on the regular. I guess when you're underground the weather isn't really a concern. Bugs might be a problem, but I hadn't really seen any flies or wasps around, so perhaps not.

I asked – Mosquitoes don't exist. Chalk one up for the Gods of Erd.

Opal eventually made polite 'I want to leave now' noises, and I gave her an opportunity to bow out. The party was going to go on for hours yet, and Balin had finally gotten up the courage to go chat with Annie. The two of them were having a grand old time doing some kind of jig while one of the other miners played a cross between a fiddle and a banjo.

I sighed and stood up from my bench, popping my abused back and neck as I did so. No point in sitting around hoping to get drunk on beer with a lower alcohol content than cough syrup. Opal had given me some direction, and it was time to meet the muffin man, the muffin man, the muffin man.

I peeked through the small ordering window into the kitchen.

"Hello! Bran? Are you there?"

There was a *bang!* followed by some swearing from a pair of doors to the left, and Bran emerged rubbing his head. His black hair was cut into short, wavy locks and he was one of the first dwarves I'd seen without a helmet. Instead, he wore some kind of mesh hairnet. Food safe! I liked it!

"Aye, what do you want – ah..."

"It's Pete."

"Right, Pete. Kitchen's closed. I'm doin' clean up. The keg for the party is out front. Help yourself, and if it's empty – tough."

"Actually, I wanted to talk to you about food."

Bran stopped dead in his tracks and eyed me suspiciously. "You lot already got your meals. No seconds."

"No, I had a question."

"I'm not tellin' how I make me special sauce, and I'm not sellin' either. Now, git." He waved me off.

"You don't understand! I want some sugar." I winced. Phrasing, Pete!

Bran scowled. "If you're here to beg, you can shove off too. If you didn't get any cake, it's not my problem. Do I need to call the guards?"

"I want to make stuff with it!" I huffed. "I'm not begging!"

Bran paused. "You know how to cook?"

I nodded vigorously. I wasn't near as good a chef as Caroline, but I was a deft hand at a variety of different desserts and alcohol-based dishes. It was something that any vintner or brewer kind of just... fell into. You've got all these fancy drinks around, why not try making food with them? Or learn how to make a meal that pairs well with that '95 Pinot Noir?

Bran gestured around the kitchen. "This is my space. I don't need any two-copper amateurs tryin' to break things in it. If I need extra hands, I get them from Grim." He grabbed a rag and started wiping counters.

I looked around. Now that I was inside, I could see that this kitchen was incredibly well appointed, with a surprising amount of gleaming stainless-steel and porcelain. This place stood out like a sore thumb in the otherwise plain and untidy camp. It was clear Bran considered this his castle.

"It is a nice kitchen. Oh, and I don't need the recipe for your secret sauce. I'm pretty sure I already know it."

Bran stopped, as though struck.

"There's no way. That's me own special secret sauce!"

"Sure. It's a pretty standard bechamel sauce," I began listing ingredients on my fingers, "with butter, flour, milk, salt, and pepper. Melt the butter in a saucepan, then add the flour and stir. The paste that forms is called roux. After it gets bubbly, add some warm milk along with salt and pepper. Stir until thick, then serve."

Bran grew pale. "That's, that's... just a normal white sauce. You're a chef, good for you, now get out of me—"

I interrupted him as I continued. "Ah, but I was pretty sure you added something else. I was wondering what it was, but now that I'm in your kitchen I can tell." I pointed to an *extremely* well-stocked spice rack. "Nutmeg!"

Bran coughed as though struck. "How... how..."

It was simple, actually. Nutmeg was often used in bechamel sauce back on Earth. It was a wonder spice used in medicine, cooking, and even as a poison. It was also an incredibly common ingredient in sauces and drinks. I was struck by a pang of desire for some of my wife's old fashioned nutmegged wine, then banished the thought.

"So, did I guess right?"

"Aye... Aye you did." Bran scowled at me. "Fine, you guessed me recipe. Shouldn't have been too hard. I doubt I'm the only one that's ever made it. It doesn't mean I'm going to let you use my kitchen."

"Ah," I held up a finger, "but what if I told you a way to improve the sauce?"

Bran's eyes narrowed to slits.

"I'm not doin' it." Bran crossed his arms.

"What!? Why not!?"

"It's an insult to the Sacred Brew."

I shook the tankard of beer I'd brought in from the mess hall. "It's just beer!"

"*JUST* beer!? Ya lunatic! Tha sulphur must have damaged yer head!"

"It's food! It can be used as an ingredient just like any *other* kind of food! Besides..." I dropped my voice to a seductive lilt. "Don't you want to know how it tastes...?"

Bran licked his lips. I could see I almost had him, so I gave one last push. "And, if nobody else is using it to cook... you'll have a *truly* secret sauce."

Bran groaned. "But beer isn't *like* goat milk or water. It's for drinkin' and celebratin'! I can't just use it to cook with! The ancestors never made it for that!"

I scoffed. "You can't tell me that for certain. For all you know other dwarves have been using beer to cook forever!"

Bran shook his head. "Nobody uses beer ta cook. Beer is *beer*, not some simple *ingredient*!"

"Well, you're a chef. This is a chance to make a new dish, and aaaaaaall you have to do is pour that tankard of beer into this pot over here." I pointed at a stainless-steel pot filled with milk. My recipe wasn't too different from a regular Bechamel – there was just one tiny added ingredient.

Pete's Special Beerchamel Sauce Ingredients

Butter
Flour
Milk
Salt & Pepper
Nutmeg
Lager

"I-I-I-" Bran's hand was actually shaking.

"Bran." I grabbed his shoulders and shook him slightly. "This is an opportunity for you to improve your craft. As a chef, do you truly think food is disrespectful? Or is it an art form, and an *honour* to bless it with the Sacred Brew of the dwarves?"

Bran looked me in the eyes, and his gaze slowly grew firm. "Aye. Yer right. It *is* an art. One I've spent over two hundred years perfectin'. It *would* be an honour to use the Sacred Brew to improve it even further."

Ugh. *Two hundred years*!? HOLY SHIT! No wonder dwarves got so hidebound!

Bran took the mug from me, and with one shaky hand, poured the beer into the pot. He added some butter and erdroot flour to a saucepan and began stirring it. "So, what did ya call this? Beka-meal? Me secret sauce was just based off o' standard white sauce."

"White sauce is fine, but I like to call this one... *Beerchamel*." Really though, this was just an excuse to see if cooking with it would improve the quality of the local swill! Thanks for the opportunity, Bran!

Five minutes later we both stared at a bowl filled with an off-brown sauce.

Bran reached a shaky finger in and scooped a bit out. He closed his eyes, took a deep breath, and then licked his finger. He actually *moaned* with pleasure, his jaw working as he tasted the sauce.

"It's amazin'. It's like me regular sauce, but with the tang o' the brew. The miners will go crazy over it!" He looked panicky for a moment. "Just, don't tell them what it's made with!"

I scooped some out and took a curious lick for myself.

It had the soft, nutty flavour of a good white sauce, with the added tang and bitter taste of beer.

The bitter, *awful*, taste of dwarven ale. I felt something crunchy and spat it out.

"Is that... a stick!? Was this in the beer!?"

"Aye, it's good for you. Lots of vitamins. This is amazin' stuff, Pete!"

"It's alright." Ok Pete, do it now! While he's distracted with delicious new food! "You know, that Blessing cake was really tasty – you're a pretty good baker, Bran. Tell you what, I know a few recipes for meals and desserts that I'm willing to bet you've never seen before. I'll give them to you in exchange for using your kitchen, and maybe... the use of some sugar?" I tried my best to look casual, but I waited with baited breath.

Bran nodded. "You're welcome to use my kitchen again if you want to show me any other recipes! Oh, but," he gave an apologetic shrug, "no sugar. It's too expensive for me to use for playin' around."

"Ugh. Fine." Well, at least I obtained access to the kitchen. I also learned two things tonight: this beer was just as awful in food as in a mug, and I could get some sugar if I invented something impressive – like Annie.

There was a raucous cheer from outside, and I heard Balin's voice raised in anger. There were shouts of "Brawl!"

"I need to go back up my buddy. Thanks for the use of the kitchen Bran, it was good talking to you." I held out my hand to shake.

Bran fist bumped into it. "Good workin' with you Pete. Thanks for the new recipe!"

I stared down at the hand turkey in abject horror.

They *fist bump*!?

CHAPTER FOUR
A MOP AND A WHISTLE

I miss my wife and daughter...

It's been a week since I reincarnated into Minnova, in the dwarven country of Crack, on the planet Erd. Erd is the dwarven word for *dirt* – I guess it's common throughout the multiverse to name your planet after mud. I hope the country is called Crack because it has a crack, not because it sells crack, or because it smells like crack.

Back to moping – or mopping in this case. I'm almost done cleaning out the unigoat stalls. It took nearly the whole week to do it, and I think I managed to avoid getting anything nasty in the process. No conditions and no back strains. Must be that famous dwarven constitution, or my vitality of twelve.

"Who's a good goat, Billy? You are!" I rubbed the neck of the unigoat beside me. These guys really helped me get over losing my wife and daughter. I know they aren't really gone, it was actually me who died, but it's still a depressing feeling.

That's right... I died. It took a few days for that to really sink in after the whole 'reincarnated as a dwarf' business. Honestly, I'm not really worried about my wife and daughter. Samantha already had a job lined up, and I knew Carol's plan was to go cruising. I could see her now, sitting on the deck of a cruise ship, in that itsy-bitsy polka-dot bikini I always liked to tease her about. Her luxurious French fork beard and Imperial moustache fluttering in the breeze...

By my beard! Now I'm doing it too!! Focus Pete, this place is getting to your head!

"Hello Peter!" An alto voice called out. I peeked around the wall to see Opal approaching the stables.

"Hello Doctor! Are you headed to one of the other camps?"

"Yes, we just had a runner arrive. There's been an attack of stoneants at Peak Brother's Mine. The miners broke into a cavern full of them. They fought them off but there are a few injured. Nothing too serious, but I'll be heading over to do some quick check-ups." She hefted a large doctor's bag and a fairly heavy looking satchel.

"Stoneants?"

"Yes, they're dog-sized ants with a grey mottled carapace. Some of them can get much larger. Still no improvement to your memory then?"

"No," I intoned. I went into one of the stables and brought out a large longhaired off-yellow mountain goat. He had a single horn curling up out of its forehead and a *most* unfortunate name. "Here, Piddles has been looking feisty for a while now. He should get you there fast enough."

"Thank you, Peter. How has your quest for sugar been going?" Opal asked as I helped her saddle up the goat and pack the saddlebags. It was well known in the camp by now that I was trying to get an achievement big enough to grant me access to some sugar.

"I've got some ideas." Which was overselling it. Grim swore he'd force me to eat goat shit if I tried to mess with the minecarts again. I'm a pretty good amateur chemist after two decades of beer and wine making, but mechanics were never really my strong suit. Case in point...

"Did your 'steam engine' and 'still' not work out?" Opal asked, looking at the sad hunks of metal in an empty stall. I'd spent about three days putting them together out of scrap metal, and at this point they were the only thing more pathetic in this camp than the beer.

"No," I sighed. Sammy was always the handy one. I don't know who she got it from – probably my dad. He was always disappointed that I wasn't interested in putting together old cars with him, but I was more into my malts and mixes. Dad died two years ago. He never got to see his granddaughter get married. Come to think of it... I'll never get to walk her down the aisle. A single tear swept down my moustache and I wiped it away before Opal could notice.

"Well, good luck." Opal broke me out of my reverie as she pounded down the path leading to the other camps. She narrowly avoided a large cart being pulled up the hill by a pair of anemic-looking unigoats. The dwarf on the cart shouted in a high scratchy voice, "Hey, I'm driving 'ere!" as she thundered past. The cart was quite eye-catching. It was an enclosed wagon with coloured scarves and paints adorning it. It had really odd sides, with what looked like double doors. A sign on the top proclaimed it *Whistlemop's Wonders*. The dwarf looked really odd too. He was extremely short, even for a dwarf, and he had no beard! Sacrilege! Instead, he had a supremely well-maintained blonde walrus moustache, thick glasses, and was completely bald. Instead of armour, he was wearing a garish suit with a mishmash of rainbow hues and exaggerated edging. It was a crime against fashion, and it was amazing.

"What're you staring at, beardie? You never seen a gnome before?" The gnome, because that's what he was, asked as he pulled up to the stables. His voice was somewhat high pitched, and had a bit of a Cockney accent to it.

"A-Actually, I was just admiring your wonderous moustache." I prevaricated. There were more than dwarves here? Were there humans too? Elves? Dragons?! The problem with being an 'amnesiac' around a bunch of alcoholics is that unless you know what questions to ask, you end up with giant gaps in your knowledge base. Doc Opal mentioned a school of some type. I really need to get my hands on some books after I finish solving the beer problem.

Suddenly, a slightly transparent blue box superimposed itself over my vision with a *Bing!*

Stat Increased: [Charisma]!

Your charisma has increased by 1! Your new charisma is 9!

"By my beard!" I shouted, startling the gnome. He'd been twirling his moustache with pride, and he turned to me in shock.

"What is it now!"

"I was.... Just thinking about how amazing it is to have a trader here. I haven't seen one... ever?" The gnome nodded at me with a quizzical look.

"I'll admit there're not too many traders that come out to the mines. Mostly the miners come in to Minnova!" The gnome chuckled. "However, I'm trying to earn my fifth Milestone in order to get my first Specialisation. I'm going to try and hit every camp and settlement around Minnova. See if that gets me anything!" The gnome explained excitedly, hopping off the carriage and narrowly avoiding a goatpie. He frowned at his boots and scuffed them on the side of a wagon wheel.

"Are you Titled then?" I asked as I handed him a rag. Once you had a Blessing you could start earning Milestones. They were small buffs for doing what you were already doing. If someone with a Title earned enough Milestones, they would get a Specialisation. The combined term for Blessings and Milestones was *Abilities*. It was kind of game-like but made sense for an 'intelligently designed' world.

"Yessir, I'm a Titled [Peddler]!" He nodded at me in thanks and got to buffing his boots, which were promptly muddied again. A [Peddler].... I still wasn't up to snuff on all the different Titles. I knew if you got a single Blessing from a God it came with two benefits. I only knew three Blessings so far due to the people here at camp.

Barck the God of Spark and Innovation – His Blessing granted a small bit of health regeneration and luck.

Tiara the Goddess of Matter and Possessions – Her Blessing granted your body and possessions some durability.

Lunara the Goddess of Order and Law – Her Blessing granted a cloak of shadows and the ability to sense motives.

A second Blessing from any God let you choose a Title based on the path you wanted to take. The Blessings and Titles played to your strengths since you earned them for feats or deeds in that God's portfolio. Annie liked tinkering with things to increase efficiency, so naturally she got Barck's Blessing. That would help her be a better tinker, and if she ever got a second Blessing it would likely be something related to that.

In short if you liked working with plants, animals, healing or inventing, you were more likely to earn Barck's Blessing and be better at what you were already doing. Same went for all the other Gods.

There were eight total Gods and one day I'd need to remember them all. Especially since my [Otherworlder] Milestone apparently made it easier for me to earn Blessings and Milestones.

"Whose Blessings did you need to become a [Peddler]?" I stepped back as the gnome fiddled with the side of his carriage.

"That would be Aaron and Tiara!" The gnome stepped back as, with a whizzing sound, the sides of his carriage sprang open. A wide variety of goods were displayed on racks and shelves within. "But where are my manners? My name is Whistlemop and Whistlemop's Wonders is open for business!!" He pulled a small chain on the side of his carriage and a cheery whistle like a train horn sounded out around the camp. He looked around expectedly for a moment, and then another minute. I coughed.

"Where is everyone?" Whistlemop asked, looking around.

"Well.... This is the City of Minnova Reform Mine. Nobody here really has much money. The only person who might have been interested was the dwarf that just left."

"Ah.... What a waste." Whistlemop sighed, crestfallen. He looked absolutely devastated as he peered back down the large hill he had climbed up to get here.

"It's not too bad Whistle-mope, there's nearly a dozen camps around here." I clamped my hand over my mouth. Damn that low charisma!

"Excuse me?" He asked as he arched a wispy eyebrow.

"Uh, I was wondering what goods you have for sale? It's a pretty impressive collection!" I desperately changed the subject as I went up to the now open side of his carriage. It was indeed impressive. He had pots, pans, scissors, needles, threads, cloth; just about anything a person would need. Then there was the more esoteric stuff: gadgets and gizmos, a couple of oddly coloured stones, as well as a bunch of different hunks of vegetable matter. Whistlemop came alongside me, a bit leery as he realised I wore manacles around my wrists.

"What's all this?" I asked, waving over the hunks of greenery. There were vines, flowers, herbs, and some suspicious-looking squashes. I looked about desperately for some hops, but was only left with disappointment. Did those cabbages have eyes? Did one just *wink* at me!?

"Dungeon materials." Whistlemop re-assumed his flowery peddler persona. "I have some of the best goods straight out of Greentree dungeon. Fresh caught by the finest adventurers! I can assure you that you will not be able to get dungeon materials more cheaply or efficiently than through Whistlemop's Wonders!"

"Uh huh," I muttered distractedly. "What does all this stuff do?" I held up some vines and a gourd. Whistlemop leaned up to look more closely.

"Well, the yellow vines provide a rather slippery fluid. They've been in demand recently, and I heard there's a new lubricant being made with it. That increases the price of course." I nodded at that. Annie's invention seemed to have caught on at the other mining camps. "The red vines are rather interesting. If you light one end on fire, a bright burning light travels along until it reaches the end of the vine. It's been quite popular with children!" Hey, that was neat; kind of like a sparkler! "The gourd I can't discuss in polite company. Suffice it to say, you wouldn't be interested in it."

"Uh... Ok? What about this blue vine?"

"Ah, that one provides a sweet sap. It's the most expensive thing on my cart, I'm afraid." He snatched it from my suddenly rigid fingers. This was the sweet sap vine! I needed it!

"How much is it!?" I nearly shouted, stepping forward.

"One gold for a metre!" Whistlemop stepped back, sudden concern in his eyes and a quaver in his voice. I calmed myself and hunched my shoulders, tugging anxiously at my moustache. There was no way I could afford that.

"Do you have a sweet tooth, young dwarf?" Whistlemop sounded almost apologetic. "I understand you're at a hard time in your life, but look up, you have many years ahead of you. Work hard and you're guaranteed to earn a Blessing at some point. A few Milestones later and you'll earn enough to eat all the sweets you could desire!" Whistlemop reached up and patted me on the shoulder. "You said there are a few camps around here, right? Could you point me in their direction? I can't give you any Sweetsap Vine but I can provide some small recompense for your time."

Whistlemop and I bent over a small map that he pulled out from his jacket. I spent the next ten minutes or so pointing out where all the camps were and the best routes to get to them. Whistlemop was a pretty nice guy, and probably had way higher than a nine in charisma. When we were all done Whistlemop thanked me and went to his cart to rummage around. After about two minutes of that he emerged from his cart and stalked towards me, holding something in his hands.

His voice was aggravated as he demanded, "What's the meaning of this!?"

CHAPTER FIVE
GLASS HALF-FULL

Two Minutes Earlier.

Whistlemop of the South Crackian Mops rummaged through his cart. The young dwarf named Pete had been very helpful, and it was only right that he receive recompense. Perhaps seeing his hard work rewarded would help put him back on the straight and narrow! Whistlemop picked up and tossed aside a small figurine of a badger. Nope, nobody liked badgers, they were vicious annoying beasts and he always regretted purchasing that case of them.

Whistlemop paused as he activated one of his Abilities, [Relative Value]. While he was unable to see the true price of items, he could determine when an object would be more meaningful or valuable to a customer. He always had a knack for connecting customers with just the right product, and it was nice to see the Gods agreed. He paused as his eyes alighted upon a vase in a pile of glassware off to the side. The lack of sunlight down here meant that outside of the dungeon, flowers didn't exactly thrive. The only things growing in Minnova, other than in the dungeon, were various mosses, lichens, fungi, and the ubiquitous erdroot. He personally preferred a fine imported tea to the beer the dwarves made, but to each their own.

What confused him was that [Relative Value] was pinging, indicating the vase held incredible value for Pete. That was when his

[Sense Deals] started going off as well, meaning the vase could hold incredible value to him too.

What on Erd was going on? Whistlemop grabbed the vase and stalked out to stand in front of the young dwarf.

"What's the meaning of this!?"

—"Wha-what do you mean?" I stammered, backing up. Had I done something wrong? Don't reduce my charisma score, Whistlemope! I have none to spare!

"Are you a [Cultivator]?" Whistlemop demanded.

"What, like Wuxia?" Were martial artists a thing here too?

"What in the Firmament's name is a woo-shoe? No, a Titled [Cultivator] for plants and gardens!"

"No... I don't even have my first Blessing!"

"Well then," Whistlemop held up a glass object, confused, "why on Erd is this vase so valuable? I can't for the life of me figure it out!" I took a moment and looked at it. It was round and made of clear glass, with a narrow base that swelled up in a curve to a wider opening at the top. It was a pretty standard flower vase. There was nothing remarkable about it other than the excellent quality of the glasswork. It was about twenty centimetres tall, and six centimetres wide.

"I don't know, it's just.. a... vase...." I paused, looking at it more closely. It vaguely resembled something important, what was it? Then I realised and grabbed it from Whistlemop's hands. "IT'S A PILSNER GLASS!" I shouted, staring at it in wonder.

"A what?" Whistlemop asked, standing on tiptoes to peer up at it.

"You were sent to me by the Gods." I whispered, closing my eyes and rubbing my cheek on the smooth glass of the vase. It was a perfect pilsner glass. It would certainly hold more than a pint, but that was fine; the beer was so low in alcohol content that it didn't matter. What *did* matter? I finally had something proper for the beer in the mess hall. Any kind of lager made in the Plzeň style was a *Pilsner*, and a Pilsner *glass* was excellent for any kind of lager.

Plzeň is a city in Germany famous for their unique flavour of beer. What exactly made Pilsner beer different was a topic of study for ages, but the secret was eventually revealed to be the local aquifer. The water being used by brewers in Plzeň was incredibly soft compared to other locations in Germany, and it was resulting in a smoother, softer beer. Soft and hard refer to the mineral content of water. Hard water has a lot of minerals, especially calcium and magnesium; soft water has very little. Between hardness and acidity, modern brewing put a lot of effort into getting the water just right. Since Dwarven water came from underground rivers it was naturally hard, which gave their brew a rough mouthfeel.

"I need to try this right away," I muttered, staring into the crystal of the glass. "What time is it?"

"Um, almost noon," Whistlemop pulled out a small pocket watch and peered into it. There was a painting of another gnome with pink hair on the inside of the lid. He poked me in the side as I turned to the mess hall. "What is it? Isn't it just a vase?"

"Come with me, I'm going to change the world of dwarven beer forever." I grabbed Whistlemop and dragged him towards the mess hall. We met up with a few other dwarves as the rest of the mine began to wind down for lunch. Lunch was a very important meal for dwarves, because it had beer in it. A few dwarves gave me the side eye, but I noticed Annie staring at me rather intently as I pulled Whistlemop into the mess hall. I've gained a bit of a reputation as a weirdo the last few days. Thankfully everyone has been very kind about it; they've been giving me some grace after my 'near-death' experience. A line began to form behind me as I went up to Bran to receive lunch. They were indeed serving Light Brew today! As he started to pour my ration of beer into the allotted tankard, I stopped him.

"Not that, Bran. I brought my own tankard today! Pour it into THIS!" I triumphantly held up the vase. Bran paused and looked at it, and the customary chatter of the mess hall stopped for a moment.

Dwarves have a really nice laugh. It's full-hearted and comes from the gut. Their noses get all red and their moustaches crinkle up (unless they have a Fu-Man-Chu). All of which didn't help the sting as the entire mess hall burst into guffaws. My face reddened but I resolutely held the vase – no – the *Pilsner glass*, up to Bran.

"Finally decided yer' a delicate flower Pete?" Bran grunted between peals of laughter. Tears poured down his brushed and braided beard. "Have ya spent too much time in tha' fertiliser this week?" The room erupted into fresh howls of laughter.

"Just give me the keg." I growled, elbowing Bran aside and pouring myself a drink. I did so carefully, ensuring that extra air wasn't poured into the drink to interfere with the bubbles. The beer slowly filled the glass, creating a perfectly crisp head that rose as I poured. I've been pouring beer for decades and I'm pretty good at it, but getting a perfect head is a science unto itself.

When you make beer, it involves a few central steps. The first and most important is the selection of the malt. Modern beers often use a combination of barleys and other cereals, but any starchy plant would do. Heck, rice beer is quite popular in some parts of the world, including the United States, where it's a main ingredient in their 'world famous' Budweiser. Dwarves use the tuberous erdroot that's ubiquitous in Crack to brew their beer. Erdroot is a starchy vegetable used to make everything from bread to beer, and while it has a musty flavour, it's healthy and filling. The malt is roasted, then ground into a powder called grist. The grist is heated in water in a step called mashing, where the starches are converted into sugars.

After mashing is complete the resulting slurry is filtered, leaving a liquid called *wort*, which needs to be boiled for sterilisation. During the boiling stage, hops are added for flavour and preservation. I doubt the dwarves have hops. It's more likely they add a combination of herbs. Herbed beer is called *gruit*, and it was the most common beer on Earth for thousands of years. I've personally never had a good gruit, and dwarven True Brew is just another in a long list of awful gruits.

The final stage is to cool the wort and pour it into a vessel with some yeast in order to cause fermentation. Fermentation is just a yuppie term for 'yeast eats sugar and makes alcohol' which is where the actual beer comes from. The fermentation process creates carbon dioxide as a by-product, and the carbon dioxide is trapped as tiny bubbles within the beer. When the beer is poured, those bubbles rise to the surface. Proteins within the beer grab onto the bubbles and rise up with them. Those proteins act kind of like soap in a soap bubble, preventing the bubble from popping. Those bubbles gather at the top of the beer as a foamy 'collar' and voila – you have head!

Oops! I was so distracted by my thoughts that I almost missed the correct timing. I stopped just as a half-inch of head reached the top of the glass – a small head for a lager. A low alcohol content or a bad batch can cause that, and I would accuse dwarven beer of both of those crimes. I let out a breath I hadn't realised I was holding in and stepped back to appreciate my pour. The bubbles at the bottom of the glass rose slowly to the top, and the head remained perfectly steady. A pilsner glass is specially designed to ensure that the bubbles rise from the narrow bottom, and the broad rim keeps the head in place. The metal tankards the dwarves used were wide and flat, and Bran did a pretty rough pour, so any head was lost by the time we sat down to eat and drink.

I leaned down and took a deep sniff of the glass. One of the benefits of a good head is that it captures the flavours of the beer, and you can appreciate the ingredients that went into it. Light Brew smelled roughly of... mushrooms? Something earthy anyway. A rare choice but understandable given the environment. The transparent glass of the vase revealed the beer in all its glory, and it was foggy, a clear sign of contaminants. I paused as I realised the room had gone silent.

"What's that?" The dwarf behind me asked, leaning in. His brown moustache stood out in a bristle, and he had muttonchops. It was a weird choice for facial hair, but... dwarves. I was pretty sure his name was Tim.

"It's a head," I replied, guarding the glass.

"Ahead of what?" Tim pushed closer, watching the bubbles rise. "Were you sniffin' tha beer?"

"Um.... Yes..." I stepped back as a bevy of dwarves starting to gather around and stare in rapt fascination at my oversized glass. Is it a bevy? What would you call a group of dwarves? A beard? "The foam on top captures the smell of the beer, and the bubbles subtly change the flavour when you drink."

"Can I try?" Tim asked reverently, reaching for the glass. His hand was slapped down by Balin, who had appeared next to me.

"None of that!" he shouted as I smiled appreciatively at him. "He's obviously gonna let his best bud Balin have tha first taste!" My smile flopped.

"Nobody is drinking it but me!" I shouted. "But you can all try it after I get a chance!" There was a clamour and the dwarves began to fight over who would be first. As the fists flew, I took another sniff of the glass and slowly sipped. The bubbles exploded on my pallet, and brought with them the nutty...

Rancid...

Awful taste of the beer. Yep. It perfectly brought out the flavour of the Light Brew lager alright, in all its terrible glory. I sighed and finished the glass off, no sense in wasting bad beer. It was going to take more than some simple glassology to fix this piss. As I washed my glass out, a line quickly formed up with Balin at the front. A few black eyes and bloody lips were visible, and I think I saw a couple bodies being stuffed under benches. Eh, not my problem.

My fellow dwarves took turns drinking from the vase as I poured, each copying my motions in turn. Sniff – pause – small sip – small sip – and chug. Their expressions were rapt, and the mood was nearly religious. It kind of freaked me out, honestly. I love my wine and beer, but I don't *love* my wine and beer. I reserve that for my wife's flowing beard.

Dammit.

Meanwhile, underneath a table in the mess hall, a pair of eyes glittered. A magnificent moustache twitched up in a smile at the unmistakable scent of gold.

CHAPTER SIX
BE MINE

Grim sighed as he scratched his signature into another injury report form. He stretched his neck and glanced at a small painting up on the wall. It was of a demure-looking dwarf with pink braids in a Verdi beard, a chainmail skirt, and a pink leather jerkin. He just wanted to go home and spend some time with his wife... Fighting amongst the miners was nothing new, but it rarely grew so vicious. There had been eight black eyes, fourteen contusions, two concussions, and a broken arm. Doctor Opal had been ready to rip someone apart until Bran presented her with a slice of cheesecake and ushered her away.

All that... over a vase...

Grim turned the piece of unassuming glass over in his hand. It appeared completely ordinary. Similar to a dozen other vases he'd seen over the years. So much chaos over this. Solen would be proud. He hadn't been there to see it, but apparently it all started after Pete did something with the vase.

Ever since Pete's accident with the sulphur he'd been a thorn in Grim's side. Between the minecart incident, the goat shit getting tracked into the mess hall, and now THIS! It was almost worth it for the city to simply exile him instead of dealing with his indenture. Pete's only saving grace in this matter was that he hadn't been the direct cause of the fighting.

It was the fault of this simple piece of glassware...

Grim went up to the door of his office and locked it. He had a small cabin to himself in the camp, and it contained only three rooms. An office, a bedroom, and a bathroom. It was nothing compared to the mansion in Minnova where his wife resided, but it was a home away from home.

Grim glanced around to make sure nobody was watching and opened his beer cabinet. He took out a small keg brought in fresh on goatback this morning and popped the cork. He placed the vase on his desk and poured beer into it, then placed his chin on the table. Grim stared deep into the depths of the amber liquid bubbling in the glass.

"Reveal to me your secrets...." Grim intoned. He looked around guiltily, before dropping a dozen flowers he'd bought from the [Peddler] into it.

—"Fer tha Firmament's sake, would ya' stop that awful racket!" A crotchety voice shouted behind me.

I paused in the middle of a well known dwarven mining song from Snow White, my pickaxe raised up in the air. I hadn't realised I was singing aloud. I smiled sheepishly at Tim, whose bristly moustache twitched in irritation. He grumbled and turned back to his own work. I dusted some gravel out of my beard and resumed swinging my pickaxe, shifting my singing to the copyright free *Drunkard's Prayer* while I worked.

"Heigh-ho, anybody home?"
Bring the pickaxe back, and *swing* *CLANG!!*
"Meat nor drink nor money have I none!"
Bring the pickaxe back, and *swing* *CLANG!!*
"Yet will I be merrrrryyy. Heigh-ho, anybody home?"

I was woken up this morning by Grim, who confiscated my pilsner glass and sent me out mining. I think he wanted me out of the camp while he tried to figure out what to do with the glass. I really hoped I got it back, as it's the only real reminder of home that I had right now. Whistlemop disappeared sometime after the second brawl, and he wasn't there in the morning. I hoped he didn't get dragged into a ditch somewhere. His wagon was gone, so I assumed he travelled on to the next camp.

AN ADVENTURE BREWING

It was pitch black in the mining tunnels, and the only light was from a cage on top of my helmet. It held a small stone that gave off a warm yellow light. Balin simply said it was a *solstone,* as though that was self evident. I'm beginning to think he isn't the best teacher. Solstones were apparently inside every light fixture in the camp, which solved the electricity mystery. I'm probably going to need to ask Doc Opal how they work.

I glanced up at Balin as his slightly shaky arm swung a pickaxe down onto his foot. A couple of hungover curses later and he was back to swinging his pick with a bit more care this time. His handlebar moustache was practically droopy, and he kept bumping into Annie. I turned back to my work after determining nothing more was injured than his pride. Score one for steel-toed boots and padded socks!

"Heigh-ho, anybody home?"
Bring the pickaxe back, and *swing* *CLANG!!*
"Meat nor drink nor money have I none!"
Bring the pickaxe back, and *swing* *CLANG!!*
"Yet will I be merrrryyy. Heigh-ho, anybody home?"

Balin was the winner of last night's drinking competition. That was before the evening devolved into more fighting. First, there were the *purists*, who believed beer should be drunk from a tankard as the ancestors intended. Then there were the *vasists,* who believed my pilsner glass was a gift from the Firmament brought to them by a lucky fool. The vasists won the fist fight, but I'm not sure how I feel about that as *the fool* in their dogma.

We were in the tunnels beneath our camp, and I was finally off of goat doody! I finally felt like a real dwarf! Down in the deep with my companions, seeking the motherlode! A team of dwarves going out on a mining expedition is called a dive, and my dive-team consisted of Tim, Balin, and Annie.

The tunnels were kind of neat. The mine was a single shaft, about four metres tall by four metres wide, that extended for hundreds of metres diagonally into the Erd. That main shaft always had a couple dwarves digging it deeper as minecarts are pushed along tracks hammered into the stone. Speaker John walked along the shaft and 'spoke' to the stone in order to find out where the metal was. Once we knew where to dig, a dive-team of dwarves grabbed some pickaxes and 'dove' down off the main shaft. The physical labour really helped clear the mind. Last night, I finally bonded with my fellow dwarves. We sang awful drinking songs, drank awful beer, and then had an awful night as I held Balin's hair back while he threw up into Tim's helmet. I hope he washed it... All told it was a lot of fun! It reminded me of frosh parties when I was back in college, or some of the benders we used to have at Beavermoose Brewery. I almost got drunk myself, but I just couldn't stomach enough of the Light Brew to really get buzzed. Plus, people kept stealing my glass.

Dwarven society is still really alien to me. The laws – the *Ordinances* – are all quite egalitarian as far as I can tell, and everyone follows a strict code of honour. Crime is nearly non-existent and most of my fellow *Reform* miners are vagrants or committed petty 'crimes' like begging for beer. Dwarves don't really hold grudges or hate people for very long. You have a big fight, knock each other out, and then get shit-faced together until morning. It's hard to stay angry at someone when you spent half the evening holding onto each other while singing *Bawdy Blondebeard*. Speaking of which, dwarves are excellent singers. Whodathunk? Annie edged away from Balin and came up to me while I worked.

"I've got a good collection of ore here, Pete." She murmured, her eyes looking down at her blonde beard. She was surprisingly demure; last night I had seen Wreck stop her from power-bombing another dwarf that had decked Balin. "Can you help me carry it up? I don't think Balin or Tim are really capable right now." I glanced at Balin, who was currently banging the handle of his pickaxe onto the rock wall, and Tim, who had a suspicious fluid dripping out of his helmet and down his back.

"I think you're right about that." I started filling sacks with ore. Tin-ore is heavy, and it's a lot of hard work pulling it up the dive-shaft. I filled two sacks and started hauling with Annie following close behind.

"Did you know Balin before you came to the mine?" Annie asked between laboured breaths.

"No, I was a vagrant before. Honestly, I still don't remember much from before the accident. Watch your head here." I ducked down as the dive tunnel became shoulder height. That's about one metre, or three feet in freedom units.

"You got along pretty well even before your accident." Annie paused, grunting as she lugged her bags through the tight tunnel.

"We were both vagrants, and I think he feels sorry for me."

"Well, he tried to stop you from going into that freschie, but you brushed him off. I think he feels guilty that he didn't just thump you in your fool head."

"Hey!" We both stopped as we shared a gasping laugh. Sweat poured down my face and onto my Garibaldi beard. It was getting pretty dirty, and I looked forward to giving it a wash and wax back at camp. Dwarves care a lot about their beards, and Balin had been gushing about going to a *beardysalon* if we ever went to Minnova.

"So, Annie," I asked, as we resumed our ascension. "How did you end up in the City of Minnova Reform Mine? You don't strike me as a wandering vagrant, or a layabout for that matter." She was silent for a moment, and the only sound was our footsteps echoing in the dark tunnel.

"I was experimenting with a new kind of beer vessel at my father's brewery." She started, haltingly. "I was always bothered that so much of the fizz in our beer was lost, and I wanted to see if a properly sealed and pressurized vessel would help. I made some small-scale models and they worked fine, so I had some full-sized versions custom made."

By my beard! She was a fellow beer snob! I always wondered why I was reborn here. Maybe the Gods sent me to her! Now wasn't the time to ponder that though, as Annie was clearly in pain.

"Did something go wrong?"

"The pressure inside the larger tanks was higher than I accounted for." She paused, her voice cracking. "One of the vessels blew on the brewery floor. Three workers were injured and the blast damaged my father's brewery and the shop next door."

"Dear Gods..."

"A [Judge] found me guilty of negligence, and I was sentenced to work in the mine to pay for the damage to the city streets. My father was required to pay the merchant next door as well as the injured workers. I left the city the next day, and I don't even know if my father was able to keep the brewery." I was pretty certain she was crying, and I really regretted asking. I covertly glanced back to see her wipe her eyes with her beard.

"What will you do?"

"I'm trying to end my indenture early. Now that I have a Blessing, I'll get a Title and make something to turn my family's fortune around. It was my honour, not my father's, that was tarnished. I need to make things right!" She resumed moving forward, steel in her eyes. I could see why Balin liked her. She was smart, strong-hearted, and honourable. A perfect specimen of dwarf. The silky blonde beard helped too.

We walked in companionable silence for a while. When we could hear the sound of minecarts echoing down the dive tunnel, Annie stopped. "Pete, I'm sorry about dumping all of that on you. I actually had a reason for asking you to come with me." She set down her bags and walked up to me in the dark, the light on her helmet nearly blinding me as she looked into my eyes. "You're really a nice guy. Nobody else seems to have noticed, they all think you're a fool." Hey, I resemble that remark!

"Uh, where are you going with this?" I asked, stepping back slightly. Was this what I thought it was?

Annie leaned in closer, whispering now. "I just didn't have the courage, but after last night I decided to go for it." What happened last night!? My mind whirled, trying to recall. "I know that you're just the right dwarf!" Her voice grew firmer.

No, Annie! I'm a – was a – married dwarf! Besides, my best buddy is in love with you!

"Peter, would you-"

Waaaait!!!!

CHAPTER SEVEN
A DWARVEN HANDSHAKE

Moments before.

Annie Goldstone struggled in body and mind as she pulled the bag of ore up the pitch-black dive tunnel. Her conversation with Pete had brought back some bad memories, and she was embarrassed by her tears. Her father never blamed her for the accident, and only told her that no matter what came to pass, he would always love her. Their family had owned that brewery for generations, the recipe for their beer faithfully followed since the First Brew. The fact that they might lose it, simply because one unfilial descendant had decided to tweak the brewing process, would be seen by purists as divine retribution.

Punishment from the ancestors for daring to try and improve upon perfection.

They were wrong! Annie knew it in her bones, and in her heart. Beer could be improved! There was no such thing as something that was completely perfect. Perfection was always in the eyes of the beholder when it came to art, and there was no arguing that beer was an art! The other dwarves at the brewery all claimed she was odd, to think that beer could be better.

She glanced up at Pete and narrowed her eyes. There was another odd dwarf. He said the wrong things, acted the wrong way, and yet with a single vase he completely upended the dogma of a dozen dwarves. Pete's pilsner glass was a revolution in beer drinking technology. She still wasn't sure if it was simply his 'luck of the fool' though. He hadn't made the vase, or even designed it, he simply found it and decided to use it as a glass. The question was... why?

Thoughts of the beer glass brought her mind back to last night, and her cheeks reddened. The image of Balin, his handlebar moustache coated in foam and a look of joy upon his face, was etched in her mind. He was kind and personable, a great dancer, an even better fighter, and had a lovely singing voice. He might be a vagrant, but in her conversations with him she learned he was simply searching for a place to call home. His clan had perished in a monster stampede, and he was now looking for a place to settle down. He'd been begging for food in Minnova when the guards picked him up and dropped him in the Reform Mine. Balin was a hard worker, and apparently an accomplished carpenter. There was a lot of wood in Minnova due to the dungeon, and Balin hoped to use his mining stipend to buy some tools and get work around the city.

After she fought to protect his honour last night, Annie realised something.

She had fallen in love with that handlebar mug. With his jolly laugh and bright emerald eyes.

So, she found herself getting ready to ask his best friend for help courting. If she knew one thing, it was that no dwarf courtship could survive without acceptance from the clan, and right now Pete was the closest thing that Balin had to one.

She cleared her throat as they approached the main tunnel. It was time for action. "Pete, I'm sorry about dumping all of that on you. I actually had a reason that I asked you to come with me."

Annie set down her bags and walked up to Pete, looking him in the eyes. "You're really a nice guy. Nobody else seems to have noticed, they all think you're a fool." Yes, he would surely help her!

"Uh, where are you going with this?" Pete asked, pulling back slightly from the glare of her solstone.

Annie leaned in closer, whispering. She didn't want anyone else to overhear. "I just didn't have the courage, but after last night I decided to go for it." Annie rushed her next few words, her courage failing. "I know that you're just the right dwarf!" Indeed, if it was Pete, Balin would trust him to stand in for a clan member! She was barely able to keep from shouting the rest. "Peter, would you allow me to court Balin?"

"No, you can't!" Pete said nearly simultaneously, holding his hands up.

"What?" Annie asked, shocked.

"What?" Pete replied, looking confused.

Annie couldn't believe it! Why would Pete immediately reject her as a match for Balin? She was under no illusions about herself. She was quite average looking for a dwarf. Her beard was never able to get that full fluff that was the current style, and she was just a little too tall and her nose slightly crooked. However, she took care in her grooming, was smart, Blessed, and came from a good clan. She never would have imagined such immediate and vocal rejection. Why?!

"Peter, would you allow me to court Balin?"

"No, you can't!" I replied desperately. I really didn't want to get mixed up in romance right now. I was still getting over losing my family, and I just wasn't ready for a new relationship.

"What?" Annie asked, her face falling.

"What?" I replied. What did she just say?

"I don't understand!" Annie huffed. "Why not? You should tell me at least that much!"

"Wait, go back a moment. Did you say you want to court Balin?"

"Yes, and you denied it!" Annie placed her hands on her hips. She stepped forward aggressively, her blonde beard shoving against my chest. Wow, Annie was tall. "On what grounds!"

"No grounds, no grounds, I thought you said something else!" I was an idiot! What was I thinking? I was a brain-addled fool with a charisma of nine! Why on Erd would someone confess to me?

"So..." Annie looked confused. "What did you think I said?"

"Nothing!" I quickly changed the subject. "So, Balin eh? Is it the moustache? It's the moustache, right?"

"Among other things." Annie actually blushed! Balin, you lucky dog!

"Well, you can't leave it at that. Tell me what you like about my Balin and then we will decide if you're worthy." I said that last bit in my best big-bad-dad impression, a stern look upon my face. Heh, 'my Balin,' as if I owned him. Why was she involving me with this? I hadn't even done this dad-with-a-shotgun routine on Sammy's first boyfriend. I raised her well and respected her decisions.

Then the floodgates broke. Annie stammered about Balin's beard, his kindness, his wit, and his prowess in a fight. Then she got more determined and talked about his talent, and his possible place in her father's brewery as a barrel maker. Then she described in clear detail the wonder of his strong dwarfly pecs.

"Hooooold it!"

"Yes?" She asked, pausing in her breathy description of 'corded muscle that shines like mithril.'

"Yeeesss..." I stopped to think for a moment. This was actually a really good opportunity if I played my cards right. Annie was from a well-established family in Minnova. Not to mention the fact that her father owned a brewery. Ok, possibly owned a brewery. It was still the first real chance I had to get into the beer breweries of Minnova, and I wanted in! I knew from experience that getting established was as much luck as perseverance, and I wasn't going to waste this opportunity! Especially when provided on a blonde-bearded platter! "I'm willing to help you court Balin... under one condition."

"What condition?" Annie asked, her voice businesslike. "I swear on my honour that I will fulfil any reasonable request."

"I want a recommendation to your father's brewery when we all get out of here." I said firmly. "For Balin and I. You said you want him to work there? Well, I want to work there too."

"Why? You haven't exactly hidden your dislike for beer..."

"It's my dislike for the current True Brew. There's a lot of room for improvement, and I want to help. I think you're on the right track with the pressure vessel, and I may have some ideas there."

"You..." Annie paused, her face twisting into a strange expression. "That – I – You... Were you a brewer? I thought you forgot everything."

"I... remember some things." It wasn't a lie; I remembered most things too. "I remember that I love beer, but not this beer."

"The Two Brews are all there are... all there have been since Mordag brewed the First Brew." Annie said, confused. "Some tinker, but never change."

"Well, I've seen others." I said, my eyes gleaming. "My tongue has beheld the tart of sours and the creams of stout."

"You're crazy!" Annie said, stepping back.

"Crazy for beer! Are you in or not?" Annie stopped and thought for a long moment. She ran her fingers through her beard and glanced down at me a few times before finally coming to a decision. "Fine, but I reserve the right to fire you for foolishness."

"I get a minimum of two months and at least a single full brew."

"Deal." Annie spat in her hand, grabbed her beard and held it up to me. Ewwwwww, what? She watched me expectantly and I realised she was waiting for me. Do I *have* to?

I spat in my hand and grasped my beard. Annie grabbed my hand in hers and said in a reverent tone, "Our Beards Are Joined, Our Words Are One."

"Our Beards Are Joined, Our Words Are One." I repeated along, feeling the spit squelch between our fingers. Yuck. She let go of my hand and I surreptitiously wiped the spit off on my pants.

"What now?" I asked.

"Can you bring Balin to the knoll behind the camp tonight after dinner?"

"Are you going to kill it? The gnoll, I mean."

"What?"

Sigh. You'd think *Dungeons and Dragons* puns would land in a fantasy world. "Fine... I can do it."

"I plan to tell him my desire to court him, as well as the benefits I can bring. Could you please discuss it with him afterwards?"

"Oh, I'm sure he'll give it some serious thought." I smirked, thinking about the longing looks he'd sent her way. Balin was going to freak!

The two of us nodded at each other and walked into the main tunnel. A grumble of dwarves was pushing a cart up the tunnel, and we chucked our bags inside. That's right, I decided to start referring to a group of dwarves as a grumble, since that was the sound they inevitably made. The trio grunted at the added weight and resumed their trek upwards.

"Want to grab a sandwich?" Annie asked.

"Absolutely."

We followed behind the cart, ascending upwards to an eternally starry sky. My future looked bright.

CHAPTER EIGHT
THE ELEMENTS

It's been a couple of days since Balin and Annie got together. Balin nearly fainted when Annie talked to him, and I think my hand propping him up was the only thing that kept him from keeling over. He'd flapped his mouth a few times and I'd pulled him away before he could go all in without consideration first.

Apparently, that was part of my 'job' as a stand-in for Balin's clan.

He and I had chatted about Annie's proposal, alongside the deal I had arranged with her. His eyes had grown wide at that, and he'd congratulated me on the good deal. Apparently he was looking for carpentry work in Minnova before he was tossed into the Reform Mine. He never imagined he would get a romantic relationship AND a job out of his stay.

So they had talked, and now the whole mine knew they were a thing. I was surprised to learn just how well-liked Annie and Balin were in the camp. I'd been so focused on my own predicament that I hadn't really spent much time paying attention to other things. Balin had one of those outgoing personalities that did so well in an organised environment. Like the popular kid at school or that one guy in the office. You know the one, who makes stupid jokes that for some reason everybody laughs at, and always seems to cross certain social boundaries but never gets in trouble? Yeah, screw that guy. Balin was like that, but cool.

Which brought me to my current predicament.

"From the top, Peter."

"My name is Peter Samson. I'm 48 years old."

"Where are you from?"

The Okanagan, Canada, British Columbia, the year 2023. Instead, I replied, "I don't remember."

"Where are you now?"

"The City of Minnova Reform Mine, in the country of Crack."

"What year is it?"

"Uh... I forgot." Damnit Balin, did we not even go over the year?

"What day is it?" That's an easy one!

"Yearday." I smiled, like a child finding the correct answer on a test. The days were named after the Gods here, just like home! It went: Tiday, Arday, Yearday, Archday, Solday, Lunday, Barday, Miday.

Doc Opal sighed as she removed her glasses and massaged the bridge of her nose. Her beard style was somewhat different from the other dwarves – close-cropped with a faintly pointy moustache. It was also shock white, which I guessed was an effect of age or stress. She was the first dwarf I'd seen with earrings, a large golden bangle hanging from her left earlobe.

We were seated at a table in the mess hall. The rest of the dwarves were all out working, and I was getting tutored. There were no medical emergencies that required Opal's attention, and she decided to put some serious effort into my 're-education.' Apparently, word had come down from administration that since this 'Peter' trouble-maker had been injured while on the job, he needed to be properly taught at the camp's expense. There weren't any Titled [Hypnotists] in the city, so it fell on Doc Opal.

We started on the basics, like numbers, letters, times and days of the week. I can't believe Balin and I never covered those, but I had more important concerns at the time, like beer. Each day was thirty-two hours, each hour was sixty-four minutes, and each minute was sixty-four seconds. Most things in Erd seemed to be based off of the Gods, of which there were eight. So eight days of the week, an alphabet with thirty-two letters, et-cetera.

This was where I discovered that I wasn't speaking English. The dwarven runic alphabet was *nothing* like our letter system, and it gave me a moment of cognitive dissonance as I realised I was reading the runes, but wasn't really *reading* them. It was more like I could understand the meaning in my head without actually comprehending each letter, and I was doing the same with speech. It was likely a side effect of my [Otherworlder] Milestone. Speaking of Milestones, my stats had changed a bit after the past few days. My charisma went up to ten after my first few lessons with Opal. I guess the combination of my deal with Annie and my lessons have paid off! I'm finally an averagely charismatic dwarf, which isn't saying much.

"What can you tell me about the Fundamental Elements?" Doc Opal continued, leafing through some papers.

"Like water, earth, fire, and air?" I asked, confused. Did they have those here too?

"What? No, why on Erd would fire or water be an element? I mean the Fundamental Elements of creation."

"Sooo atoms?"

"Adams?" Opal shifted through her notes. "We don't have an Adam in the camp. Is that someone from your past?"

"No, never mind. What are the elements?" I sighed inwardly.

"They are Matter, Aether, Magic, and Nether."

"They are Matter, Aether, Magic, and ma-mag-magic?!" I gaped. Wait, magic was real here?! How had nobody told me that yet!?

"And Nether." Opal frowned. Screw nethers! Well, I mean, yes that's what they're for, but also screw nether! I wanted to hear more about magic!

"Wait! Magic! Is that how the solstones work? I thought it was just weird physics!"

"Yes. I can't believe you've forgotten so much. Any runestone, such a solstone, is infused with a small amount of Godly energy, the Elements are one such example. They are as follows."

Opal placed her hand over her heart and recited a verse.

> "Tiara of Matter is all that has form,
> Aaron of Aether the heart of the storm.
> Archis of Magic is all that's unseen,
> And Yearn of Nether is all in between."

We spent the next hour going over the Elemental Gods of the

Firmament. They represented all the 'stuff' that made the Firmament actually exist. I already knew Tiara, but the rest were new.

Tiara as Goddess of Matter was the God of everything physical. Rock, stone, metal, if you could touch it, it *matter*ed. Nyuck. Her Blessing gave your body and everything you carried [Strength of All].

Aaron was the God of Aether, which was anything you could feel but not 'touch.' That's air, fire, all gasses, smoke – I could go on. His Blessing granted [Move in Aether], for a slow fall or glide, or faster swimming – apparently water was a bit matter *and* aether. Aaron also gave the ability to [Sense Deals], which must make shopping fun. Poor guy, it had to suck being the *gassy* God.

Yearn was the Goddess of Nether. I was a bit fuzzy on her, and she sounded sketchy as hell. She was everything that 'is-but-isn't' as well as 'nothingness'? Fundamental forces like gravity, atomic attraction, magnets and so on might fit the bill. I assume particles still exist, but Doc Opal didn't know what I was talking about when I tried to discuss it. Her Blessings were [Nothingness] and [Sense Emotions].

Finally, there was Archis, the God of Magic – OMG magic. His Blessing gave [Manasight] and [Sense Secrets]. I liked both of those, so I was aiming for his Blessing. Apparently, it was *required* to use magic effectively. Doc Opal gave me a very technical explanation of magic that I understood none of. I did nod along while imagining shooting fireballs and lightning bolts, though.

"How would I go about getting a Blessing, Doctor? Especially from Archis!"

"Well, there are several different ways to do that, but they all have the same basic idea. Thank you, Bran." Opal smiled as Bran walked over and presented her with an amazing piece of cake. It was some kind of white fluffy thing with whipped cream on it, and it looked sooo delicious and moist. I'd been obsessing over beer since I got here, but that's because alcohol was my life for so long. While the food has been healthy and filling, I was still a modern man; I wanted my junk food dammit. Did pretzels or peanuts exist here? I could totally make beer and pretzels a thing.

Opal continued. "The first thing you need to do is gain the attention of a God."

"Gain a *God's* attention?" I asked, my eyes focusing on her fork as she gently carved into the slice of cake.

"Yes, scholars are divided on the best way to do that." Opal said, her eyes closed as she *mmm'd* slightly around a mouthful. Damn, Opal! You're really selling that cake! "Some say it's by luck, others by hard work, others by ingenuity. One thing that everyone can agree on is that you must complete some great work within the God's portfolio. Make sure you get a Blessing you want though, since you can only have two!"

"Is that why a lot of miners get Tiara's Blessing?"

"Yes, spend a lot of time diligently working with rock and stone and you'll earn Tiara's Blessing. Similarly, sailors often get Aaron's Blessings, students gain Archis's, and great lovers and friends gain Yearn's."

Interesting. Not as interesting as the cake that Doc Opal was devouring, but interesting nonetheless. It looked like I needed to go to school or perhaps discover some kind of new magic if I wanted Archis's Blessing. Could my knowledge as someone from another universe help? I wonder if that's why I could earn cakes – *dammit* – earn *Blessings*, more easily.

"How important are Blessings?" I asked, as Opal started thumbing crumbs off the plate into her mouth. I could practically taste the cream, and I wiped a speck of drool off my moustache.

"Very important. Most careers won't accept you without at least one. They're seen as a rite of passage to adulthood in society. We can live up to five hundred and twelve years after all. If you can't earn a Blessing in all that time, what have you been doing?"

That made sense. If a Blessing was a clear way of indicating a person's hard work, then you'd definitely need one for any kind of advancement. It was kind of like a college degree from Earth. Wait...

"Five *HUNDRED* and twelve *years*!?"

"Yes?" Opal said, her eyes widening as I caught her licking the plate clean. She blushed and coughed as she put the plate down. "Barring disease or a monster attack, the average dwarf will live to be over five hundred years old. Some greybeards are seven hundred and sixty-eight or older. I'm three-hundred ninety-eight years old myself."

Hundreds of years!! I was only forty-eight... that meant... carry the one... Four hundred years?!

I was going to live four-hundred and sixty-four more years, on *average*!?

"How long do humans live?" I had to know, was this normal?

"An odd question. Humans and beast-kin live to be around one-hundred twenty years old, though they are more likely to fall to disease. They are also more numerous. Elves live to be around four-thousand. Gnomes are about the same as dwarves. Only the dragons are infinite." Hey cool, there are dragons! Also beastfolk, humans, gnomes, and elves.

All this talk about death made me think back to my own. I'm finally getting over the loss of my family. My wife and I were married for over twenty years, and in all that time we had our ups and downs. It was especially hard when Samantha was born. We barely had any time for *us* in between the business and the baby. We'd go a whole week with barely a word other than *your turn*. The whole 'reincarnated as a dwarf' thing was so unreal that I've emotionally decoupled fairly easily. This was a new world, and I'm a new dwarf. I was going to need to forge new relationships, and that would likely include a new family. Balin's my family for now, and Annie will be soon, I guess. Speaking of which, in all the fiction stories I've read, there should have been a hot elf babe by now. One with a pencil moustache and goatee...

Dammit.

"Let's talk about the Fundamentals of Life, next" Opal said, nodding to Bran as he came to collect the plate. She smiled sweetly at him, and brushed a few crumbs from her beard. "Delicious as always Bran."

"Thank you, Opal. I tried something new with the batter." Bran's eyes crinkled at the compliment.

"Well, whatever you did, the cake was especially fluffy today."

The two shared a companionable silence over the empty plate for a moment. I coughed. Now that I knew a bit more about Dwarves, I recognized the incredible number of romantic entanglements in this camp. It's like I died and reincarnated into an episode of *Dwarves of*

Our Lives. Nyuck. Bran walked back to the kitchen and Opal turned to me.

"Where was I? The Fundamentals of Life – " Opal was interrupted as a grumble of dwarves made their way into the mess hall. They clinked and clattered as they deposited their equipment, and a cloud of dust was given off as they grabbed sandwiches and beers. Opal frowned. "Let's finish this outside. Come join me for a walk." She stood up and made to leave. I followed her, nodding to a few of the dwarves as we passed by. They nodded back, and I even got a few smiles; indeed, a ten charisma was where it's at. I didn't see Balin or Annie, so I guessed they must still be in the mine, on a dive perhaps.

"Where are we headed?" I asked as we walked down the road.

"Over there." Opal pointed to a small ridge just outside of the camp. "We're going to finish talking about the Fundamentals, but I want to show you the city too, and more importantly, the Dungeon... "

CHAPTER NINE
GREENTREE DUNGEON

I walked with Doc Opal up the rise and looked down over the cavern. We were located fairly high and close to the outer edge, and behind us I could see the side of the enormous cave reaching up into the 'sky' above us. Great pillars dotted the landscape here and there and a faint purple glow emanated from the centre of the cavern where the city stood. I think I really love my new home here. It's... beautiful in a way that's hard to describe. The combination of the purple light and the flowing bands and spots of luminous moss was magical. Faint spores filled the air as well, slightly sparkling. The combined effect was breathtaking.

Doc Opal let me marvel for a while before catching my attention and pointing down towards the city. I could make out dozens if not hundreds of carriages making their way in and out of the main gates. We were too far away to make out any real details, but it was certainly bustling!

"That there is the city of Minnova. We are one of many cities in the caverns of Crack. Our population is only matched by the capital city of Kinshasa."

"Soo, I've been wondering what that means. Why Crack?" I turned a distracted ear her way, my eyes still taking in the wonders of the cavern stretching out below us. Were those giant mushrooms off to the right of the city walls?

"The Great Crack is a massive rent in the continent of North

Erden. It was formed aeons ago by a war between the first race, the dragons, and the Gods."

"A war? With the Gods? How did that work?" I was paying full attention now.

"Poorly," Opal said with a grimace.

"What happened?"

"In their arrogance, the dragons were smote down from the sky. Their descent to Erd created the Great Crack, which now contains the majority of the dwarven race on this continent. Modern dragons are mere shadows of their former selves; their children are masters of magic, but nothing like they once were. They're a long-lived race, but none from that time still exist. They have all died, or secluded themselves away from all memory."

We sat in silence for a moment and looked down on the beauty of the place. A few structures set seemingly at random in the cavern below denoted the location of other small settlements and mining camps. I could barely make out a few wagons travelling between them. I wonder what happened to Whistlemop?

"What about that shadowy place? Is it beyond our borders? Must I never go there?" I pointed to the mushrooms I spotted earlier. There was a massive grove of them, and I could see some actual trees poking out as well. There were a lot of people on the outer edge of the grove, yet it gave off a forbidding feeling. It also sloped downwards, like it was going deeper into the Erd. The trees looked to be... yew maybe? They had that middling tall but broad look that I would associate with a yew or monkeypod.

"Where? No." Opal laughed. "That's what I wanted to show you. It's the breadbasket of Minnova, Greentree Dungeon."

I nodded. "Balin mentioned it before. What *is* a dungeon?"

"They are places of strong mana that the Gods used as lynchpins to create the world. All of the Fundamental Elements are strong there, as are the Fundamentals of Life. What we call monsters are amalgamations of life and the elements that are born spontaneously in those places. People are drawn to dungeons for riches, for Blessings, for Milestones, and to keep the monster populations down."

"You mentioned that before, what are the Fundamentals of Life? Are they Gods too?" I continued to watch the dungeon. Was it anything like a fantasy dungeon, with bosses and mazes and whatnot? If my [Otherworlder] Milestone was translating properly, that seemed likely.

"Indeed," Opal answered, before she recited another verse.

> "Solen of light brings all chaos to bear
> Lunara of night brings the order we share
> Midna of spirit gives thought to our whims,
> Barck gives us spark and grants life to our limbs."

That solved one mystery – solstones were named after Solen and infused with his Fundamental of chaos and light. On the flip side, Lunara was order, which was dark. I argued with Opal about that one – It offended my fantasy sensibilities that the God of Chaos was the 'God of Light,' and the Goddess of Order was the 'Goddess of Night.' Chaos and dark were bad, and light and order were good, so order should be light, right? No fantasy pantheon was complete without a good ol' God of light-smiting! Opal disagreed.

"Chaos is not inherently evil, although pure chaos can be seen as such. If any God has a portfolio that could be described as 'evil' it would be Yearn of Nether, though she is also Yearn of Love. You see, light is the culmination of freedom. Nothing can truly contain light, and it goes where it will. Darkness is the still water of creation, an ever-present thing that fills our lives without thinking about it. Law is much the same."

"Okay, I understand it, I just don't like it. Next question. I noticed that each God gives two Abilities with their Blessing, and I heard each of the Gods is tied to a single aspect of civilization. Like Tiara and possessions. What about those?"

Opal nodded. "You are correct. Each God represents an Element or a Fundamental, but also a Pillar of civilization. All together the Elements, Fundamentals, and Pillars form the Firmament. However, unlike the Elements or the Fundamentals, the Pillars have actually changed over time to match the values and morals of the world."

"What are the Pillars now?"

"Taira is Possession, Aaron is Exchange, Archis is Knowledge,

Yearn is Relationships, Solen is Freedom, Lunara is Law, Midna is Communication, and Barck is Innovation."

While she spoke, there was a commotion down near the dungeon. I swear it was my imagination but I thought I heard... roaring? It was really hard to see clearly from this far away. "No fancy poem for the Pillars?" I said distractedly. Was that mushroom the size of an elephant... moving?

Opal sighed. "No. They are often seen as secondary since they contain an aspect of mortality. It *is* usually easier to earn a Blessing through appealing to a God's Pillar though." She paused. "Pete... are you paying attention?"

"Ahhhh!!!" I shouted, pointing.

"What?!" Opal whirled to peer in the direction I was looking.

"There's a giant mushroom thing!" As we watched, the mushroom waded into the crowd outside the dungeon and tiny figures were tossed like ragdolls. Then there was a flash of light and a *BOOM!!* that we heard all the way to where we were. An enormous fireball lit up the side of the mushroom and it reared back, smoking (OMG, magic). There was another flash of light and the top half of the mushroom fell off, bisected. The mushroom continued to struggle but was quickly swarmed over by little dots.

"A mushfolk," said Opal. "A big one. They are one of the primary monsters on the outer edge of Greentree. You can't see it from here, but the dungeon goes deep into the ground. There's an entirely different world down there, with enough aether to form lakes and a sky."

"Are there lots of monsters like that?" I shivered. That thing was *huge*!

"Not really, no. Most mushfolk are quite small and are mostly dangerous in large groups. The real danger is when you get deeper into the dungeon. That's when some of the more vicious creatures begin to appear."

"Like killer cabbages and peashooters?"

"Among others. I'm glad to see Balin wasn't completely remiss in your education." In the distance, smoke rose from the fallen mushfolk. Opal frowned. "Large mushfolk like that are rare. They're a defensive response from the dungeon. I suspect the council will limit expeditions for a while."

"Is that bad?"

"We get most of our fruit and vegetables from the dungeon. We may need to start importing goods from the human lands or other dungeons, and Titled [Porters] are expensive." She noticed my mouth opening and cut me off. "[Porter] is a Title that grants the ability to carry goods long distance without spoilage."

"So, what do the Blessings of Solen and Lunara give?" I asked, bringing us back to our original conversation. There didn't seem to be much left to see down by the dungeon.

"Solen's Blessing grants [Darksight] and [Dangersense] – "

"Wait, I thought Solen was *light*, why does he let you see through *darkness*?" I interrupted. Opal tutted.

"He grants your eyes an inner light, now stop interrupting and listen."

"Yes, mom."

"I'm not your mother, Peter. I refuse to believe you are *that* addled. Where was I... Lunara's Blessing grants [Shadowcloak] and [Sense Motive]."

"Those sound neat. How about Midna and Barck?"

"I have Barck's Blessing myself." Opal smiled. "I received it after several years of apprenticeship to another Doctor. Barck is the God of life and living things. The grass, the harvest, your body, that mushfolk. All of them contain the *spark*. He is also the God of innovation, because to live is to grow and change. His Blessing grants [Regeneration] and [Good Luck]."

"So, he's the one responsible for food and technology?" At last! Someone to blame for the shitty beer! That's right Barck, you heard me! I don't care if it's blasphemy! As the God of Innovation, you should be ashamed!

"Sort of. You see, after the Gods made everything in Erd, they stopped creating new things; they let us mortals shape the world."

"Why is that?"

"Erd was a gift to us, the children of creation. The Gods gave us many gifts; from life, to thought, to Blessings and Titles. However, the Gods say the most important gift they ever gave us was choice. Whenever you receive a Blessing, you always have a choice to receive it or not, and whenever you receive a Milestone, Specialisation, or Title there are always a few choices."

"So... Barck didn't invent apple pie, but he made apples and people made it into pie?"

"That's about right." Opal agreed. Ok Barck, maybe you're off the hook. Looks like it's the dwarves' hidebound traditionalism limiting their beer technology. Down below us, bits and pieces of the mushfolk were being carted away, and a brightly coloured procession was coming out from the city. I pointed at it.

"What's that?"

Opal peered down. "It looks like the Lord of Minnova has come to see the event. Likely to determine if there's a need to lock down the dungeon for a while."

We talked about the Lord for a while, and I was unsurprised to learn that dwarves had a feudal society with a King and everything. However, there's an added complication since there's an actual *God* of law. A lot of the abuses that cropped up back in Earth's feudal society simply didn't happen here. A truly corrupt noble would never be able to hold onto a Blessing of Law and would be unable to compete with a Lord that could. Additionally, there were Titled Paladins whose whole gig was to find those that abused the law and smite them with holy darkness – yay, smiting! I could only imagine a dwarf in goth leather with black eye shadow and spiky plate mail, holding a whip and spanking someone while shouting 'Repent Harder!' Heh. We watched the procession approach the group by the mushfolk and then there was a general milling about. I turned back to Opal.

"You mentioned Midna?"

"Yes, she's the Goddess of *Spirit*. Spirit moves the spark."

"Something like mind and thought?"

"Exactly. Many animals have spirit, as do all the mortal races. Few plants do, and fewer beings of matter or aether."

"Hold on, beings of matter?"

"Yes, such as golems or summons." Now there was some sweet fantasy! Would I be able to summon golems when I learned magic? Ooooh! Or an alcohol elemental! Because I'm learning it, magic. If I got to choose, then I was turning all the Gods down until I got Archis's

Blessing. I'm giving you all the middle finger with my soul right now Gods! Except you, Archie. Blessing, please. I was distracted, and barely caught the end of what Opal was saying.

"Midna's Blessing grants [Soulsight] and [Truespeech]."

"What? Who, where? Why [Truespeech]?"

"As I said," Opal sighed, "Midna is the Goddess of Spirit and Communication, and it is by her gift of thought that the races created writing and words."

"Do the different races have different writing then?"

"Yes, though gnomish is mostly a dead language now, and the beastfolk largely speak the human tongue."

"Why is that? Assimilation?"

Opal paused and looked at me askance. "Every time I think you are a fool you reveal deeper intelligence and learning. I'm surprised you even know that word, and I grow curiouser and curiouser about your past. You are correct. The gnomes have been living with the dwarves for so long they adopted our language as their own. The beastfolk are enslaved by the humans, and their language only lives on in their own far-flung tribes."

"Ugh, slavery is a thing? I thought Solen was the God of Freedom?"

"Freedom has no meaning in a world without bondage and vice versa. He was once Solen of Service, for in our earliest days service to one's tribe, community, or family was more important than freedom. The root of bondage is *bonds,* is it not?"

"I still don't like it, *again*." I frowned.

"Ah, but then we would be discussing philosophy, not history." Opal smiled. "I'm not being paid for that. Slavery is illegal in dwarven lands either way, and perhaps one day it too will be history."

We finished the lesson by talking about Titles and where people learned magic. Eventually, Opal looked at her pocket watch and made noises about heading back. I stretched, yawned, and got a notification.

Bing!

Stat Increased: [Intelligence]!

Your intelligence has increased by 1! New intelligence is 11! Score!

As we made our way down the ridge, a dwarf from the camp came running up to us. I didn't know his name, but I recognized him as a fellow member of the chain-gang.

"Doctor!" He was panting as he ran up to us.

"What is it?" Opal came to attention, her gaze growing professional.

"Grim needs ya right away. You too, Pete! All 'ands down to tha mine!"

"What's wrong?" I asked, as we began running.

"There's been an accident, a rockslide. Balin's been trapped!"

I ran harder.

CHAPTER TEN
MINER ACCIDENT

We ran to the tunnels as fast as possible. Doc Opal quickly peeled off ahead; I guess she has a higher agility stat. I gasped at the dwarf running beside me between panting breaths.

"What happened?"

"Balin got sloppy. He was wantin' to finish 'is indenture quicker now tha' Annie's in the picture. He, Annie, and Wreck dug too deep on a dive withou' waitin' fer proper mine supports. He shouted about finding a freschie, and we all came ta see, but then there was a rumblin'."

"Dear Gods." I whispered, dreading what came next.

"Annie and Wreck were with 'im. He pushed tha two of 'em outta the way when tha 'ole roof caved in. He's trapped in a damn freschie!"

That was bad. It was beyond dwarven-beer bad and into beard-caught-in-a-drill press levels of bad. Walking into a freschie, or newly opened cavern, was what had nearly killed me. I'd barely been inside for a few moments, and Balin was stuck in one.

There was a good chance he was dead. I ran harder... damn stubby legs!

We pounded down the main shaft, a couple other dwarves joining us as we ran. The entire mine was rushing to help, and there was soon a pack of us. I grabbed an abandoned minecart as we passed by.

"Everyone push!" First one, then two, then the rest understood my meaning and we pushed the minecart up to speed. The main shaft

AN ADVENTURE BREWING

stretched nearly a kilometre and the current dives were down near the bottom. We needed a vehicle or we'd all arrive too tired to help. "Now, jump!" With a shout, the entire grumble of dwarves leaped into the minecart. One dwarf was slightly too slow and didn't quite manage to make it on. Someone, Tim I realised, reached out and grabbed his beard, dragging him behind. We rocketed down the passage, the unfortunate dwarf kiting behind us and swearing at the top of his lungs.

"We're comin' up on tha end!" The dwarf that had fetched me shouted. "Every dwarf brace fer impact!" He grabbed the brakes and sparks flew as the minecart came to a screeching stop.

With an ear-shattering *BANG!!!* the minecart hit the blocks denoting the end of the tracks. Dwarves were catapulted into the tunnel with a bevy of expletives and shouts of "By Barck's Beard!" And "Solen's Socks!"

Why socks?

I rolled to a stop, my ego bruised more than my body. There's that dwarven vitality again! Up ahead there was a commotion down a dive tunnel, and we ran down it to see Annie, Wreck, and a few other dwarves hammering their picks on stone and desperately moving rubble. A few dwarves hung from the ceiling, manoeuvring large wooden blocks in to act as supports. They wore something more closely resembling leather overalls than the leather armour I was used to. The front pockets were full of tools and the overalls hooked into ropes strung along the top of the tunnel.

Annie saw us approaching, and her pickaxe stopped mid-swing. Her eyes weren't filled with tears, though there was a tinge of panic in them. She was 100 percent desperate, serious efficiency.

"Pete!" She called as we sprinted over.

"How long has he been in there?" I went to grab a pickaxe and Annie stopped me.

"Nearly ten minutes! Go help Wreck!" Wreck was pulling rubble off of the cave-in as fast as possible, her beard glistening with tears. Our grumble fell in beside Wreck and soon a daisy-chain was passing stone from dwarf to dwarf out to the minecarts. We worked in silence, the only sound the occasional orders from Grim, who arrived a few minutes after I did.

Wreck muttered beside me. "It's all my fault..."

"What are you talking about?" I asked, grunting as she passed me an especially heavy piece of granite.

"Balin and Annie were talking about their plans after the mine. I told them their best bet for early release was to find a gem cache or new vein. Speaker John can find veins pretty easy, but he can't see freshies, so they're the best bet for striking it big. Balin and Annie were so excited by the idea that we dug at random, pushed too hard, dug too deep, went too fast..." Fresh tears began to run down her cheeks. "If he dies it'll be all my fault... Oh, Annie."

"Stop it, Wreck!" I snapped at her. "It's not your fault! It was an accident, and he's not dead yet!" Wreck nodded at me with sunken eyes.

Grim yelled out a change in line. The fresh dwarves, myself included, were moved up front to the cave-in and began hammering on the rubble with picks. Wreck was shifted to the back of the line, her hands ragged. "Go see Doc Opal, you can't work like that." I told her. She nodded blankly at me. Not good. I'd seen a friend in shock once after a bad lacrosse accident and she had all the hallmarks of it.

"Doc Opal!" I called, waving her over. "We need you." Opal ushered Wreck away with soothing words. I redoubled my efforts, now first in line.

Balin was my best friend here in Erd, and he was the closest thing I had to family. He cared for me from the moment I came here, full of patience and kindness. We were going to go to the brewery together and I was going to show him the wonders of craft beer. A stone slipped and landed on my foot, but I barely noticed as I grabbed it and passed it to the next dwarf in line. After a few minutes I could feel my stamina bottoming out. My leather gloves began to fray from the sharp rocks, and my fingers were bleeding. I gritted my teeth and paced myself, falling into a familiar rhythm. I played lacrosse and rugby in high-school, and I learned a lot of mental tricks to keep going even when exhausted. A game of rugby lasts over an hour, and your legs and back are burning by the end of it. I bent my knees and put my head down like I was back in a scrum, and began to *heave* I put all my willpower, all of my focus into it. The chaos around me became nothing more than a dark blur as I struck stone and passed it back.

Strike and pass.

Strike and pass. Someone was hitting my shoulder but I ignored them.

Strike and pass. I'm coming buddy.

Strike and pass.

That was when I saw a bright blue light and there was a *Bing!*

Blessing Granted: [Tiara]!

Your hard work and effort for the sake of a friend have gained the notice of Tiara.
As you move the earth, the earth now moves with you.
If you receive Tiara's Blessing your body and possessions will gain the **[Strength of All]**.

Do you accept?
Yes/No

Just a few minutes ago I had sworn to never accept any Blessing before I received Archis's. I didn't even know how Tiara's Blessing would interact with magic. I didn't care. I could feel my body beginning to flag. I needed that [Strength of All]. I mentally clicked on 'yes.'

Blessing Received: [Tiara]!
You have accepted the Blessing of Tiara!
You have received the Blessings **[Strength of All: Self]** *and* **[Strength of All: Held]**!

Strength plus 2! Your new strength is 14!
Vitality plus 2! Your new vitality is 14!

A faint light erupted from my skin and I felt my muscles shift. There was shouting around me, but I didn't care; I felt like I could take on the world! Suddenly there was another *Bing!* and a second notification popped up.

New Quest: A Friend in Need!
A friend needs your help. Will you rush to their aid?

This is a timed quest.
Time remaining: 6 minutes.

Reward: +0.2 Strength

<u>Do you accept?</u>
Yes / No

What on Erd was this goatshit? A quest? Nobody mentioned *quests*!? Did that mean Balin had less than six minutes left? Did that mean he was *ALIVE*?! I mentally clicked on *Yes*, and a timer appeared at the edge of my vision and began ticking down. I clenched my fists and felt the power coursing through me. I shrugged off a hand on my shoulder. Grim shouted something, but I didn't care. I pushed him aside and stepped onto the pile of stone keeping me from my brother. I dug my hand into the rubble and barely felt the sharp stones. My breath came easier as I dug in my feet and *heaved,* ripping a small boulder out from the wall of stone without the aid of my pick.

There were shouts of alarm as the entire pile shifted, but I ignored them. My gloves felt more like gauntlets than leather, and my fatigue was *gone*. The line couldn't keep up, and three dwarves quickly took up places behind me. The silence was broken as the entire grumble of miners began a chanting refrain to the rhythm of the work. Their voices echoed down the flickering tunnel in a mesmerising bass tone.

> Down in the deep,
> Tiara's Keep,
> No dwarf to ever find.
> Hear now the stone,
> Rumble and groan,
> Shift and crack and grind.
> Dive in the dark,
> Killing your spark,
> Riches upon your mind.
> Be ever bold,
> Silver and gold,
> Treasure to be mined.

Down in the deep,
Tiara's Keep,
No dwarf to ever find.
Hear now the stone,
Rumble and groan,
Shift and crack and grind.
Beg to the Gods,
You sorry sods.
The luck you seek is blind.
Now strike your pick,
Now make it stick,
No dwarf left behind.
Down in the deep,
Tiara's Keep,
No dwarf to ever find.
Hear now the stone,
Rumble and groan,
Shift and crack and grind.
Strike! Heave!
Strike! Cleave!
Strike! Heave!
Strike! Cleave!

With a crash, a section of stone fell away, revealing a small portal into the darkness. There was a cheer before Grim instantly hushed the crowd.

"Balin!" I shouted into the darkness. Stale air hit my face, but it felt wet and breathable. The timer on my quest still read two minutes. Did we make it in time? I listened with desperate hope.

Silence was my only reply.

CHAPTER ELEVEN
THE OATH

I stood on the rubble, peering into a pitch-black hole. I prayed to the Gods and looked at the timer. It was still ticking down those two minutes. I tried calling again. "Balin! Can you hear me!"

"Pete?" A hushed voice croaked. Balin was alive! "Yer not me head playin' tricks?"

"We're comin' Balin!" I began to pull stones away from the hole, taking care not to collapse it inwards.

"Are Annie an' Wreck safe?" Balin's voice was weak, too weak.

"They're fine. You're the only one in danger right now. Are you okay?"

"My leg is trapped. I can hear water. I think this is a river shaft." Balin coughed. "I can breathe, but it hurts to move." Now Annie and Wreck were beside me, helping pull stones aside. The dwarves in overalls set up supports to ensure the pile didn't collapse. In a few moments Balin's head came into view. His face was slick with sweat. Annie went to grab him, but Doc Opal shoved her aside and took charge.

"Are you hurt?" She asked.

"The rocks landed on my leg. I'm pinned." Balin groaned. "I could feel it bleedin, but not anymore."

"Then your femoral artery isn't punctured, or you'd already be dead." Opal said. "I need him clear, and we will probably need a [Healer]. Grim?"

"I already sent for him." Grim elbowed into the group.

"Good. I can buy some time. We can't move you yet, Balin. This is going to hurt, but you're strong."

"Aye," Balin said. Opal placed a small stone on his head and there was a green flash. Balin whimpered, but his face got some colour back. There was a *Bing!* and the timer in my vision vanished as another blue box appeared.

Quest Complete: A Friend in Need!
You did it! Good job!
Gained 0.2 strength. Your new strength is 14.2

I mentally shoved it aside; I didn't have time for notifications right now. Opal called over her shoulder, "I only have enough sparkstones to last five minutes. Where's that [Healer], Grim?"

"I used a commstone! They should be here soon!" Grim replied.

Minutes ticked by, with Opal continuing to press sparkstones to Balin's head whenever he grew listless.

Then with a resounding *crack* and a blinding flash, two figures appeared in the tunnel.

One had a long braided white beard with a series of knots and beads in it. He was completely bald and wore a white robe with gold filigree. He adjusted a pair of silver glasses on his nose as he blinked in the bright light of the tunnel.

"Where's the patient?" he said with a quavering voice.

"Over here, Healer Bastion!" Opal motioned. He stumbled up the pile and I reached over to give him a hand. He gave me an appreciative nod and bent over Balin.

"Who's in charge here?" asked the other dwarf. She wore the dark leather armour I'd come to expect from dwarves, but she had a leather skirt! It was the first skirt I'd seen; most of the miners preferred the protection of pants. You'd think skirts would look weird on dwarves, but it fit quite nicely with the rest of the outfit. A single pauldron made of greenish glass hung over her left shoulder. She had a braided grey ponytail and a pleated beard; her eyes were flint as she surveyed the tunnel.

"I am. Mine Leader Grim, ID 32498." Grim stepped forward.

"Thank you for bringing Healer Bastion, Displacer Ruby. We have a single dwarf named Balin trapped under the rubble."

"Current status?" The – [Displacer]? A teleporter maybe? – walked over to the hole we'd made and examined it. In the meantime, the [Healer] took Balin's temperature and measured his heartbeat.

"Stable, last I checked," Opal said, and Healer Bastion nodded. "I don't know if we can remove these rocks without causing further injury."

"I've got it. Clear a space."

While a couple dwarves rushed to obey, Displacer Ruby placed her hand on Balin's chest. I helped Healer Bastion down the pile to a section of rapidly cleared tunnel. A few rags were laid down as a makeshift bed and the [Healer] sat down next to it.

"Ready, Bastion?" Displacer Ruby called down.

"Ready!" The white-robed dwarf spread his hands out.

"Now!" With another *crack* Balin vanished and appeared on the bed. He screamed, and the [Healer] immediately placed faintly glowing hands on his chest. A soothing green light seeped into Balin, whose scream turned into a breathy moan. It was hard to see through the dark leathers, but it was clear that his leg was not just broken but really messed up. At this point Balin slumped over unconscious, and Doc Opal held his head up while Healer Bastion continued to pump green – mana? – into him. As time went by, Balin's face grew pink and healthy, and his leg twitched as it healed back to its former self.

"He'll be fine." Healer Bastion stood up. "The council will expect a report, Mine Leader Grim."

"Aye, I know." Grim looked completely dejected. I knew he was already in hot water over *my* accident and the Pilsner glass incident. I hope he doesn't get into big trouble.

"Well, we are all lucky to not see kin die tonight," Displacer Ruby said, walking up to Grim and placing her hand on his shoulder. She turned and faced the group. "Excellent work everyone! I am proud to call you fellow dwarves!" The crowd gave a few muffled cheers, but we were too tired to really build up steam.

We...

Did...

It –

I passed out. The last thing I saw was Doc Opal's panicked face as she reached out to stop me from toppling over.

Balin woke in darkness. His first terrified thought was that he was back in that cave, his foot trapped beneath the rubble. Was Annie alright? Was he dead? That was when the blanket fell off and he recognised the infirmary. Annie held his hand from where she lay crouched beside the bed. She was fast asleep, her beard gently swaying as she breathed in and out. Her face was drawn and haggard, but a smile of relief was etched upon it.

Truly, he was a lucky dwarf. Pete, Annie, Wreck, he had made some incredible friends and companions in this camp. After the monster stampede, he had been lost, completely adrift in the world. This mine had reignited the jolly fire in his heart, but it had also nearly snuffed it out.

It was time to leave. He could simply run away, but he couldn't leave Annie, and Pete still needed him. The lovable dope with the beer complex was like his old dog back home. His dog's name had been Peedee, and the way Pete looked at him with trusting eyes was just like old Peedee. Balin sat up and looked at the most beautiful dwarf he'd ever known. Indeed, it was time to leave. He would talk to Pete and see if they could put their heads together and come up with a plan.

He closed his eyes, and the comforting darkness whisked him off to sleep.

I hummed the tune to 'Sweet Child O' Mine' as I sat upon the ridge looking over the caverns. Sammy always loved Guns and Roses, though I was more of an AC/DC man myself. I wonder how you're doing now, my sweet child.

Two days have passed since the tunnel incident.

We were lucky. The freschie was part of an underground stream that connected to an opening in the mountain far above us. Oxygen was carried down the stream into the caves, just enough for Balin to survive. There were no gemstone deposits or iron veins. No treasures worth my friend's life. This event drove something home: I'm in a fantasy world now. While swinging my pick is fun, and singing dwarven drinking songs late into the morning is a riot, the life of a miner is fraught with danger.

My quest for sugar and obsession with fixing the local beer had led me astray. I hadn't even thought about getting out of the mine, because it was the only place on Erd I knew. In a way, this small camp and the grumpy dwarves who lived here had become my place of refuge. But their cheerful smiles belied a life where a simple accident could spell doom.

Balin and I needed to get out of here.

I looked up. Somewhere far above us was an entire above-ground world, and eight Gods that ruled over everything. One of them had even given me the strength and wherewithal I needed to save a friend. I raised my voice. "Do you hear me, Gods of Erd? I know you're watching – at least Tiara is! Thanks for the Blessing, it really helped!" I gave an appreciative bow. "Now hear me! Dwarves are big on honour and tradition, right? Well then, I swear an oath! Balin and I *will* be free within the year! I will make that happen no matter what!"

Bing!

New Quest: An Ore-Able Time Part 1/10!
You're stuck in a mine! Are you willing to mine your way to freedom?
Ore Collected: 0/100 Tonnes
*Rewards: [**Power Pick**]*

Do you accept?
Yes / No

Were these quests directly from the Gods then? It was nice to know that someone up there cared, but mining would take too long! I hit *yes* just in case, then went back to pacing.

There was a complication – the cost of Balin's [Healer]/[Displacer] emergency call was quite high. Balin was determined to be at fault because he didn't follow proper safety procedures, and the cost of the call was added to his indenture. It was going to take him decades to get out now. I needed to do something big, and I needed Balin to help me. If I did it alone, it wouldn't count towards Balin's indenture, and his was even bigger than mine now.

What could I do though? Minecarts weren't my expertise, and it was pretty clear that most of my beer making skills would go to waste here. Bran had made it clear that amateur beer-brewing *wasn't* happening in *his* kitchen!

If only there was an easier way to mine! [Mattershapers] existed, but getting them to mine with Abilities was wasteful and expensive. [Wizards] or [Aethershapers] could use magic or Abilities to throw fireballs at the wall, but that was just as likely to kill everyone in the tunnel, and once again – *too expensive*. Typical! Millions of shapers for defence, but not one mage for mining.

Surely there was a modern solution I could steal. Mining drills? Not an engineer. Dynamite? Nitro was likely to get me killed. Modern efficiency paradigms applied to synergistic competencies? Too buzz-wordy. I switched to singing some "Knockin' on Heaven's Door" as I brainstormed ideas.

Something tickled the back of my mind as I sang a line about putting guns in the ground. I *wasn't* going to introduce guns, that was for sure! Gunpowder was explosive, but it wasn't really...

I jumped to my feet.

GUNPOWDER!!

Could it work? We already had sulphur and a ready-ish supply of saltpeter. I paced in circles and contemplated, my mind whirling with possibilities. I was in the middle of formulating a plan when a voice called to me from the camp.

"Oy, Pete! There's a Blessin' party with yer name on it! Bran's got sugar for ya! You comin?"

Barck's Beard! Did they say sugar?! I rushed down the hill, my thoughts momentarily forgotten.

Freedom could wait, there was beer to save!

CHAPTER TWELVE
BICYCLE RIDE

"So," Bran piqued. "Why have you been so desperate for sugar?"

I was in the kitchen with Bran, Balin, and Tim. Annie was talking to Opal outside in the mess hall and Wreck was still a wreck. She was already drunk and splayed out on a bench. Speaking of the mess hall, it was full of cheerful dwarves awaiting a Blessing cake.

Unfortunately, the cake was a lie.

I'd commandeered the allotment of sugar for my own nefarious purposes. Sorry, my kinsmen, but it's booze before bros. I waited almost two weeks for this moment. I know that isn't a lot, but when you're dying of thirst in a desert, you take what you can get. Furthermore, just like the pilsner glass, I was going to make this a resounding success.

"Well, Bran, I'm about to ruin this keg of beer."

"Wuzzat?" Bran placed his hand protectively on the small keg sitting on the counter beside me.

"Yep, I'm going to use this sugar to make some bad beer." I looked around the well-appointed kitchen and nodded with satisfaction. Bran's kitchen had absolutely everything I could possibly need. Several dozen copper pots of every shape and size, as well as a multitude of shining spoons, ladles, and measuring cups hung from a rack suspended over an enormous central island. There was a block of knives on the wall that were incredibly sharp and nasty looking –

leave it to dwarves to have superior cutware. Hot and cold water were piped in, and there was a cold storage area for fruits and vegetables. I have no clue how all of those worked in detail, but according to Bran they were made by Titled [Enchanters]. They could use sigils and magic stones from monsters to create long lasting effects.

"Now why would ya want to make bad beer?" Tim asked, curious. We had grown a bit closer after the minecart incident, and while we weren't *friends,* I'd call us good office buddies.

"Aye, who in their right mind would want bad beer?" Balin agreed.

"Well, when the beer is already terrible, making it bad is an improvement!" I said with aplomb.

"THA BEER AIN'T BAD!" the three of them cried in unison.

"Yer still off yer rocker, Pete!" Bran opined. Tim nodded in unison.

"Pete, don't do this," Balin moaned, pulling his beard with both hands. "I barely managed to keep ya alive, and now yer aimin' to get us both killed!"

"Well technically he saved 'yer life too," Tim pointed out.

"And now I want to save this beer, by ruining it!"

"Pete, fer your own sake, I recommend you not give everyone bad beer for that Blessin' party," Bran said seriously. "My first week as chef I made a bad sandwich, and I woke up strung halfway up to the roof. Took me ages to get down."

"I must. Fer Pete's sake!" I retorted, grinning.

"What?" Balin raised a querulous eyebrow.

"It's – my name – I – you know what? Be quiet, I'm brewin' 'ere!" I turned to the pot of sugar in front of me. It was from a type of sugar vine in Greentree. They took the vine and crushed it to remove the sap and concentrated it into a syrup. That syrup was dried out and processed to form sugar crystals. It's exactly how cane sugar was made back home, and it tasted almost exactly like it too. It was perfect. I grabbed an apron from a hook and tied it around my back. It almost felt like home; I shook my head. This was home now.

"I'm going to make some simple syrup first." I turned to Bran. "Can I have a pot, please?"

"I'm not givin' you a pot till yer good and proper." He said, handing me a beard and hair net.

Right! I have a giant beard now! There'd been a distinct lack of hair in my food up till this point, and I was reminded that dwarves took beard hygiene very seriously – even if they were total slobs with most everything else. I put everything on, and Bran gave me a once-over before he nodded his approval. I filled a large pot with water and placed it on the stove. The stoves used simple charcoal, because that was significantly cheaper than an enchanted stove and did the job just as well. I told Bran that was a good way to die from carbon monoxide poisoning, and he claimed dwarves were usually unaffected by 'foul erdly aethers.' Unaffected as long as they didn't run into a freschie full of sulphur that is.

Making simple syrup was *simple*. Nyuck.

Simple Syrup Ingredients
Sugar

Water

Boredom

Take a pot of water and add lots of sugar (technically it's equal parts sugar and water). Stir it until the sugar dissolves completely and let it boil. The convection currents will take care of the majority of the work from then on. As the water boils down, the sugar and water concentrate into a thick sweet syrup.

It can take a few tries to get it right; the sugar granulates at the last stage if you aren't careful. I did this a lot when I was living alone, so it was pretty easy for me.

Tim leaned over the pot. "Why syrup?"

"Sweeteners can be added to beer at any stage. Some prefer to do it right before fermentation in order to add a distinct flavour to the beer. You can add fruit sugars, maple syrup, caramel, any kind of sweet liquid really. Once you pour it into your wort it's called an adjunct, and they are one of the main ways to add flavour to beer."

"I know those words," Bran nodded.

"I've never heard any of that," said Balin.

"It's not what tha ancestors intended." Tim made a gesture across his chest. Some kind of ward against evil?

"What's a maple syrup? Is it sweet?" Bran's eyes sparkled and flicked briefly to Opal through the kitchen window.

"It comes from a maple tree. None of those in Greentree?"

"Nah," said Tim. "I know all tha trees in Greentree. No maple."

"Ah well, it's really good on pancakes." I could really go for pancakes or a good old fashioned rodeo pancake breakfast.

"What's a pancake?" Bran pulled out a notepad. "And where are ya gettin' all these recipes from?"

"Uh.... I don't remember?" The three of them rolled their eyes.

"How do you know so much about the trees in Greentree, Tim? Why are you even here, what did you do?" I changed the subject as I poured the sugar into the pot and stirred.

"I like trees, and I was caught embezzlin'." Tim said, and then refused to say more. Well, to each their own, and in a gold and law-centric society like the dwarves', that was a fairly serious crime.

We sat in silence for a while, watching the water refuse to boil – we had to stop watching this pot. I decided to continue my craft brew lesson while we waited.

"Adding pure sugar to the wort is often done in the Belgian fashion, using what is referred to as candi sugar. Candi sugar is a type of beet sugar that's been toasted and caramelized. It makes for a strong brown beer called a dubbel."

"What's a Belgia?" Balin frowned.

"Isn't beer already brown?" Tim's brows furrowed.

"Uh, a human city. It's different, Tim," I replied.

"You've been above ground?!" Bran asked in shock.

"Explains so much," Tim grumbled. "Human society mucked his spirit."

"Aye, me parents warned humans would rot yer head," Balin agreed. Hey! "Did ya learn all this stuff from them? I didn't know they drank tha brew o' tha Dwarves."

"Aye, they drink that swill they call spirits." Bran said sagely. "And plain water..." The three of them shivered then turned to look at me.

"Uh, I don't remember?" They rolled their eyes again.

By this time the pot had a merry boil going, and I gave it a lazy little stir.

"You can also add sugar at the bottling stage as a priming sugar or during secondary fermentation."

"'Fraid none of us are brewers, Pete. You've lost us." They nodded. I sighed.

"Well, I'm doing none of that, because I'm not brewing beer. I'm ruining it." The water was getting thick, and it would soon be time to turn off the heat. "Do you have any spices or fruits I could use, Bran?"

"Aye, I have some. Mostly for Opal though." He opened the cooler and I leaned in behind him. "I got apples, some strawberries, basil, thyme—"

"Hold tha phone!" I interrupted. I reached over his shoulder and grabbed a few round yellow fruits before he could stop me. "You have lemons?!"

"Tha phone?" muttered Tim. I ignored him.

"These change everything!" I was originally going to add the simple syrup into the beer. The sweetness would help with the awful flavour and the thickness of the syrup would help with consistency. It would turn the beer into an awful root-beerish concoction, but it would be tastier. Like I said – terrible to bad. If I had lemons though... I could do something far better! A Radler! A Bicycle! I turned to my pot and grabbed a knife. I hummed a song as I cut into the first lemon.

Pete's Lemon Radler Ingredients
Simple Syrup
Water
Lemon Juice
Lemon Slice
Bad Beer
Rosemary
Ice Cubes

Huzzah, Freddie Mercury! *Everyone* who ever sang about bicycles – thanks for the save!

Bran blocked my way as I went to cut more lemons. "I can't let ya do that, Pete, that's fer Opal's Lemon Meringue."

"Come on Bran, it's all in the name of good beer! Besides, Opal is going to love it, and I'll let you share the credit with her."

Bran stroked his beard thoughtfully. "Opal will love it, ya say? Alright, you get one shot but you're payin' for the lemons if it doesn't work out. They grow well in Greentree but they're expensive."

"You won't regret it!" I grabbed another pot and squeezed the first lemon into it.

"I already am..." he muttered.

"So, what is it?" Balin asked.

"I'm making a *radler* – er, a bicycle. Do you know what a bicycle is?"

The three of them looked at me with disdain.

"Everyone knows what a bicycle is, Pete," Balin scoffed.

"Aye, gnomish contraption made with good dwarven aluminium," Bran nodded.

"I love a good mountain bike meself," said Tim. We turned to stare at him and he reddened.

I turned back to my preparations. "Anyway, the story goes that a group of humans were out biking when they came to a small bar. They went in for a beer but there wasn't enough for all of them. The barkeeper asked if they were thirsty for some lemonade instead, and they said 'why not both!' The bartender mixed the beer and the lemonade together and a new kind of beer was born! A bicycle, or *radler* in the human tongue, is especially good on a hot afternoon or after a long day's work. It's usually made with lemonade, but any citrus fruit will do. I'm partial to some *pamplemousse* myself!"

"Lemonade?" Balin asked, peering into the lemon juice filled pot as I added some of the syrup and a bunch of water.

"A gnomish drink," Bran said, knowingly.

"Pimple-moose?" Tim muttered.

"Grapefruit. Don't worry about it." I stirred the pot and tasted it – then sighed in pleasure. Tasty, tasty, lemonade. I grabbed the keg and three dwarven hands stopped me.

"Are ya sure Pete?" Balin's tone was filled with concern.

"Absolutely. Now let me finish this, it's my party!"

I grabbed a tankard and poured it roughly three-quarters full of beer then added the lemonade. A bunch of the carbonation was washed out, but there was barely any bubbly anyway. I added a sprig of rosemary from Bran's spice rack and a single slice of lemon. There weren't any ice cubes, but that was fine.

I toasted the trio, "Bottoms up!" then drank deeply.

The sweet and sour taste of lemonade poured down the back of my throat, mixed with the slight fizz of the ale. I sighed in pleasure; the lemonade took the edge off the rancid taste of the gruit, and all the extra water reduced the grit. It wasn't good, but it wasn't terrible anymore – it was plain old bad beer. Balin and Tim looked at me suspiciously as Bran poured himself one. He took a deep drink and paused as he smacked his lips.

"Its... good!!" He said, looking surprised. Balin poured himself a tankard and tried it as well, his handlebar moustache twitching as he drank. The two of them looked at me and then back at the beer.

Bran sighed. "There's goin' to be another fight..." But his eyes steeled as he glanced Opal's way. "Well, let's do this!"

We brought the beer up to the distribution table and Bran cleared his throat. "All right, everyone! Pete's got a treat for you all tonight! Line up and grab yer tankards!" There was some confused mumbling as all the dwarves queued up and we started pouring radlers.

After three minutes a tankard was thrown across the room. After five minutes, the first dwarf was tossed out a window. Then the true pandemonium began.

"Ya can't put lemons in tha beer!"
"It's delicious!"
"Spits in tha face o' the ancestors."
"That glass too, are ya'll touched by Yearn?"
"TIM! Shut yer gab!"
"Make me!"
"Someone, hold him down!"
"ARRGHGHHH!!! ME BEARD!!!"

I nodded at the brawl and sipped from my tankard. A successful evening all around. A bright blue box grabbed my attention with a *Bing!*

Blessing Granted: [Yearn]!

Your ability to gain the love and hatred of many people at once has gained the notice of Yearn!
May you survive long enough to continue your great work.
*If you receive Yearn's Blessing you will receive [**Nothingness**] and [**Sense Emotions**].*
If you receive Yearn's Blessing you will be eligible for a Title.

Do you accept?
Yes/No

I hummed some *Sugar, Sugar* as I mentally clicked on "No." Doc Opal told me I could receive a total of two Blessings, and I wanted a certain precious someone. So come on, Archie! I'm waiting for you! Are you watching me right now, in your big God house in the sky? Give me some of that magic!

Somewhere Else.

On the side of a cliff stood a white stone gazebo. Mist fell from a great waterfall that stretched beneath it, vanishing into the clouds below. A black mountain rose up behind it, seeming to touch the sky. A circular marble table covered by a complex game-board sat in the centre of the gazebo, and a group of eight figures were arrayed around it in plain wooden chairs. Each of the beings had distinct features, but their bodies shifted in strange patterns, seeming more like a collection of concepts than a physical thing.

"Has everyone chosen their piece?" a crisp masculine voice asked. His voice was a sharp growl that seemed to cut the very air. He clacked his fingers upon the table with the staccato of long nails, or claws.

Light poured out from him, obscuring his exact form in a chaotic halo of power. There was a chorus of assent around the table.

"A dragon again, Solen?" a young girl giggled in reply, pointing to the game-board. The speaker's face seemed to shift back and forth between age and race, her true form lost in the entropy of it all. Her voice aged in mid-sentence as she continued, becoming a scathing alto. "Those scaly shut-ins are never useful."

"You'll see, Midna," Solen growled back, a fire flickering in the back of his throat. "It will be different this time. You all know the rules. No interference, and no direct contact. All agreed?"

"I have concerns about a particular aspect and wish to discuss it." A figure wearing the robes of a scholar stood and the attention of the room shifted to him. Soon a heated discussion was underway.

On the other side of the table, a short figure covered in gems and jewels elbowed her neighbour and whispered in brusque feminine twang, "Well Barck, I got the jump on you with Peter Samson. You're going to miss your chance."

"I don't think so, Tiara," a deep, gravelly voice replied. A smile winked from behind a bushy green beard.

Tiara scoffed. "Well, I think you've lost before we've even begun."

"Ah, but I got an advantage."

"No doubt he will give you a chance sooner or later, but how is that an advantage? There's no guarantee Archis won't get to him first."

There was a pregnant pause as Barck gave a knowing glance.

Tiara gasped. "You wouldn't!"

"Aye, I would."

"That's against the rules!"

"There's a loophole."

"Who cares if there's a loophole! There is always—!" Tiara dropped her voice to a hiss, wary of eavesdroppers. "There must *always* be a choice."

"I've paid too much ta lose this chance, and my Chosen cannae *afford* ta lose this chance. I'll have ta force it if it becomes necessary."

"What if there's a penalty?"

"I don't care. The reward will far outweigh any personal cost." The short, squat dwarfish looking being smiled self-assuredly.

"If you say so, but I can't imagine *anything* worth *that*."

"You're simply lacking in imagination, a character fault."

"Hmph, you'll pay for that remark!"

The conversation across from them came to an end. An accord was reached.

Solen's gravelly voice spoke again. "We are agreed?"

"AGREED."

They all called as one, "LET THE NEW ERA BEGIN!"

Beneath them, the mountain trembled.

CHAPTER THIRTEEN
INTERLUDE – VILLAINOUS

"Allo! Welcome to tha Glassworks!"

Ralph Ralphson of Ralph and Ralph Glassworks turned to the door as the bell rang. He put down the piece of stained glass he was working on and looked at the customer standing on the other side of the counter. Ralph pulled at the long braids of his goatee as he put on a bright, welcoming smile.

"Can I 'elp you?"

The customer in front of him was different from his usual fare. Ralph was used to noblemen and clergymen coming for clear glass for their windows or the occasional wine glass for a gnomish oligarch. He also had a few dwarves come in for a one-off or two, but that was about it. He'd never seen a gnomish tinker-trader come in the door, and certainly never one that looked so... wild.

"Do you do requests?" the gnome asked in a squeaky voice. He kept looking over his shoulder like he was afraid of something.

"Aye, of course! What are ya lookin' fer?" Strange customer or not, gold was gold, but Ralph wondered why this gnome looked so twitchy. Was he a thief? Ralph raised his guard; he wasn't getting robbed today!

The gnome placed a vase on the counter. "I want a copy of this."

"Aye?" Ralph dropped his guard and examined the vase, flipping it over to look at the maker's mark. "Hmmm... It's got a maker's mark from Kinshasa. I can make it. Any changes ya want made, or do ya want it *as is*?"

"Yes... make it as clear as possible, lose the colouring." The gnome pulled at his moustache as he thought.

"Aye, anythin' else?"

"Can you add a handle? Like a tankard?"

"Uh... yes?" What an odd request. Did the gnome plan on drinking water from the vase? That struck Ralph as strange, but then Gnomes liked to drink weird things. They preferred their coffee and tea and juice to a proper brew. Ralph shuddered. Perhaps this was some new way of drinking leafy flower water. "Anything else?"

The gnome fell deep in thought for a while. He hummed and hawed, while Ralph took the vase and measured it. This would be a simple order, and he could knock it out before lunch. He was looking forward to meeting some of his mates in the bar for a game of hammercup soon.

"Add some etching. I want it to say, 'Whistlemop.'"

"'Whistlemop?'"

"Yeeesss – No." The gnome's voice grew firm. "'Official Whistlemug.'"

"'Official Whistlemug?'" What was a *Whistlemug*?

"Yes, in gold, with a drawing of me." The gnome grinned maniacally.

"That'll be a lot more expensive." Ralph paused in his work. He could already see his early evening disappearing. He pulled out a notepad and took notes. This one was going to be a pain; he could tell already. "Anything else?"

"On the other side put 'The best way to drink a beer.'"

"'The best way to drink a' – WHAT?!?" Ralph put down his notepad and stared. Was this gnome insane? Well, if he was, Ralph needed to ensure that he would get paid for this job. Far be it from him to stand between a gnome and a bad idea. "I'm gonna need pay up front."

The gnome stepped outside without a word. Ralph sighed in relief, that was possibly one of the oddest requests he'd ever received. Why on Erd – The gnome entered again with a small cart filled with bags. His eyes glowed with avarice as the gnome placed a bag on the counter. It clinked and a few coins fell onto the wood. "I sold everything. *EVERYTHING*. I don't want one. Make it a thousand."

Ralph stared at the gold rolling around on the counter in front of him. What was he getting himself into? Then again... gold was gold. "Alright, Mr. Whistlemop, you're the boss!"

The gnome began to laugh – a high pitched cackle – and Ralph soon joined him. Their cackles echoed down the tiny Minnovan side street, disturbing a couple of sleeping cats who yowled in protest.

***

He sat under a table, nursing his eye and his grudge. This could not be, this would not stand!

He drank from his tankard, and revelled in the taste of nostalgia, herbs, and millennia of dwarven traditions. A stick crunched between his teeth and added extra texture. The True Brew was perfect, and nothing could tell him otherwise. Every dwarf knew in their bones that beer was the greatest drink ever created, and nothing could improve upon it. Even Light Brew was a bastardization of the First Brewer's creation, let alone some swill made with lemon water! A tankard splashed down to the ground beside him, and the awful smell of lemon mixed with beer came with it. He shuddered, and his grudge grew deeper. Tim shut his eyes and tried to shut out the world; perhaps this was all a nightmare and he'd wake up beside his beloved Sofia.

For the umpteenth time tonight, Tim wished he'd kicked the pot of syrup off the oven and drowned Pete in the beer. He pulled a hand-mirror out of his jacket pocket and glanced at his face. His beard, his glorious beard that Sofia adored, shaved half-off. Tim could even see his chin beneath the stubble. To shave off another dwarf's beard was the most incredible of insults, and it hadn't slowed the brawl even a little. Not a single person had raised a hand to stop the carnage. He'd been utterly alone in his misery. Even Pete, the Godsbedamned *bastard* that Tim had considered a friend, hadn't raised a finger to help. He glowered at the disfigured image before him, hating it just as much as he hated Pete right now.

Oh, Sofia! How he missed her. How he needed her. Her breathtaking, supple curves. Her mahogany complexion and amber highlights unmatched by any in all of Crack! Oh Sofia! There was nothing he loved more than to drip oil down her sides and rub it in; his fingers caressing leather as he inhaled her intoxicating and exotic scents. Truly, there was nothing better than his Sofia.

Indeed, his desk had been more precious than his own life. He'd poured every ounce of his spare gold, and even some of the city's own funds into her. Was it not important that the front desk clerk of City Hall show the power and majesty of Minnova? How better to do that than with fine woods and oils from the dungeon? He'd showered Sofia with so much love that he'd received the Blessing of Tiara! He'd thought everyone in the City Hall would share in his joy!

Instead, the Head Administrator had confiscated his desk and thrown him into this blasted Reform camp. Told him to 'learn some temperance.' This awful, wretched, *prison* that had spawned a threat to all that was dwarven. Tim's jaw grew tense as he stared deep into his hand mirror. He pulled out a belt-knife and began to shave. First the jaw, then the muttonchops – first he shaved it short, then he shaved it off. When there was nothing left but a moustache, he shaved that off too.

The image that stared back in the mirror was a stranger, a mockery of the dwarf he was. His Sofia wouldn't even be able to recognize him when he came home to her. Something inside of Tim *snapped*. *Pete* was the architect of all this. Pete, who seemed so nice. Pete, who pretended to *care*. Pete, who knew nothing about what it meant to be a dwarf and blamed it all on some convenient *amnesia*. But Pete was a liar, a *DECEIVER*. Even now the fighting continued. Good dwarves fighting over the very root of what it meant to be a dwarf. There were always fights, but they were small things, like:

Who brought in the most ore that day?

Who had the prettiest beard?

Who was more poncy, elves or dragons?

These were the everyday fightin' words of dwarves all around

Crack; the days of Blood-Feuds were over! Yet today, he was witnessing a terrible thing – a *real* fight over the taste of beer.

Oh, Peter Samson may have them all fooled with his fop routine, but Tim knew the sharp mind that hid behind those glazed eyes. Pete wanted to ruin what it meant to be a dwarf? Well, Tim would throw it all away, and then *stop* him. He would sacrifice *himself* so that no dwarf would ever need to fight like this again. He should've realised it earlier – with all Pete's strange words and mannerisms – that a monster lurked in their midst. He giggled giddily as fear and righteous wrath warred in his heart. Oh Sofia, if only she was here! He would do this all for her! Even if it meant he might never see her again.

There was a *Bing!* and a notification appeared.

Blessing Granted: [Yearn]!
Your mortal curse has gained the notice of Yearn, who sees your empty heart.
Fill it with vengeance and become a terrible enemy!
*If you receive Yearn's Blessing you will gain [**Nothingness**] and [**Sense Emotions**].*
If you accept Yearn's Blessing you will be eligible for a Title!

Do you accept?
Yes/No

With a hooked smile, Tim mentally clicked on 'Yes.' His teeth flashed as he went through the four Title options; his decision was simple and immediate.

Title Gained: [Swindler]!
A [Swindler] can steal not only gold, but the spirit and spark of their mark.
Just don't get caught!

Blessing Evolved: [Strength of All: Held] becomes [Steady Hands]!
Your hands are firm and unshaking no matter the situation. Your charisma increases by 4 when bluffing, and you are immune to telltale signs of lying.

This Ability is always available.

Blessing Evolved: [Nothingess] becomes [Distraction]!
A spirit divided is ripe for the taking. Your ill-gotten gains will cause problems unless you can keep attention elsewhere. Increases the chance that a mark will become distracted when they're talking to you. Keep in mind that you may need to set up the distraction yourself.
This Ability is always available.

Milestone Gained: [Lost Reason]!
If you can't find a fool to rob, make your own! While you're working a mark, you can reduce their wisdom by four for an hour. Successive uses on the same mark will increase the duration of the effect up to a maximum of eight hours.
This Ability can be used once a day.

Beneath a table in the middle of a brawl, a newly Titled [Swindler] laughed and laughed and laughed.

Nobody heard.

CHAPTER FOURTEEN
FROM THE DIARIES OF PETER SAMSON

I started this diary to keep track of *The Project*. I also noted down important events and doodled a lot in the margins. Honestly, this thing is a mess and I hope nobody ever reads it. I plan on burning it after making a good copy of any relevant notes.

Excerpt from the Diaries of Pete Samson: First Dwarf on the Moon.

22nd Day of the 1st Month, 7997

The creator of dynamite was so distraught by the carnage his invention wrought that he started the Nobel Prize. The Winchester-gun-guy's wife went similarly insane and built a crazy house. I don't want to go nuts, so I spent the entire last month contemplating the ethics of gunpowder. Yesterday, I made up my mind – I talked to Grim, and I have permission to start my gunpowder project with Balin.

My biggest concern is guns, and based on my research they are *unlikely* to become a problem. A *lot* of adventurers and soldiers have Tiara's Blessing, which gives strength to 'held' and 'worn' items – but ammunition doesn't count. That means bows and crossbows just aren't used outside of hunting for food. Adventurers use melee or magic, full stop. Heck, there are *magic-cannons* that barely see use outside of siege warfare. Ammunition can be enchanted, but it's so cost prohibitive nobody does it.

My next concern is that gunpowder could give any random dwarf on the street a way to kill people. But then I studied monster biology with Opal, and there are some monster acids and other terrible readily available alchemical concoctions that make pistols look like a joke when it comes to murder.

Even if Minnova put a thousand guns in the hands of dwarven infantry, there was still one big roadblock: real magic. I watched a lot of fights at the distant dungeon over the past month, and stuff got crazy down there. I saw lightning strikes, earth spikes, fireballs, tornadoes, water dragons, you name it. Simply put, guns and gunpowder are never going to be an instrument of death here – they're simply too inefficient. Those thousand dwarven soldiers with guns would run into one [Mattershaper] or [Stormcaller] and they'd all be toast. Non-magical bullets would bounce off magic armour and mages could kill hundreds in an instant.

On the other hand, nobody puts [Mattershapers] in a mine! That's where mass produced gunpowder could really pay off. In fact, most of my research has led me to believe I'm on the right track.

Honestly, I may have missed some possible source of death and destruction, but I have enough evidence to salve my conscience. I swore an oath to get Balin out of this mine, and gunpowder is our ticket out. Please be good, Erd!

Excerpt from the Diaries of Pete Samson: Mine Magazine's Dwarf of the Year Award.

1st Day of the 2nd Month, 7997

My first new month in Erd!

Mining is going well! Speaker John found two new veins and we just finished clearing them out. Both my strength and vitality actually went up by one with all the heavy lifting! With the bonus two from my Blessing, there's a noticeable difference!

My other stats refuse to go up. I assume that's because I haven't been doing much other than working on getting gunpowder and mining.

From the Diaries of Pete Samson: A Man Among Dwarves

7th Day of the 2nd Month, 7997

Annie left today.

Balin is working like a dwarf possessed. He's 100 percent on-board with my project now.

From the Diaries of Pete Samson: Professional Pooperscooper

10th Day of the 2nd Month, 7997

Saltpeter ingredients:

- Poop
- Urine
- Straw
- Time

My nostrils have ceased to work. My life is a fog of nasal agony. The sulphur merely killed old me; this makes new me *want* to die.

Four more months of this? It had better work! Sorry, not sorry, Balin. This is all for your sake!

Excerpt from the Diaries of Pete Samson: Number One Friend

13th Day of the 3rd Month, 7997

Several new Dwarves joined us in the camp this month.

As a result, our dive team got broken up. Tim managed to convince Grim to bring him on as a secretary, and now he's running around doing errands. Balin stayed, and Annie's friend Wreck got moved onto my dive-team along with a couple new dwarves.

Most of them are quite nice! I actually struck up a friendship with one; Sam's a musician, and a ton of fun. It's great having another dwarf that loves singing during dives!

Since Tim is dealing with a lot of the camp logistics, he offered to get the charcoal I need for gunpowder.

You *rock*, Tim!

From the Diaries of Pete Samson: A Dwarf Freschie out of Luck

27th Day of the 3rd Month, 7997

Guess who has two thumbs and found a freschie?

NOT this guy!

Some other *lucky bastard* who isn't even important enough to get a name in the footnotes of my diary found a freschie. *He* was smart enough to keep out of it, and guess what?

It was full of gemstones. That lucky son-of-a-billygoat!

He packed up and left yesterday after a little farewell party.

Some dwarves get all the luck. It's enough to make me start praying to Barck meself!

From the Diaries of Pete Samson: Owner of the Death Note

16th Day of the 4th Month, 7997

Tim.

Timothy.

Timmie.

If Tim even *is* his real name. Your name is in my note, Tim!

He *still* hasn't gotten the charcoal I asked for! It's been over a month! I keep getting sidetracked when we chat, but I'm going to nail him to the wall next time.

From the Diaries of Pete Samson: A Man Among Dwarves

28th Day of the 4th Month, 7997

I completed the first Ore-Able Time Quest and got the next one in the chain!

Looks like the amount I need to mine increases each time. No other quests since; I wonder what causes them to appear? It seems to be based on life-altering or life-defining moments, and they're all from Tiara so far. Probably because I have her Blessing.

I wonder what Quests Archie will give me?

Come on, carrot-top! Bless me!

From the Diaries of Pete Samson: The Mental Mountain

31st Day of the 4th Month, 7997

Lessons with Opal are going great. I'm pretty close to being smarter than the av-er-age dwarf!

In fact, my intelligence went up again!

I can finally say it with pride – I absolutely *am* smarter than a dwarven fifth-grader.

From the Diaries of Pete Samson: The Ironed Chef

9th Day of the 5th Month, 7997

Just a couple months left on the saltpeter. Then I just need the charcoal and I'm good to go! Tim says it'll be soon.

I burned my hand in the kitchen today. I was showing Bran how to make lady-fingers, and I foolishly reached into the oven and picked up a baking sheet with my bare hands. It wasn't too hot yet, so it could have been way worse.

I blame all my fancy new stats and Blessings making me a wee bit overconfident.

Bran just says it's more evidence that I have a low wisdom.

It's above average, I'll have you know!

From the Diaries of Pete Samson: I said Pru-no Means No

4th Day of the 6th Month, 7997

Things have been uneventful, and I'm getting bored.

Now that I have access to the kitchen and most of Bran's ingredients, I want to make some other kinds of alcohol. As a master of the brewing arts, doing so will be child's play.

Fermentation is the trick for every kind of alcohol. Wine, beer, ginger-beer, they all have the same basic step of 'let sugar and yeast ferment for a while to make alcohol.' As a result, you can make just about any kind of alcohol as long as you're willing to let something sweet ferment for a while.

The easiest alcohol to make is mead, but that requires honey, and Bran doesn't have any; no bees in Greentree, apparently. That left two kinds of beer. Unfortunately, we can't get the required ingredients for the one I really want to make right now, but Bran's looking into importing some of the ingredients I need for my other option: the vilest, most gut-wrenching alcoholic beverage that has ever existed anywhere in the world.

Pruno.

From the Diaries of Pete Samson: Dwarf with an Achy Breaky Heart

13th Day of the 6th Month, 7997

The fruit Bran ordered from Minnova finally arrived, so we sat down and made some pruno. It isn't *beer* so he was fine with making it in the kitchen.

Pruno, better known as *prison hooch*, or *prison beer* is a kind of alcohol that absolutely anyone can make with almost zero effort. Throughout history it was brewed in ziploc bags, tote bags, garbage bags, and toilets. When you're stuck in prison, alcohol is worth its weight in gold, and the taste doesn't matter.

Personally, I think pruno is a crime against alcohol.

But in this case, I'm desperate, so I broke out my best Garth Brooks and sang some country as I got down to some serious prison blues. Besides, the idea of making a real bag of prison pruno while in a figurative prison appealed to my adventurous side.

Making pruno is dead simple compared to actual beer. Honestly, it's more like prison *wine* than beer. Take a bunch of mashed fruit – oranges and lemons with some raspberries are best – and put them in a ziploc bag with some water, juice, and sugar. The next step is getting some yeast to start the fermentation process. Technically there's yeast everywhere, and you could get lucky with just the yeast on the fruit, but that is more likely to rot than ferment. Prisoners usually just stuffed a couple pieces of bread into the bag instead. Baking bread doesn't always kill the yeast, and there's often enough in a couple pieces of bread to jump start the brew.

Dwarves obviously don't have ziploc bags, but Bran did have a pot with a clamp-down lid I could use, as well as some proper baker's yeast. Keeping the fermenting alcohol free from any outside air is important for proper brewing, and the pot worked perfectly for that. The resulting slurry of water and fruit looked like a pot of horrific punch.

I need to release pressure from the pot every few days to keep it from going boom like poor Annie's setup, but that'll be easy.

The final step for pruno is to let it sit somewhere warm for a few days. In a prison that was commonly done with warm 'water' in a toilet. Yech. Bran promised to keep my pot next to the stove.

Now I just need to wait three or four weeks, and I'll have a new kind of alcohol! Maybe it'll help keep my mind off our excruciating gunpowder experiment.

From the Diaries of Pete Samson: Messenger with an Olive Branch

20th Day of the 6th Month, 7997

I've never made pruno before, but I really should have been able to guess that it would stink to high heaven. I managed to convince Bran not to toss the pot by giving him a recipe for macaroons.

Not that I could smell it. My nose is so damaged by this point that I can't even smell Bran's new garlic-and-beer goat-stew with mushrooms. He's been experimenting with more beer recipes, and I'm so proud of him! Though he does prefer learning new sweets to feed Opal. I think he's *sweet* on her!

Bran's unrequited love aside, I now have to move the pot of pruno out of his kitchen when I pop the lid to release pressure.

I think I'll leave it one more week. I can't *wait* to see what a fermented slurry of fruit and sugar tastes like after sitting in a pot next to a stove for two weeks.

From the Diaries of Pete Samson: Trend *and* Record-setter

23rd Day of the 6th Month, 7997

Another miner got a Blessing today! Bran says this has to be some kind of record. Usually they come in spurts, but there's been a new Blessing at least once a month, sometimes more.

You could say we're living our *Blesst* life here in the City of Minnova Reform Mine!

I'll see myself out.

From the Diaries of Pete Samson: Dwarfy Princess

28th Day of the 6th Month, 7997

We don't talk about pruno.

From the Diaries of Pete Samson: That-uncle-who-always-gives-socks-for-Christmas

3rd Day of the 7th Month, 7997

My agility went up by one! I think it's because I'm finally used to these stubby legs. I still can't jump properly, and I'm not going to win any gymnastics competitions, but at least I'm not toppling over when I try to put on my padded socks.

Seriously, these socks are amazing. I would fight a horde of monsters to get at these socks – or even more terrifying – wade into Walmart on Boxing Day.

From the Diaries of Pete Samson: Member of the Eh Team

7th Day of the 7th Month, 7997

777! Our gunpowder experiment is coming to an end! I think we only need one more week!

I can't wait to make some explosions and then walk away without looking at them!

From the Diaries of Pete Samson: A Man Among Dwarves

14th Day of the 7th Month, 7997

It's time. Tomorrow the saltpeter will be ready.

CHAPTER FIFTEEN
A SALTY BALIN

I yawned and stretched, my arms still sore after yesterday's intense dive. I turned to my bunkmate and called out. "Mornin! Time ta wake up!"

A groan was the only reply as I jumped out of bed and shook myself awake.

"Rise and shine! Today's tha day!" I pulled on my clothes as Balin levered himself out of his bunk bed. Our small cabin smelled faintly of bad BO and vomit. A collection of cloves and fruit in the corner were a gift from Bran after I'd bribed him with a recipe for spiced tarts. The makeshift potpourri only partially helped.

"Yer too damn chippy in tha morning, Pete." Balin blinked crusty red eyes. "It's barely tha break o' day! I dunno how ya roped me inta this."

I went to the small basin, filled it with water and began combing my beard. "Because Annie got out five months ago and yer desperate. How ya doin?" There had been another Blessing party last night with a plain old cake, this time for a miner named Drawl. I don't really know Drawl since I've been so busy with *The Project*.

"I'm fine. Jus' give me a moment. Where's me socks!"

"Well, good morning, fine, I'm Peter. Nice ta meet ya!" I gave Balin a chipper grin as I brushed in the last of the beard oil.

"Solen's Socks, Pete. Even after seven months, I barely understand ya." Balin lumbered over and washed his face in the basin. "Especially this Barck-brained scheme of yers."

"You'll understand today." I pulled on my boots and squared my shoulders. "Meet you at the pens!" Time to see if the last six months were worth it! As I stepped out of our cabin into the eternal twilight of Crack, I gave my Status Sheet a glance.

Status: Provided by the Firmament

Name: Peter ~~Phillips~~ Samson
Age: 48
Conditions: None
Race: Dwarf
Blessings: [Strength of All: Self], [Strength of All: Held]
Titles: None
Milestones: [Otherworlder], [Power Pick]
Strength: 15.2
Vitality: 15
Agility: 12
Dexterity: 11
Wisdom: 12
Intelligence: 12
Perception: 13
Charisma: 10

Quest Complete: An Ore-Able Time Part 1/10!

You did it! Don't you feel amazing?
*Gained [**Power Pick**]!*

New Quest: An Ore-Able Time Part 2/10!

You're stuck in a mine! Are you willing to mine your way to freedom?
Ore Collected: 33.3/200 Tonnes
Reward: +0.2 Strength, +0.2 Vitality

I freaked out when I got *Ore-Able Time* 2 because the count dropped back down to zero. I was worried that I'd lost all my work, but I think the count simply reset. I hated it because it felt like I was re-starting from scratch.

Some subtle questioning of Doc Opal had revealed that quests are unique to me. I suspect it may be that 'gain Blessings and Milestones more easily' portion of [Otherworlder] again. I tried [Power Pick] for the first time yesterday and it does what it says on the tin. I am HE-DWARF and my pick HAS THE POWWEERR!! My pick strikes can shatter mountains, or at least very large stones! Speaking of Blessings, I pulled up another two blue message boxes. It seems I'm 'Mr. Popular' with the Gods this year.

The first one was from a few months ago.

Blessing Granted: [Solen]!

Your dedication to gain the freedom of a friend has gained the notice of Solen.
Let freedom reign!
*If you receive Solen's Blessing, you will receive [**Darksight**] and [**Dangersense**].*
If you receive Solen's Blessing, you will be eligible for a Title.

Do you accept?

Yes/[No]

The second one was from yesterday.

Blessing Granted: [Midna]!

You have fully immersed your spirit in a new world and gained the notice of Midna.
Let your spirit grow to touch the spirit of others, Otherworlder!
If you receive Midna's Blessing, you will receive [Soulsight] and [Truespeech].
If you receive Midna's Blessing, you will be eligible for a Title.

Do you accept?

Yes/[No]

I chose *No* for both of them and planned to continue doing so. So

AN ADVENTURE BREWING

far, the only Gods that hadn't Blessed me were Lunara, Barck, and Archis. I likely haven't done anything innovative enough for Barck, and haven't learned enough for Archis. Lunara, I don't understand. Haven't I been a model citizen of this new world?

I dodged some dwarves headed to the mines as I made my way to the goat pens. We nodded at each other though one out of the trio glowered at me, the nerve! Bran had turned radlers into a daily option on the menu and I was dwarf non-grata among some of the chain gang. It wasn't even my fault – Doc Opal was the one that suggested it!

"Hello, Piddles! Who's a good boy? You are! You are!" The unigoat pens were mostly empty with only the off-yellow unigoat remaining. I gave his coat a brush as I glanced over at the reason I was here: a large trough sitting to the side. Balin and I had dedicated the last few months of our lives to that trough, and it had been a trough life.

While I'm not a mechanic and certainly no expert miner, I am an amateur chemist. You have to be if you want to be a successful brewer or vintner. Many years ago, back when I was fiddling around with my first meads in university, I spent some time on YouTube watching chemistry videos. One that always stood out to me was of a redneck knee deep in chicken shit talking about making gunpowder. I thought it was really neat and tried making some gunpowder in my own backyard. In retrospect, I was probably on a list, but it was a lot of fun at the time! All I needed was some saltpeter, sulphur, and charcoal. I had intimate knowledge of a local supply of sulphur, and charcoal *should* have been abundant, so all I needed was some saltpeter. Thankfully, there was a ready supply nearby!

The required ingredients for saltpeter are super-ripe animal poop, urine, straw, and some way to contain it all. The goats were happy to provide the poop and straw. The dwarves, with some encouragement and lots of beer, were willing to move the latrine to the goat pens. Balin and I had to promise to keep the pens clean for a year, and I think he may resent me a little for that, but it will all be worth it...

I was not planning to see what *An Ore-Able Time Part 10* looked like!

I checked the trough and it was gently steaming with a white crust on top. It looked ready to go! The mixture needed about six months or so to 'ripen' and we'd been out here daily, mixing and observing. While there was a massive amount of goat shit here it wasn't actually going to provide too much saltpeter. Thankfully I only needed to do this once.... I hoped.

Balin arrived at this moment with gumboots and a clothespin over his nose.

"Do you have gloves?" I asked.

"Aye." He passed me some heavy gloves. Our next few steps were pretty dangerous so we needed to be careful.

Balin and I began to shovel the white crusty top of the trough into a spigotted barrel. It held a good amount and was only about half full after we were done. We added some straw then filled the barrel with water. Balin and I took turns stirring for the next few hours as other dwarves came and went to the mine, giving us strange looks. They could laugh all they wanted now – soon we'd be unveiling a revolution in mining technology! Eventually we turned the tap and emptied the barrel into a large metal pan which we placed on a fire.

Boil and filter. Boil and filter. Boil and filter. Eventually, the only thing left was a clear fluid filled with crystals.

That was when the blue box appeared with a *Bing!*

Blessing Granted: [Tiara]!

You have brought forth a hidden material and gained the notice of Tiara. Hard work and dedication are often their own reward!
If you receive Tiara's Blessing for a second time, its effect will be strengthened.
If you receive Tiara's Blessing, you will be eligible for a Title.

Do you accept?
Yes/No

I mentally clicked on *No* and the notification flickered away, but Balin began to glow. He closed his eyes, and a feeling of ecstasy passed over his face. He opened his eyes and stared at me.

"Pete! We did it! I got a Blessin' for it!"

"Congratulations!" We danced and hugged for a moment before we broke apart in disgust; both of us were covered in faeces and reeked. "We did! It's not perfect, but it should be good enough for the next step!" We danced for joy. Seven months of raking through goat poop, and we'd been suitably rewarded!

"So, what is this stuff? What did ya call it? Salty Peter? Why's it named after you, couldn't we call it Salty Balin?" We both paused and considered that before we shuddered. "Mebbe not."

"It's also called potassium nitrate!" I smiled at the result of our months of hard work: A collection of white crystals in a metal pan.

"Ah, potassium nitrate! Right, right. Wait—" Balin's eyes grew cloudy, and he grabbed my shoulder. "Didja say potassium nitrate?" His grip tightened, a far off look in his eyes.

"Yeah? What's up Balin? Ow! That hurts!"

"Follow me, Pete."

Balin led me a short away from the camp, closer towards the side of the cavern wall. There was a large cave mouth there, separate from the main mine. He led me inside and we activated the solstones on our ever-present mining helmets. The inside of the cave was *filled* with a white powdery substance on the floors and walls.

"Wow! A saltpeter mine! I can't believe this is here!" I gaped as I looked around, if there was this much potassium nitrate, we'd be fine for years! We didn't need to do that stupid trench anymore!

We...

Didn't...

Need...

I turned to look at Balin, who was advancing on me with murder in his eyes.

"What's wrong? We got *Saltypeter*, so why are ya... Salty, Balin?" I gulped. Then I ran – twelve agility, don't fail me now!

CHAPTER SIXTEEN
PETE THE DWARF

"So." Doctor Opal applied some poultice to the swollen eyes of the dwarf in front of her. "What did you do this time?" She was sitting at her usual spot in the mess hall. There were no emergencies in any of the mining camps, and she was having her usual afternoon sweets. A half-empty tankard in front of her smelled faintly of lemons.

Peter smiled sheepishly at her. "I ran into a door."

"With both eyes?" She asked, raising an eyebrow. She daubed some more poultice and Peter winced.

"With both eyes."

"Does this have anything to do with why Balin set fire to that awful dung trough you two have been working on?" Opal held down a smile on one side of her mouth. Her close-cropped white beard twitched as she fought a full grin. This afternoon had been quite the spectacle. The trough had been an inferno, with flames roaring nearly ten metres high. Balin was lucky he didn't get seriously burned. That hadn't stopped him from prancing around the trough screaming 'BURN, YA TIARA-DAMNED DUNG HEAP! BURN!' It had been an entertaining sight for the few dwarves around to see it happen. Most were going to come back from their daily mining expedition to find nothing but a pile of smoking wood and some antsy goats. Balin probably should have let the unigoats out before he lit a bonfire next to their stables, but he clearly hadn't been in his right mind. Thankfully, nothing else was damaged.

"Kind of..." Peter looked downcast, the near-blinding optimism of the past few months gone from his face. "I messed up a little."

Opal laughed outright at that. "A little! I don't think I've ever seen Balin that upset, and you've been moping like a broke gnome since you got here! What happened?"

"I wasted a lot of our time. The trough did what it was supposed to do, but I didn't realise what I needed was already available." Peter looked completely crushed as he clenched his fists a few times. "I cost Balin a lot of time and effort, all because I thought I knew better than everyone else. I should have just *asked*."

"Yes, ever since you recovered you have been a bit standoffish." Opal nodded, as she reached over and grabbed a strawberry off a plate. "All 'the beer is bad' this and 'there's a better way' that. It's grating."

Peter flushed, an amusing sight with two black eyes.

"I'm sorry. I thought.... I don't know what I thought." Peter looked lost as he rubbed at his neck. "I have all these ideas and all this knowledge, but I can't use half of it."

"Because everyone would thump you for trying?" She'd gotten a good thump or two in herself over the past several months. There'd been that disaster with the molasses, and don't even get her started on the noodle incident! Opal shuddered, no need to remember *that*!

"No. I just don't quite know how to do most of what I want to try. I'm wasted without a chemistry kit, or a brewery or winery to work with." Peter grumped, thumping his forehead on the table. "I feel like I have this huge opportunity to do great things for the world and I'm just not cut out for it."

"Now you're whining, not a good look on you." Opal tutted. "Besides, that's egotistical don't you think?"

"I know." Peter's voice came out muffled from his face down position on the table.

"Well, Peter, if it will make you feel better, nobody is expecting you to save the world!'" Opal delivered the line with all the panache she could, laying a hand on Peter's head and peering imperiously down at him. Then she couldn't stop herself from laughing till she nearly fell off the bench.

"Good thing. I'd probably be late to the apocalypse." Peter peeked up and smiled back at her.

"I hear Balin got a Blessing out of your little escapade." Opal wiped some tears from her eyes as she continued laughing. "So your time spent as the mine's resident swine wasn't completely wasted."

"That's nothin' much..."

"Nothing much!" Opal stared agog. "It can take decades of hard work to earn a Blessing! It's something every mortal strives for! A mere six months of hard work for a Blessing is nothing!" She patted Peter on the shoulder. "Balin will realise that when he calms down. He really came out ahead in this whole thing."

"That does make me feel better." Peter took a deep breath. "You're the best Opal."

"Of course, Peter. Now, begone. I want to finish my snacks in peace." Opal shooed him away.

"Doctor's orders?"

"Doctor's orders! Shoo!" Peter made his way out of the mess hall, a spring back in his step. Opal watched him go and tapped her finger on the table. She hoped Pete got some good luck soon. At the same time, her stomach hoped that Pete and his unending supply of sweets recipes would be stuck in this mine for a long, long time.

I stepped out into the dimly lit street running through the camp. The cool twilight air of Crack cleared my mind and gave me the emotional space to think. Okay Lunara, maaaaybe darkness isn't so bad after all.

I could always trust Doc Opal to make me feel better. She was the smartest dwarf in this whole mine, and it showed. She was right, of course. Our time hadn't been a waste – Balin got a Blessing, and I spent the last six months learning everything I needed to know about my new life. Besides, the saltpeter mine would run out one day and I had proven there was another way to get it. That was more than enough for me!

I paused for a moment, as something else Doc Opal said kicked in. I *have* been a bit standoffish. Maybe it's because I see dwarven society as backwards and stuck in tradition. The part of me that's still Pete from Canada feels like the old guard needs to 'move outta the way'! That's the wrong way of looking at it. In many ways dwarven society is a lot better than what we had back home. I shouldn't be judging it. I should be doing what I can to fit in first.

I'll start by laying off the 'bad beer' and 'bad BO' complaints. It doesn't endear me to anyone and doesn't further my goals. I also need to start learning dwarven customs with the intention of actually following them, instead of simply observing them with clinical interest. Finally, I need to think of myself as a *dwarf*, rather than as a human stuck in a short, shaggy body.

I'll eat with my hands and like it! I'll comb my beard five times a day and fuss over braids! I'll swear by the Gods and jealously guard my socks! I won't shudder when I think of beards as *sexy*! That's right, I'm a *dwarf* now, and I need to dig deep into my heart and fully become the dwarf my mother raised me to be! BY MY BEARD AND FOR MY ANCESTORS!

No need for self-delusion though, my mother was a Newfie hippie, not a dwarf. Love ya mom, wherever you are.

Bing!

Stat Increased: [Charisma]!

Your charisma has increased by 1! Your new charisma is 11!

My feet bumped against a door, and I realised my musings had brought me back to my cabin. I couldn't hear anything inside, but I knocked just in case.

"Hey, Balin, you in there buddy?" There was a moment of silence before a forlorn voice came through the flimsy wood.

"Aye, Pete. Come on in."

"Listen, I wanted to apologise for stringing you along the last few months. I really thought this was the only way to get what I wanted. Sorry." I swung open the door and stepped inside. It was dark so I flicked on the light – a small solstone hanging from the centre of the ceiling – and opened the shades. Balin was curled up in his bed, facing the wall.

"Nah, I overdid it, Pete. I'm sorry. I should have been 'appier about getting a Blessin'. I was just a bit miffed we spent half a year scrapin' goat shit fer nuthin'."

"If it makes you feel any better, I don't think the time was wasted. That deposit won't provide enough potassium nitrate if my plans take off."

"Really?"

"Yeah, the trough was a good proof of concept, and we can say it works fer sure."

"That's good ta hear. What's next?"

"Tim just needs a bit more time to get us the charcoal. He's running some supplies for Grim." Poor Tim. It's been weird having a beardless dwarf around. Everyone else has been avoiding him since he started shaving it, and I feel bad about it. It got cut during the radler brawl, and I guess the loss drove him crazy. Maybe a year or two or ten will help him get over it, and he'll regrow a good old-fashioned dwarven beard. I brushed my own and shivered at the thought of losing it.

"Yer *still* willin' to wait? That's..." Balin's eyes grew concerned. "Never mind. Is there enough silver left fer tha rest of what we need?"

"I think so." The silver came from our 'pay.' Each month we were given a small portion of our earnings to spend on personal items. The rest went to our indenture.

"Well, let's talk about it." Balin slid out of bed and I got a look at his face.

I started to wheeze, guffaw, and then laugh the deepest belly laugh I'd had all year. I could feel my anxiety and worry melting away with that laughter. Balin stood there, dumbstruck as I laughed and laughed.

"What's so funny?" He demanded, grabbing a mirror. "Arrggh, me face!"

"You only have half an eyebrow! And your moustache!" I laughed harder. One of Balin's eyebrows was scorched clean off, and the other only had half remaining. His handlebar moustache looked like a burnt candle wick.

"This is all yer fault, Pete! Annie loves my moustache!"

"Hey, I didn't start the fire! You did, and she 'loved' your moustache! Past tense Balin!"

For the second time in a day, I was chased by my friend, but this time it was all in fun.

CHAPTER SEVENTEEN
EH

I sighed as I laid my pickaxe against the wall.

Balin came over and took the ore I had mined and placed it into a pair of sacks. "Isn't this so much nicer than shovelin' shit?"

"Sure, but it's killer on my joints." I stretched.

Balin heaved the sacks over his shoulder and dragged them up the dive to the main tunnel.

"I saw tha fire. Is yer thing almost finished?" A rosy-cheeked dwarf with an enormously bushy red beard asked. His beard was almost as big as he was, and I think all the dwarves in the mine were jealous of it. His curly red hair could barely be contained in his mining helmet.

"Yep. I tell you, Sam, it'll be a real *banger* when it's done!"

"If ya say so, Pete. Be careful, I've got five silver on you two not dyin' before it's done."

"Oh, we'll be fine – wait." I paused, slowly turning an arrested gaze in Sam's direction. He continued picking obliviously at the wall. "Is there a betting pool on us dyin'?" Those ingrates! Here I was working towards making mining a better job for dwarves everywhere!

"In me defence, I put money on you livin'." Sam chuckled and I turned back to my work while Balin lugged the sacks up the dive tunnel. Sam arrived in the camp about four months ago. He was brought in for 'repeatedly breaking noise Ordinances.' He's been in and out of Reform Mines for centuries. All the mining personnel already knew him, and he's good friends with Speaker John. I love him for many reasons, but one specifically.

"So how are ya doin' today, Sam?" I put my pick down and wiped some sweat from my brow. Mining was hot and hard work!

"Eh, I'm doin' alright." Hee! Sam says 'Eh' more than a Manitoba farmboy! When I first heard it, I had a sudden intense pang of homesickness, but now it's more a warm dose of nostalgia. His giant red beard and slight prairie accent mean I get to spend all day with a squat, friendly, lumberjack.

"Glad to hear it. Let's keep it that way. Blast incomin'!" I readied a [Power Pick] by focusing my thoughts into the pick. The pick began to glow with a grey light before I brought it down on the wall. With an ear-splitting *CRACK!!* an enormous portion of ore was blasted off the wall. I was pelted with a few stones, but nothing bigger than a pebble. The glow on my pick petered out, and I wouldn't be able to use it again for around another four minutes. [Power Pick] was a fairly common Ability, and using it enough could net things like [Fast Power Pick] or [Infinite Power Pick].

"I still can't believe you and Balin got yer Blessin's in less than a year here," Sam griped, as he helped me shovel rock powder into bags. "Ya know, it took me nearly fifty years in tha mine ta get my Blessin'."

"That long?"

"Aye, turned 'er down though! Hah!" Sam had a deep belly laugh. He was the only other dwarf I knew that had turned down a Blessing. Apparently, it wasn't too common.

"Why didja turn it down?" My shovel got stuck in a mound of stone dust and I struggled to lift it out. Tiara's Teats, you'd think dust would be light, but it's still rock!

"Eh. I didn't want anythin' from Tiara. All her Abilities are about bein' greedy fer stuff or fightin'. I'm a lover! Not a fighter! And I don't want to spend all me days in the mines. This is just a sacrifice fer my art!" He struck a pose. Sam is a Titled [Maestro] – that's someone Blessed by Solen of Freedom and Midna of Communication. As for how he's an artist?

Bagpipes. He plays the bagpipes. That's also why he's here.

To be honest, I *love* the bagpipes. I'll take a lovingly rendered *Amazing Grace* any day of the week, and I'm an aficionado of the band

Dropkick Murphys. Dwarvish bagpipes take it to the next level though. I think it's the giant gouts of fire and the fact that you can hear it in your bones. I actually taught Sam *Scotland the Brave* and that was partly how we hit it off so well. Apparently, bagpipes are seen more as an 'instrument of war' – like a bugle – and there aren't too many dwarves that treat it as an art form.

"I can see Midna, but how did you catch Solen's attention?"

"Oh, I broke outta the camp about a dozen times. They always brought me back, but it was enough!" The two of us laughed, and then continued working. After a few minutes, Sam began to hum, and I joined him. The sound of *Scotland the Brave* soon echoed down the tunnel. We continued like that for a while until a returning Balin broke up our duet.

"Can you two keep that racket down! All o' Pete's singing was bad enough, Sam! Now yer doin' it, too!" Sam and I laughed and soon Balin joined in. He didn't actually hate our singing. We were pretty good, if I said so myself!

"You should learn the words and join us, Balin!" I said.

"Ay, come on, don't be a stick in the mud!" Sam smacked him on the back and Balin shook a fist.

"If ya keep askin', I'll do it, and then you'll both regret it!" According to Wreck, Balin had serenaded Annie at one point. Neither of them ever spoke of it, and Wreck's only explanation was a haunted look in her eyes. Maybe we'd stop asking Balin to sing....

"By tha way, our shift's about done. Grim said come on up." Balin grabbed the bags we'd filled and slung them over his shoulder.

Sam arched his back with a *crick* as I collected all our tools. "Ach, sweet freedom, thank Solen! I'm getting too old ta be down these tunnels!"

"Maybe if you stopped playin' your pipes at midnight, they'd stop throwin' you in here!" I joked.

"Nah, they're just jealous o' my panache. Everyone knows City Hall is full of crotchety bureaucrats and stuffed up nobles."

"Shush! You don't want to add insultin' a noble to yer charges, Sam!" Balin said with panic in his eyes.

"Ach, who cares, Balin? Those fops are gonna get what's comin' to them one day. You mark my words!"

The three of us marched up the dive tunnel while Balin and Sam bickered about royalty. It was good natured, if a bit pointed. Balin's a royalist and Sam thinks they're unnecessary. He believes your average dwarf deserves better representation. I really want to teach him the wonders of parliamentary democracy, but I think I'll keep to beer instead of politics for now.

We arrived at the surface and met up with a few other miners. We all said our 'hellos,' did a headcount to ensure everyone was still kicking, and then the whole grumble headed over to the mess hall. It was bacon and egg sandwiches for lunch today, and I was ravenous.

As we walked into camp, Wreck came alongside Sam, Balin, and myself.

"How was yer day? Did Sam break you with his singin' yet?" she asked.

"Oy!" Sam cried in a tone of faux hurt. "You had the day off, so you can't talk!" The rest of us laughed.

"Actually, Pete taught him another new song. Both of 'em won't shaddup!" Balin whined. There were some general notes of commiseration from the other miners as we made our way into the mess hall. There were two kegs of beer, one of which had a little picture of a lemon affixed to it. I noticed that nearly a quarter of the dwarves chose to drink from the radler barrel. There was also a marked reduction in angry remarks and muttering. I think the mining crew has grown used to the idea.

Over the past half a year I put a lot of thought into why there was such a big reaction to the radler, and why dwarves didn't cook with beer. The first problem is that beer is a major part of dwarven tradition. Dwarves are very clan- and ancestor-oriented, which means they consider heirlooms sacred. Add some fairly complex racial tensions to the mix and it means that beer is something of a institution, like maple syrup or hockey. Altering beer was like altering the Constitution, or conflating European football with American football. Cooking with it was like taking grandma's homemade apple pie and using it to make cobbler – it might be delicious, but granny would die a little inside, you *monster*.

The second problem was that I wasn't actually a brewer! Becoming a registered Brewer was as close as a dwarf could get to a

Title without actually receiving one, though there *was* an actual [Brewer] Title too. A Brewer was as respected as an Engineer or Doctor back on earth. Some families have been Brewers for literally thousands of years! Amateurs just *don't* mess with beer here, like you wouldn't even dream of trying to play at Doctor. That's why there's no craft brewers.

Of course, on the other end of the spectrum you had dwarves like Wreck. I noticed she had poured herself a tankard of the regular beer, and as we sat down, I caught her attention.

"You don't like the radler, Wreck?"

"I told ya, Pete. I don't really like lemons."

"Ya like regular beer, eh?" Sam asked. He had a tankard full of radler and swore by it since the first time he drank it. Leave it to a dwarf like Sam to go all in on something new.

"Nah, it's just beer. It tastes better than water but it's just another kind of chemical. I don't see why everyone is so worked up," Wreck replied. At the other end of the table a couple of dwarves stared at her incredulously and shifted slightly down the bench.

Right, there was a third camp that simply didn't care. They were a minority, but some of the dwarves didn't have any real attachment to beer in the first place. Weirdos. We ate the rest of our food interspersed with chats about the daily dive and the *trough-incident*. Then Balin caught everyone's attention and pulled us all in conspiratorially.

"'Ave you noticed that Bran seems off?" He asked in a hushed tone. We all turned to look over at the kitchen window. Bran was handing out sandwiches, but he did indeed look a bit... off. His regular good-natured smile was gone, and he barely acknowledged the 'hellos' and 'thankees' he was getting.

"I'll go check. I want to talk to him anyway." I picked up my now empty plate and made my way over. "Hey, Bran? Why the raisin face?"

"Oh Pete." Bran turned to look at me. "I'm just worried. Opal's sick."

Eh?

CHAPTER EIGHTEEN
CODDLED

"How is she doin'?" I asked. Sam, Wreck, Bran, Balin and myself were all clustered outside of Doctor Opal's Cabin.

"It's a cold," said Bran. "She started coughin' this mornin', and she was out of it by lunch time."

"I'm goin' in to check on her." Wreck opened the door and stepped inside. The rest of us moved to go in as well, but Wreck spun around and firmly shut the door in our faces.

"Alone!" she hissed as the door closed. "Opal doesn't need a bunch of gawkers!"

The rest of us stood bereft for a moment.

"How bad is it?" Sam broke the silence.

"A slight fever, but nothin' serious," Bran replied.

Phew! I'd been worried about her since Bran looked so down. In a world with magical healing and God given [Healers], illness must not be a real problem. Of course, being sick sucked no matter what. That did bring up a good point though – I posed the question to Sam, since he seemed to be most likely to know.

"Couldn't she just get the [Healer] to fix her? What was his name? Bastion?"

"Aye, she could." Sam nodded. "But it would be expensive, and [Healers] are always busy. She'll be better before he even has time to see her."

"What if she can't pay for it?" I could feel the Canadian habit of promoting public health care rise up within me. "Opal said we pay a lot in taxes, why isn't healing covered?"

Sam shrugged. "Not enough dwarves get sick. Besides, a dwarf can always get indentured if needed. Work fer tha city in a mine like this fer a few years and they'll square you with the [Healer], no matter how much. It's a big headache, and not worth it fer a common cold."

That made sense. Even in our world you wouldn't go to the doctor for the common cold. Well, unless it got really bad, or your two-year-old was up all night with hacking coughs. I felt a little melancholy at that. I haven't really thought of Caroline and Samantha recently. I guess that's why I got the Blessing notification for my 'spirit adapting fully' or whatever. I still miss my family, but I don't have time to dwell on it. I have new friends, new goals, and no real regrets from my last life. Well, maybe a few.

"She said that she'll be fine. I tried goin' in, but I know nothin' about helpin' sick folk." Bran said, a note of depression in his voice. "She said, 'I'm the Doctor here, Bran. I'll be fine.' I just wish there was somethin' I could do."

While I was distracted with thoughts of my old family, the rest of the group finished up their discussion and started to head back to the mess hall. All except for Wreck, who was going to stay behind with Opal. It sucked that there wasn't anything we could do for the kindly [Doctor]. She always worked so hard taking care of us. Then something tugged at my memory – my wife, sick in bed smiling as I made her favourite medicine.

"Ya comin', Pete?" Balin asked, tapping me on the shoulder.

"Sorry, Balin. I was just thinking."

"Uh oh."

"Hey! It's not that bad! My ideas are all great!"

"My moustache would disagree." Balin scowled and twirled the scorched strands of his moustache while he glowered at me.

"Then there was that pot of horror…" Bran shuddered.

"We *don't* talk about pruno. And Balin, all the time we spent on the saltpeter trough was kind of great."

"What? How."

"Because it was *grat*ing."

Sam laughed and Balin grinned, but Bran just groaned.

"I pray daily that the Gods strike you down," he grumped.

"Well, excuse me, Bran! Here *I* was considering sharing a recipe that might help Opal." I scoffed. "I guess you don't want it!"

Bran feigned desperation. "Did I say strike you down? I meant that I pray daily for your good health and happiness! Do you really have a new recipe for me, Pete? Somethin' to help Opal feel better?"

"Yeah, it's something I made for my wi – for a friend." I was thinking of an old recipe that I used to make for Caroline. I made it for the first time while we were engaged, and ever since then it was something she asked for whenever she was sick. It was an old British drink called caudle. "To the kitchen, gents!"

"What are we makin'?"

"I'm going to ruin some beer!"

"Not again!" Balin sobbed.

"What do you mean again?" Sam asked.

"You'll see! Follow me!" I pointed in the direction of the mess hall and headed towards it, a skip in my step.

"I have nightmares from the last time this happened...." Balin muttered.

The four of us were wearing aprons and standing in the kitchen, with a pot on the stove and a keg of beer on the counter beside us.

"Oh, hush! It went perfectly!" I said as I poured some beer into the pot.

"Tim lost his beard, and half the camp got injured!" Balin protested.

"Tim's fine," I replied.

"Nothin' about that dwarf is fine..." Sam muttered. "I think he's been stringin'... never mind."

I ignored the three of them. I had caudle to make! There were a couple variations on the drink, and I planned to cook up the heartiest version. I grabbed a set of beard nets and passed them around.

"Alright, Bran. Time to get started."

"Aye, what do ya need first?" Bran pulled out a little recipe book and began to take notes.

"First, I need some eggs and sugar."

"Sugar again..." Balin muttered.

"Help or get outta the way, Balin." Bran pushed Balin aside and got the eggs out of the cooler. He pointed Balin towards the sugar.

I poured a few cups of beer into the pot and set it to boiling. Then I cracked a few eggs into a bowl and whisked. "I'll need some breadcrumbs too."

"Got it!" Sam grabbed a nearby loaf and crumbled it into a bowl. "What are we makin'?"

"It's a drink called caudle." Caudle was an interesting drink that sounded vile when first described but tasted quite nice. It had its roots in England in the early 1300s where it was originally given to mothers suffering from postpartum pain. It's the origin of the word *coddled*, since you would bring caudle to the ill and injured. I was going to make a slight variation on it that included bread for added texture and nutrients.

"Do we need fish, then?" Bran scratched his head. "Fish oil is good for the sick, but I don't think it'll taste good in beer."

"What?" I paused in my mixing.

"Ya said it's got *cod* in it," Sam pointed out.

"I heard that too." Balin nodded.

"No, it's cau-*dle*. It doesn't have fish in it."

"Dunno why you'd call it that if it doesn't have fish in it," Bran said as he scribbled more notes. "No cod around here anyway."

"Aye, it's weird." Balin and Sam nodded in agreement.

I grumped, "Am I makin' this or not?"

"Not is better," Balin quipped.

"Anything more, Pete?" Bran and I ignored him as we continued working.

"I need cream, salt, and saffron if you have some."

"What's saffron?"

"It's a spice." Come to think of it, saffron was the 'most expensive spice.' I seriously doubted they had any in a mining camp, no matter how big a sweet tooth the resident doctor had. "Grab the nutmeg, that'll work too."

"Aye, got it." Bran opened up the cupboard and pulled out some containers while Sam grabbed the cream. The three of us watched the pot as it came to a simmer, and I poured the eggs and cream into the beer.

"The first step in caudle is to add some cream and eggs to warm beer or wine."

"Wine, eh? Is it an elvish recipe?" Sam asked.

"Makes sense," Balin mused. "Elves are weird. Comes from livin' thousands of years."

I ignored them, whisking until the beer mixture turned foamy.

"Next, add some breadcrumbs or oatmeal, and sugar. Something starchy and something sweet." I mixed in the breadcrumbs and the sugar and whisked a while longer. "Finally, a sprinkle of salt and some spices!" I added a pinch of nutmeg and salt and gave the mixture one final whisk. It was roughly the colour of caramel and had a milky, foamy texture.

"That doesn't look half-bad. I'm a fan of both milk *and* beer, and that's milk *with* beer!" Sam actually smacked his lips.

"I admit it does look tasty," Balin said.

"It smells quite sweet. I think Opal will love it. Makes people feel better, you say?"

"Absolutely. I made enough for everyone to try, so give me some tankards." I poured out five mugs and everyone stared into the milky foam of their mugs with trepidation.

Balin took a sniff. "It smells like nutmeg."

Sam and Bran did the same and voiced their agreement.

"Alright, bottoms up! Cheers, eh! To Opal's health!" Sam held up his tankard and we all clinked mugs. There was a brief moment of silence broken only by the faint sound of chugging. Then four dwarves took a satisfied gasp at the same time.

Balin's eyes were wide with surprise. "It's delicious!"

"I could get used ta this!" Sam crowed.

"It has a light and fluffy texture that makes it easy to drink, but enough body that it feels like eatin' a meal." Bran rubbed his beard, now with a slight patina of milk foam. "The sugar makes it sweet and easy to drink while the bitterness of the beer keeps it from bein' too much like a dessert. Opal will love it!"

"Aye, it feels nice and warm in me stomach, and tha alcohol helps settle ya! It's perfect fer relaxin'!" Sam sighed with pleasure.

"I need ta get sick more often!"

"Alright! I'm glad you all like it." I calmed them down and grabbed the remaining tankard as Sam's hand reached for it. "The rest of it is for Doc Opal. Bran, do you want to take it to her?"

"Aye, Pete. Thanks!" Bran grabbed the tankard and made his way out of the kitchen.

I looked at the now-empty pot. "Should I make some of this for everyone else?"

"NO!!!" Balin and Sam both shouted in horror.

"It was just a thought..." I muttered.

Hopefully, Opal would be better soon, and things would go back to normal.

Now I just needed that damn charcoal!!

CHAPTER NINETEEN
CHARCOAL

"Pete, any word on the charcoal?"

"No, not yet Balin."

"Ugh, what's takin' so long!"

"I don't think we have enough silver yet. I'll talk to Tim."

"I still don't know why we asked him to do it! He was embezzlin' from City Hall!!"

"Tim's a reformed dwarf! Isn't that the whole point of this mine? I choose to believe in him."

"You just feel sorry that he got shaved at yer Blessin' party."

"There's nothing wrong with a clean shave. He has a very distinguished cleft-chin."

"You don't believe that."

"No comment. He'll come through."

"Harumph. Do you want me ta handle it instead?"

"No, it's fine. Your help with the … *shovelling* was more than enough, leave the rest up to me. I got this!"

"If yer sure…"

"Tim! How's the charcoal supply coming along?"

"Hey, Pete! Sorry I haven't been around. I've been dealin' with inventory for Grim. What do ya need?"

"Charcoal?"

"Right. I'm afraid I don't have any good news. The supplier wants more silver."

"Haven't I already given you—"

"It just isn't enough yet, Pete. You don't know how all this works. My hands are tied by higher powers. It's complicated getting supplies out here, and charcoal is expensive now that Greentree is closed. Did you hear?"

"No, what happened?"

"A lot of monster movement and big mushfolk coming out at the fringes. It's dangerous."

"Wow. Is the city safe?"

"There's talk about a possible monster stampede. Anyway, just bring me next month's silver and I'll deal with it."

"I... *sigh* fine. Thanks for the help, Tim."

"Of course, Pete. What are friends for? I'll see you at the mess hall, it's steak for dinner tonight!"

"Thanks for the caudle, Peter! It helped a lot!"

"You're welcome, Opal! I'm glad you liked it!"

"Any luck with your venture?"

"Not yet, I'm just waiting for the last few pieces to fall into place."

"Make sure you give some more recipes to Bran before you go."

"Absolutely, I'm rooting for you two."

"What!?"

"Nevermindexcusemebye."

"Hi, Tim!"

"Hey, Pete! Sorry, I can't stick around. Runnin' an errand for Grim right now."

"There's something I need to talk to you about."

"Is it important, or can it wait?"

"It's important to *me*! Where's my charcoal!?"

"Geeze, Pete! I'm working my tail off here and doing your shopping on the side. There's no need to get all mad at me because things aren't working out! It's not *my* fault."

Sigh "Sorry, Tim, I'm just... starting to get antsy."

"That's okay, Pete. I understand, and I forgive you. I sent off the last bit of silver, and I promise that I'll let you know as soon as I hear back from the supplier."

"Can I help with anything?"

"No, no, I've got it handled. You focus on you. By the way, are you up for another game of hammercup after dinner? You won last time, so I want my revenge!"

"Sounds great! You're goin' down!"

"You'd better practise, or I'll crush you with my new technique!"

"Will do!"

ping Our pickaxes rang in the darkness of the dive.

"Why are ya still stickin' around here, Pete? Didn't ya have a grand plan to get out?"

ping

"Yeah, but we're still waiting on our charcoal, Sam."

ping

"Eh? Just nab some from a [Peddler] the next time one comes through."

ping

"We already put a lot of time and money into asking Tim to do it. It should be arriving any day."

ping

"Pete... That's— are you sure Tim is lookin' out fer your best interests? Mebbe you should leave it to Balin?"

ping

"Pass me that sack, would ya?"

"Aye..."

"Alright, Pete. Here's your monthly silver."

"Thanks, Grim!"

"What have you been using it for? I know you two've been squirrellin' it away for your grand plan."

"Yeah! We need it to buy the last ingredient for our experiment."

"What on Erd do ya need that much silver for? I've given ya at least a full two months' pay since ya finished with that Tiara-damned trough! You said you needed some sulphur – I've got some set aside – and Balin was yellin' about 'salt-somethin'. What else do ya need?"

"Charcoal."

"What? You've been waiting for that!? I can just get you some in a few days, Pete!"

"What!! Really!? I could have just asked *you* this entire time!? Why didn't I!?"

Bing!

Stat Increased: [Wisdom]!

Your wisdom has increased by 1! Your new wisdom is 13!

Grim gave me an odd look. "Aaron's Arse, Pete. If it gets you out of my camp even a day sooner, I'm more than happy to get you all the charcoal you need! Just leave your silver with me and I'll deal with it."

"Thanks so much, Grim!"

"Aye. There'll be a bit of a delay cause of tha' new year, but I'll have it to ya within the week. Now get out."

I stepped out of the mining office elated but confused. I slapped the sides of my cheeks a few times and considered washing my face. Why had I gotten a bonus to wisdom just for realising I could ask Grim to do my shopping? Then my eyes widened.

Charcoal! I had charcoal! I was finally going to make some gunpowder and get out of this prison and into a proper brewery! Huzzah! I practically skipped down the hallway and ran into Tim as I launched myself out the door.

"Sorry, Tim!"

"What are you jumpin' around for? You got the silver for this month?" Tim put out his hand. I paused for a moment, confused, then was immediately distracted – I had great news to share!

"Yeah, I got my silver, but more importantly!" I smiled massively and struck a pose. "Grim is gettin' me charcoal!"

"What!?" Tim cried. For a moment, shock and anger seemed to play across his face. I blinked, because that couldn't be right. Then he smiled and nodded. "I'm happy for you! What's your next step?"

"That's a secret!" I put a finger up to my lips. "Can't be too careful with corporate spies!"

"Corporate spies? This is a *mine*." Tim quirked an eyebrow and rubbed at his hairless jaw. His bald chin still gave me the willies. Maybe it was a leftover reaction from previous dwarf Pete, or a wonky atavistic factor like with arachnophobia. Either way, Tim didn't deserve my scorn or distrust over something silly like a shaved beard – even if it did make him look like Lex Luthor with a mullet!

"I'll see you later, Tim!"

"Alright. So long, Pete." Tim turned around and left. It may have been my imagination, but it looked like he was scowling as he went into the mining office. Ah well, I had more important things to worry about, like the creation of gunpowder!

I practically floated on air down to the mess hall for dinner. At last, after so many months of waiting, I had charcoal! I passed Sam on the way and waved at him to follow me.

"I got what I needed, Sam!" I patted him on the shoulder as he fell into stride beside me.

"Really? Opal was finally able to getcha a decent sense of humour? That's great!"

"Hardy har."

"I'm glad it worked out. Remember that I got money on you not dyin', so stay safe." Sam smiled, but he was limping and I noticed a slight tear in his thick leather trousers. I slowed down and he paused to catch his breath.

"Speaking of 'staying safe,' are you alright?"

"Just got caught in a small rockslide on a dive. Nothin' big, but my leg did get pinned. I have [Sense Danger] so I got out of the way in time. Balin and Wreck pulled me out." Now that I looked more closely, he did look a little shell-shocked.

"Did you break anything?"

"Nah, just some cuts and bruises. Maybe a small sprain. Nothin' to worry about, eh?" Sam struck a pose. "I'm one of the strongest dwarves around! Don't ya worry about me, son!"

"Glad to hear it." At this point the two of us reached the mess hall and we made our way inside. Now that I had charcoal it was time to start phase two of making gunpowder with poop: the crapshoot.

I had a slight problem. Well, it was more of a *big* problem that could be solved with time and experimentation – I couldn't recall the exact ratios required to make gunpowder. I knew that saltpeter, sulphur, and charcoal were the main ingredients, but not how much of each to add to the mix. I was going to need to try a bunch of different ratios and pray I'd stumble on the correct one. I was literally shooting in the dark with crap. I lost over seven months so far, and I hoped I wasn't going to spend another seven playing with measuring cups. Sam poked me, and I realised that I'd reached the front of the dinner line.

"Hi, Bran. What's for dinner?"

"I've got some roast serpent along with gravy and chitlins and some mashed erdroot."

The plate of food was incredibly appetising. The roast serpent looked like a perfectly circular beef steak with a slightly orange tint to it. It was well marbled, and had a single bone in the centre – probably the spine? The gravy was dark brown and steaming, and it smelled like Thanksgiving. Caroline always made the most incredible turkey, and I swore her stuffing was superior even to grandma's. I'd probably never have another Thanksgiving again... As for the rest of the meal, erdroot was boring and I wasn't a fan of chitlins. They were really healthy, but I just didn't like eating something that once contained poop. *Especially* after the past year.

"No vegetables?" I asked, as he finished spooning the erdroot onto my plate.

"*You* want a balanced diet? Drink yer radler. It's got plenty of vitamins." Bran pointed at the radler barrel.

"Ah yes, the dwarven food groups. Malt, meat, cheese, fruit, and beer."

"Not fruit and beer. It's fruit *with* beer." Bran grinned at me, and I grinned back. He leaned in and whispered to me through a cupped hand. "I mixed turnips into tha' erdroot, and beer into the gravy. Don't tell anyone."

"I understand." I nodded back, sagely. I still couldn't believe that Bran had to *trick* the entire camp into eating their vegetables. There were never simple veggies on the side. It was always some veggies hidden in a sandwich under a slab of roast beast and coated in sauce. It amazed me that every dwarf didn't have gout after a couple hundred years of this diet. "Anyway, can I borrow the measuring cups we talked about?"

"Oh, are ya finally ready to get started?"

"Yep, I can probably start as soon as next week!"

"Congratulations! Somethin' to kick off the new year!"

"Right, Grim mentioned that too. It's the new year, huh...." I took my plate and made my way to our regular table.

It had already been a full year since I arrived on Erd. How time flew. It felt like just yesterday I was still playing chess with Sammy, or cuddling with Caroline on the couch while we read books and drank wine. I chuckled as I remembered my first day on Erd, when I had sprayed beer all over Balin and Grim. Now Balin was the closest friend I'd ever had, and Grim still couldn't wait to get rid of me. I had a mentor in Opal, a comrade in Bran, a friend in Tim, a gruff and affectionate uncle in Sam, and a cautious co-worker in Wreck. I'd carved a place out for myself, and obtained new goals and new skills. Where there had been a hole in my heart at the start of the year, there was now the start of a warm and comforting feeling.

I was soon surrounded by friends at the table as we discussed our future plans and current gossip. Sam and Balin got into a drinking competition as Wreck and Doc Opal talked about beard oil. We discussed plans for the new year celebration, and our resolutions for next year. After a half-hour Tim joined us and we got into a rousing game of hammercup. We were joined by a couple other miners and soon there was a whole cheering squad. Sam crushed all of us, and some cups. I still think it's a terrible game and a waste of good tankards. I needed to teach everyone some Earth drinking games before I left. We ended the night with a toast. Nearly a dozen tankards rose in unison.

"To the Firmament!"

"To charcoal!"

"Fer the ancestors!"

"Fer Crack and Minnova!"

"I want a Blessin' too, dammit!"

I clinked tankards with Tim and the two of us nodded at each other before we took a deep drink; him of regular beer, and I of radler. Indeed, it was good to have friends! Next week I would start mixing gunpowder and then it was just a matter of time until I was free to explore this fascinating new world.

But first, maybe I could do something special for everyone to kick off the new year.

CHAPTER TWENTY
RIBFEST

Canadian celebrations follow one of four main formats. A pancake breakfast, a picnic lunch, a pizza party, or a barbeque dinner. But I wanted to cook something a bit more dwarven, so the first three options were out.

But a goat meat barbeque? That was dwarven – a favourite in fact.

The dwarven unigoat is used as a beast of burden as well as a common pet. They were frightfully intelligent, needy, vocal, and lived for over eighty years. They were kind of like parrots that way, and owning one was a long-term commitment. Dwarves don't eat unigoat, but that doesn't stop them from enjoying the taste of regular plain-old two-horned goats. I'd seen a few massive herds covering the landscape in the distance on occasion.

Speaking of pets, there are several cats in camp. They keep the rat population down, but nobody really owns them. They're just a part of the landscape. Dogs existed, and people knew about them, but they were considered more of a human thing.

I considered the problem of pets as I swung my butcher's cleaver and hacked off another side of ribs with a *thwack!* I love meat too much to go vegan, but twenty dwarves' worth of ribs sitting in a small kitchen was enough to give *anyone* chronic veganism.

thwack! "Urp."

"If you throw up on the ribs, I'm tellin' everyone you ruined the party," Bran opined.

"I'm good, I'm good."

Thwack!

"Then pass me those ribs. I need to stick em' in the cooler before we throw them in the fire-pit."

Thwack!

"No propane or propane accessories? For shame!"

"Dunno what propane is. I use charcoal. And I'm surprised you know the meanin' of shame."

"It's a barbeque thing. You know, if you have charcoal, why did I have to go buy my own?"

"We aren't allowed to give camp supplies to any miners tryin' for a reduced indenture. Also, you refused to tell me what you needed." Bran glowered at me.

"Ah... that wasn't very wise. I should have told you."

Thwack!

"It's a secret, Bran," Bran said, mocking my voice as he brought down his cleaver with an aggressive *thwack!* "I can't tell anyone but my dive-team, Bran." *Thwack!* "Oh, but I'll ask Tim for help, because *that's* such a good idea." *Thwack!*

"Aww, are you jealous, Bran? I thought your only love in life was Opal!"

Bran grumbled. "I'm glad you finally got what you wanted. Maybe I'll have some peace in my kitchen when you're gone."

Thwack!

"Owch. You know Grim said the same thing?"

Thwack!

"Aye, you have that effect on any right-thinkin' dwarf."

"Sam and Balin seem fine."

"Like I said," Bran chuckled.

I gave a mock gasp. "I'm going to tell Sam on you."

Bran brandished his cleaver and gave a wicked smile. "I'd like to see him try anythin'."

"I put my gold on Sam."

"Pete...." Bran's tone turned sweet as simple syrup. "Are you tryin' to get kicked out of me kitchen?"

Thwack!

"Umm, no?"

AN ADVENTURE BREWING

Thwack!

I stared deep into the molasses sitting in the barrel before me. Bran bought it on the promise that I'd teach him how to make molasses cookies, but I really wanted it for something else. Molasses was one of those ingredients that didn't look complex, but actually had a long and storied history. I couldn't even look at a container of the stuff without thinking about the fact that it'd murdered a couple dozen people.

The Great Molasses Flood occurred in 1919, when an enormous vat of molasses exploded and drowned an entire neighbourhood in Boston's North End in scalding molasses. A wave over eight metres high had swept down the main street at over 50 kilometres per hour, smashing through walls, cars, and people. Nearly two dozen killed, over a hundred injured, and an annihilated town that stunk of molasses for years afterward. I shivered, imagining what it would be like to drown in boiling sticky gunk, desperately clawing for a spoon to eat myself free. Were there any other foods that could claim those kinds of numbers? Other than fast-food burgers, of course. Was this barrel a ticking time-bomb, waiting to kill every dwarf in the mine?

"Pete?"

Was there *magical* molasses in this world? Could it form into a molasses slime – a brown gooey creature of death? Would such a slime reach a brown liquidy pseudopod out and suck adventurers into a sweet, sticky end? Why was it called mole-asses anyway? It wasn't as though hairy burrower butts were appetising in any way, shape, or form.

"Pete!"

"Oh, sorry, Bran. What's up?"

"You asked *me* to come see this new sauce of yers."

"Ah, yes. I was just considering the molasses."

"There somethin' wrong with it?"

"Nope, it's perfect. Tell me, Is there such a thing as magical molasses?"

"Maybe? Probably? Never seen it though. Why?"

"No reason."

"Uh huh. Can you tell me what we're makin'? I usually just grill the ribs with some smoked gravy."

"Yeah, it was actually the liquid smoke that gave me the idea to make this. I want barbeque sauce."

"I just said I make sauce for tha barbeque."

"No, it's a special kind of sauce. I haven't seen you make it yet, so let me know if it already exists when we're done."

"I can do that."

"I strongly doubt it since I'm adding beer." I bit my lip in chagrin. All my best barbeque sauce recipes used beer in them, and I was pretty sure the dwarven swill was going to ruin it. Bran looked happy though, if a bit worried.

"Everyone loves the beer sauces, but I don't know how much longer I can keep it hidden." Bran sighed. "I should tell everyone at the barbeque and see what happens. I think they'll be fine with it."

"Me too. You didn't change the brew, or add anything to it, you just used it to make delicious foods. Like I said, your ancestors would be proud of you."

"Thanks, Pete. Now show me this sauce!"

I shuffled around the kitchen island and grabbed some onions and tomato sauce. "Welcome to *Peter Samson's Cooking School*. We're making a beer-based barbeque sauce today. We don't have much to work with, but a little improvisation never hurt anyone. This sauce is a common favourite from back home."

Pete's Budget Beerbeque Sauce Ingredients

Cayenne Pepper
Onions
Ale
Tomato Sauce
Garlic
Molasses
Liquid Smoke

Salt & Pepper

"Where's that? Did you remember where you came from!?" Bran gave me an excited look. Shit, I was still supposed to be amnesiac. I needed to get around to another cover story or stop making slip-ups like that.

"Uh, no. I remember a lot of foods, drinks, and recipes, but not much else." I gave my best piteous expression. Bran didn't look completely convinced, but he gave a sad nod.

"Maybe you loved 'em the most, so you remembered 'em the best."

"Makes sense. Anyways, take all these onions and sauté them. I need to mince a ton of garlic," I said in a rush, shoving the onions into Bran's arms.

We worked in companionable silence for a while, the only sound the simmering pop of onions in butter. Pretty soon my eyes were streaming, and my beard was covered in blubber. By Midna's Mullet, it was *awful*.

"Bran," *Sniff* "How high does your vitality need to be for onions not to bother you?"

Sniff "Has to be over twenty-four."

"Dear Gods, that's so high!"

"Higher than needed for most poisons, aye." *Sniff*

"Argh." Curse you onions! Your power was unfathomable! Minus one fer the Gods of Erd!

We stepped outside to wipe our eyes and took a minute to air out the kitchen while the giant mass of onions cooked. I looked up into the twilight of Crack and considered my last year here. Was I really doing the right thing? Should I just ignore the beer and the cooking, and simply mine my way to freedom over the course of the next decade?

I looked over at Bran, who was gleefully pacing in anticipation. My heart grew firm as I considered my time with him in the kitchen. How many more dwarven *artistes* were hampered in their craft by millennia of stagnant thinking? Annie, for one. If my only mark in this world was a thriving craft beer industry and *A Bran, a Can, and a Plan* cookbook, I'd die a happy dwarf.

"Time to dive back in and stir the onions. Should be good now, Pete."

"Alright, let's go!"

We stepped back into the kitchen, and the scent of steaming onions and freshly diced garlic wafted over us. We took deep breaths in unison and let them out with satisfied *aaahhs.*

"Now *this* is why we cook." I nodded with satisfaction.

"Speak for yerself! I cook 'cause I love it."

"You cook because *Opal* loves it!"

"Shaddup. What's the next step?"

"We need to empty those vats of tomato sauce you bought into one of the giant sauce pots, then toss in the onions and garlic. Pour in the beer and molasses, then warm it up – but don't boil it."

"Aye, got it." Bran was efficient, and soon the mixture was steaming on the stove top.

"Okay, now we add a bunch of vinegar and sugar, some salt and pepper, and a pinch of *scary spice* – the hottest of the Spice Girls." I hummed a little *Wannabe* under my breath as I considered various powders in Bran's well-stocked spice-rack.

"What spice girls?" Bran asked, pausing in his notes.

"You know. Posh-paprika-spice, Sporty-jalapeno-spice, Ginger-spice, Baby-chili-spice, and Scary-cayenne-spice."

"Why would you think of those as girls? I only know paprika, ginger, and cayenne."

"Well, we're adding cayenne – oooh, and a little paprika, because it's awesome." I added a few pinches of the red powder, then dumped in a fistful, followed by some salt and a lot of pepper. "Spicy is good."

Bran nodded. "Aye, I like spicy."

I dipped a spoon in and took a taste. I was greeted by the warm undertones of tomatoes mixed with garlic, and the sweet and sour flavour of molasses and beer. It was *marvellous,* even in spite of the slight bitter aftertaste of the ale. I closed my eyes and imagined sitting on my patio at home in June. The sun played through Caroline's hair as she laughed at one of my awful puns. Sammy clamoured for the first ribs off the barbeque. I took another taste of the sauce and sniffed, tears welling up in my eyes. It's the onions dammit! I passed a spoonful to Bran and he tasted it.

"Guh, it's delicious! Barck's Beard, I'll never be able to go back to smoked gravy ever again!"

"And it isn't even done yet! The final step is going to involve that liquid smoke you've got squirrelled away."

"Aye, don't use too much, though. It's expensive." Bran passed me a small glass vial filled with a black liquid.

Liquid smoke was made by condensing the smoke from a woodfire, and the *Wright* way to make it was created by an *Ernest* pharmacist. Nyuck. *Ernest Wright* was only a teenager when he first discovered smoke condensing in the stovepipes of the print shop he worked at. Years later as a pharmacist he recreated the phenomena, and then sold it as a food additive. Apparently, it was invented by gnomes here on Erd, though Bran couldn't tell me when.

I added the smoke drop by drop until I finally had that sweet, smokey, tangy taste of good BBQ sauce that all Canadians knew and loved. I passed a spoonful to Bran and his eyes crossed.

"It's hot! And *delicious!* The taste of the beer compliments tha woody taste of the smoke. The spicy cayenne and paprika give it a bite that gets covered with the sweet aftertaste of the molasses! I love it! It's thick, tangy, and *amazin'!*"

"So, it's new?"

"Aye!"

I grabbed a pair of goat-hair brushes and handed one to Bran.

"Alright, let's start brushin' sauce on ribs, and cook us some meat! We've got dwarven bellies to fill and a new year's party to start!"

"Now you're talkin'!"

Grim finished up with his speech welcoming the new year and thanking the various Gods for all the Blessings they'd given out. That was followed by a round of toasts to Minnova, Crack, the Gods, and whatever other excuses could be found to drink some more. Why on *Erd* were there so many speeches in a mining camp?

I grinned at Bran, who grinned back. We each flipped a set of ribs in unison, and the fire beneath roared to life as fresh grease poured onto the coals.

I watched as one of the new miners was tossed out a window by Balin for cutting in line. The barbeque sauce was a hit. The ribs were a hit. The ambiance of an enormous charcoal fire-pit filled with roasting ribs was a hit.

I nodded at Bran and gave him a fist bump. Then I dodged out of the way as one of the charcoal briquets sparked.

Three hours of constant grilling later, we were done cooking all the ribs. The entire camp went insane over them, declaring the new barbeque sauce to be the greatest thing since Bran's original secret sauce. Grim even came up and told Bran he was going to buy some more liquid smoke to ensure we never ran out.

Bran was over the moon. I poked him in the side as he stared blankly at the stage.

"Do you want to tell them?"

Bran nodded. "Aye, I will." He walked up to the stage and hopped up. The clamour in the hall died down as the miners began to notice him standing there. Then the cheering and hooting and hollering started. Bran bowed and the cheering grew louder.

"THANKEE EVERYONE! DID YOU ALL ENJOY YER BARBEQUE?"

The crowd roared.

"I WANT TO THANK PETE FOR HELPIN' MAKE ALL THIS." Bran pointed in my direction and everyone turned and cheered again. "AND I WANTED TO MAKE AN ANNOUNCMENT TO ROLL IN THE NEW YEAR!"

He waited until the noise died down. Then he took a deep breath and continued in a more level tone.

"I realised over the past year that I was wastin' one of tha greatest gifts our ancestors left us. I put it in the secret sauce first, then my gravy, and a few other meals too. It was the base of the sauce on the meat and it always makes everythin' taste a million times better."

One of the dwarves in the back of the room gasped, and everyone turned to look at him. He stammered.

"Is – is – is it... WATER?"

A voice from the front called you. "YA IDJIT! Water is in EVERYTHIN'!"

"What!? You take that back!"

"I'm stuck in a mine with a bunch of *morons!*"

"Yer not stuck in here with *me!* I'm stuck in here with *YOU!*"

"SHADDUP!!!" Grim roared, and the volume clamped back down. "Bran was talkin'! Let him speak – or do you lot want to eat bread with cold meat every day?"

There was a general noise indicating that was a terrible idea, and Bran coughed and continued. "The ingredient... was *BEER.*"

There was shocked silence, then one dwarf put his hand up. Bran pointed at him.

"Bran? We already knew that. Any dwarf can tell when there's True Brew."

Everyone nodded.

"Aye! It tasted great with everythin'!"

"It was a brilliant idea, addin' beer!"

"Yer ancestors would be proud of you usin' their gifts in such a great way. It *did* make everythin' taste a million times better!"

"Yer a genius, Bran!"

The entire mess hall broke into affirming shouts. Bran glanced over at me with wide eyes, and then basked in the appreciation.

I thought back to the fighting over my radler and smacked my forehead. No fair!

I taught everyone some *Auld Lang Syne* and Grim even let Sam play his bagpipes.

We laughed, drank, ate, and sang the last night of the year away.

Should all yer old pals be forgot,

and never thought upon.

The flames o' love are all put out,
and fully past and gone.
Ya kiss yer silver, rub yer gold,
And never leave the mine.
Didja ever once reflect,
On times gone by.

I rubbed at a spot where a ring wasn't while we sang, and even drank several tankards of regular True Brew.

Today proved that change *was* possible. One year down. Several hundred to go. Phew.

CHAPTER TWENTY-ONE
BOOM?

It's been half a week since the new year, and today was the day. I got time off work from Grim, I had some basic chemistry supplies, and most importantly: I had charcoal!

So now I was sitting in the kitchen with some measuring glasses and a bunch of bags of saltpeter, charcoal, and sulphur. The next step was to –

"BY THE UNHOLY YAMS OF YEARN! WHAT IN THE NETHER ARE YA DOIN' IN THE KITCHEN WITH ALL THIS DIRT AND SHIT?!"

"Sorry, Bran."

20 minutes later

I was sitting in my cabin with some measuring glasses and a bunch of bags of saltpeter, charcoal, and sulphur. The next step was to –

"BARCK'S BEARD, PETE! WHY ARE YA STINKIN' UP OUR ROOM?!"

"Sorry, Balin."

20 minutes later

I was sitting at a table in the common area of the camp with some measuring glasses and a bunch of bags of saltpeter, charcoal, and sulphur. The next step was to –

"TIARA'S TEATS, PETE! DIDN'T YA SAY THIS STUFF WAS DANGEROUS? GET OUT OF THE CAMP!"

"Sorry, Grim."

20 minutes later

I was sitting at a makeshift workstation far away from the camp with some measuring glasses and a bunch of bags of saltpeter, charcoal, and sulphur. The next step was to –

I paused and looked around. No dwarf appeared to angrily demand my immediate eviction, and the only sound was the beating of my excited heart. Alright! It was time to get cracking on my escape plan! That's right, I never planned on using gunpowder to earn enough silver to end my indenture. I was always planning to blast my way free from this prison and escape to the town, smash into a bank, and steal enough gold to live the next 400 years in peace.

Muhahaha! The fools have handed me their own doom! DOOM!

I put some saltpeter into the first measuring pot and sighed. No escape from Alcatraz for boring old Pete. As much as I wanted to use my 'superior technological knowledge' to get all OP and stuff, I found it unlikely to succeed. I strongly suspected that a police force that had a teleporter and who knows what other crazy magic was way above my ability to deal with. Besides, there was a good chance I'd make actual long-term money with gunpowder.

So, I sat down and got a trio of containers. I filled one container with saltpeter, another with charcoal, and the last with sulphur. The first step was to grind these down and then measure them out into portions.

I paused.

20 minutes later

I was sitting at a makeshift workstation far away from the camp with some measuring glasses and a bunch of bags of saltpeter, charcoal, and sulphur and a MORTAR AND PESTLE. The next step is to grind each of the three components into a fine powder. First, I scooped the saltpeter into the stone bowl and began grinding. Honestly, it's kind of relaxing. There's a groove to it, where your arm finds just the right motion and then you can watch everything turn into dust. After around ten minutes of grinding my arm didn't even feel tired and I wondered anew at my high vitality. Being a dwarf is AWESOME!

After the first saltpeter grinding, I dumped the resulting white powder into a separate bucket. I was going to try a couple different mix ratios so I'd need a lot of saltpeter. As such, back to grinding! The grinding of the pestle and the psychedelic purple light of the cavern brought to mind an old Judas Priest song – *Grinder*. I started a more rhythmic pounding with the pestle and started singing to the beat.

Soon I had all the saltpeter I needed, and after carefully cleaning out the bowl and the pestle in a soapy bucket, I started on the charcoal. Over an hour had passed, and even my muscly arms were starting to get tired. I decided to push through and finish the charcoal before taking a break. I waited *months* for this charcoal, and I wanted it done yesterday. My arms were burning at the end, but I got all the charcoal done. I wiped the sweat from my brow and sat down in a heap.

I stared up into the stars and thought about my future. I didn't plan on becoming some kind of mining magnate. I wanted to brew beer. No matter where gunpowder goes, I'm not going to let it take over my life. I'll probably just leave it all to Grim and ask him to stick any excess gold into my account. He's a stand-up guy, and he'd probably appreciate the chance. Maybe Tim, if Grim can't do it.

"Whatcha doin', Pete?"

I looked up, startled, as Balin appeared before me like magic. Which in a world with real magic is an incredibly stupid statement. "Just some grindin', Balin. Do you want to do it?"

"Not with you." Balin eyed the buckets and pots with wariness. "Will I need ta shovel that saltypeter again?"

"No, I did that already. There's just the sulphur."

"Ah, you don't want to work with tha stuff that almost killed ya?" Balin winked at me. "I understand. Let yer good friend Balin do it fer ya." He walked over and began scooping sulphur into the mortar.

"AHHHH!" I screamed.

"What!?" Balin stopped with a jerk.

"Clean that first! You'll kill us both!"

"WHAT!?"

I grabbed the mortar and doused it in the soapy water and began rubbing it down. "I have been talking about how this works for months, Balin!"

"Pete, I'm a carpenter, not an [Alchemist], I dunno how this stuff works." He paused and seemed struck by a terrible realisation. "YOU WERE MAKIN' IT IN OUR ROOM?!"

"I know what I'm doing." I muttered petulantly. To be fair, that had been a terrible idea. Then something he said caught my attention. "Alchemists?"

"Changin' the subject again... Aye, there's Titled [Alchemists]."

"Do they change lead into gold and stuff?"

"Not unless they want every miner in Crack to come an' murder 'em. They make potions and salves and such. What yer' doin' here looks a lot like alchemy to me."

Huh. Well, maybe I could make a book on modern chemistry and sell it to the alchemists. Then again – world of magic – so everything I knew could be completely wrong. I took out the mortar, dried it and handed it back to Balin.

"Here, now do it. We are making a low explosive, that means that each of these ingredients can react violently with each other. We have to be really careful and make sure nothing gets bumped or mixed that we don't intend to."

"Thank ye fer tha explanation." Balin took the bowl, filled it with sulphur and began grinding. I had to show him the technique, but he picked it up quickly. My man Balin is a quick learner and good with his hands. Annie will be pleased. By his *hard* work. At the brewery. Nyuck.

"Have you heard from Annie, Balin?" I asked as I turned my eyes towards the purple glow of the city. We couldn't see Minnova from where we were, but the glow of the central crystal was an ever-present reminder of where it lay.

"Nah, can't get visits. I'd need ta wait until tha next vacation day."

"When's that?"

"Two years."

"Excuse me?"

"Sam's bagpipes wreck yer ears? I said two years."

"Oh, I heard you, I just thought that was insane. Two years?"

"Aye, it's normal. Most of us are out before that though." Balin paused and shook his shoulders. "By my beard this is tough work, Pete!"

"Whining about physical labour? Are you an elf?"

"Shaddup!" We grinned at each other and he went back to work. Soon there was a third bucket full of ground sulphur and it was time to start.

The next step was the most dangerous. It was time to mix the three ingredients together. One misstep and the entire mixture could go boom right between my fingers. I admit that I was shaking a little bit.

"How are we doin' for time, Balin?"

Balin shrugged and thought for a moment. "I came right after me shift. We missed lunch – thanks fer that – so we've got about an hour or two till dinner."

"I wasn't even trying to *hit* lunch, so I don't mind if I *missed* it."

"What?"

"Just give me the mortar, Balin."

I didn't know the exact ratio needed, so I started by putting the saltpeter into a measuring cup. Then I stared at the cup.

20 minutes later

Iwassittingatamakeshiftworkstationfarawayfromthecampwithsomemeasuringglassesandabunchofbagsofsaltpeter,charcoal,andsulphur,amortarandpestle, and A SCALE. I rushed through the now-familiar thought process and sighed mightily. By the *Gods*, I was bad at this.

You do chemistry portioning with a *scale*, not *measuring cups*.

I didn't know the exact ratios, so I was going to start with a 33/33/33 then do a 50/25/25 and finish off with a 75/12.5/12.5 for each of the different ratios. If it wasn't one of those, then this was going to take forever. With shaking fingers, I added some water to the mortar along with some carefully weighed portions. Then I started grinding. If something was going to go wrong, it was going to happen here – explosively. The water helped lower the chance of an explosion and made the gunpowder into a paste.

The first set of ratios went off without a hitch and I started the next one. It took the rest of the hour as Balin watched in trepidation with the occasional, "You got this, Pete!" and, "Don't die! Sam has money on ya!" I finished three sets of 50/25/25 and started on the 75/12.5/12.5s. When I completed the final mix, I heard a *Bing!* and a blue box appeared before my eyes.

Blessing Granted: [Barck]!
You have invented something incredible and gained the notice of Barck.
Your passion and ingenuity will change the world.
If you receive Barck's Blessing, you will receive **[Regeneration]** *and* **[Good Luck]**.
If you accept Barck's Blessing, you will be eligible for a Title!

Do you accept?
Yes/No

Huzzah! That message means that I got it right! It must have been the 75/12.5/12.5! I mentally clicked on "No" and turned towards Balin. "Balin! We did it!"

"Are ya sure? Nothin' happened."

"I know it must have! I got a Blessing from—"

In the corner of my vision, a blue box began to blink.

Blessing Granted: [Barck]!
You have invented something incredible and gained the notice of Barck.
Your passion and ingenuity will change the world.
*If you receive Barck's Blessing, you will receive [**Regeneration**] and [**Good Luck**].*
If you accept Barck's Blessing, you will be eligible for a Title!

Do you accept?
Yes

Didn't I hit 'No,' on this already? What was happening? Where had the "No" gone? As I watched, the blue box changed again.

Blessing Granted: [Barck]!
You have invented something incredible and gained the notice of Barck.
Congratulations, your invention could change the world!
If you receive Barck's Blessing, you will receive [Regeneration] and [Good Luck].
If you accept Barck's Blessing, you will be eligible for a Title!

You have 10 seconds to decide
Yes

"What!?"

"Somethin' tha matter Pete?"

"I—"

You have 9 seconds to decide
Yes

"Balin, somethin's wrong!"

You have 8 seconds to decide
Yes

"Are we gonna die? I don't wanna die, I finally got a girlfriend!"

You have 7 seconds to decide
Yes

"No, I can't hit "No" on this Blessing!"

You have 6 seconds to decide
Yes

"Who hits "No" on Blessin's?"

You have 5 seconds to decide
Yes

"Sam does!"

You have 4 seconds to decide
Yes

"Sam's a loony bard!"

You have 3 seconds to decide
Yes

"I turned down all the Blessin's. I want Archie's!"

You have 2 seconds to decide
Yes

"Wait, *ALL* the Blessin's? How many elfin Blessin's have you turned down Pete?"

You have 1 second to decide
Yes

"NOOOOO!!!"

Blessing Received: [Barck]!
You have accepted the Blessing of Barck!
You have received the Blessings [Regeneration] and [Good Luck]!
Vitality plus 2! Your new Vitality is 17!
Perception plus 2! Your new Perception is 15!

"ARGGHHHHH!"

CHAPTER TWENTY-TWO
TITLED

"Pete? Peeete. Peter?"

"Go away, Balin."

"Aye, I can do that, but tell me you're alright first."

"I'm fine. I just need some space."

"Alright, I'll head to the mess hall. You come tell me when you're ready to talk."

"Ok. Thanks."

"I dunno what's goin' on, but I'll keep it between us. Don't worry."

Balin stood up and left me where I lay, staring at the stars. I had fallen to the ground and I wasn't planning to get up.

Ever.

I looked up at the blue boxes in my vision, uncomprehending.

Blessing Received: [Barck]!
You have accepted the Blessing of Barck!
*You have received the Blessings [**Regeneration**] and [**Good Luck**]!*
Vitality plus 2! Your new vitality is 17!
Perception plus 2! Your new perception is 15!

Title Gained!
Your Blessings from Barck and Tiara can be merged into a Title!

Merge Blessings?

Yes/No

What just happened? I'd finished making gunpowder and received the Blessing I'd half expected. I'd hit "No" because I wanted magic and I *needed* Archis's Blessing for that. Instead of vanishing, the prompt had forced the Blessing on me instead.

I rolled around on the ground and screamed into my helmet.

WHERE WAS MY CHOICE!?

Opal was very clear in her lessons that the single thing the Gods were always constant on was choice. Choice about Blessings, choice about Titles, choice about Milestones, choice choice choice.

SO WHERE WAS MY CHOICE, BARCK!?

What WAS this shit? Was it an Otherworlder thing? Had I run through my allotment of allowed 'Nos'? Was Barck just the absolute *asshole* of the Gods?

You have accepted the Blessing of Barck!?

NO, I DIDN'T!!!

I rolled around on the ground and screamed into my helmet a bit more. I did have the presence of mind to avoid bumping into any of my bowls full of gunpowder. Just because I was royally pissed didn't mean that I'd completely lost my head. Honestly? Screaming into a metal helmet full of beard is a great stress reliever. I've used a pillow before but it wasn't quite the same. The acoustics of the helmet were just perfect.

Eventually I sat up with a sigh and glanced over at the harbingers of my doom. The seven pots full of gunpowder mix sat demurely on the table, unaware of the great injustice they had brought upon me. My chance for magic, gone. I couldn't believe it – I pinched myself, then bit my tongue. Ow! Nope, not a dream. There goes that hope. Seriously though, what just happened? Opal was adamant when she talked about choice and the Gods.

Could this... get me in huge trouble? Am I cursed by the Gods and so they removed my choice? I don't think I should tell anyone about this ever. I hope Balin is on the up and up. If he went back to camp and told everyone, 'Pete got a Blessin' forced on 'im by Barck,' I could get the dwarvish inquisition coming after me! I never expected the dwarvish inquisition! I think Balin's got my back, and he did say he'd keep mum, so I'll trust him for now. I looked back over the Title notification while I considered weeping.

Title Possible!
Your Blessings from Barck and Tiara can be merged into a Title!

Merge Blessings?
Yes/No

I contemplated hitting "No" as a screw you to Barck. However... could that mean I'd never have a Title? I didn't even know Titles existed a year ago, but I knew they were important.

Well, looks like I'm getting a Title. I had to hope there was some reason to this madness. Maybe I was destined to save the world, and the Gods chose me? By my beard, I hoped not. If anyone comes and tells me I'm the *chosen one*, I'm going to *choose* the other direction. If a demon king showed up to start the apocalypse, I'd just invite him to the pub to have some drinks until it all blew over.

Might as well get this over with. I mentally clicked on 'Yes.' With a *Bing!* another blue box appeared, followed by four more.

Title Gained
Please choose two Blessings to combine into a Title!

Possible Title: [Immortal]
Combine Tiara of Matter and Barck of Spark
*[**Strength of All: Self**] and [**Regeneration**] will combine into the Title*
*[**Immortal**]*
*An [**Immortal**] combines a strong body with incredible regeneration. An [**Immortal**] stands on the front lines and commands others with a strong voice and undying flesh.*

Accept [Immortal]?
Yes/No

Possible Title: [Alchemist]
Combine Tiara of Matter and Barck of Innovation

[Strength of All: Self] and *[Good Luck]* will combine into the Title *[Alchemist]*

An *[Alchemist]* is a master of the material world and needs a strong body and stronger luck.

An *[Alchemist]* crafts and brews mixtures that can heal, harm, or bring about miracles.

Accept [Alchemist]?
Yes/No

Possible Title: [Slaver]

Combine Tiara of Possessions and Barck of Spark

[Strength of All: Held] and *[Regeneration]* will combine into the Title *[Slaver]*

A *[Slaver]* has a strong whip and a stronger life force that grants the ability to dominate others.

A *[Slaver]* can turn the spark of another into their own possession.

Accept [Slaver]?
Yes/No

Possible Title: [Gambler]

Tiara of Possessions and Barck of Innovation

[Strength of All: Held] and *[Good Luck]* will combine into the Title *[Gambler]*

A *[Gambler]* trusts in the heart of the cards they hold, but is able to make their own luck.

A *[Gambler]* gambles not only with Gold, but can gamble with Fate itself.

Accept [Gambler]?
Yes/No

Opal never really went over all the different Titles; I'm not sure she even knows them all. Honestly, I kind of tuned out anything not related to magic, and I'm regretting it now. Seriously, a [Slaver] that made people into possessions? Tiara, you're one scary Goddess.

I slumped into the chair I'd lugged out here, because this was going to take a while. I needed to examine this from a couple of different perspectives. Did I get a Title here because the Gods had some deeper plan for me, or was there something else at play here? Why Barck in particular? I never had this happen with all the other Blessings. Was there something special about Barck?

I'd have to worry about those possibilities later. Eyes on the prize, Pete!

First was [Immortal], and I'd be lying if I said it didn't appeal to me. Just the name made it sound incredible, let alone the description. Undying flesh? Hell yeah! If I was going to live in a world with magic and monsters, then a Title that increased my survivability sounded like a pretty hot deal. I bet the ability to get easy Milestones from [Otherworlder] would allow a Title like that to snowball pretty hard. I put [Immortal] in the *likely* pile for now.

Next was [Alchemist] and it felt a bit too... on the nose. 'Can craft and brew mixtures' would sound like a dream come true under other less forced circumstances. Plus, I could only *imagine* what a 'miracle' beer would look like! Could I craft beers that counted as potions? Could I use magic ingredients to create magical beer for people who got ACTUAL GODSDAMN MAGIC, BARCK?! Either way, this class felt the most like *me* and I put it on my *under protest* pile.

[Slaver]... should I even consider it? I don't know how I feel about something like [Slaver] being an actual Title with powers granted by the Gods. I thought back to my conversation with Opal on it. Solen was the God of Freedom, so it *kind* of made sense that there would also be an aspect of the Gods that opposed that. The choice was there, you just had to choose to ignore it... Opal had mentioned the Gods were a reflection of 'society,' and Solen used to be of Service so it seemed modern society simply valued freedom more than bondage. Depending on the bondage of course, no kink shaming here. I put [Slaver] in my *never* pile. Even if it was out of spite at this entire situation, I wouldn't be able to live with myself if I became a [Slaver].

Finally, there was [Gambler], and here was the difficult choice. First off, the reference to 'heart of the cards' bugged me. Were these messages based on my own memories? I used to think they were standardised, but that felt really personal. The alternative was that my notifications just made an Earth pop culture reference and that had some uncomfortable connotations. I do love some gambling now and then – especially mahjong or poker – and I could always beat Caroline and our friends. A Title dedicated to making me rich could be just what Doc Opal ordered. However, what really caught my eyes was that a [Gambler] could gamble in 'Fate' with a capital 'F.'

If Fate was a thing here, I strongly suspected I wanted nothing to do with it. Nothing good could come of putting 'Otherworlder' and 'Fate' together in the same sentence. Would becoming a [Gambler] trap me in some terrible Fate, or give me the power to avoid it?

I decided to do what all sensible men – uh, dwarves – do when facing a conundrum like this. Go ask a woman.

"[Alchemist] or [Immortal]," Doc Opal said firmly.

"Are ya sure? What's wrong with [Gambler]?" I asked.

I was standing at the goat pens with Doc Opal. She'd just arrived back from a call to one of the other camps and I was helping her remove all the tack from a grey unigoat.

"It has terrible connotations and can result in ruin just as much as success."

"What about this 'Gamble with Fate' thing?"

"Grim has me on standby for your 'Spontaneous Combustion' so I believe you gamble with Fate already."

"Oh."

Opal smirked.

"I could always grab [Slaver]. Maybe put a collar on Bran and have him beg for recipes?" I asked as I unbuckled one of a dozen buckles.

"If you pick [Slaver], I will stop being your friend."

"Awwww, we're friends?"

"To my dismay, that appears to have become the case."

"Thanks Opal." I grunted and heaved as the two of us removed the saddle. We moved it into the tack closet and took a moment to catch our breath. Opal turned to me with a questioning gaze as we locked the unigoat in a paddock labelled "Dusty."

"I admit to being confused by this. I thought you wanted the Blessing of Archis."

"Uh, I decided I wanted [Regeneration]. It sounded too good to pass up." I attempted a bald-faced lie and I regretted it instantly, Opal deserved better, but I was really spooked by this whole thing.

"True, you do tend to walk a razor's edge." Opal eyed me but didn't seem to suspect anything.

"So, your recommendations are [Alchemist] or [Immortal]?"

"Yes. [Immortal] is a popular Title due to the vigour it provides. Many greybeards are Titled [Immortals], and it is a trusted Title. [Alchemists] can get a bad name if they mess with poisons or toxic fumes, but potions are always in high demand. Also, I think you'd have a gift for alchemy."

"Hmmm... Alright. Thanks Opal."

"Take some time to think about it, and congratulations!"

"Yaaaaaay." I gave a half-hearted cheer and made my way back to my gunpowder station.

I wasn't going to think about it. I'd made my decision. I'd made it even before I talked with Opal, but she'd helped me come to terms with myself.

I glanced over at one of the blue boxes, and with a firm feeling in my heart, I mentally clicked on 'Yes.'

With a jolt, the powers of an [Alchemist] flowed into me.

CHAPTER TWENTY-THREE
BOOM!

So. I'm an [Alchemist] now.

I'm also sitting in my room with a radler, staring at a wall. Why? Because I don't want to spend another hour looking at blue boxes. A Title came with some big benefits plus the choice of a Milestone, and I didn't particularly feel like making another big decision right now – I was kind of bummed out. I was doing my best to put a smile on my face and power through things, but I really wasn't doing well. My dreams of magic had just been snuffed out, and I was possibly on some God's hitlist.

"So, tell me again. You've been gettin' Blessin's for months?" Balin asked. He'd brought me a plate of dinner that was sitting half-eaten on my bedside table.

"Aye, everyone but Archie and Lunara now."

"Archie?"

"Archis."

"And ya turned 'em all down?" Balin's voice was incredulous.

"All of 'em. I wanted Archis's Blessin', because I wanted to learn magic."

"Oh." Balin paused and scratched at his head. "Why?"

"Because it's *magic!* So, I turned all the other Gods down."

"Then you got Barck's Blessin'."

"Then I got Barck's Blessin'." I sighed and took a drink of the radler. By all the Gods but Barck, I needed a stronger drink.

"So, what happened?"

"The Blessin' had no way to turn it down, and then I was forced to take it."

"That's... not normal Pete." Balin looked extremely uncomfortable. "Are ya sure? Choice is the most important thing to the Gods."

"There was a countdown and everythin'." I said plaintively. I was taking a risk, talking about this with Balin, but he'd saved my life once already and vice versa – plus I was a stand in for his clan with Annie. I *needed* to talk to someone, and he was practically family. Keeping stuff bottled up is never a good idea, and I didn't know enough to judge this situation. I was terrified that a forced Blessing was a punishment for evil or that it would mark me as an outsider.

"I don't think I've ever heard tha like." Balin pulled at his newly regrown handlebar moustache and thought for a while. "Ya may need to go see a [Prophet]."

"That sounds like a Title. Is it for a specific God?"

"Aye, Lunara and Midna, but they can speak for any or all of tha Gods."

"Under the circumstances, would it *really* be a good idea to see someone like that?"

"Why not? Yer havin' God problems, so go talk to a God botherer."

"What if I'm cursed by the Gods, or they accuse me of blasphemy?"

"What's *blasphemy*? Another way to ruin beer?"

"Nah, it's when you... defame the Gods I guess?"

"Oh, like insultin' a noble? That's always a bad idea, lot of laws about that." Balin hummed and hawed. "I've never heard o' blasphemy. Is it somethin' you learned in the human lands? You mentioned you were up there once."

"What?" That seemed strange to me. How could a world with Gods not have blasphemy? "I mean, doesn't the church get angry at people when they insult the Gods?"

Balin choked back a laugh. "Why?"

"Because it would threaten their authority or somethin'."

"Pete, the Gods don't care if you insult them." Balin laughed.

"They... don't?"

"Half of the time we swear it's at the Gods!"

"Oh." I had noticed a lot of Godly Arses, Beards, and Yams and such. "Why don't the Gods care?"

"Because they're Gods!" Balin sputtered. "I need ta get Sam in here to talk to ya. He knows a lot more about this stuff."

"Sam does know a lot of weird stuff. Any reason to ask him and not say, Doc Opal?"

"He's all about politics and the machinations of the Gods. It's a Blessed of Midna thing."

"Is that why you two keep arguing over politics?" Last week, Balin had put Sam in a headlock after he'd sung an ode Titled *Tha Queen's Comley Beard and Shapely Rear'd*.

"Aye, Sam thinks the nobility isn't needed anymore. I say if it was good enough fer the ancestors, it's good enough fer us! Tha greybeards have hundreds of years of wisdom, so it makes sense ta listen to em. Just look at Doc Opal!"

I sat upright at that. "I didn't know she was a noble."

Opal was indeed quite different from most of the other dwarves in the camp. She had a more cultured accent, and she didn't involve herself in any of the fights or quarrels. She was a calm pool in the chaos of daily life here.

"Not officially, but damn near. She's not a true noble yet, but she's as close to one as a dwarf like you or me'll meet. She'll probably be made one if she keeps doin' so much good work."

"You can be *made* a noble!?" I asked in surprise. "I figured you had to be born into it."

"Course! Dwarven nobles are chosen by the greybeards! I hear human nobility is chosen by birth. Stupid way to do things; nothin' special about bein' born!"

Well, that was interesting. Maybe I could become a dwarven lord or duke sometime in the future?

"Anyway, we were talkin' about the Gods. They don't care if we insult them?" I asked.

"Nah, it would be like gettin' insulted by a fly."

"I mean, we smush flies."

"Ok, mebbe not the best example." The two of us shuddered in unison, imagining a giant godly hand descending to smush a recalcitrant dwarf. "Pete, the Gods don't need to worry about their power or authority or anythin'. They're *Gods*."

I mulled on that a bit. As a proud agnostic from Earth, my only belief in God up until this point had been polite *dis*belief. Then in less than a week I'd died, reincarnated, and been exposed to *very real* Gods who granted magical powers.

"Back to the main issue, Balin. Am I cursed? Or is Barck punishing me fer somethin'?"

"I doubt it, Blessins' are a gift. My best guess would be that you needed that gift? Like when a kid asks fer a present and you want to give it to them, but mebbe what they really need is padded socks."

I had an aunt who always gave socks for Christmas. I hated that aunt. "Then why don't the Gods do that all the time? If they know better, just do it. They're Gods, wouldn't they always know better?"

"Dunno. I'm not a God, Pete. Talk to Sam, or a [Priest]. Mebbe Barck needed ya to take it, and now he owes you a favour!" He slapped me on my shoulder. "Some people never get a single Blessin', Pete. They're a privilege! Trust that Barck had a reason for it and see what happens."

Hmmm... if all went to plan, I'd be in Minnova soon. I could talk to a [Prophet] or [Priest] there. Hopefully it wouldn't get me mixed up in some crazy politics. Speaking of which...

"Does the church get involved in government at all?"

Balin sipped on his beer before answering. "Pete, [Politician] is a Title granted by the Gods, so [Priests] don't *need* to get involved. Besides, the Gods don't really worry about what we're doin'. Except you apparently." He gave me some side-eye as he said this.

"So that's a yes?" I asked. Balin thought for a while before answering.

"Only time I've ever heard o' [Priests] or [Paladins] getting involved with the government was to deal with a corrupt Titled [Judge] or [Politician]. I mean really, really corrupt. Lunara doesn't look kindly on anyone with her Blessin' floutin' the law."

Well, what a change from Earth. I guess the trope of an evil or overbearing church doesn't work when the Gods are very real and always watching. No blasphemy charges for Pete! Huzzah! That was one problem solved, but now I have another.

"Will it be easy for me to see a [Prophet] when we get to Minnova? How about a [Priest]? What's the difference?"

"A [Priest] is a holy-dwarf that gives out beneficial Conditions, while a [Prophet] is more of a mouthpiece or messenger. I imagine it'll be easy to see a [Priest] but hard to see a [Prophet] – there's usually only one [Prophet] in a city like Minnova." Balin shrugged. "What did the notification say, anyway?"

I thought back and recited from memory as best I could, "You have invented something incredible; your invention could change the world. Then a bunch of blah-de-blah."

Balin shifted uncomfortably. "Pete, I've been helpin' you with this, and yer practically me brother."

"Thanks, Balin."

"That said, I want ta dump you and yer *gunpowder* in a dive tunnel and seal it up. That notification makes me *very* worried."

"Why?"

"Didja not read it? 'Could change the world?' Pete, when a God says yer goin' ta change the world, they *mean* it."

I stuck out my jaw and bit my upper lip in response. I already knew that gunpowder could change the world – I just really, really, hoped it would be in a good way.

Balin studied me suspiciously, "You've been sayin' this stuff will be useful fer minin'. What is it, really? I understand powder, but what's *gun*?"

"The easiest way would be to show you. Come on."

I lead Balin out of the room and over to my makeshift workstation. I'd left everything behind, but there was no real weather or animals out here, so it was fine. We made our way over a ridge and down into the basin.

"So, this is it..." Balin said, as he looked into the bowl.

"Yeah, be really careful with it. This stuff is dangerous."

"Is it a good idea ta bring it into the mine then? It's already plenty dangerous in here."

"Well.... You'll see. This stuff has a lot of uses outside of the mine too. Like fireworks."

"What are those?"

"It's a bright, shining fire in the sky."

"Magic can already do that."

"I know. I've seen it. Thanks for the reminder!" I grumbled. "It's different, you can make beautiful shapes and stuff out of it." Come to think of it... I didn't really know how to make fireworks. Maybe being an [Alchemist] would help with that. I eyed the four blue boxes I was ignoring – I'd get to them eventually. "Alright, let's do this. I need to see if it actually works, and I want to show you that we didn't waste the last year of our lives."

"Aye, what do ya need me to do?"

"Just stand over here, and I'll do the rest." I walked us a very good distance away from my workstation; over another ridge and further away from camp. Hopefully the distance and the rocks would keep anyone from coming to investigate the noise. I put Balin a safe distance away and placed the bowl down.

"Uh.... I need a way to light this." Damn! I had no way to do it safely! There wasn't too much in the bowl, but it would still make a pretty big bang.

"I'll go get a taper from Bran." Balin ran off.

While I stood twiddling my thumbs and waiting for Balin, I realised there was a small problem. I didn't know how to make a fuse... I knew it involved fabric, but that was about it – this could be an issue. Then again, the valuable thing was the gunpowder, and I didn't necessarily need a fuse. Even Barck the Bastard agreed with me on the value of gunpowder! Soon enough, Balin crested the ridge and came down with a smouldering piece of wood.

"Will this do?" He asked, as he ran up to me.

"Yep! It's perfect!" I emptied some powder onto the ground a few paces away and then washed the bowl out. It was enough for a nice *bang* but not enough for anything serious – I didn't want to chance a real explosion. I grinned at Balin as I stood beside him. "Are you ready for me to rock your world?"

Then I threw the taper onto the pile of powder.

There was a sharp *BOOM!!* and a bright flash of light and heat. I could feel my eyebrows singe and I was momentarily blinded. Odd... maybe I'd put down a bit too much powder?

"ME MOUSTACHE!!! PETE!!!"

"Sorry, Balin!"

CHAPTER TWENTY-FOUR
BLOOD AND VINEGAR

"I can't believe ya burnt me moustache off twice!"

I rubbed some more burn ointment on my face and passed the jar to Balin. We'd decided to sneak some of the kitchen's and do it ourselves, rather than go face Opal. Bran had a small first aid kit in the kitchen, and I'd used it a couple of times for small burns or cuts I got while baking. He'd raised an eyebrow when he saw us, but didn't pry further.

"I didn't know it was goin' to be that bad!" Honestly, I hadn't – I never actually reached the *gunpowder* step when I played around with this back home. I'd seen some videos on the internet, but that had been a bigger *boom* than expected. Well, all the better to earn some gold!

"Do you believe me now when I say it's worth a lot?"

Balin nodded excitedly. "All that without magic? Aye, I can believe it, it's got quite a kick!"

"Almost as much as a Moscow mule!"

Balin paused as he morosely pulled at his scorched moustache in the mirror. "I know a mule... what's a Moscow? You use some strange words sometimes, Pete."

"It's a drink with actual alcohol. I can't wait to see a pub full of dwarves with a drink that's higher than 10 percent. It'll be a riot."

"I dunno if starting riots is a good idea, Pete."

"No, I mean it'll be hilarious."

"Riots aren't really funny."

"You sayin' you don't like a good scrap? Then what was that business with the stools and the buckets last week?"

"Ok, I guess it can be a *bit* funny. Least it wasn't as bad as yer noodle incident." Balin grinned at me and I grinned back. For all his straight shooting, Balin could get really riled up when it came to the things he cared about. *I* don't really get angry, and I'm more of a 'flight' person in a 'fight, flight, freeze' scenario. I don't *avoid* conflict – I just don't see a point in dealing with it mano-a-mano. I'd simply leave the situation and figure out a way to crush my enemies later when they least expected it.

I applied a little more salve to a slightly blistered cheek and nodded into the mirror. Yep, vengeance was a dish best served as a surprise party. Like the party the senate threw for Caesar. Now there was a sharp group of individuals who knew that the best thing for a party was a Bloody Caesar! Speaking of Bloody Caesars...

"Are there clams down here, Balin?"

"I dunno. I just got to Minnova. I don't think the dungeon would have 'em. You can probably get some imported."

"How about Worcestershire sauce?" Unlikely, but I should ask.

"War-chest-sire sauce? That somethin' about the King again?"

"No, Worcestershire. Wor – Chester – Shire Sauce"

"Wooster-sher?"

"No, nonono. Wort – Chess – Tchure."

"Warty Chest Tire sauce? Sounds vile."

"Midna's mullet, Balin, that's all wrong."

"You can't even pronounce it tha same way twice yerself!"

I ignored Balin's insult to my pronunciation of the world's greatest sauce. Worcestershire sauce was a wonderful invention from the city of Worcester and probably didn't exist here. It was fermented – just like beer – and made with anchovies, molasses, vinegar, garlic, tamarind and a mix of sugar and spices. It's delicious on meats and other treats. It's also one of the main ingredients of the national cocktail of Canada: the bloody Caesar.

A bloody Caesar sounds even more vile than a caudle if you can believe it, but it makes for a tasty treat on a hot summer day. It was invented in Calgary and it's a common drink at the Stampede. Heck, I must have drunk nearly a half-dozen Stampede Caesars when we went to see the Muttin' Bustin' rodeo. Watching small children get thrown off of sheep is amusing, but only for the first ten minutes. It's *very* amusing for *hours* if you're slightly buzzed on Caesars.

I doubted that I'd ever be able to make Caesars on Erd, though. The Worcestershire sauce was bad enough, since I didn't know how to make it, but the rest of the ingredients were pretty exacting.

Canadian Bloody Caesar Ingredients
16oz Drinking Glass
Lemon Juice
Celery Salt
Tomato Juice
Clam Water
Worcestershire Sauce
Tabasco Sauce
Celery Stalk
Ice Cube

First, take the 16oz glass and dip the rim in lemon juice before coating it with celery salt. Then add one shot or so of vodka to the glass before filling it with Clamato. Clamato would be easy enough to make myself since it was just tomato juice with clam water in it. But... no clams. Finally, add a spoonful of Worcestershire sauce and a spoonful of tabasco, then garnish with a celery stalk and some ice.

Voila! A bloody Caesar!

"Pete?" Balin was waving his hand in front of my face.

"Huh?"

"What are ya thinkin about when yer eyes go all blank like that?"

"Just... the past." I thought I was over it, but I guess twenty-odd years aren't going to disappear in a few months.

"You rememberin' somethin'?" Balin's voice was hopeful.

"No, maybe, not really." Even if it was only to Balin, I needed to come clean about my amnesia soon. I was starting to feel like a real heel. "I'm sorry you got hurt. Maybe becoming an [Alchemist] will give me something to keep us safe the next time we do this."

"Dunno about a *next* time..." Balin muttered.

I waggled my slightly singed eyebrows. "You'll keep coming back for the good company if not the good silver. Now, do you want to go ahead and set up a meeting with Grim? I want to finish one last thing here and then I'll follow along."

"Aye, I can do that. I got somethin' to discuss with Grim anyway." Balin checked his face one more time in the mirror and made his way out.

It was finally time to look at the blue boxes I'd been putting off.

Title Gained: [Alchemist]!

An [Alchemist] crafts and brews mixtures that heal, harm, or bring about miracles.

Short and bittersweet, just like my dashed dreams of magic. I flipped to the notifications about my new Blessings and their descriptions appeared with a *Bing!*

Blessing Evolved: [Good Luck] becomes [Flash of Insight]!

Sometimes all an aspiring [Alchemist] needs to make an experiment succeed is the right idea. You gain a flash of insight regarding a subject of your choice.
This Ability can be used once a day.

Blessing Evolved: [Strength of All: Self] becomes [Flesh of Stone]!

Playing around with alchemy can be dangerous. You can reflexively turn your flesh into stone for 4 seconds to avoid nasty burns or explosions.
This Ability can be used once an hour.

Those looked neat, though [Flash of Insight] felt more limited than [Good Luck]. Maybe the power lay in *choosing* when I'd have a lucky moment rather than generally better luck? I needed to think about that one. The once per day limitation was way more limited than [Power Pick].

[Flesh of Stone] looked awesome. Having the ability to turn my body into stone felt enough like real magic that I felt a little better about this whole thing. Plus, an extra layer of protection in a world with real monsters couldn't hurt. Maybe I'd use it in the next bar fight if someone tried to punch me in the nose again.

Next came another big decision.

Milestone Gained: Titled!
Gaining a Title has granted you the ability to choose a Milestone! Please accept one of the following:

Possible Milestone: [Determine Ratios]!
Why waste time measuring when there is alchemy to do! With a simple glance you can determine the exact weight and composition of a material. This Ability is always available to use.

Accept [Determine Ratios]?
Yes/No

Possible Milestone: [Burning Finger]!
An alchemist is never complete without their alchemical cauldron and flame. You can produce a small jet of flame from your index finger to light objects on fire.
The Ability can be used once per minute.

Accept [Burning Finger]?
Yes/No

Possible Milestone: [Stabilise Mixture]!
Chemical reactions can get out of hand, and an alchemist can be well served by halting them in their tracks. You are able to make an unstable mixture reach perfect equilibrium. It will no longer react violently unless you force it to do so.
This Ability can be used once per minute.

Accept [Stabilise Mixture]?
Yes/No

Possible Milestone: [Perfect Recall]!

Never forget how you made that one particular meal again! You can always perfectly recall any recipe that you completely learned in the past. This Ability is always available.

Accept [Perfect Recall]?
Yes/No

By this point I'm absolutely sure that these notifications are based on my own thoughts and actions. These Milestones were all relevant to the event that granted my Title. Unfortunately, they were also... kind of boring?

I needed to measure the ratios for gunpowder so I got [Determine Ratios].

I needed to start a fire so I got [Burning Finger].

I needed the gunpowder to not explode in my face so I got [Stabilise Mixture].

I couldn't remember the correct formula for gunpowder so I got [Perfect Recall].

They were all exactly what I needed while being simultaneously meh. Give me more stuff like [Flesh of Stone]! It looked like Milestones just gave inherently weaker abilities compared to Blessings.

I needed to choose something that would serve me long-term. Pretty soon I was going to be making beer. *That* was my goal, and the gunpowder was a stepping-stone. That meant [Burning Finger] was out; making fire with my fingers was cool and all, but that was easily replaced.

Same problem with [Perfect Recall]. I was confident in my memory when it came to brewing and mixing alcohol. [Perfect Recall] might point out a few nitty-gritty-details, but it wasn't going to help much with a craft I'd spent twenty years honing.

That left [Determine Ratios] and [Stabilise Mixture]. [Determine Ratios] was clear enough; a big part of beer brewing is getting the exact ratio right for the grains in the malt and the *adjuncts* – the extra flavours in the wort. [Determine Ratios] would help me to get it perfect every time. However, it was another Milestone that could theoretically be replaced with some proper tools.

On the other hand, if [Stabilise Mixture] allowed me to force fermentation to stop it could have a lot of uses in beer making. During primary fermentation, yeast converts sugar in the wort into alcohol, and the exact ratio converted is called *attenuation*. There was a science to perfect attenuation, you didn't always want it to be 100 percent. If I could use [Stabilise Mixture] to control the exact attenuation of a batch, it would open up some interesting new ways of brewing.

And of course, gunpowder could always go boom in my face – which made my decision easy. I focused on "Yes" for [Stabilise Mixture], and there was a *Bing!* as another blue box appeared.

<u>Milestone Gained: [Stabilise Mixture]!</u>
Chemical reactions can get out of hand, and an alchemist can be well served by halting them in their tracks. You are able to make an unstable mixture reach perfect equilibrium. It will no longer react violently unless you force it to do so.
You can use this Ability once per minute.

Well, that was done. Time to go talk to Grim.

"Hey, Balin–"

There was another series of *Bings!* as a series of blue boxes labelled "Quest" appeared in my vision. Solen's socks, not more decisions!!

I pulled a brush through my beard and gave my armpits a quick sniff.

Right. I was as ready as I was ever going to be – no point in putting things off.

I walked up to Grim's office and knocked. I didn't see Balin about, so I guess he was already inside.

I'd needed a moment to get prepared for this, and Balin had offered to go ahead. I was thankful, as it probably meant Grim was already mostly up to speed.

A voice came from inside. "Who's there?"

"Pete, sir. Is Balin there?"

"Aye, come in."

I pushed open the door and made my way inside. Grim was seated behind his desk, looking *grim*. Nyuck. Balin was on a small chair in front, and he waved as I entered.

Grim turned to Balin. "I'll talk to City Hall. They'll handle it."

"Thankee Grim."

"What's up?" I asked, taking a seat next to Balin.

"Balin had a concern about somethin' goin' on in the mine. Nothin' ta worry yerself with."

I shrugged. "If you say so. Thanks for seein' us."

Grim's face grew a shade less grim, "No problem, Pete. I heard yer little experiment go off, so I assume you two are here ta talk gold?"

"Yes, sir!" Balin and I said in unison.

Grim nodded and his straight-edge moustache twitched back and forth. "I've already heard some from Balin, Pete. How 'bout you tell me yerself?"

I looked at Balin. Was my shame safe, Balin? How much did you tell him? Balin waggled his eyebrows at me. I'd take that to mean my forced Blessing was a secret for now. I could accept that Balin didn't think it was a big deal, but he was a pretty forward-thinking dwarf. I already had a reputation as a bit of a weirdo, and I didn't want rumours that even the *Gods* thought I was weird.

"Okay. I used the charcoal you got me to finish making my gunpowder."

"Why 'gun'-powder?" Grim asked.

"I've been wonderin' meself," Balin said. The two of them turned to look at me. Uh...

"I don't remember." The old standby! "I just remember it having that name. Maybe the person who taught it to me was named *gun*?"

The pair gave me a disbelieving look.

"Doesn't matter." Grim pulled out a form from his desk and laid it on the table. "Alright. Name: Peter Samson. Invention for consideration: 'Gunpowder.' Ingredients: 'Potassium Nitrate, Charcoal, Sulphur in 75/12.5/12.5 ratio' Date created: 4th day of the 1st Month, 7998."

"Wow, 7998 already. Time sure flies. Is there anythin' special planned for the year 8000? An event like that only comes around once every eight thousand years!" I chuckled. Balin and Grim turned to look at me, and Balin put his face in his hands.

"Pete, nobody told ya' about tha octa-millennial?" Grim asked, his scowl deepening.

"I mean, I'm pretty sure Opal taught me," I fidgeted. Hey you try learning about an entire world in under a year! "But there's been so much goin' on and I've been kinda distracted lately." Grim and Balin exchanged a glance that I couldn't quite read.

"Hrmm... To answer your question, yes." Grim put down his quill, "There are celebrations planned at the Capital. They'll last for an entire year. I'm planning to go with my wife and her family. Perhaps you'll have an opportunity ta go yerself." He smiled – a rare occurrence.

"Have they finally announced 'em?" Balin asked, sitting forward on his chair.

"Aye. There'll be gladiatorial combat in the colosseum – I hear they're bringin' in some nasty monsters fer 'em ta fight." Grim hummed and hawwed. "Some art and culture competitions. I think it'll be a good chance fer you to get yer memories back, Pete. There'll probably be a [Hypnotist] or two there."

"Good idea. Thanks, Grim." I lied. It all sounded *awesome*. Hopefully I'd be able to convince Annie and Balin to go.

"Now, where were we?" Grim looked down at his form. "What's the use of this powder, Pete?"

"It can be used fer rapid mining and it has some other uses." I was never going to talk about most of those uses, though I might try to make fireworks – especially with a big celebration happening soon.

"Use: Mining and other. How do we make it work?"

"Um... I think you take some barrels, fill 'em with gunpowder, and then light 'em?" I wasn't too sure about that. I'd never actually seen or heard of how gunpowder was used in mining other than video games. "I know that it works best in enclosed spaces."

Grim put his quill down. "You don't sound very sure, Pete."

"I'm... kind of not. Gunpowder is very powerful and it can move a lot of rock at once, but I'm not sure about the engineering of it."

"That's fine." Grim made another note. "I can get the [Engineers] to work on it, but your share of any gold for the invention will be reduced."

"As long as it's enough to get me and Balin out, I don't care."

"Good. Balin mentioned that it's explosive? How ya gonna set it off? Some dwarf just needs ta stand next to some exploding barrels and toss on a taper?" Grim muttered darkly, "you volunteerin'?"

"It just needs a fuse."

"A *fuse*?" Balin and Grim asked in unison. Tiara's Teats... I had forlornly hoped that fuses or some kind of analog already existed.

"I can probably figure it out. I'll just need some supplies." I could *maybe* figure it out. Hopefully my new [Alchemist] powers would help, but I had my doubts about anything provided by *Barck the Bastard*.

"You go ahead and do that. Let me know when yer ready to show it off." Grim nodded and set the paper aside. "We're done with that. Anythin' else to report before I boot you two from me office?"

"Oh, I got a Title!" I seemed to recall Opal saying we were required to report those. "I'm a Titled [Alchemist] now!"

"Good fer you." Grim turned to look at his work. "Yer dismissed."

Balin got up and the two of us turned to leave. As we made our way out the door, Grim called out.

"Pete, if ya need any supplies, do it through me. Got it? Don't go givin' any more silver to Tim."

An odd request, but sure. "Yessir!"

"Good. I don't want to hear about any fights at yer Blessin' party. Got it? I've got an errand in Minnova and won't be here."

"Yessir!" I lied. There were always fights. He knew that and I knew that.

"Now, git!"

Balin and I made our way out of the office. Him oddly stressed, me buzzing with hope. Soon!

CHAPTER TWENTY-FIVE
FLASH OF INSIGHT

"Well, gentle-dwarves, do you have any ideas?"

I was down a dive tunnel with Wreck and Sam. Balin had the day off to explain our gunpowder to the engineers. Grim only sent his report off yesterday, and I was impressed by the fast turnaround.

I used [Power Pick] on a particularly difficult section of the wall, and then turned to check on Sam. He'd just come from lugging some sacks up the dive tunnel and was lying wheezing on the ground.

"What about a candlewick?" Wreck asked, as she filled a sack with the ore I'd collected.

"Eh, probably not, Wreck," Sam said from his spot on the floor. "Candlewick'll be too slow."

"It's a good idea, Wreck. I'll try it anyway."

"It'll be too slow," Sam complained.

"Nobody asked you, Sam," I retorted.

"Ya literally just—"

"I'll try the candlewick, maybe soak it in oil or somethin' if it's too slow. Come on, Sam, yer the [Maestro]. Don't you have an idea or two?"

Sam mulled it over while I helped Wreck fill the bags. "You said it needs to be a rope or somethin' that burns fast, but not too fast?"

"Aye, and at a constant rate." I didn't want to light the thing and have it streak to the end! No sudden bangs for Pete. Fast and steady, that was the ticket.

"'Fraid not, Pete," Sam shrugged.

"I think that would be way slower than the candlewick Sam, it's a terrible idea."

"What?" Sam went over his words and then guffawed. "Hah! You got me!" Wreck didn't even grin, but I think I saw her eyes roll.

"What about guts?" Wreck asked after a few minutes of silent work.

"Guts?" Sam and I asked in unison.

"Aye, some dried-out guts. Mebbe with an accelerant."

"Oh! Like an instrument string!" Sam exclaimed. "Doused with somethin' flammable. That could work... I shoulda thought of that!" He slapped Wreck on the back and she turned around and kicked him in the shin.

"I'll add it to my list. Thanks, Wreck."

Seriously, the work was mind-numbing sometimes, and the only thing that kept it fresh was the fact that I did it with some friends.

Oh, and the mining songs. Wreck and I grabbed our bags while Sam got back to mining while singing a song I'd taught him. It echoed joyously along the rock and stone as we made our way up the dive tunnel.

Brothers in the dive rejoice!
Swing, swing, swing with me.
Raise your pick and raise your voice!
Sing, sing, sing with me.
Down and down into the deep,
Will we find Tiara's Keep?
Diamonds, mithril, gold and more,
Hidden in the mountain store!
I am a dwarf and I'm digging a hole.
Diggy diggy hole, diggy diggy hole!
I am a dwarf and I'm digging a hole.
Diggy diggy hole, digging a hole!

That song had gotten more popular in the past few months than *Tiara's Keep*, which was the first mining song I'd ever heard down here. Sam especially loved it, and I couldn't wait to hear it on the bagpipes. Maybe I could write a punk rock version. Speaking of which, I suspected dwarves would be big fans of *rock* music. Nyuck.

Soon we were up around a bend and I couldn't hear him singing anymore. Wreck wasn't a big talker, so we dragged our bags up in silence. I had some time to think and it suddenly struck home that I was going to leave the mine soon. That was a sad thought – this place had become a second home.

Doc Opal was like a beloved aunt to me, and her lessons were probably going to be the only thing keeping me alive.

Sam was a loveable gruff father-figure, and I looked forward to jamming with him on his pipes when we got out. His indenture was for a year and a half, so he'd be out in about a year.

Bran's been like an older brother or a cousin. He had that 'I'm tolerating you because mum requires it' feel down to an art.

Tim was... Tim. He was like a buddy that... I owed money.

Something tugged at my memory. Something about Tim and money. I shook it off as I tripped on a rock. Careful, Pete. Don't want a concussion right before the big escape!

Grim was the angry grandpappy who yells at clouds. He secretly loved you, but hid it with a constant stream of criticism. We love you too Grim, you incorrigible bastard.

Balin and Annie would be out with me, so nothing to miss there. I'd have to marry Balin off to Annie eventually, though. *sniff* They grew up so fast!

Wreck... I turned to look at Wreck as she walked up the tunnel beside me. I didn't really know Wreck. She was the introvert of the group and while I'd say we were friendly; it was hard to say that we were *friends*. I regretted that, as she and Annie had been besties. Well, no time like the present.

"So, Wreck, how are you findin' mine life?"

"It's fine."

"Do you miss Annie?"

"Aye."

See? What am I supposed to do with that? Well, every friend group needs the strong silent type. I compared the single sack I was dragging up the tunnel with the two Wreck had hanging on her shoulders. Yep, the strooong silent type.

"Are you goin' to come and find us when you get out? We'll all be at Annie's brewery, hopefully."

"Probably." She hesitated. "Maybe."

"Maybe what?" Now I was curious, was she playing hard to get? I could get behind a tsundere dwarf, especially one with such a marvellous... stringy beard. Alright, Wreck didn't have the most marvellous of beards.

"Depends on a couple things."

"What things?" I edged closer and put on a winning smile.

"Things."

My smile twitched. Fine, keep your secrets.

We reached the end of the dive tunnel, and Wreck hoisted both her bags into a passing minecart. I tried to toss mine in as well, but my arms were too weak from dragging the heavy sack up the tunnel. Without a word, Wreck grabbed it from me and tossed it into the minecart as easily as the first two. She turned to face me as the minecart whizzed off. She grinned, and I realised for the first time that Wreck had a very pretty smile.

"You should work those weak arms as much as you work yer mouth, Pete!"

Oof.

I put down the sack of materials and sat down at my makeshift workstation.

It was finally my day off, and Grim had been kind enough to get me everything I needed. There was even a small vial of methanol with a label that said, "ABSOLUTELY DO NOT DRINK, FOR MEDICINAL PURPOSES ONLY" and another hastily scrawled note that said "DO NOT ADD TO THE BEER, PETE." Puh-lease, any high school chem kid knows not to drink methanol. I'm *ignorant*, not *stupid*. I did wonder if they used nasty additives here; most methanol back on Earth had all kinds of added stuff to prevent 'experimental drinking.'

I was surprised to learn that alcohol existed in a form other than beer. With [Alchemists] around, it made sense to have distilling techniques. I was further surprised that the dwarves weren't using distilling to make stronger alcohol, but then again... I wasn't.

There were four different ideas for my makeshift fuse.

1. Some gunpowder wrapped in cloth.
2. A candlewick, just for Sam.
3. A rope soaked in oil.
4. Some guts soaked in alcohol.

If none of those worked, it was back to the drawing board. Or I could give up a lot of gold and set the [Engineers] on it.

I tried the candlewick first, and... it was a candlewick – it burned nowhere fast. I needed something that moved a little quicker so I could make a long fuse. Once the fire got anywhere near the powder it could blow, so short fuses were out – no using Grim as a fuse. Heh.

Next, I tried wrapping some gunpowder in a long, thin, cotton sheet; I made sure to use [stabilise Mixture] just in case. It took a while, but it actually looked like a fuse when it was done! I lit one end on fire, and it worked great! At least it worked great until it reached a section where I'd poured a bit too much gunpowder and the entire thing went up in an instant. I imagined going up in an instant with it and instantly shelved the idea. It did create a stereotypical hissing fuse, but it was just too risky.

Next, I tried the rope soaked in oil, and it worked... okay. When I lit it, the fire travelled at a nice rate along the rope, but it was kind of stop and go – I needed consistency.

Finally, Wreck's big idea! I soaked the guts in alcohol for a while and then dried them at low heat in the oven while Bran angrily tapped his foot beside me. I think he was worried I would blow up his kitchen; can't imagine why. When it came time to test it, the makeshift fuse worked exactly as intended! The fire burned merrily down the string of guts at a fairly constant rate.

Perfect! I had a working model, and a massive problem. There was no way a string of guts mixed with methanol was cheap or easy to work with. Wreck would be happy to know her idea worked, but it just wasn't right for me.

I hummed a little *Boom Boom Pow* from the Peas as I brainstormed, and then made a small *tsk* as I remembered something. I had [Flash of Insight] and this was the perfect time to use it. I was *loath* to use anything from *Bollocks Barck*, but 'waste not want not.'

I activated [Flash of Insight] and for a moment, nothing happened. Typical Barck, garbage God, garbage–

Suddenly my head rocked as knowledge exploded in my brain and drained out through my eye sockets. Everything around me and everything I'd seen or heard in my entire existence spun through my head. I collapsed to the ground, but the only thing on my mind was the rampant fractal patterns wracking my cerebellum. Then, as a series of mental switches clicked into place, I gained an insight.

I already had what I needed. I'd known about it for a year. Whistlemop's red vine.

Also, eat shit, Barck. Ugh.

CHAPTER TWENTY-SIX
DAS BOOT

Tim frowned into his tankard as he took another drink of the True Brew of the dwarves.

Nothing was going to plan anymore.

"How's it goin', Tim?" The Great Deceiver asked.

Tim put on his brightest and most winning smile. "Great, Pete! Congratulations on getting your Title!"

He couldn't believe it. How could the Gods possibly favour this dwarf? The rest of the room raised their tankards in a toast, and Tim shivered as he smelled the telltale rank odour of lemons from many of them. The rot was spreading fast.

A few months ago, barely one in ten dwarves would have been willing to admit their attachment to this radler. Now, nearly a third of the camp was drinking it nightly.

It had been going so well! He needed to act more decisively now that his plan had ended in failure. He'd initially been using only his new Blessings to distract and trick Pete into giving up all his silver. However, he'd eventually decided to use his Title Milestone, which went far beyond a simple swindle. Tim pulled up his Abilities and read them over for the hundredth time, trying to see if there was any possible way to deal with the current situation.

[Distraction] – A spirit divided is ripe for the taking. Your ill-gotten gains will cause problems unless you can keep attention elsewhere. Increases the

chance that a mark will become distracted when they're talking to you. Keep in mind that you may need to set up the distraction yourself.
This Ability is always available.

[Steady Hands] *– Your hands are firm and unshaking, no matter the situation. Your charisma increases by 4 when bluffing, and you are immune to telltale signs of lying.*
This Ability is always available.

[Lost Reason] *– If you can't find a fool to rob, make your own! While you're working a mark, you can reduce their wisdom by four for an hour. Successive uses on the same mark will increase the duration of the effect up to a maximum of eight hours.*
This Ability can be used once a day.

Tim shivered as he read the last Ability; it was truly powerful. It explained why so many classes based off of Nether were restricted or banned outright.

He'd been so close! Pete had trusted him, even though that fool knew the reason he was here in the first place! Pete didn't even realise the dangers posed by one of the *Beardless*. Everyone knew a beardless dwarf was one with nothing to lose; to trust one was madness!

Tim growled softly as Sam and Balin lifted Pete into the air and threw him face-first into the cake. Everything about Pete was simply undwarvish. From his hatred of beer, to his lack of respect towards Doctor Opal or Speaker John – he treated them like friends or colleagues! The worst part was that they seemed to humour him; Speaker John had even tried a radler! Tim could understand Doctor Opal being seduced – her weakness to sweets was legendary. But Speaker John was one of the most respectable and most dwarvish dwarves Tim had ever met, and even he was being swayed by the Great Deceiver!

Tim didn't buy Pete's lies about amnesia. Pete knew too many things to be truly addled in the head – too many new and dangerous things. As a Titled [Swindler], Tim could tell Pete was covering something up. Something big. Tim would reveal it to everyone, and Pete would be outed for the monster he was!

How, though? Pete no longer needed to give him silver, and recently, Balin never gave them any time alone together. He was also

AN ADVENTURE BREWING

being run ragged by Grim, who had him on errands constantly. Tim sat and thought for a while as the party devolved into the regular brawl.

Perhaps it was time to do something a little more... direct. Tim looked down at the object clutched in his hand. Yes... when the time was right, he would use it and see if Pete was truly a *dwarf*.

"Hey Tim! You want some of this cake?"

"Sure Pete! I'd love some, give me a moment!" Tim got up and put on his best smile. A lying smile to go and greet the biggest liar in the camp. It was pure poetry – it was *justice*.

It was time for my Title party! There wasn't too much of a difference between a Title party and a Blessing party. Titled people were given a lot of respect, and the Blessing party was the last opportunity for their friends and family to dunk on them. Hence why I was currently face first in a cake while someone dumped beer on my head.

I was a slimy, creamy, gooey mess – it was marvellous. I could tell a few people still didn't really like me, but I think I've finally managed to fit in.

"Ya love puttin' yer foot in yer mouth, dontcha, Pete? Have some boot to go with it!" My thoughts were interrupted as Sam dunked a – thankfully clean – boot into the cake and then jammed it in my mouth. It tasted like metal, leather, and a rather delicious almond cream. Bran had outdone himself.

I took a moment to appreciate it as I grabbed a handful of cake and crammed it into Sam's beard. "At least I can appreciate a good dessert. That noise you call music proves that you have *no taste*!"

The rest of the cake clattered to the ground as I launched myself at him. Sam dodged out of the way, and we took a moment to stare each other down. One of the dwarves in the crowd looked forlornly at the cake on the floor and then at the empty dessert plate in his hands. Oopsie.

"Ooooooooohhhh!!!!"

"Brawl! Brawl! Brawl!"

"Hit him with a fist *Sam*pler!"

"Give him the ol' one, two – three, four, five!"

The crowd got worked up as we circled each other. I think I saw Balin collecting bets on who would win. I threw the first jab, and Sam blocked it with his arm.

"You'll need ta do better than that, boyo!" He cried, as he drove a foot at my shins. I sidestepped and tried to sweep his feet out from under him, but Sam was solid as an oak. He came at me in a rush, and I threw a series of jabs at his weaving head. I even connected on his chin with a little uppercut.

Sam stuck a shoulder in my chest and *heaved*. "Let me teach ya what it means ta be a *real* dwarf!"

Then we were clinching, and it was a mad scramble until he shoved some cake up my nose. I jumped back, disoriented, and slipped on the remains of the cake just as he swung a haymaker that brushed past my head. My legs came up as I went down and one of my feet nailed Sam right between the legs. There was a general *groan* from the entire room as Sam collapsed with a wheeze of 'Foul!.'

It took a moment for everyone to realise we weren't getting up. I'd rung my head pretty well on the wooden floor, and Sam's other head had been rung pretty well too. Hands propped us up and carried us over to a bench. After a few minutes of staring daggers at each other I took a quavering step up onto a nearby table.

"Sam has challenged me with this boot!" I declared, holding up the offending article of clothing. "So, I challenge him in turn! We shall both drink from a boot, and may the best dwarf win!"

There was sudden silence, and then a mutter spread around the room. Eyes flicked back and forth, and a few dwarves stepped away. Had I said something wrong?

Then Balin thumped another boot on the table and said in a loud voice, "You heard 'im! Let's give these two jokers the BOOT!"

The room cheered and the strange silence passed. Sam and I plunked down on opposite sides of a table with a boot in front of each of us. The boots belonged to Grim, who had agreed to allow us the use of them for pranks this evening before he ran off to Minnova. The fool!

"Do you understand the rules, Sam?" I bared my teeth in a malicious grin. Behind me, Balin massaged my shoulders and there was a general clamour as a half-dozen dwarves began to cheer for me.

"Child's play!"

Wreck was currently on Sam's side, and it looked like she was examining the boot for tricks. Where was the trust? Sam also had a cheering section, and his looked a little bigger than mine. Ah well, it's not the size that counts. It's winning.

"We fill the boots to the top, and then drink. Winner is the one that drinks the fastest with no spillage!"

"I've been drinkin' beer longer than you've been alive whippersnapper!"

"Too bad yer age has made you infirm, old man!"

"I'll empty this boot and shove it in yer rear before you even get halfway!"

"I think you'll choke on it! Too bad all your piping hasn't left you with better plumbing!"

"Some [Alchemist], the only thing you ever make is bad puns!"

"Better than a [Maestro] who only ever mastered his own instrument!"

I held out the boot toe first and nodded at Sam. He lifted his boot and we held the tips of the toes together. Speaker John materialised out of the crowd, his plaited beard swinging, and he placed his hand on our boot tips.

"On your marks! Get set! Go!" He raised his hand and we raised the boots to our lips.

Sam and I both chugged as fast as we could. I gave it a moment and then slowed down. I wanted to relish the moment, because...

I knew the trick to drinking from a boot.

Sam was so engrossed in his drinking that he didn't see me rotate my boot as I drank. Drinking from boots is an art form that started among the nobility in England. Lords and their knights would escape to remote hunting lodges, where they then drank competitively from their riding boots. The practice was picked up as a hazing ritual by the German military before it eventually became an Oktoberfest tradition. Obviously, they don't use real boots anymore, but the technique is the same.

Once you start drinking from the boot, a small vacuum begins to form in the toe. At the same time, an air bubble begins to travel up the boot from where you're drinking. When the air bubble reaches the toe, the vacuum releases and all the liquid in the toe washes out in an instant, creating a wave of beer.

Which meant I got to thoroughly enjoy the moment an eruption of beer smashed into Sam's face. He sputtered and coughed, his eyes blinking furiously as the beer drenched him. Meanwhile, I took my time slowly rotating the boot as I drank. The trick was to turn the toe roughly ninety degrees just as the air bubble hit the vacuum. I pulled it off with long-practised aplomb, and enjoyed the glower that Sam sent my way as I slowly finished off the rest.

I slammed my boot on the table with an *ahhh* of appreciation. Not of the beer – which was still shitty – but of my sweet, sweet, lemony victory. My cheering squad went wild; Sam's did too, but mostly in mockery – dwarven fans were a fickle thing.

"You thought you could defeat the master?" I asked, quirking an eyebrow.

"Ah, shut it!" Sam grumbled.

Then we shook hands and grinned. I grabbed a hunk of cake off the floor and Sam got ready to dodge, but instead I turned to a quiet corner of the room. I'd noticed a friend staying out of the party, and we couldn't have that!

"Hey, Tim! You want some of this cake?"

"Sure, Pete! I'd love some. Give me a moment!" Tim got up and put on his best smile.

I shoved some cake into it.

That was when the food fight started.

CHAPTER TWENTY-SEVEN
INTERLUDE – ADMINISTRATIVE WOES

"Mine Leader Grim, ID 32498, you have been called to give your report to the Head Administrator."

The imposing greybeard in front of him glowered down from a raised desk. The desk was fine mahogany with leather padding and brass buttons. A tiny sculpture of a mushfolk sat in one corner alongside a tankard that read "Champion of 7408" in tiny, faded script. The dwarf sat forward in his plush velvet chair and tapped his fingers on the desk in a staccato rhythm as he glowered briefly down at Grim. Grim knew the desk was a recent acquisition, confiscated from an official caught embezzling.

Grim sighed with jealousy. He wanted one. He idly tapped a shoe as the Head Administrator read over the paperwork – probably with Abilities like [Verify Authenticity] or [Check Spelling]. Dear Lunara, did Grim ever want [Check Spelling]… He straightened as the greybeard harrumphed.

"Yes, Sir?"

"Your paperwork mentions this 'Peter Samson' rather a lot…" The Administrator stroked his grey streaked beard, which reached all the way to the floor. It was knotted and pleated in a dozen different ways; a rather old style. The younger generations preferred not to step on their beard while they walked – younger being anyone under the age of six hundred. "I noticed that name before, in a medical report. One moment. [Find Reference]." He reached down and pulled open a drawer, withdrawing a file folder. "Indeed, ten gold for the services of Doctor Opal as well as a sparkstone. In addition, partial medical fee responsibility for no less than two brawls. That ten gold feels insufficient. From the report, it appears Doctor Opal has been spending a significant amount of time with him."

Grim interjected. "Yes, but the mental rehabilitation is not added to his indenture. As per Mining Manual V. 342, Section 4, Article 13, Subsection A: All injuries obtained by a labourer within the City of Minnova Reform Mine while not following regulations are to be added to the labourer's indenture. Subsection B: Any recurring injuries or required rehabilitation after a significant injury will be paid for by the City of Minnova Miner's Rehabilitation Fund."

"Yes, but those funds are MEANT to be used for the citizens of Minnova! Not vagrants!" The Administrator thundered, pounding the desk with his fist.

"The codes do not specify that! Peter Samson was injured in a Minnova Mine and is therefore due recompense from the Minnova Miner's Rehabilitation Fund!" Grim replied, his voice raised in kind.

"Bah, and now you want me to send Statustician Diamond for him as well!"

"*As I said*, there are multiple reports concerning the possibility of an illegal Title at the mine. We suspect him to be a victim in the matter!"

The two of them glowered at each other for a moment before the Administrator sighed and slumped into his chair. "Do you feel that the city of Minnova would be well served by exiling this 'Peter Samson'? We can continue to pay for his medical bills, but he appears to be a troublemaker."

"Sir, I feel that removing him from the city is an extreme course of action. He has not purposefully instigated any of the brawls. They all stem from his experiments with beer."

"Yes. Tell me about that." The head administrator eyed the trophy on his desk and glowered, like a man reminded of his youthful indiscretions.

"Following labourer Peter Samson's near-death experience, he began claiming that beer is 'bad.' He has been mixing it into other

AN ADVENTURE BREWING   197

drinks, and using it in cooking." Actually, he'd been claiming it was terrible, but no point in telling this old codger that.

"How strange. Was he of the same opinion before?" The Administrator furrowed his eyebrows in consternation. A dwarf that didn't like beer? Preposterous!

"No, sir. He was picked up on a City of Minnova Civil Infraction 4218: Begging for Beer In An Unsightly Manner."

"Sir, in my opinion Peter Samson is not a danger to the city of Minnova and should not be exiled. He is a kind and hardworking dwarf and was responsible for saving the life of a fellow in the incident with miner Balin. He is also in the middle of a project that I believe will be quite valuable for the city." Grim swallowed as he said this. He was putting his neck on the line for Pete here, but he honestly felt it was necessary. Pete did not deserve exile. Sure, he was a bit of an addled fool, but the Pilsner glass was rather interesting and the beer sauces were delicious. Also, while he'd never admit it.... He kind of liked the radler. plus, Doc Opal would have his head if he kicked out the source for all of Bran's new sweets recipes.

"Quite valuable you say. Is this the 'gunpowder' project my [Engineers] have been working on? Stupid name, that."

"Aye."

The Administrator grumbled as he shuffled around some paperwork and thumped his stamp a few times. "Very well. That brings me to the next thing, Mine Leader!" He growled.

"Yes, sir!" Grim straightened. What was it this time?!

"Is my daughter doing well?" The Administrator's gaze softened as he looked over to the side of the room where a painting of the Administrator and two female dwarves hung. One of the pair had a set of pink braids in a Verdi beard that Grim knew quite well.

"Lustre is doing very well, Sir."

"Do you have plans to give me a grandchild any time this century?" The Administrator arched an eyebrow. Grim choked.

"Assuming I can get enough leave to see her, sir?"

"I'm sorry, son. You know I can't do that. If you want a serious position in city administration you need to spend some time on Mine Leader duty. Finish your tenure, get a Title, and then we'll talk."

"Aye, sir."

"Would you like a drink?"

"Actually, I have to get going soon. We 'ave another Blessin' party, and I can't keep missin' those. Especially since they all seem ta end in brawls lately."

"Another one? [Find Reference]. That makes three Blessings this month! That's unheard of!"

"Yes, sir."

"Interesting... Interesting..." The Administrator tapped his fingers on the desk. "Well, go on then. I won't keep you from your work any longer. Peter Samson will stay at the City of Minnova Reform Mine, and may the Gods have mercy on your soul."

"Thank you, sir. And with regards to Statustician Diamond?

"I'll send her with the [Engineers]. Now get out of my office."

Grim bowed as he made his way out of the office. Dwarf Lord Rodson could be a stick-in-the-mud conservative sometimes, but he was always fair and followed the rules. Grim considered him a reasonable father-in-law as far as fathers-in-law could be concerned. As he stepped over the threshold there was a *Bing!* and a bright blue light appeared in his vision.

Blessing Granted: [Lunara]!
You have performed a favour for the Gods and gained the notice of Lunara.
May your spirit and spark ever toil in accordance with the law.
If you receive Lunara's Blessing you will gain [Shadowcloak] and [Sense Motive].
If you accept, you will be eligible for a Title!

Do you accept?
Yes/No

A Blessing!? So soon? By Lunara's Lace, how fortuitous! He thought it would take years to earn another Blessing from Lunara! Getting a second Blessing from the same God was always an order more difficult. Grim grinned through his straight-edge moustache as he went to mentally click on 'Yes.' Then he paused. His legs beginning to quiver.

Wait, what? He had performed a *favour* for the Gods? He thought back through the meeting just a moment before. There'd been nothing of great import, no great revelations, and no great plans.

What had he done?!

What in the Firmament had he done?!?!

Opal sat down in the mess hall and swirled her drink around in its tankard. She took a small sip and sighed. She was alone – most of the camp was out mining, but she could hear the clink of dishes in the kitchen as Bran prepared for dinner. Opal looked deep into the slightly golden foam and took a deep chug of it before slamming her tankard on the table.

Truly, this *radler* was delicious. It had a sweet citrusy flavour, but the texture and after-taste was the beer she knew and loved. The Brew of the dwarves had been around for nearly ten millennia. None had dared change it much, though some dwarves did create Light Brew by accident around five millennia ago. A brewery had forgotten a few kegs in a cold storage cave and when they went to fetch them, most were ruined. One keg, however, had lost the dark colour of Ale and turned into something else.

"What did Pete call it?" Opal mused as she took another sip. "A lager." She personally preferred the sweeter Light Brew to True Brew. Almost all Light Brew in the city was made using yeast from that very first keg. In fact, the same was true of nearly all the beer in the city. Dwarven Master Brewers owed their craft to the First Brewer, and in recognition they all used the yeasts from that very first batch, Light Brew being the exception of course.

Opal peered into her tankard, which was now nearly empty. Exception – there was the problem. Was it an exception, or had Light Brew happened so long ago that it had been given the opportunity to grow? The fight after the radler incident had been vicious. She'd fixed at least a dozen black eyes and a broken arm. Someone had even shaved another dwarf's beard! It was unheard of! Poor Tim would take years to grow back his cropped beard, if it ever grew back the same at all. Several miners were still not quite on speaking terms, and that was simply not the dwarven way anymore. Some had been ready to declare a Feud on the spot! She didn't know what was going to happen if Pete ever got free from the camp and brought his ideas down into the city. There could be actual civil unrest.

All over beer. Opal shook her head, scandalised at her own thoughts. It was beer! The Sacred Brew of the Dwarves! And yet... and yet that was all it was. If beer disappeared tomorrow, dwarves would still be dwarves. They'd wake up in the morning and work hard, follow the laws as set forth by the ancestors, and find something new to fight over in the mess hall. Then they would shake hands, laugh, and do it all again the next day.

What could be done, though? At this point beer was one of the most sacred traditions. Entire family lines were dedicated to the protection of the yeasts and malts of the First Brewer. Proud adventurers went into the dungeon each day, risking their lives to bring out the herbs and spices used to flavour the wort. All 'As-the-First-Brewer-Intended.' What, did they think the First Brewer was a God? He was simply another dwarf Blessed by Tiara and Barck – though the first to be granted a Specialisation related to beer. If such a miracle could happen once, surely it could happen again?

"Everythin' alright, Opal?" A voice asked by her side. She turned to see Bran standing next to her table carrying a cream puff on a delicate plate. Truly, she was spoiled here. When she'd first gotten the job as camp Doctor, she'd worried the food would not meet her exacting criteria. She'd considered bringing her own personal chef but wanted to fit in with the miners as best as she could. She'd sat down for her first dinner expecting to be disappointed and had been pleasantly surprised instead. The roast beef had been succulent and the erdroot had actually been moist instead of powdery. The two had combined so perfectly with the beer that had she'd wondered where she was. This was camp fare?! She'd burst into the kitchen to see the chef and run right into Bran, knocking him over and covering him with gravy. At the time she'd made some imperious excuses, but she was *still* a bit embarrassed about the incident.

Pete had even been influencing her Bran. All the sweets were one thing, but Bran has revealed that he was even using beer in his cooking. Beer again... at least the sauces were delicious, and the ribs had been something else.

"Everything's fine, Bran. Thank you for the dessert. Could I have another radler, please?"

"Aye, one more radler comin' up. You're gonna be the heaviest drinker in camp soon, Opal!"

"Well, if you keep making such delicious concoctions, what choice do I have?" The two of them laughed as Bran went to pour her another drink. Opal watched him as he worked. He'd lost a lot of his angry edge in the sixty years since they'd started working together. She took her fork and broke off a piece of fluffy pastry, spooning it into her eager mouth.

She was aware of his feelings, and the two of them had danced around the issue for years. She could tell that Bran was too ashamed of his past as a reformed dwarf to make any serious advances. She wasn't a noble or anything, but she came from a very prestigious family with a lot of Titled individuals. She'd been raised as one of the elites since birth, and her work here in the mines was merely a stepping-stone to higher things. Bran... was not. There was no real shame in doing time in a reform mine, but Opal knew the miners rarely felt the same way.

However, if she was honest with herself... she quite liked Bran. Opal blushed and hid it in her tankard. He was kind, well groomed, and had a sweet smell from all his work in the kitchen. He had a jolly laugh and got along well with others. He was probably the most liked dwarf in the entire camp, even if you included Balin. But now was not the time. She had to focus on her work as camp Doctor until she was done with her tenure. Surely, she could stay strong until then? *After* she returned to Minnova, she would sit down and have a chat with Bran.

Time. She just needed time. Maybe she would talk to him tomorrow.

CHAPTER TWENTY-EIGHT
A WIDER WORLD

Tomorrow was the big day!

I sat on my bed, lost in thought. I'd put in a hard day in the mine, and Grim had dropped by partway through the day to announce the [Engineers] were coming tomorrow. He had a big stash of the red vine – which was apparently called *sparkvine* – and the [Engineers] were providing the mining plans.

Depending on the results of tomorrow's test, Balin and I would be free.

It was hard to imagine. Well, I mean it was easy to imagine. Me in a brewery making sweet, sweet liquor. I purred as I scribbled in the small notepad Grim had given me. I looked down and realised that I'd been doodling Barck's name in the margins like a lovesick schoolgirl. Except with guns and little skulls and various other instruments of death.

I'd caught myself doing that a lot recently, just... happily thinking about the casual murder and destruction of Barck and everything he loved. I love revenge as much as the next guy, but I never had a deep-seated hatred like this before. I wonder if it's a dwarvish thing, or if I've simply never been screwed so hard. I'm not sure, because so far, all the dwarves seem to get over stuff with no real hard feelings. Either way, I'd try to deal with it and just punch Barck metaphorically in the face when I finally got a chance to chat with a [Prophet].

Back to what I was doing – looking at quests and pondering a mystery.

Quest Complete: An Ore-Able Time Part 2/10!
You did it! Don't you feel amazing?

Gained 0.2 Strength! Your new strength is 15.4!
Gained 0.2 Vitality! Your new vitality is 17.2!

Bing!

New Quest: An Ore-Able Time Part 3/10!
You're stuck in a mine! Are you willing to mine your way to freedom?
Ore Collected: 123.4/400 Tonnes

Rewards: +0.2 Strength, +0.2 Vitality

Do you accept?
Yes / No

New Quest: Striking it Rich!
You're broke! Find three treasures buried beneath the Erd! Diamond, gold, gems and more!
Treasures discovered: 0/3
Rewards: [**Sense Quality: Gems**]

Do you accept?
Yes / No

Those were the quests from Tiara. Next came what I assumed was the first Barck quest – may he rot in the Nether.

New Quest: The Father of Necessity!
You're broke! Create new uses for gunpowder and earn some gold!
Uses created: 1/5

Rewards: [***Quick Measure***]

Do you accept?
Yes / No

I chuckled as I hit "No" on the quest. *Eat shit*, Barck. The little guy strikes back! Honestly, I think the only person *truly* hurt by denying quests would be me. Don't care, it felt great, and I really didn't want to mess around with gunpowder more than I had to. I'd *probably* accept the rest of Barck's quests though, maybe. I doodled some thorns and bloody knives in the margins.

Next came what I assumed was my main [Alchemist] quest... and a mystery. I read it again and again, and I still couldn't believe my eyes.

New Quest: Dwarven Influencer Part 1/10!
The dwarves need your help. Influence 2,500 dwarves with your otherworldly alcohol knowledge.
Dwarves influenced: 2500/2500

Rewards: [Ingredient Scan]

Do you accept?
Yes / No

What on Erd was this? A quest to teach dwarves about beer? It was simply the most ridiculous thing I'd seen since I got here, and I saw a dwarf put a helmet on a rock to keep it safe.

Jack is really attached to his pet rock.

This confirmed some of my suspicions and added some more. The Gods must be involved in my reincarnation here. *Obviously* the Gods were involved in my reincarnation, but I meant in a more direct way. Some of the events and dwarves in this mine have really pushed me in a brewing direction, and now a quest like this? Heck, Annie – the only dwarf in all of Minnova that wanted to change brewing – was waiting for us when we got out.

I... needed to think about it. On one hand, I'd been working towards improving dwarven beer already. I loved alcohol and brewing, and it was my whole life back home aside from my family, but I was kind of being *forced* into it here. On the other hand, a whole new world where every drink I made was new and exciting to everyone and I had the *Blessings of the Gods* to do it? That's...

I shivered, whether from excitement or a bit of terror I couldn't tell. I put down my notepad and laid down on my bed, deep in thought. I didn't even notice when Balin came in, muttered something, and turned off the lights. I just continued to stare at the wall, thinking. I thought about influencers and Gods. I thought about Erd and Earth. I thought about beers and beards. I should have gone to sleep but my mind just wouldn't stop. Deep into the morning I pondered, and in my soul, I slowly solidified my answer.

You know what? If the Gods wanted me to brew beer, *fine*. I should be dead, and I had been given another opportunity to spend hundreds of years doing what I loved. So, thank you Gods! I'll be your reluctant hero in this quest to free beer from the shackles of dwarven tyranny! I'll influence every dwarf on this planet if that's what it takes! You guys may be pushy assholes, but you're not all that bad.

Except you, Barck. Go eat goatshit.

I went to click on "Yes" and paused at another thought. There were only 30 or so dwarves in the camp... So why did it say 2500 dwarves were already influenced? I mentally hit "Yes" while I considered the problem.

Bing!

Quest Complete: Dwarven Influencer Part 1/10!
Keep up the great work!

Gained [Ingredient Scan]!

I was about to check out [Ingredient Scan] when another quest appeared.

Bing!

New Quest: Dwarven Influencer Part 2/10!
The dwarves need your help. Influence 5000 dwarves with your otherworldly alcohol knowledge.
Dwarves influenced: 5000/5000

Rewards: +0.2 Perception, +0.2 Vitality

Do you accept?
Yes / No

The counter ramped up to completion almost instantly. I'd influenced 5000 more dwarves? I thought these quests reset to zero...? Had I really influenced over 7,500 dwarves? What was going on? I hit "Yes."

Bing!

Quest Complete: Dwarven Influencer Part 2/10!
Keep up the great work!

Gained 0.2 perception, new perception is 15.2!
Gained 0.2 vitality, new vitality is 17.4!

Bing!

New Quest: Dwarven Influencer Part 3/10!
The dwarves need your help. Influence 10,000 dwarves with your otherworldly alcohol knowledge.
Dwarves influenced: 10,000/10,000

Rewards: +0.2 Perception, +0.2 Vitality

Do you accept?
Yes / No

I started to rapid fire "Yes" as panic set in. I'd never left the mining camp! How had I influenced thousands of dwarves!?

Bing!

Quest Complete: Dwarven Influencer Part 3/10!
Keep up the great work!

Gained 0.2 perception, new perception is 15.4!
Gained 0.2 vitality, new vitality is 17.6!

Bing!

New Quest: Dwarven Influencer Part 4/10!

The dwarves need your help. Influence 25,000 dwarves with your otherworldly alcohol knowledge.
Dwarves influenced: 25,000/25,000

Rewards: +0.4 Perception, +0.4 Vitality

Do you accept?
Yes / No

Bing!

Quest Complete: Dwarven Influencer Part 4/10!
Keep up the great work!

Gained 0.4 perception, new perception is 15.8!
Gained 0.4 vitality, new vitality is 18!

Bing!

New Quest: Dwarven Influencer Part 5/10!

The dwarves need your help. Influence 50,000 dwarves with your otherworldly alcohol knowledge.
Dwarves influenced: 50,000/50,000

Rewards: +0.6 Perception, +0.6 Vitality

Do you accept?
Yes / No

Bing!

Quest Complete: Dwarven Influencer Part 5/10!
Keep up the great work!

Gained 0.6 perception, new perception is 16.4!
Gained 0.6 vitality, new vitality is 18.6!

Bing!

New Quest: Dwarven Influencer Part 6/10!
The dwarves need your help. Influence 100,000 dwarves with your otherworldly alcohol knowledge.
Dwarves influenced: 34,435/100000

*Rewards: [**Carbonate**]*

Do you accept?
Yes / No

I was hyperventilating at the end. Looking at part 6 it was clear the count *did* restart from zero, so... ninety... one hundred... six thousand... ONE HUNDRED, TWENTY-SIX THOUSAND, NINE HUNDRED AND THIRTY-FIVE DWARVES?!? I almost yelled out loud and then remembered it was way too early in the morning for that. How had I influenced that many dwarves from here!? Was this some kind of *Truman Show* shit, and I was actually in a soap opera or on reality TV? It would explain so much – but no, that couldn't be it. More likely my radler had made it out into the wild somehow. Maybe Grim talked about it outside, or Doc Opal, or heck, even Speaker John.

The sweet embrace of sleep called to me. Now that I'd made the important decisions, I could worry about the number conundrum later. As I finally felt my eyes droop shut with exhaustion, I took one last moment to look over my new Ability, and my massively improved Status.

[Ingredient Scan] – *An alchemist often needs to forage for their own ingredients, whether in a field or a market. When you use [Ingredient Scan]*

you can scan a 200-metre zone around you for a particular ingredient. If any amount of the selected ingredient is present, you will learn its exact location and amount.
This Ability can be used once a minute.

Status: Provided by the Firmament
Name: Peter ~~Phillips~~ Samson
Age: *49*
Conditions: *None*
Race: *Dwarf*
Blessings: *[Flesh of Stone], [Flash of Insight], [Strength of All: Held], [Regeneration]*
Title: *[Alchemist]*
Milestones: *[Otherworlder], [Power Pick], [Ingredient Scan], [Stabilise Mixture]*
Strength: *15.4*
Vitality: *18.6*
Agility: *11*
Dexterity: *11*
Wisdom: *13*
Intelligence: *12*
Perception: *16.4*
Charisma: *11*

Huh, my birthday passed. Happy Birthday to Meee. I was starting to feel like some kind of Olympic athlete with my massive vitality.

I wonder if that means more hit points or whatever analog to it exists in this crazy world.

I wonder why my charisma is still so low.

I wonder why Barck sucks so much.

What if something goes wrong tomorrow?

I hope Sam wins his bet and I don't die.

I wonder what the [Engineers] are like?

How does Bran keep his beard so well groomed in the kitchen?

Will I like Minnova? Will I fit in?

[Carbonate] looks pretty amazing if it is what I think it is.

Maybe I should have accepted the gunpowder quest...

Plagued with thoughts and concerns about a suddenly wider and stranger world, I fell into fitful sleep. Today was the big day!

CHAPTER TWENTY-NINE
FANCY DRESS PARTY

I shuffled impatiently as we stood at the entrance to the camp. Soon, Balin and I would either be spending the next few years mining, or we'd be free. We were joined by Speaker John, Doc Opal, and Grim. Almost all the Titled dwarves in the camp were here except for Whisperer Gemma. The rest of the miners were watching from behind us back in the camp. They had the day off from mining, and they weren't going to miss the show. I grumbled as I saw Sam taking the last bets on 'does Pete die today.' Balin was stiff as a board beside me.

"Come on, Balin. Don't be nervous. This is a once in a lifetime opportunity!" I nudged him and he almost tottered over.

"Because we're gonna die right after?" he squeaked.

"Nah, because we're going to meet a lot of Titled people at once!" One of the most important lessons I'd learned in my life was the power of networking. That one famous guy who loved Beavermoose and talked about it on air was all it took to make us rich. Hard work doesn't hurt, but making it big comes from knowing the right people and a little bit of luck.

We were about to get the right people served up to us on a silver platter – the lead [Engineer] and his entire posse, plus some dwarves from City Hall with a capital C and H were coming. In other words, it was time to schmooze!

"Put the cinnamon back in yer shirt." I adjusted Balin's necktie and pulled out my beard brush. He had an incorrigible tangle in his beard and it took me a while to get it out. I also took a moment to consider his poor lopsided handlebar moustache. Ah well, maybe he could earn pity points for sacrificing his own facial hair to the cause.

"It stinks like cinnamon!" Balin hissed.

"That's the point! Better to smell like cinnamon than smell like a dirty miner!" I glowered at him until he acquiesced and returned to his nervous fidgeting. It was clear that he found the suit very uncomfortable. I brushed my own wavy brown beard and locks and checked my outfit.

When I'd heard from Grim that we had a whole parade coming through, I'd asked to borrow some proper business attire. He'd raised an eyebrow, then obtained a pair of 'fashionable' clothes for me and Balin. I was currently dressed in a white shirt and three-piece suit made out of some kind of linen. It was dark blue with a small stripe down the side and an understated checker pattern. Then, because dwarves, it had some chain sewn into the jacket, and the vest was made of thick leather. There was also a set of leather greaves and a shiny leather skullcap with fur lining and a feather in it. It was a mix between an adventuring outfit and a pin-striped suit from the prohibition era.

I loved it. It beat the heck out of wearing stinky faux-armour all day. Now I could wear *snazzy* faux-armour!

Grim coughed as a line of unigoats came up the trail in the distance.

"These are some important people. I expect everyone ta be on their best behaviour. Got it?"

"Do you know any of them, Grim?" I asked.

"The head [Engineer] is a gnome named Copperpot. He has a few gnomes and dwarves workin' under him that'll be comin' as well. A couple of 'em are Titled, but I don't know 'em."

"Anything to know about Copperpot?"

"He's sharp as an axe and likes straight talk. He'll hate you."

"Ouch. He must love you."

Grim chuckled. "Nah, he hates me too. He hates almost everybody. Comes from bein' thrice specialised."

"So, he's got... at least fifteen Milestones?" I counted my own – four. One more to go until I could Specialise!

"Aye, takes hundreds of years ta get that many. Most Titled never even get *one*! He's an [Arcanomechanical Civil Engineer]."

"A whosawhatsitnow?" That was a mouthful equal to Worcestershire! Civil Engineer was obvious, but what was Arcanomechanical? "Is that the word for magical engineering?"

Doc Opal leaned over. "Arcanomechanical. He works on integrating magic with civil engineering projects and designs magical buildings."

Wow, that sounded cool. I seemed to recall something similar called *arcanepunk* back on earth – or something like that.

"What Blessings make an [Engineer]? Archis and whom else?" They needed Archis for magic, and he was the god of knowledge so that made sense. Maybe the other God was Barck?

"No, Lunara and Barck. Why?" Speaker John asked. He put some bows in his beard braids today! Looking good, John!

"What!? How can he do magic if he doesn't have Archis's Blessin'?" I asked. Doc Opal looked struck for a moment.

Speaker John nodded as he replied. "It's a common misconception by most of the non-mage community that the Blessing of Archis is required to do magic. Indeed, [Manasight] is necessary to perform any kind of work with Mana."

"I'm sensing a *but*!" I was growing excited. Could this mean what I thought it meant!?

"Yes, some rare specialisations can grant either a lesser form of [Manasight] or a way of doing basic magic without it."

"I didn't know that," Opal mused.

"That doesn't surprise me." John nodded. "Most of your training would have been physical and practical in nature."

"Yes, we didn't really cover magic. Just enough to know how some magics interact with the healing process." Opal shrugged. "Sorry for leading you astray there, Peter."

"Wait, so I can still learn magic? Even as an [Alchemist]?" I was practically vibrating now.

Speaker John smiled. "Eager to learn the deep ways of the world,

Pete? Mana can do things Abilities can't, but it requires a lot of training! And you'll need a bit of luck getting the right Specialisation."

Don't Care! Magic! My mind buzzed with ideas for getting the right specialisation. Since everything seemed to be based on the moment, maybe I could try using some of that Arcanomechanical stuff in the beer-making process. Perhaps that would get me something like [Arcanomechanical Alchemist] – that would be *sweet*!

At the possibility of getting magic again I could feel my anger at Barck unravelling. Then I furrowed my brow and held on to it. It wasn't just about the magic – Barck had taken my choice, and until l got a decent explanation for that, I was going to remain on the 'I hate Barck' train. Maybe I'd forgive him if he taught me how to get a magic-based Specialisation.

"Why is someone so important coming out for this?" I asked, as the procession slowly moved closer.

"He said he wanted to meet you." Grim's grin was sharp as a shark's.

Oh.

Great.

The procession slowly made its way into view. There were just over a dozen people in the group, from some fairly heavily armoured dwarven guards, to someone in a shocking amount of red, to what looked like people wearing doublets with weird poofy pants. What were those kinds of pants called? Bombasts? That seemed appropriate for the occasion!

They were accompanied by a brightly coloured cart with glowing letters carved into its side that were visible even from this distance. I think they were sigils, and they were clearly doing something magical to the cart – it didn't jostle or wiggle an inch as it came up the rocky path.

"Here they come," whispered Grim. "Engineer Copperpot is the one leading, and the dwarfess in the magenta hauberk chainmail is

Statustician Diamond from City Administration. They're the big names in the group." Well, that answered the 'what to call a female dwarf' question.

"A statistician?" I whispered back. "Is she here to audit the experiment?"

"No, a [Status-tician]," Doc Opal replied in Grim's stead. "She's quite nice, I like her."

Speaker John adjusted his braids and pulled out a hand mirror. He fiddled with his moustache and straightened his collar. Oho!

"She's very pretty too?" I asked, ensuring John could hear.

"Oh, very. She has a gorgeous red beard and a temper to match. She also plays a mean game of hammercup. She went to university with John, didn't she, John?" Opal nudged John in the ribs and he started.

"Huh? Oh yes, Statustician Diamond is very intelligent and good look— I, I, I mean good at her work." He blushed. Wow, I'd never seen Speaker John be anything other than stoic and taciturn. This was amazing!

"How well do you know her, Opal?" I asked, keeping an eye on Speaker John.

"I met her on the job, and we got to talking," Opal said. "I'd call her more than a work acquaintance but not quite a friend. She's well-spoken and well-read, with a delightful sense of humour, and she enjoys sweets – though not as much as me. Is that a box of chocolates I see hiding behind your back, John?"

John coughed and turned as magenta as the approaching dwarfess. He shuffled around to better hide the gold-rimmed box behind his back.

"What does a [Statustician] do?" I asked, as the parade entered the final approach to our rise.

"She works with City Hall to find and catch criminal Titled. She can read Status Sheets, which allows her to search for illegal or restricted Titles," Grim interjected.

"Those exist? What are they?"

Speaker John spoke up, desperate to change the subject. "A-hem. Most banned Titles arise from Yearn of Nether."

"Well, that seems unfair. Why single her out?"

"It's simple," John continued, his voice turning scholarly. "Most Nether Blessings provide a Title that is the manifest opposite of the Blessing it is paired with. The most common examples would be Nether and Possession combining to create a [Swindler] or Nether and Freedom creating a [Jailer]."

"Huh, interesting. Does Diamond like her dwarves smart, Doc?"

"Oh yes, we've talked about it at length over tea and cakes. She also likes dwarves that aren't afraid to accent their look. She likes colour, Diamond does." Opal winked at me and John turned practically purple as his hands pulled at the brightly-coloured bows in his beard.

"Shut it," Grim hissed. "They're here."

"Wait," I asked, in dawning horror as the group crested the hill up to the camp. "Can she read Abilities too?" I had that [Otherworlder] Milestone! Solen's Socks, there was never a handy lead sheet for blocking magic x-rays around when you needed it!

"Aye," answered Grim.

I tamped down a surge of panic. Just don't act suspicious, Pete. And besides, literally everyone knows you're an [Alchemist]. Unless they think I lied...

We all stood to attention as the first unigoats approached. The guards came in first and split around us. Half of them went to stand between us and the camp while the rest stayed with their charges. There were eight plate-clad dwarven guards, four gnomes, and three dwarves.

The gnome at the front of the line hopped off his unigoat. He had a shock white moustache that drooped down to his shoulders, and a tiny goatee. He also had the largest set of coke-bottle glasses I'd ever seen, complete with more glowing sigils. He wore a grey doublet and a set of brown bombasts. He also had an honest to the Gods *beanie*, complete with a tiny propeller that slowly spun in a lazy circle.

"Administrator Grim." He nodded at Grim as his eyes swept over us. He had a voice that was creaky with age, but firm and confident.

"[Administrator]!" Doc Opal's eyes were wide from shock. "Grim, you cabbage. You never said a word!"

Grim smirked slyly but didn't reply.

"Opal, as enthusiastic as ever." The elderly gnome nodded at her.

"Hello, Engineer Copperpot. I haven't seen you since my doctorate days."

"I heard from my colleagues that your thesis was a marvel." He smiled at her.

We were joined by the magenta-dressed female dwarf. The reddish-purple of her hauberk and her silver plate accents were offset by an incredibly fiery beard shaped into twin drills. Her hair was similarly coloured, with fine ringlets.

"Opal!" she cried, opening her arms. She and Opal shared a brief hug before she turned to Grim.

"Lustre sends her regards, Grim. I ran into her outside Lord Rodson's office."

"Thankee, Diamond. Is she doin' well?"

"Looks chipper as ever. I'm excited to see this mine where the Blessings fall like rain!" Diamond's eyes roved over the camp.

"Oh, it's unbelievable, Diamond!" Opal rolled her eyes. "Another party nearly every month."

"You poor thing." Diamond poked Opal in the side. "Have they been fattening you up?"

"Enough Diamond, we have business to do." Copperpot interrupted. He stepped in front of me and regarded Balin, who had been dead silent this entire time. "You two are the ones behind this operation?"

"Yessir!" I held out my hand and he shook it. "Peter Samson. Thank you so much for takin' the time out of your schedule to come and see us. This is an exciting opportunity, and we're lookin' forward to seein' your plans." Balin just nodded and made a slight leaking sound. Come on Balin, pull it together!

"Yes, I did take time out of my schedule." Copperpot nodded, his face turning serious. "It's a shame the recipe you sent us was worthless."

Excuse me?

CHAPTER THIRTY
BOOMDUST

"Excuse me?" I couldn't believe my ears. This pint-sized, over-moustached, propeller-capped egghead thought gunpowder was worthless? "Do you have the correct recipe?"

I wanted to follow up with 'and did you do it right?' but figured now wasn't the time. It was possible Copperpot was using a high-pressure sales technique. I could feel my old business brain clicking into gear. I was a little rusty, but skills honed for that long didn't disappear overnight. It did feel nice to be back in my element!

"Hmmm, well the recipe you gave Grim called for potassium nitrate, charcoal, and sulphur in a 75/12.5/12.5 ratio." The gnome listed off the ingredients on his fingers. Opal and Diamond were chatting off to the side, and Grim was listening in on us. The other gnomes and dwarves were unpacking a bunch of machinery and barrels from the red wagon.

"That's correct. We tested it and it worked out great." I turned to Balin for approval, and he nodded stiffly.

"Well, we did too, and it was barely worth our time." The gnome adjusted his glasses and scoffed. "I'm afraid that we can't give you much for it as is."

"What happened? Can you explain? You can see from my colleague's poor moustache that he suffered greatly when we did our test. We had a pretty big bang!" I pointed at Balin, who turned white as a sheet. Sorry for putting you on the spot bro!

"I see." Copperpot leaned over and peered at Balin's face. "Well, the problem was with the recipe you sent."

"We used the exact same recipe you just told me, how was it a problem?"

"Well, that depends. Were you the one that came up with the formula?" He turned a predatory gaze my way.

I opened my mouth to go with the old standby – amnesia – and paused. This guy was super smart, like magically super smart. Lies weren't going to work, so let's go with half-truths. "I made my first batch a few weeks ago. The sulphur ignites the charcoal, and the potassium nitrate acts as a catalyst. The resulting burn happens so fast that it causes an explosion." That was the most I could bullshit with my limited chemistry knowledge – I didn't really know how gunpowder worked.

"Hmm..." He peered over his glasses, "Well, that's a rough approximation. I'm surprised you were able to come up with it. There is, however, a problem." He walked over to the carriage and beckoned me to follow. Grim came alongside, clearly interested in the proceedings. Balin stayed behind as we walked, and I hoped he hadn't fainted on his feet. Copperpot beckoned to a young gnomesswearing a white smock-frock and leather apron as we approached. She had a bright, eager smile, and for a moment I was painfully reminded of my daughter. "Lillyweather, the gunpowder please."

"Yes, Professor." She nodded and went into the cart. She came out with a small red cask inscribed with white letters. I leaned over to read them; they were various symbols of skulls and flames and such.

"Are those WHMIS— I mean safety symbols?" I asked. They certainly had that look. "Wait! This is a cask full of gunpowder!" I took a step back as Copperpot carelessly handled the cask. "Be careful with that! [Stabilise Mixture]!"

"You made this recipe, and you can recognize hazardous material symbology? You must be trained, but your folder said you were a hapless drifter..." Copperpot pulled at his moustache. "I sent a message to Kinshasa's Administration, and they said your records are essentially nonexistent. No schooling, estranged from family, and recently arrived in Minnova from Gomba. It also said you were suffering from amnesia, is that no longer the case?"

"No, I still can't remember anything about my life in Crack from before I arrived in the City of Minnova Reform Mine." I shook my head sadly as I spoke another half-truth. Gomba, eh? Good to know where my body originally came from! "By the way, how should I address you? She called you Professor, and Doctor Opal mentioned something about a university?"

As we talked, Copperpot took us away from the group to a small rise. "Don't worry too much about the barrel, I had an [Alchemist] use [Stabilise Mixture] on it already. As to your question, Copperpot is fine. If we're going to work together, I'd prefer to avoid a situation where the extra seconds required to say, 'Engineering Professor Copperpot look out!' results in a lost limb." He winked at me.

Oho! The 'serious but with a sense of humour' type. I'd been worried Copperpot was one of those overbearing academic types, but this I could work with. Copperpot dumped some black powder out of the small barrel onto the ground. Instead of asking more questions I simply quietly observed, while ensuring Copperpot could see me absorbing everything he did. He smiled softly, and continued his work until there was a small mound.

"Step back a bit."

I took a couple large steps back and he gave a wheezing laugh. "Hah! Not that far. You'll see." He pulled a small red-tinged stone out of his pocket. He tossed it towards the pile and muttered "[Safety Shield]." We were suddenly surrounded by a translucent barrier as the red stone landed on the pile, and...

Not much happened. The pile sparked, then caught fire, and was consumed with a gout of flame and billowing black smoke. It was more of a *fwoosh* than a *bang.*

Grim's voice came from right behind me and I almost jumped. "That's not right. It made a big bang when Pete set it off before."

"Yes, well that was because the recipe was wrong. Who purchased the charcoal?" Copperpot asked as the barrier fell away.

"I did," Grim said. "Was there somethin' wrong with it?"

"The opposite actually. I don't think you realised because it's so commonly used, Grim, but you bought *fireash* charcoal." Copperpot held out an admonishing finger. "Pete could have been badly injured!"

AN ADVENTURE BREWING 221

"Ach, you're right! I never even thought about it!" Grim smacked his hand against his helmet and it rang like a bell. "I'm sorry, Pete."

"Excuse me, what's fireash?" I asked.

"It's a Minnovan export," Copperpot said, as he waved over Lillyweather and handed her the small cask. "A treant tree-monster in the dungeon that rapidly and furiously combusts if ignited. It's where sparkvine comes from as well. If a Fireash corpse is properly treated, it can be used to make charcoal that's famous for its intense flame."

"And Grim gave me some to make gunpowder!?" I asked in dawning horror.

"Yes. That *is* the danger in asking a layman to purchase your experimental supplies." Copperpot looked at me disapprovingly. "Why did you ask Grim to do it anyway?"

"I asked Grim, because..." I paused. "Because..." At this point we'd been joined by Diamond and Opal who had come to see what all the smoke and sparks were about.

"Sunnuvanannygoat!" Opal actually squeaked as I swore out loud. "Tim never got me any charcoal! He owes me back that silver!" I turned towards the camp, trying to see if I could spot him. It had been a couple weeks since Grim bought the charcoal and Tim had never once mentioned returning the silver I'd given him! I know I've been distracted, but he could have at least made an effort.

"I see," Diamond said, looking me over. "I think it's as you said, Grim."

"Looks like." Grim nodded.

"What are you talking about?" I asked, as I turned back to the group.

"Can I see your Status Sheet, Pete?" Diamond asked, coming over to stand beside me.

"Uh." I took a step back. "That's kind of a personal question there, Diamond. We should get to know each other first, maybe over some beer? Or maybe a radler? Have you had one?" Like Yearn I was letting this maroon menace look at my Sheet!

"Is that the drink Opal was just telling me about? I'd love to try some, but no, I just want to see if you have any Conditions. If it makes you uncomfortable, I can assure you as per Section 4, Article 15 of the City of Minnova Ordinances, I am not allowed to look at anything other than what I have received permission for – unless you are suspected of a crime, of course."

"So you'll only look at my Conditions? Why?"

"We think someone has been using a spirit-alterin' Ability on ya, Pete," Grim said. "Balin came ta me a while back complain' that you were makin' some real bad decisions. Givin' yer silver away and makin' foolish mistakes. I didn't think to much of it, but Balin was insistent. Then Sam and Doc Opal came forward with concerns of their own. Sam thought it was some form of wisdom-alterin' Ability, and Opal backed him up. All dwarves are required to report any new Blessin's or Milestones to tha' mine supervisor, but sometimes they can slip through the cracks. We got protocols fer when we suspect somethin' like that happened, and I sent fer Diamond here."

"What!" I looked over at Balin in shock, but he was still out of it. "Why didn't anyone tell *me*!?"

"Forcefully breaking someone out from any kind of mind manipulation can be dangerous without proper preparation." Doc Opal pulled at her beard. "Diamond is here to assess you and look for the culprit."

Holy shit! "Will you be able to tell by looking at my Status Sheet?"

"Yes, mind manipulation doesn't show up when you look at your own Conditions, but if someone else knows to look they can see it." Diamond nodded. "May I proceed?"

"If you can promise it's just to look at my Conditions. I don't like the idea of someone staring at my internal workings."

"Very well"

Bing!

Milestone Used
A [Statustician] has asked to look at your Conditions.

Do you accept?
Yes/No

I mentally clicked on *Yes* and hoped I wasn't making a terrible mistake. Diamond looked me over then nodded. "Yes, it says [Wisdom Loss: Recovering]. Would you take me to the dwarf in question, Grim?"

Grim nodded. "Aye, follow me. I've had Whisperer Gemma watchin' him."

"Who was it!" I demanded angrily. Who in the camp disliked me enough to do something like that? I thought back on the conversation we'd just had. "Was it Tim!? Why would he do that!?"

"Not sayin' till we're sure, Pete. We're dealin' with it. You stay with Engineer Copperpot." Grim and Diamond headed towards the camp with two of the guards.

"Well, that was interesting." Copperpot nodded sagely. "Are you ready to go to the mine and test the boomdust?"

"*Boomdust*?" I asked, my mind still reeling. Was it Tim? How could he do this to me? Dwarves were generally bullheaded, but kind-hearted and forgiving, weren't they? This threw my entire Erdview into question. But maybe it wasn't him at all!

"Yes, gunpowder is a stupid name. Nobody can tell me what a gun is, and you're clearly not a reliable source at the moment. You can keep gunpowder as the name for your recipe, but I'm calling the fireash variant boomdust!" He turned to his assistants, who had fully unpacked the carriage by this point. "Everyone move out! Into the mine! And be very careful with all the equipment!"

I snapped back to reality. "Hoooold it! I still get money from *boomdust, right!*? Even if I sent the wrong recipe, my original experiment was correct. Do I need to get a lawyer?"

"Boomdust was completely your invention, even if you got the recipe wrong. Don't worry, you'll still get paid, but I get my name on it as a co-inventor." He winked.

I nodded. "Well, that's alright then."

Copperpot gave me a wide smile. "If that's everything, are you ready to make a really Big Boom, Peter?"

I cheered up a bit. Who could turn down a capital 'B' Big Boom?

"Lead on, Copperpot!" I followed, deep in thought, as we made our way into the mine.

CHAPTER THIRTY-ONE
BIG BOOM

I walked in silence while Copperpot ordered his grad students around. Lillyweather notified me that most of them were staying on as research assistants because Copperpot was the biggest genius this side of Nikola Tesla.

There were a lot of boxes and barrels to be moved, and every time I thought they were done, a fresh set of supplies came out of the magic wagon. After several minutes, a giant drill took shape on the minecart tracks and Copperpot went to inspect it. For a brief while, there was nobody to talk to except Balin, but he wasn't much good for anything just now.

That meant I had a moment to digest the news about my mind being attacked. And wow, did I have a lot I needed to unpack. I'd been completely wrong about dwarves from the start. Doc Opal had said I was being standoffish, and I thought I'd gotten over it, but I was just now realising the real root of the issue. It wasn't a case of culture shock, or a problem with my modern sensibilities clashing with dwarven hard-headedness. It was a problem with *me*, and it wasn't the first time.

Back when I was in college I had a lot of buddies, especially after my mead side hustle swung into gear. They ranged from good friends to hangers-on to those just trying to get free alcohol. There were two people that really stood out though – Michael from London, and Jebediah from Texas. In a sea of West-Coasters they were the only two with really heavy accents. Well, there *were* numerous Japanese, Chinese and Korean students, but Jeb and Michael each had an accent all their own.

Michael had the thickest British accent you could imagine, of the deep and husky David Attenborough variety. Put him in a miniseries about the royal family and he'd make a believable King of England. Michael milked that accent to the nines, and was incredibly popular with a certain subset of girls on campus. Everyone talked about how smart and cultured Michael was.

On the other hand, Jeb had the most stereotypical, hillbilly, Texan accent that I'd ever heard. It made him almost impossible to understand and people judged him horribly over it. Incest jokes and chainsaw massacre cracks followed Jeb around for the entire four years that he was in college with us. People always assumed Jeb was dumb, and nobody ever wanted to work with him on group projects.

The worst part was that it was in fact the exact opposite. Michael was dumb as rocks, and nearly failed every course. On the other hand, Jeb was a business whiz, and when I figured that out in second year, I took advantage of it to get his help whenever I was struggling. He was happy to trade some tutoring for a bottle or two of whiskey mead. Jeb would leverage people's prejudices by playing up the 'dumb hillbilly' act until he pulled the rug out at the last moment. People were so blinded that they didn't see the person behind the accent until it was too late.

Last I'd heard, Michael was a used car salesman in Bradbury, and Jeb became the accountant for my own Beavermoose brewery, and half the other vineyards in the Okanagan besides. I thought I'd learned my lesson about accentism then, but it was rearing its ugly head again.

I'd been severely underestimating the dwarves. Their accents and demeanours and my own prejudices about them from years of dwarves in pop culture were making me judge them as a race rather than as people. Whether it was treating Balin like he wasn't smart enough to keep up, or bossing Bran around in his own kitchen, or thinking Tim was a simpletim, it was clear I'd fallen into bad habits.

Right here and now, some gnomes and dwarves that were obviously way smarter than I'd ever be were setting up a massive science experiment. It was humbling, and it was a humble pie I needed to eat right now, or I was going to get blindsided over and over again.

Stat Increased: [Wisdom]!
Your wisdom has increased by 1! Your new wisdom is 14!

See? Even the Gods thought I'd been a dumbass, and it was time to make some changes. I turned to Balin, who was riveted to the proceedings.

"Hey Balin? Balin? Baaaalin?" I waved my hand in front of him.

"Aye, Pete?"

"I wanted to say thank you for lookin' out for me with the mind thing. I have something to tell you when we get out of here. It's about my past."

"Uh, ok. You remember something?"

I nodded. "I'll tell you when we're free."

Balin nodded back, and as he turned away, I pulled out a comb and brushed my beard. Yes, life as a dwarf was just... perfect.

"Well, what do you think, Peter?" Copperpot approached while I was talking to Balin and broke into our conversation with the practised ease of someone in upper management. He pointed at the drill his students had assembled. "Isn't it glorious?" "Pete is fine. It's a nice piece o' machinery. Does it run on magic?" I looked it up and down. It was as shiny and fancy looking as a '67 Mustang. I had some basic tinkering knowledge from my work with stills, but this was beyond me. I was now *very* glad I hadn't wasted a lot of time on my makeshift steam engine.

"That's correct and incorrect." Copperpot pointed at some stones set in a container at the base of the drill. "The drill runs off of the raw mana contained in cores taken from monsters within the dungeon."

"So why do we use picks instead of drills like this when we mine?" Gods, it would make this work a lot easier.

"A pertinent question. It's due to expense. There is a limited supply of cores, but a somewhat ready supply of ne'er-do-wells with picks." Copperpot's eyes glittered with his not-so-subtle jab. "That's also why goats are still commonly used for transport, and charcoal for most cooking."

"I'll have you know that a simple miner can have a *higher perspective* that an academic might lack," I retorted as I stood at my full height. Copperpot was fairly short, even for a gnome, and only came up to my stomach.

"They make up for it with a *miner* pro-spective," Copperpot shot back.

"I disagree," I countered. "When you're in a mine, you learn some of the best *prospecting*."

"Hah, well played, sir. I tip my beanie to the superior wordsmith." He made a small bow and Grim stifled a groan from behind us.

"How in Yearn's Yams are you two gettin' along so well?"

Copperpot and I looked at each other and grinned.

"You're just not twisty enough to understand, Administrator Grim," Copperpot said.

"Thank the Gods for that," Grim muttered.

We went back to ignoring him.

"Excuse me Professor, and Alchemist," a bright voice interrupted.

"Yes, Lillyweather?" Copperpot nodded at the gnomess who had appeared beside us.

"Could you step aside, please? We're going to move the drill now."

"Of course. This way, Pete."

We moved over as the gaggle of grads pushed the drill down the mine track. I could see some little wheels spinning underneath it. Neat.

We let the drill cart get far ahead of us before we followed after. The long, straight nature of the main mineshaft meant that sound echoed terribly up and down the tunnel. It had been impossible to concentrate, let alone chat, with the rumble of the cart travelling down the track. The walls down here were strung with solstones and a slight orange glow outlined everything. It smelled of damp stone and future dreams.

"What's the plan?" I asked, curious to see how the engineer had solved the mining problem.

"I'll explain later, I need to do some due diligence."

As we made our way down, Copperpot stayed busy by checking the walls and the rafters. He pulled out a notepad and took notes in it every few metres. By the time we reached the end of the tunnel the grad students already had the drill up against the mine wall and were preparing to power it up. Copperpot gave it a once-over and then declared it ready.

"Excellent! It is time to sup from the bounty of Tiara's Teat! Start up the drill!"

Ew.

The drill started up with a whine and dust poured into the tunnel. Everyone had masks on except Copperpot. The beanie on his head whirled and the dust eddied around and away from him. I stood beside him to take advantage of his personal protective equipment; the boss always had the best PPE.

"Can you tell me the plan, now!?" I shouted over the roar of the drill.

"Boomdust shows the greatest power when it is fully contained!" Copperpot shouted back. "We're going to drill some deep holes and then pour boomdust in! If our calculations are correct, that should provide enough force to blast the rock apart!"

"I thought the drill was expensive! How is this better than using the mining picks!?"

"While it won't replace picks for dives, the main tunnel is always the most expensive part of any mining operation! If this method can significantly reduce the time for carving the main tunnel, it offsets the cost of the drill!" Copperpot smiled wolfishly. "Also, fireash charcoal and sparkvine are primarily Minnovan exports, so if this gets adopted everywhere it means a lot of gold for the city!"

"Don't forget, Balin and I!"

"Yes, but it'll take a while!" Copperpot chuckled.

I could live with that. I had hundreds of years to wait!

The drilling continued for about fifteen minutes while Copperpot checked and double-checked each step. Eventually the drilling stopped, and the grad students took some red barrels and poured their contents into the holes. I subconsciously backed up.

"Want me to use [Stabilise Mixture] on those?"

"If it will make you feel better. It's not really necessary though," Copperpot said offhandedly. I did – it made me feel better.

Eventually the barrels were all emptied and the holes were capped. Everything was cleared away and a long string of sparkvine was wheeled up the mineshaft. We followed behind while Copperpot ordered cleanup and the last few safety procedures. Soon enough we were standing back under the light of the stars.

"Alright! We should be safe here!" Copperpot handed me the end of the sparkvine. "Would you care to do the honours, Pete?"

It was do or die. Copperpot handed me a small red stone he called a 'firestone – a flame-infused aetherstone' and I held it up to the sparkvine. It sparked and a small flame hissed down the line. We waited with bated breath, and just as I was beginning to worry the whole thing had misfired –

BOOM

I felt my ears pop, and while no dust poured out of the tunnel, the ground did feel like it shivered. That may have been my imagination though.

"Good work everyone! Shall we go see the results?" Copperpot pointed into the tunnel and we all descended back into the Erd.

CHAPTER THIRTY-TWO
TANNINS

The end of the tunnel was over a kilometre away, and we were taking it slow.

"Rafter crew! Check on the supports!" Copperpot shouted. The overall-clad dwarves I'd seen during Balin's rescue got to work climbing the walls as we made our way down the tunnel. "Excellent, I don't see any real damage to the tunnel structure..." Copperpot leaned in, and I could see his glasses telescoping outwards.

"What do you think? Was the experiment a success?" I was nervous, and Balin wasn't helping, as he rubbed his hands and practically jittered beside me. I could understand – we were about to see if he'd be with his lady love next week, or next decade.

"Well, the boomdust certainly went *Boom!*" Copperpot smiled.

"Broke my ears," grumbled Grim.

"It was quite loud, Professor," Lillyweather said from beside us. "Perhaps next time we should have ear covering even when we're outside the mine?"

"Yes, I didn't take into account the focusing nature of the tunnel on the sound. Make a note of it please, Lillyweather."

"Yes, Professor."

The party continued down the tunnel like that for a while. The rafter crew would go up and check the wooden supports, Copperpot would examine the walls with his glasses, and everyone would take notes. Every once in a while, someone ran down a dive tunnel to see if they'd been affected.

I looked around and realised we were actually stuffed in here pretty tight. Between the four guards that had come with us, the five grad students, the four-man rafter crew, Grim, Balin, and Copperpot, we were standing shoulder to shoulder at times.

I held Balin back so we weren't in the way. I didn't want to cause any problems at this stage, not when we were so close. Grim stayed near the front and helped Copperpot direct the rafter crew. One guard peeled off and stuck to us. I didn't want to shoo him away, so I did my best to ignore him and turned to Balin.

"Do you think it worked?" I whispered.

"Sounded like it ta me, Pete," Balin hissed back. "I still can't believe ya made somethin' like that."

"'We.' *'We'* made it, Balin!"

"Say what ya want, but it was yer idea, Pete."

"What matters is that we both get credit for our indenture."

"True enough. I can't wait ta see Annie again!"

Eventually Copperpot came back to chat with us, a bored Grim following behind.

"Everything good?" I asked.

"Yes, I wanted to ensure the rafter crew was competent enough to spot any problems. They have proven their excellence, and I am confident enough to leave them to their work."

"Don't want to make 'em nervous, eh?" Gods knew I'd had difficulty with that when I first became the boss. I'd checked every employee's work, ensured every single job was done to exacting standards, and practically ridden my first workers until they'd nearly quit. Thankfully, Caroline sat me down and explained what an ass I was being before it was too late.

Coach, instruct, and then leave it to the proven professionals. *Don't micromanage.*

"Nothing quite like a bigwig standing below while you hammer on the ceiling to give someone the shakes," Copperpot agreed. "Now that we have some time, what was this radler that you and Statistician Diamond discussed?"

"It's a mixture of..." I shut my mouth with a *clack.* Wow, I'd been giving out a *ton* of recipes for free lately. I was so used to getting anything I wanted off the internet that I'd forgotten even *basic* information could hold value. On Earth, I'd just look up a radler recipe online, but here I was the only resource. Except for Bran and a few other miners that had probably guessed by now, but I had ways to silence them. Having a sharp mind like Copperpot trying to ferret out my secrets was really helping me get my A game back! That or the freaking *recovering loss* of my wisdom!

"The exact recipe is something I worked out with Bran. It's currently a trade secret," I practically purred. "It's been successful enough that I'm considering some investors. If you're interested, we could discuss –"

"It's just lemonade mixed with beer," Grim interrupted from behind us. Copperpot laughed out loud.

"Barck's beard, Grim!" I whirled on him. "Why would you do that!?" Grim just gave me another shark-tooth grin.

Copperpot wiped some tears from his eyes. "Sorry, Pete. Looks like the lemon is out of the bag on that one. Still... lemonade and beer?" He pulled at his moustache. "Lemonade is more of a gnomish drink. I'm surprised that a dwarf was willing to, ah, contaminate their sacred brew with it."

"I did hear that gnomes don't drink much beer."

"It isn't unheard of, but no – it's too sour for our tastes. Most gnomes prefer dry flavours like teas and coffees though some prefer the sweet sugary taste of juice."

We chatted about tea and coffee for a while as we walked. Copperpot came from a family of gnomish oligarchs that owned a tea business in Minnova. They were one of the main distributors of teas and coffees to all of Crack. At first, I was desperately imagining glorious cappuccinos, but then a thought slowly began to take form in the back of my mind.

"Copperpot, what if I could make a less-sour beer? Or one with more 'gnomish' flavouring?"

"That would be interesting. How?"

"It's complicated, but I could probably whip up something acceptable." I considered what was safe to tell him without giving too much away. If I played my cards right, I could gain Copperpot's interest.

Right now, that outvalued any money I could gain from the information as long as I didn't give too much away.

I decided to start with some background science. "Since your family sells tea, do you understand the concept of tannins?"

"Hmmm... I've heard of them but can't say I'm overly familiar. It's not my area of study, though it is part of my family's business."

"What do you know?"

"I know they're in plants, but not much else."

"Let's see if I can explain... You understand that acids are sour, correct?"

"Yes, obviously." Copperpot looked askance at me.

"Well, tannins are chemical compounds that make the tart flavour associated with black teas. They're bitter and astringent and leave your mouth and tongue feeling kind of dry. On the other hand, sour is a taste that leaves your mouth feeling watery and puckered, like some fruit teas."

"Oho, you know some of the secrets of tea!" Copperpot jabbed a finger in my direction. "Were you trained somewhere?"

"Actually, I know about it because I'm interested in brewing. Tannins are important for beer brewing too."

"Truly? How so? I wouldn't think that beer has much in common with tea." Copperpot's eyes sparkled with academic interest.

I squared my shoulders and spoke authoritatively. "First, you need to understand that tannins are a natural part of most vegetation. They are a preservative, and they form an outer coating on plants to help them survive winter. You get a lot of them on grapes, which is why red wine is often so dry."

"You've had wine? I haven't even had any. It's very expensive." Copperpot raised his curly eyebrows at me.

"Uh, so I've heard, anyway. When you mash your malt, it adds some tannins into the wort. Those tannins stay in the brew and help keep the acidity of the beer from overwhelmin' your taste buds. The erdroot used in the local malt doesn't need to survive winter, so it's got no tannins in it. That makes tha beer a bit one-dimensional." Most beers get their tannin from the husks of the plant used to make the malt. Rice beer has some of the most tannins in it, and wheat beer has some of the lowest. Here in Crack, the lack of any tannins in dwarvish beer was just another thing to dislike about it.

"Interesting. I don't really know what mash and wort are, but I can extrapolate them well enough from the context."

"Ah, sorry. Do you need me to explain?"

"No, that's quite alright." Copperpot looked me over. "Pete, you seem to know a lot about flavour, and you're quick on the uptake. Are you looking for work when you complete your indenture? My family might be interested in someone with a unique point of view."

Score! While a job working for a gnomish oligarch family sounded appealing, it wasn't really what I wanted. It made for a nice failsafe though.

"No, sorry. I want to work in a brewery."

"A brewery, really? How do you plan to get into one? They are very selective in who they employ," Copperpot pointed out. "Most are kept within the family."

"I have a friend that's letting me work at hers."

"Well, that's a lucky break! Praise Barck!"

Ugh, I'd rather not.

After an interminable amount of time filled with constant stops to check the integrity of the tunnel, we reached a location coated in fine dust.

"Alright everyone! Keep a sharp eye out!" Copperpot commanded. "We've reached the blast zone, and I want you to take note of every single detail! Leave nothing out!"

Every grad student had a notepad in hand in an instant, and the sound of furious scribbling soon filled the tunnel. I was getting incredibly bored, and Balin and I had taken to discussing our plans upon leaving the mine. He wanted to go straight to Annie's, and I wanted to scope things out for a day or two first. However, our discussion was suddenly interrupted by a pair of blue boxes that popped into my vision.

Bing!

New Quest: First Encounter!
You have disturbed a monstrous brood! Can you survive long enough for help to arrive?
This is a timed quest.
Time remaining: 16 minutes.

Reward: +0.2 Vitality

Do you accept?
Yes / No

New Quest: Prove Yourself!
You are encountering monsters for the first time! Show off your otherworldly prowess and slay them!
Monsters Slain: 0/10

Reward: [Basic Slash]

Do you accept?
Yes / No

HOLY SHIT! I accepted the two quests then turned to Copperpot and opened my mouth to shout a warning. How could I tell him without revealing my secrets?! Quick brain, think!

"Copperpot! I was just thinking, could a blast like that disturb any local animals?"

"I suppose," Copperpot mused. "I had Speaker John check the blast zone ahead of time, but if there were any freshies, he wouldn't have seen them. The only thing we'd need to worry about around here are – "

"STONEANT!" A shrill feminine cry came from slightly down the tunnel. We yanked our necks around just in time to see some dust-coated antennae quaveringly peek out from behind some rubble.

CHAPTER THIRTY-THREE
STONEANTS

A stoneant looked very similar to a regular ant, if a regular ant was the size of a Gods-bedamned Rottweiler. It had a hard grey exoskeleton with significantly more spikes than your average ant deserved. A serrated set of pincers, and a pair of fuchsia compound eyes completed the set. It otherwise looked and behaved like a regular ant, complete with an obsessive desire to defend its nest.

A nest we'd just blown a hole into.

"Hold tha line!" a dwarf in plate mail shouted. He swung an axe and sheared the antenna off a stoneant specimen with a head nearly as big as its body. It was double the size of the other stoneants, and I clinically wondered if it was a soldier ant. The four guards stood shoulder to shoulder with their shields up, swinging their axes with abandon. Every once in a while, one of them would shout out an Ability. Shouting isn't necessary to activate Abilities, but it feels really good.

"[Advanced Slash]!"
"[Wide Cleave]!"
"[Flaming Axe]!"
"[Meteor Hammer]!"

That last one made a fairly large explosion as a burning hammer spun into the mass of insects and blew up. Wind rushed down the tunnel back towards us and we were momentarily blinded as the dust picked up. The hole in the chittering horde had already filled with more ants by the time I finished clearing the dust out from my eyes.

"This could be bad," Copperpot observed.

"*BAD?* Are ye mad?!" Grim exclaimed. "There's too many of 'em! We must 'ave blasted into a nest!" He turned to run back up the tunnel then paused. "We'll never outrun em! We need ta stick together!"

"Yes, the guards should be fine. I can protect myself, but I am worried about my students." Copperpot looked at Balin and I. "And I do hope you don't die."

"Oh, don't mind us. I think we're both in shock. Balin?" I went to poke him in the side. Except... he wasn't there.

"Ya buggers!" Balin smashed a pick he'd gotten from who-knows-where onto the head of a stoneant. It scrabbled through a guard's legs, and he barely stopped it from chomping on a cowering dwarf in coveralls. "You tryin' to keep me from mah Annie!?"

"Balin's fine, I guess?" He smashed a soldier ant into the wall and stood back-to-back with the plated guards. I knew Balin was good in a fight, but holy *scrap*! I pointed up at the roof of the tunnel, "He's fine, but we're not!"

A stream of ants advanced along the ceiling, bypassing the shield-wall. The first wave dropped ineffectually onto the line of guards and were promptly torn apart. The second wave landed behind them and charged at the unprotected grad students. Lillyweather cried "[Safety Shield]!" and a dome of translucent light surrounded them. The ants smashed their pincers futilely against the shield, which quivered.

"Not good. That won't last longer than a few seconds." Copperpot pulled out a small vial and tossed it at the ants. It exploded over the backs of a half-dozen of them, and they keened as their carapaces melted.

"By the unholy Yams of Yearn! What was that stuff?" I cried as the ants' bodies smoked and fell apart. Balin stepped forward and finished the last of them. Lillyweather's shield winked out a moment later and the students scrambled towards us.

"Acid taken from a pitchervore. Guard Captain Morris, this isn't working!" Copperpot shouted at the line of guards.

A dwarf with an especially impressive set of pauldrons turned his head. "We need a more defensible position! Engineering Professor Copperpot, get everyone back and into a dive tunnel!"

"Damn! Pete, Administrator Grim, you two know this mine, where can we make a stand?"

I held up a hand. "I was just minin' this section. There's a dive two tunnels up – about a hundred metres back. It has a narrow opening, but we pulled a lot of ore out of it, so it should fit everyone."

"Good, we'll head for that. Grim, is help on the way?"

"I've already called fer reinforcements with my emergency commstone."

"How long?"

"The entire camp is comin' down the tunnel. Maybe ten minutes?" Grim rasped, his voice tight with fear.

I looked numbly at my 'Survive' quest; thirteen minutes remained, so that was about right. At that moment an especially large soldier ant crashed over the guards and launched itself at us. Copperpot shouted "[Safety Shield]!" and he, Grim, and several students were enveloped in grey light. That didn't help Lillyweather, who was holding up the rear. The ant landed beside her and turned a pair of wicked mandibles in her direction. It lunged, and Lillyweather screamed.

My body moved unconsciously. Every fibre in my being was yelling at me to run away, but as Lillyweather cried out, all I could hear was Sammy crying for her daddy. I reached out and pulled Lillyweather into my arms as the mandibles closed around us.

"[Flesh of Stone]!"

Balin gasped, his arms aching. His pick had been torn from his hands by a worker stoneant, and a lucky grab for a guard's spare axe had been the only thing that saved him from a vicious strike by a soldier stoneant twice his size. His return riposte had cleanly sliced the offending pincers in half and ichor now dripped from his clothes.

"Yer doin' great, greenhorn!" One of the guards shouted as he activated an Ability that tore a line through the mass of stoneants.

"Thankee!" Balin heaved and his axe cut through another couple of workers in a single blow. "I've got lots of practice swingin' an axe!"

"Haha! He's a natural!" Another guard laughed heartily as an enormous soldier stoneant crashed into him. "[Shield Wall]!" he shouted, and the ant was repelled with a clang of metal.

Balin glanced around at what he assumed were official Titled [Guards]. The majority of the stoneants were being rebuffed by the oddly cheerful wall of steel. Thankfully, Lunara City Hall had sent them to ensure nothing went wrong. It looked like they might be able to hold the ants here long enough for everyone else to escape up the tunnel.

An ant dropped onto his back from above, and Balin ripped it off with an "Argh!" He was fast, but it wasn't fast enough to keep the ant from biting into his shoulder. The chain sewn into the suit kept his arm from being torn off, but he still received a nasty gash.

"Gods *damn* this *damn* suit!" Balin wanted to rip the fool thing off, but it was the only thing he had that resembled some form of armour. "I never shoulda let Pete talk me into wearin' it!" Wait... where had that stoneant come from? Balin looked up.

A solid stream of stoneants was climbing along the ceiling. The guards hadn't noticed because their plate helmets kept them from looking up. Any ants that landed on them simply bounced off their armour, but the real problem was...

"[Safety Shield]!" Lillyweather's cry caused Balin to whip around. The students were being assaulted by nearly a dozen stoneants. He rushed to their aid as a bottle crashed into the heaving mass of insects and they began to smoke and melt. With a guttural cry, Balin waded in and cleared out the remaining ants. He stood and struggled for breath in the acrid smoke as a dozen more ants began to crawl along the walls.

"Guard Captain Morris, this isn't working!" Copperpot shouted.

The dwarf standing at the head of the formation turned his head and shouted back. "We need a more defensible position! Engineering Professor Copperpot, get everyone back and into a dive tunnel!"

Balin braced to receive the new wave of workers as they dropped from the ceiling. He swung his axe in arc after arc just as he'd learned as a carpentry apprentice. He imagined them as trees, felled in a single swing.

A pincer came at his face and Balin blocked it with a forearm. It bit deep, but the bracer built into the suit kept it from taking his arm. He killed the offending insect for the insult.

Suddenly, an enormous soldier ant barrelled over the guards and past Balin. He felt it brush by him, and the world fell into slow motion.

A translucent shield popped into existence around Copperpot and bumped into Lillyweather.

Lillyweather screamed as she tumbled back and fell towards the gigantic stoneant.

Pete reached out and grabbed the gnomess in his arms.

The two of them were engulfed by the enormous pincers.

"NOOOOOOOOO!!!!" Balin cried. He wasn't going to lose his family to monsters again! HE'D SWORN HE'D NEVER LOSE ANYONE EVER AGAIN!

A set of pincers grabbed Balin's ankle from behind and he kicked viciously, tearing free. Another jaw clamped onto his arm, and he simply whipped the stoneant up and used it to bludgeon another out of the air as it launched at him. Balin swung his axe at the enormous soldier stoneant's back and it bounced off the heavily armoured exoskeleton.

He wasn't strong enough. He hadn't been strong enough to save his sister. He hadn't been strong enough to save Pete. He hadn't been strong enough to save his mum.

Balin wept tears of rage at the unfairness of it, at the world, and at the Gods.

Bing!

Time seemed to fall into slow-motion as the notifications appeared in Balin's subconscious.

Blessing Granted: [Yearn]!
Your deep love and righteous rage have caught the attention of Yearn.
May your strength be used to protect those you love!
*If you receive Yearn's Blessing, you will gain [**Nothingness**] and [**Sense Emotions**].*
If you accept, you will be eligible for a Title!

Do you accept?
Yes/No

YES. He barely glanced at the words, making choices almost purely on instinct.
Bing!

Blessing Received: [Yearn]!
You have accepted the Blessing of Yearn!
*You have received the Blessings [**Nothingness**] and [**Sense Emotions**]!*

Charisma plus 2! Your new charisma is 20!
Wisdom plus 2! Your new wisdom is 14!

Title Gained!
Your Blessings from Yearn and Tiara can be merged into a Title!

Merge Blessings?
Yes/No

YES.
Bing!

Title Gained
Please choose two Blessings to combine into a Title!

Possible Title: [Destroyer]
Combine Yearn of Nether and Tiara of Matter.
*[**Nothingness**] and [**Strength of All: Self**] will combine into the Title [**Destroyer**].*
*A [**Destroyer**] can crush steel in their palm and destroy stone with a thought.*
*A [**Destroyer**] fears nothing and wears terror as a cloak.*

Accept [Destroyer]?
Yes/No

NO.

Possible Title: [Swindler]

Combine Yearn of Nether and Tiara of Possessions.
*[**Nothingess**] and [**Strength of All: Held**] will combine into the Title [**Swindler**].*
*A [**Swindler**] can convince anyone to give up all they have in return for nothing.*
*A [**Swindler**] manipulates the spirit just as easily as the truth.*

Accept [Swindler]?

Yes/No

NO.

Possible Title: [Butler]

Combine Yearn of Relationships and Tiara of Possessions.
*[**Strength of All: Held**] and [**Sense Emotions**] will combine into the Title [**Butler**]*
*A [**Butler**] cares for the spirit, spark, and home of the one they choose to serve.*
*A [**Butler**] can cook, clear, and clean at great speed without a single broken plate.*

Accept [Butler]?

Yes/No

NO.

Possible Title: [Knight]

Combine Yearn of Relationships and Tiara of Matter
*[**Strength of All: Self**] and [**Sense Emotions**] will combine into the Title [**Knight**]*
*A [**Knight**] is a shining hero to the weak and a fearsome enemy to the strong.*
*A [**Knight**] can turn the tide of battle and bring hope where all is lost.*

Accept [Knight]?
Yes/No

YES. Balin didn't even read the description, choosing based on the name alone.

Title Gained: [Knight]!
*A **[Knight]** is a shining hero to the weak and a fearsome enemy to the strong.*

Blessing Evolved: [Sense Emotions] becomes [Challenge]!
You can twist the emotions of a monster and demand they face you in a battle of arms or wits.
This Ability can be used twice per hour.

Blessing Evolved: [Strength of All: Self] becomes [Heroic Moment]!
*A true **[Knight]** can wield incredible strength at just the right moment. For five minutes your strength, vitality, agility, and dexterity are increased by 12.*
This Ability can be used twice per day.

Bing!

Milestone Gained: Titled!
Gaining a Title has granted you the ability to choose a Milestone!

Please accept one of the following:
Possible Milestone: [Staunch Bleeding]!
No small scratch will stop a knight! You can staunch your wounds and prevent them from bleeding further.
This Ability can be used once per hour.

Accept [Staunch Bleeding]?
Yes/No

NO.

Possible Milestone: [Resist Acid]!
Armour cannot stop the burning corrosion of acid, but your body will! Your body becomes resistant to the caustic effects of most acids.
This Ability is always available.

Accept [Resist Acid]?
Yes/No

NO.

Possible Milestone: [Basic Cleave]!
Even when facing a horde of enemies, a knight does not falter. You can cut through many enemies in a single blow.
This Ability can be used once per minute.

Accept [Basic Cleave]?
Yes/No

NO.

Possible Milestone: [Shining Armour]!
A knight is a beacon in the dark, sometimes literally. Your body is encased in a set of shining golden armour. The armour disappears if it is removed.
This Ability can be used once per day.

Accept [Shining Armour]?
Yes/No

YES!

The world snapped back into focus. Balin roared, "[Heroic Moment][Shining Armour][Challenge]! Turn and face me ya bastard!"

The soldier stoneant opened its slavering maw and a pair of bodies clattered to the ground with a *crack!* It wheeled on Balin, opening a pair of jaws to a span thrice his height. Balin's axe swung upwards in a blur, and the ant nearly flipped over as an enormous crack formed on its face. It screeched and reared back down, jaws snapping, but each wicked pincer was caught in a shining gauntlet.

"I'll never let you take 'em from me again!" With a ferocious burst of strength, Balin wrenched sideways, and the stoneant's head was torn from its body in a spray of ichor.

CHAPTER THIRTY-FOUR
LAST STAND

I shook my head, which was still ringing after the giant stoneant had bounced me off the floor. I didn't think I was dead. My body was no longer made of stone and I could still feel Lillyweather wrapped in my arms. The afterlife had better not just be a string of Pete ending up in the body of different Petes throughout the multiverse...

The soldier stoneant had thrown us aside after someone, Balin I think, yelled at it. Balin! I sat bolt upright. Lillyweather slumped over, but I caught her before she hit the floor. Something wet splattered against my pants – a quick glance revealed her left leg was completely mangled.

I hadn't been able to cover her completely, but at least she was still breathing.

"Copperpot, Grim! I need you!" I screamed, then looked wildly for Balin. He'd distracted that monster! A moment later and I would have died! What happened to him!?

"Fer Crack and Annie!" came the answer, and I goggled as a dwarf clad in shining golden plate-armour smashed an axe into another giant soldier ant at the front lines. The ant was carved nearly in half, and the golden dwarf continued to take on the biggest stoneants in turn. *Balin?* The guards adjusted their formation to support him, and the stoneants were driven back.

"Pete!" A hand shook my shoulder. "We need ta move to that

tunnel! Guard Captain, we're retreating!" Grim lifted Lillyweather onto his shoulder while Copperpot examined her leg. "NOW!"

"Aye, Sir. Everyone, orderly retreat!"

Copperpot grabbed my arm and pulled as the party began to fall back up the mine tunnel. The timer on my quest still read over nine minutes until help arrived. I couldn't fully parse what was happening. It was one thing to watch distant specks blast apart stick figure monsters at the dungeon, but it was another to have a swarm of giant fantasy ants trying to eat you. I was just Pete from Canada! I wasn't ready for this! How tha nether did fantasy transmigration protagonists just... jump right into things? Is that why they were always teenagers? I was way too set in my ways to suddenly become an action hero, even if my stats were way higher than earth Pete's!

As we ran, I grabbed a discarded minepick and held it in one shaking hand. Having a weapon helped calm my monkey nerves, and my breathing evened out. The others quickly outpaced the three of us as Grim was still carrying the gently bleeding Lillyweather, and Copperpot and I weren't going to leave him behind.

After about a hundred metres, the guards called out to us. "Ants incomin'!"

I glanced back to see four more worker stoneants headed in our direction. Two headed towards Grim and Lillyweather, and two jumped at Copperpot – the smaller target. Dumb choice.

"Hmph, [Arc-Welder]." A scintillating torch of energy erupted from one of his fingers and sheared through the two ants. Their corpses hissed and spit as the ichor in their bodies evaporated from the intense heat. While that was fascinating to watch, I still had two insect problems to deal with as I stepped into their path. I pulled my pick back as the first one launched at me, and I batted it out of the air like a baseball. It flew across the tunnel and smashed into a wall.

Then the second stoneant was on me, and I barely held it back with my pickaxe. I fell onto my butt as it snapped its pincers at my face and its spiked legs scrabbled, tearing at my suit. Out of the corner of my eyes, I saw the first stoneant groggily pick itself up and stumble back towards me.

"Yer just a bug, so.. get... squished!" With a grunt of effort, I shoved the ant off me and onto its concussed kin. The two of them fell over in a tangle of limbs and took a moment to get back up. That was all I needed.

"[Power Pick]!" I cried. My pick gained a faint glow and I brought it down on the pair of them. They practically exploded and I was showered in goo.

"Can't you cast some spells or somethin'?" I asked Copperpot, as we turned and continued running.

"No, I don't know how," Copperpot explained between gasping breaths. "I have a limited form of [Manasight] that allows me to work mana into my engineering projects. I'm too old to be learning everything required for shaping mana into spells."

"What use is [Manasight] if you can't cast magic?!"

"Since when is anything good in life that easy? Most mages receive Archis's Blessing because they put in the years of study necessary to use mana, not the other way around. Now shut up and run!"

We passed the first tunnel, and the grad students up ahead turned into the second. We caught up to Grim and flanked him until we also reached the dive and jumped in.

"Everyone here?" Copperpot asked, looking around.

As far as I could see, all the grad students as well as the support crew were in the carved-out cavern, and Grim was laying an unconscious Lillyweather against the back wall. The cave was five metres by five metres, and only had one small entrance tunnel. A dwarf could barely fit into it, which meant the ants would only be able to attack in pairs.

"I think that's everyone." I walked through the entrance and peered back down the tunnel. "Ugh, another bunch of workers are headed our way." In the distance a gleaming form smashed into the wave of ants in order to buy time for the guards to retreat. *Damn, Balin. What happened to you?!*

The oncoming ants approached the entrance to the dive and Copperpot leaned out. "We can't have their bodies blocking the entrance before the guards get here. I'm going to incapacitate them. Can you kill them, Pete?"

"Uh..."

"We're out of time. I'll take that as a yes." Copperpot held out his hand. "[Lubricate]!"

Instantly, the ants slipped and slid, their feet unable to find purchase. They wildly flailed their limbs and two of them were even impaled by their fellows.

"Fer Crack!" I yelled, psyching myself up. I ran forward to the first of the ants, which was on its own and struggling to stand. I plunged my pickaxe into its head, and it twitched twice then fell over dead. I wrenched the pickaxe free then killed another, and another.

As I turned to the tangled pile of struggling stoneants I felt an intense burning sensation in my leg. I looked down, horrified – a dying stoneant had clamped its pincers onto my thigh. Then it thrashed, and I screamed in agony. My vision flashed with pain and shock as my leg collapsed out from under me. I brought my pickaxe down onto the monster's head over and over again.

"You Netherspawned thing! Get off me!" The ant finally loosened its grip and died, but my injured leg was pinned beneath it. By all rights I should have lost my leg and fallen unconscious, but I was quite literally twice as durable as the average dwarf. Beside me, a few ants crawled clear of the tangle and skated over to get a bite in edgewise. Blood pooled around my leg and sweat poured down my face.

Bing

Condition Gained: [Bleeding]!

*You have gained the [**Bleeding**] Condition!*
You will die if not treated!

I was going to die.

Then the ants were dead, and a sprinting guard grabbed me as they ran by.

"Good job, boyo!"

"Yer buddy is one heck of a fighter!"

"Ach, his leg is all cut up, someone tell tha boss!"

"Make sure tha [Knight] can get free. No dwarf left behind!"

All I could do was whimper in pain and relief. Then I passed out, again.

"Pete, how are you doing?"

I blearily opened my eyes. "Copperpot?"

Bing!

Condition Lost: [Bleeding]!
*You have lost the **[Bleeding]** Condition!*

The sound of combat came from right nearby, so I couldn't have been out long.

"I applied pressure to your leg until [Regeneration] knit the flesh shut. You probably would have died of blood-loss without it. Praise, Barck."

Argh. Please tell me I didn't owe my life to Barck now. I'd prefer to have died to the stoneants.

"What's happening?"

"The guards are taking turns fighting at the entrance and your friend Balin has finally come down from his [Heroic Moment]. Lucky timing on that! He checked on you and then collapsed over there." Copperpot pointed to a golden figure sprawled on the floor a little way over to the side.

I checked my quests.

Quest: First Encounter
You have disturbed a monstrous brood! Can you survive long enough for help to arrive?
This is a timed quest.
Time remaining: 3 minutes.

Reward: +0.2 Vitality

Quest: Prove Yourself
You are encountering monsters for the first time! Show off your otherworldly prowess and slay them!

Monsters Slain: 5/10
*Reward: [**Basic Slash**]*

Only three minutes left. We could do this!

"How's Lillyweather?"

"Not good. We applied a tourniquet to her leg, but she's still unconscious, and she doesn't have [Regeneration]; her only Blessing is from Lunara."

I felt a cold pit in my stomach. "Is she going to die?"

Dark silence was my only answer.

"Gods."

A few more minutes passed. I checked my quest every few seconds, willing time to go just a little bit faster. The guards continued to slaughter ants at the entrance to the dive. The constant sound of crunching carapace matched the rhythmic beating of my heart.

Time remaining: 3 minutes.
Time remaining: 1 minute.

"Big one incomin'! I think it's a brood-guard!" The soldier at the front called. "Barck's Beard, it's huge! Everyone back from the wall!"

The guards ran back down the tunnel and formed a shield wall at the entry to the cavern. A swarm of ants followed and were beaten back by axes, boots, and expletives. Stoneant bodies soon formed a pile of the dead that blocked the entryway, and there was a moment of blessed peace.

"We might have a reprieve..." I whispered into the deathly silence.

Copperpot groaned. "Never say things like that! They're called stoneants for a reason!"

A crack formed above the tunnel, then another as shards of stone fell from the ceiling.

The guards gathered into formation and the captain raised his hand. "Here it comes!"

An enormous pincer ripped through the ceiling of the cavern, and I had a moment to contemplate my existence as I stared up at an elephant-sized ant with dripping mandibles. It must have taken up every bit of the main tunnel to get up here. It roared and purple fluid sprayed over the party.

"[Aegis]!" The guard captain cried out, and a shield similar to Copperpot's sprang up, though it was much wider and only faced one direction. The fluid sprayed against the shield and fell to the floor where it hissed and spat on the stone. "Watch out for its acidic venom! Concentrated fire! Ready.... and *THROW*!"

The enormous brood-guard opened its mouth to blast us again. At the exact moment that it prepared to fire, it was struck in the face by four throwing hammers. It reared back and screeched in pain. In that instant, a multitude of workers crawled into the hole it had made and attacked.

The next few moments were a chaos of screeching and swarming ants. I swung my pick with abandon, though I could barely summon any strength. I killed one ant with a lucky hit as Balin got shakily to his feet and picked up his axe. He and I stood back-to-back and swung with adrenaline-fuelled fury as we killed ant after ant.

"[Power Pick]!"

"[Challenge]!"

The rafter crew grabbed their tools and jumped into the fray. At least half a dozen stoneants fell beneath my pick and a notification popped up in my vision, but I didn't have time to read it. I couldn't keep this up for much longer. The guards all pulled out another set of hammers and got ready to throw. The brood-guard loomed back through the hole in the ceiling and opened its mouth to attack.

There was an odd whistling sound, like a car whipping past, then a roar as bright light and fire filled the entire main tunnel. The brood-guard screamed and spasmed as its body was cooked alive.

Time remaining: 0 seconds

Quest Complete: First Encounter!
Congratulations! You're alive!

Gained 0.2 Vitality! Your new vitality is 18.8!

CHAPTER THIRTY-FIVE
BURN IT WITH FIRE

It turned out Diamond was a fairly powerful mage.

In fact, I had a front-row seat as she wiped out the entirety of the swarm by herself. The guards kind of helped, mostly by acting as meat shields while she rained down various forms of fiery destruction. Balin stayed behind to rest and recuperate, but my regeneration had me back at full health. Honestly, it was pretty amazing, and I was dwarf enough to admit Barck had given me something nice there.

My first experience with real magic was leaving me both amazed and disappointed. It was certainly awe-inspiring, but there were fewer, 'Oh, fires of Gehenna strike down my enemies,' and a lot more drawing. In order to cast magic, Diamond traced patterns in the air with a crystal-tipped wand, and a glowing trail would be left behind. Those lines of power coalesced into a series of symbols that transformed into magical fire.

"Copperpot, this is going to get us killed!" I hissed as a trio of fireballs rocketed through the air barely a dozen paces away.

Why were we immediately walking back down the tunnel while the attack was still ongoing? Because Copperpot was a *massive nerd*.

"One moment." Copperpot leaned over and examined something on the wall. "We still need to check whether or not the boomdust experiment was a success, and we can't let something like an attack by a nest of monsters distract from that." He took a few notes while I twiddled my thumbs and worried about Lillyweather. Doc Opal had hissed and shouted and transported her back to camp a few minutes ago. She was still alive – and they'd called for the [Healer] – but it was going to be a near thing.

"Why can't we do this later? I was almost eaten!"

"With all the guards here as well as Statustician Diamond, we don't need to be concerned. Last time we were ambushed and had a large number of non-combatants. We now have overwhelming firepower and no civilians."

"Except us, and the volunteers." I looked around at the two dozen miners that were killing any worker ants that got past the guards and the fire.

"If you volunteer to fight, you're not a civilian anymore – you're militia. The City of Minnova Ordinances are clear on that."

I stopped in my tracks. "I'm not a volunteer! I'm management!"

Copperpot snickered. "All the more reason to ensure this entire thing goes off without a hitch. You had a question that you wanted to ask earlier?" Copperpot closed his notebook and put it in his pocket before turning to face me.

"Oh, we're doin' this now? Fine, how does magic work? It's... not quite what I expected." I waved my hand toward the intricate light show.

"Well, explaining things to an amnesiac should make for a fun thought experiment, so why not? Do you know what the elements are?"

"Matter, Aether, Nether, and Magic."

"Correct! I read Doctor Opal has been training you, and she's done a fairly good job as far as I can see. Matter is the physical, Aether is the immaterial, Nether is the space in between, and Mana makes it what it is."

"I get most of that. I just didn't really understand Doctor Opal's explanation of magic." I pursed my lips. "How does 'mana make it what it is'? Also, I thought the element was magic?"

"Ah, technically mana is the actual Element, and magic is how it can be manipulated. They are often conflated. Let's take this rock as an example." Copperpot held up a piece of grey stone. "It's almost all matter with no aether in it. Nether keeps it from breaking up into a bunch of smaller rocks."

I translated the lesson into basic Earth chemistry as Copperpot talked. Matter and aether were different forms of atoms, and nether was forces – or not, because that was all Earth knowledge and physics might not even exist here!

"The entire stone is filled with a slight amount of mana." Copperpot continued, breaking my train of thought. "You can't see it without [Manasight], but the mana is what makes it *rock* rather than any other kind of matter."

I thought about that for a moment. "So, mana is the flavour? It's what makes chicken taste different from beef?"

Copperpot chuckled, "Yes! I've never heard it put that way before, but that's pretty close."

"How does magic work then?"

"Do you see the diagrams Diamond is drawing in the air there?"

"Yes." We watched as she completed a rather large set of glowing circles that resolved into a curving flame that arched back and forth down the tunnel. It practically evaporated everything inside it, including another enormous brood-guard.

"Those are concentrated mana, which even someone without [Manasight] can see."

"I *do* see!"

"She's drawing the mana out of her own body using the wand as a wooden spoon and using it to cook the surrounding aether into a new spicier flavour." Copperpot smiled, "This is a useful analogy!"

"Drawing it outta her *body*? That sounds dangerous."

"It absolutely is! People that use magic without understanding it can draw out too much mana, and it isn't pretty."

I shivered, imagining a dwarven body losing everything that made it 'dwarf.'

"What are the symbols for?"

"It's a lot of math and specific arcane patterns that tell the mana what flavour it needs to be. As a fire mage, she then forces that mana into the surrounding aether to transform it from savoury air-flavoured aether to hot fire-flavoured aether."

"I thought she was a [Statustician]?"

"What? No, well, it's complicated." Copperpot pointed to a portion of the tunnel and shouted. "Rafter crew, that needs to be shored up!" I waited patiently as the rafter crew went up and repaired some damage the blast had done to the existing rafters.

"The blast damaged the tunnel further back than I was expecting. That's good, as it means the boomdust has more power than we first thought," Copperpot mused under his breath before turning back to me. "Where was I? Ah yes, a fire mage. [Statustician] is Diamond's Title, but her school of study is fire magic."

"So, you don't need a specific Title to use fire magic?"

"A Titled [Aethershaper] could achieve similar effects, but it wouldn't be magic. They have Abilities that allow them to change the mana of the aether directly, without needing to shape their own mana first. It's more elegant, but limited. 'Mage' refers to anyone with [Manasight] who decided to learn the magic formula necessary to change their mana and force it into their surroundings."

"Can you tell me some more about those magic formulas?" Those were what I needed to learn to do magic on my own!

"Yes. Learning all the necessary arcane formulae for any kind of magic is a long and difficult process, so most mages focus on a single school to study. Diamond is a fire mage because fire is a powerful school. Also," Copperpot leaned in to faux-whisper conspiratorially, "I don't know if you noticed, but she likes red."

"I HEARD THAT, you old curmudgeon!" Diamond called from ahead of us. Copperpot chuckled.

"There are many schools of magic – too many to list – but they all work the same. There's a lot of maths involved because it isn't just enough to memorise the symbology, you need to take into account the ambient mana as well."

"That... sounds complicated."

"It is. It's why most mages are in school for nearly fifty years or more. It's also why dragons and elves usually have more powerful mages, as they simply live longer." He shrugged.

We walked in silence for a while as I mused on this new information. I wasn't that hot at math, and the thought of putting in fifty more years of schooling right as I entered a new world was horrifying at best. Plus, I may have never earned Archis's Blessing anyway.

Honestly, at this point I'd mostly cooled off about Barck's Blessing. I would have died today without it, and it really did fit me pretty well.

I still had a ton of questions for a [Prophet] later, like: was the forced Blessing the Gods' way of saying, 'Nobody else wants you'? In the meantime – regardless of the reason – Barck remained a bastard in my books for stealing my choice.

We eventually reached ground zero, and it was...

"Wow..." whispered Diamond.

"By tha Grace of Lunara..."

"Tiara's Teats!"

"Muh leg!" We all turned to one see one dwarf beating in the charred head of an ant that had somehow survived our initial onslaught. Some of the miners hustled him back up to our base camp in the dive tunnel.

"This certainly exceeded my expectations," Copperpot mused.

"Who cares? It worked!" I hollered. I grabbed Copperpot's hands and danced around, laughing. "It worked! Haha! We're free! Someone go tell Balin! It's amazin'! Hell yeah, boomdust!"

An enormous hole had been blasted out of the mountain, and carved a cylindrical cavern roughly the size of a double-decker bus. The area was filled with rubble and dust and the charred bodies of ants. The guards were guarding a large crack in the wall filled with more scrabbling stoneants. It was mostly worker ants attacking at this point – the soldiers and brood-guards had all been in the first few waves.

Copperpot extracted himself from my grasp and smiled. "Don't get too excited, Pete. We still need to complete our report. Celebrations are for the tea shop afterwards."

"You mean the bar! Come on, Copperpot! Give me a cheer!" I could barely contain my excitement as I took it all in.

He harrumphed and then pumped his fist. "What did you say? Hell yeah? An interesting turn of phrase. Hell yeah, boomdust!" I joined in and our voices echoed off the rocks until Diamond turned an angry glare in our direction.

Copper coughed and pulled out his notebook. "Let's stop and check the integrity of the walls, I don't want anyone getting crushed. I wish I had my students for this, but I don't want to risk any more of them." His glasses telescoped outwards and he began writing.

Some time passed while the rafter crew did some raftering, Engineer Copperpot did some engineering, the guards did some guarding, and Diamond did some... diamonding? Diamonds were made with time, pressure, and heat, and she definitely upped the heat around here. I ended up helping Copperpot take some measurements after I got bored. Apparently, tape measures were universal.

Eventually everything was done, and Copperpot waved to the Guard Captain and Diamond. "Everything is good to go! You can head in now!"

"Aye sir! I'll leave two guards and the militia here with you, the rest of us will go deal with the queen."

"Make sure Diamond doesn't destroy anything important or load-bearing! It's not too often that we get to come in the back side of a nest like this! Leave something for the research teams!"

"I know what I'm doing, Copperpot," Diamond huffed, as she followed the guards into the crevice.

The rest of us watched them go. The miners, mostly armed with pickaxes and thin leather armour, moved in to block the opening. A few ants trickled out, but it was clear from the sounds echoing from the hole that the hive had more pressing concerns.

"What's the queen like?" I asked, as I chewed my lip.

"The queen isn't actually that big a deal." Copperpot said, as he sat down on a rock to rest. "She's an immobile baby factory. The bigger problem will be the several brood-guards she'll have with her."

"Will Diamond be able to handle it?"

"Oh, Diamond is *exactly* the dwarf needed to handle something like this. A narrow space with a limited number of enemies that cannot receive further reinforcements, and no need to worry about causing fires? She'll take them apart."

"I thought you said not to damage anything load-bearing?" I sat down beside Copperpot, only now realising just how tired I was.

"That was just to tweak Diamond's beard. Nothing in there should be really flammable. The ants build with saliva and stone. We just need to wait for them."

Indeed, it was barely half an hour before the ants stopped trickling in, and then Diamond and some banged-up guards emerged from the tunnel. They carried one injured guard, though they didn't seem overly worried.

Diamond smiled as she approached. "Alright, Copperpot. We're done. We have an injured member, so we need to head up. I'll leave the clean-up of the site in your expert hands." She walked away, whistling.

Copperpot turned to watch her leave. "Damn, she got us. Alright, Pete. Go grab a mop and start cleaning."

"Excuse me?"

CHAPTER THIRTY-SIX
LOOSE ENDS

"You alright, Balin?"
"Aye, Pete. I'm glad you aren't dead."
"So am I."
"*So am I!*" Sam nuzzled a bulging leather bag that clinked as he rubbed it.
"Rude," Wreck opined.
"Gold is gold!" The three of us retorted.
"I admit none of us had 'Crazy Pete's experiment summons monsters' as part o' the bet. I still won a good chunk off ya livin'." Sam said as he deposited the coin-purse into his pocket.
"They don't really call me 'Crazy Pete,' do they?" I asked, as my eyebrows furrowed. An impressive sight when you have eyebrows as bushy as a squirrel's tail.
"Uh..." Sam looked away.
"We're all glad ya lived, Pete," said Wreck. She even patted me on the shoulder.
We were standing around Balin's cot in the infirmary. The infirmary was a small alcove off to the side of Grim's office, and I recognized it as the room I'd arrived at when I reincarnated here. I looked around with a small amount of nostalgia. The plain grey walls with slight adornment, the musty smell of earth and dwarf, and the cheerful voice of Balin were all the same. The only thing missing was–
"I want a full report! Number of wounded and supplies used!

Healer Bastion has been held up at the dungeon, so I want constant updates on Lillyweather's status! You, guard, I want you on the dwarf we discussed until I say stop, got it?" Grim was in fine form. He had managed to escape unscathed from the initial attack, and had taken charge of the entire operation. He was the picture of efficiency, no different from the day I'd first arrived.

"Yes, sir!" The guard saluted.

I turned back to Balin. "I can't believe you went full Super Saiyan!"

"Sayin' what?"

"No, I – um... I can't believe you turned into a real-life knight in shining armour!"

"Me neither." Balin was actually *moping*. "I know how you feel about yer thing now Pete. I wanted somethin' that would make me a better carpenter fer Annie. Now I've got a bunch of fightin' stuff that's no good fer anyone."

"Och, but Baaaaalin." Sam nudged Balin. "Annie was expectin' some kinda labourer. Now she's got an 'eroic knight to sweep her off 'er feet. Imagine what her daddy will say, eh?"

Balin's face actually turned beet red. "Errr..."

"Annie, my love!" Sam swept Wreck off her feet, and she squeaked. "I, the shinin' golden knight of Minnova, have come to court ya! I shall slay a hundred monsters in yer name if you so desire!"

Sam hit the floor with a *thwack* as Wreck's fist connected with his jaw.

"Well, Balin, what are you goin' to do?" I asked. "You were amazing out there – even the guards said so. Will you become an adventurer in the dungeon?" I couldn't imagine it myself. The thought of going toe-to-toe with a bunch of giant monsters again left me with a cold sweat. I was going to have nightmares about this for *months*.

"I dunno..." Balin mused. "Adventurers make a lotta gold, but it's dangerous work."

"You'll be a hero from the tales," Sam gasped from where he was curled up on the floor. "Save me from this monster!"

"Rude." Wreck continued kicking him for good measure. Balin and I ignored the byplay.

"Am I interrupting?" Copperpot joined us with the guard from before.

"No," Balin and I said in unison.

"Yes!" Sam wheezed.

"I have to head back to the university, so I need to leave now. Diamond will be staying behind until her work is done."

"That's too bad. We'll miss you, Copperpot." I held out my hand.

"This isn't a forever goodbye." Copperpot smiled jovially. "I need to stay in touch to discuss your proceeds, and I want to hear more about your ideas for tea and beer."

"Oh, Gods," Balin groaned. "Tell me he doesn't want to add tea to beer."

"You were there when we discussed this, Balin." I raised an eyebrow.

"Only in body."

"I wanted to share the news myself," Copperpot continued. "Based on the experiment, I can unequivocally say that you'll be receiving enough to end your indentures."

"Huzzah!" I pumped my fists.

"Congratulations!" Sam cried.

"Yaaay," Wreck monotoned.

"Here's an invitation card, Pete." Copperpot handed me a small piece of cardstock. It was similar to a modern-day business card, with Copperpot's name done up in beautiful calligraphy. The card shimmered slightly when I flipped it over.

"Is this magical? It looks and feels different from regular paper." This was the first real magical artefact I'd personally handled in Erd, and it was... anticlimactic. An enchanted business card? Really?

"Indeed. It's been enchanted with mana that proves it's the real thing." Copperpot nodded. "Helps my security keep out anyone that doesn't have an appointment."

"Aw, I need an appointment? We were in a life-and-death battle together!"

"Heh, I'll make sure to let them know to expect a crazy dwarf."

"Hey!"

Copperpot pulled out a pocket-watch. "It's time for me to go. So long everyone, and congratulations on completing your indenture Balin, Pete." He nodded at the two of us and made his way out the door.

"We did it, Balin!"

"That we did."

We smiled at each other for a long while. It had been a painful and arduous journey, but we were finally going to be free. I was finally going to see the wider world and experience the rest of my new life. Balin and I would head to Annie's brewery, he'd get a fiancé and I'd get tools. I could see from Balin's eyes that he was dreaming about the future, too.

"Ahem." A brusque cough broke our reverie.

"Yes?" I turned and looked at the guard, who had remained behind after Copperpot left. He had on his full set of steel plate armour, and the only thing I could make out were some glinting black eyes and a bushy black beard coming out from under his helmet.

"Grim's orders. I'm yer guard fer a while. Name's Brock" He shrugged apologetically.

"What? Why? Has Pete done somethin?" Sam was on his feet and in between me and Brock in an instant. I blinked at his sudden ferocious attitude. "I protest, he's been tha picture of a good and lawful dwarf!"

"No, it's not that." Brock brushed Sam aside like he was a child and looked me in the eye.

"The dwarf named Tim was placed under arrest while you were preparin' tha boomdust. Durin' tha chaos of the stoneant attack he managed to escape."

"What!" Balin and I cried in unison.

"Eh?" said Sam as he tumbled to the side.

"Rude."

"Tim actually was a [Swindler], then."

"Aye." Brock nodded. He and I were walking through the camp back towards my cabin. "Statustician Diamond checked 'im. He had tha' [Swindler] Title and an Ability called [Lost Reason]."

"That sounds dangerous. Does it make you lose a reason or lose your reason?"

"Dunno. I'm not paid to understand that. I'm paid ta keep ya safe right now."

"Are they sure he's still in the camp?"

"Aye. Tha manacles woulda told us if he left. They think he might be hidin' in tha mine, so they're searchin' there." Brock said as he stepped aside to let some miners carrying a brood guard carcass get by. The carcass was singed and burned, and ashes fell from it as it bounced on their shoulders.

"I can't believe we killed those." I shuddered, remembering the moment the brood guard's monstrous head had burst into our dive tunnel and showered us with venom.

"We kill bigger stuff in tha dungeon all the time!" The guard clapped me on the shoulder. "Besides, I heard ya threw yerself into a soldier ant's mouth ta save that gnome lass! Good on ya!"

"Thanks." My mood grew cloudy at the mention of Lillyweather. She was the worst injured, and was still holed up in Doc Opal's cabin. Every once in a while, we could hear screaming and weeping coming from it. Healer Bastion had been called for, but a massive wave of monsters had erupted from the dungeon, and he'd been tied up for hours. I said a small prayer to the Gods, even Barck, hoping she'd make it through.

I took the lead, and we walked in silence for a few minutes, Brock about half a pace behind me – it was incredibly distracting. I tried to ignore him, but someone in full plate-armour walking right behind you was not a quiet or subtle thing. I finally broke and did a stutter-step back to come abreast with him.

"I... Honestly, I kind of thought of Tim as a friend up until earlier today. It's a lot to parse that he's some kind of mind-manipulating, netherspawned, backstabbing, [Swindler]," I admitted.

"That's not uncommon." He nodded. "[Swindlers] make friends first, then hit ya with their Abilities. They're good at makin' people trust 'em."

"Con artists." I scowled at the thought. I'd hoped that the straight-laced dwarven society would be free from such people, but I'd recently learned my lesson about monoliths. It was hard, but I could see Tim doing something like this. "I did feel Tim's behaviour had been a little too heel-face-turn, but I really wanted to believe I'd won him over."

"What's that?"

"Which?"

"Con artist, and 'heel-face-turn'"

"A *con*fidence artist is someone that's good at gettin' people to trust them. They earn your confidence through kindness, trickery, or simply exploiting yer greed. After you trust them fully, they take you for all you're worth."

"Sounds familiar." The guard nodded. "They like ta go after the young or the elderly?"

"Yeah, it can get bad. What have you seen?"

"A common one is ta send a letter pretendin' to be a grandkid. Askin' fer a spot o' money cause' yer in trouble."

"That or pretending to need someone to sell something valuable for a commission?"

"That's another one, aye. You have some guard experience!"

"No, just movie— er, moving around a lot gave me plenty of exposure to that kind of thing."

"I can see that. What about tha other one? Is it a wrestlin' move? Like ya stick yer foot in his face and knock 'im over?"

"Close! A heel-face-turn is a villain that suddenly decides to become a good guy for no real reason. It came from wrestling, actually!" The best example from Earth would be the Grinch.

"Oh! Like when Murder Machine decided ta split with tha Wreckin' Crew and joined up with Kid Crusader 'cause he fell in love wi' a floffle?"

"Uh.... Sure?" While I didn't understand anything he'd said, the WWE lover in me understood every word. "Murder Machine with tha steel chair?"

"Yeah!" We high-fived, and then Brock remembered he was on duty and got back to looking serious. After a roundabout walk, we arrived at my cabin without any incident and I went to open the door. I stopped just as my fingers touched the knob. My room would be the stupidest place to hide, but ...

"Is this where I say, 'Thank you for your hard work, Brock. You can go now'?" I pointed at my eyes and then at the door.

"Sounds 'bout right," Brock raised his voice as he nodded and pulled out an axe, "yer safe in yer own room of course."

"Of course." I nodded and stepped to the side. "I imagine Tim must be hiding somewhere in the tunnels."

"Probably. Whisperer Gemma is searchin' 'em right now with tha rest o' tha guards. I'll be waitin' 'round outside. Have a good sleep," Brock said as he lined up with the door.

"I'll see you around!" If this was all for nothing, we were going to look like a couple of idiots. Well, like I always said, 'better idiot than dead.'

I've never said that before in my life – I was a sheltered child.

"[Charge]!" Brock smashed forward in a blur, his axe cleaving the door in half as he burst through the doorway. There was a scream and a smash, followed by the sounds of grunting and swearing.

I peeked inside. My bed was turned up against the opposite wall, and pieces of the door were scattered through the room. Brock was lying on the ground, and beneath him, locked in an arm bar and tapping one hand on the floor, was Tim.

That sonnuvanannygoat.

CHAPTER THIRTY-SEVEN
CLOSURE

"You don't understand! He's lyin' to you all!"

Guilt.

"He's been insultin' everythin' about bein' a dwarf since the accident!"

More guilt.

"He's gonna destroy generations of beer makin'!"

Extra guilt.

"I just did what I had to!"

I looked up at that, feeling a pang of anger rather than guilt. How *dare* he! He'd swindled me and messed with my head, and it was what he *had* to do?!

"Be silent, Tim. We aren't here to listen to your justifications. We are here to release any ongoing abilities on Alchemist Peter and provide him with some closure. As per Nation of Crack Ordinances Ver. 1130, Chapter 16, Section 8, Subsection 2, you may choose to voluntarily surrender any goods and repair any damages done to the injured party in order to reduce your sentence." Diamond held her hand up to forestall Tim's sputtered reply. "Do not think of wasting the final opportunities provided to you by the law."

Tim nodded, his eyes downcast.

"Very well, release any of your abilities of Alchemist Peter first."

Tim held up a hand, and I actually felt a weight come off my mind. It felt like everything suddenly snapped into focus, and I could finally stop stealing glances at Diamond's lovely twin drill-curl beard. Ugh, I'd been under this for *months*? Jerk!

"So, what now?" I put forward. Diamond, Brock, Tim, Grim, and two other guards turned to look at me. Diamond twirled her beard for a moment before answering.

"Tim's psych profile, as well as his interrogation and examination of his Status Sheet, indicate there is a chance for rehabilitation." Diamond's tone turned sharp. "You and he both agreed to allow for an arbitration, and right now he is *wasting* it!"

"I thought... I dunno. That'd I'd have an opportunity to throw rotten tomatoes at him or somethin'." I mimed a tossing motion.

"Where would you get a barbaric idea like that?" Diamond shook her head.

"What a waste of good food," Grim muttered.

"See! He's a mad-dwarf!" Tim shook his cuffs plaintively.

"Hey!"

"ENOUGH!" Diamond smashed a plated hand on the table, and we all jumped as the wood cracked. "Tim, silence! Alchemist Peter, you may ask five questions!" She turned to look at Tim. "You will speak only when questioned and may only answer the question. Any further outbursts and I'll personally see you put on the lowest level of the Capital Prison!"

She dropped thirty-two silver coins, a tankard, and a small keg of beer on the table. "Here is the evidence that we collected from him, now let us perform this arbitration *properly*," she practically hissed.

"Fine. Tim, have you been fakin' everything? Were we ever friends at all?" I asked.

"Maybe. Until you mixed lemonade into the True Brew, when you began—" He was cut off as Diamond harrumphed. "Until you made the radler."

Diamond nodded at me, which I took to mean he was telling the truth. Diamond had approached me late in the evening to inform me of a possible "arbitrated closure." She had deemed the situation appropriate for one and was giving me the option. If I took it, Tim's sentence for having a Banned Title would change from life imprisonment to a chance at supervised parole. The entire thing would take place under a truth spell, which would tell Diamond if Tim lied. The idea was to provide me closure in a controlled space.

So, we had been friends for a short while. That... was nice, but it also made the resulting betrayal hurt even more.

"Why?" I asked in a pleading tone.

"Why what?"

"Why did you do all this?"

"Because you—!" Tim took a deep breath. "Because I consider you a threat to our traditions and way of life."

"That doesn't even mean anythin'!"

"It does to me."

I rubbed the bridge of my nose. It was like arguing with someone on the internet. He wasn't going to change his mind in this short time. Speaking of time.

"When did you start messin' with me?"

"Not until the third month. I'd been doin' a simple swindle for a while. I wanted to slow down yer 'gunpowder' plan. If it was anythin' like tha radler it could be nothin' good. I wasn't sure I wanted to use my abilities on a fellow dwarf, but I decided to do it when I saw Speaker John drink some of yer radler."

Diamond nodded at me again. "Two more questions, then Tim is allowed one."

"Tim, why in Yearn's name were you in my room?" Grim coughed and hid a grin. He'd been at Tim's initial interrogation. Why the hell was that funny?

"I was going to see if true dwarven blood ran in your veins."

"You were going to knife me!?" I looked at the evidence but the only thing of note was the tankard.

"No prevarication." Diamond warned, her voice dark.

"I was goin' ta make ya drink tha True Brew till you admitted it was good."

"What!?"

Grim actually sputtered and ran out of the room. The sound of supressed laughter echoed briefly in the hall before the door swung shut. Diamond glowered at the door and nodded at a guard, who locked it. She turned to Tim. "Continue please."

"I figured I could bring ya back with enough of Tha Brew. You might be the Great Deceiver – "

Diamond's fingers snapped and Tim's voice was cut off, though his mouth continued to move. I shook my head. "No, let him finish." She nodded and snapped her fingers, and he was suddenly audible again.

" – give you a chance to prove you were a true dwarf. I'd lost the chance to stop yer experiments, but maybe I could convince ya to give up yer ways."

I looked at Diamond. That couldn't be true. It was nuts! She shrugged and nodded.

I slumped back in my chair. No wonder she'd set this thing up. Tim wasn't a monster – he was a misguided IDIOT. That and a howling hypocrite. My heart grew a little stony at that. He'd stolen from me, and I was beginning to remember that he'd stolen from the city coffers too. He was justifying things to himself, but the reality was only one of us had truly broken dwarven law and tradition, and it wasn't me.

"Why didn't you just talk to me?"

"Because you were so full of yerself that you never gave me tha time of day."

Ugh. Diamond looked at me and nodded, then shrugged. "Those are your five questions, Alchemist Peter. Tim, you may ask your one question."

Tim turned to look at me, his bald head wrinkled with thought. We sat in silence for a few minutes until he finally spoke.

"Are you actually Peter Samson?"

Wow. What a loaded question, and frighteningly sharp. Diamond looked confused at the question. Sweat beaded on my forehead, but I had an easy answer.

"I am, and always have been, Peter."

Tim looked at me suspiciously and then at Diamond. She nodded and he hung his head.

"Very well, Alchemist Peter, you may make one closing statement."

It was my turn to think for a while. I looked at the three guards, who were clearly bored out of their minds, and considered the problem.

Did I forgive Tim?

No. It was too soon.

Was I mad at him? Kind of. He'd scammed me, and used abilities on me that were so vile they made his entire existence illegal. That was kind of sad in a way. I thought back on my incredibly racist great-grandpa, who'd gotten into a lot of trouble towards the end for his opinions on the First Nations and the Chinese. Tim was.... kind of like my grandpa. Hidebound, afraid of change, and lashing out in the only way he could. He hurt those around him, but in his own mind it was a misguided attempt to save people.

I sighed; I almost wished he *had* tried to knife me. That would have made this all so much easier.

"Tim, you were one of the few friends I can remember. If you were truly my friend, then rather than forcing it on me you'd have tried to make a beer that I would actually enjoy. I didn't choose to dislike the True Brew, it's just tha way I am."

Tim was downcast as the Guards removed him and took him away. I stared down at my feet and wondered if I really *was* the monster he claimed. Hmm... nope, he was just nuts.

Diamond grimly shook her head after we were the last two dwarves in the room. "I don't understand why he didn't just declare a Feud. That would have been legal and avoided all of this."

I looked up. "What's a *Feud*? I've heard that word before."

"Usually, dwarven families and businesses deal with conflicts like this with a Feud. The party that declares the Feud sets the Challenge, and the challenged party declares the Contest. It can be anything from combat in the arena, to a crafting competition, to a foot race."

I scratched my cheek. "That's a strange tradition."

Diamond shook her head. "Dwarven feuds used to last generations and involved the wholesale slaughter of entire clans. The Ordinances set strict rules on them to keep our society from fracturing every time some curmudgeon took offence."

"There *are* a lot of curmudgeons in the world." I stood to leave. "If that's all, I have to go say my goodbyes."

"Yes, we're done here. When are you leaving?"

"Tomorrow morning."

"You there, Doc?"

"Yes. Come in."

I entered Doc Opal's cabin and paused. Lillyweather was asleep on the bed. I flinched as my eyes ran over her injuries.

Her left leg was missing below the knee.

I dropped my voice to a whisper.

"Is she okay now?"

"Yes. Healer Bastion came an hour ago and we managed to save her life. She needs some rest for now, but she lost her leg." Opal's voice was clinical, but I could hear the anguish behind her words. "Unfortunately, a full regrowth of the limb far exceeds Healer Bastion's mana capacity."

Gods. I felt awful. It wasn't my fault, but it had been my experiment, so I felt a little responsible.

"Is there anything I can do?" Perhaps I could find a better Healer?

"No, Copperpot has it handled. Leave it to him. As her mentor, he bears the most responsibility and obligation."

We both looked at her for a while before I spoke again.

"I came to say goodbye. Balin and I leave in the morning."

"Oh. That soon?" Doc Opal got the weirdest look on her face as she rubbed at her chinstrap beard. It was a mixture of delight and annoyance, hope and despair at the same time. "I will be.... sad to see you go."

"I'll miss you too Doc. Thanks for everything, especially the use of your supplies."

"Of course, Peter. Thank you for the sweets, and for brightening Bran's kitchen."

"I hope we meet again."

"We will eventually, surely. Balin said you plan to move to Minnova."

"Balin has a big mouth. And don't call me Shirley."

"What?"

"Goodbye, Opal."

"I'm really going to miss you, Sam."

Sam smiled as he leaned in and gave me a giant hug. I could feel tears wetting his beard.

"I'll be out before ya know it, eh?"

"Not too soon, I value my eardrums."

"Good luck out there, son, yer goin' ta need it. If you get stuck, go look for a dwarf named Drum at tha Rusty Battleaxe. Just tell him Sam sent ya."

"Goodbye, old man."

"So long, Pete."

I peeked around the door.

"Goodbye, Grim – "

"I don't care! Get out! Beggone, Agent of Solen!"

"I'll miss you!"

"I'll miss you with my AXE if you don't get out of my mine!"

My teeth flashed in the darkness of the hallway as I retreated. I'd need to send something special to Grim. Maybe a couple kegs of my first beer, to share with everyone.

---

sniff "I can't believe yer leavin'!"

I held up a handkerchief, nonplussed. "I didn't realise it meant that much to ya, Bran."

sniffle "You always had so many amazin' ideas." *honk*

"You're a great chef, Bran. You know enough now to start making yer own recipes."

"But now I got nothin' to sell to make enough silver fer lemons!" *sob*

"YOU WERE SELLIN' MY RECIPES!?"

Bran opened up a drawer and revealed the contents. My eyes widened.

CHAPTER THIRTY-EIGHT
GINGER I CAN'T BELIEVE IT'S NOT ALE

"I've got all our stuff packed up, Pete," Balin said, tossing his sack onto the bed.

"Are you sure? I don't want to forget anythin' important when we leave tomorrow."

"Because we have sooo much stuff."

"Hey, speak for yourself!"

"I've got everythin' you own packed into a tiny little sack."

"Touché. Is that really everything you own?"

"I'll need ta go an' get my stuff from City Hall later. I got some tools and things that were put in storage while we were in the mine."

"Alright, I'm just about done too. We just need to wait for Bran. Want to go see the stuff we made?"

"That's the weird bucket ya been playin' with, right? What did ya say it was?"

"It's my going away present for everyone. It's a drink called ginger-pop."

"I've never heard of pop. At least it's not one of yer bastardised beers again."

"Uh, sure."

"Pete..."

"Before you judge me, let me tell you how it happened! It all started three weeks ago. I was in the kitchen with Bran and..."

Three weeks before Pete and Balin left the City of Minnova Reform Mine

Our gunpowder test was going to happen soon, likely without a hitch, and I was going to be free. Before we left, though, I wanted to leave everyone in the mine with one last present – an actually decent beer. Unfortunately, I had to tiptoe carefully around the issue, as making bootleg beer would probably set some dwarves off.

That didn't mean I couldn't cheat! The pruno had failed, which was perhaps a blessing in disguise, but there was one other kind of beer that would be incredibly easy to make. Even better, it could be disguised as something other than beer until it was too late. I'd asked Bran to get me some ginger, and while expensive, it was going to be *totally* worth it! I'd been busy with my experimenting when it arrived, but I finally had an opportunity to make use of it!

"Muhahaha."

"Pete, yer doin' that creepy laugh again."

"Sorry, Bran."

Bran thunked a pile of groceries on the kitchen counter and went to put on an apron. "I got the ginger ya asked for, and ya can have as much sugar as ya want."

"Finally! That took forever! Thanks again for letting me use all the kitchen supplies."

"Er, *cough* sure. So, what are ya makin' this time?"

"It's a special drink called ginger beer – ginger ale – ginger *pop*."

"I've never heard of pop."

"It's a fizzy drink with some alcohol – kind of like beer, but it isn't beer."

"You're sure? I don't want ya makin' unlicensed beer in my kitchen. That's against city and guild law. I thought ya were tryin' to get *out* of here."

"Absolutely. Not a single brewer in all of Minnova would call this beer."

"That's good." Bran shuffled his feet. "Is it sweet? Will Opal like it?"

"I can guarantee she may even like it more than radlers, and I'll even leave you something special."

"What is it?"

"My ginger bug!"

"What is it?"

"Sigh. Watch and learn, Bran. First though, you'll need to help me grate this ginger."

Bran eyed the brown pile warily. "That's a lot of ginger. Are ya goin' to use it all?"

"Not right away. The first thing I need to make is the base for the ginger pop, and that's going to take a week, at least. Wash your hands first, though, you filthy animal."

"I dunno why yer so obsessed with that." Bran shook his head. "I already told ya that dwarves don't get sick much."

"You have such a clean kitchen, and obsess over your beard, so why does a little thing like washing your hands bug you? Just call me old-fashioned. Now wash." Bran grumped about 'old-fashioned' but complied, giving his hands a good scrub with soap and water. It looked more and more like the clean kitchen was less of a cleanliness thing, and more a 'Bran likes a clean and organised space' thing.

In the meantime, I began grating my ginger. As any good Canadian could tell you, Coke was better than Pepsi, and ginger ale was the best. Not the shameful faux-Canadian stuff that only pretended it had ginger, but the real deal. I was going to make ginger beer, which took a bit of time since it needed to ferment first.

Pete's Ginger Ale Pop Ingredients
Ginger
Water
Baker's Yeast

Bran sat down and the two of us grated ginger for an hour. It was nice just working on a brew again. I'd been making so many desserts and sweets in this kitchen and been so busy with the mining and gunpowder project, that I'd forgotten the glorious feeling of making a beer. I was planning to make enough ginger beer for the entire camp, so we needed a lot of ginger. And honestly, ginger beer can really take any amount of ginger and still be palatable.

"Alright, that's it for the ginger. Pass me the bucket."

Bran passed me a large bucket, and I dumped in the ginger along with several cups of sugar. I added a gallon or so of water, just enough to dissolve all the sugar. Then I pulled out a ladle and stirred. "Baker's yeast, please."

Balin passed me a hunk of something that looked a lot like butter. I was used to dry instant yeast for my beers, but it would do. I added a spoonful to the mixture and stirred it in.

"Alright! Done!" I shook my hands off and went to wash them.

"That's it?" Bran asked, surprised. "I thought it would take more time." He peered into the bucket. "Looks.... boring."

"What we've made here is something called a 'ginger bug.' We're going to spend the next week feedin' it."

"Kind of like a sourdough bug?"

"Sure, it's quite similar. We'll need to ensure that mould stays out of it by adding enough yeast, keep it nice and hydrated, and feed it some more sugar and ginger every day. We'll know it's ready when it starts to bubble a lot." I tied some cheesecloth on top of the bucket and then took the bucket to an empty section of the kitchen. I wanted my bug to stay somewhat warm, and the pantry would have been too cold.

"This is a weird drink, and I saw ya make caudle," Bran chuffed.

"Trust me, Opal is going to love it. It just needs a week to grow."

"I don't like tha sound of drinks that 'grow'..."

"It's ALIIIIVE!!!!! Muhahaha!!!"

"Creepy laugh again, Pete."

"Worth it!"

The cheesecloth on top of my bucket rippled slightly from the bubbles rising through my ginger bug. I'd been coming into the kitchen every day to add another few cups of sugar and ginger to the bucket.

The slurry of ginger at the bottom of the bucket was gently waving as carbon dioxide from the fermentation process bubbled in the bug.

"We're ready for the next step, Bran. We're going to need your big pot to make some gingerette." I held up my hand as Bran opened his mouth to ask the inevitable question. "A gingerette isn't a pretty dwarf maid with a red beard, it's just a hot ginger tea with a bunch of sugar."

"Easy enough." Bran nodded and pulled an enormous cookpot onto the stove. It was the one he usually used to cook chili for the work crew. "We're goin' to need a lot o' ginger though."

So we began grating.

And grating.

And grating.

And grating.

Finally we had an enormous yellow mushy pile that I scooped into the pot. I added several cups of sugar and stirred while Bran juiced some lemons.

"Lemons again?" He moaned.

"Grapefruit could work too, and I wish I had some jalapenos but lemons are what we have." I started up the stove and we sat and chatted while we waited. I stirred it every once in a while until it came to a merry boil, then turned it off. We cleaned and re-organized the kitchen while we waited for the pot to cool.

"Here comes the hard part. We need to strain this." I looked at the large strainer, and considered the problem of lifting the enormous pot to run the ginger water through it.

"I got it." Bran said, as he grabbed the strainer and waved it around in the pot until a vortex formed. With a deft hand he scooped all the ginger out of the mix and dumped it out into the compost. I clapped appreciatively at the sight of a master working at his craft.

"Next step is to add the lemon juice and... this!" I held up the bucket and pulled off the cheesecloth. The brown slurry inside the bucket bubbled and popped. Bran took a step back in horror.

"Ugh, that's almost as bad as that *pruno*..." He gasped.

"Hey! We don't talk about pruno! And besides, It's fiiiine." I poured most of the liquid out of the bucket and into pot, though I left the slurry at the bottom untouched. "Now add the lemons."

Bran shrugged and added the lemon juice while I took a moment to thank my dutiful bug.

"You can keep adding sugar and ginger to this bucket to keep the bug alive if you want to, Bran."

"I think I'll see how this turns out before I try that, Pete."

"Suit yourself." The next step was to pour the gingerette into a bottle and let it undergo a kind of secondary fermentation called 'bottle conditioning.' Unfortunately, Annie's predicament meant I didn't trust the barrels commonly used for brewing, so everyone would need to be happy with flat ginger beer. It was what they were already used to, so no real big loss.

"Now we wait another two weeks! Hopefully it will be ready before we go!"

—"And then one thing led to another, and here we are!" I finished the story with a flourish, pointing at the large barrels filled with ginger-pop.

Balin looked at them suspiciously. "This won't start another fight, will it? We're leavin' tomorrow morning and I really don't want ta get in trouble right before we go."

"It's not beer, and its only ingredients are ginger and sugar." I shrugged, "I can't imagine that we'd see anyone come to blows over it."

"If ya say so."

But he didn't sound convinced.

"Now help me get these barrels to the mess hall. We have our farewell party to get to!"

"...and I want to thank Pete and Balin for their hard work this past year!" Grim's voice echoed through the full mess hall.

The crowd roared and cheered and jeered. Balin and I stood

proudly on the stage as our manacles were removed, and we were officially signed out of the mine.

"Do you two have anythin' to say before you go?" Grim looked like he really didn't want to do that, but it was tradition. He'd let us know ahead of time to prepare a speech if we wanted. I nodded and walked forward.

"I want to thank you all for being an amazing crew! You had our back so many times, and I'm going to miss every one of you. Both Balin and I had our lives saved by the good dwarves of the Minnova City Reform Mine, and I'll never forget you! To commemorate our freedom and to thank you, I prepared a special drink as a present for all of you!"

"Not more radler, I hope!" A dwarf in the crowd heckled.

"He said it was a present, not a disappointment!" Sam roared from the back. Thanks Sam.

"This is something new, called 'ginger pop'! There isn't any beer in it at all. Bran has it in the pot at the back, so go and enjoy it with dinner!"

The dwarves murmured and jostled into place, eventually forming a cursing line. Bran and I began serving the ginger pop. The first dwarves through the line took a few sips and raised their eyebrows. A couple of them even drained their mug and got back in line. I smiled with pleasure. Yes indeed, I had finally made a decent 'beer' for the dwarven populace, and it had nothing to do with beer, so nothing could possibly go wr–

"Hey, this stuff tastes even better than beer!"

"What did you say!?"

"You heard 'im. This is great!"

"You take that back!"

"Make me!"

"Yer' mother!"

Then the fists began to fly.

Grim's voice was the last thing I heard before I ducked under a table. "Tha father o' chaos, Solen 'imself must have sent ya to destroy my camp! PEETE!!!"

Oops.

Balin and I stood at the entrance to the City of Minnova Reform Mine and looked down the path towards the city. The entire camp had lined up to say goodbye, and there was a heady mix of cheering and happy well wishes to send us off. It had taken a year, but I was free.

The incident with Tim made me realise something. My original plan was to go to Annie's brewery and start a revolution in beer. That plan needed to change. I would start slow and take my time getting to know the dwarven brewing process. Then I'd make a few *small* changes to get the dwarves interested in the possibility of different brewing methods. Just like Annie thought, even a small thing like better carbonation could be a big change.

I turned to Balin.

"Are ya ready to go, buddy?"

"Aye, that I am. Let's step into our future!"

"Okay, but watch where you're stepping, Balin."

We each took a step forward. There was a squelch and the stench of cat shit.

"See? I told you."

"PETE!"

CHAPTER THIRTY-NINE
BROTHER MINE

"Pete, can we take a break?" Balin groaned and collapsed to the ground in a heap on the side of the path.

I moved to the edge of the road and leaned against the rock wall. The terrain was actually incredibly craggy, with canyons, ridges, and weird crevasses. It felt kind of like walking on an enormous grey-brown glacier. The only reason we weren't horribly lost was the well-maintained road down to the main highway. It was a pretty gruelling hike, with the occasional sheer cliff to either side – though it did make for fantastic views. We were currently on one such section, with a ridge rising above our heads, and a drop-off stretching down nearly twenty metres on the other side of the road.

After our goodbyes, we'd been freed of our manacles, given a small bag of silver each, and sent on our merry way. My bag had over one hundred silvers in it, which was actually a pretty decent amount. I hadn't expected that much, since removing our indenture was essentially an advance on any gold the city earned from boomdust. Imagine my surprise to learn that Bran had been selling my recipes to earn silver for all the sugar and lemons. I'd been angry at first, but then he'd pulled out nearly ninety silver and handed it to me. A small tear came to my eye at the thought.

Then I poked the prone Balin in the stomach with my foot.

"Bah, you big baby. We've still got hours ahead of us. You can't be givin' up already!"

"Psh. I'm a bigger *dwarf* than you'll ever be," Balin wheezed.

"I'm bigger than you think." I mimed with my hands and he snorted.

"That what ya tell tha ladies?"

"Just the ones with red beards."

"Don't let Speaker John hear ya say that!"

We both laughed and then paused as the reality of our newfound freedom crashed down on us. There was a non-zero chance that we'd never see Speaker John again. Balin sat up and placed his back against the wall, then pulled out a canteen full of ale. He took a dreg and held it out.

"Ya want some?"

"No, Bran gave me my own."

"Radler?"

"What do you think?"

"That he was out o' ginger pop."

We grinned at each other.

"To freedom!"

"Praise Solen!"

We each took a drink then wiped our moustaches clean. Balin's handlebar had finally started to grow back in a little bit.

"What've ya been thinkin' about, Pete? Yer broodier than a mamma cat with a whole clowder o' kittens."

I stayed silent for a moment as I gathered my thoughts. I'd thought a lot about what I was going to tell Balin, and eventually decided he was owed the whole truth.

"Do you remember what I told you in the mine tunnel?"

"What? Nah, I was there in body–"

"But not in mind, yes, I know. I told you I remembered a bit about my past."

"That's right!" Balin snapped his fingers. "Are ya ready to tell me? Why couldn't ya just do it in the camp?"

"I can't perform when people are watching."

"Yer a dirty-minded little horny goat, ya know that?" Balin glowered at me.

"No I'm not! Anyway, I figured there might have been surveillance in the mine."

Balin thought about that for a moment before he nodded. "I know Whisperer Gemma can hear things from far away. There might have been magic on tha cuffs too, but I don't think so."

"I thought the cuffs were just designed to tell Grim if we left?"

"Aye, but they *could* have had listenin' or trackin' magic on 'em."

"But you don't think they did?"

"Nah, expensive and tha Reform Camp ain't that kind of place."

"They would have caught Tim more easily, if they did."

"There's that."

We both grew morose at the mention of Tim. He'd been carted out a few days ago, headed to the Capital Prison. He'd undergo 'rehabilitation' there, whatever that meant. I just prayed that it didn't mean brainwashing or some other kind of mental manipulation. Knowing that kind of stuff existed here made me incredibly wary of what other nasty tricks were going to catch me by surprise.

"Are there enchanted items that block mind-manipulating effects, Balin?" I doubted they cost... a mere hundred and twenty silver, but I could start saving.

"Like a [Swindler's]? Aye, but they're expensive. Most Nobles have 'em."

"That makes sense."

"Pete?"

"Yeah?"

"Yer stallin'."

"No, I'm Lenin – never mind. You're right. Are you sittin' down?"

Balin waved his hands in his general 'already sitting down' vicinity and arched an eyebrow.

"Alright. Balin.... I'm a human."

Balin choked, and then chortled, and then coughed. His face went through a couple of odd contortions before it finally settled on 'amused.'

"I dunno what I was expectin', but it wasn't that! Pete, I'm a forward-thinkin' dwarf, so if ya identify as human that's okay. I had a cousin that identified as an elf – cut his beard and shaped his ears. I know that greybeards can get stuffy about it, but it's – "

"No, I mean I am a human," I interrupted. "My spirit is human."

"Like I said – "

"No. I died, Balin. It would be more accurate to say I was human, and now I'm a dwarf. The Gods or whatever put my spirit in the body, er... spark, of Peter Samson with all my human memories intact."

Balin went really quiet. His face slowly lost the amused expression and his mouth became a more serious line.

"Are ya serious?"

"Deathly."

"Pete... that's..."

"Ridiculous? I know, but it's the truth." I calmed the rising tension in my voice and took a deep breath. "My original name was Peter Phillips, and I'm from another universe. All the odd things I've been inventin' and my weird references are because my memories are from a completely different world."

Balin was really quiet for a bit and I gave him some time to think. It was a lot to take in at once, and honestly, I don't think I'd have ever believed it. On Erd though, magic made the impossible possible. Balin took a few deep swigs of his canteen before he spoke.

"Opal never talked to ya about death, did she?"

That was an odd segue. "No. It... never really came up." I sat down beside him and took a deep drink from my own canteen.

"If ya knew, you wouldn't talk about this, not even with me."

"Do I sound insane?"

"No... it's believable." Balin dry-washed his hands and looked up into the sky for a few moments before he continued. "Here on Erd, when we die our spirits are reborn within a new spark."

"Like reincarnation?"

"Aye, that it is. You know it?"

"My world had.... similar ideas. Go on."

"Yer spirit gets a new spark. But tha loves and the hates, tha personality, who you are? That's all part of yer spirit and it comes with."

"You're saying that people are defined by their nature, not their nurture?"

"That's right."

"You know this for sure?"

"Of course. It's all part of Tha Firmament. When yer Blessed by tha Gods, they get ta choose where yer spirit goes when you die. The un-Blessed are split amongst all of 'em."

"So... Barck and Tiara get my soul when I die?" I didn't think I was really comfortable with that. I'd gone from agnostic, to theist, to 'the Gods own my soul' in pretty quick succession this past year.

"Nah, they just get ta choose where ya reincarnate."

"I'm guessing you usually don't keep your memories?"

Balin snorted. "That would make fer some weird births."

"My goodness! This is most uncomfortable! Please, just shove me back in?" I mimicked an offended baby.

"See, you *are* a dirty-minded little horny goat," Balin chuckled, but it was a pained laugh.

I ignored the jab. "I'm guessing it's all set up so the Gods can put the right spirit in the right place at the right time." I paused and pulled at my beard for a moment. "Do the Gods have 'favourite' spirits?"

"That's about right. Some spirits have been around since tha start o' this world."

Phew. That was something to take in. "Only some?"

"Aye, sometimes tha Gods make new ones. Or..." he trailed off.

"Or?"

"Or they get them from other worlds."

"Ah."

"Ah. They don't usually keep their memories though."

"Usually?"

"Never, more like."

"So... I shouldn't talk about it because... it marks me as something special."

"Aye, very. We really need ta get ya to a priest."

We sat for a while, Balin and I. Friends now, hopefully friends in the future.

"When?" Balin's lip quavered as he asked.

"After my accident in the sulphur freschie," I replied, quietly.

Balin held his arm over his eyes and took a deep breath.

"I never really knew ya before that. We'd spoken a few times, but Peter Samson was a hard dwarf ta like."

I didn't say anything. What could I say under the circumstances?

'Oh, I'm glad you didn't like the dwarf whose body I snatched'?

"So ya never lost yer memories." Balin's question was more of a statement.

"No...I never had them to begin with."

"Doc Opal will kill ya if she ever finds out."

"Nah, those lessons weren't wasted. I owe her, and you, a lot. I never meant to lie to you, Balin. Everything I've said and done has been real."

A few tears did spring to Balin's eyes then and trailed down his cheeks to wet his beard. I admit to some drippage myself. Can I just say that crying and sneezing with an abundance of facial hair is a singularly awful experience?

"Thanks fer trustin' me with this, Pete."

"I had to, Balin. Yer the only family I got here."

We shared a hug and then sat there, drinking silently. Eventually Balin cleared his throat and spoke up.

"I should tell you 'bout my family...."

We sat there and talked for about an hour. About the past. About the future. About who we were and would become.

Then, as one, we stood and took our first steps into that future before the Firmament and the Gods.

As brothers.

Somewhere else.

On the side of a cliff stood a white stone gazebo. Mist fell from a great waterfall that stretched beneath it, vanishing into the clouds below. A black mountain rose up behind it, seeming to touch the sky. A circular marble table covered by a complex game-board sat in the centre of the gazebo, and a group of figures were arrayed around it in plain wooden chairs.

"It's unacceptable!" one of the beings bellowed in a stately feminine voice. Her skin was the colour of a warm summer's night, and each of her ebony hairs was perfectly in its place. Ethereal jewels adorned her neck, and a gown of gossamer moonlight fell from her shoulders and flowed to the ground. Her pointy ears marked her as an elf, though no elf ever born could ever match her otherworldly appearance.

Her fist pounded the table with a *CRACK*. The mountain trembled at the impact and for a brief moment the waterfall lifted into the sky.

"He *forced* that Blessing on him! If we start allowing that, we'll soon face Negentropy! The rules are there for a REASON," she roared.

"He hasn't technically broken *any* rules," a cultured voice drawled beside her. The woman wheeled on a man reading a book. "Why aren't you the most upset about this? He would have chosen *you*, Archis!"

The being pushed some glasses up his nose. His skin, hair, and eyes were all white, with golden highlights in the hair at his temples. He wore a superbly tailored but simple scholar's robe covered in pockets. Each pocket contained a book or writing instrument. He appeared human at first glance, but he radiated power and knowledge no mere mortal could match. "You assume I even wanted him, Lunara. Besides, I already knew this was going to happen. I made a deal."

Lunara scoffed, "Why would you agree to that? What deal could possibly be worth the soul of a Chosen Catalyst?"

"Because we followed tha strands o' his fate." A gruff voice interjected. "He'd have been dead long before he got that Blessin'." A shaggy head of dwarven appearance peaked over the lip of the table. A pair of black eyes, gleaming with whirling galaxies and the stoked flames of a forge, glowered at Lunara. A thick and curly green beard bristled with barely contained emotion.

"It doesn't matter." Another voice cut in. A being with bronze skin speckled by faint blue scales stood up from his seat. A mane of silver hair parted around a pair of azure horns on his forehead, and he opened a mouth filled with razor-sharp teeth as he spoke to the shaggy haired God. "Barck, you have broken our most fundamental rule, and there must be consequences."

"Shut it, Solen! I paid for his soul and had tha' right to claim it!" Barck growled.

"Paid too much for it, I say." A being with the delicate ears and beady nose of a serval stretched his lips in a Cheshire smile. A pair of antlers stretched over his head and his cheeks were shaggy as an elk's. He wore the fine silks and vest of a merchant, and every inch of him spoke of great wealth. His soft voice was carried on a breeze that brought it to every ear at the table. He appeared every inch the beast-folk, though his bearing marked him as more.

Barck narrowed his eyes. "I paid what I thought it was worth, Aaron."

"You still haven't given him the chance to win it back," Aaron countered.

"I haven't denied him that chance either!" Barck retorted.

"I approve," another voice broke in. All eyes turned to face a being sitting at the foot of the table. Her form was at first that of a small human child, then an old elven woman. She became a mother grieving the loss of a child, and then a grandmother broken by years of toil. "Archis's Chosen are always so boring and this one amuses me. Let Barck keep him."

"Of course, Yearn likes him," Lunara muttered.

"I'm fine with it," a tiny being sitting on raised chair put forward. She wore the overalls and leathers of a hard-working miner or farmer and wore the guise of a gnomess. Her earthy hair was done up in a pair of pigtails, and her skin was weathered and tanned. Her simple appearance was belied by her skin, which was studded with gems, "Barck was acting in the Chosen's best interests, and he did technically own Pete's soul already. What do you think, Midna?"

"Don't ask me, Tiara!" A disheveled being waved her hand dismissively. Her disheveled appearance stood out from the rest of those gathered, and her blonde mullet swayed as she shook her head from side to side. She wore the guise and clothing of a human adventurer. Not the kind that fought monsters, but one of the original explorers. Her leathers were worn with hard use, and her pouches bulged with curios. "I agree that Barck broke the spirit of the laws, but he did so within them. I say leave the punishment to Solen."

"Fine. We will put it to a vote." Solen held up his hand. "On the punishment of Barck for violating the Absolute Right. Hands up for Yea."

Four hands went up. Three stayed down.

"I thought you approved of it, Yearn!" Barck roared.

"I changed my mind," the small elven girl giggled.

Solen counted on his claws, "Four yeas, three nays, and my abstention. The yeas have it. Barck, for violating the Absolute Right of Peter Samson, you are sanctioned. The game-board is hidden from you, and you may not know the movements or status of any other Chosen. You may not grant them quests, nor speak to them through any means."

"Bah!" Barck spat to the side. "I dinnae care."

"I know. So, in addition, I levy one generation of souls against you."

Tiara gasped, and Barck stumbled back as though struck. An old woman's wheezing laughter turned into the mocking roar of a female dragon at the foot of the table as Yearn cackled.

"That is a bit much, Solen." Archis raised a perfectly arched eyebrow.

"Do you want to Host, Archis?" Solen hissed, and smoke curled from his draconic nose.

"Once was enough for me, thank you."

Solen turned to the Barck. "Your sentence is passed. Leave my pavilion."

"You're going to regret pushing me out. Ya may have blocked me from tha board, but I'm playin' a higher game," Barck shot over his shoulder as he stood up and marched out.

Barck stepped down the stairs, and an opaque gleaming rainbow shell enveloped the gazebo behind him. He began to walk around the mountain, humming to himself. He opened his hand and a glass appeared in it. The glass was quite tall and oddly shaped – it looked more like a vase than a tankard. A golden image of a cheerful gnome was etched upon it, and Barck frowned and ran his hand over the etching. The image disappeared and was replaced with a golden relief of a dwarf raising his tankard in a toast. Barck smiled, and in an instant, the glass was filled with amber liquid. The faint scent of lemons wafted from the glass, and rich vapours poured down over the mountain.

"Aye, this makes all tha trouble worth it. Barck raised his glass and took a drink that lasted an age.

CHAPTER FORTY
INTERLUDE – HEART TO HEARTS

Several months before Pete and Balin left the City of Minnova Reform Mine

"'Scuse me, Opal?"

Wreck opened the door a crack and peaked inside the Doctor's cabin. She had left Pete and Bran behind at the door for a few reasons, not the least of which was that the two of them were stress-inducing.

The room was dark and smelled of medicine and sweat. Opal had a fairly well-furnished room considering the locale. Her floor was a rich red carpet, with designs that were somewhat out of date, but still chic. Her walls were covered in tapestries that showed the dwarven body, everything from nerves to muscles to bones. A spare cot shoved to the side was clearly for long-term care, and a workstation with shelves filled by medicines, notes, and mana stones took up one entire wall.

A hearth burned merrily on the other wall, filling the small room with warmth and light.

Opal was a lump under the covers in a corner bed. She was faintly shivering, and her head turned towards the door at the sudden intrusion.

"Is that you, Wreck?" Opal croaked, as she was wracked with a coughing fit.

"Aye, Doc. Can I come in?"

"Of course." *cough* "Is it that time of the month again?"

"Aye."

"Alright, come on in."

Wreck opened the door wide and shoved it shut behind her. Opal struggled to sit, and Wreck walked over to help her up. While Doctor Opal still had many years ahead of her, it was at times like this that she showed her age.

"Thank you, Wreck. Give me a moment." Opal reached under her bed and pulled out a small ornate rod and twisted it. A sigil on the rod began to glow, revealing a motif of a dragon boxed into an upside-down triangle. "Alright, we can talk."

Wreck's entire demeanour shifted, and her stance grew more relaxed. "How are you doing, Opal? Bran was really concerned. He's absolutely sure that you're dying."

Opal sighed and sunk back into her cushioned bed. "Bran tried, and he's a dear, but he fusses so."

"Of course, he does. He's completely smitten with you."

"You're one to talk!"

"That's a separate issue, and one I don't care to discuss right now."

"Fair." Opal hunched over as she was wracked with coughs. Wreck patted her on the back, her face growing concerned.

"Have you had a tonic?"

"I finished off the last of it this morning."

"I can mix some up for you. May I use your workstation?"

"You don't need to do that."

"No, no, I insist. You stay there and I'll make sure you're taken care of. Our family owes you so much, and you need rest. I know what I'm doing."

Opal chuckled, "A small understatement."

Wreck walked over to the workstation and began mixing ingredients. Her hands were a blur as she mixed and poured. Opal pulled out a handkerchief and blew into it as Wreck poured the mixture into a large empty bottle labelled 'Tonic.' After the bottle was full, she filled a small pot with some of the liquid and placed it on an apparatus atop the workstation. The apparatus began to glow red hot, and Wreck picked up a wooden spoon and began stirring.

"It'll take a while to heat up, Opal."

"That's alright, dear, thank you. How are you finding the mine?"

"It's alright, though it's quite a bit more boisterous than I had expected."

Opal chuckled.

"I can see how you'd think so, but I assure you this isn't normal."

"None of this situation is normal."

"True."

The two sat in silence as the tonic heated up. Wreck eventually stood and began doing some tidying up, putting away the Doctor's clothes and tossing her unmentionables into the laundry.

"How are you, really?" Opal's voice was filled with concern as she watched Wreck work.

"I'm... doing well, considering the circumstances."

"I still don't think what happened to you was fair."

"That isn't for you or me to decide. Dwarven law applies to all dwarves, no matter their status. That is how our government functions."

"You know that isn't really true. The nobility takes certain liberties all the time." Opal pointed out, her tone growing harsh.

"That is them. I am me. And I choose to follow the laws."

"And, we are all the better for it." Opal's tone switched to motherly. "Your grandfather is proud of you, you know."

"Then why did he send me here, so far away from the Capital?"

"For the same reason he gave you illusion enchantments and manipulated the government logs. To keep you safe."

Wreck stewed for a while, then went to remove the slightly steaming pot. She poured it into a cup and brought it to Opal. Opal took a deep sip and sighed.

"It's time for your monthly recharge, right? The chest is under my bed."

Wreck fished under the bed and pulled out a plain wooden chest. She opened it to reveal a glittering mound of fingernail-sized manastones. She pulled one out and fiddled with a necklace hidden under her shirt. For a brief moment, there was a flash of platinum-blonde curls and a pair of umber eyes before Wreck once again stood in the Doctor's cabin, her nondescript stringy beard and dull gaze unchanged from moments before.

"That amazes me every time I see it," Opal murmured. She held a now empty cup up to Wreck, who took it.

"Thank you for agreeing to be my grandfather's agent in this, Doctor," Wreck said. She walked over to a basin and washed the mug before placing it back on the rack.

"It was an honour to serve his grace."

There was a knock at the door, and the two of them jumped.

"It's me, Doc. I got something to make you feel better. It's somethin' new called caudle," Bran's muffled voice came through the wooden door.

"One moment, Bran!" Opal picked up the rod and nodded at Wreck. "Thank you for your help, Tourmaline." She twisted, and the dragon pattern disappeared.

"Sure, Opal." Wreck nodded and walked over to open the door a crack. She leaned outside and grumbled, "Shaddup, Bran. Doc Opal's restin'."

Several more months before Pete and Balin left the City of Minnova Reform Mine

"Well, Balin. What do you want to do?" Annie looked down at the dwarf she loved. The two of them were up on a ridge away from the camp. Not so far that their magical manacles would activate, but far enough away that they wouldn't be disturbed.

"I'm stumped, Annie. They said ma indenture would be near fifty years now." Balin sighed, his head upon her lap. Her beard tickled his forehead and she laughed as he batted it aside. "Tha's more than what workin' hard can fix."

"Well, you are a skilled labourer. You could try and join one of the rafter crew?" The rafter crew put up the mine supports. They got more time off their indenture as they were in a more skilled position. As a carpenter, Balin could join them, but it was also a more dangerous position.

"I wouldn't be caught dead in those pocket-pants." The two of them laughed before Annie grew sombre.

"You nearly were, caught dead that is." Annie wrapped her arms around Balin's head, and he sneezed as her beard caught in his nose. "Thanks be to the Gods and Pete that you survived." A tear nearly squeezed its way out from an eyelid before she took a deep sniff and stopped it.

"I'm fine now." Said Balin. "That which doesn't kill ya makes ya stronger!" He puffed out his chest before he too grew sombre. "I don' want to take any more risks, Annie. Not when I got so much ta lose now."

The two sat in silence for a while before Balin spoke back up. "Pete's got an idea he told me about. I don' think I like it..."

"What is it?"

"He said I'd need to shovel shit for 'alf a year, and then we'd be out in a couple months."

"What?!" Annie sat bolt upright, her knees shifting. Balin's head slipped off her lap and bounced on the ground. "Sorry!"

"By my beard! Owch!" Balin cradled his head and rolled around.

"What do you mean, in a month?" Annie asked, as she placed Balin's head back in her lap and patted it.

"Owwww... I dunno. He said he's got a grand plan. He knows 'ow to make somethin' that'll make enough gold to break both our indentures. Said it would change minin' forever."

"Do you believe him?"

"Well, I thought he was crazy when he wanted sugar fer tha' beer. Look where that went."

The two of them thought back to the radler incident. Bran had lemonade available every night now. He said it would protect against scurvy, and it was in every dwarf's best interest to drink some. They all knew what it was *really* about though, and he wasn't fooling anyone with that 'doctor's orders' spiel.

"Balin..." Annie paused, this was perhaps her best opportunity to tell him.

"Aye, Annie?"

"I got word from Grim today." Annie took a deep breath. "The city administration has allowed for the reduction of my indenture."

"Annie! Tha's great!" Balin sat up, a look of joy on his face. "Was it tha grease?"

"Yes, nearly every mine in Minnova is using it now." Annie's face flushed with pride. It was her first successful invention, and soon everyone would be using it. "I'll be leaving within a few weeks."

"Oh... I'll miss ya."

"I know, I'll miss you too." Annie's voice grew resolute. "I'm going ahead. I need to see how the brewery is doing and get things ready for when you and Pete get out. I don't know what's been happening for the past year, and I'm worried. I suspect most of the workers will have left, and my family can't run that whole brewery alone."

"Alright. I'll make sure Pete doesn't bring the whole camp down in the meantime."

"Luck o' Barck with that, Balin!" Annie laughed. "I'll take a dozen grumpy workers over a single Pete!"

"Hah! Luck o' Barck to you too, Annie, not that you'll need it. You'll do well. I know it!"

The two of them watched a line of carriages slowly wind into the city far in the distance. Soon they would all be there, free dwarves once again.

PART TWO
THE BREWERY

CHAPTER FORTY-ONE
MOUNTAIN CLIMBING

"Balin, give me your hand!"

"I can't reach it!!"

"You got this! I believe in you!"

"How aren't ya tired yet, Pete?"

"Easy, my vitality is 18."

"That's disgustin'! How!?"

"I'll tell you later. Focus on climbing." I pulled and yanked Balin up on the boulder with me. I turned around to look at our goal. Only another hundred metres or so to go.

We'd found a section of road that had gone around a large... hill was the correct word, but mountain felt more appropriate now. We'd figured that a climb over the 'hill' would save us several hours of travel.

Dumb, dumb, dumb.

"Watch it!" A rock slipped as I walked and bounced towards Balin's head. He swore and ducked underneath it.

"Barck's beard, Pete! This was a terrible plan!"

"You agreed to it!"

"It looked easy from down below," Balin muttered, as he struggled to draw in breath. Balin's vitality wasn't nearly as high as mine. The climbing was hard, but without several bags of ore, the actual effort was pretty much a cakewalk. For me, anyway.

"Aye, but think of the view we'll get from the top!" I trudged upwards, while this time I ensured that my feet were on steady stone before I took each step.

I waited for Balin at the top and we crested the hill together. The 'horizon' stretched before us; we were even higher than the ridge at the mining camp. This hill was about halfway to Minnova, but most important – the main highway lay directly beneath us.

A few other travellers and carts were on the road, even this far off from the city. We were high enough that they looked like ants from here. I shuddered slightly at the thought of ants and turned to Balin.

"Do you need to rest for a bit?"

"Aye. Gimme a moment. I need a drink."

He grabbed his flask and took a deep drag.

"You know, water would probably be better in this case."

"Did ya bring any?"

"Eh... no."

"Me neither," Balin groaned. "We do have lots of beer, though. Nice of Bran ta do that fer us."

"Alcohol isn't that great for dehydration, it's a diuretic."

Balin sighed as he took the flask away from his lips.

"Pete, if you want ta keep a low profile, ya shouldn't be usin' words like 'diuretic.'"

"Hmmm... that's a good point."

"What's it mean? Alcohol gives ya tha shits?"

I chuckled.

"No, it means that your body uses a lot of water to flush out the alcohol. Do you know anything about the liver?"

"Aye, it tastes good when ya spread it on bread."

"Ugh. Your liver is the organ responsible for removing toxins from your body."

Balin's face pinched up. "Pete, I know ya don't like beer, but callin' it toxic is a bit much."

"Oh hush. Doc Opal was a good enough doctor that I have little doubt dwarves are aware alcohol is bad for you." I wagged a finger as I spoke.

"I've heard that's true fer humans." Balin nodded. "But it's not too bad fer us unless ya completely ignore raisin' yer vitality."

"Really?" I considered what he'd said. Vitality gave stamina, but it also provided resistance to disease and poisons. Dwarves had a naturally higher vitality, which made them more resistant to alcohol. That made the fact they were total lightweights even weirder. Maybe more of the alcohol crossed the brain barrier than normal? Then why hadn't I been affected by dwarven alcohol even when my vitality was still around twelve? A mystery. I gave up thinking about it after a moment and continued the biology lesson.

"Your liver metabolises the alcohol into something your body can handle before it gets dumped into your urine. What little alcohol that's left stays in your blood, but a lot of it also aerates through your lungs. All of this requires water though, which means alcohol makes you thirsty."

"Mah lungs!?" Balin held his hand up to his mouth and breathed out before smelling. "Is that why yer breath smells bad after beer?"

"No... that's because nobody brushes properly. I don't know why we don't have massive cavities."

"What's brushin' yer beard got ta do with it?"

"And you call me a dirty goat."

We chuckled together for a moment before I continued.

"There're ways to test how much alcohol is being removed from your body. In my world there are machines called breathalysers that can detect the amount of alcohol coming out of yer lungs."

"Neat! They tell ya how drunk ya are?"

"Yes, kind of."

"So, you'd know how much more before ya pass out?! Ya could party all night with that!"

"That's... not... sure. Yes, you could use it to party all night." I pulled out my own canteen and took a drink. "Here, drink some of mine, it's got a lower ABV."

"What's ABV?" He took my tankard and looked at it suspiciously.

"It stands for Alcohol By Volume. My radler has almost half as much alcohol as yours since it's watered down."

"That makes sense." He took a couple of deep drinks and then exhaled with pleasure while he wiped his beard with his arm. "Now that yer not hidin' it, yer full of neat stuff!"

Dwarven ale had a very low ABV, close to 1 percent, while most modern earth beers were closer to 6 or 7 percent. That made dwarven ale pretty close to mediaeval beers, which fit with my assumptions about their brewing techniques. Mediaeval brewers only cared about having *just* enough alcohol to ensure the drink was sanitary. Water was often contaminated, and a peasant couldn't run to the store to buy soda. That was one of the things I hoped to change when we got to Annie's brewery. With my higher vitality, I could barely get drunk on regular dwarven ale.

"Alright let's try and hit the main highway before we take another break. Are you better now?"

"Fresh as a dwarven househusband." He waggled his eyebrows at me.

"Please tell me that's not a real saying."

"I won't lie to ya, Pete."

The trip down the hill was fairly uneventful. The main highway was nearly ten metres wide and paved with some kind of rough granite. It intersected several paths to other mining camps, and we slowly met up with more travellers as we walked. It was usually other miners or mine personnel, but the occasional company of armoured guards marched by on patrol, their armour clattering as they marched. Balin called them the 'Highwatch' and it was their job to keep the roads clear of bandits and monsters. We chatted with some of them, though most were either in too much of a hurry or too tired to make good company.

The trickle of travellers turned into a flood, and soon we were simply one of dozens travelling towards the city. There were miners carrying picks and shovels, merchants on their carts laden with food and goods, and adventurers. Oh, the adventurers, now there was something out of pure fantasy. I saw a few dwarves in basic leathers, their bandoliers full of throwing axes and hammers. There were gnomish mages decked out in robes and magical accoutrements, their eyes crackling with magic. Plate-clad warriors carried axes and swords bigger than they were, alongside every other kind of weapon you could imagine. They all radiated power and menace, and everyone gave them a wide berth. I even saw a single elderly bearded human dressed as a mage go by in a cart. He was travelling with several dwarves and they passed us by in an instant.

I turned my head to watch them go. "Are there a lot of humans in Minnova?"

"Nah, just a few oddballs. There's more of 'em in tha capital."

What surprised me the most though, was the sheer variety of bodies on display. Yes, they were mostly gnomes and dwarves, but they were nearly as varied as humans back on earth.

There were black and brown-skinned dwarves, and some with pink or green hair. I saw one black-skinned warrior with a massive broadsword walk by who had an afro for a beard. He met up with his party and high-fived a gnome who looked like an evil wizard from a kung fu movie, complete with East Asian features and a Fu Manchu. There were tall dwarves, short dwarves, dwarves in armour, dwarves in robes, and dwarves that were nearly naked. A dwarf had passed by wearing nothing but a loincloth and an incredible series of tattoos. I think he caught me staring, because he winked and wiggled his butt as he walked away.

"Balin," I pitched my voice low and asked the burning question on my mind. "Why were all the dwarves in the mining camp white?" I'd gotten used to the basic whitebread beard combo from the mine, but I'd been sorely mistaken thinking that dwarves all looked like that.

Balin shrugged, "Crackian dwarves are mostly pale-skinned with dark hair. The city has all sorts though."

"Why would dwarves have dark skin when they live underground?" I watched the afro-bearded dwarf as he walked off into the distance.

"They're from South Erden, near tha equator. Down there, they actually live on top o' tha mountains, and it gets hot. They're mostly here for tha dungeon. Greentree is a good dungeon fer new adventurers."

I thought back to Opal's lessons.

"There are three inhabited continents, right? North Erden, South Erden, and Drakken?"

"Aye, though only dragons live on Drakken."

"We focused on North Erden in my lessons… South Erden is mostly savannah, right?"

Balin nodded, "and full o' some of tha scariest animals in tha world! Some of those beasties can even kill monsters!"

"Are there lions? A big yellow cat with a giant fuzzy mane?" I asked excitedly. I loved lions – they took second place on my 'coolest animal' list to the all-powerful moose.

"Sort of. There's pinsirs, which look like big mountain cats. They got six legs, stripes, and a mohawk."

"Whew, sounds nasty." It wasn't a lion, but it might do.

Balin clapped me on the back. "We've faced a stoneant swarm! Ya won't find anythin' nastier outside of a dungeon!"

We eventually hitched a ride from a passing cart full of faintly rotting cabbages. It was driven by a crotchety gnome named Gimbletack – no wonder he was crotchety – and he had been willing to give us a ride into town for a couple of coppers. Balin said it would be nice to walk, but I was itching to enter the city I'd only seen at a distance. Minnova was still a fair ways away, through gullies and over small hills, and I just didn't want to be stuck walking all day. I enticed him with the prospect of seeing Annie a few hours sooner.

Gimbletack was a terrible conversationalist. I tried coaxing some small talk out of him, but it always ended in disaster.

"How long have you been a cabbage farmer?"

[Translated from angry toothless gnome] "I have been cabbaging longer than you prime specimens of dwarven youth have been alive."

"Wow. Is it fun?"

[Translated from angry toothless gnome] "It is about as fun as this conversation, you handsome and intelligent dwarf."

"Do you take cabbages to any other cities, or just Minnova?"

[Translated from angry toothless gnome] "If you ask me any more questions, I will most certainly make you walk."

That was about the gist of any conversation, except with a lot more gummy swearing. Thankfully, the cart ate up the road, and we arrived at the outskirts of Minnova well before evening. Balin fell asleep partway through, but I was barely even tired and I was too excited. We went up a small rise, and there it was: the city of Minnova.

Even from over a kilometre away, the walls rose up into the sky.

They stretched for several kilometres to either side, and I could see hundreds of plumes of smoke from cook fires and forges. The centre of the cavern was several hundred metres above us, and an enormous purple crystal embedded in it poured light into the cavern. A few clock towers and several steeples peeked over the wall. The bustling sounds of the city were audible even from this far away. I took a deep breath and inhaled the scent of civilization. It was glorious.

I shook Balin, who was gently snoring, and he awoke with a yawn. "Hey, you, you're finally awake! Look, we're here!" I quipped.

"Aye, we made it, Pete." Balin sat up and looked around. He smiled as his eyes fell on the approaching walls. "There it is, our new home. Tha city of Minnova."

[Translated from angry toothless gnome] "I'm so *very happy* to be back."

CHAPTER FORTY-TWO
AT THE GATES

We passed by the dungeon of Greentree as we approached the city, and I could feel the hairs on the back of my neck rise up.

The boundary of the dungeon was a sudden and imposing wall of wood. The dark greens and purples of the treeline loomed towards the road. There was a palpable feeling of menace to the place. Birdsong, hoots, and roars echoed out from the forest. Several adventuring groups were stationed outside, and they all seemed on high alert. Defensive structures dotted the landscape around the half-kilometre diameter copse of trees.

A large *crack* caught our attention and several treetops deeper in the woods swayed. Birds erupted into the air and the forest went silent, but for the sound of more crunching wood moving deeper into the dungeon.

[Translated from angry toothless gnome] "Verily, the adventurers do a most excellent job keeping the dungeon contained."

"We heard about a possible dungeon break back at the... mine. Is it looking likely?"

"Lunara's lace, I hope not." Balin shivered beside me. I patted him on the shoulder as we passed by.

[Translated from angry toothless gnome] "By the grace of Barck, no monster stampede shall befall us."

Gimbletack snapped the reins and urged his donkey on faster. Our eyes never left the dungeon until we were well past. Hopefully, we'd never come near it again.

The last kilometre to the city was packed with travellers. There were even roadside stalls and whole caravans. Then I had my first glimpse of dwarven children; they looked a lot like short human children. Sort of.

"Balin, those kids have moustaches."

"All kids have moustaches, Pete. You took care of tha unigoats long enough that I woulda thought ya knew that."

"Arggh. No, I mean do all dwarven children have moustaches? Or are those just some gnomes that have aged really well?" I whispered hoarsely and pointed towards a small group of children playing what looked like a cross between cricket, croquet, and MMA. A pitcher tossed a small rubber ball at another child who hit it with a makeshift mallet. The 'batter' ran back and forth between a pair of sticks while the other children tried to tackle them and another group defended. There was a lot of punching and kicking involved.

Balin leaned over to look. "Ah, they're playin' hitball. I love that game! Ta answer yer question, all dwarven children 'ave moustaches. Beard hair doesn't grow till they're at least thirty."

I continued to watch the game in fascination. The higher base vitality of dwarves seemed to make small scraps possible without serious injury. While I watched, the pitcher got hold of the ball and beaned the runner in the head with it. There was some cheering and then the teams switched places. Some of the children ran in front of the cart and Gimbletack had to pull on the reins to prevent an accident.

[Translated from angry toothless gnome] "Pray move out of the way, dear children! Your mothers must be so proud that you were born from their bodies'!"

Crisis averted; I turned back to Balin. "That looks fun. We should play sometime!"

"I used to! I was tha all-star pounder fer my town's junior team!" He thumped his chest and flapped his arms. "Go Shadow Crows, ca-caw!"

"Go Shadow Crows, ca-caw!" I copied him and we both burst into laughter.

[Translated from angry toothless gnome] "I do so enjoy talking about sports."

Up close, Minnova was even more impressive than it had been from far away. The city walls rose up nearly twenty metres. They were made of smooth stone, and I couldn't see a single seam. The outside of the city was a flat plane with dozens of tents and wagons set up, but no permanent structures. There were cooking fires and a massive milieu of grubby looking people. There were a few children here and there, but it mostly looked like adventurers and vagrants. I actually saw a couple of humans among them.

A gnomess bard stood on a makeshift stage made of wooden pallets in the middle of a ring of wagons. Her instrument was some kind of mix between a lute and a guitar, which until I am told otherwise is now called a glute. She was singing something that reminded me deeply of *Sweet Home Alabama,* and I lost myself for a while.

"Gimbletack, who are all those people?"

[Translated from angry toothless gnome] "They are upstanding adventurers and nomads who lack either the coin or the desire to enter the city."

I broke out of my reverie. "It costs money to enter the city!?"

Gimbletack hauled on the reins. [Translated from angry toothless gnome] "I am not overly concerned about your monetary situation, but you had better be able to pay me."

We paid Gimbletack, who spat and trundled off, then stood in line to enter the city. There were two main lines, one for pedestrians and another for merchants. Gimbletack had moved into the merchant line, which was moving rather more quickly than our own.

I looked back at the way we'd come. The mining camp was so distant that it couldn't be seen. Here in the centre of the cavern, the ground slowly sloped upwards far off into the distance. It was like being in the middle of an enormous lumpy bowl.

"I can't imagine a road this well maintained simply goes to the mining camps. We must have travelled over fifty kilometres and there wasn't a single pothole."

"Tha highways connect tha cities of Crack to tha capital so they need ta be in good shape. This one connects to tha city of Gungu."

We made small talk with the dwarves next to us as the line moved towards the gate. The general sentiment was worry about the state of the dungeon, and excitement about the upcoming octa-millennial celebration. A couple guards checked every traveller and cart as it came into the city, but the line still moved fairly briskly. At one point, there was some yelling from the guards and a small commotion on the merchant side of the line.

[Translated from angry toothless Gnome] "My cabbages!"

Soon it was our turn, and a severe looking dwarf in plate mail frowned as he waved us forward. A crest of a tree under a mountain marked him as part of the Minnovan city guard. His nameplate read, 'Captain Hammer.' Some faintly rotting cabbages were strewn around the front of the gate, and a rather tired-looking dwarf in overalls was sweeping them up.

"Names and identification please."

"Pete Samson, and Balin Roughtuff, Captain Hammer." Balin handed over the paperwork that Grim had given us. The guard perused the documents, his brow furrowed.

"Yer from Minnova Reform Mine? Don't plan on causin' any trouble, I hope."

"No, sir."

"You got someplace to stay?"

"Aye, a friend has some jobs lined up for us."

"Which friend?"

"A-Annie Goldstone."

I watched the byplay for a while as Balin got more and more flustered. He really didn't do well with authority figures. After Balin started describing his marital plans in detail I decided to cut in.

"Captain Morris said we should give our regards." The guard captain had indeed said that before he left. Apparently, he really liked the way we'd sacrificed ourselves for others, and he especially liked Balin. He'd been making noises about Balin joining the city guard, but Balin had his heart set on the brewery.

Hammer's entire demeanour changed instantly. "Oh, ya know tha Captain?"

Balin smiled. "Aye, he saved our lives durin' a stoneant attack."

"I heard about that! Wait..." He thought for a moment and then held up a finger. "Balin! Yer tha [Knight] tha boys were talkin' about!"

Balin flushed. "I dunno about that..." he mumbled.

"No need ta be so humble!" Hammer slapped Balin on the back. "I heard ya took down a soldier stoneant tha size of a giant mushfolk in a single swing!" Balin turned crimson as a crowd of curious dwarves gathered behind us. Hammer waved his arms expansively. "Gained yer Specialisation in tha middle of a fight, got a rare Milestone, and then beat back a whole horde by yerself!"

There were some *oohs* and *aahs* from the crowd while Balin squirmed. I enjoyed watching it. Balin was a great guy, and he deserved some recognition. Plus, this could be good advertising!

"Aye, he was a knight in shinin' armour!" I declared.

"Pete, shut it!" Balin hissed, but it was too late. The crowd began to chant for him to show off the Ability until he was left with little choice.

"[Shining armour]!" There was some cheering, followed by some angry yelling from the line we were holding up. Hammer dispersed the crowd and then turned back to us.

"Yer good to go. Enjoy yer time in Minnova!"

Balin turned off his armour, and glowered at me. I shrugged my shoulders in mock innocence as we walked through the massive gates into the grand city of Minnova.

It was like walking into a fantasy village from the Middle Ages. Back home, one of my favourite places to vacation was the Austrian city of Salzburg. Salzburg had wide foot-passenger-only streets lined with quaint old buildings and metal signs that hung over the sidewalk and announced the business or address. They also had the most amazing beer halls and pubs.

Minnova was just like that, except short. Nearly every building was only a single story. A lot of them were nearly completely open-air. I saw an open-air beer garden, where a full-blown party was in swing complete with a band and dancing. Passersby were pulled into the festivities. A sign outside said *The Awful Floffle*. The street we were walking on was wide and covered in flat cobblestones. A drunk pottered out of the bar and threw up into an odd ditch on the side of the road. I realised with a start that it was a rudimentary sewer and storm drain system.

Overall, the city was a mix of old Europe and pure fantasy. Where did everyone live, though? There was no way this city had enough housing for all the people I could see. There were a handful of taller buildings, but they seemed to be very wealthy houses, or important locations like churches or clock towers. Then I saw a party of dwarves open the door to a nearby house and immediately walk down some stairs. Of course! They were dwarves, the city was mostly built underground!

Finally, there were the cats. There'd been a few in the mine, but they were *everywhere* in Minnova. Every shape and size and colour could be seen hanging from roofs and meandering the alleys. At least there weren't any of those ones with the fluffy white hair and smooshed-up faces. Dollars to donuts, those were the absolute worst kind of stuck-up cat, and nobody in their right mind liked them.

Balin took out a piece of paper and read it over. "Annie's in tha western quarter. We'll need ta go to tha main square and then turn left."

"Lead the way, Balin!"

"Alright, follow me!"

"Oooooh, let's go in here!" I pointed at what looked like a stereotypical coffee shoppe.

"Gods dammit, Pete!"

Somewhere else

In a dark space, stood a white stone gazebo, and mist rose from several incense bowls surrounding it. A black mountain rose up in the darkness, seeming to touch the sky. A circular marble table sat in the centre of the gazebo, and a group of cloaked figures sat around it in ornate wooden chairs.

"Dark days approach, and none shall be able to stand them," said the first figure.

"Woe are we, to be here at the end of days," said another.

"Truly, these events shall lead to the death of our world," said a third.

Another spoke up, their voice light and melodious. "All know of the dwarf king's competition. I was disturbed to see it, and more disturbed by the sudden interest."

"We shall be there to stand against it. Our children shall be the bulwark against this abomination the king has wrought."

"What word is there of the young upstart? Has she been suitably chastised?" The first turned to look at a silent brooding figure, the tallest of them all.

"She... 'as not truly recovered." The tall figure ground out, their respectful tone belying an undercurrent of shame and anger.

"Hmph, it was the will of the ancestors that the explosion occurred." The first figure bowed his head and clasped his hands. "We are but their instrument."

The refrain was repeated by all assembled.

"THE WILL OF THE ANCESTORS."

"At least there are some that stand against the darkness," the second figure piped up. "Like that chap Whistlemop!"

"Indeed! His wares are how the future should be approached! An innovation that brings forth the colour and essence of the brew, but does not intrude upon what makes it the True Brew." The first figure nodded sagely as he regarded the assembly. "Are there any others that bring forth a concern to the Honourable Guild of Brewers?"

"Ma boys caught a beer smuggler," one figure put in, the sneer evident in their gravelly voice.

"Excellent, were they properly dealt with?"

"As we always 'ave. They won't be a problem again."

"Very good."

Another figure put up a hand and said in a cultured accent, "The cost of erdroot has gone up by an unacceptable amount."

"Yes, people are panic-buying in preparation for a dungeon break.

We will do what we can to manipulate the market," the first figure said, with more confidence than they likely felt. There was a lengthy pause before he spoke again. "Anyone else?"

"Are we done yet?" a figure that had been gently snoring up until this point, asked in a quavering tone. "Did your wife pack the treacle tarts, Browning?"

"Oh yes, dear Shalea's tarts are always the highlight of these meetings," another heretofore silent figure put in. There was a general murmur of agreement.

"Can we get some lights on in 'ere?"

"Midna's mullet, these theatrics are bloody daft, Browning."

"How did you deal with that smuggler, Drum?"

"Gave 'is address to City Hall, heh heh."

"Hah! He'll be payin' taxes fer decades!"

A dim lamp was lit in the centre of the table, as the first figure pulled back his hood, revealing a grey-bearded and balding dwarf. He sighed the deep sigh of a long-suffering friend that has put up with your shit for far too long. "Yes, I have the tarts, Malt. She packed them especially for you."

Browning put a doily-wrapped box on the table and the grumble pulled back their hoods to reveal a collection of ageing dwarves and dwarvesses. One of them pulled aside the wall hanging of a black mountain and opened up a secret door. Bright light streamed into a bevy of curses and shouts as he called up the stairs, "Bring us a round of drinks, the meeting is breaking up!"

"Aye sir, Master Brewer!" a young voice called back down, and the door was closed again to general relief.

"Fine, I guess we're done for the night." Browning moaned and massaged his temples. "To close, in the matter of Annie Goldstone, the engineering report is available at Pewtership & Pewtership."

"So, it was an engineering failure?"

"Yes and no. Young Annie was so sure of her work that when she had the vats commissioned, she did not get them looked at by an [Engineer]. She was worried about espionage." Browning frowned, "A foolish consideration. Who among us would dare to change the brewing techniques of our ancestors?"

"Did you know, I heard she put lemonade in her beer when she first got back?" Malt whispered.

"Ugh, foul. Truly?"

"Interesting, isn't it? But she 'asn't since."

The grumble nodded their general agreement around mouthfuls of tart. It was a shame what had happened to her, but hopefully with that young firebrand cooling off, the next few centuries would be just as quiet as the last.

CHAPTER FORTY-THREE
ROUGH AND TUFF

I sipped on my coffee and sighed. Then I took a deep sniff of the scent of roasted beans and cream and sighed again.

The rich aroma reminded me of a dark roast, while the thick texture and flavour was closer to a cappuccino. I swished the dark liquid around in my mouth and savoured the mouthfeel of the tannins. It burned slightly going down the back of my throat, but it was a nice burn. A good cup of coffee can ignite the taste buds and invigorate the mind, and this was a *damn* good cup of coffee. I'd asked for a latte, but the barista didn't know what that meant – I was drinking the 'house special' instead.

"Dunno how ya can stand that," Balin muttered. He was drinking some ale from a repurposed teacup, and I think I saw the barista shudder every time he took a sip. A passing waiter gave Balin a sharp look, before he sniffed loudly and started cleaning a table.

"Well, Balin, we need to take a moment."

"Couldn't we do it at Annie's? Why'd you choose this place?" He waved his hand, gesturing at the inside of the gnomish café.

"We should make a battle plan before we go see your future father-in-law, Balin."

"Oh... I didn't think of that."

"Of course not, that's your best dwarf's job! Your job is to be hopelessly and foolishly in love. Also, I didn't choose to come here, I just followed my nose." I finished off my cup of coffee and gave thanks to Tiara that coffee existed here. "This is the life."

"It's not bad. Better'n a mine."

"Really? I figured it wasn't your... cup of tea." I pointed at the slightly foamy tea cup.

"Harr harr." Balin took another sip. "A fire an' a comfy chair beat a hard bench and cold stone."

While I had been following Balin, agog, the scent of coffee and pastries had overwhelmed my every sense, grabbed hold of my appetite, and seduced me across the street into a quaint little gnomish café called *Joejam Cuppa*. We'd bought our drinks, slumped down into a pair of plush leather recliners, and relaxed after our long journey. We'd also taken the opportunity to use their washroom and change our clothes. Grim had let us keep the fancy suits, and Doc Opal had fixed all the tears and cuts as a going-away present. A small wash up in the sink and we were a pair of fiiine-lookin' dwarves.

That's right, a sink – with running water. And a toilet – a flushing, porcelain throne. With a *bidet*. I'd sat upon it and was for a brief moment the king of all I surveyed. It was Glory. I forgave all the Gods for every slight and every wrong done to me since I'd arrived on Erd. Indeed, I sold my soul for running water and a flushing toilet and would do it again in a heartbeat.

"One sec while I refill this." A couple other gnomes had come and gone, and I didn't want to overstay our welcome. But one cup wasn't enough.

I made my way up to the front, got a fresh cup of deliciousness and sat back down. "Alright Balin, let's talk about what we're going to do at Annie's."

Balin looked up from where he was nose-deep in a tart.

"Mrmph?"

"You wanted to introduce yourself to Annie's father as a carpenter, right?"

"Mrhmhm." He nodded, his mouth still full of pastry.

"Do you... still want to do that now that you're a [Knight]? I'm absolutely not the dwarf to deny a fellow dwarf's dreams, but has your new Title changed anything?"

Balin thought for a while and turned his head from side to side while he chewed. He swallowed and licked his lips before he answered.

"I'm... not sure, Pete. I still want to, but I dunno if it's tha best I could do fer Annie."

"Captain Morris did say that you were gifted at fighting. I... don't know enough about Dwarven society to tell if that's more or less appealing to a future father-in-law than a carpenter."

Balin clicked his tongue a few times. "Well... carpentry is often a business fer tha whole family line. It makes good money. Sons learn from their fathers, and daughters from their mothers, and tha whole family earns silver cuttin', shapin', and installin'."

"That sounds a lot like my world too. Families are even given the last name 'carpenter.' I'm guessing it's respectable?"

"Aye, it is. At tha other end o' tha beard, becomin' an adventurer or a famous warrior makes that family line in tha' first place."

"So... adventuring is more prestigious and valuable. Assuming you don't die."

"That's tha hard part."

"Don't die Balin."

"I'll try fer yer sake, Pete."

We clicked our cups in a mock toast.

"I'm your best dwarf, Balin, but I don't think I want to say anythin' that may push you one way or the other. My advice? Ask Annie before you make any serious decisions. She's the one who will suffer the most if somethin' happens to you in the dungeon."

"Aye..." Balin's brow furrowed.

"Can't hurt to introduce yourself as a Titled [Knight], though. I could be your squire!"

Balin held his nose up, imperiously. "Fetch me mah arms, squire."

"I can't milord! They're already attached to yer torso!" We both chuckled.

"What about you, Pete? Now that I know yer... you know, I understand why ya knew all those weird foods and drinks. What are yer plans?"

"That depends..." I sighed. "I had this grand dream of sweeping in and making massive changes to the brewery, but there's no way that's gonna fly. I've learned my lesson on that. I think I'm just going to introduce myself as a hard worker and do what I can to earn some trust."

Balin snorted. "Addin' lemons ta beer is one thing, Pete. Dunno if ya have that much to teach a real brewer."

I held up one hand with all my fingers showing and quirked an eyebrow. Balin looked at it quizzically. "Wha's that?"

"The number of different brews I've made."

"Five brews? Tha's pretty impressive, Pete. We only really have tha two, so that might be worth something. There might be some grumblin', but if they're good brews, it could be worth gold." Balin sipped his beer thoughtfully.

"Not five. Five hundred."

Balin spat his beer all over my face.

"Five hundred brews?!" He passed me a napkin while he goggled at me. I wiped my face clean then glanced down at my shirt with trepidation. Thankfully, my beard had kept the suit safe. It would have been awful to show up at the brewery in beer-stained clothes.

"Yes. Give or take."

"Pete... what in tha Nether were ya?" Balin's eyes grew even wider in his awestruck face.

"I was a master brewer. Famed throughout the land." Well, that was a *bit* hyperbolic, but it wasn't completely untrue.

"By tha firmament, yer not jokin'..." he whispered.

"No, quite serious. Alcohol was my life."

"Weren't ya human? How long did humans live on yer world?"

"Same as here."

"How did ya make so many brews then?!"

"I just... tried everything." I began counting down my fingers. "Stouts, pilsners, lagers, ambers, coffee ales, amber ales, IPAs, goses. That doesn't even take into consideration the nearly infinite number of adjuncts that can be added to the wort." I glanced up at Balin, whose chin was about to hit the floor. "You should close yer mouth, Balin. You look like a beardfish."

He closed it with a *clack* and leaned over the table. "Pete, ya can't just waltz into Annie's brewery and say, 'I know more beer recipes than there are master brewers in all o' Crack!'"

I paused for a moment, arrested. "Wow, that few?"

"It's a closely guarded family business. Most o' tha brewing families have been around fer thousands o' years!"

"I mean, I knew that, but I didn't realise it meant there were barely any brewers." I waved my hand dismissively, pushing the discussion aside. "Well, I realised I couldn't just waltz into the brewery, which is why I stopped here to discuss this before I suffered an 'axe-ident.'"

"This is serious, Pete. Yer a walkin' fireball waitin' ta go off!"

"I know," I sighed. "Between the Radler, the ginger beer, and everything with Tim, I'm not going to make waves if I can avoid it. I think I still have the potential to make Annie a lot of money, even with small changes to start."

Balin sat back in his seat and took a deep breath. "Ar'right. You've put some thought in, I can see that. Now, how do we introduce ourselves?"

"I was thinking... as kin?"

"Really?"

"If you're okay with it. I... don't really have any attachment to my family name." I felt myself flush and hid it behind a fake cough.

"If ya want ta be a Roughtuff, Pete... I'd be happy to have ya. No, my ancestors would be proud to have ya." Balin teared up, and we shared a handclasp over the table.

"Peter Roughtuff," I mused. "It doesn't sound too bad."

"We'll need ta get it recorded at City Hall." Balin grinned.

"We can do that eventually, first let me tell you about some of my ideas for the future prosperity of the Roughtuff clan."

"Nothin' too grand to start, right?"

"Nope! I want to start with bubbles!"

"Bubbles?" Balin asked, quizzically.

"It's something that Annie was already working on. There's barely any carbon dioxide in the local brews. The beer in the mine barely had any."

"Ah. I did notice that tha beer in tha mine had less bubbly than usual."

"There probably isn't that much in the first place. There's a lot of reasons for that, and I'm pretty sure I can guess some of them, based on Annie's unfortunate accident."

"Really?"

I glanced around to make sure we weren't being overheard. The shop was busier now, and the staff were studiously trying to stay away from our table. I leaned in and lowered my voice anyway. "Yeah, I know some of the history of beer, and dwarven beer seems to be quite similar to my world's original method."

"How can ya tell?"

"The flavour, the body, the carbonation, and some of the stuff Annie said. I'll tell you one thing – when we get to her brewery, I can almost guarantee there will be a bunch of giant open vats that they use for primary fermentation."

"Words, Pete, make this easier for me. What's tha problem?"

"The old methods for beer result in a mostly flat beer. It's why everyone was so amazed by my pilsner glass. The narrow shape let what little carbonation there was create a head, which isn't usually visible." I missed that glass. Grim had never given it back. Apparently, they'd decided it was not worth any more fighting in the camp. I needed to go get another one here in town.

"How are ya' goin' to fix it?"

"There're a few methods. Annie had the right idea for one of them."

Balin smiled brightly. "She is a smart one!"

"That she is, but there are a dozen errors she could have made. I had to custom design lots of fermentation vessels, so I can help her make it work."

Balin whistled. "She may not be allowed to."

"Maybe, but it's something that I can do that is more Annie than me." I tapped my finger on the side of my nose.

"I see. You'd be usin' yer knowledge, but everyone would think it was Annie." Balin nodded his head. "Smart."

"Right? If that succeeds, I can get Annie to put in a good word with her dad."

"After that?"

"I want to improve the clarity of the beer." I pointed into Balin's cup. "Do you see the stuff left on the bottom of the cup?"

Balin peered into the cup. "Aye, that's tha body o' tha beer. It adds some chew to it."

I shuddered. "That's not supposed to be there, and it can make the beer far more sour than it needs to be. It should really be filtered after fermentation or dealt with before it gets into the wort. That's a small change that can massively improve the body of the beer without affecting the flavour too much."

Balin tapped his fingers on the table as he thought about it. I finished off the last of my coffee as he did so. It was no Tim Hortons, but it would do – Joejam had a loyal new customer. Oh caffeine, how I missed you.

"I think that might work, Pete."

"I put a lot of thought into it. I've got a few other ideas, but they can wait. I'll need Annie's dad to trust me first." I sighed, lamenting that I couldn't simply grab the reins of power.

"What are some of those ideas?" Balin asked, as he chewed on the crud at the bottom of his cup.

I shuddered again. Ew. "Well, branding would be a good start."

"Branding? Like goats?"

"Same idea. I noticed that there's a maker's mark on most of the beer casks, but nothing that really said 'THIS BEER WAS MADE BY THE GOLDSTONES.'"

"What would that do?"

"A few things, but most importantly, it would help me bring something to this world. Something I didn't notice in the streets while we were walking here. Something more dreadful than even boomdust."

"What's that?" Balin leaned in, his voice quivering in trepidation.

"ADVERTISING."

CHAPTER FORTY-FOUR
THIRSTY GOAT BREWING

"Is this it?"

"I think it is, Pete."

"There could be multiple places in Minnova called 'Thirsty Goat Brewing.'"

"I think that's unlikely."

"Minnova's a big place."

"Not that big."

"But it could be possible."

"Aye, but this is probably it."

"I could go in incognito and scope it out, make sure it's the right place."

"Annie would spot ya right away."

"I could wear a disguise?"

"You got anythin' to use fer one?"

"I could go buy one. We still have over a hundred silver."

"Seems a waste of money."

"For a little info on your future family before you meet them? Could be useful!"

Balin sighed. Honestly, if it wasn't for Balin's intense desire to see Annie, it would have taken us all day to get here. Minnova was an amazing town from the perspective of a non-native, and I could have window-shopped and toured the attractions for hours.

During our short trip through the city centre, I'd seen magic devices, armour and weapon shops, street performers, strange plants, strange animals, strange food, strange people, and more. It was like watching a fantasy movie from my childhood with all my childhood wonder left intact. City hall, at the dead centre of the city, had been a massive, multi-storey building with intricate carvings and a gigantic clock face on the front. There looked to be some kind of mechanism as well, but I'd barely looked at it for a moment before Balin had grabbed my ear and pulled me down a side alley.

Now we stood just across the street from Annie's brewery on a busy side street. Minnova's roads were very easy to navigate – Annie's brewery was on 4th Street South-West, just off of Main Street West. The numbers counted down to the main street, and every city block was nearly exactly square. It was horrifically well organised, and anyone from the Okanagan would have found it to be overbearingly OCD. All of the streets in rural Canada were named after famous people, so you just had to go down McCurdy, turn on Craig and then you'd find Webster Street. Except of course, Craig Street actually turned into Hemlock Street at Hartman... Alright, maybe numbered streets were more practical. Still, where was the sense of *adventure,* Minnova?

The brewery was a tall, single-storey, red-brick building that took up nearly half the block. The walls were weathered with age, though one side of the building was clearly new. A wooden sign hung over the door – a drawing of a goat with its face buried in a tankard that read *Thirsty Goat Brewing*. There were several shuttered windows, and a single step up to an ornate wooden door.

This street seemed to be a random collection of shops and businesses. To the left of the brewery was a general store called *Knicknack's*. It had a large picture window, and I could see various tools and hardware inside. A few dwarves and gnomes filtered in and out of the store, carrying everything from fishing poles to buckets. To the right of the brewery was a rather plain stone compound with no signs or obvious habitation.

"Pete, I'm going in," Balin said, his voice firm with conviction.

"Alright. Let's do this." I nodded and the two of us walked up the front step together.

"Wait, Pete. I changed my mind."

"Nope." I gently dwarfhandled Balin through the door.

The inside of the brewery was a rather standard front foyer for any shop. The room was well furnished with wooden walls and rafters and plush green carpet. A counter stood to one side, with a line of casks on the wall behind it. The rest of the walls were lined with various pieces of brewing paraphernalia. Some fairly standard magic solstone lamps gave a bright, cheery yellow glow to everything. The feeling was kind of like a pub, and I think that was on purpose. I didn't see any actual place to sit and drink, but perhaps one of the side doors had a tasting room.

The brewing equipment littered around the room was quite close to what I expected. There were several giant wooden rakes for stirring mash, some kegs, a few ladles, and a big barrel that was clearly a mash tun for stirring hot mash. Several awards were hung here and there, though most of them were from a few hundred or thousand years ago. A line of portraits ran along one wall, which ended with a painting of Annie and a rather severe looking blonde dwarf who I realised must be her father. I was about to go get a closer look when a voice called out to us.

"Welcome to Thirsty Goat Brewing, nice to meet you!" The bright cheery voice brought our attention to a dwarfess standing behind the counter. "I'm Aqua, how can I help you?"

I did a double take. This was the first dwarf I had seen that wasn't in some kind of armour. She was wearing what appeared to be an actual white sundress! No, wait, she was also wearing silver armguards inset with bright ruby roses. Her blue-coloured pigtailed beard framed a cute feminine face, and her hair was up in a ponytail with a dainty circlet in front.

I strode forward confidently and held out my hand. "Hello! I'm Peter Roughtuff, and this is my brother, Balin Roughtuff. We're friends of Annie's."

"Oh! *The* Balin and Pete?" She shook my hand vigorously, and I took an unconscious step backwards as her businesslike smile turned practically feral. I recognized that smile from my wife's friends... "Welcome to the brewery! I was told you'd be around sometime this week."

"Aye, we sent a letter to Annie letting her know we'd be out."

"Well, congratulations on that! Annie's been waiting with bated breath for your arrival." Her smile got even wider. "And the boss has been waiting with even more anticipation than her!"

Balin gulped and I stepped gently on his foot. Don't go fainting on me Balin, keep it together!

"Yes, Balin and I have been looking forward to comin' here ever since Annie mentioned the place."

"Annie seemed to think you'd be out sooner? She managed to get out of the mining camp quite quickly after all!" Aqua looked us up and down, and I could feel the unsaid question: 'what took you so long?'

"We had some complications." I shrugged. "What matters is that we made it out and made some good connections too."

"Well, you'll need to tell us all about it!" Aqua pointed towards a door behind the counter. "I'd invite you into the brewery, but Annie and the boss are working on a brew right now."

"Ooooh, can we watch?" I asked. I was really interested in seeing the actual brewing process and comparing it to what I knew about ancient brewing.

The first beers on earth were actually made by the Chinese nearly ten thousand years ago, using rice as a malt with honey and flowers for sweetener. The Mesopotamians are usually credited with the first western style beer, and we actually have archeological evidence of their brewing process from 4000 BC. The Mesopotamians used barley to make their beers, as well as a type of barley bread called bappir. Their brewing process was quite close to how beer was made all the way up into the 1800s, and I was itching to compare it to the dwarven method. Although, of course...

"I'm afraid I can't let you onto the brew room floor." Aqua shook her head sadly. "You may be friends of Annie's, but the brewing process is a secret held within the Goldstone family."

"I understand." I'd expected as much, actually. "How did you get involved with the brewery? You don't appear to be a Goldstone." I pointed to the paintings on the wall. Aqua turned to look at them and shook her head.

"Oh, nonono." She laughed, a merry tinkling sound. "I'm no Goldstone, though my father's family has worked in the brewery for two generations now. He's Mr. Goldstone's right-hand dwarf. I'm just the clerk, but I do know the whole process. I have to, since I order all our supplies."

"Are there a lot of dwarves working here right now?"

"Well, the Goldstone family is much reduced of late. There's Mr. Goldstone and his cousin John, as well as Annie and John's son Johnsson." She started to count on her fingers and I held out a hand, stopping her before she could continue.

"Sorry, say that again? Did you say Johnson Johnson?"

"John's son is named Johnsson, yes."

"That's..." I tried to keep my face from breaking into a grin.

"Oh, it's not that bad. I have a friend named Potter Pottersdotter."

I choked. "Am I allowed to laugh at that?"

"Oh, please do. She hates it." We snickered, and even Balin let out a strained chuckle.

"Anyone else? Or is it just you, your father, and the Goldstones?"

"There's also Richter. He's kind of new. He's from down south. His family immigrated to Minnova recently, and his father actually saved Mr. Goldstone's life. He's been working in the brewery since he was a lad."

"Define... *recently*." I was suspicious of that word when it came from the mouth of a dwarf.

"About one hundred years, give or take." Yep, there it was.

I think I had Aqua's number at this point. She was probably the company gossip, and the most sociable to boot, so if I wanted my advertising idea to go to plan, she was the best place to start. She struck me as the kind of dwarf that would talk for hours if you got her started.

"Thanks for telling us all this Aqua," I gave her the best smile I could muster with my middling charisma, "we're hoping that we can fit in here, especially Balin." I gave her a wink and she tittered.

"Oh, Annie has been pining, so I think the boss won't have any choice in the matter!"

"Hah! Yes, I remember when my... friend's daughter was like that. It was impossible to tell her no!" We both laughed at Balin's expense, and he turned around to study the paintings on the wall. That didn't stop us from spotting his red cheeks and we laughed a little harder. Eventually though, Aqua turned her attention to me.

"What about you, Peter? Are you going to ask the boss to hire you too?"

"Yes, I hope so. I'm actually a Titled [Alchemist], and I almost have my first Specialisation."

"Really?! Annie didn't mention that!"

I nodded. "I earned it by tinkering with powders, but my real love is brewing."

Aqua chewed her lip. "The boss could use another hand. Annie helps a lot, but it's hard with just the two of them and the hired hands." She bobbed her head slightly and continued. "My dad is a hard worker, and he's got Tiara's Blessing, but he doesn't have any Abilities to help with brewing."

"Well, if Mr. Goldstone needs a hard worker, Balin over there is the hero of the City of Minnova mine! He's a Titled [Knight] and he saved a dozen dwarves from a stoneant attack."

"What!?"

"Oh yes, indeed! He's even got shining armour! I told him to sweep Annie off her feet, but he's too shy." I whispered the last in a faux sotto-voce.

Aqua leaned in conspiratorially, her eyes sparkling. "Goodness, I'd pay gold to see that!"

"Yer gonna pay fer this later, Pete," Balin groaned.

I studiously ignored him. "It's alright. We have quite a lot of gold coming in from our project." Eventually, but she didn't need to know that.

"Annie mentioned that, can you talk about it?"

"Perhaps over a drink..." I said, waggling my eyebrows.

"Of course! I can't take you into the brewery itself, but you can come into the tasting room and have a drink. We use it as a mess hall." She led us to another side door and opened it, motioning us inside. The inside of the room had a few picnic style tables and a giant mural of a drunk goat on one wall.

I glanced up at the cock-eyed caprid. "You know, I've been wondering why this place is called the Thirsty Goat..."

"Oh, that's because of Penelope-the-Five-Hundred-and-Fourth."

"Penelope-The-*What*?"

"Over there. Come say hello, Penelope!"

That was precisely the moment that a waist high, pure white unigoat rammed me in the gut.

"Oooh..." Aqua hissed. "Sorry, that's just how she says hello."

Maaaaah!!! [Translated from Prima Donna Goat] "Prithy who art thou, trespasser?!"

All I could do was bleat back.

CHAPTER FORTY-FIVE
MEET THE GOLDSTONES

"Dad, this is Balin and Pete. The two I told you about."

Aqua had let us hang out in the mess hall until the whole brewery arrived for dinner. Penelope had been escorted back to her pen while I nursed my injured dignity.

The dwarf in front of us was clearly Annie's dad. I'm not just saying that because Annie was standing there calling him 'dad.' Just like Annie, he had a flowing blonde beard, though he had a small tie at the bottom. His head was shaved clean with a short blonde mohawk and a series of tattoos. He was dressed in fine white linen and practical leathers. He was the tallest dwarf I'd seen so far and had muscles on top of his muscles. If he flexed, he was liable to take out a window when the buttons on his shirt exploded off.

I was happy he was even willing to meet us. No father is going to be over the moon when their daughter comes home from what was essentially prison and says, "Daddy, I met the nicest man in jail and we're going to be married and I'm going to have his babies and he and his crazy amnesic buddy are going to come stay at our house!"

Balin and I were going to have to tiptoe carefully for the next few weeks.

"Nice to meet you, Mr. Goldstone." I held out my hand. He looked at it and then took it in his meaty appendage. He squeezed, but it was a companionable grip rather than the expected bone-crushing crunch of a future father-in-law. I had expected a bit more... vim.

"So, you're the 'reformed dwarves' my Annie met in the mine?" His voice was a deep bass, gravelly but warm.

"Yes, sir. We don't deny it. Balin and I had a rough start to our time here in Minnova, but Annie really helped us turn our lives around. We owe her and the city of Minnova a lot, and we want to show it with the sweat of our brows." I glanced at Balin and widened my eyes slightly.

"Er, aye, sir! I'm Balin." Balin opened a white knuckled fist and held out his hand as he spoke, his voice unsteady. "I-I'm truly fathered ta meet the honour she talked so much about!"

I twitched, but Goldstone's gaze softened.

"She talked about me, did she?"

"Aye, sir. She's right proud of her pap. Told me all kinds of stories about how happy she was havin' ya as a dad while she grew up." Good Balin!

Goldstone stood a bit straighter and puffed out his chest.

"Said she was proud ta be a brewer, and I said there was nothin' I'd like to do more than help her succeed at that dream." Balin grew calmer as Goldstone's appreciative tone penetrated his terror. He'd been a total mess when we hashed out his opening speech together. He thought he'd stumble over it, or that Goldstone wouldn't appreciate prevarication. I told him that no dad would turn down hearing about how much his daughter gushed about him.

Balin continued, "She said ya were a Dwarf with an honour none could match. She also said no dwarf could match ya fer tha stinkiest breath in Minnova."

Nooo!!! Off script, Balin! Off script!

Goldstone stared at Balin and I awaited some kind of reproach, but instead he patted Balin's shoulder and roared with laughter.

"She always hated how much I love pickled fish!"

"I'm a fan of it meself!"

"Oh really? What's yer favourite?"

"I'm partial to King's Kippers."

"Ha ha! A man of taste!"

I stared incredulously at Aqua, who simply shrugged. Annie held her face in her hands. This was our first introduction to 'The Boss' – Mr. Jeremiah Goldstone.

"So ya want to be a brewer, do ya?" Goldstone held up a mug full of the Thirsty Goat's finest True Brew. Which was to say, not that great. They didn't make Light Brew at all, which was my preferred dwarven poison.

"Not me, sir. I want to work as a labourer and carpenter." Balin toasted him and the two took a drink. The rest of us clinked our mugs in the middle and sat down at the oversized picnic table.

Goldstone rubbed his beard. "That could be useful. Do you think an extra hand would help, John?"

He turned to regard another pair of dwarves that had joined us in the mess hall. We all sat at a single table, and Aqua had brought in a couple cans of pickled herring to munch on. Balin and Jeremiah were happily digging in while the rest of us held in our gag reflex.

"It's getting a bit much fer just me, Johnsson and Richter." John was quite similar in features to Jeremiah, which made sense for cousins. He was less muscley, and his hair was in a braid, but other than that, they both really had the Viking motif down pat.

"Aye, Boss." Johnsson was the splitting image of his father, though he had gentle blue eyes to his father's harsh green gaze. His beard had the shine of product in it, and I think I spotted some eye-shadow. "The hours are getting difficult, and with most of the other workers gone, it's gonna be hard to keep up with the celebration."

"Ay agree." A deep bass echoed agreement, and we all turned to regard the last to join the group. Richter was a giant of a dwarf, and his beard and hair were a massive mop of dreadlocks. His skin was a dark brown, almost black, and he spoke with something like a cross between an African and a Spanish accent. "Tha work is too much with just da tree of us, Boss. I've been tryin' ta do some of da repairs on da barrels, but I'm no carpenter."

Jeremiah's eyes grew cloudy. As a former businessman, I knew that look. Money troubles, and bad ones. The walls were repaired, and sales ongoing, but the general feel of this place set off all my small-business-owner alarm bells.

After a moment Jeremiah put forward, "I could ask Tom to help in the Brewery."

"That's a bad idea," Annie put in. Jeremiah turned to face her as she continued. "Tom is almost always busy dealing with orders, supplies, and management. If you pull him away from that it will hurt more than help. He's so busy he doesn't even have time to eat." She gestured towards an empty spot and everyone nodded.

"Speaking of which. Did your father hear anything from Master Oak about the repairs?" Jeremiah aimed this question at Aqua, who sat at attention instantly.

"I did! The price he quoted was far too much. He said, 'Sorry, but with the octa-millennial coming up my time is at a premium.'"

All the dwarves around the table except Balin and I groaned. We both looked around in confusion. Annie filled us in.

"Preparations for octa-millennial celebrations are swamping all the local guilds and craftsmen. Everything is far more expensive than usual, which is a... problem."

Balin nodded. "If it's some simple barrels, I can do it."

Jeremiah's shoulders slumped, though it was hard to tell with his massive delts.

"That would save our lives, Balin. You've arrived just in time, thank you. Welcome to the team." He smiled broadly at Balin, who choked as he inhaled a kipper.

"Really Daddy? Can he stay?" Annie's face beamed with joy. Jeremiah glanced at his daughter and patted her on the head.

"You like him, and that's enough for me."

I call bullshit.

"I call bullshit," John said. "Just last week you were... er." He glanced at Balin, apologetically. "Something changed your mind, what was it?"

Jeremiah shrugged. "Captain Morris."

Oh. Ooohhh! A piece clicked into place.

"I'm guessin' you spoke to him recently?" I asked.

"That I did. He's a drinking buddy of mine" Jeremiah grinned widely. "He had a lot to say about you two!"

"Wait, what is he talking about?" Annie asked.

"Oh, dear Gods, can I tell her?" Aqua practically squealed.

"Tell her what?" Johnsson asked.

"It's nothin' really." Balin blushed into his mug.

"Balin did a thing," I said.

"A thing?" Annie raised an eyebrow.

"It was a big thing." Jeremiah nodded.

"Ay think ya can do away wi' da suspense, Boss." Richter pointed a finger at Jeremiah.

"Fine. Spoilsport. Morris says Balin was instrumental in saving the lives of over a dozen dwarves. He gained a new Title in the middle of a crisis and held off an entire army of stoneants nearly by himself." Jeremiah's grin took up nearly half his face. "They're calling him a hero in the guard house."

"WHAT!?!" Annie roared. The rest of the table – except Aqua – looked on in shock, while I nodded smugly.

"So yes, I'm fine with him working here. He's proven his dedication and willingness to do right. You on the other hand..." Jeremiah turned to look at me and I gulped, but I sat straight and held my head high.

"Balin is my brother. You don't need to feel obligated to hire me on, but I am a Titled [Alchemist], and I do have some experience with brewing."

Jeremiah raised an eyebrow. "Annie said you've been suffering from amnesia."

"Yes, sir. I honestly don't remember a lot about people, places, or things, but I can remember a lot about brewing. I'd be happy to prove it to you."

"You understand that our brewing is a family secret. The fact that you have knowledge of brewing makes me trust you *less*, not more." Jeremiah's gaze turned stormy. It was a storm I'd weathered before. Jeremiah had nothing on the Canada Revenue Agency.

"I do, sir, but I place my beliefs in *people*, not Titles or memories. Right now, Balin and Annie are the two dwarves nearest to my heart, and I'd do whatever it takes to help them."

Jeremiah looked deep in my eyes, and I met them unflinchingly. After a moment, he nodded. "Morris told me about that gnome lass you saved. I'll give you a chance, but you only get *one*."

It was a beautiful day.

The birds were singing – there were no birds here.

The sky was blue – there was no sky.

The grass was green – the grass was brown scrub.

I had a beautiful woman by my side.

"Aaron's Arse! Penelope, stop trying to eat my pants!"

I shooed away the frisky goat and continued doing what I was apparently cursed by the Gods to spend my eternity doing.

Shovelling goat shit.

I hummed a little *Highway to Hell* as I dodged a headbutt to my crotch – I was getting good at that – and started up the hose. Penelope made a graceful pirouette over the water as I aimed at her.

Maaaah! [Translated from prima donna goat] "You missed me, peasant."

"What's that, Penelope? You want me to give you a bath!?" I placed a thumb over the hose, spraying it out in a wide arc. The water doused the pure white goat and she bleated in horror. She shook herself off and pawed the ground.

MeeeHEEH!!! [Translated from prima donna goat] "Insolence! I shall have you beheaded, varlet!" She lowered her head and charged.

I think I saw Annie walk by shaking her head, but I didn't care – I had to show this stuck-up nanny-goat who was boss around here. I rushed forward and met Penelope's charge head on. We met with a *bang!* in the centre of the little goat pen in the back of the brewery. Did you know dwarves have hard heads, especially when they're wearing a helmet? Penelope didn't. Her single curled horn bounced off my steel skullcap and she reeled backwards.

Bleeeh!!! [Translated from prima donna goat] "Treachery! You are a gifted jouster!" She stumbled back and stared at me unsteadily.

I decided to seal the deal. I had prepared carefully for this day. After a solid week of shovelling shit and taking shit, I had decided the time had come to put this pampered princess in her place. I reached behind the fence and pulled out a bag and a tankard.

"Want to make peace over some goat treats and beer, Penelope?"

Her eyes sparkled as she stared deep into my own. Our souls briefly touched, and in that moment, we understood each other. Guy to goat, caprid to cicerone.

Maaaah. [Translated from prima donna goat] "Truly, I was mistaken. I recognize you now as a man of culture!"

"Penelope!"

Meeehaa! [Translated from prima donna goat] "Peter!"

We met in the centre of the pen – this time in a hug. I pulled her tight, tears in my eyes. She bleated happily and ate my cravat.

"Yearn's Yams, are ya romancin' tha goat, Pete?"

"Bugger off, Balin."

I resumed my work and was soon mopping up the last of the mess. I needed something more to do than menial chores or I was going to go mad. I'd pitched my ginger pop to Jeremiah, but he wasn't going to do anything with my ideas until I proved myself. As soon as I was 'allowed onto the brew floor' we'd talk. I could try and do something with the ginger pop myself, but I really wanted to do it as part of this brewery, dammit!

Problem was, I wasn't really part of this brewery until my probation was over, which could take months. It was months I wasn't willing to spend, not while beer was still stuck in the mire of dwarven tradition! It was time for drastic measures, so I went and found Balin during my break. Penelope happily capered behind me as I stalked through the mess hall. Balin was carrying a bunch of planks and whistled while he worked. I'm glad he fit in so well, and honestly, I really liked everyone here. They were all quite welcoming, and we got along great, but I was still kind of an outsider. If my plan succeeded, that would hopefully change. "Balin, we need to talk."

"Hey, Pete. I see you've made up with Penelope."

"Oh yes, we're best friends now. Which is why she'll do this for me. Say hello to Balin, Penelope." I grabbed Balin's beard and Penelope butted him in the knees, knocking him to the ground. She *maaaah*-ed cheerfully over his head while I sat on his chest to keep him from running off.

"Ow! What was that for, Pete!?"

"I know you and Annie have been keepin' secrets. You're terrible at it. Spill!"

"I don't know what yer talkin' about." Balin's eye's shifted slightly up to the left and his voice rose an octave.

"You can't lie to your brother, Balin. You don't have it in you. I know it's about the brewery's finances, now give it!" Jeremiah had been spending more and more time in his office with Annie, and I knew a shipment of bad beer had been returned. Things weren't looking good, but I wanted to know just *how* bad.

"So, ya knew." Balin's eyes filled with pain. "I would have told ya, Pete, but Annie asked me not to. The brewery's got maybe a month left before tha bills are too much."

I whistled. "I guessed as much. Don't worry about it too much, Annie has the right to protect her father's secrets. What matters is what you and I know but they don't."

Balin's eyes widened. "That's right! *You!*" He lowered his voice. "Yer from *another world*! Do ya have any ideas ta save us?"

"I just might!" I gave my widest smile and held up a sheet of paper. "We're going to win a drinking contest."

CHAPTER FORTY-SIX
GAMBLIN' DWARF

"You see, Balin, the main ways to earn money quickly are stealing, winning the lottery, or gamblin'. We already won the lottery with gunpowder, but all the advance went to our indenture. That leaves us with stealing and gamblin'."

"I think yer gamblin' here, Pete."

"Naww, I disagree. I have a monstrously high vitality, and dwarven ale doesn't affect me much. I'm nearly guaranteed to win this competition, which makes it practically stealing." I grinned at Balin, who simply shook his head.

"It says here ya needed to sign up yesterday."

He pointed to a slip of paper, which read:

Barck's Bounty Beer Brawl:

A drinking competition sponsored by the Lord of Minnova
In cooperation with Minnova Casino and the City of Minnova

The first ocata-millennial Crack Drinking Competition approaches!
Who will we send to represent Minnova?
Compete with Minnova's best and prove your worth!
Top three will go on to represent Minnova at the Capital.
The last one standing wins!

First Prize: 72 Mithril
Second Prize: 12 Mithril
Third Prize: 12 Gold

Inquire at Minnova Casino for more information.
The competition will take place on the 8th Day of the 2nd Month, 7998.
All entry forms must be completed by the 32nd Day of the 1st Month, 7998.

Currency converted at twelve copper to a silver, twelve silver to a gold, and twelve gold for one shiny-blue mithril coin. For small purchases, there were tiny bits of melted and misshapen copper coins called *bits*. A single silver had roughly the same buying power as a ten-dollar bill back home. That meant the first prize was over one-hundred *thousand* dollars.

I held up a copy of my completed entry form for Balin to see. "I signed up earlier this week. I read about it on the Adventuring Guild notice board – neat place by the way. I've been thinkin' about it all week."

Balin read over the form. "There's a fifty-silver entry fee!?"

"Yep. I used my own money, so don't worry about it." Fifty silver could go a surprisingly long way in a mediaeval society if you were willing to subsist on nothing but erdroot, bread, and beer. I didn't want to subsist on erdroot, bread, and beer, dammit.

"Don't worry about it!? Pete, we may need that silver soon!"

"No, we need it *now*. You need to spend money to earn money, Balin. Any capitalist could tell you that."

He sighed and scratched his head. Balin had mellowed a lot over the last week. He'd achieved his short-term goal – meeting Annie – and the next step was to obtain her family's approval for a courtship. Right now, things were too up in the air for that conversation to happen. Speaking of which!

"Listen, Balin. If we earn enough money to save the brewery, think about what that will mean for Mr. Goldstone. We could probably skip right past the 'Are you a good match for my Annie?' step and jump straight to 'Will you please marry my daughter you marvellous bastard?' step."

I had several reasons to be so confident. I'd noticed that drinking was social rather than competitive, and dwarves mostly drank to enjoy the taste and experience of the beer. I'd asked around, and apparently drinking competitions just weren't a thing – chugging was disrespectful to the beer. On the other hand, people back on Earth were competitive about everything, and beer drinking was an art. Some of my techniques were unheard of, at least according to my discrete questioning of Aqua.

I could see Balin wavering. "I dunno, Pete. I don't want it to look like I'm buyin' her."

I gave it one last push. "Balin, Annie will be crushed if the brewery goes under. She still feels that the current situation is entirely her fault. Tell me you won't do whatever it takes to help achieve her dreams?" I barely kept my voice from oozing schmooze. There was no *real* need to convince Balin here, but I wanted him on board. He would be loath to accept a 'handout' from me unless he was involved in the enterprise somehow.

Balin nodded a few times. "Ya know what," His voice grew firm, "yer right, Pete. I was even thinkin' of goin' to tha dungeon and earnin' gold that way. If ya think you can win, we should do it."

"You're in?"

"Aye, let's do it."

"Good, because I need you to go get every penny you own and bet it on me."

"WHAT!?"

On the day of the competition, we left early to buy me some semi-formal clothes. We made some polite excuses about 'goin' on a walk' to Aqua – which was true – as we left the building. I wanted to look good, but still be comfortable. I'd done a lot of drinking competitions in my time, and even won some of them too. I knew all the tricks, and one of them was an expanding waistband. I didn't want to limit myself with a big belt, and dwarven outfits almost always had rigid armour accoutrements like a heavy leather belt or girdle.

So I got a comfortable set of dark brown pants with a simple slip tie knot. They had the pinstripes that were the current height of fashion, as well as some leather greaves and deep pockets. The shirt was a soft white linen with three buttons at the top and a small ornate plate over the heart. The suit jacket was dark brown and a bit more armoured, though only with simple leather vambraces and shoulder guards. The usual cravat was replaced with a fashionable leather gorget that was more of a weird tie than an actual armour piece. All told, it was the least armoured I'd been since I arrived in Minnova.

"I don't like goin' without armour," Balin muttered. He wore his good armoured suit, which Aqua had kindly starched and ironed for him. He was quite snazzy in it, and I think I spied Annie nabbing him and dragging him off to a dark room when he'd first worn it into the brewery.

"Are you serious? You have an Ability that grants you armour anytime you need it."

"Aye, but that'll only work once."

"You only need it once!"

"Still...."

"You look fine, and besides, nobody is going to attack us at a casino."

Balin silently stared at me. I stared back. I began to gently and desperately shake my head 'no,' and he made a slightly sad face and shook his head 'yes.'

"Nooo nonono.... please tell me there won't be fighting. It's a fancy casinooo..." I moaned.

"There'll probably be a brawl at some point, Pete. How long have ya been a dwarf now? How often did Grim's whinin' ever stop us from havin' a row?"

"I just thought things would be civilised at such a distinguished venue..." I had to stop a slight whine from entering my voice.

"Oh, it is. You'll get a pair of silver knuckledusters to tha back o' tha head instead of plain iron ones."

"I'm glad I have *you*, then."

"You'll be fine. Ya always could handle yerself in tha mine!"

"You may have missed it, Mr. Born Fighter, since you were always in the thick of it. I spent most brawls hidin' under Opal's skirt."

"Ooooh, I hope Bran never finds out. He'll be right mad at ya." Balin winced.

"It's a figure of speech, Balin. Opal doesn't even wear skirts."

Evening arrived, and we made our way to the casino. Between the two of us we'd collected just under twelve gold to bet. I still had about half my initial hundred-odd silver, and we'd earned quite a bit more from our work at the Brewery. We wanted to work for plain room and board, but Jeremiah refused, saying 'free work' had no real value. Balin and I were pretty sure Annie and Jeremiah would try to stop us from using our gold this way, so we'd kept it under wraps. It would be a nice surprise for them later!

The casino itself was one of the very few multistorey buildings in the city. Anything over a single storey seemed to be limited to official city structures, religious buildings, or clock towers. It made for rather easy navigation, as landmarks were simple to spot. The casino was a beautiful beige-granite castle-like edifice, with light shining out of nearly every nook and cranny. There was so much obvious magic and power on display that it practically hurt to look at it.

I'd come by earlier for my entry form but hadn't really explored. I'd taken to staying indoors and chatting with Aqua while I worked myself to the bone in the brewery. She was an absolute landmine of information. Not a goldmine, since I had to pay incredibly close attention to every word I said around her. Aqua was a Blessed of Midna and had access to [Truespeech] which gave her some small insight into truth and lies. It wasn't a true lie detector, but it provided a bit of context for why so many dwarves were straight-laced. It was a survival strategy for dealing with a sizable population of empaths.

Out of curiosity, I'd asked Aqua if human society was similar. She'd claimed human society was simply so fast and loose, and humans so capable of self-deception, that trying to separate fact from fiction was impossible. I filed that under 'make my own judgements later.'

Balin and I joined the throng entering the casino. We were swept alongside armoured sequined dresses, mithril plate, and black leathers until we were brought before a couple of guards. They looked us over, pronounced us acceptable, and then let us in.

If you've never been inside a casino before, they're almost always a giant open room. That provides the perfect acoustics to hear when someone wins big. The idea is that it fosters a feeling of shared excitement.

It's also really loud and crowded.

There were tables filled with dwarves everywhere. There were dice games, roulette games, some kind of peg games, tumble games, and a lot of other games I'd never seen before. There was an abundance of beer, a notable lack of cards, and at least two ongoing brawls.

A cat scurried underfoot, and I lifted my leg to let it pass. Barck's Beard those things were *everywhere*.

"Balin, where are the card games?" I had to exercise my self-control to keep from yelling at the top of my lungs just to be heard. I'd figured a few games of blackjack or poker would help cool my nerves. An easy win was in the bag, but performance jitters were completely normal. Not that my wife had ever complained about my performance.

"Why would ya want cards in a gamblin' hall?" Balin asked, confused. "'Please accept my condolences that ya' lost all yer gold?' 'Congratulations on bein' a lucky bastard?'"

My eyes widened. "Wait, you're saying that playing cards don't exist?"

"What dwarf would want ta' bet on paper? The only thing worth bettin' on is cold, hard, cash!"

Literally cold and hard! Every table and every game seemed to involve the use of gems. There was a roulette that had a pair of diamonds rolling around in it. One brightly lit game had gems of different cuts falling down pins. They flashed and twinkled like the gamblers' starstruck dreams, before landing in a slot that said, "House

Wins." A few games of cups were ongoing with dwarves trying to guess which cups had what gems hiding beneath.

"Dear Gods, It's nothing but gems!" I filed *playing cards* into my valuable innovations pile alongside *chess*, *go*, and a myriad of other games. "What are people supposed to compete in?"

"Dice, mostly. Have ya' ever played Liar's Dice?"

"Aye, the drinking game version mostly." Liar's dice was a fun little game that was easy to play, but hard to master. Each player got a cup and six dice to play with. You'd spin the dice inside the cup and then plant it upside down on the table, trapping the dice underneath. You were allowed to look at the dice under your cup, and then had to state how many of a specific number of dice were likely to be under all the cups at the table. For example, I might say "I think there are three fours under all the cups at the table. The next person could either call a 'bluff' or had to increase the chosen number or the number of dice, say to 'four fours' or 'three fives.'

There were a few monkey wrenches. Sixes counted as any number, and the dealer would always throw a cup of six dice down as well, but didn't need to guess. Additionally, if you called 'bluff' or if someone called 'bluff' on you and you were wrong, you lost a die. Dwarven dice seemed to be large cut gems, but it was otherwise what I was used to.

"Do you want to play a round? Ooh, is that Yahtzee!?" I asked. It would probably help my nerves to do something I was used to. I wasn't *nervous*, but I was anxious about bringing home the bacon. Mmm.... Baaacon.

Balin shook his head and pointed towards an enormous sign that read, 'Drinking Competition.' "I don't want ta chance ya gettin' knocked out. Let's head over, Pete."

"Alright, time to go win a hundred mithril." I rubbed my hands together and strode confidently towards the stairs.

"Seventy-two."

"Same difference!"

CHAPTER FORTY-SEVEN
THE COMPETITION BEGINS

The competition banner hung over an enormous spiral staircase that led deep underground. Balin and I followed the throng down into the deep as we circled the granite stairs. We were preceded by a string of red arrows that read, "Colosseum This Way."

"Balin, is there really an entire colosseum under the casino? Nobody told me about it when I signed up."

"Aye, a big one. People bet on fights there." He answered. "They use it fer other events too, like this drinkin' contest."

"Fights like dwarf versus dwarf, or monster killing?"

"Both. There's magic on it ta keep fighters from takin' mortal wounds."

"Well, that's... neat." I didn't know if the thought of bloodsports being popular made me sick to my stomach or excited.

"Besides, nobody even really gets hurt, since the casino has their own [Healer] on staff, and he's real strong too."

I eyed him with sudden suspicion. "How do you know all this? I thought you were new to Minnova, too."

Balin shuffled his feet. "I came down earlier. I was thinkin' of competin' here to make money fer tha brewery."

"It would probably be safer than the dungeon." My thoughts drifted back to the mine. "Could the casino [Healer] help Lillyweather?"

Balin shook his head. "Nah, you'd need a [Healer] with a Specialisation fer bringin' back limbs. None a' those in all of Crack, as far as I know."

"But there might be."

"Aye, maybe in Kinshasa, but more likely Copperpot will get her a good magic prosthesis."

"Wait, that actually sounds awesome! Like a hand that could fire magic blasts?" I mimed a certain red-armoured superhero.

"Aye, and more. A lot of adventurers end up gettin' em." He pointed around the crowd, and now that I was looking for it, I could see a lot of heavily armoured and muscled dwarves with silver, gold, or brass limbs that I'd initially taken for armour. With a closer inspection they looked like cyborg limbs from a movie, with properly moving musculature and everything.

"Do adventurers ever get them on purpose?" I could imagine a metal limb would be a massive advantage if it packed enough magic.

"Sometimes." Balin nodded. "Usually it's like Lillyweather, and they lost an arm or leg to a monster. There's a lot o' competition between magic engineers, tryin' ta make 'em better an stronger."

"I'm going to go out on a *limb* and say that engineers competing in a magic *arms* race are *humerus*?"

"No."

"Do they cost an *arm and a leg*?"

"Please stop."

The colosseum was in an enormous cavern under the casino. It looked a lot like the colosseum in Rome – circular with a ton of arches. The walls above and around us were covered in beautiful stone and crystal formations. I'd seen pictures of crystal caves on the internet, and it looked a lot like that. The crystals were all a solid white, but lights had been set up to dye them silver and gold. When combined with the marble stone of the colosseum it made for a really rich backdrop.

I looked around and spotted my quarry.

"Balin, the betting booths are over there. Go put all our gold on me to win."

"Are ya sure, Pete? I've never done any drinkin' competitions meself, but there's gotta be some real competition."

"They briefed me when I signed up, so I know what to expect. There's a knockout round to start where everyone competes to drink a beer as fast as possible with no spillage. The top hundred do it again, then the top fifty. The top ten move on to the actual competition later tonight. I practised last week and it seems I still have my old skills from Earth, and I was no slouch."

Which was odd, come to think about it. Some of that had to be muscle memory and these were all new muscles. Maybe my spirit was affecting my body and vice versa? That could explain the high alcohol tolerance too.

"I dunno.... I've heard a good drinker can put away a jug of beer and not even feel it." Balin frowned.

"Well, Balin, I could drink two jugs and not even feel it. Let me tell you my regular drinking competition routine. Last night, I drank a ton of water. That got me nice and hydrated, and also expanded my stomach. For breakfast today I had a couple glasses of beer, enough to get tipsy, alongside a heavy breakfast of yoghurt, eggs, and your horrible fish."

"What!? Yer' already drunk!? Aaron's Arse, Pete!" Balin clutched his coin-purse and held it tight, clearly having second thoughts about betting it all on his crazy brother.

"Let me finish!" I waved him down and continued. "I'm fully sober now, but you can think of the morning drink like priming my body's pump. My liver has been clearin' alcohol out of my system since this morning, so it's ready and raring for more."

"Huh, that makes sense."

"Additionally, tha heavy breakfast will help absorb the alcohol. Then, I have my secret weapon." I leaned over and revealed the contents of my pocket. Balin peaked inside.

"Is that... butter?"

"Shhhhh!!" I clamped my hand over his mouth as I noticed a few dwarves peer curiously in our direction. "It's my secret weapon!"

"What, will ya' rub it on yer' opponent's mug and make him slip and spill?" Balin's voice was decidedly amused.

"Nah, I'm goin' ta eat it."

Balin held his hand over his mouth and turned slightly green. "Urgh, why?"

"It's a secret technique from a country called Russia. Their spies would eat a big stick of butter before going to parties. They'd be able to drink with everyone while still staying sober. The body still absorbs the alcohol, but much slower, which means you get drunk later instead of right away."

I now knew that to be an old wives' tale, but I'd internalised it in college, and the ritual was almost as important as the technique.

"Wow, Pete." Balin raised his eyebrows. "Ya really prepared!"

"I'm not taking any chances. I want that prize, and I want onto the brewing floor. I'm sick of waiting." I thought about it and sighed. "If you're really worried, bet on me getting into the top ten. We'll make a lot less money, but at least we'll cover our bases. Now go and put the money down, I need to get checked in."

We went our separate ways and I headed towards a big sign that said, "Competitors Here."

The dwarf at the entrance led me and three others to the competition grounds. The centre of the arena looked exactly like I expected, with rows and rows of seating overlooking a massive sand floor. There were multiple entrances for gladiators and monsters, as well as various interesting gadgets that I couldn't quite place.

"Ugh. I don't like sand." I grumbled.

There was another sight I'd come to expect from dwarven society – a hundred long picnic-style tables. Each table was packed with dwarves of all kinds, and the atmosphere practically thrummed with anticipation.

Our guide, a black-and-white-armoured dwarf by the name of Urist Mchost, seated the four of us at our respective tables. "The first heat starts in about twenty minutes. You may take the time to prepare or meet with your fellow competitors. Any questions?"

"None from me. Thank you, Uric!" I waved goodbye and turned to face my first competitors. They weren't really anything to look at. Most were wearing some semblance of an armoured suit just like mine, though mine was the only one with an expandable waistline.

Amateurs. This competition was in the money bag.

I pulled out my stick of butter and munched on it. The dwarves around me edged away, and a couple turned green, but I didn't care. I gagged a bit as I swallowed; it had the slightly rancid aftertaste of goat product. I'd searched for regular bovine butter, but the only varieties I could find cost nearly ten times as much as the goat variety.

After another five minutes or so, the stands began to fill with onlookers. I could tell a few were bookies from the way they watched and took notes. Most were family members, based on all the banners and hooting and hollering. There were paper signs, leather signs, solstone-embedded flags, and a gnomish family with a gizmo that let out puffs of smoke that formed the word "Beatbox." The aforementioned gnome, whom I immediately wanted to meet, was seated four tables over from me. I could tell because he pulled out a megaphone and called back to his family. He was middle-aged, and wore some kind of spandex suit, complete with a dozen fans and bottles strapped to his back. A cooling apparatus maybe? I noted him down as a serious competitor.

Some of the other dwarves at my table waved at various people in the stands, and I searched for Balin. Eventually I managed to pick him out of the crowd, and I waved until he waved back.

I started up some small talk with the others at my table. They were reluctant at first, but one fellow – who was clearly already drunk – took me up on the offer. Soon we were all sharing our favourite beer stories and having a grand old time. Most weren't really here for the money, they just wanted to say they'd taken part in the competition to choose Minnova's greatest drinkers. Honestly, I could really get behind that. Some of my fondest memories were hanging out with my buddies at big events like Oktoberfest, and what could be bigger than celebrating a octa-millenium?

"Thar's ma son an' waif." A dwarf named Thatch, who had the

thickest accent I'd encountered so far, pointed to a pair of dwarves sitting in the stands. They waved back at him, and he blew a kiss. "Ma son ain't ten yars auld. Looks laik 'is father 'e do."

"He's going to be so proud when you win this competition." I winked cheekily, and Thatch laughed.

"Nah, I don' 'spect ta win. Just fer fun."

"It's a lot of silver to spend on fun, but it is once in a lifetime." Besides, who was I to talk, considering the amount of money I'd spent over the years on expensive drinks at fancy places that sold subpar alcohol.

"Meh," Thatch shrugged. "Gold is gold."

That floored me. I'd heard the saying used a lot in dwarven society, but this was the first time it'd been used in a fashion that clearly meant 'Gold is *only* Gold.' It was an ethos I'd had closer to the end of my life back on earth, when I could afford to impulse buy expensive stuff, or randomly go on vacation. In my constant struggle for money over the last few months, I'd forgotten what that was like. Hopefully I'd get it back once I was brewing full time.

"ATTENTION ALL COMPETITORS!" My thoughts were interrupted as a dwarf up on a balcony overlooking the arena caught everyone's attention. His voice carried far more than it should have, and I suspected some magic or Milestone was involved. As one, every person snapped their eyes up to look at him. He smiled widely, and continued as the crowd grew silent. "As the Lord of our fair city, it is my pleasure to welcome all of you to the City of Minnova's first champion beer drinking competition!"

The crowd roared its approval, and I focused in on the small figure dressed in red. He wore some kind of ruby encrusted outfit, almost like a crimson version of Elvis's signature suit. He had an enormous black beard, and his eyes actually *glowed*. A trio of steel-clad guards stood on the balcony with him. He swept his hand over the crowd and continued.

"This octa-millenium is special! We celebrate not only the continued prosperity of dwarf kind, but the invention of our Sacred Brew! Even now, the other cities of Crack are scouring their populace for the greatest drinkers among them. They think they stand a chance!"

The crowd booed and jeered at that, and he waited for them to quiet down before he continued.

"But we know the truth! From amongst you, we will find the hidden gem that will show the true might of Minnova! Now, prepare to drink, and MAY THE TREE TOWER!"

The crowd roared back "MAY THE TREE TOWER!" and I joined in the fun. I guessed it to be the town motto, likely based on the motif of the dungeon. I found it interesting how much of the local culture was based around Greentree dungeon. I would have thought there would be some distrust or dislike, but it was clear the city was massively proud of their super-dangerous, death-filled dungeon of doom. It was at that moment that I got another quest. I had been putting off my previous ones, and I was going to need to deal with them soon.

New Quest: Championship Road Part 1/2
You're on the road to becoming the greatest drinker in Minnova. Prove yourself!
Make Top Ten in Barck's Beer Brawl.
Rewards: +0.2 Vitality

Do you accept?
Yes / No

As I accepted the quest a veritable flood of servers entered the arena, each carrying a platter laden with drinks. One came alongside our table and handed a tankard to each of us. He then walked to the head of the table and raised his arm.

"In a moment, I will drop my hand. Each of you will drink your beer as fast as possible. Any spillage will disqualify you. The top drinker at the table will move to the next round."

We all nodded and took hold of our drinks, placing them at our lips. The host looked at his watch, and after a few seconds, dropped his hand.

The technique for fast drinking varies from person to person, but its essence can be boiled down to: don't breathe, and don't swallow. The trick is to expel every bit of air in your lungs and then open your mouth as wide as possible. This opens up a muscle in your throat called the epiglottis, and lets you pour the beer directly down your esophagus and into your stomach. If you can avoid gagging, it allows you to drink incredibly fast. The world record is only one-and-a-half seconds to drink an entire litre of beer. The record for a pint is half a second.

I wasn't that good. It took me almost three quarters of a second to chug the pint.

I slammed my mug down on the table and looked around. Everyone else had barely taken their first sip. A couple of them even stopped and stared at me with wide eyes, though Thatch continued chugging merrily away.

I glanced at the host, who stammered. "The winner of this table is Peter Roughtuff!"

Hail to the king, baby!

CHAPTER FORTY-EIGHT
ALL IN

I said my goodbyes to Thatch, who merrily went up into the stands to sit with his wife and son. He didn't care in the slightest that he'd been the last to finish at our table.

"Guid lachk thar, Pete."

"Thanks, Thatch. Hope you enjoy the rest of the show."

"Dontcha warry. Ay will."

And so, the top one hundred drinkers in Minnova went on to the next round. The staff came out and moved tables around as a grumble of dwarves moseyed around the Lord. All the royals, schmoozing up there while us poor bastards were boozing down here. Thankfully, a bunch of them were moving up to the bookies and handing over large sacks of cash to place their bets. It was time for the big money to hit the table now that the top hundred were chosen.

Speaking of royalty, I hummed a little *Smooth Criminal* while I waited at the sidelines. Based on how that first round had gone, this was indeed practically stealing. I sent a silent thank you to those lords and ladies up there for their generous donations to the 'Get Pete on Brew Duty' fund. Hopefully not too many of them bet on me. Speaking of which, I should have toned down that first round... I'd slow down a bit for round two.

The next round went fairly similarly to the first. A hundred tables were reduced to twenty-five and four competitors were invited to sit down at each one. The drinks were brought out and the same spiel was made. This time the Lord himself – not Jesus, the other Lord – held up his hand and dropped it. Everyone else was so enthralled with watching nobility announce the start that they almost missed it. I actually choked when the dwarfess sitting across from me *swooned* when the Lord flashed us a smile. Thankfully, I kept it down and managed an easy three-second drink. The other dwarf at my table who moved on to the next round was named Jim.

Jim didn't talk much.

I turned to wave at Balin up in the nosebleed section, and he was surprisingly easy to pick out of the now growing crowd.

Because of the massive sign that said, "Go Pete!"

I could juuust make out splotches of blue and blonde on opposite ends of the sign.

Shit. We'd been made.

"You're sure they're up to something?" Annie asked. "I want you to know that I trust Balin unequivocally." Her voice was steadfast, with nary a quaver of doubt.

"I can understand that." Aqua nodded, as the two of them shadowed the pair of well-dressed dwarves just ahead. "But Pete's been super suspicious the past couple days. You must have noticed Balin was talking nearly a whole octave higher all morning."

Annie sighed the adoring sigh of a fiancé. "Yes, I did notice. He's a darling, and completely incapable of hiding anything from me."

"Well, Pete is more than capable of hiding lots." Aqua shrugged and paused to peek around a corner as Pete and Balin continued down the main thoroughfare, completely unaware of their shadows.

"What makes you say that?" Annie raised an eyebrow.

"It's simple!" Aqua waved Annie on and the two ducked behind a stall before they slowly slunk up the street. "Everyone has things they want to hide, and little white lies they tell everyone every day. That's just a fact!"

She began to list examples on her fingers as they waited for Pete and Balin to stop staring at an extremely fancy gnomish contraption that created roadside sugar sticks.

"The dinner is delicious. That dress looks good on you. Of course, we're best friends. I'll be home on time. I'll always love you."

"Ow." Annie winced at the last one. "You can tell when people lie about that? That feels more like a curse than a Blessing."

"You learn to live with it." Aqua shrugged. "Culturally speaking, we're pretty good with being blunt most of the time. If you hate something Balin is wearing, would you just tell him?"

"Absolutely. I want him to look as good as I think he looks!"

"See? I don't run into trouble with most of our kinsmen, because they usually tell me straight. The lies are still there, but they're small."

"Well, that's good, isn't it?"

"We're also partial to throwing punches when the honesty is a bit *too* straight."

"So? That's good too!"

"If you like a good scrap, Annie, but not everyone does!" The two of them ducked behind a cart as Balin glanced in their direction. "The people I trust the least are those that don't tell any lies at all."

A few dwarves gave them curious looks, and Aqua shooed them away.

"What?" Annie said, confused. "That doesn't make sense. Why would the most honest people be the most suspicious?"

"Because they're weasel-wording around my Blessing, which means they're trying to keep a secret. The fewer lies they tell, the bigger the secret. Pete *never* lies. He's hiding something *big* and I want to find out what it is!"

Annie chewed her lip. "Do you think it's a threat to the brewery? Should I just ask Balin?"

"I don't know. It might cause a rift, given how close those two are. That's why we're doing this. That's odd..."

"What? Wait, where did they go!"

"They just went into the casino. Quick, let's follow!"

Balin jingled the gold in his pocket as he waited in line to bet. He was uncomfortable putting so much money on a gamble, but then he'd never been the gambling type. Pete was absolutely certain though, and last time that had paid off with dividends.

Balin really hoped this went well. He didn't want to see Annie lose hold of her dream. But if it did happen, he'd be there for her. He already knew what it meant to lose everything, and people hurt the most to lose. They'd survive if the brewery closed, and maybe even find something else. Pete did have that ginger pop thing, and they probably didn't need to be part of the Brewers Guild to make it! Life would go on.

"What are you thinking about, Balin?" A feminine voice asked beside him.

"Oh, I was just thinkin' that no matter what happens, we'll be okay, Annie." He turned and smiled at the most beautiful dwarf in the entirety of Crack. The flowing gold of her beard always gave a warm feeling in his heart, and the crinkles at the sides of her eyes when she smiled were the brightest part of his day.

"That's nice. What're you doing here?"

"Pete's lookin' ta win tha competition so we can save tha' brewery. I'm puttin' our gold down..." He trailed off.

"Yes?"

"Annie, is that really you? I'm not hallucinatin'?"

"Oh, yes."

"That Aqua beside you?"

"Uh huh!" The blue haired little *minx* waved cheerily.

"Uhh..."

"Tell me more about this gold you're putting down."

Annie glowered at the red-faced, lovable goof in front of her. She couldn't believe it. Every penny he and Pete owned, put down on a bet – for *her* brewery! She wasn't sure if she should kiss him or boot him in the rear.

"Secrets, huh?" Annie gave Aqua a *look*.

"Fiiine." Aqua squirmed. "I'm still suspicious."

Annie turned back to Balin. "You said Pete is sure he can win?"

"Aye. It sounded like he's got some good ideas too."

"Why was he so certain?"

"Um. Dunno."

"Lie." Aqua pointed out.

"Durnnit! He's won a lotta drinkin' competitions and thinks he's got a good chance." Balin's voice rose a slight octave.

"Truth." Aqua smirked.

"How's that possible, Balin? The only drinking competition I know of is this one, and my family provides the beer to nearly a tenth of the city. Well, used to provide." Annie grimaced at the thought.

"Um... Uh... I – I cannae..."

"Is it something Pete asked you to keep a secret?" Annie asked. Her heart reached out at his obvious distress. Balin truly was a terrible liar.

"Aye..." Balin deflated, giving her a piteous look.

"Oooh, tell us!" Aqua moved in closer, and Annie stomped on her foot. "Owieee!!"

"Alright. We won't push it. Sorry, sweetheart." Annie considered the problem as guilt weighed heavy on her heart. Pete and Balin were willing to bet every penny they had for her future. She had returned that love and sacrifice with suspicion. Well, some of it was Aqua's fault – most of it really, but even so!

Annie reached into her pocket and jiggled her coin purse. She had all the money for next month's bills in there; over ten mithril. Between the interest to the bank for the cost of the walls, the bad beer, and general operations, it would last a month or two at most. She needed at least three months to convince some of the old hires to come back and start up a plan to get people buying their beer again. She was positive she could do it.

She just needed time.

Trust, and time. She made her decision as they were called up to make their bets.

"Give me the gold, Balin."

"Annie, we—" Balin began to protest.

Annie pulled out her coin purse and thumped it on the counter.

"Let's add it to the pile. We're screwed either way, so let's put our hope on Pete. Top ten, right? Aqua, go get a roll of paper. I'll go get some paint. Balin, go get some seats. We have some cheering to do!"

I sweated as Aqua and Annie waved from the stands. We were going to get such a talking to.

I was currently seated with four other dwarves, waiting for the next round to start. The tables had been set up for the final fifty, which meant ten tables of five. The fastest from each table would go on to the top ten.

A dwarf seated at the table beside mine chuckled, a deep bass, "Ho, ho, ho," that brought immediate thoughts of Santa to my mind. He was also built like Santa, with a white beard and jolly red nose. I would describe his figure as... rotund; he was practically a sphere! "Yer distracted, lad!"

"Just a bit." I pointed up at the sign.

"Ho, ho, ho, it's nice ta be loved, isn't it?" He pointed at a small clan of dwarves that were doing the flippy sign thing that happened at football games. A series of wooden panels swapped between red and black to make moving images. They eventually settled on, "Rum Tum Rumbob."

"That it does. Are you Rumbob?"

"Aye, that I am. Nice to meet you. They're here ta see me win this!"

I held out my hand for a companionable shake. "I'm Pete. I'm here ta win this too!"

Indeed, the competition was actually serious now. I could see people going through meditation routines, stretches, and various superstitious rituals. This was a real gathering of weirdos, for sure. It made sense though; drinking competitions weren't really a thing, so any fast and big drinker was going to be different from your average dwarf. If you've never met a Guinness Record holder, they're often just a little crazy. 'Eat the most hot dogs in one minute' wasn't something a fully sane person would attempt.

Beside me, Rumbob began burping a song, and a dwarfess that had introduced herself as "Gemgem" began hyperventilating with an extreme look of concentration.

Yep, a real collection of weirdos. I was probably the only normal dwarf here.

I took another bite of my butter.

The next while was a blur of activity as the hosts came and delivered their amber payloads, and the competitors squared off. Then the Lord killed the mood with a long reverential speech. "The city appreciates," "Generations will remember" and other such nonsense. None of that mattered as much as the moment and the malt. I peeked a glance at Rumbob and we nodded at each other. I could see Beatbox was still in, and Jim looked as bored as ever. This was the moment of truth.

I'd asked a host about the odds on me making it to the top ten, and it was just over three to one. I thought it was high for just top ten, but apparently some of the dwarves in this competition were nobility and other nobles were betting big on them for the sake of solidarity. If I won, we'd go home with over thirty gold. It would be enough to help, but I doubted it would be enough to save the brewery. I'd still need to get first place.

The Lord raised his hand and my attention snapped towards him. I exhaled and opened my mouth wide. A half beat later, he dropped his hand and I poured the tankard directly down my throat.

Bing!

Quest Complete: Championship Road Part 1/2!
Congratulations! You've stepped onto the bottom rung of fame.

Gained 0.2 Vitality! Your new vitality is 19!

New Quest: Championship Road Part 2/2!

You're on the road to becoming the greatest drinker in Minnova. Prove yourself!
Make Top Three in Barck's Beer Brawl
Rewards: [Adjust Taste]

<u>Do you accept?</u>
Yes / No

[Adjust Taste]!? Booya!

CHAPTER FORTY-NINE
SCOUTING THE COMPETITION

Welcome to the WWB! The World's Worst Beer!
Ten people enter.
One winner leaves.
A MATCH FOR THE AGES!!

The 'Goliath,' Rumbob! His jolly "Ho, ho, ho" is the last thing you'll hear before his massive fists POUND you into the floor!

The 'Heartbreaker,' Emerelda! Her green eyes and raven tresses are a trap to catch the eye while she CRUSHES your spirit!

The gnomish 'Demon of Artifice,' Beatbox! Don't let his small frame fool you, his DEVILISH good looks are only matched by his HELLISH intellect!

The 'Basic Bitch Warrior,' Jim! *Pause for effect.*

The 'Pink Panic,' Raspberrysyrup! This adorable gnomess has cooked up a hearty serving of PAIN and it's time for dinner!

The 'Crackian Bear,' Chuck! The MIDNIGHT of his skin is only matched by the BLACK of his heart, but he'll give you the BRUISES to match!

The 'Tiny Tank,' Tania! Heavy armour's her fame and MAKING YOU CRY is her game!

The 'Aptly Named' Brewski! What monster names their child after bad beer? Find out when mummy runs into the ring and DESTROYS you!

The 'Great White' Lord Samuel! You'll learn to respect yer elders after he teaches you a LESSON you'll never forget!

Finally, the 'Cicerone,' Peter Roughtuff! The master of a thousand brews and the CERTAIN champeen!!!!!

YEAAAHHHHH!!!!

The crowd goes wild! Peter! Peter! Peter! Peter!

"Pete?"

Pete! Pete! Pete!

"Pete!"

"Huh, wuzzat?" I turned away from the massive trophy filled with mithril coins that had been set up on the stage. I had pro-wrestling on my mind ever since my conversation with Brock, and I totally needed to go catch a show with him after this business with the brewery was done. Rumbob stood beside me with a big smile on his white-bearded face.

"Ho, ho, ho! Yer distracted again! Are ya planin' to give me an easy win?"

"Fat chance!" Erm... maybe not the best word choice there. "Uh, no chance?"

"Ho, ho, ho! No worry! I am what I am, and I'm proud of what I am. I know you meant no harm, so no Feud required." He winked.

"Phew. Thanks, Rumbob. Yeah, I am a bit distracted. I really need to win this."

"Ahh.. you seek to bring Minnova glory by competin' at the octa-millennial?"

"No."

"Hmm, you desire the fame that comes with bein' the first in all'a history to win this event!"

"Nope."

"You... have spent many years preparin' yer body and mind for this final test and seek to prove your worth to one of the lovely lads or lasses up there?"

"Oh, definitely not. I just want the money."

"Ho, ho, ho! Often the simplest answer is the correct one! Did you truly have such a need that you were willing to be a misfit before the entire city?"

"Aye. My friends really need the money, and I want to prove to them that I have what it takes."

"I can see from their waving and shouting that they already believe that you have what it takes, my stylish competitor." Rumbob pointed up to the stands, where Aqua was singing a cheer song that she must have just made up. My ears coloured with embarrassment, and maybe a little appreciation.

"Woah, woah, woah. Hold on a moment." I dodged out of the way of a builder as he put a couple more finishing touches on the stage. "Did you say 'misfit'?"

"Why yes! I know most of these fine dwarves and gnomes." He pointed towards Beatbox, who waved, as well as Chuck, Emeralda, and Jim. "They are my compatriots – comrades at arms in the art of deep and fast drinking! The pro-drinker's ways are unpopular, though not illegal. This is our chance to shine in the sun and reveal to all the glory of the drinking competition! Ho, ho, ho!"

"Truly a noble goal, sirrah!" I gave him a thumbs up.

"I'm glad you think so!" He gave me an off-kilter thumbs up in return.

The ten winners were killing time on the sand of the arena floor while we waited for the competition to begin. I would have thought there would be a ceremony or some kind of back room for us to relax in, but apparently the organisers and the betting public wanted the maximum number of eyes on us at all times. I felt like a fish in a bowl, and I could feel a cold sweat trickle down the small of my back.

Over a hundred overall and leather-clad workers had descended upon the stadium like a swarm of ants – I shivered at the thought of ants – like a *plague of locusts*. A massive stage with a ring-shaped table appeared. There were ten chairs set up inside the ring, each facing out towards the stands. The stage stretched out to the Lord's box seat, and at its foot, a large podium had been set up for the trophy.

It was all incredibly grandiose, completely overdone, and absolutely magical. I couldn't wait.

"I have to ask, since you know Beatbox, what are all those contraptions on him, and are they legal?"

"Why don't you ask him yourself? Beatbox! Come greet our new friend, Pete!"

The gnome finished strapping on another set of spinning fans and made his way over to where we were standing next to the stage. Like a lot of gnomes, he looked almost childlike, with tiny proportions and big eyes. He also had a large horseshoe moustache and slicked-back grey hair, which made him look like a certain wise-cracking wabbit in disguise; I had to hold back a giggle.

"Heya! Rum-Tum-Rumbob! Looks like my win may not be set in stone!" He shook Rumbob's hand and then turned to look at me. His voice was a rapid-fire alto that I could barely keep up with. "It appears Minnova has a brand-new master degenerate. I saw you throw back that beer like nobody was watching. Amazing stuff! It was practically an art! You'll need to teach me your technique."

"Ho ho, ho, Beatbox! Give the lad a chance to get acquainted first!"

"Aw, you hush up, Rumbob. Your wife and dozen children are all the attention you need. I'm amazed she let you compete. You think she'll actually let you take them all to the Capital if you win? She must be keeping an eye out for any of your neighbours so she can off them before they get the chance to gossip about your depravity."

"Oh?" Rumbob leaned in, his face growing sinister. "I saw that cheering device up there. Aren't you still sanctioned by the Tinkers Guild for the last time? Are you even allowed to do any tinkering? Could I reduce my competition by sending a simple message?"

Beatbox growled. "You wouldn't dare! Besides, my daughter put it together. I didn't have a single hand in it. I'll rat to your [Doctor] about your drinking habits if you even touch a commstone."

"Try me, droopy."

"Ohhh, you'd like that, wouldn't you, henpeck?"

"I'd grind you like malt, shortstack."

The two of them were practically forehead to forehead at this point.

cough "Hello? Excuse me?" The pair turned to look at me, and I waved. "Still here."

"Ho, ho, ho, That you are! Sorry about that Pete, Beatbox and I are old rivals."

"No worries, and I'd love to give you some drinking lessons Beatbox! Come by the Thirsty Goat some evening and I'd be happy to have you!"

"The Thirsty Goat, huh?" Beatbox looked up to where Aqua was currently in a scuffle with a group of dwarves all dressed in pink. "I thought I recognized that blue mop and fiery charm. A shame what happened to them." He and Rumbob both looked at me with pity.

"No worries. I'm here to make sure things get back on track."

"Ah!" Rumbob smacked his fist into his palm. "The money! You plan on puttin' tha mithril towards tha Thirsty Goat? Truly a noble goal! Ho, ho, ho!"

"Indeed! It would be a shame to lose such an excellent ale!" Beatbox nodded. "Now, you have a question?"

"Aye. What's all... this?" I waved my hand, encompassing Beatbox's gadgets.

"My personal perspirators? They're perfectly legal by the letter of the competition."

"So... what do they do?"

"They reduce my internal thermal coefficient while providing adequate dermal hydration."

I parsed that for a moment. "They keep you cool and sweaty?"

"If you want to be pedantic."

"Uh huh. Anyways, anything I need to know about the competition?"

Rumbob clapped me on the shoulder. "An excellent topic of conversation! I know most and can point them out to you!" He pointed to where Chuck, Emerelda, and Jim had gathered to chat. "Chuck there lifts kegs for fun, and likes drinkin' them in one gulp if he can. He's got a mean right hook to watch out for. Emerelda may not be the fastest drinker–"

"Good enough to make the top ten!" Beatbox interrupted. Rumbob rolled his eyes and continued.

"She may not be the fastest drinker in our group, but she can keep going forever. She's also got a head harder than a rock, and she isn't afraid to use it. Then there's Jim."

"Yes indeed, there is Jim." Beatbox nodded.

"What about Jim?" I asked, curious. Perhaps he had some great secret that made him stand out, because Midna's Mullet, that dwarf could *wallflower*.

"He likes beer." Rumbob shrugged. "He's pretty good at not getting noticed."

"I noticed." The three of us laughed as Jim turned to look at us, perhaps having heard his name.

"The others I only know by reputation. Tania over there is a rather famous adventurer, and I'm desperately glad no weapons are allowed inside the ring. She's famous for an insatiable drinking habit and for ending more brawls than she starts. Lord Samuel is an actual stuffed-shirt noble, and he's probably had more kinds of alcohol than every other person in this colosseum combined. He was a fierce colosseum fighter back in his youth, but he retired after old age caught up to him."

"I've seen him drinking one of those human alcohols. I think he may have even had... wine," Beatbox added, with way too much aplomb and emphasis for something like wine. Barck's Beard, I wonder if there's something screwy with the wine here too.

"Those are all the ones I know. Do you have anything to add, Beatbox?"

"There's Raspberrysyrup," Beatbox practically growled.

"She looks nice." I gave the pink-pigtailed gnomess a onceover. She reminded me a lot of that pink-haired little Sailor Scout from back when Sammy had her 'magical-girl' phase. The look was completed by a ruffled dress and a cheerful demeanour.

"Ah, yes." Rumbob's face darkened. "I was trying to ignore her."

I could sense the grim undercurrent. "Why?"

Beatbox pointed up to the stands. "If you look over there, you can see the bodacious blue beauty of Thirsty Goat Brewery beating a posse of pink perfumed posers with their own signs."

"I see that." I made the connection immediately. "They're wearing the same pink! Is that her family?"

"Her hangers-on," Rumbob grumbled.

"Her groupies," Beatbox grumped.

"What's wrong with that?"

"She's not a drinker," Beatbox whined. "She's a [Maestro]."

"Again, what's wrong with that?"

Beatbox stamped his feet, which was absolutely adorable. "Beer is serious business! Our reputation is bad enough without turning drinking into... into –"

"A show?" I raised an eyebrow and waved my hand around the packed colosseum.

"Ho, ho, ho!" Rumbob pulled at his white whiskers. "He's got us there, Beat-boy."

"She's just using her drinking skills to garner fans! It's not – It's not – It's not fair! Dammit, I had to be a closet speed drinker for years and she just... does it out in the open!"

"You're just angry she's prettier and more popular than you are," Emerelda broke in, as she joined us. "Besides, if you're not careful you'll end up sitting with them." She pointed towards a dozen or so dwarves at the front of the stands. They were all in traditional leather and mail armour, and they were carrying placards that had slogans like: "Beer isn't a Game" and "The Sacred Brew Needs You."

"Who're those posers?" I asked.

"The Honourable Guild of Brewers," Rumbob sighed. "They're in charge of all the breweries in Minnova. They're not fans of competitive drinkin'." Ergh, that sounded a lot like Tim. I was nearly guaranteed to butt heads with them at some point.

"Are they powerful?"

"Not really. They take themselves pretty seriously, but their own traditions keep 'em from pushin' their weight around too much. They always stink like onions, too."

"And shortstack sounds just like them!" Emerelda added.

"Yearn's Yams, Emerelda, this was a private conversation!" Beatbox kicked the dwarfess in the shins.

She smiled cheerily and put her hand down on his face, pushing him away. She turned to me, and I was struck by what an absolutely charming permed beard she had. Her eyes sparkled as she looked me up and down. "You're a cut above the rough crowd I'm used to in this field. I'm Emerelda. Nice to meet you, handsome." She held out her hand, and I smiled as I took it.

"I'm Pete. Nice to meet you too. You're a good bit better looking than these two, too."

"Ha, flatterer! Don't let these two try and hoodwink you. Rumbob here is almost impossible to knock over, and those contraptions make

Beatbox slippery and a pain to keep grappled. Rumbob is weak to tickling under his left knee, and Beatbox can't handle having his moustache pulled."

"Hey!"

"Ho, ho, ho! Says the lass with a glass jaw!"

The three friends laughed and jostled good naturedly. The trickle of cold sweat falling down the small of my back was slowly turning into a river.

"Why... why are you all giving me so much advice on how to fight?"

"Didn't ya read tha competition rules?" Emerelda asked.

"Indeed, all the relevant information can be found there." Beatbox nodded.

I pulled out the paper with the competition rules on it and quickly read down to the offending sentence.

'Top three will go on to represent Minnova in the Capital. The last one standing wins!'

"Ho, ho, ho! Surely you realised. It's called a 'Beer Brawl'!"

I stared in shock at the page. Oh, come on! What's in a name?

"Makin' sure yer beer doesn't spill while a gnome is chewin' on yer toes is always the tricky part!" Rumbob continued, incredibly unhelpfully.

Oh, nooo. Where was Doc Opal to hide behind when I needed her!

CHAPTER FIFTY
THE BARCK BEER BRAWL

Okay, Pete, you've got this. It's just a small curve ball!

First, let's run down my stats and Abilities.

[Flesh of Stone] was essentially a second life.

[Flash of Insight] could give me the correct course of action in a pinch.

[Power Pick] would come in handy if I... thought of a mug as a pick? Doubtful, but worth a try.

[Ingredient Scan] wouldn't be much help. I'm still dying to go to the market and test it, which should be possible later this week.

[Strength of All: Held] should help with holding onto my tankard.

The ever awesome [Regeneration] would ensure I couldn't get taken out in one hit.

Finally, my high vitality meant it'd take a lot to knock me out. Then there was this handy dandy new Milestone, courtesy of a Quest that I'd been purposefully avoiding. I pulled up my notifications.

<u>Quest Complete: Prove Yourself!</u>
You may not have demonstrated any prowess, but you put on a good show.

*Gained [**Basic Slash**].*

I've been putting off any thoughts about the stoneant incident, and

I think the only thing keeping me from getting some PTSD has been the absolute rollercoaster of the past week. [Basic Slash] should work fine with any weapon – including a chair – and would likely come in clutch.

[Basic Slash] – *Add an additional four strength to an attack with a melee weapon.*
This Ability can be used once per minute.

It definitely had a heroic feel to it. An awesome Milestone that was practically necessary to become an adventurer.

I also hated it and originally never planned to use it. Balin took to combat like... well, a dwarf to combat, but it just wasn't for me.

Finally, I had a secret weapon that I just couldn't bring myself to use. Opal had been loose in her description of Specialisations. It wasn't that the stuff you were doing at the moment you got your fifth Milestone determined the available Specialisations, instead...

Specialisation Possible!
Please select 5 Milestones to combine into a Specialisation!

You have selected [Otherworlder], [Stabilise Mixture], [Power Pick], [Ingredient Scan], and [Basic Slash].

Merge Milestones?
Yes/No

I hadn't accepted yet, but the option was there. I'd asked Copperpot about it and he'd said most people just went for their Specialisation as soon as they hit five Milestones. A Specialisation was just that powerful. However... the four Specialisation options you'd get were always based on the selected Milestones. In other words, this current set of Milestones was likely to get me some combat-related Specialisations.

I couldn't bring myself to do that. Not with [Carbonate] and now [Adjust Taste] right within reach. If I could get some kind of magic Milestone, that would be even better. But according to Copperpot, stuff like that was more likely to show up after my first or second Specialisation.

"NOW ANNOUNCING THE MAIN EVENT!"

My attention was pulled to a tuxedo-armoured dwarf with a megaphone of some kind standing next to the trophy. I was with the other contestants, kneeling underneath the Lord's box as he imperiously surveyed the coliseum.

"THESE TEN CONTESTANTS WILL COMPETE TO DETERMINE THE GREATEST DRINKER IN ALL OF MINNOVA."

Muh ears!

"THE RULES ARE AS FOLLOWS! THE TEN CONTESTANTS WILL TAKE THEIR SEATS WITHIN THE RING! THE LORD HIMSELF SHALL HIT THE GONG TO BEGIN! FROM THEN ON, THE GONG SHALL SOUND EVERY TEN SECONDS! A CONTESTANT THAT LEAVES THE RING OR IS UNABLE TO FULLY COMPLETE A DRINK WITHIN THOSE TEN SECONDS WILL FORFEIT!"

Alright, there was the trick. If I could keep someone from finishing their drink within ten seconds, they were out. That was actually very beneficial for me, since I could just pound down a drink in one second and then spend the next nine to eighteen seconds dodging.

"LET'S HEAR IT FOR THE TOP TEN!"

The stadium roared, and I do mean ROARED. It sounded like a very happy bomb had gone off. Every seat was packed, and I could barely make out my cheering squad now. The only reason I could pick them out was the giant collection of pink banners sitting behind them. Spoils from the fan wars? Raspberrysyrup kept giving me angry glances, and I tried to ignore them. Not my fault!

The four pro-drinkers, as I'd come to learn they were called – Beatbox, Emerelda, Jim, and Rumbob – glowed with pride. I was happy for them, especially as a newfound cultural appreciation for competitive drinking could be very lucrative for us!

"NOW FOR A WORD FROM OUR TEN CONTESTANTS!"

OY! Nobody said anything about a speech!

Rumbob was first and said some platitudes thanking his family and the Gods for the opportunity. Beatbox was quite the same. The crowd cheered dutifully after each short speech. It was like listening to the Oscars, except these competitors actually meant those thank-yous.

The only standout was Raspberrysyrup, who did a whole song, dance, and pose. Complete with an "I wuv you my adoring fans, make sure to come see my concert next week!" There was a mix of cheers and stunned silence – I was right that advertising wasn't really a thing. She glared at me as she turned off the stage, and I winced as I realised those pink banners up behind Aqua were probably part of her ad package.

Then it was my turn, and my stage fright vanished as I took a deep breath and reached down into my CEO and marketing lizard brain.

"HELLO MINNOVA! ARE YOU THIRSTY!?"

The crowd roared their approval. Good start, good start!

"I HOPE YOU LIKE THE TASTE OF TEARS! BECAUSE YOU'RE ABOUT TO SEE A LOT OF 'EM!"

Laughter, good. This was definitely a crowd that was used to the showmanship of pro-wrestling. I could work with this.

"I HOPE NONE OF YOU PAID FULL PRICE FOR THOSE SEATS, BECAUSE YOU'RE ONLY GOING TO USE THE EDGE!"

More scattered cheers, and then a growing swell of laughter as the crowd got it. The hidden benefit of [Otherworlder] was that all the old jokes were new again!

"I'M PETER ROUGHTUFF, AND I'M HERE REPRESENTING THIRSTY GOAT BREWERY! IF YOU AND YOUR PALS WANT TO DRINK WITH A CHAMPION DRINKER AFTER THE COMPETITION, COME DROP BY THIRSTY GOAT BREWERY, WHERE WE DON'T KID AROUND WITH BEER!"

Unlike Raspberrysyrup's pitch, the crowd wholeheartedly approved of my approach. There was a lot of shouting and raised fists. I pumped my fist as well and pointed towards a shell-shocked little blonde figure up in the stands. Annie waved nervously as the crowd turned towards them and cheered some more.

Bing!

Stat Increased: [Charisma]!

Your charisma has increased by 1! Your new charisma is 12!

Score!

It took a minute for the MC to calm the crowd, and then it was time for the last few speeches. I wasn't really paying attention; I needed to get into the zone.

I pulled out my second-to-last bar of butter.

"Nice speech, Pete," Rumbob sotto-voce'd as we walked down the stage towards our seats.

"Thanks, Rumbob."

"I'll need to come to the afterparty at Thirsty Goat."

"The more champions, the better, Rumbob. Especially when they're going to be drinking with the winner."

"Why, thank you for the support!"

"I was talking about me!" We both laughed as we pulled out our chairs. Rumbob was seated at my left and Brewski was on my right. We were inside the ring of the table, which was about ten metres in diameter; it was fairly big, but not massive. Each seat had an assigned host standing outside the ring with a collection of tankards and a keg. They would be putting a tankard at each spot every ten seconds.

"Barck's Luck, Pete."

"You too."

I took my seat, and we all turned to look at the Lord. He held up his hand and the crowd fell silent. Then he took up a massive hammer in one ruby-gemmed glove and swung it.

GOOONGGG

The crowd cheered, the first tankard was placed before me, and I breathed out, opened wide, and drained it. Then I ducked under the table.

Rumbob's fist flew over my head as Brewski ran through my now ex-chair and plowed into Rumbob.

"[Immovable]!!"

And bounced. The two of them swore in various forms of Godly clothing and body parts, before they met with a crash on top of the wreckage of my chair.

There was a brief pause as they each struggled to gain control of the clinch. Which was exactly when a certain no-good villain cheap-shot Brewski with a [Basic Slash] to the knee. My tankard exploded on his kneecap, and he roared with pain, which gave Rumbob the opening he needed.

Rumbob got Brewski into an armbar then held him tight. Rumbob was massive, and he applied that leverage to keep Brewski in check while he happily downed his first drink. Brewski struggled and swore, but his lonely drink lay just out of reach, undrunk.

GOOONGGG

Rumbob dropped the now despondent Brewski. I snuck a hand out to grab my next tankard, but was arrested as a hand like a vice clamped around my ankle.

"Sorry about this, Pete!" Rumbob yanked me out from under the table and held me upside down. I struggled as he reached over and grabbed his new drink, unphased. He lifted it to his lips just as a hollering Beatbox ran over and tossed a chair our way. Rumbob lifted me up as a makeshift fleshy shield, but I had an escape ready to go.

"[Flesh of Stone]!!"

Rumbob cried out an oath and dropped me as I became too heavy to hold. That oath was drowned out by a howl of pain when my statuesque body fell on top of Beatbox. The two of us crashed to the ground, but I jumped right back to my feet as I ended [Flesh of Stone]. Beatbox stayed down and Rumbob was busy with his drink. I ran back to my spot and downed the beer. Ugh, it was even more sour than usual! Was it the butter affecting my taste buds? No time to think!

GOOONGGG

I ran around the ring, Rumbob on my tail. Up ahead, I saw Jim sitting in his chair and drinking as everyone ignored him. I could feel my wisdom resist the compulsion to look away from him, and I was uncomfortably reminded of Tim. They even had the same name-ish!

Which was why I grabbed the smashed remains of a nearby chair, and called the only war cry I knew as I went in for a [Power Pick].

"Fer Crack and Annie!"

"Did he just yell 'Fer Crack and Annie?'" Aqua asked, as they watched the carnage unfold. The volume was magically amplified to ensure everyone could enjoy the action, and Pete's warcry had echoed through the colosseum.

Pete had done well surviving the first ten seconds; they'd been worried he would be knocked out right away. Two competitors were already down, and Pete was about to take out a third. He might even make the top three at this rate.

Annie had turned pink after Pete's little speech earlier and was slowly turning crimson as sections of the crowd looked their way again. Some titters rose above the general volume of the fighting, and Annie hunched down into her chair.

"Hey! That's my line!" Balin cried, in feigned indignation. "Ouf!"

He doubled over as a fist propelled by desperate embarrassment found his solar plexus.

Jim went down without a sound. It turned out that [Power Pick] worked fine as long as the weapon was pick-like. Such as the back of a chair broken into a basic uppercase 'T.' I turned towards my seat, and realised that... I was too far away. Rumbob had met up with Chuck and the two of them were tussling for control in the centre of the ring, while Tania and Emerelda whaled on each other with their fists. My tankard of beer was way on the other side....

"[Flash of Inspiration]!!" My head ached with the flow of knowledge as my mind considered everything I knew and saw. I'd practised it a bunch recently, and avoided falling over from the shock. The answer came instantly – the rules didn't say I had to drink my own tankard! I reached down, breathed out, and drained Jim's now unattended tankard.

GOOONGGG

"Have at thee, varlet!" A voice to my side wheezed out, and I doubled over as a leg found my gut. The leg was followed up by a fist to the side of my head that bounced off my ornamental skullcap. The attack flowed into a smooth kata, and I realised with horror that Lord Samuel had me in some kind of combo.

"[Expert Combo]!"

I was struck a half dozen times and my head swam as his fist came up to meet my nose. The only thing keeping me up was my high vitality. I thought I heard the gong ring again, but it was just *my* gong getting rung. I saw his knee coming for my forehead, and there was nothing I could do to avoid it when...

AAA-AAA-AAHHHHHH!!!

My eardrums practically burst, and Lord Samuel fell back, clutching his ears. Raspberrysyrup advanced on us, her voice magically enhanced by an Ability of some kind. She continued to scream at the top of her lungs, and Lord Samuel cried out in pain. I felt [Regeneration] pull me back from the cusp of unconsciousness, and I jammed my fingers into my ears. Lord Samuel fell to the ground beside me; I guess his old ear-bones couldn't hold up against a sonic attack. With Lord Samuel down, Raspberrysyrup aimed her full might at me, and I was forced to use the only weapon I had in hand. I reached up and stuffed my last bar of butter into her open mouth.

Then I ran, and drained an unattended tankard of beer as I went. Raspberrysyrup desperately clawed at the wad of butter in her mouth as she tried to drink, but was unsuccessful.

GOOONGGG

Up ahead, Tania's fist found Emerelda's chin, and the poor dwarfess toppled like a statue. Tania's plate armour was barely even dented. She turned towards me, her feet slow and plodding. I fled, and she activated an Ability.

"[Advanced Charge]!"

I'd seen Brock use that skill – it was a straight line! I sprang sideways and felt a mass of metal rocket through where I'd been standing. Tania crashed into the table as I scrambled to my feet. I had zero confidence that I could take her out, so I ran to where Rumbob and Chuck were duking it out. I ducked past them and grabbed another tankard and downed it. Chuck and Rumbob took a short break to drink as well, and Tania downed hers at the last second.

GOOONGGG

Tania and I each immediately drained the next mug as it was placed, and I used my precious second or so head start to try and make some distance.

I dodged and weaved, but she cornered me with the confidence and skill of a primal hunter. She raised a plated fist to bring it down on my head, and I had to make a decision. If I chose to Specialise, I could get a new pair of Blessings. That could be enough to turn the tide, but I would be pigeonholed into a combat Specialisation.

I watched the fist inch towards my nose and closed my eyes. No. There would be other opportunities to save the brewery, and I was done getting yanked around by circumstances. I would not sacrifice my future in this world on a split-second decision.

That was when a struggling Chuck and Rumbob tripped over Tania and all four of the final competitors fell in a groaning heap.

GOOONGGG

CHAPTER FIFTY-ONE
AND THE WINNER IS

Four competitors, four mugs of ale. Chuck grabbed my foot and Rumbob thumped him in the nose. Tania tried to clinch Rumbob's neck, but his girth prevented it. I used [Basic Slash] with my fist on Chuck's fingers and broke his grip. Finally we were all forced to disengage as we reached out and desperately grabbed at various handles.

"[Disarm]!"

Tania's gauntlet pounded into my wrist, and my fingers shook. [Strength of All: Held] kept me from dropping the mug, but it was enough to cost me a single desperate second as I regained my grip. I breathed out and –

GOOONGGG

I stared in disbelief at the half-full tankard at my lips.

A host called me out from the ring and I rolled under the table. Adrenaline kept the sound of blood beating in my brain and the crowd was like the roar of the sea in my ears. Everything had that surreal feeling that came with a major win or loss.

That's right... I'd lost by half a second. Fourth place, not even the top three. Wreck had been right, I just... wasn't strong enough. I was the fastest drinker here, but I still lacked the level of personal power necessary to compete at the very top of dwarven society. I was still a young dwarf.

The competition continued. Chuck got taken out by a double-team of Rumbob and Tania, and then the two of them suddenly stopped in mid-combat. Rumbob held up a hand, and called over the MC. The gong was paused during some whispered conversation, and then the MC pulled out his megaphone.

"EVERYONE! THE TWO REMAINING CHAMPIONS HAVE DECIDED TO CHANGE THINGS UP FOR FIRST PLACE! THEY WANT TO SEE WHO CAN TRULY DOWN THE MOST!"

The crowd muttered confusedly for a while.

"THEY SAY IF WE ARE GOING TO SEND THE BIGGEST DRINKER IN MINNOVA, IT NEEDS TO BE THE ONE WITH THE GREATEST LOVE FOR THE BREW!"

That got the crowd cheering. A short intermission later, Rumbob and Tania sat across from each other on a small square table in the centre of the ring. The Lord dropped his hand as the first drinks hit the table.

There was no more gong, simply one beer after another. The crowd grew silent as the conga line of empty beer mugs grew longer and longer. My eyes grew wider and wider as each empty mug hit the table. Where the hell were they keeping all that beer? Then I heard it. I was standing close enough to the action that I caught their whispered cheats.

"[Expand Stomach]"

"[Compress Fluid]"

"[Remove Poison]"

"[Subspace Gullet]"

They had Godsdamn *drinking* Abilities!? This competition had been rigged from the start! What kind of cockamamie weirdass God handed out something that made your stomach bigger!? Barck, *it was probably Barck.*

In my indignation, I almost missed the moment Tania let out a massive burp and collapsed to the sandy floor. Rumbob stood and thrust both fists into the air. The crowd went wild.

My place was just beside the podium, a grinning Chuck at my side on the third-place riser. I wasn't completely despondent – all wasn't lost. Rumbob and some of the rest had agreed to come to the afterparty at the Thirsty Goat, which was sure to help drum up business. We should have won a good amount of gold on our bet, and I'd done some free advertising.

I might not have managed to get onto the brewery floor this time, but slow and steady won the race. I looked up for Balin, Annie, and Aqua, but didn't see them. They were probably at the Thirsty Goat getting things ready for the party. I'd need to apologise later for getting their hopes up. To be fair, I hadn't told them about any of this initially, but still.

The Lord came down on stage to personally present our awards. The massive trophy filled with mithril got handed to Rumbob, who lifted it up into the sky to the cheers of the crowd. There were similar cheers as Tania and Chuck were handed small wooden boxes. The Lord made some speech about Minnova being proud of its sons and daughters, but I was busy thinking about my next move.

That was when the pilsner glass landed in my hand.

I stared at it. It was indeed my vase-shaped pilsner glass with a faintly familiar gnome etched in gold on the side. My eyes snapped over to the Lord, who was still talking. His voice echoed through the Arena, but he didn't need a megaphone, it was just... easy to hear him.

"–thank Whistlemop's Fineries for being a major sponsor as well as providing these genuine Whistlemugs for the top ten!"

Just down the line, Brewski gave a tiny fist-pump and I could make out his whisper.

"Score! These are from the first run! I can sell this for serious gold!"

I stared down at the glass in a fresh round of disbelief. Whistlemug?!

I pulled up a quest that I had been curious about for a while now.

Quest: Dwarven Influencer Part 6/10
The dwarves need your help. Influence 100,000 dwarves with your otherworldly alcohol knowledge.
Dwarves Influenced: 74,324/100,000

Rewards: [Carbonate]

I watched with anticipation as the Lord handed Tania a mug.

"Thank you, my Lord. I've been wanting one of these, but my adventuring in Greentree kept me from obtaining one. They're always sold out!" she said cheerfully.

The number ticked up to 74,325.

HOLY SHIT!

I'd been wondering why my quest numbers were so high! It was because a certain Whitle*rat* had been selling my pilsner glass!

The Lord continued down the line and handed a glass to Emerelda. She smiled and nodded, but this time the counter didn't tick up. She was coming to the after party, so I'd ask her more about it there. If my suspicions were correct, I may have just discovered another avenue that I could extort – I mean collect – gold from.

I strode towards the Thirsty Goat alongside Rumbob, Beatbox, Emerelda, Tania, Chuck, and Jim. The pro-drinkers were a great crowd, and we had some wonderful discussions about the future of competitive drinking as we left the stadium. Tania and Chuck fit right in and were overjoyed at having met some fellow drinkers. Jim was a bit sore about my cheap shot to the back of his head, but I explained my experience with Tim and he understood.

A parade formed behind us as Rumbob walked down Main Street carrying his massive trophy. Word had spread that the champion drinkers of Minnova were headed to the Thirsty Goat for a party. I spent most of the walk chatting with Rumbob, who was apparently a rather well-known [Tavernic Matchmaker].

"Your work is seriously just hooking people up in taverns?" My mind fought to connect the enormously rotund and jovial white-haired Rumbob with my internal image of the matchmaker from Mulan.

"That's an interesting way of puttin' it." Rumbob thumbed at his fourth chin in thought. "I'd say it's about right though."

"What does that even look like?"

"He grabs their heads, knocks them together and says, 'Now, KISS!'" Beatbox quipped and dodged a playful swat from Rumbob.

"It's mostly about puttin' folks at ease. Find a quiet tavern, sip a few drinks, and then just talk. I do have some Abilities that help too. Got a nice one after I 'hooked up' my thousandth couple!"

"That can't be all there is to it."

"There's also makin' sure they've got compatible families, and similar expectations. Lotta young folks don't ask the right questions when they're fallin' in love!"

"I can understand that. You need to make sure everyone wants children, and that they put the toilet paper roll the right way up."

There was some general laughter. Come to think of it, I was probably the youngest person here.

"Enough about me though." Rumbob's smile turned cheeky. "Tell me, Pete. How did you get involved with the Goat?"

"I was in the Reform Mine a while back with Annie," I admitted.

"Ah, a reformed dwarf. Are ya pinin' over her? I heard your little war cry!" He slapped me on the back with a guffaw.

A bead of sweat formed on my forehead. Shit, Balin was going to kill me. "She actually got romantically involved with me brother, Balin. I was just copyin' his war cry."

Beatbox leaned in and tittered. "That's going to be a fun little misunderstanding! My daughter is already cheering you on." He pointed to a small crowd of gnomes that were walking in the parade. A mousy-haired gnome girl waved back energetically. "Everyone in the drinking community knows the bashful blonde firebrand, Annie Goldstone! Has yer brother been killed by Jeremiah Goldstone yet?"

Rumbob held up his hand. "Let me check, [Sense Connections]." After a moment, he nodded. "Yer strongest connection is over by tha Thirsty Goat. Assumin' that's him, he's still alive!"

"That's hard to believe!" Emerelda put in. "Do you remember that time Goldstone locked a suitor in a barrel and mailed him out of town?"

"They never proved that!" Beatbox chided with mock indignation.

Oh Gods... Goldstone. I'd dropped a massive party on them with zero warning. I needed to check how much gold we'd made too. First place had eluded me, but we should have won a fair bit, nevertheless. "I need to go check in!"

A massive crowd met us at the entrance to 4th Street. Multiple dwarf-standard picnic tables lined the streets, and I could see gnomes from the general store helping out as waiters. They were passing out Thirsty Goat beer, as well as cured meats, fish, and other goodies from the store. The crowd roared a welcome as we arrived, and Rumbob held up his trophy for everyone to admire.

"Drinks are on me!" He bellowed, as he poured a small pile of mithril into the hands of a shocked gnomess in an apron. She stuttered and then ran back into the brewery. The various dwarves and gnomes cheered their approval and started up a chant of "Rum Tum Rumbob!"

A table was emptied for the champions and we took a seat to much back slapping and arm punching. Drinks were brought out and Rumbob led the toast to Crack and Minnova. I begged a moment to go see Goldstone and went to the front door. I took a deep breath, squared my shoulders, and walked in.

"It's Pete!!!" was the first thing I heard, and I was promptly knocked over by a blue bowling ball.

What in tha nether?

"Gerroff me, Aqua!" I struggled as her beard tickled my nose. *Achoo!!*

I escaped from Aqua's smothering hug and stood up just in time to meet Annie's eyes. She stood there in a serving apron with her arms folded. Her long blonde waves were done up in a style vaguely reminiscent of a certain galactic princess. Penelope stood beside her and *maah*-ed a happy greeting.

"Penelope, go say 'hello' to Pete," Annie said.

Penelope came over and nuzzled my knees while I tickled under her chin.

meeeeh [Translated from Prima Donna Goat] "How art thou, fine sir?"

"Good to see you too, Penelope."

I grinned widely as I looked back at Annie, whose lips were now a thin, frustrated line.

"Since when were you two such good friends?"

"I-I'm sorry." My smile slipped. "I tried, but I didn't quite make it. I'm sorry for getting your hopes up."

"Are you kidding!?" Aqua blurted. "Do you know what –"

"WHERE IS HE!?" The tall and muscular form of Goldstone burst in from the mess hall. You wouldn't think something as short as a dwarf could loom, but Jeremiah Goldstone certainly could.

"Er, Mr. Goldstone, I can explain..." I backed up as he advanced, and winced as his arms went back –

And then scooped me into a giant bear hug.

What?

"You did it! We've nearly sold our whole stock, and Annie brought back enough to keep us running for a couple of months! I'm still going to kill that girl for betting all our money, but you did it!"

What!? I turned an incredulous look over at Annie, and she shrugged and mouthed 'top ten.'

Goldstone continued. "I talked to everyone about it, and we've decided that you're serious enough about this that we can let you into the brewing hall. Heck, you've done enough to practically consider you a partner!" Goldstone pounded me on the back and roared with laughter. "Only practically, though!" He gestured to the wooden portal that contained my wildest dreams.

WHAT!?

"Do you want to go in?" He gave me a mischievous wink.

WHAT!?!

I stared at the door, which just a moment ago had seemed out of reach. I looked at Goldstone and raised my eyebrows in a plaintive 'really'? He waggled his back, 'Aye.'

I put my hand on the doorknob, turned it, and walked inside. Hold tight beer, I'm finally on my way.

Somewhere else.

In a gazebo on a mountaintop, a bearded ivory figurine moved across the board.

CHAPTER FIFTY-TWO
PONG

While Pete was being shown into the Thirsty Goat

Rumbob tipped his head and strained his ears. He had excellent hearing, courtesy of a high perception honed by listening in on couple's conversations. "Did you hear somethin'?"

"That high pitched screaming sound?" Beatbox frowned slightly as he looked towards the brewery. "Yes. It sounds like my daughter when she sees a particularly good deal on wrenches."

"Sounds more like Erd's most excited kettle to me."

"I think it's coming from inside the Thirsty Goat. Should we go check it out? Or vacate? They did have something explode here last year."

"Nah, I'm sure it's fine." Rumbob took another sip of his beer. Agh, it was wonderful getting a batch fresh from the brewery. Rumbob liked fizz, and there was a lot of extra fizz the closer you drank to the source. Sadly, it wasn't too often that breweries threw a party with product straight from the barrel. The earthy and sour flavour of Thirsty Goat beer complemented the bitter tang of the grout at the bottom of his mug. Then of course there were the tasty nuts from the general store. Rumbob chewed happily while he watched Emerelda and Tania take part in a boisterous arm-wrestling match.

This was the first time he didn't feel ashamed sitting in public amongst a bunch of other pro-drinkers. No snide remarks for 'wastin' tha brew' or angry mutters about 'drinkin' too fast to enjoy it.' All it had taken was a single word from the King that he wanted the 'greatest drinkers in Crack' to compete at the octa-millennial. He smiled as his eldest son attempted a bashful conversation with a blushing gnomish waitress. Now there was a match that would have been frowned upon just a scant few millennia ago!

Rumbob shook his head. Dwarven society needed a touch of spring cleaning. He'd noticed more and more young dwarves were unhappy with the matchmaking system and the current status of the nobility. They wanted to fall in love and for society to damn well keep their noses out! As a matchmaker, he was inclined to agree. Too often a good match was ruined by a noble who couldn't keep his hands to himself, or a grandmother that had too much to say about the potential groom's beard.

Speaking of change, Rumbob looked over as Pete stumbled out of the brewery, a grin plastered to his face. He recognized that smile, but it was usually reserved for the first time a pair held hands. Rumbob quite liked Pete, and he was on a rather meteoric rise within the city. Perhaps his little Tiger would be interested in him? She was partial to dwarves that broke the mould, especially since she started listening to that crazy Raspberrysyrup's 'pop' music...

"What's the matter, Pete?" Jim asked, as Pete stumbled to their table.

"I-I – "

"Gaht somethin' in yer eye?" Chuck chuckled. His accent was very reminiscent of Richter's deep South Erden bass.

"Maybe one of those nipples..." Beatbox muttered. Chuck was dressed in the shirtless style of the southern continent, and his bright orange spade beard stood out against the pitch black of his skin. Chuck grinned wolfishly and flexed his muscular pecs in reply.

Rumbob waited patiently for Pete to speak. That was something he was good at, after all.

Briefly, he wondered what the future held for this shining star in front of him. Whatever it was, Pete had certainly not chosen an easy path.

I stuttered a few more times as I gaped at Rumbob and the rest. Only moments ago, I'd been hashing out ideas for my next attempt at entering the Thirsty Goat, and now...

"I... I got into the Brewery," I whispered in shock. "Goldstone is letting me on to the brew floor."

"Ho, ho, ho! Congratulations! Did you go inside yet?!" Rumbob clapped me on the back. "I did. And then... I got a Milestone!" It had come out of nowhere, no quest or anything! "Then Annie kicked me back out and told me to socialise."

There was a shocked silence at the table for a moment, and then several cheers, both verbal and mug.

"Ho, ho, ho! Congratulations! Didja choose [Bottomless Barrel]?"

"Uh, probably. How did you know? There are a couple options, but [Bottomless Barrel] is *amazin'*."

"A few of my friends have it, there's a lotta nobs and brewers with it. If it's the Milestone I'm thinkin', one of the options is always [Bottomless Barrel]." Rumbob nodded.

Beatbox leaned into the conversation. "Careful with that one. The beer it makes has to be drunk right away, so you can't make multiple kegs. It's meant to ensure you don't run out of beer at a party."

I shook my head and looked over my notifications.

Bing!

Milestone Gained: Generous Host!

Getting 800 people drunk on your brew at your party has granted you the ability to choose a Milestone!
Please accept one of the following:

Possible Milestone: [Project Voice]!

Never again worry if the people at the back can hear your voice. Grants a significantly increased volume of voice.
This Ability is always available.

Accept [Project Voice]?
Yes/No

Possible Milestone: [Bottomless Barrel]!
You can touch a container that contains no more than forty-eight litres of non-magical liquid and grant it a touch of infinity. For the next one minute, any drink you pour out of it does not reduce the liquid level. If the liquid is not poured into an appropriate container or imbibed within the next twenty-four minutes, it disappears.
You can use this Ability once per hour.

Accept [Bottomless Barrel]?
Yes/No

Possible Milestone: [Quicken Steps]!
The host often has to be in two places at once, but that isn't always possible. Increases agility by 4 for walking and running. This Ability lasts for 24 minutes when used.
You can use this Ability once per hour.

Accept [Quicken Steps]?
Yes/No

Possible Milestone: [Game Face]!
No matter who you are talking to or how you are feeling, you always appear your best. Grants a bonus 4 charisma to appear calm and you are immune to Abilities that sense emotions.
This Ability is always available.

Accept [Game Face]?
Yes/No

Off to the side, Emerelda and Tania started a small brawl that began to rapidly expand. A grim-looking Goldstone walked past carrying a bench. The conversation at the champion table stopped for a minute as several dwarves were politely given a seat.

"The notification says I threw a party that got more than eight hundred people drunk on my brew. I think it's because I'm officially a part of the brewery now? And I threw the party?" I watched Goldstone stalk back inside with a broken bench. "But Annie and the others did all the work!"

"Aye, but as far as everyone here knows, you threw it, m'boy!" Rumbob chuckled. "Intent can matter fer Milestones!"

"That doesn't seem fair."

"Gods don't need ta be fair!"

"Don't need to tell me that," I muttered darkly, and then drained my mug. I shuddered a bit as the foul gruit hit my gullet, but the moment passed.

"Who cares! I'm in! I did it!!!" I roared as I got up onto the table. "YOU HEAR THAT MINNOVA!!! I *DID* IT!" I roared out to the crowd.

"Don't let Goldstone hear that!" someone shot back. There was general laughter and some cat-calling.

"Ugh, I don't even care. This calls for some drinking games!" I spun and looked down at my cadre of new friends and acquaintances. "Who here plays beer pong?"

I was met with a bevy of confused glances.

Beatbox was the first to ask the question. "Pong?"

"This looks like a waste of beer," Beatbox opined, as he brought another half dozen mugs over.

I wasn't allowed back into the brewery until after the party. Annie wanted me to 'mingle and drum up more interest.' I could do that, though I was really itching to get onto that brew floor. In the meantime, I commandeered a table for us to play one of Earth's most famous drinking games: Beer Pong.

"It's not a waste, Beatbox. We're going to be drinking it."

"I thought you said it was for a game?"

"It is for a game. A drinking game!"

"Drinking isn't a game," someone shouted from the curious onlookers.

"We just came from a drinking tournament, ya idjit," someone else put in.

"What did you say?"

"Yer head as daft as yer beard? You heard me!"

I ignored the small scuffle that ensued as I explained the rules to everyone else and finished setting up the board.

"The first thing we need is twenty mugs of beer. We put ten o' them into a triangle shape at each end of the table." I set up the first set of ten mugs in a style reminiscent of billiards, and then moved on to the other side of the table. "You can see I've staggered the cups and left about two thumbs width in between each tankard."

I looked up to see a crowd of nearly a hundred dwarves and gnomes watching in rapt attention. Good, good. I kept an eye on my quest to influence people with my otherworldly knowledge. I was hoping that drinking games would count as well. It was still ticking up, but no big jumps.

"I'll need three willing volunteers to play! Champions?" I turned to my table, and an eager Beatbox thrust up a quivering hand. "There's one. Anyone else?"

Emerelda and Chuck raised their hands, and I pulled them all over to explain the rules. At the same time, a gnomess ran over from the general store with a set of four small wooden balls.

"Ah, thanks, Spruceleaf!"

"You're most welcome, Peter! It's on the house from my old man! He says thanks for all the business!" The green-haired young woman said brightly, before running off to continue serving tables.

"I'm always game for games, Pete." Emerelda winked and flexed her fingers. She sported a fresh new black eye, and her black garibaldi beard and walrus moustache were smeared with a spot of blood from a cut lip.

"And ah'm always up far tryin' samthin' new!" Chuck added. He and Emerelda sized each other up with competitive grins.

"Alright then, let's get this party started. Here are the rules." I handed one ball to each player. "Beatbox, you and Chuck stand on the other side of the table there. Emerelda, you stand beside me here. Notice that when you stand like this, there's a triangle on the other side of the table with the point facing you."

"I think I get it! Are we supposed to throw the balls into the mugs on the other side of the table?" Beatbox put in.

"Bingo!" I sent a double-fingered point his way.

"What?" He scrunched up his brows in puzzlement.

"Uh, yes. That's correct."

"No, what's Bingo?"

I looked down at the small, middle-aged gnome with grey whiskers and a few liver spots on his receding hairline. 'My spotty dog's name-o' died on my lips. Thank the Gods for my higher charisma.

"Something I like to say when someone's right. It's just a me thing. Don't worry about it. Anyways, you were correct! The objective is to toss your ball into the cups on the other side of the table. When you get it in a cup, your opponent needs to drink it! The first team to fall unconscious or drink all their cups loses!"

"Clear ta me." Chuck nodded and Emerelda cracked her knuckles as I got ready to take the first shot. A few other tables were set up around us so people could sit and drink while they watched us play, and I saw another table being set up for a second game.

"Oh, one last thing," I mentioned, as I lined up my throw, "no Abilities, since that would make it too easy." I made a lazy toss, and the ball spun through the air to land directly to the side of the triangle. Huh, that was odd. I wasn't an expert at this back home, but I was certainly a semi-pro. How had that missed?

"Who needs Abilities when you have a high dexterity?" Beatbox asked, as he easily flipped his ball into a mug on our side. Emerelda took the drink with a *hmph* and downed it in a single go.

"Don't hold me back, Pete!" She grumbled, as she easily dunked a ball on her turn.

I quickly checked my dexterity. It was eleven. Balls. Chuck easily landed his first shot, and I took a drink. This was not going to go well.

Play continued back and forth, and after another botch, I managed to land the ball most of the time. More of that 'spirit affecting my spark' as I was beginning to call it. After the first six mugs were drunk on each side, the cups were rearranged into a diamond shape. Beatbox and Chuck started to miss the target more often by that point, and the game became competitive. There was even a cheering section!

Okay, my cheering section may have mostly consisted of *maaahs* but that counted!

While we waited for Beatbox to go through a pre-throw routine that included drunkenly asking his wife to "kiss his balls" – ugh – I turned to Emerelda.

"Hey, what's up with the Whistlemugs?"

"You didn't know about them?"

"I was living in a cave for the past few months. Literally."

"Ah. They're sold by Whistlemug's Fineries, and they've been really popular."

"Oh, *reaallly*?" I hissed, like a pissed off cat. One such feline burst out from under the pong table and hissed in reply before running off.

"Aye, they're nice and clear so you can see your brew, and the shape makes the bubbly really pop!"

"Dwarves really like the bubbly, huh?"

"Some. No, a lot."

"Annie had the right idea then." I rapped my fingers on the table as Chuck got the crowd into a cheering frenzy for Beatbox's shot.

"What's that?"

"Oh, just thinking."

We stepped to the side as Beatbox finally took his shot. It bounced off the rim of a mug and fell to the floor. Emerelda immediately stepped up and unceremoniously tossed her ball. It landed square in a mug and the crowd crowed with laughter as Beatbox drank it with chagrin.

I gave her a fist bump as she turned back to me. "Did you already own one, then?"

"Yes. They're quite expensive, nearly five silver, but I think they're worth it. Rock collectors are going wild over them!"

That was fifty loonies! And he must have sold tens of thousands! Argh! I needed to see this for myself!

"Would you be interested in showing me to Whistlemop's? I'm curious after your description."

"Oh? *Yer* askin' *me*? That's new. Sure, I'd love to!"

Alright, it seemed likely that if someone bought a Whistlemug when they already owned one it didn't affect my quest, but I wanted to make sure. I'd need to do a little testing, but this could be a useful benchmark to check how quests were tabulated.

The game was a massive success, and soon there were several tables playing. Oh, and we lost.

"Sorry, Penelope."

mournful maaaaaah [Translated from Prima Donna Goat] "I don't understand what is happening, but my disappointment in you is immeasurable and my day is utterly ruined."

CHAPTER FIFTY-THREE
THROUGH THE DOOR

"Three hundred five mugs of beer on the rack, three hundred five mugs of beer! Take one down, swirl it around, three hundred four mugs of beer on the rack!"

If dishes were wishes, I'd own this whole damn brewery.

Pick up the mug, rinse the mug in scalding hot water, look for the soap.

Fail to find the soap. Because apparently, MOST DWARVES DON'T USE SOAP!

Put the mug on the drying rack and move to the next mug.

The party had ended sometime around noon the next day. Pong was a big hit, and I was slightly bothered that it didn't count towards my otherworldly beer knowledge quest. At around five in the morning, the last beer from the brewery got hit with my new Milestone every time it came off cooldown.

[Bottomless Barrel] was super neat and an absolute joy to use. I've had fun with my Abilities, and they've even saved my life, but [Bottomless Barrel] just felt the most *me* out of everything I'd received on Erd. I could touch a bottle of Romanée Conti red wine, pour it out to a dozen people, and never use a drop of wine in the bottle. I imagined my expensive alcohol collection back on Earth, with its forty-year-old whiskeys, rare wines, and specialty craft beers. A skill like this would have allowed me to share those delicacies and still have a full bottle!

It was a shame that opening a bottle was a countdown to destruction for the drink within. Uncorking introduced oxygen to the drink, which allowed for an oxidization reaction to occur. It was the exact same process that created rust, with a similar outcome. The flavour would slowly be destroyed, and in some cases, all that was left after oxidation was pure vinegar. I could use a trick involving a nitrogen-filled barrel, but there was no guarantee nitrogen even existed here. Then again, it would be a bit too much of a cheat to open a bottle, use [Bottomless Barrel] and then re-bottle it with no possible downside.

I paused in the middle of placing a mug on the rack. Wait... could I actually do that re-bottle trick? I popped open my Status Sheet. As I did, a few 'failed quest' notifications popped up. One was expected, but the next few were a surprise.

Bing!

Quest Failed: Championship Road Part 2/2!
Looks like you hit a speed bump on the road to success.

Bing!

Quest Failed: An Ore-Able Time Part 3/10!
You don't plan on mining ever again. Some dwarf.

Bing!

Quest Failed: Striking it Rich!
Gambling is a terrible way to earn money when there are gems to be mined.

Failing *An Ore-Able Time* and *Striking it Rich* was a surprise. In video games I was used to taking a hundred quests and letting them sit on the backburner. The thought that they would simply fail on their own had never occurred to me.

It did make sense. Now that I was officially in the brewery, I wasn't ever going to complete that quest. It was a massive, subconscious, 'abort quest' in my soul. Those two had probably been Tiara's quests? Sorry, yer worship!

On to the rest of my Status Sheet! Let's see if it had what I was looking for.

Status: Provided by the Firmament
Name: Peter ~~Phillips~~ Samson
Age: *49*
Conditions: *None*
Race: *Dwarf*
Blessings*: [Flesh of Stone], [Flash of Insight], [Strength of All: Held], [Regeneration]*
Title: *[Alchemist]*
Milestones: *[Otherworlder], [Power Pick], [Ingredient Scan], [Stabilise Mixture], [Basic Slash], [Bottomless Barrel]*
Strength: *15.4*
Vitality: *19*
Agility: *11*
Dexterity: *11*
Wisdom: *13*
Intelligence: *12*
Perception: *16.4*
Charisma: *12*

Yep, there it was. I popped open [Stabilise Mixture] and gave it a read through.

[Stabilise Mixture] – *You are able to make an unstable mixture reach perfect equilibrium. It will no longer react violently unless you force it to do so.*
You can use this Ability once per minute.

Would that allow me to keep a drink from being oxidised? The Ability seemed to have two parts; the second part was clearly focused on explosives, but the first part specified 'allowing an unstable mixture to reach perfect equilibrium.' Oxidization was essentially an instability within the alcohol. If I re-corked a drink, could I use [Stabilise Mixture] to prevent it from going bad? I HAD to check. I may have just discovered the first synergy in my skills! Who doesn't love cool synergies?

Sure, it wasn't big or fancy – or freaking magic – but unlimited expensive alcohol with no downsides!? I almost dropped a mug before I refocused my attention. Some experimentation could wait; Annie was letting me on the brewery floor as soon as the dishes were done. At least I was better off than poor Balin, who was going to be fixing tables outside till next week.

"Three hundred mugs of beer on the rack, three hundred mugs of beer! Take one down, swirl it around, two hundred ninety-nine mugs of beer on the rack!"

"And here it is!" Annie swung open the door and let me onto the brew room floor. I had been inside for a brief, incredible moment yesterday, but now I had the time to fully appreciate it. I took a deep sniff, and the scent of boiled wort and musty malt assailed my nostrils. I closed my eyes and thought back to my first commercial brewing room.

Caroline's cheerful laugh echoed in the large, mostly empty warehouse. "Ha! I can see under my skirt on the floor. Why is it so shiny?"

"Careful! You'll slip, and I don't want to spend the next eight hours in Emergency!" I glowered in mock disapproval.

Caroline stuck her tongue out at me. *bleh* "I'll be fine, worrywart."

"I'm not worried about you." I walked over to pat her burgeoning belly. "Is our little girl kicking yet?"

"Mmmm." Caroline closed her eyes and leaned her head into my shoulder. "Not yet. The doctor says it'll be soon though."

We stood there for a moment until Caroline pulled away. "You're avoiding the question, why does the floor of our brewery look like an ice rink?"

"Well... It cost a bit extra, but I got the concrete sealed. With all the spills in a brewery, we want to keep the concrete floor from staining or cracking, so I had them put epoxy over top."

"Was it expensive?"

"A little, but we need it to be up to code anyway."

"Keep to the code?"

"Arrr, that's right, me hearty!"

The two of us shared a hug as we gazed upon the gleaming rows of fermentation tanks in Beavermoose Brewery.

That damn floor had been way too expensive but had also been so wonderfully easy to clean. It was the first thing that came to mind as I looked out over the brew room floor here. The dirty, dirty, brew room floor. There was mud caked in places from spilled beer mixed with dirt, and while it certainly wasn't a pigsty, it was nothing like the pristinely clean brewery I remembered. I knew that most dwarves weren't that big into hygiene, but this was just ridiculous. I'd kill for Bran's obsessively clean kitchen right about now.

The floor was an enormous slab of grimy, off-yellow granite, while the dusty walls were made of a combination of wood and stone. A warm yellow light shone down from several solstones set in the rafters. A large brick fireplace with a chimney up to the ceiling sat beneath a copper-bottom boiling tank at the centre of the room. The pungent aroma of coal smoke added to the various earthy scents wafting through the space.

Still, even with the slight patina of dirt and grease on everything, it was the most beautiful thing I'd seen in this life. Most of the usual brewing equipment was there, alongside rows upon rows of barrels and kegs. A few things were missing, but I could fix that soon enough.

Thankfully, all the equipment was clearly well maintained and in top shape.

There were three other dwarves hard at work and they all looked over as we entered. There was the braided Viking John, and his pretty-boy son Johnsson, alongside the massive Richter. They were busy levering a large wooden trough from the boiling kettle to one of the many open-topped fermentation tanks. Looks like I'd guessed right about the open-air tanks. Score one for Pete.

Bing!

New Quest: Middle Management!
You're on the bottom rung of the company, can you go one higher? Become a manager at the Thirsty Goat Brewery.

Rewards: +0.2 Charisma

Do you accept?
Yes / No

That had to be Tiara. I hadn't seen her in a while.

I hit "Yes" as Annie cleared her throat for attention, "Ahem, we have decided that Pete is going to join us on the brew room floor."

There was a moment of shocked silence, and then Johnsson gave a hoot and a holler.

"That's great! Welcome to the family, Pete!" He came over and gave me a pound on the shoulder. He was covered in sweat and grime from a day of hard labour, and he positively exuded 'thank the Gods, someone my age' energy.

"Thanks, Johnsson, it's great to finally be a part of this brewhaha!" I gave him a friendly pound back. He looked confused for a moment, though John gave a small snort from where he was locking the trough into place.

Richter came over and shook my hand.

"I sah ya workin' 'ard wit tha priss, ya?"

"Priss? Do you mean Penelope? She's not that bad!"

"Yer brudda's in love wit' tha biggest troublemaker in Minnova. I tink tha Roughtuff clan 'as a ting fer punishment."

"Excuse me!?" Annie protested as the rest of us laughed. Her cheeks grew more and more crimson as the laughter grew until she finally pulled back a fist and swung at Richter. He deftly dodged with the grace of long practice, and her punch connected squarely on the laughing face of Johnsson. He went down with a squawk, and the rest of us laughed harder.

Annie turned to me, her eyes promising murder. "Do you want me to show you around, or should I leave you with these louts? Maybe we could go wash more dishes?"

I stopped laughing and stood to attention. "Yes, ma'am! No, ma'am!"

"That's what I thought. The rest of you, we have two large orders to fulfil within the month, and someone just emptied out all our stock! We need those three batches done by tonight! Pete bought us a few months, don't waste it!"

Johnsson and Richter scrambled back to work, though John took his time. He gave me a wink as he passed. He struck me as the silent and thoughtful type compared to Jeremiah Goldstone's jolly giant.

"Alright, Pete, let me show you around. I will remind you that all of this is confidential." Annie's voice carried a tinge of warning. "The methods of beer creation are a secret passed down from generation to generation, and jealously guarded by the traditional brewing families and the Honourable Guild of Brewers."

"Oh, those guys?" I thought back to the angry figures I'd seen in the distance at the colosseum. "They seem a bit... uh..."

"Set in their ways?" Annie sighed, "Don't I know it. You said you know how to brew?"

"That would be correct." And an understatement.

"Can you tell me what everything in here does?" She waved her hand around the room.

"Absolutely, but is this your tour or mine?" I waggled my eyebrows.

"Humour me. Balin said some stuff that has me curious, but he clams up whenever I push."

Uh oh. That wasn't good. Communication issues like that could be a problem in a relationship, and I was the direct cause. Well, Annie had let me into the heart of her family, so maybe we could let her into the Roughtuff clan's.

"Let me talk with Balin."

"Does it have something to do with your 'amnesia'?" I could practically feel the air quotes in her voice and winced. Yeah, that excuse had been wearing thin recently.

"Sort of. I promise it'll make sense."

"Fine. Do you want to do the honours?"

"Sure."

We dodged out of the way as Richter walked by carrying a giant bag full of Erdroot. He dumped it into a metal hopper and went to get another sack.

I pointed to the hopper. "That there is the grist mill, and it's where you mill the Erdroot into malt." The hopper dropped into a large grinder, and Johnsson got to work turning a crank nearly as tall as he was.

"That's right. We get most of our Erdroot from local farms, but it's gotten a lot more expensive. The price dropped back down recently, but that may not last for long."

"Do you take turns on the crank?"

"No, Johnsson does most of it since he's the youngest. I think he's looking forward to giving someone else a chance." She grinned maliciously.

"Um."

"What about this?" Annie directed me to a pair of large apparatuses. One was the copper-bottom boiling tank and fireplace combo while the other was a large wooden barrel. They were nearly thrice my height and equally as wide. They were empty at the moment, though I could see leftover bits of gunk inside. A ramp led up to sturdy scaffolding constructed around the two barrels, and a complex series of pipes ran back and forth between them. John was busy shovelling coal into the fireplace.

"Easy enough. You put all the milled malt into that wooden barrel, which is the mash tun. Next, you boil water in the copper brew kettle beside it. Then you pipe the hot water into the mash tun to make your wort."

"Yes, that's all correct." Annie's eyes narrowed. "And all classified.

I need you to have that conversation with Balin about your amnesia sooner rather than later."

"I will, I promise." I pointed to an enormous wooden spoon up on the scaffold. "Who stirs the mash?"

"Richter mostly. He's tall enough and strong enough for it. My dad used to do it before, and then Richter's father."

"What happened to Richter's father?"

"You'll need to ask him," Annie said coolly. Oops, some kind of history there. I pointed back at the copper tank.

"Next, you pump the wort back into the brew kettle, where you boil it for a few hours. During this phase you add some flavours and bittering agents."

"Correct again. Do you happen to know what we use?" She asked sweetly, but I could sense the slightly bitter undertones. It was clear that the secret ingredients were a touch more sensitive than everything else.

"No idea." I shrugged. I left the 'they suck though,' unsaid.

She sighed in relief. "Well, that's something at least. Dad buys the ingredients and puts them into sacks." She pointed to a series of brown burlap bags lying against the scaffolding. "You'll just dump it into the boil, so don't worry about it."

"Aww, not even a clue?"

"No, we need to keep some things secret."

"Fiiiine," I whined, petulantly. "After you boil the wort, it gets filtered through the hopback and chilled before it goes into one of the fermentation tanks. Or it should, but I don't see any equipment for that. The last step is to add some yeast and wait."

"What's a hopback?" Annie asked. "You're mostly right, but we don't chill the wort, it just gets pumped through those troughs into the fermentation tanks to cool."

"Ugh, that's the no-chill method. And no hopback? That explains so much."

"What are you talking about?" Annie asked as her eyes gleamed with curiosity. That's right, Annie was a rebel who believed there could be a better way to make beer. Well, two could play the 'mysterious secrets' game.

"I'll tell you, but you need to do something for me first."

"What?" Annie folded her arms in the universal 'I'm about to deny your silly request' pose.

"Get me a pair of mops and buckets and I'll tell you while we work."

Her arms fell to her side in confusion. "Why mops and buckets?"

I looked around me and said, "Because if there's anything I've learned recently, it's that all good things in this world start with cleaning up shit."

CHAPTER FIFTY-FOUR
THE BREWING OF YEASTERYEAR

"Why the long face?" I asked as I pushed the mop around the dirty floor. I couldn't really say I was cleaning – it was more like I was artistically moving mud around.

"I'm... still digesting what Balin told me," Annie said, her eyes a little hollow. Her golden tresses and silky beard were wrapped up in nets, and we were both in grubby leather work-armour. She'd spent an hour or so talking to Balin about my reincarnation, and seemed a bit wobbly over the whole thing.

"I wasn't talking to you. I was talking to Penelope. Do you want a goat treat, princess? Who's the only clean thirsty goat in Minnova? You are!" I rubbed her head and presented the aforementioned treat.

maaaah!! [Translated from Prima Donna Goat] "Your obeisance is acceptable, knight."

Annie slopped some water in my direction, but it was half-hearted. John, Johnsson, and Richter did their level best to ignore us. They were busy making beer as fast as they could, so their distraction was understandable.

Their lack of hygiene was less so.

"Pete... were you –" Annie began with a note of trepidation.

"Ixnay on the ebornray ewerbray," I interrupted.

"What? By Midna's Mullet, so much about you makes sense now."

"Am I supposed to take that as a compliment?" I leaned seductively on my mop and blinked my eyes coquettishly. I'd tried this move in the mirror a while back, because... well, because I was curious. It turned out that dwarves can indeed do coquette, though it's kind of like getting assaulted by a barbershop.

"Ugh, never do that again."

"You know you like it." I flexed my biceps.

"I'm marrying your brother."

"That poor soul. I tried to warn him."

"Excuse you!? You tried to warn him about what!"

"I can't say! You'll mop the floor with me!" I covered my face with my arms in faux fear.

"I swear to the Gods, if you utter one more pun within this building, I'll –"

"You'll pun-ish me?"

The rest devolved into soap suds and screaming. Only some of it from the goat.

"There. Done." Annie stretched her back and sighed with relief.

"It's acceptable." I nodded. We'd mopped, dusted, cleaned, buffed, and then done it again. It had taken a whole day and a half, but we were finally done. The building practically gleamed.

"By the Gods!" Johnsson screamed as he slid across the shiny floor and smashed into some barrels.

"Yep! Looks great. We'll need non-slip footwear though." I pursed my lips.

"I can see that." Annie mused. Richter had gone to help Johnsson up and slid into him instead. The two of them now looked like a pair of penguins trying to polka on ice. "Now that we're done, do you care to explain why I just wasted a whole day being a maid?"

"Because Balin has a thing for maids?" I deadpanned.

Annie sputtered and blushed. Hah! Got 'er!

"No, you idiot. Why was this such a big deal? I was only willing to go along with it because of what Balin told me, and I'm still not sure I can believe half of it."

"Hmmm... there's a limit on what I'm okay tellin' you here." I nodded in the direction of the flailing duo.

"That's fine, what can you tell me?"

"Well, it all comes down to how you ferment your beer." I took off my shoes and walked along the floor towards the fermentation tanks. "Take off your shoes, guys. Just go barefoot for now."

Johnsson and Richter looked chagrined as they untangled themselves and removed their shoes.

"Aaron's Arse, this is goin' to be ungodly hot on my toes next to the oven," Johnsson complained.

"You'll survive," his father said, as he carried over a large bag of coal. "Or would you rather be back on crank duty?"

"Nah, my back needs a day off. Toasty toes are fine."

Annie and I found a somewhat secluded spot among the fourteen fermentation tanks. They were a sight to see. Each square tank a two-metre tall open-top wooden structure with a copper liner. The copper was all quite shiny, and I was again taken aback at how dwarves seemed to treat maintenance so seriously, while they outright ignored sanitation.

The fermentation tanks were something to smell too, as they had a pretty pungent aroma. About half of them were full, and two were nearing completion. I could tell by the crusty white layer on top. It kind of looked and smelled like a four-square metre slab of cream cheese gently floating on a bubbly pond.

I waited a moment to ensure the three droppers of eaves were busy with their work before I began my explanation. I was almost giddy with joy – I was finally talking shop with another brewer. This was my first step on the path to introducing dwarf-kind to mastery of the craft of brewing!

Annie poked me in the side. "Why do you have that silly smile on your face? Are we starting, or what?"

"Right, right." I took a deep breath. "To start, how many of your batches fail? One in three? One in four?"

Annie frowned. "About one in four. How did you know that?"

"An educated guess." I pulled over a large wooden step stool and climbed up so I could see into the tank. As Annie joined me, I pointed to the white scum on top of the beer. "You are using what my world refers to as the open-fermentation method. It was used for millennia, and it has some rather severe limitations."

"What limitations? Wait, you said 'used'! Does that mean you found another way?" Annie's eyes grew brighter. I was struck. I hadn't realised until just now how much energy and intelligence had been lacking in her demeanour. The stress of nearly losing the brewery and the inability to experiment on her brewing had taken its toll.

"Yes, and you actually had the right solution." I smiled at her and softened my tone. "Annie. You weren't wrong. There was a better way."

"I... I..." Tears welled up in her eyes, and she banished them with an aggressive wipe of her armoured forearm. "I don't have time for this. What limitations?"

"It all comes down to yeast." I shrugged at the segue and continued.

"Yeast?"

"Yup." I pointed back at the white scum on top of the tank. "Yeast! Your brews keep failin' 'cause of a yeast infection!"

"Yuck! What? Beer is made from yeast, why would it infect it? That sounds disgusting." Annie gagged slightly.

"You're right in some ways and wrong in others." I grabbed a small ladle from a nearby hook and scooped up some of the white scum. It burbled slightly in the ladle and Annie leaned in to examine it. "Yeast is a single-celled fungus that likes to eat stuff. In the case of our lovely tanks of wort here, it wants ta eat the sugar inside. It turns that sugar into alcohol as well as carbon dioxide. That's what's makin' all the bubbles."

"Yes, I know all that," Annie said, as she poked the contents of the ladle with her finger. It jiggled slightly, and popped.

"I figured, let me pontificate here," I chided in my best professorial tone. My wife always hated that tone; she said I was beersplaining. "In open-top brewing like this, a layer of yeast forms on top of the wort, providing a slight seal against the elements. It isn't perfect, obviously, since the bubbles eventually push up through."

"Johnsson once had a whole chunk pop up onto his face when he was checking progress," Annie chortled.

"Hah! Well, in my world –" I stopped short. "I can't keep calling it 'my world' since this is my world now. My old world was called Earth."

"Earth? What does that mean?"

"It means dirt."

"Erd means dirt too, do all worlds name their planet after dirt?" Annie asked incredulously.

Wow, déjà vu.

"On Earth," I continued, "this white goop is called Kräusen and it's an important ingredient in open-top brewing." I dumped the contents of the ladle back into the tank and held the ladle out at arm's length. "This spoon tells me that it's pretty much the same here. After the hot wort is poured into a fermentation tank, you let it cool, and then skim some of the Kräusen into it from another tank."

"That's right." Annie nodded.

"We call that top-cropping. Not to be confused with crop-topping, which is what we call it when a daughter utterly disappoints her father."

"We call that method 'Ancestral Seed' because –"

"Oh hell, naw. Ew, stop." It was my turn to gag.

"What? It's a perfectly natural –"

"No! You're ruining it! Stop it! Stahp! I beg you!"

"By the Gods, you are such a child!"

"I'm only forty-nine! Am I explaining this or not!?"

"Yes!"

I mentally and physically shook myself and took a deep breath. "Before I was so horrifically interrupted, I was talking about top-cropping. The massive benefit of using Kräusen is that you can skip the yeast-washing step."

"What is yeast-washing? I thought we were discussing limitations, not benefits."

"I'm getting there, patience my young padawan." Annie looked like she was about to say 'what' but clenched her jaw instead. I cleared some space in the Kräusen and stirred with my spoon. The amber brown liquid was quickly filled with fine specks of debris. "This sediment is called 'trub,' and it's made from bits of dead yeast called 'lee' as well as leftover bits and pieces from the bittering agents you boiled into the – is that a stick?"

Yes indeed, a stick had bobbed up to the top of the wort. Annie reached in and grabbed it before I could react and tossed it down to the ground. "Yes, don't worry about it. You don't need to know the secret ingredients."

"That was a stick! And we just finished cleaning that floor!"

"Continue."

"Ugh. Actually, yeast washing isn't important, but that stick is part of why your brews keep failing. It's because there is yeast everywhere, and the horrific state of this brewery means that a lot of foreign yeasts are contaminating your brews."

"What? How? The only yeast we put in is the Ancestral See—" Annie frowned.

"Don't!" I put my finger up in a shushing motion and widened my eyes.

Annie rolled her eyes. "The only yeast we put in is the 'Kräusen.' How are other yeasts getting in?"

"I'm pretty sure I saw Johnsson spit into one of these tanks earlier." I'd been ready to murder him.

"It's for good luck!"

"Well, it's adding the yeast from his spit into the brew. Yeast is also able to get airborne, and it can stick to all the various contaminants that were in here. All that dust we took off the rafters? It had yeast in it, and I can guarantee it was getting blown into these tanks. All that mud? It had yeast in it, and then it got on your clothes, onto your hands, and then into the wort. The junk stuck to your unwashed brewing kettle? It had yeast in it! Heck, you're probably getting bacterial contamination too, which is causing the sour aftertastes. If you do it on purpose, you can make a *sour*, but by accident it just tastes bad."

"Oh." Annie's eyebrows drew together in concentration. "We can keep everything washed. We always figured the boiling was sufficient for sanitization, and we didn't want to contaminate the taste with soap."

"Hmm... no, you'd want to use a food-grade sanitizer. I suspect we will need to talk to an [Alchemist]."

"Aren't you an –"

"Wrong alchemist."

"If the yeast is airborne... I can think of a few ways to keep the air clean in here.... I need my sketchbook." Annie's fingers began to tap on the side of the tank, and I recognized the far-off look of a nerd deep in thought. "How will we know if it worked?"

"Well, for one thing, you aren't going to get a good Kräusen on a contaminated beer. So, if you've got a good Kräusen, you know the beer yeast is thriving."

"That makes sense. We call beer without it "bastard beer" because the Ancestral Seed di –"

"I got it! I got it!" I held my hands over my ears and Annie grinned wolfishly. Damn, she got me. "The long and short of it is that if you want to improve the quality of your beer and reduce waste, this brew floor needs to be clean and sanitised at every step, and kept that way."

"That's going to be expensive."

"More or less expensive than the wasted batches? Besides, the lack of contaminating yeasts means that your beer will probably taste better too. All without breaking any traditions." I practically purred the last sentence, and Annie twitched. Yeah, I figured that would be the right button to press.

"There's nothing wrong with following the traditions!" Annie replied, but her heart wasn't in it.

"But think of the possibilities! So many ways to improve your beer. I can help you with your tank designs. I know a way of using the environmental yeasts to make special 'lambic' beers."

"No! You will not tempt me, minion of Yearn!" Annie jumped off the step stool and began to walk back to the entrance. I stalked after.

"They'll call you the 'second brewer' and all will know the name Goldstone."

"I'm not listening!"

"I'll teach you the secret of stouts, and the process for porters. Take my hand Annie Goldstone, and I'll –"

"I'm sorry to break up this family tiff, but we are out of Erdroot and we are busy with the current batch." We were interrupted by John, who didn't look sorry at all, and was in fact grinning. "Would you two please take your conversation to the market and obtain us some more?"

Annie and I stopped, flustered. We turned and looked at each other.

"Sure?"

CHAPTER FIFTY-FIVE
THE GRAND MARKET

"[Ingredient Scan: Hops]" I looked down the row of produce, but nothing really 'pinged' in my vision. Sigh, another bust.

"You do know that you don't need to speak Abilities out loud to use them, right?" Annie remarked.

"Yeah, yeah." I paused as we passed by a rack of roots of some kind. "Hey, we should order some ginger from Kinshasa, and I can start making ginger pop! Did Balin tell you about it?"

"He did. One thing at a time, Pete – focus on the beer for now." Annie picked up some leafy-greens, frowned, and tossed them aside. "Ugh, this is rotten. How can you sell rotten food like that? Do I need to complain to City Hall?"

[Translated from angry toothless gnome] "My cabbages!"

"Oh, hey, Gimbletack! How are you doing?"

[Translated from angry toothless gnome] "I assume you will pay for that wasted produce, you lovely youngsters!"

"What did you say about my mother!?" Annie balled up her fists and moved in. I grabbed her collar and dragged her away. She had a higher strength, so it was a struggle, but I had better leverage. I tossed a few coppers to Gimbletack for the wasted produce and waved goodbye.

"Just ignore the cantankerous old gnome, Annie. The best vengeance will be outliving him."

"By Lunara's Lace, I don't think so! I'm reporting him for substandard vegetable produce the first chance I get!"

I paused, "Is that actually a thing?"

"City of Minnova Ordinances Ver. 315, Chapter –" Annie began in a huff, but I cut her off.

"Of course, it is. Why do you even know that?"

Annie squared her shoulders proudly. "I memorised all the Ordinances related to food or drink. I wanted to make sure nothing we did at the Goat could run afoul of city law."

I clapped. "Good fer you! I never really bothered learning all the laws back when I owned my own company."

Annie's face was a rictus of horror. "How could you not know the laws!?"

"They were more what you'd call *guidelines* than actual laws."

"Don't you dare tell my father that." Annie hissed. "He'd have you out of the brewery faster than you could say, 'I'm a reincarnated master brewer.'"

"Nah, Balin and I are a packaged set, and he loves Balin." I looked around, quizzically. "Speaking of Balin, where did he go?"

"He needed to get his saws sharpened. They got a bit dull while he was in the mine, and all the woodworking lately chipped one of the teeth." Annie pointed to an open-air blacksmith just down the street. "He's over there."

"Well, let's go get him. I'm not carrying a dozen sacks of erdroot by myself."

We trekked down one of the four main streets that demarcated the Grand Market Square of Minnova. The Grand Market was a literal square about four blocks wide and long, with an open central plaza. City Hall was a towering edifice to one side, with the Cathedral of the Gods at the other. A uniform series of shop-fronts lined the outer Main street and the central plaza was a massive combined bazaar and farmer's market. The enormous purple crystal that lit the entire cavern hung directly over the market and bathed everything in a soft lilac light. The effect was magical, and that didn't even take into account the literal magic on display everywhere.

Annie had explained the politics of the Grand Market on the trip here, and it was like nothing back on Earth. The major Guilds and businesses all had the opportunity to bid on a spot at the Market each year. They didn't bid anything as simple as gold, oh no; they bid a percent tax on all the goods they sold within the Grand Market. The highest bidders got the fancy physical Main storefronts on the outer street. The losers had to sit out with the travelling traders and local farmers in the plaza, but *still had to pay their bid taxes.*

The result? The Market was cut-throat, and companies could and would go under if they over-bid, but the possible profits were monstrous. Everybody shopped in the Grand Market, and there were nearly a million people in this city. A sewer system, [Healers], a cat infestation, and high vitality kept the population from getting wiped out by plague while underground housing kept living space from becoming an issue. Back in its mediaeval heyday even old London only had around half a million residents.

Suffice it to say, the place was packed, noisy, smelly, and amazing. The scent of spices and sweets and smoke and sweat was intoxicating, and I had to physically hold myself back from a stall selling some kind of glazed meatbun. When an odd amalgam of steel and bones walked by, I pointed it out with excitement.

"Is that a golem?"

Annie looked it over. "Yes, a fairly standard porter type."

"That's amazing! Why don't we have a golem? It would beat lugging sacks and barrels and erdroot around ourselves!"

"We used to..." Annie's voice was chagrined. Oops! Landmine!

"Uh... what's that!" I pointed at a flurry of motion overhead. A series of what looked like electrical streamers were whizzing by. They covered nearly every colour of the rainbow, and looking at them made my soul itch in my eyes. I blinked and rubbed at my eyelids vigorously. "Argh! What in Midna's Mullet are those!?"

"They're spirits, summoned by a [Summoner] and contracted to perform tasks. They're good for scouting and communicating, and they can possess and animate small objects. Those ones are probably looking over the bazaar for any interesting goods. Don't look at them too long, you'll hurt your spirit. They're almost as expensive as the golems."

"Don't need to tell me that." I looked away and noticed a kiosk in the plaza that was selling runestones. "Ooooh, I should buy some. I'm rich now!" I started to walk over, and Annie grabbed my sleeve.

"What?"

She shook her head, her visage grim. Then I remembered – Balin and I had given all our gold to the brewery, and I hadn't gotten any more money from the city for my boomdust yet. I was completely broke.

"Noooooooooo!!" I raged quietly as Annie dragged me over to a shop with a sign that declared it to be *Battlehammer Battlegear and Blacksmith*.

I begged to stay outside. While the inside of a dwarven forge was certainly interesting, I was pretty sure I'd just seen a miniature dragon walk by. Besides, you've seen one fantasy dwarf forge in an MMORPG, you've seen them all. Plus, it was really hot in there!

"Do you promise not to wander off?" Annie asked.

"Absolutely. Cross my heart and hope to die."

"What kind of weird oath demands wishing for death," Annie murmured as she went in to fetch her beau.

I stayed outside and cooled my heels for a while. I played a little 'spot the human' while I waited. I'd seen four so far today: two elderly men, a young woman, and an armoured adventurer. I had to wonder how they dealt with all the carbon monoxide from the coal fires down here. That was when something in a nearby alley caught my attention.

"Ooh, what's that?"

"I cannae believe that was so expensive!" Balin grumbled. "Outrageous prices! It woulda cost half that back in me own town."

"They're the best, and you paid extra for fast service." Annie shrugged. "I don't want you using substandard tools, that's how injuries happen." She petered off. "I should know."

Balin gave her a soft look and took her hand in his. "Yer makin' tha most of it. The brewery is gettin' back on track, and it's lookin' more'n more like tha person ya need forgiveness from tha most, is you."

Annie sighed and nuzzled her beard into Balin's armoured shoulder. "You're right, Balin. I just... worry that I'll mess everything up again."

"Nah, yer tha Annie Goldstone that made the new lubricant being used by half the mines in Minnova."

"That's true. It's a shame it wasn't more valuable." Annie turned to look around them and frowned. "Where's Pete?"

"Where did ya leave him?"

"Right there! Gods, he promised –"

"Hey guys!"

"AHH!" The two of them cried out and spun around. "PETE!"

"Uh, yeah?" I stepped back in shock.

"You said you wouldn't move!" Annie pointed her finger accusingly. Balin was taking big, angry gulps of air.

"I'm a stranger in a strange land, not a child. Besides, I'm still here." I pouted. Where was the trust?

"You're right, I'm sorry." Annie's shoulders dropped in defeat. "What do you have there?" She pointed to a sheet of paper in my hand.

"Oh, yeah! I found it in the alley over there, it –"

"Ah, Annie Goldstone is it not?" A voice from behind interrupted and we turned to see a grumble of dwarves in traditional leather and chain-mail. Their beards were all similarly done up in a neat knotwork that I was beginning to recognize as the more archaic style, while their helmets had *actual horns*. Every bit of them stunk of power and privilege and... onions? I admit I stared, a little agog, until Balin stepped on my foot.

"Master Brewer Browning," Annie said, her voice curt and cold. "I greet you on this most auspicious day. How do you fare?"

"Quite well, young Goldstone. How is your father?"

"He's doing well. We've been very busy."

"Yes, I heard about that." The dwarf glanced my way, and I realised his gaze carried a mix of contempt and hate. What the heck had I done to get stuck in this guy's craw!? "That beer drinking competition was a black mark on the history of brewing in Minnova, and the Guild is considering censuring the Thirsty Goat for its participation."

"You can't do that!" Annie shouted, and then switched gears to her usual matter-of-fact tone. "The King himself approved of that contest. To censure us for our participation would be lèse-majesté."

"Hmph. I don't think you're one to talk about breaking traditions. Especially when you're depending on a pair of 'reformed dwarves' to save your brewery."

That was a low blow, and I especially didn't like the implication that this jerk had done some research on me. I hadn't exactly been laying low though. Annie was turning white, and Balin looked ready to pop, so I decided to butt in before a brawl broke out.

"Actually, we were just here to buy some erdroot. We're running out of beer faster than we can make it and right now you're keeping us from our sacred duty of crafting the True Brew," I said in my best 'Why Yes, I'm the Manager, Ma'am' voice.

"You'll find that it'll take more than winning a silly contest to get the dwarves of Minnova to continue drinking your beer. Besides, I sincerely doubt any brew you make will be True," Browning sneered. He then brushed past us, and his stony-faced entourage followed.

"Who were those assholes?" I whispered when they were out of earshot. "And why do they smell like onions?"

"Some of the Masters of the Brewers Guild," Annie spat out. "They were the ones that forced Dad to agree to send me to the Reform Mine. It damn near broke his heart. Holier-than-thou bastards, the lot of 'em. Resting on the laurels of their ancestors and never striving to grow. Their traditions require them to carry onions in their breast pockets."

"Wow, I hate them already."

"I've never liked tha sort me'self," Balin added. "Want me to armour up and deck 'em? Let me Feud him in the *face!*"

"Don't you dare! But, By Barck's Beard, I pray our next brew goes so well I can shove it in their smarmy faces," Annie growled.

"Meh. Bugger Barck, let's make our own luck. Sanitization is a good start."

"Let's hope so." Annie's quirked an eyebrow. "What do you have against Barck?"

"Oh, Pete think's he's cursed by Barck," Balin said off-handedly.

"Hey, the specifics of that are still a secret!" I rammed my hand over Balin's mouth and his eyes bugged out in horrified realisation.

"WHAT?!" Annie rounded on me and advanced. I backpedalled and held out my hands in a calming gesture.

"It's not a big problem, I was going to deal with it eventually! I've been so busy. I just need to go to the church and talk to a [Prophet] and it'll all be fine."

Annie hauled me up by my gambeson and pitched her voice low so it wouldn't carry through the market. "You think you're cursed by the God of beer and you want to *work in MY BREWERY*!?"

"Uh..." Put that way, it was pretty bad. "Yes?"

"The cathedral is right there!" She pointed across the square at a looming golden edifice, and just barely managed to keep from screaming. "Go have a heart-to-heart with Barck and you're not coming back until it's done."

Sigh. Looks like it's time to go and meet the maker.

'Cause he's the God of craftsmen. Nyuck.

CHAPTER FIFTY-SIX
MEET THE MAKER

I was never a church guy before. I mean, I grew up in what could best be described as a heavily Christian household, but I was always more of an agnostic myself. That didn't mean I wasn't appreciative of all the art and culture surrounding religion. Heck, going to cathedrals was always on my bucket list whenever we jetted to some new country on vacation. Whether it was a golden temple in South Asia or an imposing gothic edifice in Europe, they all carried the same feeling of reverence and history.

None of which could carry a candle to the Cathedral of the Gods in Minnova. The epic Latin refrains of 'O Fortuna' pulsed in my mind as I beheld it. At least, the parts I could remember; I was pretty sure 'gopher tuna' wasn't Latin.

The casino had been covered in magic, and the Market was something straight out of fantasy, but the Cathedral was something else. I paused in wonder at the bottom of the first step, looking up and up and UP nearly to the roof of the cavern. The cathedral was made of some kind of white stone with black detailing and every square centimetre was etched or carved in some way. A rainbow curtain of light hung in the air around it, an aurora that bathed the artistic surface of the cathedral in cloying light. Flickering shadows of humans, elves, dwarves, gnomes, and dragons cavorted upon majestic frescos. A pair of belfries with crystalline bells sat far above, and as I gawked, they chimed a song that filled my heart and soul with peace.

Bing!

Condition Gained: [Calm]!
You have gained the [Calm] Condition!
Your wisdom and perception are increased by 4.
You are less likely to be frightened.

Well, that was something. Was it magical, holy, or some other kind of effect? Not that I was angry about a lower blood pressure right now. This was my first time walking into a church feeling like I was there to beat up the pope.

If I was honest with myself, I'd mostly gotten over the whole [Alchemist] Title thing. The Blessings had saved my life, and [Alchemist] kind of suited me. But I was still pissed at Barck for forcing it on me. Every person on this rock got a choice except me, and I was seriously considering giving him a one-two to the jaw if we ever met.

A constant flow of worshipers streamed in and out of the church. I was surprised to see some were completely unarmoured, wearing pure white robes and gold filigree cloaks. I assumed they had to be clergy. My assumption was corroborated when a pair of dwarves exited the church carrying a small blonde moustached baby. They paused to converse with one of the more elderly, white-robed figures. He made some kind of gesture and said something I couldn't hear over the din of the market. There was a faint glow around the baby, the parents smiled and bowed, and the group broke up. That must have been one of the [Priests] Balin mentioned.

Well, time to stop procrastinating. I climbed up the stairs and passed through the double doors, which were flanked by a pair of dwarves in whitish-blue plate mail. I recognized it as mithril and managed to avoid gawking. Those pieces of armour had to be worth millions of gold! The pair looked me over as I walked in, and I guessed they were using an Ability on me. I shivered – what kind of soul-stripping powers could a pair of guards for a Church have? It made me glad that intrusive spirit manipulating stuff was illegal, at least according to Diamond.

Surely a *Church* wouldn't do something *illegal*. Right?

The inside of the cathedral was somehow even more impressive than the outside. It reminded me a lot of the Sistine Chapel, with paintings covering nearly every single surface. Except these paintings were moving, acting out scenes within. An enormous organ sat against one wall – at least, I thought it was an organ? I wasn't sure because it actually looked more akin to bagpipes the size of a semi-truck.

There were several massive statues stationed through the church, each depicting a single God replete with their own magical effect. Aaron's statue was a human with a swirl of water surrounding it, arcs of multi-coloured liquid spinning up to the ceiling. Lunara was an ebony elf cloaked in darkness that practically had substance, while Solen was some kind of weird, fangy, frilly person that was impossibly bright to look at. Finally, Barck was a verdant statue of a dwarf off to the western side of the church, with an enormous silver tree growing out of the base. Those were all the Gods I could make out from the entrance.

There must have been hundreds of people in here, and I was stumped about where to start. Should I go to the statue of Barck? Maybe I could grab a white-robed acolyte and say, "Hi, I'm here to see a [Prophet]." Gutsy, but it would probably put me in a line half a kilometre long. I doubted Annie would let me back into the Goat until I figured stuff out, and I didn't want to be here for hours.

I dithered for a moment until the problem was suddenly solved for me.

"Hello, Peter Roughtuff?"

"Uh... yes?" I looked around and then down at a short gnome in white robes. "Can I help you?" My eyes narrowed. "Check that, do I know you?"

"You are expected. Prophet Barnes will see you now." He turned and went into a side alcove, then popped back out and waved at me to follow.

Well... Yay? Shit? Score? Damn? There was possibly a word here that captured my simultaneous feelings of relief and gut-churning dread, but I couldn't put my finger on it. I was expected!? I swear if they bring me in front of the congregation to announce I'm the new [Hero] anointed by the Gods I was going to blow this building to kingdom come. Inner Peace, Pete. You're calm as a cucumber. *Inner Peace.*

I peeked into the alcove and looked up and up and UP. First, apparently, I had to climb a couple hundred stairs.

The white-bearded dwarf with traditional knots and pleats stood up from his rather plain wooden desk and smiled as I entered the room. He was wearing the same robes as the rest of the acolytes, but with even more gold stitching. His voice was leathery with age as he spoke. "Ah, the hero of the hour!"

I almost turned around and bolted. The [Calm] Condition was all that kept me from bowling over the acolyte behind me and jumping out the nearest window, the fall be damned.

"Hello, [Prophet]." I smiled back and made a small bow like I'd seen the dwarven couple do below. He nodded in return and held his hand up to make a sign that kind of looked like a W. His pointer and pinky fingers were held straight up with his ring finger down. His middle and thumb fingers met in the middle. It kind of looked like crackling tongues of fire.

"Come in, come in. Thank you, Paddlefoot." He waved the acolyte out and invited me to take a seat. The door swung shut behind me, cutting off a joyous shout of "HEY, I JUST GOT A BLESS –!" The [Prophet]'s office was made of the same whitish stone as the rest of the temple, but was otherwise quite utilitarian. Besides a few beautiful tapestries, it looked like nothing so much as a standard middle-management office and not the ostentatious throne I'd expected. Then again, perhaps a [Prophet] was essentially middle management for Gods?

"I heard from the acolyte that you were expecting me, Prophet Barnes?" I began.

"Right to business! Yes, yes, we were." The [Prophet] leaned back in his leather chair and steepled his fingers. There was a moment of stretched silence while he observed me. A couple papers rustled and shifted on the table from a slight draft.

"Um... can I ask why?"

"You can." He smiled. Shit, did I just get dad-joked by a multi-centenarian?

"Why?" I kept my tone firm, but a little plaintiveness may have leaked in.

"Because I knew you were coming." He grinned.

"Now yer just playin' games."

"Hah! Guilty. You looked like you needed some levity. To answer your question, Barck told me you would be coming by. Your visit is the final and most important task on my plate today lad, so your presence means I'll soon be free. I plan to go and have a couple drinks with my brother – he's visiting from the capital, you see. Thank you for not coming late!"

Right, that made things easier. "Well, I'm here. Why did you want me?"

He shrugged his shoulders. "I don't know. Why did you come?"

"Seriously?"

"I'm not a [Telepath]."

"So, you don't have any messages for me?"

"No, not at all. I was simply told you would be arriving."

"Well, you asked me to come. I figured there would be something."

"Not in particular. Should there be?" He leaned forward and smiled.

Wow, what a loaded question. "I kind of wanted to talk to Barck..."

"There is a statue downstairs. He will hear your prayers." Prophet Barnes pointed a finger down through the floor. We stared at each other, at an impasse.

I stood slowly out of my chair. What in tha' Nether was this? "I guess I'll go downstairs then?"

Barnes nodded and bent his head to sign some papers. "You do that. Blessings of the Gods be upon you, child."

"Uh... thanks, you too."

I made my way to the door without taking my eyes off the [Prophet]. He ignored me and continued his work. I opened the door behind me and stepped through, but he never moved.

And then I was falling.

Prophet Barnes chuckled as he heard the scream and the door snapped shut. [Pinnacle Portal] was such a fun Ability.

He finished off the last few pieces of paperwork and stood up, stretching his stooped back as he did so. The rusty joints popped and cracked; these young upstart [Healers] just weren't as good as he remembered. Back in his day, the head [Healer] would have been able to fix his rheumatism in a heartbeat! Maybe he was getting a bit too old to stay hunched up in this draughty office for hours on end. It was time to see about getting one of the younger [Prophets] to replace him.

Barnes hummed a merry tune as he stepped out the door and into the hallway leading to the stairs. The new Whistlemugs sweeping Minnova's drinking scene were going to be a fun surprise for his brother! His Grace always loved interesting new ideas.

Pete was nowhere to be seen. –

Thankfully, the ground broke my fall. I bounced a few times, and scraped a knee, but the grass provided a nice cushion.

The... grass.

I felt it beneath and around me, the slightly wet crispness of it against my skin. It had the earthy scent of cuttings when I mowed the lawn for Caroline. It was the prickly texture on my back as I played cloud animals with Sammy. For an instant, I was back on Earth, and I nearly wept.

I stayed there for a while, staring up with watery eyes at a grey sky filled with mist. There was a sun up there somewhere, so I wasn't underground anymore, and definitely not in Kansas. It was glorious.

A dull roaring sound filled the air, but it didn't sound like an animal or civilization. Maybe a waterfall? I eventually stood up so I could have a better look around. My current location was on the side of some hill or mountain, with a black wall of stone just a few dozen metres ahead and a sheer drop another dozen metres behind me.

There wasn't a single animal or tree to be seen. Just waist-high green grass, boulders the size of houses, and a black cliffside shrouded in white.

That was when I heard it: the sound of footfalls. Each a thundering boom that drowned out the ever-present roar. I looked around wildly and saw an enormous shadow sweep through the fog just beyond the cliff.

"HELLO MR. PHILLIPS"

Bing!

Condition Lost: [Calm]!
*You have lost the [**Calm**] Condition!*

Bing!

Condition Gained: [Terrified]!
*You have gained the [**Terrified**] Condition!*
Your wisdom and perception are decreased by 4!
Your agility and dexterity are decreased by 4!
Fight, freeze, or flee!

Holy *God*zilla! Only now did I realise that years of cartoon myths and tiny nativities had primed me for Gods to be regular sized people. My ears ached and nearby boulders quaked, as the voice avalanched across the mountain.

"OR SHOULD I CALL YA PETER SAMSON? OR PETER ROUGHTUFF? YOU'VE EARNED SO MANY NEW NAMES IN SUCH A SHORT TIME."

A craggy face loomed out of the mist, twenty stories tall. His beard was a shuffling canopy of trees, His moustache a sweeping mat of cattails, His skin a vibrant mat of blooming algae with the texture of cowhide. His eyes were a galaxy, and I tore my gaze away before my soul fell into their emerald abyss. The rest of Him was lost to the mist, His titanic mass a shifting shade amongst the depths. My eyes just barely perceived Him for what He was. He was a dwarf, but He wasn't. He simply *WAS*.

Bing!

<u>Stat Increased: [Perception]</u>!

Your perception has increased by 1! Your new perception is 17.4!

"I UNDERSTAND YA WANT TO PUNCH ME IN THE FACE? I COULD LEAN IN AN' GIVE YOU A CHANCE."

I may have peed a little.

CHAPTER FIFTY-SEVEN
ROCKET DWARF

The wall of greenery that was Barck sidled closer as he presented a cheek. My boots shook. I'd seriously been contemplating punching *that* in the face!?

"AYE, OFFER'S OPEN!"

Did he just read my mind too!?

"YEP."

I don't think so! I imagined the dirtiest, most twisted stuff that I could from the internet. Real unigoats and four-dwarves-one-mug kind of shit. Take that!

"I'VE SEEN IT ALL, PETE. YER NOT GOIN' TA SHOCK ME WITH YER' VANILLA CRAP. ARE YA READY TO CHAT? WE DON'T HAVE FOREVER. I MEAN, I DO, BUT I DON'T LIKE WAITIN'."

I deflated. This was not at all how I'd foreseen this meeting going. I briefly considered taking him up on his offer but... eldritch unfathomable being. I decided against taking a swing.

"So, you're Barck," I began.

"THAT'S RIGHT. GOOD JOB."

More like an eldritch unfathomable *wise guy*. Must be where Prophet Barnes got it from. Well, two could play at that game!

"And you're all Barck, no bite, right?" I gave a sick smile. Hah! Take my dad-fu!

He paused. "THAT'S A NEW ONE."

"I hope you liked it. Please don't smite me." I shivered slightly in terror, gathered every last bit of bravado I had, and continued. "Before we start, I need to know. Why did you force me to become an [Alchemist], Barck? I thought choice was important to the Gods. Seriously, W-T-F?"

"AH, YEAH, I DID THAT."

"Yes! Yes, you did!"

Barck continued while I chuffed. "ARCHIS AND I FIGURED YOU'D DIE TO THA STONEANTS OR GUNPOWDER WITHOUT IT. IF IT MAKES YA FEEL BETTER, I GOT PUNISHED BY THA OTHER GODS FER DOIN' THAT."

As a Canadian, I was incredibly offended by the lack of an "I'm Sorry." But...

"You're right. I would have died without it," I sighed. "So, I guess you're partially forgiven. Hearing you got punished for it does make me feel a bit better, actually. What happened?"

"I'M NOT ALLOWED TA HELP YOU AS MUCH ANYMORE. AND SOME OTHER STUFF."

"Wait, that's more like me getting punished! How is that fair?!"

"TOUGH."

Have you ever wondered what it would be like to chill with Jesus?

The guy sounds like an awesome hang. Never need to make a beer run – he can make water into wine. If you run out of munchies – BOOM infinite fish and chips. If you break your spine doing a stunt while he holds your beer, no worries – Jesus has got yer back!

Barck was a pretty awesome hang, and I quickly lost my [Terrified] condition. There were two big problems though.

"SO, THEN I SMOTE HIM."

"Hah! In front of everybody!?"

"THEY WERE TALKING ABOUT IT FER CENTURIES."

"I thought the Gods didn't care about our piddly human insults?"

"NAH, I HATED THAT GUY. HE GOT WHAT WAS COMING TO 'IM. I GOT HIM OUT OF THE KARMIC POOL AS FAST AS I COULD."

Barck lifted a Whistlemug the size of an aircraft-carrier from the cliff beside me and took a drag. The scent of lemons washed over me. I still couldn't believe Barck drank my radler! I took a sip from my own Whistlemug and frowned at it, both at the mug and its contents.

The other big problem was that I was in Heaven, or the Pinnacle, or whatever, and still drinking shit beer.

"Barck…?"

"ASK, MORTAL. PERHAPS I SHALL ANSWER."

"Why are we drinking this awful beer?"

"WHAT!?" I winced as a boulder crashed along the slope and then flew past overhead. "YOU DARE CALL THE SACRED BREW AWFUL! THIS MOST HOLY OF BEVERAGES WAS BLESSED BY MESELF!! PROSTRATE BEFORE ME AND I MAY FORGIVE YOU."

Barck drew himself up. The trees of his beard shifted and cracked as a suction of wind nearly ripped me from the cliff. The twin galaxies of his eyes flashed crimson, and somewhere far off in the distance his monumental fingers cracked as he flexed them.

Back when I was in kindergarten, I put a tack on my teacher's chair. Yes, it was an awful and terrible thing to do, but if my favourite cartoon character could do it, why couldn't I? It turned out that having an adult scream bloody murder and come bearing down on you with death in their eyes was a lot less fun when it was for real.

This was kind of like that, but a million times worse.

"I..I.. I apologise, yer Godliness!" I supplicated into dogeza as best as I could. This was how it was done, right? I put my hand into the same holy sign I'd seen that asshole Barnes make. "Please forgive this mortal for he has sinned."

"NAH, I'M JUST SCREWIN' WITH YA, PETE. IT'S GOATSHITE!"

What? My face betrayed my shock.

"YEAH. MEBBE IT'S ABOUT TIME WE GOT TO BUSINESS." Barck put down his mug and his expression turned serious. "YOU PROBABLY HAVE A LOT OF QUESTIONS, AND I HAVE A FEW ANSWERS."

"Not a lot?"

"THERE'S RULES. I CAN ONLY TELL YOU SO MUCH, AND I'M BLOCKED FROM A LOT RIGHT NOW."

"Ok… can I make a small request first? Talking to you like this is giving me an awful crick in the neck."

"OH, LET ME FIX THAT."

I stepped aside to let him drop down next to me. Instead, the next instant, I was snatched up by a craggy fist and felt a massive pull as we accelerated upwards. The hand holding me felt vaguely mossy, and I swear something was moving in it. The ride was bumpy, but only lasted a few seconds, and then I experienced something I never expected to feel in this life or my last.

Weightless.

Barck opened his hand and I floated away, my arms and legs flapping uselessly. Down below me, a blue and green orb floated in a vast ocean of stars. A pair of other, smaller orbs sat closer to us, spinning in a lazy circle around what had to be Erd. I could count three enormous continents down below. From up here, the clouds looked like rivers, flowing across an azure canvas.

"Oh my God..."

"YES?"

I ignored that. My chest swelled with childish glee. I was in space. I freaking *loved* space. Heck, when Caroline and I had gotten married, I'd walked into the church to Holst's *Jupiter, the Bringer of Jollity*. The refrain crescendoed in my heart as one of the moons swept by behind us.

"HAH! I KNEW YOU'D LIKE IT!"

"It's amazing!" I turned to look at Barck and did a double take. He floated off in the distance, where I could comfortably see all of him. He must have been nearly a kilometre away for that to be possible, but his voice was clear as ever. He wore an armoured suit in the classical style, and his hair was done up in traditional knotwork. If I didn't know he was the size of a mountain, I would have assumed he was a regular green-haired dwarf. He looked like an old man sitting in a black leather recliner made of stars, and his gaze upon the world was positively paternal.

"IT'S ONE O' ME FAVOURITE SIGHTS."

"Do you come up here a lot?"

"SOME O' THA TIME. WE MOSTLY STAY IN THA PINNACLE. WE'RE IN THA' FIRMAMENT RIGHT NOW, SO IF ANYONE IS LOOKIN' WITH A TELESCOPE, THEY'D SEE US."

He waved towards the northern continent.

"ALLO JACK. NOBODY WILL EVER BELIEVE YOU." He snapped his fingers and some clouds moved to cover a portion of the northern continent. I was bemused; Barck seemed to jump between serious, joking around, and angry at the drop of a hat.

We simply sat and enjoyed the view in silence for a while. "Honestly, I just thought you were going to shrink down to my size, this is so much better," I admitted.

"WE DON'T DO THAT."

"Why not?"

"THAT WAS SOMETHIN' YER GODS DID. MADE IT EASIER TO TALK TO 'EM AND EASIER TO RELATE TO."

"That sounds right." Hold on a tick, there was a rather major revelation in that sentence. "Wait –"

"DIDN'T WORK OUT TOO WELL IN THA END."

"Wait –"

"HARD TO BELIEVE IN SOMEONE THAT'S JUST ANOTHER GUY IN A TOGA."

"HOLD IT!"

Barck paused and *Harumphed.* A hurricane started somewhere over the southern coast from his breath alone.

"Um, I mean, excuse me please, yer Barckliness. You said, your Gods, as in my Gods, as in – there were actually Gods on Earth?"

"AYE. WHO DO YOU THINK SOLD ME YOUR SOUL?"

I rocked back on my heels – an incredible feat in zero-G. "Sold you my *soul*!?"

"YOU DIDN'T KNOW?" He quirked an eyebrow the size of a bus.

"NO!!!"

"HALF-BAKED, AMATEUR, HAS-BEENS," Barck grumbled. "THEY MADE A GREAT WORLD BUT THEY'RE SHITE GODS."

"SOLD YOU MY SOUL!?"

"YOU WERE EXPENSIVE. I HAD TO PAY YOUR GOD A RATHER PAINFUL SUM."

"I was an agnostic! I didn't believe in any God! Did some God just get my soul by fiat!?"

"SURE, YA DID. DIONYSUS? AEGIR? DU KANG? THA GOD O' WINES, BEERS, AND ALCOHOL? YOU WERE ONE O' HIS MOST FERVEROUS FOLLOWERS. YOU SPREAD HIS WORD YER ENTIRE

LIFE AND DEDICATED YER BODY TO HIM IN DEATH. HE WAS LOATHE TO GIVE YOU UP, BUT I MANAGED TO CONVINCE 'IM."

Huh, they did bury me in wine grapes. Wait, don't get distracted! *"SOLD YOU MY SOUL!?"*

"DON'T GET LUNARA'S LACE ALL IN A TWIST."

Barck waved his hand, and I blacked out.

A dozen beings sat in a space that had no real borders. Each of them was more of a concept than a physical thing, their forms not tied down by anything so mundane as geometry.

"So, what have you brought us, *screecrackle*" The last bit sounded like a mix between a modem and high-pitched static.

"It's a new invention created by one of my souls." One figure said, holding out a strange box. "It's pure technology, no magic at all."

The item was passed around to all those assembled, and they pronounced it a fine thing indeed.

"Another one o' my favourite souls lost everythin'." One figure grumbled. "Same problem, they're amazin' at inventin' but no head fer gold."

"My humans had a similar problem," another voice put in. "They solved it with something called 'patents.'"

"How does it work?" a figure that appeared to be an embodiment of the concept of pasta and meatballs asked.

"I created a magical gift that prevents anyone else from making or selling the same thing for an inventor's lifetime."

"Seems short. Mortal lives are a candle in the wind," another being with far too many metaphysical tentacles purred.

"Aye, perhaps five or six generations would make it better," another voice said.

The assembled agreed it was a very fine invention, and a very fine idea.

AN ADVENTURE BREWING

Another time, another space, another assembly.

Barck called for attention, "Look at what one o' me favourite souls made! They called it beer! I LOVE this stuff!"

A metaphysical mug popped into existence in front of all those assembled. They each took drinks in their own turn and kind.

"It's okay," A snake the size of a universe proclaimed.

"I'm not a fan," said a mass of energy.

"Tastes like something my people make, too. I've been letting it stew until it improves. Would you like to try?" said a four-armed being with eight limbs and sixteen hands and thirty-two mouths and sixty-four legs and one-hundred-twenty-eight ears and –

"Aye! Absolutely!"

Another set of mugs went around, and drinks were had by all.

"This is even better than mine! I can't wait till they make it!" Barck chuffed.

"How soon?"

"Ach, I dunno. I gave em' one o' those [Patent] Blessin's so it'll be a while. Hopefully they won't rest on their laurels!"

"Next, try the wine! It's new!" The assembled beings cheered.

Barck sighed. "Hey there, *screech crackle pop*"

"Ah, what has you down, my short-statured friend?"

"All the alcohol here is so damn good, but it's gone stagnant on my world."

"If you're feeling down, try some of this mead. It's to die for!"

"That doesn't really make me feel better. I want my spirits to enjoy some real spirits!" The being slammed his mug down on the floor.

"What's gone wrong?"

"Well, you see, do you remember that patent idea from way back?

I made it corrupt any unlicensed alcohol, but... I think I made it last too long."

"What is it, my short-statured friend. You have had more to drink than usual." The being in a toga raised an eyebrow and took another gulp of wine.

"Yeh, I've had an epiphany." Beer dripped down a beard that was knotted in a traditional non-Euclidean manner. Barck sighed and took another drink.

"Do tell." The being in a toga eschewed refilling its glass and drank straight from the bottle.

"If my souls won't make better alcohol, I'll be stuck drinking tha same few drinks forever."

"That is a terrible problem, you have my condolences."

"So, I had a great idea, you give me one of yours, and they can make proper drinks!"

It turned out even Gods could spit-take.

"Ten thousand souls, not a single one less."

"Grrr, you drive a hard bargain." Barck growled. "Fine!"

"You must ensure he gets the chance to win his soul back."

"Of course. I've been doin' this longer than you. I know tha rules."

"You aren't exactly known for following the rules, my short-statutered friend."

"Bah! All that matters is that 'is soul won't be held down by that damnable Blessin'."

"Take good care of him."

"Don't worry, I 'ave a good spot fer him. I've placed my most treasured souls there."

AN ADVENTURE BREWING

My eyes popped open, and I dry heaved into space. If I lost my lunch here, some poor explorer far in the future was going to find the oddest space-junk ever.

"SO, THAT'S IT." Barck said, morosely. "THAT'S WHY YER HERE."

"I'm here because... of – of – *patents*?" I croaked. I couldn't tell if that was fascinating or incredibly dumb.

"AYE. THA DWARVES WERE SO USED TA' NEW BREWS NOT WORKIN' CAUSE OF IT THAT IT BECAME A TRADITION NOT TA TRY. LIGHT BREW WAS A HAPPY ACCIDENT A WHILE AFTER THE PATENT ENDED." He shrugged. "TURNS OUT LIFE PLUS FIVE GENERATIONS WORKS GREAT FER HUMANS BUT AWFUL FER DWARVES."

"The elves..." I whispered, horrified.

"WORSE." Barck nodded. "THANKFULLY THA DRAGONS ARE TOO LAZY TA INVENT ANYTHIN'. I DON'T GIVE OUT THA [PATENT] BLESSIN' NOW, BUT THA DAMAGE WAS DONE. AND AS AN OUTSIDE SOUL YOU AREN'T AFFECTED BY ANY PATENTS STILL LAYIN' AROUND."

"So my quest, to influence the dwarves. The reason I'm on Erd and have a second chance at life – it's all because you want new alcohol? Why not just ask someone like Annie? Not that I'm complaining, mind you!" Yeesh, talk about your deific revelations: alcohol was *literally* my reason for existence.

"YOU SEE, AFTER CREATION WE GODS CAN ONLY MAKE MILE-STONES AND BLESSINS,' OR THINGS THAT OUR MORTALS HAVE INVENTED. IF WE JUST TOLD YOU WHAT TO DO THEN YER NOTHIN' MORE THAN AN EXTENSION OF OURSELVES. INSTEAD, WE PROVIDE THE FIRMAMENT AND THE GIFTS, AND MORTALS PROVIDE THE INNOVATION. NO INNOVATION MEANS..." Barck created a Whistlemug with a *pop* and filled it with beer. He took a sip and frowned. "NO NEW ALCOHOLS."

"But why me?"

"WELL, THAT'S A WHOLE OTHER STORY. TA BE BLUNT, IT'S 'CAUSE YER GOD SAID YOU WERE AMONG THA BEST."

"I sincerely disagree."

"YER NOT DEAD, YER IN A BREWERY, AND YER JUMPSTARTIN' STUFF WITHOUT EVEN BEIN' INVOLVED." Barck counted down on his fingers. "AND *YER* THE ONE THAT WANTED TA '*SAVE BEER*'."

Okay, maybe I could agree a little.

"Why all this rigamarole then? Why not just throw me in the brewery and send a [Prophet] at me with a message."

"IT'S A LITTLE MORE COMPLICATED THAN THAT. YOU SEE, AS MY CHOSEN –"

"LIKE HELL!"

"YOU'LL NEED TA BE MORE SPECIFIC, PETE. WHICH ONE?"

CHAPTER FIFTY-EIGHT
THE BOOZEN ONE

"I'm not going to be your chosen one." I harrumphed and crossed my arms. There were very few things I would never budge on, and this was one of them. Chosen ones lived a life of conflict and pain, and their stories always ended with some kind of sacrifice. I had zero interest in that. Several hundred years of brewing and good eating followed by a death surrounded by moustachioed great-great-great-great-grandbabies sounded just fine. Assuming I ever married again. Maybe great-great-great-great-grandnieces and nephews?

Barck pulled his beard. "IT'S NOT THAT KIND OF CHOSEN!"

"Well then, what kind is it? Keeping in mind that you kind of need to earn my trust here, Mr. Forced Blessing."

"PETE, DOES ANYTHIN' ABOUT ME SOUND LIKE THA WARRIOR HERO TYPE? WHAT KIND OF CHOSEN DO YA THINK I'LL NEED?"

"You're a skyscraper-sized omnipotent deity made of landscape! I have no appropriate point of reference here."

Barck grumbled for a moment. I thought I heard him mutter something about 'whiny mortals' under his breath. "FINE, LET ME PUT IT IN TERMS YOUR FEEBLE MIND WILL UNDERSTAND. LET ME TELL YOU ABOUT THE GREAT GAME."

"Oh, *woooow*. Hearing the words 'Great Game' from a God makes it *soooo* much better."

"I'M NOT LUNARA. I UNDERSTAND SARCASM."

"Good fer you."

Barck's eyes narrowed. "DO I NEED TO SMITE YOU?"

I quickly sat in seiza, then began pinwheeling in space. "Listening."

"BETTER. IN A WORLD WITH REINCARNATION, YOU CAN GET STAGNATION. THA SAME SOULS GOIN' THROUGH THA SAME CYCLES. THE GREAT GAME IS TO BREAK THAT CYCLE. DO YOU SEE?"

"I... think I do. You summon souls from outside the cycle to introduce change."

"THAT'S RIGHT. YOU AREN'T A CHOSEN 'ONE,' YOU'RE ONE OF EIGHT CHOSEN 'CATALYSTS.' EVERY EIGHT THOUSAND YEARS WE COMPETE TO SEE WHO CAN SUMMON A SOUL THAT WILL BRING FORTH THE MOST CHANGE."

"Good or bad change?"

"DEPENDS. USUALLY GOOD, BUT YOUR MORTAL CONCEPTS OF GOOD AND EVIL ARE OBVIOUSLY LIMITED. THERE HAVE BEEN SOME DEMON KINGS, BUT THEY MUST STILL BE PLACED IN AN EXISTING MORTAL VESSEL, WHICH LIMITS THEM GREATLY."

"I hope I'm one of the good ones." I joked, but there was a pit forming in my stomach. This felt a lot like responsibility.

"I CAN GUARANTEE THERE WILL BE SOME THAT FIND YOU TO BE THE OPPOSITE."

"I guess... like Tim, or those Honourable Whatever of Brewers."

"THOSE IN POWER WILL OFTEN FEAR CHANGE. I WOULDN'T WORRY, THOUGH. THE OTHER CHOSEN WILL BE RUNNING INTERFERENCE."

"Well, that's nice. Can you tell me about them?"

"NO. THAT'S ONE O' MY PUNISHMENTS. I CAN'T KNOW ANYTHIN' NEW ABOUT THEM OR WHERE THEY ARE."

"But you could tell me what you already know." I waggled my eyebrows.

"NO."

"In that case, will the others be told about me? That seems like a major handicap." I frowned. I was going to have seven other people out there with all my intimate details? That was almost as intrusive as social media.

"SOME THINGS. WE ARE FORBIDDEN FROM REVEALING YOUR NAME OR LOCATION DIRECTLY."

"Well, shit. At least tell me they aren't trying to kill me."

"SPEAKING OF REWARDS."

"Godsdamnit!"

"I CAN'T. IT'S IN THE RULES." Barck deadpanned. "THE CHOSEN CATALYST THAT IS ABLE TO INFLUENCE THE MOST SAPIENTS WILL RECEIVE ONE WISH."

"Worse still. Can we wish for more wishes?"

"NO. IT COULD BE TO GO BACK TO THEIR ORIGINAL WORLD, TO LIVE FOREVER, RAISE THE DEAD, OR GAIN VAST POWER."

"What about makin' someone love me?"

"PERVERT."

"Just asking." I sighed. "What I'm hearing is that I have seven targets on my back." This was almost worse than being summoned to kill some world devouring monster. At least the monster wasn't incentivized to seek and destroy me personally. I would just be another tasty treat amongst all the carnage.

"YES AND NO. VERY FEW OF THE EIGHT SUMMONED THIS TIME WOULD BE INTERESTED IN KILLING YOU."

"Barck, if you're trying to make me feel better about this whole thing, you're making it worse. 'Very few' is significantly higher than zero."

"NOT ON THE SCALE OF ALL NUMBERS. ALL I CAN SAY IS THAT YOU ARE UNLIKELY TO RUN INTO ANY THAT WOULD WANT TO KILL YOU. HISTORICALLY, WINNING THE GREAT GAME BY KILLING ALL THE OTHER CHOSEN IS A POOR WAY TO AFFECT CHANGE. THE GAME IS JUST OUR WAY OF MAKING THE PROCESS OF CHANGE INTERESTING."

Now it was my turn to narrow my eyes. "What's in it for you?"

Barck smirked. "CAN'T SAY, BUT IT WILL NOT BE SUPERIOR TO AN ETERNITY OF HIGHER-QUALITY ALCOHOL."

"I can toast to that."

"NOT WITH THIS SHITE."

We eventually made our way back down to 'The Pinnacle' as Barck called it. The gigantic misty black mountain that was this world's version of Olympus. Barck said it 'STANDS ABOVE EVERYWHERE IN ERD AT ONCE AND ALLOWS US TO SEE ALL.' Which just gave me visions of creeper Gods using it to peep.

I sat back down on my grassy hillock, with Barck mostly obscured by mist again.

"So, you can't tell me anything about the other seven, you can't give me free Abilities, and you can't give me any awesome gear either."

"I COULD DO EQUIPMENT, BUT YOU EXPRESSLY SAID NOT TO GIVE A REVELATION TO THE [PROPHET] ABOUT YOUR STATUS."

"Yeah, nope, I don't want that much attention. I'll hold that as a card in reserve, to be played in only the most dire of circumstances."

"SUIT YERSELF."

"Can you tell me about Earth's Gods?" I admit I was curious.

"NO, BUT I DID MAKE SOME ARRANGEMENTS WITH ARCHIS THAT YOU'LL PROBABLY LIKE."

"Archie!?" My ears perked up at that. "What is it?"

"GET THA NEXT TIER IN YER INFLUENCE QUEST, AND YOU'LL SEE. USE IT FOR YER SECOND SPECIALISATION."

"Anything else?"

"YES." Barck snapped his fingers, and I received a new quest.

New Quest: The New Brew!

Can you create a new dwarven brew for the first time in millennia?
The odds are against you, but you will surely persevere!
New Brews: 0/1

Rewards: One Karmic Reversal

Do you accept?

Yes / No

I hit 'yes.' "Didn't I already make ginger beer? Shouldn't that count?"

"YOU SAID SO YOURSELF – IT WASN'T GINGER BEER, IT WAS GINGER POP. INTENT MATTERS. BESIDES, I DON'T LIKE GINGER."

"Booo. What's this Karmic Reversal?"

"THINK OF IT AS A TEMPORARY UNDO BUTTON FOR FATE."

"Phew, sounds powerful. Can you really give me something like this?"

"IN THE SCHEME OF GODLY GIFTS, SOMETHING THAT REVERSES FATE FOR A MOMENT IS FAR WEAKER THAN SOMETHING THAT CAN ALTER ITS FLOW."

"I don't know enough about fate to understand any of that." I said with complete confidence.

Barck chuckled. "I WOULDN'T EXPECT YOU TO. THE LAST THING I WAS ABLE TO GIVE YOU WAS A PLACE YOU'D FLOURISH AND GIFTS TO HELP YOUR COMPANIONS ALONG THE WAY."

"Hey yeah, apparently the number of Blessings people were gettin' at the mine was pretty high." Grim had waxed on it vociferously – at length – for *hours*.

"NORMALLY A MORTAL MUST PERFORM A GREAT FEAT TO CAPTURE OUR ATTENTION AND BE WORTHY OF A BLESSING. RIGHT NOW, ALL OF OUR EYES ARE UPON THE CHOSEN, WHICH MEANS WE ARE MORE LIKELY TO HAND OUT A BLESSIN' SO LONG AS THE ACTION MEETS THE MINIMUM REQUIREMENTS."

"So... I could look for other people with lots of Blessings happening around them to find out who the other Chosen are?" If I was flying blind, I could at least put out some feelers.

"YES. I ALSO PLACED YOU AMONG SOME OF MY MOST FAVOURED SOULS, AND THEY WILL BE OF GREAT HELP TO YOU."

"Oh, who? No wait, let me guess. Annie, Copperpot, and... Bran?" I listed out the three I thought were the most innovative souls I'd met so far.

"GOOD GUESSES. TWO OUT OF FOUR."

"Hah, score!" I pumped my fist. "Which two?"

"ARE YOU SURE YOU WANT TO KNOW? THEIR PREVIOUS LIVES WILL HAVE NO BEARING ON THEIR CURRENT ONE, AND IT MAY CHANGE HOW YOU PERCEIVE THEM."

"I'm good with spoilers. Hit me." I paused. "Not literally."

"I UNDERSTAND FIGURES OF SPEECH AS WELL AS SARCASM. MY FAVOURED SOULS WERE BRAN, ANNIE, WHISTLEMOP, AND TOURMALINE. THE OTHER GODS HAD SOME OF THEIR FAVOURED PRESENT AS WELL, BUT I CANNOT SAY WHO. THEY WERE ALL PLACED TO INFLUENCE YOU IN A SPECIFIC DIRECTION. I COULDN'T AFFORD TO LOSE YOU AFTER TIARA STOLE THE MARCH ON ME WITH HER EARLY BLESSIN', WHICH WAS ANOTHER REASON I FORCED MINE."

"Ok, those make sense. Question, what is the difference between souls and the Fundamental of Spirit? You keep saying soul, but everyone I've spoken to says spirit."

"A SOUL IS THA METAPHYSICAL CURRENCY OF US GODS. WHEN IT MANIFESTS UPON REALITY, IT DOES SO AS SPIRIT. ERDIAN MORTALS ARE NOT TOO CONCERNED WITH THA DIFFERENCE SINCE THEY'LL USUALLY JUST BE REINCARNATED"

I mused on the fact that the Gods viewed my existence as *currency*, then got distracted trying to figure out who the other favoured souls around me might be. Balin was almost guaranteed to be one. Maybe Tiara's, or Yearn's? Grim for Lunara. Doc Opal for Archis? "Hey, were any of your favoured souls ever famous people? And wait a second, Tourmaline? Who the heck is that!?"

"TO YOUR FIRST QUESTION, YES. WHISTLEMOP IS THE SOUL THAT INVENTED BANKING ON ERD. HE IS TECHNICALLY BOTH MINE AND AARON'S. BRAN IS THE SOUL THAT INVENTED BREAD."

"Phew. Sliced bread?"

"THAT TOO. ANNIE GOLDSTONE IS MY MOST TREASURED SOUL." Barck waved his hand and the mist below us cleared to reveal the inside of the Thirsty Goat, as if we were in a giant IMAX theatre. Annie was there, busy cleaning everything with wild abandon, and occasionally ordering Johnsson around. "THE FIRST BREWER." Barck's voice was full of joy and affection.

I leaned in to see. The view was crystal clear from up here. There was likely a zoom function too. I gave Barck some side-eye; creeper Gods using it to peep *indeed*.

"I CAN STILL READ YOUR MIND."

I turned away and whistled. "Sooo, anyways. Who's Tourmaline?"

"FOR THAT CRACK I'M NOT GOING TO TELL YOU." Barck waved his hand, and the mist covered the mountain once more.

"Oh, come on!!"

"NO. SUFFER, MORTAL."

"You apparently own my soul. I don't think any form of suffering can match that! Maybe I should go complain to Solen..." I paused, as my mind raced back to the visions I'd been shown. They were oddly hazy, as though my mind was rejecting the memory. [Flash of Insight]. Pain briefly spiked in my mind, and then I remembered. I pointed accusingly at Barck.

"You're supposed to tell me how I can win my soul back!"

"EVENTUALLY." Barck prevaricated.

"I would appreciate it if you told me now. Especially if we are going to have a relationship based on mutual trust and respect."

"I AM A GOD. I DO NOT REQUIRE YOUR TRUST, AND YOUR RESPECT IS INEVITABLE."

"I will sit on my ass and macrame tiny yellow ducks until the day I die." I folded my arms and levelled my most deadly threat. I'd do it too, if only to make the point that I was nobody's lackey.

"UGH, FINE. YOU MUST FIRST CREATE FOR ME AN APPROPRIATE STAGE. SOMETHING GRAND ENOUGH TO WARRANT ME SUMMONING AN AVATAR. I WILL THEN COME TO YOU IN A FORM YOU DO NOT EXPECT AND CHALLENGE YOU TO A GAME. IF YOU WIN, YOU WIN YOUR SOUL BACK. IF YOU LOSE, I CONTINUE TO OWN YOUR SOUL UNTIL THE NEXT CYCLE. YOU GET ONE CHANCE PER CYCLE, NO MORE, NO LESS."

"Works for me. How grand?"

"THAT'S FOR ME TO DECIDE. 'DO NOT EXPECT' KIND OF REQUIRES THAT."

Damnit! Well, the octa-millennial was coming up. I could probably do something with that.

"IT'S ABOUT TIME FOR YOU TO BE GETTING BACK." Barck waved his hand, and my feet began dissolving into light. I panicked for a moment, and then realised he probably wasn't going to be killing his 'Chosen.'

"Wait! Do you really have nothing else you can help me with?"

"HMM, WHEN YOU ARRIVE BACK ON THA FIRMAMENT, LOOK FOR A FRIEND IN NEED."

"That's it?" My legs had now vanished up to my knees; white light streamed from my thighs and down the mountain.

"YOU HAVE ALREADY MET ONE O' THA OTHER CHOSEN."

"What? Who!?" I was now specks of light up to my neck, and I craned an ear up to hear.

"AND THA WHITE GOAT IS YER OLD WIFE."

"NO! *REALLY!?* YOU LIE!"

"YOU FIGURE IT OUT. NOW PISS OFF! I HAVE WORK TA DO."

My eyes dissolved, and the last thing I saw was a shit-eating grin that stretched across the horizon.

There was a flash in the Cathedral of the Gods. The statue of Barck cascaded through a rainbow of light before the entire room was filled with such brilliance that all assembled dropped to their knees in pain and reverence. Unnoticed among the chaos, a single figure fell to the floor in a corner. None saw him arrive, and none took notice as the room devolved into chaos.

The figure stumbled amongst the shoving, shouting throng. "Ugh, I still have grass stains on my pants, and couldn't he have fixed this gash on my knee? Oof! Scuse me!"

"Pete? Is that you?"

"Bran, what are you doing here!?"

"Hey everyone! This is Bran!" I announced to everyone in the mess hall.

"Hello, Bran."

"Hey."

AN ADVENTURE BREWING

"Nice to meetcha!"

"Good to see you again, Bran!"

"More mouths to feed..."

"NO! Not you, Penelope! Someone grab her before she says hello!"

When we'd first arrived back at the Thirsty Goat Annie had grilled me about the meeting with Barck. I told her everything was fine, but to keep the whole shebang quiet. No need to start a panic. Then I'd distracted her with Bran, and the two of them had gone off to chat for a while. Four hours and some paperwork later, and here we were, about to make history.

Annie stepped forward. "Pete and I have been running the numbers, and I've come to a decision. With Dad's blessing, Bran here is going to take over the kitchen. I think the success of our recent street party showed that the first step to bring back this brewery is getting more people drinking our beer. The easiest way to do that will be to turn this underutilised eating space into a full-time pub. Pete has gotten the pro-drinkers to agree to come and use the Thirsty Goat for their meetups, and with the current climate in the city, that is going to bring us a lot of attention."

She nodded at me, and I gave her two thumbs up.

"Bran is an amazing cook, and we're hoping that some of his dishes will turn the Thirsty Goat into a hot new place to eat. Pete said he has some other ideas to drum up business, so we will hopefully be very busy soon. Balin, we are going to need a lot more chairs; get to work on that. John, Johnsson, Richter, we still have over a dozen empty fermentation tanks; you'll need to work double time. We've got about two weeks to get ready while the first batch of wort ferments, so get to it!"

CHAPTER FIFTY-NINE
PRIMETIME BEERS AND BEARDS

"Oh hellooo, Barck." The gem-studded gnomess purred as she sidled up to the dwarf. He was in his usual spot, on the bluff near the top of the mountain; He said it offered the best views. He had created a plush leather recliner, like those used in gnomish cafes, and was lounging in it while staring up into the clouds. He looked miffed at being interrupted, but then, he always looked miffed.

"What do ya want, Tiara? Don't ya have some duties ya should be doin'?"

"We all felt some Godly power being used yesterday. Did you have a nice meeting with Peter?"

"Yes." Barck was as brusque as usual, and Tiara's eyebrow twitched.

"I was just checking to see if you were bored and all, with only the one Chosen to watch."

"It's goin' fine." Barck snapped a drink into existence and passed it off to Tiara. She took a sniff and drank.

"This is that new radler, right? It's okay. Nothing compared to tea though."

"It's a good start, and Aaron likes tha ginger pop. Nuts?" Barck handed over some nuts in a golden bowl. "I hope Pete introduces some better beer snacks soon. I'm gettin' tired o' nuts and pickled fish."

"Oh?" *crunch* *crunch* "Do you think he has a good chance?

He's made another move on the board, but it's nothing close to the other Chosen."

"Are none of ya' watchin'?" Barck asked, flabbergasted.

"Sort of, but the Sword God is making serious waves among the dragons, and stuff is getting pretty crazy in the human kingdoms too. Between that and our regular work, Pete just doesn't register as important."

"Bah. Not even someone from Murim is going to get those lazy lizards off their behinds."

"We'll see! How about Peter?"

"Here, I'll pass you the frequency and you can watch."

"What's happening?"

"Nothin'. He's just hangin' out and runnin' errands fer tha next week or two while tha batches ferment."

"What?! Then why are you focusing on it!?"

"Because it's entertainin'. Now shhhhhh!"

The clouds above them parted to reveal a scene happening just below in a small store in the city of Minnova.

"This is the place," Johnsson said, opening the door. "After you, Pete!"

The sign on the door read *The Bashful Beard*.

It was inhabited by several dwarves in skirts and had a line of chairs and washbasins lining the walls. It definitely reminded me of something out of a magazine from the 60s. All it was missing was a dozen chatty housewives.

"So this is the beardy-parlour you kept mentioning, Johnsson?" I walked into the building and looked around. It was fairly modern, by dwarven standards, in an art deco style with a lot of colour.

"It is. Isn't it great?" Johnsson shrugged his light blue, armoured jerkin onto a coat hook and took a seat by the window. "Afternoon, Tina, you're looking fine today! Two for today, please!"

"Oh, you. Who's yer friend, Johnsson?" The dwarfess working on a patron's moustache waved some painted nails at us.

"Oh, I'm sorry. Let me introduce you. This is Pete!" Johnsson said.

"Hi, sorry, I'm Pete," I said offhandedly, as I examined Johnsson's hanging armour. "I'm also mystified. How did you get that armour off so fast, eh?"

"Well nice to meet you, Pete. Grab a seat by the window and I'll be right with you." Tina grabbed what looked like an aetherstone on a stick and placed it up to the patron's beard. A warm breeze wafted from the stone, and the seated dwarf sighed in pleasure.

"It's nice, isn't it?" Johnsson said. "The suit only looks like armour at first glance. It's actually padded cloth and filigree. There's no actual protection at all, which makes it a lot easier to put on and take off. More comfortable too. Besides, who needs armour in modern society anyway?"

I stared at the jerkin with wide eyes. "You need to show me where you got it."

"I'd be happy to, but your beard comes first, Pete. No dwarf or dwarfess is going to be interested in you if you don't practise proper beard care."

"I know, I know. It was getting kind of ratty. You're the most put-together dwarf I've met, so I figured you'd know all the best spots."

"I do indeed. Tina is a wizard with a brush, and she'll make you the most handsome dwarf in all of Minnova."

"Hear, hear!" Tina called from her chair.

"I won't let anyone else work on my beard, and I'm always trying new styles." Johnsson flicked his beard, which was split into a three-part braid with several teal bows in it.

Eventually we were called up, Johnsson with Tina, and myself with a dwarf in clogs and a sundress named Petunia. Soon, the only sound in the shop was the snapping of scissors and the occasional sigh of pleasure. I just couldn't help myself...

"Mmmmm... the scalp massage is nice."

"Wow, this oil treatment feels so good in my beard."

"Do you want to get matching beads, Johnsson?"

"Ahhh, keep brushing right there!"

Soon all the other dwarves in the building were chuckling.

"You sound like this is yer first time getting yer beard done." Tina laughed.

"Um, yeah, ha ha..." I laughed along too.

"Alright, let's do this name-change thing."

Balin, Annie, and I were all standing at the foot of City Hall. We'd taken the afternoon to finally go and get my name changed so Aqua could file my employee paperwork.

"Before we go in, do you have all your identification, Pete?" Annie asked.

"Yep! ID, signed statement by Grim, and... huh, what's this?" I pulled a folded-up piece of paper out of my pocket and snapped it open. "Oh, hey! It's the poster I found in that alley at the Grand Market!"

"A poster?" Balin asked, leaning in.

"Yeah, I grabbed it because I wanted to start doing stuff like this too. I haven't seen ads or posters like this up anywhere, so I wanted to ask about it!"

"You'd better not put up 'stuff like that.' It's defacing private property and obnoxious signage," Annie said matter-of-factly. "City of Minnova Ordinances Ver. 315, Chapter 14, Section 17, Subsection 4. We seriously need to get you a tutor for local laws before you get us shut down."

"It was on a public street," I countered.

"Defacin' public property then," Balin put in.

"Ugh, dwarves!" I rolled my eyes.

"Yer a dwarf!" The two of them said in unison.

"Yeah, yeah..." I stood to the side to allow a pair of angry-looking dwarves access to the stairs and began to read aloud from the poster.

We call for the King and his High Lords to sign the Great Charter!
Too long have the King and High Lords ruled by fiat. We approach the octa-millennial, and a chance for great change is upon us.
Do the guilds not run the cities? Do the greybeards not hold our knowledge?
Do the barons not protect the land?

The Crack Council for Independence calls for a change to these millennia-old injustices!

We call upon the King to protect the rights of the gentry from unfair abuses by the High Lords.

We demand that justice be assured no matter the station of the offender, as is the dwarven way!

We demand that the gold of the guilds and greybeards be left in their care, as is the dwarven way!

We demand the rights of gnomes not be curtailed! Let them be free, as is the dwarven way!

Come to the octa-millennial and join us as we march upon the Castle to entreat the King!

Signed, Thad Harmsson of the Crack Council for Independence

"Psh, revolutionary drivel," Balin grumbled.

"I don't know, Balin," Annie said. "If there was better justice, then maybe the [Judges] would be going after real criminals instead of people like you and Pete."

"I suppose." Balin stroked his now completely restored handlebar moustache. "But then I wouldn't have met you."

"Gods forbid." Annie fluttered her eyelashes at him.

"Ugh, get a room, you two," I groaned. "Annie, by real criminals, do you mean recalcitrant gnomish purveyors of shoddy green vegetables?"

"Yes."

"Heh. Hey, why does it say the rights of gnomes are curtailed?" I asked, pointing at the paragraph in question. "It doesn't look that way at all."

"Most of it is traditional dwarven stations," Annie said. "Gnomes cannot become greybeards, they cannot become brewers or record-keepers, and they cannot join City Hall." She waved her hand to indicate the building beside us. "They also struggle with purchasing land in traditionally dwarven held enclaves."

"Well, that's awful."

Balin shrugged. "That's the way it's always been. I can agree with ya there, tha gnomes have been our staunchest allies forever."

"The gnomes agreed to those limitations in return for free travel

AN ADVENTURE BREWING

and taxation benefits within the dwarven kingdoms. It made a lot of sense at the time, but those laws are a bit out of date now," Annie put in.

"You know, Annie, I've noticed you seem to know a lot and your accent is different. Is it a schooling thing?" I asked.

Annie nodded. "I went to the Archis Academy for Magic when I was younger. A lot of wealthy and well-to-do families put their children through there."

"You learned magic!?"

"Yes and no." Annie shrugged. "It's mostly like any other school, just more advanced and with better connections. You learn magic in the higher years. Aqua and Johnsson went there too, though Johnsson quit before I did."

"Why did you all quit?"

"Who wants to spend the next hundred years in school? Now let's go get a number so we can get your name changed, Mr. *Samson*."

"And the STONER keeps rolling!" The announcer cried. "DOES HE EVER STOP!?!"

"Here's yer nuts, Pete." Brock's cheerful eyes peered out from his enormous bushy beard. He was wearing some black spiked armour with a lot of angry white lettering on it, much like the rest of the horde. The accompanying goggles were nearly a necessity to keep from losing an eye.

A dwarf with a short black goatee and no moustache, wearing nothing but green shorts, climbed up onto the ropes of the arena. He began yelling down at another dwarf in yellow spandex with a black full-plate helmet and a horseshoe moustache.

"Tha STONER thinks that this vermin isn't dwarf enough to compete in the ring! Send Tha STONER a real challenge!"

"Woah!" The announcer cried as the crowd booed and jeered in turn. "The Stoner has thrown down a SUPER EFFECTIVE challenge to

Electrorat! Will he take that, or is he too weak to face off against his NEMESIS after their last bout!?"

"Hah! This is great!" I exclaimed around a mouth of nuts while the yellow-spandexed figure hunched down and began to glimmer with electricity. "Is that an Ability? This makes for an awesome show!"

"No, Electrorat has some special enchantments on his armour that make that effect. He does use some aether magic too though." Brock sat down beside me and passed over a tankard. "Here you go, half-empty like you asked. Why?"

"I have something I like to add." I pulled a flask out and poured its contents into the beer. The faint scent of lemons washed out from it.

Brock leaned to look closer. "Is that some of that 'radler' I 'eard about back at the mine?"

"Yep. OOOH!!! GO STONER! MAKE THAT RAT ROADKILL!!!" I stood up with the rest of the crowd and roared as The Stoner did an elbow slam off the ropes onto Electrorat's head. His elbow 'pinged' on the yellow plate helmet and he cried out in pain as he was zapped by the contact.

"Tha STONER is smoking!!!" he shrieked as his hair caught fire.

"Hah!!" I snorted up some radler.

Brock took a swig of his beer and grumbled. "This is nothing. I wish you could have seen Tombstone's last match."

"Now, that I need to see. Tombstone is my favourite wrestler." I grinned.

"You 'ave good taste, sir!" The next few moments were a madhouse of heavy bagpipe music, flames, thunderbolts, and a lot of screaming between two half-naked dwarves.

"Speaking of Tombstones, how are things at the dungeon?" I asked while the announcer began the countdown for The Stoner, who was currently twitching on the ground as electricity coursed through him.

"May not be a monster stampede. Scouts think there may 'ave been a Boss Shift. That's a change in the boss of the dungeon ya see, so the territories are bein' swapped around. A lot of the weaker monsters are gettin' pushed to the outer edge."

"Oof, sounds rough. GO STONER! DON'T GATHER MOSS, YOU GRASS-HEAD!"

AN ADVENTURE BREWING

"Not too bad. It's an opportunity fer younger adventuring parties to get some fightin' close to tha edge where it's safest. ELECTRORAT! GIVE HIM A GOOD OLD WAVE O' THUNDER!"

The Stoner stood up at the last second and then stumbled around the ring. Electrorat came up behind him and attempted to deliver a massive suplex, but The Stoner grabbed onto Electrorat's helm with his thighs and flipped him to the ground instead. The crowd roared their approval.

"How's Balin doin'?" Brock asked as the fight devolved to some basic punches and kicks.

"He's crazy busy right now. Why do you ask?"

"Tha' boys at the guard station wanted to know. Some o' their kids are lookin' to get into this new wave of adventurers and they need a good defender. Balin's name came up."

"I know he was thinkin' about it. I'll pass on the message, but I honestly doubt it."

"That's all I can really ask fer. Thanks, Pete."

"No problem. I've been under a lot of stress after some recent events, so this is just what the [Doctor] ordered. GO STONER! GIVE HIM SOME *BLUNT* TRAUMA!" Nyuck!

"This is barbaric." Tiara complained, her mouth full of tea and pastry. "I have so much else I should be doing."

"Yer still here, aren't ya?" Barck remarked, grinning.

CHAPTER SIXTY

PETEY FIRST DATES – EPISODE 1

I stood and waved at the young gnomess as she entered the cafe.
"Hey, Lillyweather! Over here!"

The mousy-haired girl smiled brightly and made her way over, awkwardly manoeuvring around a barista as she did so.

"Hi, Peter!"

"Pete is fine. It's great to see you." I offered my hand in greeting at the same moment that Lillyweather moved in to initiate a hug. An awkward shuffle of hands, arms, and feet followed until we decided on a companionable handclasp. I cleared my throat and moved to pull out her chair.

"Thank you. It's good to see you too." Lillyweather replied. She moved to sit and bumped her foot against the table, spilling my drink. "Oh gosh! I'm so sorry. I'm not quite used to this thing yet."

She rubbed absentmindedly at her right leg. She was wearing short brown leather shorts, and her visible thigh was a matte metal the colour of porcelain.

I shook my head. "It's fine, don't worry about it. I can just go get another one. Do you have a preference?"

"Two cream and two sugar please."

"One double-double coming right up!"

Lillyweather giggled. "That's a unique way of putting it."

Quick, Pete! Make up an excuse! "Ah, yeah. It's the way I like my coffee too, so I came up with a name for it."

AN ADVENTURE BREWING

"Double-double, huh? I like it." She smiled and I smiled back. There was a brief *moment* before I took a deep breath.

"Right, the coffee." I walked over to the counter to order. Lillyweather watched me patiently for a while before pulling out a compact mirror from a pocket. She closed it with a *snap* as I walked back to the table. I placed down the drinks alongside a pair of plates; each a tower of white sponge cake and strawberries piled high with whipped cream.

"Ooooh, strawberry cake, my favourite!" She exclaimed.

"It's everybody's favourite. I just wish there was some chocolate." I sat down and took a drink from my cup. "Ahhhh... perfection."

"What's chocolate?" Lillyweather asked, as she dug into the slice of cake. She took a dainty, mouth-watering bite of the creamy concoction" *mmmmm*

"Something I ate once. I haven't found it locally." I laughed. "You've got a little something there." I pointed to a glob of whipped cream on her cheek.

"Here?" She licked at the wrong spot.

"No, here."

"Here?"

"No."

"Where is it?"

"Right *there*."

"Can you just get it?" Lillyweather pointed her chin across the table and I leaned across to wipe the cream off with a napkin. She looked slightly disappointed as she slid back into her chair.

There was a moment of silence as we ate and drank. Eventually I broke it.

"I was surprised when I got your message about wanting to meet. What's up?"

Lillyweather's face turned a slightly deeper shade of pink than her makeup. "I just... wanted to thank you. I heard about what happened at the mine. Without your help... Anyways, I'm glad you were able to take some time to meet me!"

"Of course! So, how are you doing?"

A shadow passed over her face. "I'm doing ok. I – I've been off work for a while. The college is paying for me to get some counselling and extended vacation time. Professor Copperpot got me a great prosthetic from the research branch at the university, it even has tactile sensation!" She knocked on the leg which made a sound like rapping on plastic.

"It looks great, by the way." I smiled.

"Thanks." Some of the cheer returned to Lillyweather's face. "You too."

"What?"

"Um, *howhaveyoubeen?*" She said in a rush, before taking a deep drink of coffee.

"I've been fine. I'm mostly busy with the brewery. I did get into the top ten at the Barck Beer Brawl though!"

"Really? What happened?"

"Well, you see…"

I waxed poetically about my adventures since leaving the mine while she listened with rapt attention. She laughed and I joked until the cafe got busy. Then we packed up and parted, as friends.

"So, this is the Minnova City Library, huh?" I put my hands on my hips and looked around. "I was imagining a lot more floating bookcases and stacks reaching up ten storeys." The library was normal-sized, though the stacks did reach to the ceiling. A sound-dampening red carpet stretched in between the shelves, with a few nooks here and there for readers. A squat red golem with four arms and legs walked by and picked up some books on its back before trundling off.

"At least that's magical." I nodded.

"It's naht *'Tha'* Minnova City Library, Pete. It's *'a'* Minnova City Library." Richter closed the door behind us and moved up to the front desk. His deep South Erdian accent was pitched to avoid carrying in the chill silence of the space. "Nice ta see ya, Uric."

The librarian nodded companionably, his long, braided beard bouncing on the desk as he did so. The nameplate in front of him read "Uric Mcbook."

"Evening, Richter. Are ya studyin' again?"

"Na, ahm here ta give da tourist ova der a crash course." Richter pointed at me as I slowly spun around to take everything in.

"Ah, well, make sure he knows the rules." The librarian nodded to Richter, who caught my attention and lead us away.

"Don't I need a library card?" I asked as we walked between the tall bookshelves.

"Why? Jus give dem yer ID if ya take any books. City 'All takes care of alla dat." Richter led us to a small collection of tables. A few gnomes and dwarves were seated around them with dour expressions and eyes that told of many sleepless nights. Richter indicated I should take a seat while he went and obtained something to read. He returned moments later with a leather-bound book the width of a dwarvish thigh and gently placed it on the table. The cover read *City of Minnova Ordinances*.

"Here ya go."

I shooed a cat from his chair. It yowled in disapproval before bounding away. The little fur factories were *everywhere*. "Dear Gods, do I need to read all of these?"

"It shouldn' be dat 'hard." Richter frowned. "What's yer intelligence?"

"High enough, I'll have you know!"

"Long as it's above twelve, ya shouldn't 'ave too 'ard a time rememberin'."

"Come to think of it..." I frowned. "Yer right. I haven't forgotten much anymore. I lose track of it, but don't forget as much."

"Den dis should be easy." Richter sat down beside me and got comfortable. "Da Goldstones are payin' me ta make sure yer up-ta-date on tha Ordinances. So, let's get started, ya?"

"Yes, yes. How did you end up being the one doing this?" I flicked open the first page and began to read. This was even denser than my college textbooks. "Huh, I didn't even know you could do that with a pickle, I wonder..."

"Don't try it. Tha's why it's in dere," Richter sighed. "I'm da only one really still studyin'. I come to da library a lot, so dey asked me to make sure ya were taken care of."

"Are you at the Archis Academy too?"

Richter went quiet for a moment before he continued. "Not yet. I got some tings ta work out first."

"Oh." I didn't push any further and the two of us read in silence for a while. Occasionally, I would hum or haw, and point to something for Richter to explain. Richter pulled out an old and ratty leather notebook that had 'Ricky' written across it in large letters and took some notes.

I nodded at it, curious. "That looks old. Is it from when you were younger?"

Richter paused and looked at the notebook as if seeing it for the first time. "Aye. I've 'ad it fer so long I don't even tink about it anymoar." He smiled. "It was from me da."

"Oh." I made a face like I'd sucked on a lemon. "I heard some… stuff from Annie, but not too much."

"She don't like Da, but he deserves it," Richter said in a terse voice tinged with regret. "He worked fer Mr. Goldstone nearly a hundred years after dey took us in."

"I heard he saved Mr. Goldstone's life." I angled my chair to talk, the book of Ordinances temporarily forgotten.

Richter nodded and leaned back in his seat. He pulled at his dreadlocked orange beard as he reminisced. "Mr. Goldstone was almost hit by a runaway cart. We'd just immigrated from da south then, and Da was lookin' fer work when he was passin' by and saw it. He shoved Goldstone just in time. Da broke his leg and was up fer a few weeks since we couldn't afford da [Healer]. Da Goldstones took us in and gave us a home and honest work. I went to a city school, and Ma eventually went to work at da Market."

I nodded and let him continue.

"Da rest were all goin' ta Archis Academy, and I wanted ta go too." Richter looked up at the ceiling and reached a hand to an imaginary sky. "I wanted ta learn magic."

I gulped. "I can understand that."

"Da did too, but we couldn't afford it. We were buildin' a new life here." Richter sighed. "So, when anotha' brewery offered 'im a lot more gold ta switch…"

"He didn't!" I gasped and the small collection of bleary-eyed bookworms hissed. I waved back apologetically. "Sorry!"

AN ADVENTURE BREWING 461

Richter nodded sadly. "He did. I begged him no. Dat it spit in da faces of da Goldstones. But 'e said 'One day you'll understand, me son,' and went."

"So... the Archis Academy?"

"Da money is there. I could go tomorrow; I could pass da entry test easy. But I just can't. Mr. Goldstone, Ma, all da older folk seem fine with it. 'Yer da saved me life, and I'm glad I could get 'im a good job.'" Richter smiled sourly. "But us younger ones feel betrayed. Like we came as thieves. Mebbe... mebbe one day I'll take da money, but not now." His fist tightened on the table. "So I come here and study, hopin' dat one day Archis will notice me."

"He will..." I smiled, a sick look on my face. "The Gods are always watching."

Richter scrunched his eyes and took a deep breath before opening them again. "But not everybody gets Blessed. Yer stallin' Pete, what's da City of Minnova Ordinance Ver. 315, Chapter 10, Section 4, Subsection 8?"

"Uhhh..."

The two of us continued for several hours, with Richter quizzing me and pointing out things I had missed. When it was time to leave, I checked out the *Book of Ordinance*s and made my way out the entrance. I stopped as I realised Richter wasn't following, but was still as a statue at the door.

"What's up?"

"Pete... Pete... I... I...."

Far above – in the metaphysical sense – the observers glanced up at the elderly man that had joined them, his arcane robes flapping as he lounged in the air over their heads. He was chewing on some peanut brittle and drinking an amber liquid from a tumbler glass that floated beside him.

"It's a good show," Archis commented around a mouthful of brittle. "But a twist always makes things more interesting."

Barck groaned. "Is *nobody* workin'? Who's drivin' tha planet!?"

I lit a candle, and the gentle yellow light flickered over a pair of plates filled with food. Each was piled high with a fancy salad, complete with nuts and some very expensive berries. A fine drizzle of some kind of honey completed the dish and lent it a posh air. My companion sat and gave me a questioning gaze.

"I – I'm starting to miss companionship," I said, as I wrung my beard. "I've been so focused on getting into this brewery and starting a new life that I wasn't really paying attention to romantic relationships. Yearn's Yams! I was on a date with a pretty girl earlier this week, and didn't even notice." I sighed. "She's a nice kid, and I know she's technically older than me, but she just reminds me too much of... well, I don't think we'll ever be able to be more than friends. I need to find a time and place to clearly turn her down."

I took a bite from my plate and filled two tankards with beer. I pushed one across to my date and we dug in.

"On top of that, I've been trying too hard to fit in. It's like I'm a freshman, trying to make new friends and acting like a fool to get in with them." I chuckled ruefully. "You'd think I would have learned my lesson in college."

We finished our plates, eating in companionable silence for a few minutes. The only sound in the dark room was the crunch of vegetables. I mulled on everything Barck had told me. I'd been avoiding thinking about it much because it was just... too big. *Way* too big, in every sense of the word. It was better to take Barck's advice and simply act as I had always been acting. The whole 'Chosen' thing changed *nothing*. I would simply take it as Deific approval of my utterly ridiculously awesome plan to save beer.

And then there was the opportunity to go back home, dangled in front of me like a poisonous fruit. All things considered, aiming for that was a death sentence attached to *seven possible assassins*. I would have to ignore the bait for now, no matter how much it called to me.

I spoke again, choosing my words carefully. "And some of the things that Bar – a person – recently told me have been messin' with my head. So that's why I asked you to join me for dinner tonight." I paused and brushed a spot of sweat from my forehead. "That is to say, erm. I – you – Caroline, my love, are you in there!?" I said the last in a rush.

meeeeeh [Translated from Prima Donna Goat] "What?"

A choked laugh came from a slightly ajar door to the renovated mess hall, and I stood up in a sudden motion. "Who's there!?"

I slammed the door open just in time to grab hold of a fleeing Balin, Aqua and Annie having already made it outside. I achieved a chokehold and put on the pressure while Balin flailed desperately.

"You enjoyin' peepin', bro!?"

"Pete!" Balin barely choked out. "Ya have to stop romancin' tha goat!""

"DAMN BARCK AND DAMN YOU ALL!!!"

"What on Erd did you do?" Tiara asked, reaching up to steal a slice of brittle from Archis's plate.

Barck snickered. "Nothin'. But I'm glad he didn't lock up. I knew I picked a strong one."

CHAPTER SIXTY-ONE
PETEY FIRST DATES – EPISODE 2

Bran and I sat in a restaurant, our table piled high with food. We took a few bites from each dish in turn, and then discussed.

crunch *crunch* "Too salty." Bran said.

I pointed at another dish. "I like this one, Bran."

"Too sweet, try this."

"Ugh, what *is* it?"

"Grilled cutter eel wi' a balsamic glaze."

"It's foul."

"Can't really disagree, Pete. Try tha braised roast goat and mushroom sauce."

I took a big bite. "Mmm... now *this* I can get behind. It melts in my mouth. The roast goat has a strong flavour that threatens to be a bit too gamey, but the mellow notes of the mushroom sauce counteract it perfectly. Combine that with this roasted erdroot and it almost makes me *like* erdroot. Anyway, add it to the list?"

There was a scratching of pencil on paper as Bran wrote something onto a notepad. "Aye. Needs some onions, though. Maybe some beer in the sauce?"

"Oooh! Maybe some shallots?"

"What's a shallot?"

"Sigh. More like shalnots, then. Are there any fish plates?"

"Just the cutter eel."

"Hmmm... is it because of a lack of fishes or a lack of dishes?"

AN ADVENTURE BREWING 465

"Only a few kinds of fish in tha dungeon and only cave trout in the lakes around Minnova." Bran shrugged. "You get bored of tha same grilled fish after a "few decades."

"Then we won't grill it. Add 'beer battered fish and chips' to the menu. I'll teach it to you later." *burp*

"Hmmm... We got a good mix here." Bran leafed through the notepad. "A lot more than most restaurants. What did you call this again?"

"We're doin' market research. I want to know what tha most popular dishes are in Minnova, so we have a guaranteed hit on opening night. Coupled with some of my recipe ideas and a little word of mouth, we should be full on day one."

"Here's hopin'." Bran nodded. "Maybe my new Blessin' will help with that."

"How does it work?"

"[Artisan's Luck]. It says that I make my own luck so long as I'm workin' hard."

"That's... amazing? But seriously, how does it work?"

Bran shrugged. "Dunno? I think it means that the harder I work, the luckier I get. So, if I work hard on these dishes, we might get lucky for openin' night."

"That *is* amazing! Is there anythin' else you need?" I asked.

Bran pointed eastward. "I want ta go to the place just around the corner. They make a really mean goatherd pie."

"Sounds tasty."

"It is. Ground goat with steamed vegetables like killer corn and peashooter pods. Topped with mashed Erdroot an' mixed with a ton of salty butter and garlic."

"Mmm."

"Mmm."

We rubbed our stomachs and leaned back to enjoy the feeling of a full belly.

"Excuse me..." A well dressed-dwarf in a button-up blazer approached our table. "May I ask what you're doing? Are you two actually planning to eat all this? I must ask that you pay now before any other food is brought to your table."

"Um..." I took in the massive pile of food. "Can we get this to go?"

"Do you know why I invited you into my office, Pete?" Jeremiah Goldstone asked.

"I'm guessing it has something to do with Annie moving a bunch of boxes around?"

"Shove it. You're in my way." Annie said, as she lugged a box filled with papers. I held the door open and waved her by. She grunted some thanks as she passed.

Jeremiah waited until the door swung closed.

"You're somewhat right. I actually invited you here to invite you somewhere else."

"Okay?"

"We're leaving." Jeremiah swung open the door and headed out.

"Okaaay?" I ran after. "Where are we goin', Mr. Goldstone?"

"The *Blasted Oak*."

"It's hard, havin' a child." Jeremiah lamented, his nose deep in a mug. A couple more mugs lay empty on the table beside him. His voice slurred as he spoke, and his accent was closer to Crack standard than usual. "Even when ya know she's smart as a whip and can knock most other dwarves out, all ya' can see is yer little darlin' callin' 'Daddy.'"

"I knooooow." I wept, tears streaming down my face. Nearly twice as many mugs lay beside me. I wasn't quite drunk, but my eyes were clouded with nostalgia and freshly healed pain. This was the first time I'd actually grieved for my family since arriving on Erd, and it hurt, but it was a good hurt. "They grow up so fast!" Then again, maybe – maybe I could see them again one day...

Jeremiah pulled out a locket and snapped it open. He gazed down at it tenderly, and wiped at it with one trembling finger. "And after her mother died.... my darlin' Lazuli. She's all I got left. That and my brewery."

We shared a look for a moment. Two fathers that shared a love of brewing, each feeling the hurt that came with losing the love of their lives.

"And yerrrr tryin' ta take both of those from me." Jeremiah finished, his tears turning into a scowl.

"What!?" I cried, nearly tumbling off his chair at the sudden change in topic. "That's not true, Jeremiah! I love the Goat, and Annie, and my Balin is *perfect* fer her! He's too honest to a fault, straightforward, and absolutely dedicated to his family. Yer lucky to have him fer a suitor! At least y-y–you get to see yer little girl get married!" Fresh tears poured down my cheeks.

"I thought ya didn't 'member much? Weren't you a-a-a drifter?" he asked, curiously.

I blew my nose into my beard and then stared at it, aghast. "I... I was a father. Balin and Annie know. I can't talk about it... I... I lost her."

"Gods. Gods. I'm sssorry."

"It's fine. I'm in a good place now, and yer daughter has made that possible. She's a bright dwarf, and I think she has a powerful future. Barck's Beard, she's probably one o' tha – one o' tha most beloved souls in all o' Minnova." My voice fell to a whisper. "I should know..."

"Aye. And that part's the part of what I wanted ter talk about." Jeremiah's tone grew more plaintive, as the dam that held back his emotions broke apart. "This brewpub of yers... It's too huge, er, big a change fer me. I was gettin' ready to retire a couple years back, thinkin' of leavin' the brewery to Annie. But she waz too headssstrong, too quick ta act without thinkin' things through." He smiled sourly. "Juzt like – 'er father."

"She's not like that anymore," I put in.

"Shaddup, I'm gettin' there. When that tank blew – KABLOOEY – I thought it destroyed her heart as well as that-that-that Godsdamn wall." He looked above my head, far off into a distance only he could see. "She came home from that mine still shaky and unsure of 'erself but fer one thing. She loved a dwarf named Balin and s-s-she was goin' to save her brewery. She were goin' ter make a place fer him to come home to. You two helped her find herself again, and I thank you, wanted ta thank you fer that. Thanks."

"They're good fer each other." I nodded. "Balin needs someone who's a bit more worldly."

"Annie needs someone that thinks, but is ssstill a fighter." Jeremiah nodded back. "They're a good match. But then there's *you*." He leaned across the table. "Full of new ideas and pushin' her to make rash decisions again."

"I didn't push her into that gamble!"

"*You* were the one that instigated it!"

"I only bet my own money! I didn't even tell her about it!"

"I *KNOW*." Jeremiah's roar dropped to a hoarse whisper. "I know. I also know yer takin' things slow. I heard from my buddies about yer *radler*, and how you've decided to improve on the brew."

"Because I think Annie's right."

"I... I may too. But I'm too old. Too afraid of change." Jeremiah's usually grim face turned dour. "I can't do it, Pete. So I'm lettin' her run the brewpub and make tha next few batches. I'm not going to step down, but I'm going to step back."

"You mean–" my voice bubbled with excitement.

"Aye, I'm makin' you a manager, and letting you two loose. As long as you can promise no explosions."

"When have I ever caused explosions!?" I laughed cheerfully, then noticed his glare. "When have I ever caused explosions *accidentally*?" I corrected.

Two more blonde dwarves sidled into line. A sea of pink swayed and bobbed around us with nervous excitement. A pair of massive pink posters framed the double doors to the concert hall and proclaimed "Raspberrysyrup On Tour." The mood was infectious, and more than one gnome or dwarf hollered with joy.

"Why are we in disguises?" I asked, scratching at my yellow hair. "This itches."

"Shhhhh!" Aqua hushed. "Don't scratch at that! You'll knock it off!" She adjusted my pink collar and brushed at my bangs. "Perfect, I can't tell it's you at all."

"Aye, and I can't tell if there's even a dwarf under all that pink makeup..." I poked her nose with a finger, and she giggled.

"Well, after the casino incident, you and I are public enemy number one and two." Aqua pointed at the ticket booth. A drawing depicting two dwarves, one blue-haired and one brown-haired, could be seen behind the ticketing agent. Large point font at the top of the drawing stated: "NO ENTRY."

"What!?" I hissed. "*You* stole all their signs. What did *I* do??"

"Are you kidding? You stuffed your butter in her mouth!"

"SHHHH!!!" I clamped his hand over Aqua's mouth. "It sounds so dirty when you put it that way!" Ok, I could see how the... unfortunate imagery might set Raspberrysyrup or her fans off.

"Says tha man in love with a goat!" Aqua's voice was muffled. She bit my finger and I yanked my hand back.

"Owch! I'm not in love with Penelope! No matter *how* cute her beard is."

"Sure, sure."

"Why did you even want to come?" I asked, nursing my munched digit.

"I was curious..." Aqua craned her neck around the sea of pink. "And this is new! I love new! You love new! So, I figured we could check out this new thing together!"

"I do love new." My smile widened. "I also love concerts, so let's do this!"

We made it through the ticketing booth uneventfully and found our seats near the rear middle of the auditorium. Like most dwarven architecture, the space was buried into the stone, with the ceiling sitting just above ground level. The rows of seats were inset with bright pink and white solstones, and some of the audience had sticks that glittered with light. Down beside the stage was a large open-floored space that looked to be for dancing or an orchestra – or a *mosh*. The hubbub was immense, and I had to put my head together with Aqua's to be heard.

"This looks like a rave!"

"A what?"

"A... type of concert I went to!"

Aqua's eyes narrowed. "Yer so darn shifty!"

"That's me!"

"I'll figure you out eventually, you know!"

"Good luck!"

Eventually the lights went off, and the crowd grew silent. Then, there was an explosion.

A series of pink and white smoke bombs went off with a roar, and sparks flew from the edge of the stage. A spotlight snapped onto a young gnomess in a skin-tight sequin skirt and halter top. A heavy bass beat shook the stands while an electric guitar began to whine. The crowd screamed and Raspberrysyrup nodded to the beat. Then she opened her mouth and screamed.

"LET'S GET THE PARTY STARTED!!!"

My jaw dropped and I rubbed at my ears. It couldn't be!

Aqua jumped up and down and roared with the rest of the crowd, then noticed my shocked silence.

"THIS IS GREAT!" she shouted.

I turned wide eyes her way. "YOU HAVE NO IDEA! I'VE ALWAYS LOVED THIS SONG!"

"I THOUGHT YOU'VE NEVER LISTENED TO HER MUSIC!?"

"NOPE!"

"HOW CAN THOSE BOTH BE TRUE?!"

"YOU'LL FIGURE IT OUT! ISN'T PINK AWESOME!?" I pumped my fist with the rest of the pink-festooned crowd, then said more quietly. "Found you."

Soon, Aqua and I were surfing in the mosh pit.

Barck glared at the collection of high-quality furniture that now dotted the bluff.

"Where are y'all comin' from?" he grumbled.

Lunara pointed at the lounge-chair floating above them. "I was actually looking for Archis – he left the planet on autopilot."

"We all live here too, you know," Aaron put in, then gave Tiara a *look*. "And besides, I'm done with *my* duties."

"At least Yearn hasn't found us yet," Tiara huffed, nettled.

There was a murmur of general agreement.

CHAPTER SIXTY-TWO
PETEY FIRST DATES – EPISODE 3

I leaned back in my chair and took a deep drink of beer. "Thanks for agreeing to take me to Whistlemop's cart, Emerelda. I appreciate that you remembered given that I kind of mentioned it in passing at the awards ceremony."

Emerelda smiled from where she sat across the table from me. "Honestly, I was surprised when you asked to take me out for drinks as well."

"Yes, well, I've been making some changes to my lifestyle."

Emerelda curled her beard. "Honestly, I'm usually the one that asks."

"Truly? A beauty like you?" I scoffed. "I'm surprised there aren't more dwarven gentlemen beating at the gates."

"Nah, I'm usually the one beating them."

We shared a chuckle. We were seated in a busy beer garden hosted by the Honourable Guild of Brewers. The space was a large open-air collection of tables located next to the Guild's Main store. The Guild had one of the permanent buildings on the Grand Market's main street – a single story affair with an enormous beer cellar. A raised private booth alongside the garden had a sign above it that stated "Master Brewers Only."

We spent the next hour discussing our love of the brew and all the places we'd been to drink. Emerelda had actually travelled to several different cities in Crack to try their beers. She described them as,

"Kinda all tha same." I was very careful in my own descriptions to always talk about my love for beer in the general sense. I was trying to avoid falling into the habit of lying like I had in my first year here. Eventually, I got to my reason for inviting Emerelda out.

"How do you like your Whistlemug?" I tapped the plain metal tankard provided by the garden.

"Aren't they great? I have two now, and almost nobody has more than that."

"Why's that?"

"There's a limit of one per customer." Emerelda sighed. "Ya have to sign your name. They keep a register of all 'official owners.' I think it's crazy, but they're always sold out, so it can't be too crazy."

"Huh… I was interested in grabbin' another one. My name shouldn't be on the register since I won it from the city."

"That's possible." Emerelda nodded. "I can take ya to Whistlemop's stall now if you'd like. He has a small space in the central square."

"That sounds great. Let's go."

We finished off our drinks and headed into the centre of the Grand Market.

The Market was full of knickknacks and oddities, both magical and mundane, so a little window-shopping was unavoidable. I spent nearly thirty minutes at a stall that sold talking objects made by an [Animist].

"By the Gods, why would you want a talking coaster?" Emerelda guffawed.

"Because I could hand them out? I may not be allowed to put up posters, so I need to get creative with my advertising."

"What's advertising?"

"Hmmm… think of it as forced word of mouth. It's getting the name of a business out into the community through more direct means."

"Well, a coaster that screams 'DRINK A GOAT' every time you put a mug on it *would* get attention." She chuckled.

We eventually found our way to Whistlemop's, which was a rather familiar wagon converted into a more permanent stall. The sides were filled with Whistlemugs, and the side was adorned with:

"Whistlemop's Wonders" and a newly painted "and Whistlemugs" beneath it. A pair of plate-armoured dwarves kept the large crowd at bay as Whistlemop himself handed out mugs. A gnome beside him checked IDs and put names down in a ledger.

As we approached, I folded my beard up into a fashionable leather gorget and pulled my skullcap down. I completed the makeshift outfit with some goggles and a long leather jacket.

Emerelda raised her eyebrows. "What's with the getup?"

I pulled out a compact mirror and checked my beard. "I'm doing some market research on Whistlemop, and I don't want others to know."

"Why not?" She looked me up and down and bit her lower lip. "It makes you look mysterious."

"Dwarf of mystery, that's me. Want to be my femme fatale?" I said the last while twirling my moustache.

"Does it involve a little mayhem?" She fluttered her eyelashes.

"A little chaos, a touch of bloodshed, maybe a murder," I said and sidled closer.

Emerelda laughed and smacked me on the shoulder. "Then count me in!"

It felt odd to be flirty again. I wasn't that much out of practice though, since I'd always kept it up with Caroline.

While we waited in line, we shared stories about our childhoods. Emerelda was born and raised in Minnova but liked to travel. I shared what I could, but tried to keep the topic off of my past. Emerelda was chatty, witty, and just a little too fond of violence.

I kept an eye on Whistlemop while we chatted. Every time some silver and a mug were exchanged my quest counter ticked up by one. At one point, there was a commotion as a dwarf whose name was already on the register started a fight. He was quickly subdued by the guards and then escorted out of the Market. Nobody complained, and a few even cheered. Then it was my turn.

"Name and ID please."

"Peter Roughtuff." I handed over my newly minted ID.

Nearer the wagon Whistlemop twitched at the name "Peter" and glanced my way. He calmed at the name 'Roughtuff' and barely gave me a cursory second glance.

"[Verify Authenticity]. That will be five silver."

"Guh. Aaron's Arse."

"Is there a problem?" The gnome looked down his nose at me and adjusted his glasses.

"Nope. Just thinkin' how much I'm looking forward to this." I ground out through clenched teeth. I moved up to Whistlemop, who handed me a glass.

"Thank you purchasing this one-of-a-kind Whistlemug!"

I coughed and lowered my voice to a gruff tone. "Thankee."

"Now move along please so I can serve the next person."

"Congrats on yer success. 'Ow did ya come up wit tha idea?"

Whistlemug seemed annoyed but quickly turned on a bright smile.

"It was luck, really, I needed something to drink from and had a similar object handy. I used it for my drink, and realised how perfect it was. Now, please move along. I have many customers to serve."

I coughed, feeling my rage build. So that's how he was playing it, eh? If I asked Barck *really nicely* for a smite, would he oblige? "How can I get ya some fan mail?"

Whistlemop's smile grew strained. "My clerk handles all mail. Please give it to him."

I stalked away and handed the mug to another dwarf in the line as I passed by.

"Hey, are you sure!?!" The stranger exclaimed.

"Merry Christmas." I growled as Emeralda ran after me.

"What?" said the confused but overjoyed dwarf.

"Did you figure out what you wanted?" Emerelda asked as she got alongside.

"Yeah. I need to see a gnome about a dog."

"Why a dog?"

"It's a surprise. At least, *he'll* find it surprising." I removed the costume and smiled with my teeth. Whistlemop was going to *pay* one way or another.

"Ooooh, that's a mean look. Do it again!"

We shopped for a while longer. Before we separated, Emeralda agreed to meet me again the next week for dinner, and to pass on a message for the pro-drinkers: they were all invited to opening night at the completed brewpub.

"I ship the gnomess more." Lunara said around a mouthful of sweets as she stretched in her black chaise longue.

Midna muttered, "I prefer the blue-haired one. Her spirit is more suited to his."

"Emerelda is more his style, and he'll push her in my direction," Aaron piqued.

"Yer all wrong!" Barck huffed. "His true love is obviously–"

"THE GOAT!" an elderly woman shrieked with gummy teeth.

"Yeaarrnn..." the assembled Gods moaned.

The two of us, the giant and the goof, stood in front of the building. The plaque upon it read: *The Rusty Battleaxe*. We stepped aside as a dwarf was tossed out of the building and rolled across the street into a ditch.

"Are you *sure* this is the right place?" I asked.

Rumbob laughed heartily. "Ho, ho, ho! Only one place called tha *Rusty Battleaxe* with an owner named Drum around here, Pete. He owns tha only brewpub in town. At least until yers is done."

"I think that makes him the competition." I frowned.

"Aye, and you were in tha top ten o' tha drinkin' contest. That also makes you a target."

"A target!?" I ducked as a table sailed through an open window. Most dwarven buildings didn't bother with glass, so there was no real damage done.

"Aye, a target. Tha Honourable Guild of Brewers don't like us pro-drinkers. You almost made the top three, and that's going to put you on their shit list. Drum is one o' tha enforcers for the old fusspots. It's why he runs this brewpub. It lets him keep an ear to tha pulse o' tha city, especially its undesirables."

"And I'm undesirable now."

"Aye, and new competition to boot."

I sighed. "Sam said I should come to Drum if I needed help. I trust Sam, so... let's do this." I really hoped I wasn't making a terrible mistake. I bounced from foot to foot and hummed a line from *Eye of the Tiger* before stepping through the door.

The building was a large open space, with a stairway leading up to a second row of seating. A chandelier covered in solstones lit the entire space, and several dozen tables were all full of laughing, jostling, fighting dwarves.

I had to yell to be heard. "IS IT ALWAYS SO NOISY?"

"Ho, ho, ho! YES!"

We made their way to the bar, which was staffed by a gruff looking dwarf with a shaggy black beard and an unruly mop of black and silver hair. His face was etched with scars and a black eyepatch covered his left eye. His left arm had the telltale silver sheen of a magical prosthetic. As I approached the bar, the hand made a *shing* sound, and morphed into a pick. The sharp point smashed a hole into a new keg before the bartender stopped it with a spigot.

"I need a new keg here!" He called towards a swinging door behind the bar and then faced us. "What do you two want? Ugh, Rumbob!?" His hand morphed into an axe, which he thrust in our direction. "Give me a good reason not ta gut you, eh? You get one sentence."

I gulped and paled slightly. Rumbob just looked jolly.

"Aw, come on, Drum. You wouldn't do that to one of yer best customers!"

Drum snapped his right hand, and his thumb erupted with a small flame. He pulled out a cigar and lit it before taking a long drag. "That was two sentences. Could have saved us all a lot of trouble if I'd poisoned yer beer ages ago, Rumbob."

"Ho, ho, ho! Yer too much of a perfectionist ta mess with perfection."

"At least you know perfection. Who's tha kid? Hmm... wait, aren't you—"

"Hello, Mr. Drum." I stepped forward with a winning, if slightly sick, smile. "It's a pleasure to meet you. I'm Peter Roughtuff."

"Mr. Drum was me dad. What do you want? You get one sentence." He took another pull on the cigar and blew the smoke in my face.

I kept a straight face and avoided turning away or coughing. "Sam sent me – he said you'd be able to help."

"Oh? Old Sam did, did he?" Drum looked me up and down. "How do you know him? Take a seat. Congratulations, you've earned a chat."

Rumbob and I sat down at the bar. Another dwarf came up to get a drink, and was rebuffed with a snarl and a tossed mug from Drum. I told my story, starting from the time I entered the mine, to the sulphur incident, to my first time meeting Sam, and so on and so forth. A lot had happened in the short time I'd been on Erd! Was that the Gods putting their fingers on the scale, or had it really been simple action and reaction?

Drum was frowning by the end of it. His cigar lay on the counter, forgotten. At some point, Rumbob had joined a party and the entire table was now singing a rip-roaring naughty song called *Twa Bearded Lady*.

Her beard is fine and golden brown,
It hangs in curly locks!
The other one is further down,
And quivers when she–

I winced at the mental image and tuned the rest out.

"So why did ya come to me?" Drum asked.

"I need your help looking into a gnome named Whistlemop."

"What? Tha merchant?"

"Yeah, I need to know his regular movements and where he lives. Stuff like that."

"Huh, why?" Drum drummed his fingers on the counter.

"I have... *business* with him. He kind of stole the Whistlemug from me."

"HA! Sucks fer you! Well, he's been gettin' a bit too big fer his britches. May be good fer him to get shook up. I'll need ta look into yer story though. What did you say yer name was?"

"Peter Roughtuff."

"Right, give me a few days. I'll need ta check with Sam first."

"You can get word into the city's Reform Mine!?"

"Who do ya think yer talkin' to? Course I can!" Drum stood up to leave but I stopped him before he got too far.

"Oh, well in that case. He knows me as Peter Samson. Tell him I said hello."

Drum paused, his face twitching. "What? Samson? You said yer name was Peter Roughtuff."

"Aye, I changed it."

Drum's face wrinkled. "Why?"

"No real attachment to it. I never really knew me mum or dad, and I've made a new family here in Minnova." I shrugged.

Drum drummed his fingers on the counter. Then his face twisted. Then he chortled. Then he guffawed. Then he laughed. Then he roared. He began to beat his metal hand on the counter with glee. "HAW! Never knew! By tha Gods that's the funniest thing I've heard in a goat's age! Midna's Mangy Mullet!! HAR HAR HAR!!!!"

I watched in confusion. Was this some kind of dwarven ancestral in-joke? Just when I thought I was fitting in, too...

Rumbob came over and watched curiously as tears began to leak out beneath Drum's eyepatch. "What did ya do?"

"I don't know."

Barck looked around.

"You're *all* here!? Since when!?"

The various Gods and Goddess looked slightly guilty as he glowered at them.

Midna put up her hand. "Yesterday? You and Tiara have been here the whole week and we were curious."

"Grrr... you lot have seven other Chosen ta watch, and a multitude of other souls besides!"

"But your beard twitches when you laugh," a girl that looked like a small elf put in, "and you get all pink when the dwarf ladies comb their beards!"

Barck's face slowly turned crimson from his neck upwards.

"Uh oh! He's gonna blow! Scatter!" Aaron shouted, jumping up off the mountain.

"YOU LOT!! BUGGER OFF!!!"

CHAPTER SIXTY-THREE
INTERLUDE – BRAN'S MUFFINS

B alin had worked his arse off to get most of the construction complete within a single week, and the new eating area was a thing of beauty. Though the grand opening was still a week away, the brewpub would open to take its first customers tomorrow, and everyone was celebrating. The scrumptious vanilla sponge cake added to the festive atmosphere

"So, how did you end up coming here, Bran?" Aqua said around a mouthful of cake.

Bran's eyes grew misty with reminiscence, and he shook his head.

"It just happened, is all."

Four weeks prior to Bran's employment at the Thirsty Goat.

"What's wrong, Bran?"

Bran pulled up the covers as Opal nestled into his chest. He sighed mightily and held her tight. She curled his beard while he thought for a moment and answered.

"I'm bored, Opal."

"Not with me, I hope?" Opal joked. "But you have lost a bit of your spark lately. What happened? Do some of the new miners have you down? Do I need to spike someone's drink with laxative until they get the picture?"

Opal pulled violently at his moustache, and he tickled her viciously until she stopped.

They paused for a moment and caught their breath, gasping the astringent medicinal air in Opal's cabin.

"No need ta take it that far. And besides, tha new crop are just fine. No, the problem is the old crew."

"I think I see." Opal flopped onto her back and held a hand up to the ceiling. "You've seen the sky, and you want to reach for it."

"Aye. I didn't realise it before, Opal, but I've outgrown this camp. I'm tired of makin' sandwiches for recalcitrant dwarves. I'm sick of stew, and I've had enough of erdroot. When I was cookin' with Pete, I felt more alive than I had in years." Bran's eyes looked far into a distance only he could see. "I want to cook more fascinatin' things, and make dishes no dwarf has ever seen before."

Bran grew animated as he spoke, and as he shone brighter and brighter, Opal grew more and more dour. She could see where this was going.

"You want to leave."

Her voice was flat. It wasn't a question.

"I love you, Opal, and I'll always love you, but you know yer family will never accept a middlin' Blessed of Aaron for their daughter. I need to make a name for myself."

"What if I told you I don't care what my family thinks? That Bran the mining cook is dwarf enough for me?" Opal ran a finger down his chest, and he laughed.

"Your father will roll right over, though your mum might have some words. But it's not them I'm worried about. It's me, love, I want to be worthy of tha future noble, Doctor Opal."

"If you think you aren't good enough Bran, that's not true at all!" Opal flushed with anger, and Bran smiled. Her passion was one of the reasons he loved her so much. Her love of his baking was simply another.

"Doesn't matter what either of us think. I can see it, Opal. I've gone as far as I can in this mine."

Opal held him tight, and the two of them shared a passionate kiss.

She broke apart first. "You can run away, Bran Hurler, but you'll never be able to hide from me."

"I wouldn't think of it."

Bran strode down the aisles of the Grand Market, looking to and fro for any interesting ingredients, spices, or confections. There were myriad odds and ends, but nothing that came close to the wonders he'd seen in the past few months with Pete. Between the tarts, the eclairs, and the meringue, Pete's basic recipes were a veritable fount of inspiration for scrumptious new delicacies. Bran sighed. He'd grown far too complacent in the mine and hadn't realised it until Pete widened his horizons.

Opal said Pete was headed to Annie Goldstone's brewery, but he had no idea where that was. There weren't too many breweries in the city, so he could just search them out one by one, but he wasn't even sure that was the correct path in the first place.

All his life, he went with the flow, letting life take him where it willed. First, he fell into cooking for his family after their mother died. As the eldest of four brothers, it made sense for him to take over his mother's chores while his father continued the family business of running the axe-throwing hall.

Necessity became the drive for his ingenuity. He learned new methods for braising cheap meat and sautéing mushrooms to bring out their flavour. He made soup stock out of leftover bones and vegetables and discovered the myriad ways of salt. It was never quite as good as his mother's, but every dish brought him a bit closer to her memory. The daily trips to the market and quiet moments stirring a cookpot brought some simple joy to his melancholy.

Then, they fell on harder times. His father was injured in an accident, and while City Hall provided enough to feed and shelter them, it wasn't enough to keep the hall. So the boys took to begging and then stealing; anything to avoid losing their ancestral home. First, they stole some bread. Then, they stole some gold. Then, they were caught, and as eldest, he took all the blame.

Thieving was not tolerated in Minnova. He spent several years in the Reform Mine for that, where he naturally took over most of the kitchen duties. Cooking for a half-dozen hungry mouths wasn't that different from cooking for several dozen. The kitchen was well appointed, and he had all the budget he needed to cook hearty and fulfilling meals. It was enough.

And then she arrived.

She was older, wiser, an educated miss from a well-to-do family. She shone bright and glittered with hidden depths, much like her namesake. He was smitten from the moment she entered his kitchen and demanded to speak to the chef; she found the food lacking in variety and wanted him to expand the menu.

So he'd gotten cook books, fruit, vegetables, and meats he'd never heard of, all supplemented by the doctor's income so she could enjoy the food she was accustomed to. He added basil, pepper, and oregano to supplement the ever-present salt. In one of their few conversations, he discovered she had a sweet tooth, which inspired him to bake his first pie.

It was a horror show. He threw it to the goats and swore them to secrecy.

The fourth pie was acceptable. The look on her face when she took a bite from the crisp crust and licked apples from her moustache was the moment he knew – he was beard over heels. With Opal and with cooking. So, he learned the ways of butter and sugar, how to make his crusts flaky, and his tarts tart. He became more than a simple cook; he was a chef.

He stayed after his indenture was complete, and with Grim's blessing became the head chef. He took over the logistics for the kitchen, and with that came the Blessing of Aaron, God of Exchange. The Blessing brought prestige and Opal's congratulations. The labourers came and went, but there were always the two – the cook and the doctor.

He took to telling people he was originally arrested for throwing rocks. He was a Hurler after all.

Then came Balin, and Pete, and Annie, and Wreck, and Sam. The stoneant incident. The radler. The stream of delicious pastries. Suddenly, Bran was no longer going with the flow; every day was a refreshing whirlwind of new and exciting dishes! Some of the recipes he sold to other bakeries in the city, others he kept in reserve to experiment on. For the first time in his life, he took steps on his own, and it was exhilarating.

He couldn't go back to that monotonous life, taking each day as it came and hoping that things would work out. His endeavours won him the heart of an incredible dwarf, and he would do whatever it took to ensure it stayed that way.

The problem was... where to start?

Open up his own shop? He had the gold for it. He could go to his family, but they were long gone from Minnova. Join one of the local bakeries or restaurants? There was little doubt his skills would quickly propel him to the top. Perhaps the Grand Market itself would be a good start, with a small street food cart.

His meandering brought him to the steps of the Cathedral of the Gods. The pealing of the bells gave him some [Calm] and with it, an idea. The Gods would provide him guidance!

They had not provided guidance.

Bran sighed as he pushed back against the throng of people.

He could have just been swept along with the everyone else, but that was more going with the flow. Bran was done going with the flow. He separated himself from the crowd and peeled off into a secluded corner. The space was filled with incense and a multitude of flickering candles. A fresco in the alcove pictured the Gods in judgement over the dragons, and the creation of Crack as the vain lizards were smote down to Erd. He dropped a few silvers into a nearby donation bin and lit a candle of his own.

"Erm. 'Allo Gods, it's me, Bran. Though you already knew that." He chuckled, feeling somewhat foolish. "I'm new to this whole 'makin' my own way' business, so I was hopin' to get a push out tha' door. Aaron, as yer Blessed, would ya consider giving me a sign? Or mebbe Barck, since I'm looking to change meself."

There was no answer. Bran sighed, of course there wasn't an answer. The Gods worked in their own way, there was no way that–

The world went white.

Bran stumbled, his eyes aching from the sudden radiance. The entire cathedral was rocked by a pulse of multi-coloured light emanating from the statue of Barck. The [Priests] standing near the statue got the worst of it and were all screaming in agony. The crowd was beginning to panic. Had Barck decided to smite someone? Had someone in the Cathedral displeased Him?

Bran blinked, the rainbow kaleidoscope behind his eyelids setting off new starbursts of pain. Of course, this would happen right as he was starting a new path in life. If this was how the Gods answered every prayer, it made sense that most considered it a last resort. He was just as stuck now as before, except with an excruciating headache.

Perhaps this wasn't the right moment. Maybe it was a sign that he wasn't meant to… Bran paused as a figure appeared before him.

"Pete?" As his sight cleared, the familiar figure resolved itself in his vision. "Is that you?"

"Bran?"

Bran left the table while everyone sang a drinking song about a toad and a fool, and went to look around his new kitchen.

Everything was finally ready, and he knew just where to start. He grabbed a few carrots that were set aside for Penelope and began peeling them. Pete once described something called 'muffins' and he was eager to try. With his own twist of course. Maybe some roasted honeyed nuts, or candied carrots.

Bing!

Blessing Granted: [Barck]!

Your heart of hard work and innovation have caught the attention of Barck. Bake more cakes! Cook more delicacies! Dazzle the entire Firmament with your food!
*If you receive Barck's Blessing you will gain [**Regeneration**] and [**Good Luck**].*

If you accept Barck's Blessing, you will be eligible for a Title!

Do you accept?
Yes/No

Bran smiled as he mentally hit 'yes.' It looked like he finally had his sign.

CHAPTER SIXTY-FOUR
THIRSTY GOAT BREWPUB

"Come in!" Annie waved everyone through the door. The grumble tumbled in from the lush foyer and gawked.

"Barck's Beard! What a difference!" Emerelda muttered.

"Welcome to the Thirsty Goat Brewpub!" I stood ready in my best suit, holding a set of menus to pass to the pro-drinkers as they entered. Johnsson and Richter shouted their own hellos as they rolled in a large barrel from the brew floor.

"What have you got for eats?" Beatbox asked as I handed him a menu. "More than nuts, I hope...."

Each menu item was carefully hand-calligraphed with a tiny drawing and a clearly labelled price. A little note at the bottom added: "no haggling."

"No haggling! How am I supposed to get cheap sausages!" Beatbox cried with indignation.

"We are allowed to set fix'd prices," I said with a grin. "City of Minnova Ordinances Ver. 315, Chapter 23, Section 6." I was proud of all my hard work over the past two weeks. Richter had to beat it into me at some points, but I now had almost half the Ordinances memorised.

"What are 'Pretzels'?" Emerelda asked, reading over his shoulder. "Hey! This says it uses *BEER* in it!?"

The partygoers all turned identical shocked looks in my direction, and I shrugged.

"Bran is a whiz at making meals that really accentuate the fine flavour of True Brew. Our meals aim to honour the fine tradition of Goldstone Brewery by serving beer not only as a drink, but as a form of *food*."

Beatbox nodded. "I always thought beer deserved to be food. Its true potential was wasted when you could only drink it in a mug."

There was a general mutter of agreement.

"Ho, ho, ho! Hey, Pete! It looks great!" Rumbob exclaimed, as he ran his hand across the long wooden counter. Bran smiled from the other side and nodded at the kegs positioned behind him.

"You're Rumbob, right? I'd be happy to pour a drink for tha champion drinker of Minnova."

"Thank you, I'll have a mug o' ale. First round is on Beatbox."

"Comin' right up!" Bran placed a barrel up onto a curved holder set in the counter. He popped the cork, shoved in a spigot, then began to pour into a mug. The foggy beer barely foamed as it poured into the mug, and the head was mostly gone by the time it reached the end.

"Excuse you!? Who's paying?!" Beatbox cried.

"You lost that bet with me last week."

"Fine," Beatbox grumbled.

"What is 'Fish and Fries,'" Emerelda muttered as she continued reading, "and how do I not know anything on this menu?"

Chuck grabbed a menu for himself. "Ooh, dese 'crisps' look raight tastee."

"Oh, they are." In fact, they were *damn* tasty, if I said so myself. Which I just did. I put them somewhere above Doritos but below ketchup chips. "I also have a little event planned for everyone to christen – er – *open* this new brewpub."

"That's right." Annie agreed. "We only have the three kegs right now, so we can't open up to the public yet. The next brew won't be ready for at least a week, so we decided to commemorate the opening with a little drinking competition instead." She pointed to a page on the wall behind a pane of glass. The paper was titled *Champion GOATS*, with spaces for names beneath it. "Pete says the GOAT stands for Greatest of All Time."

"Well then, I'd like to be a Goat." Beatbox said with a giant grin.

"So would Pete!" Balin quipped from beneath a booth table, where he was doing some finishing touches.

"Gods damn it, Balin!" I groaned. "Yer never goin' to let me forget that, are you!?"

Annie coughed and hid a blush behind her hand. "Aqua?"

"Yes, Ma'am?" Aqua popped up from behind the bar, where she had been stocking mugs.

"Could you take everyone's orders?"

"Sure! We *are* going to need to hire someone to do it full time, though."

"I'll put it to Dad."

"Where is Mr. Goldstone?" Johnsson asked.

"He's out with his guard buddies again. He said that he'd 'leave it all to me.'" Annie looked somewhat starstruck as she looked around the brewpub.

The new brewpub was greatly changed from the original plain mess hall. The enormous painting of a drunken goat still took up one brick wall, but the rest of the space was completely transformed. Booths lined the walls, and the original long tables were cut down into smaller four dwarf-affairs with picnic benches. The benches were much shorter than usual, but still long enough to make them unwieldy weapons; a necessity for dwarven bars.

A framed painting of Penelope was up on one wall with a nameplate, along with a mishmash of paintings displaying the countryside of Minnova. A large wooden bar took up one whole corner, with a kitchen space behind it. The kitchen was brand new and made to Bran's exacting specifications. It was nearly identical to the kitchen at the mine, though with an upgraded magic-stone oven and magically enchanted cool-room. Those had cost a pretty penny!

A set of tables in the centre of the pub were placed end-to-end to make one long table. Rumbob grabbed his now-filled mug and pulled out a bench to take a seat. He was joined by the rest of the party as everyone got comfortable.

"This looks expensive..." Beatbox mused as he ran his hands along the fine red leather covering a booth seat. "I thought you were tight for gold."

"We are, but as Pete says, 'we need to spend gold to make

mithril.'" Annie shrugged. "We want to capture a permanent clientele while the city still has its eyes on us. We're aiming to make a splash!" Her slightly manic smile betrayed her true worry about the state of the brewery's finances.

"Speaking of a splash. Does anyone know anyone that can play live music?" I added, as I brought out some small bowls and distributed them to everyone. "I want to hire someone for the real grand opening. It'll be in a day or two, after the current batch is done."

"I might. I helped a [Bard] get married just last month," Rumbob said between sips.

"Rumbob knows *everybody*," Emerelda quipped, her eyes rolling practically out of her skull.

"Everybody, eh? Well, in that case, Rumbob, I was hoping you'd put in a good word with the King for me. You see—" I was cut off as the room broke into laughter that was interrupted by the sound of loud, enthusiastic crunching. Everyone turned to look at Chuck, whose ebony face was practically buried in his bowl.

"You lot need ta trai dese crisps!!!"

Beatbox poked his bowl suspiciously. "What is it?"

"Those crinkly wafers are thinly cut erdroot, deep-fried in sunflower oil and then lightly dusted with my own custom blend of salt and spices. They're crispy, flavourful, and go great with beer," Bran said smugly.

crunch *munch*

"Mmmmm..."

crackle *CRUNCH*

"Barck's Beard, they're amazing! They're not too greasy, but just greasy enough that it makes tha beer taste that much better!" Emerelda said after her first bite.

"Ho, ho, ho! If these are tha kind of things yer' servin', I think tha Thirsty Goat Brewpub is goin' to be just fine!"

"Here's hoping," Johnsson sighed.

"Annie mentioned a competition?" Emerelda said around a mouthful of chips.

"That's right!" I nodded vigorously. "Tania and Rumbob were the only ones that got to do the *drinking* contest, so I was hoping we could do one here tonight! Speaking of which..." I looked around. "Where are Tania and Jim?"

"Tania's dealin' with Greentree," Chuck said. "An' Jim's right ova thea." He pointed to the bar. Jim was seated on one of the stools, eating from a bowl of chips.

"Ahhh!" Aqua screamed from where she was cleaning the counter beside him. "When did you get here!?"

"Aaanyways, I figured we could use the last three barrels for an old-fashioned drink off. Winner take all."

"Winner take all the what?" Rumbob asked.

"Uhhh, pride?"

"He's salty about losing the contest," Beatbox said as he took a sip of beer.

"Yep." Emerelda nodded.

"Saltier than these crisps." Balin shrugged.

"Ho, ho, ho! Pete, there is no shame in losing to a fine dwarven specimen like meself!"

"I'm not salty!" I huffed. There was a chorus of *mhms.* "But I was sad that I didn't get to do a real drinkin' contest. Would you all be willing to humour me? We only have three barrels, so we'll need to say no Abilities. The winner gets to have their name up on the GOAT board for opening night..." My voice trailed off as I looked up for everyone's approval.

The grumble looked at each other and then broke into cheers of approval.

"Of course, Pete!"

"I think you'll find that what I lack in height I make up for in pure drinking power!"

"Ho, ho, ho! It will be my pleasure to mop tha floor with all of 'ya."

"I think I'll sit this one out."

"Don't you dare chicken out, Balin!"

"The chicken is a brave and noble animal!"

"Buckaw!"

"[Golden armour]!"

"Argghh! Mercy!"

AN ADVENTURE BREWING

Bodies littered the floor.

Bran's limp form lay atop his polished counter, and Aqua was stashed somewhere beneath it.

Balin and Annie cuddled together under a booth, where they had hidden at some point halfway through the carnage.

Beatbox was similarly cuddling Rumbob, his short form nearly fully enveloped by the massive beard he was using as a blanket.

Emerelda sat on the ground at the foot of the table, and Jim lay comatose within an empty barrel.

Johnsson was sprawled on top of the table, and Richter was sprawled on top of Johnsson.

I sat on a bench, nursing an empty mug. I caressed a rectangular object sitting next to me on the table and gazed at it with reverence. I had won it *all*.

"Yep. It's all thanks to you, butter." My face turned green.

urgh "Aaron's Arse, I can't fix this garbage beer fast enough!" I ran for the washroom, and made it just in time.

Groan

Moan

"Ugh, you sound like a beached whale, Balin!" I hugged my pillow over my ears, trying to block out the piteous wailing that filled our tenement house. Blood pounded in my ears from a *massive* hangover; I needed to rehydrate, stat.

"How do ya stand this Pete! Is it like this every time ya do a drinkin' competition?"

"Aye"

MOOOAAAANNN

"Ugh, enough. I'm going to *Joejam Cuppa* for a cuppa. Do you want anything?"

"I want tha world ta stop spinnin'!"

I peeled myself out of bed and stumbled to the washbasin. I needed to get going; there was a lot to do today.

We'd used most of the gold from the competition and the big party to outfit the new Thirsty Goat Brewpub, which meant we were cash poor again. That was a problem on two fronts. The Goldstones were still on edge about money, and I couldn't exactly enact my grand plan for introducing new and improved beer on a shoestring budget. It was a plan that came with a lot of advertising but wasn't against any City Ordinances. It wouldn't break too many traditions and would make a fizzier beer with no risk of explosions.

But it was going to cost a *lot* of money – money we didn't have right now. I needed a quick cash infusion if I wanted my bigger plans to succeed, and I knew where to get one. "It's time to catch a little Whistle*rat*," I said menacingly. Ooooh, this body could do menacing really well! "It's *time* ta catch a *RAT* in a *trap*. Muhahahaha!"

"Argggh, me head! Pete!? Why are ya shoutin'!"

"Just somethin' stuck in my throat! Mu *cough* ha *cough* ha."

CHAPTER SIXTY-FIVE
THE STALKING GOAT

The crowd had thinned after his last Whistlemug sold, and Whistlemop was ready to call it a day. He still had to go and check in on the latest batch of Whistlemugs at Ralph and Ralph Glassworks, and he had an absolutely *massive* pile of gold to deposit at the bank. Yes indeed, it was a wonderful day!

"Thank you for your hard work today, gentledwarves." Whistlemop nodded to his guards. They were the best adventurers money could buy, and he paid plenty for them. They did a more than admirable job of keeping the riffraff away.

"Of course, Mr. Whistlemop."

"Pleasure ta be o' service, Mr. Whistlemop."

"I'll be heading to the bank now. Good work today, Trickledown!" He tossed a gold coin to his scribe. The young gnome caught the coin and returned a two-fingered salute.

"Another great day today, Mr. Whistlemop. Here again tomorrow?"

"No. Take the day off! I have some things to work on." Whistlemop thought for a while and then tossed another gold to the lad. "Go and have a good time, on me."

"Hah! Thanks boss!"

Whistlemop shooed the boy away. It was important to keep your employees happy. Especially when they were handling your important paperwork. He knew that a lot of nobles and wealthy merchants didn't look at things the same way, but they were *also* one really hard year away from being eaten by their employees.

One gold to buy some goodwill? That was nothing. Besides, the boy had been nearly beaten half to death by a [Berserker] last week, and this would placate him before he thought about asking for something truly terrible, like injury pay.

Whislemop closed his cart and applied a few magical defences. It wasn't that he didn't *trust* the Grand Market's guards, but certain dwarves could be curiously blind when it came to seeing a wealthy gnomish merchant's wagon being robbed.

"The bank next." He led the way through the Market to the bank. The Grand Market, being the centre of commerce in Minnova, naturally had a branch office of the Nation of Crack Central Bank. It dealt with levels of wealth that Whistlemop could only dream about. He sent his guards away at the entrance and was escorted by a smiling [Administrator] to make his deposit at a teller.

Then he went to the washroom and applied his disguise. He could have taken the guards with him to Ralph and Ralph Glassworks, but he preferred to keep the manufacturing location of Whistlemugs a secret. He trusted the guards' arms with his life, but he didn't trust their mouths with his livelihood.

After a short while, a cloaked gnome in a wide-brimmed hat with a giant red droopy moustache made his way down the bank stairs before disappearing down an alleyway. Whistlemop ducked behind a potted plant and looked back towards the bank. Nobody seemed to be paying him attention other than a white goat at the other end of the square. Whistlemop nodded and exited the alley. He made his way confidently through the Grand Market, sidestepping golems and occasionally ducking through shops to dodge any tails. His purposeful meandering eventually brought him to a side street. His steps grew quicker as he travelled towards his destination in earnest.

Then his gait skipped a beat. Down the street was another white goat, staring at him with rectangular, beady eyes. It *maaah*-ed. It couldn't be the same goat, could it? Whistlemop stared at it. It had a beautiful beard and a well-maintained, pure-white coat. It had to be someone's pet. What was it doing, standing there alone? Whistlemop stepped into another side street and picked up his pace. After a few twists and turns, he came back out onto the main street. He looked around and didn't see anything. He took a sigh of relief that turned into a gasp as he glimpsed a flash of white in the crowd ahead.

He began to run.

Through alleys, through streets. His legs carried him as fast as he could, but his agility was pathetic, and his vitality worse. He was barely faster than a dwarven child, and soon he began to flag. At every turn, he was stymied by a sinister *maaah.*

As he ran down an alley, he careened headfirst into a dwarf walking in the opposite direction. He bounced off with an *ouf* and fell to the ground.

"Excuse me sir, I-I-I'm in a great hurry if you could please..." His voice cracked as he looked up at the dwarf standing in front of him. "Peter?"

"Hello, Whistlemop. Where are you running off to?" Pete's voice grew menacing. "I was hoping we could have a little... *chat.*"

"Go-goat–" Whistlemop couldn't speak. He pointed behind him. A white form stood silhouetted at the other end of the alley.

"Oh, that's just Penelope. Come say hello to Whistlemop, Penelope!"

There was a flash of white. Then it all went black.

I stared down at the gnome sitting on the chair in front of me. We were in an abandoned building that Drum had cleared out for me. Whistlemop looked exactly as I remembered, though the stupid hat and fake moustache were new. I couldn't believe that this bedraggled little *thief* was one of Barck's most favoured souls. His eyes were furious, though his gaze turned wary as Penelope came up and nuzzled my hand.

"Good girl, Penelope. Here's a goat treat, how about you stand...

right over there?" I gestured behind Whistlemop and she happily cavorted past him. He shied away as she did, then glowered at me.

"This is kidnapping!"

"In the most literal sense of the word!" I guffawed.

"You think this is funny? I could have you arrested!"

"But you won't."

"And why would that be?"

"Because you don't want me making a fuss about your precious 'Whistle' mugs." I pointed out matter-of-factly. He scowled but didn't gainsay me.

I sat down on a chair across from him and pulled over a small side table. I set down a pair of to-go mugs filled with coffee and pushed one over to Whistlemop. "Coffee?"

"You... drink coffee?" He said suspiciously.

"Nectar of the Gods." I took a deep sip and made a satisfying "ahhh." The gnomes made coffee that was nearly as good as a Turkish brew I'd gotten from a street vendor in Istanbul. Not Constantinople.

Whistlemop glared at his own mug suspiciously.

"It's not poisoned," I pointed out.

"You think I can trust you!?"

"You don't really have a choice, and besides, you think *I* can trust *you*?!"

"Bah!"

baaaaah [Translated from Prima Donna Goat] "Your accent is terrible!"

"I – no. I can't do this." I pointed at his face. "Can you please take off that ridiculous disguise? You look like Yosemite Sam, and I just can't take this seriously."

"Who's Yosemitesam?" Whistlemop asked, as he pulled off the moustache and threw it to the floor. "Cursed thing was useless anyway, seeing that you found me so easily."

Actually, Drum's men found him. Whistlemop was terrible at disguises, and it only took a few days for them to suss out his secret route from the bank to his Whistlemug supplier. From there, it was as simple as offering Penelope some goat treats to herd him towards the pickup point. Penelope was *damn* smart for a goat.

I was *mostly* sure she wasn't my wife.

"Yes, well you are awfully difficult to meet, Whistlemop. I *tried* sending an invitation, but apparently you don't read your mail!"

Whistlemop grumbled. "My mail gets screened. You weren't important enough to get passed through to me. I'm too busy for a bunch of whiners whining about getting their hands on my mugs."

I took another sip of coffee and savoured it. The heavy roast was so thick that cream was unnecessary, and the sweet spices made sugar an afterthought. "Could be worse, they could be clambering to get their hands on your jugs."

Whistlemop's eyes narrowed and then he hesitantly took a sip of coffee. "Huh, this is the *good* stuff."

"Only the best for my dear friend Whistlemop."

He snorted. Then took another sip. We sat there in silence for a while, sussing each other out. He broke the silence first.

"I suppose you think you deserve a share of my Whistlemugs."

"Oh, what would give you the idea that I would want to talk to you about MY *Pilsner glass*," I growled. I was getting tired of people taking advantage of me. Bran at least had the decency to save up a bunch of gold for me when he was selling my recipes. Whistlemop took my idea and ran with it, and then *lied* about it to everyone. He likely had zero intention of ever paying me a single silver. Heck, if I hadn't invented boomdust, he probably would've been wealthy enough to be untouchable by the time I got out. That may have even been his exact plan.

Whistlemop shimmied uncomfortably in his seat; I hoped it was from a guilty conscience. "I would have been glad to pay you something if you asked."

"I sincerely doubt that." I looked him up and down. "You're a penny pincher." Though a kindly one, *mostly*. An odd dichotomy. According to Drum, he treated his workers well, didn't *usually* cheat his business partners, and was a fairly above-board businessman, all things considered. The sheer *wealth* offered by Whistlemugs and my status as a locked-up labourer had been too much of a temptation. "But you *owe* me."

He took a petulant drink of coffee and harrumphed.

"I don't owe you a single copper. According to the City of Minnova Ordinances, I–"

"According to the City of Minnova Ordinances Ver. 315," I interrupted, "Chapter 56, Section 12, Subsection 14, anyone that can prove a product was stolen from them can complain to a [Judge]. I think I have over two-dozen witnesses that the Whistlemugs were *my* idea, and you *stole them.*"

Whistlemop gaped at me with a shocked expression. "You know the Ordinances? I thought you were a vagrant!"

I couldn't hold back a chuckle. "I prefer to consider myself *fragrant.*"

Oh, *something* stinks here, and I'm pretty sure it's your half-cocked dwarven intellect! Tell me, have you *actually* succeeded at anything in your entire life? You should be *glad* I turned your glass into an icon!" Whistlemop snapped, nettled by my clever wordplay.

I grabbed my chest in faux outrage. "How dare you, sirrah! I've been successful at *dozens* of ventures. I'll have you know that I have *complete* confidence in my brews and my sharp business mind."

It was Whistlemop's turn to chuckle. "Oh really? Now you're a businessdwarf?"

I *pshawd.* "I've forgotten more business than you'll ever know."

Whistlemop frowned. "Oh, I did hear something about an injury and amnesia. Are you better now?"

"Pretty much."

"Congratulations."

"Why, thank you. Speaking of which, I heard about some violence at your shop the other day. Is your scribe doing well?"

"He's much better now. A visit to the [Healer] and a few days off heals most ills."

We both took sips from our coffee and *aaaah*-ed in unison.

"Where were we?"

I smacked my head. I really wasn't very good at this. "I was extorting you for gold."

"Ah, right. Well... fine!" He threw up his hands. "I'll give you fifty gold to go away and never darken my doorstep again!"

"That's pathetic! I deserve at least 50 *percent* for it." I banged the table, slightly upsetting the drinks. Whistlemop shied away and then his face turned beet red.

"Fifty percent!? You barely did *anything! I* was the one that bet my entire life savings on the Whistlemugs panning out. *I* was the one standing in front of the crowds each day selling mugs! *I* was the one putting his face out there for everyone to judge! You took *zero* risk, and you think you deserve 50 percent? All *you* did was set off my [Sense–]" He paused mid rant and looked at me, then he *stared* at me.

"Uh, why are you staring at me?" I backed up in my seat.

"You...." He reached towards me, then stopped as his eyebrows knit together. His voice grew contrite. "I got my Specialisation after I started selling Whistlemugs, you know. I suppose I do owe you for giving me the idea, and I hate that our relationship has become so strained. It truly was my fault for being greedy, I'm sorry." He bowed his head.

I stared incredulously. What? "You just used an Ability on me, didn't you. What did you see? What's your game?"

"No game. I'll give you a dozen mithril for the idea and I'm even willing to forget this entire... inconvenience."

"Yeah, I don't trust this sudden change of heart, and I think you can afford a lot more." I crossed my arms. A dozen mithril was a *lot*, and I was seriously tempted. But I was done being yanked around, and I didn't trust this. But... Barck said Whistlemop was placed here to *help* me.

"I assure you, I have not actually made that much gold." He held out a hand placatingly. "And I honestly wish to put this entire situation behind us."

I rolled my eyes. "Psh, you've made *millions* of silver. I'll bet I could even tell you how much."

Whistlemop picked up his mug and chugged the entire thing. He wiped his mouth with his sleeve and raised his eyebrows at me as he banged the mug down on the table. "Oh? Want to bet?"

I leaned in. "Yeah, why not? Let's... *bet*."

"Hah! You'll need the help of Barck himself!" Whistlemop cackled like some kind of 80s cartoon villain.

Indeed. *Indeed*....

Bing!

New Quest: Whistlebet!
You've bet everything on one gamble. Can you win it all?

Win the bet with Whistlemop.

Rewards: +0.2 Wisdom

<u>Do you accept?</u>
Yes / No

Oh, yeaaah!

CHAPTER SIXTY-SIX
WORTH THE WHISTLE

The Good, the *Baaaad*, and the Ugly – A Roughtuffian Sonnet
Cue whistling and twangy guitar plus cheesy cowboy accent.

Our scene is set inside a town of mud.
The sun hangs low and paints the world in red.
Today's the day good men will count the dead.
The dusty dirt will soon be bathed in blood.

Two shadows cut across the crimson light.
The outlaws enter from each end of town.
Sweet silence carries on without a sound.
A tumbleweed rolls past and out of sight.

As one, the two draw guns and fire a shot.
A sharp retort rings out with puffs of dust.
No life was cut to stain the ground with rust.

A noble goat comes at an angry trot.
Her angry bahs so fearsome that they fled.
The outlaws chose to go get drinks instead.

I tipped my imaginary ten-gallon hat. "So tell me... do you feel lucky, punk?"

"What?" Whistlemop said distractedly. He looked around the room, which was still the secluded building that I'd sequestered him in.

"Nothing..." I grumped. "Are you done reading the contract yet? I'm gettin' bored."

"Oh, poor you. I'm just about done. It seems... suspiciously fair." Whistlemop tapped the sheet of paper he was holding. "For a meeting that started with kidnapping, I was expecting a few more broken fingers and shouting."

"It wouldn't have even *started* with kidnapping if you hadn't forced my hand." I glowered at the little rat. He rolled his eyes and continued reading.

I'd excused myself to ask Drum for a contract. I didn't know enough dwarven law yet to do it myself, and Drum struck me as the kind of dwarf that did. He actually had several standard contracts already written up! Upon my return, I found Whistlemop dismantling the lock, the sneaky little bugger! I'd *escorted* him back to the table to read over the contract, which was missing one finishing touch.

"This contract doesn't actually discuss what I'll be giving up..." Whistlemop pointed at a large blank space for conditions.

"Yes indeed, yes indeed. Whistlemop, let's talk *business*." I crossed my fingers.

"I thought this was a shakedown?"

"It is, but I've had some time to think."

I was suspicious of Whistlemop's sudden change of heart. It felt a lot like the first time we'd met, when he'd suddenly gotten all agitated and handed me the pilsner glass. That had ended with Whistlemop becoming a household name in Minnova. So, I asked Drum what kind of Abilities Whistlemop might have. I knew that Whistlemop was a [Peddler] with his first Specialisation, so he probably had some doozies.

According to Drum, [Peddlers] were Blessed by Aaron and Tiara, which gave them [Sense Deals] and [Move in Aether] as well as [Strength of All: Held and Self]. A Titled individual got improved

Blessings, like my [Flesh of Stone] and [Flash of Insight]. [Peddlers] got [Sense Good Deals] and [Sturdy Merchandise]. Drum said that [Sense Deals] simply said there *was* a deal, but the improved version gave an idea of how much. [Sturdy Merchandise] did what it said and was an evolution of [Strength of All: Held]. [Peddlers] usually aimed for Milestones that helped with making money, and their Specialisations were focused in that direction.

So, a supernatural merchant spent a short time with me then suddenly decided he needed to get on my good side. Why?

The obvious answer was that I had a lot of otherworldly knowledge. There was a good chance he had a Blessing that told him if someone could bring him a lot of money. Even if I didn't know how to leverage my knowledge, a born merchant like Whistlemop might. Between the two of us, we could probably do all kinds of crazy things. However, I didn't trust Whistlemop enough to reveal any of my secrets. Plus, that would just be Whistlemop using me, and I wanted to be the one using Whistlemop.

Then, I'd been struck by an idea. A terrible, horrible, no good, very bad idea. I had some needs, and Whistlemop was *just* the gnome to fulfill them.

So, here I was. Ready to discuss *business*.

"Here's the deal, Whistlemop. The bet is: can I guess how much silver you've made in revenue by selling Whistlemugs. If I win, I get 30 percent of your Whistlemug profits." I'd decided that 50 percent was a bit much. Whistlemop was correct that he'd done all the hard work, and I wanted to start patching things up between us. A 50 percent cut, even on a bet, was going to cause acrimony.

"That's a sucker's bet." Whistlemop smirked. "Only *I* have ever seen those records in full."

"Sure, sure." I waved the comment aside. "But what I want isn't actually your money."

Whistlemop's face twisted in confusion. "Excuse me? I thought that was what this whole thing was about."

"Don't hurt yerself. It *was*. But then I think we both realised that there was a lot more at stake here than just Whistlemug gold."

Whistlemop flinched. It was the barest little twitch of an eyebrow, but my improved perception caught it. Ha! I got him dead to rights!

"So, here's what I really want, Whistlemop. I want your expertise. I want your glassworking facility. I want your business acumen. I want your brand, and I want *exposure*."

Whistlemop covered his chest and crotch. "You want *what!*? You pervert!"

"What!?"

"By Aaron's Arse, I refuse to allow you to brand and expose me! What in the nether is wrong with your head!?"

"Agh! Not that kind of brand! No!! Gods!! No!!"

"What other kind is there!?"

I sunk down in my chair. "Ugh... I can't tell you until our deal is complete. Do you have anything that lets you detect the value of an idea?"

Whistlemop began to shake his head and then paused. "I'm not going to tell you that."

I smirked. "Uh, huh. Well, a brand is something worth a lot of money, but only to the right person. Here's the deal. I don't want the entire 30 percent in cash; I mostly want you to *bankroll* me. You'll get 5 percent of any profit that I personally pull in, as well as free consulting, and after ten years we can renegotiate this contract. Think of it as an investment."

Whistlemop drummed his fingers on the countertop and frowned. "What if you lose?"

"If I lose, then we can look at other options."

"This seems incredibly lopsided towards me. You're even offering me a portion of your profit. What's the catch?"

I smiled, and my estimation of Whistlemop rose a tick. Drum had been correct that he was mostly an honest gnome.

"No catch. If it worries you, let me guess within a 10 percent spread. That's plus or minus 5 percent." I wasn't sure that my method would give me the exact value to the copper and a ten percent wiggle room was something I was aiming for from the start.

"Five percent spread." Whistlemop shot back immediately.

"Eight."

"Seven."

"Seven and a half. Nah, screwit, I don't want to do that much ugly math. Eight, plus or minus 4 percent. Take it or leave it. It's an auspicious number."

Whistlemop *hummed* and *hawwed* and I gave him some time to think. There was a chance Annie would kill me if I bungled this, but I would take that chance. My plan for the brewery would work without Whistlemop, but he massively increased the odds of success.

"Alright. Fine." Whistlemop nodded and penned it in. "I agree to your terms." I'd done *more* than enough legal paperwork in my past life, so the contract was easy to read over. After a bit of bickering on the conditions, Whistlemop and I both signed.

Then I spat in my hand and grabbed my beard. Whistlemop looked at my sticky, hairy, palm, then sighed and spit in his hand. He grabbed the red false moustache off the table and held it out.

"Our Beards Are Joined, Our Words Are One," we intoned in unison.

"Ugh, dwarves –"

"Want me to make you redo it with yer real whiskers?"

"– *are* such wonderful business partners!"

The final contract gave me 30 percent of all the profit on Whistlemugs, backdated one year. It contained a provision that 15 percent of it would be paid out in cash while the other 15 percent would be provided in at-cost glassmaking and equipment. I'd learned that he was building a massive factory for his glassworks, and the long-term value of free access to that might possibly exceed my profit share for Whistlemugs. In return I agreed to give him 5 percent of any *personal* ventures of mine, and free consulting.

"Alright." Whistlemop jumped up and stood next to the door. "Tell me the number so I can leave and be done with this farce. When we renegotiate, I want to focus on your consulting time and fees."

I handed him a slip of paper.

He read it and his jaw dropped. Then he fainted.

Hah! Bullseye!

Quest Complete: Whistlebet!
Winner, winner, gnomish dinner.
Gained 0.2 wisdom! Your new wisdom is 14.2!

"You need to tell me how you guessed. Especially if we're going to be business partners. Was it my accountant? That's impossible, *I'm* my accountant. Did you bribe the bank? Did you go through my list of buyers and count them individually? That would have taken *days* and already be out of date. Was it Trickledown? Did he give you the numbers? I'll have him hung on a goat and dragged through Greentree!"

I winced. "Oof, is that a punishment here?"

"For treason! Which this is!"

"It wasn't Trickledown. Calm yer moustache."

"Then what was it?" Whistlemop was red in the face and ready to pop. It looked great on him.

"You already figured it out." I shrugged nonchalantly.

"What?" Whistlemop paused, clearly distraught. "Which? Was it the bank? Those bastards!"

"Nah, it was Barck. You said it yourself, Barck would need to tell me."

Whistlemop sputtered. "Do you expect me to believe that?"

"Believe what you want."

The truth was, Barck practically *had* told me the number.

Quest: Dwarven Influencer Part 6/10

The dwarves need your help. Influence 100,000 dwarves with your otherworldly alcohol knowledge.
Dwarves Influenced: 94,225/100,000

*Rewards: [**Carbonate**]*

Since Whistlemop was limiting mugs to one per customer until his glass empire scaled up, the number of dwarves I'd influenced was going to be a pretty close match to his total number of customers. That didn't take into account the fifty-odd dwarves in the mine, sneaky people that managed to buy multiples, or those that simply weren't influenced – but it was close enough. The rest was just math, and I was pretty okay at math.

The Dwarven Influencer quests started at 2500, then 5000, 10000, 25,000, 50,000, and finally 100,000. It started from zero each time, which meant including the current 94,225 number, Whislemop had sold around 186,725 mugs. Multiplied by five silver gave – after some long multiplication napkin math – a total of 933,625 silver. That worked out to a hair under ten million Canadian dollars, the little rat bastard. Fifty gold in-*deed*! So, I wrote a conservative 900,000 silver plus or minus 4 percent and knocked the bugger out.

Hah! Who ever said maths was useless!

Other than half my friends in high school. Honestly, that [Mental Maths] Ability couldn't come fast enough...

I was interrupted from my thoughts by Whistlemop. "Bah! Fine, you win! I'll see that you are sent some financial statements later tonight at The Drunken Goat."

"The Thirsty Goat. And no, I'll come get them from you. I don't want anyone at the Goat to know about this yet."

"Whatever! Now tell me about this 'branding' and 'exposure,' so I can get something out of this ordeal."

"Hold yer horses. What was the actual number?" I was curious about how close it was.

"Are you telling me you don't actually know!? That was a *guess!?*"

"Maybe, maybe not."

"Hmph. Well, you'll find out later anyways. It was 935,345 silver."

My high vitality was all that kept me from passing out. My conservative drop down to 900,000 had nearly cost me. Heck, If I'd agreed to Whistlemop's 7 percent range, I would have gotten it wrong! No wonder he fainted. How was it so much *higher* than my initial guess? Maybe some dwarves were buying it but not being influenced?

I hid my consternation by arranging a piece of paper and pencil. Gnomes and dwarves loved drawing up plans, so pencils and paper were actually pretty cheap. I drew a very recognizable swoosh and pointed at it.

"Here's yer lesson. Let's start with a logo."

Whistlemop leaned over to look. "It just looks like a curvy checkmark."

"Ahh, but the magic is in *branding*." I did some jazz hands.

"I don't understand."

"A logo is like a maker's mark. You do know how a maker's mark works, right?"

"Yes, absolutely. A maker's mark indicates that a product is made by a specific craftsman within a city. Most city guilds will not allow someone in the same guild to copy that product exactly. Additionally, a maker's mark is a symbol of authenticity. Some Abilities can check them."

"Really? Neat. Now imagine a certain blacksmith who makes the *best* swords. Over time, his swords will become more valuable as the general population begins to accept the superiority of his work."

"Yes, yes." Whistlemop waved me on.

"Don't rush me! Over time, our hypothetical blacksmith's mark comes to mean more than the sword does. The sword is no longer what holds value, it is the *mark* that holds value. Branding," *jazz hands*, "means that you don't just sell a product, you're selling the *idea* of a product. A mythos, a *brand*."

"What would that..." Whistlemop trailed off, then his eyes grew wide.

"You see it? In the current model, if our stabby blacksmith makes armour, he has no reputation. However, with *branding* the blacksmith's *armour* is just as famous as his *swords*, because it isn't the *sword* that's famous!"

Whistlemop whispered nearly reverentially. "It's the mark."

"Right, and you're already part-way there with your Whistlemug trick. You already *are* branding, and even have a 'logo' that serves the same kind of purpose as a mark. The logo is your face, by the way. It's an ugly logo, but it'll do for now."

"Hey!"

"What I want to do, Whistlemop, is turn your work into a powerful brand in Minnova, and then move on to all of Crack. Then I want to get some exposure, which just means you showcase my products, and I'll ride your coattails with the Thirsty Goat's newest product."

"What is it?" He leaned forward eagerly.

"First, let's talk about gearing your glasswork industry up. Then we're going to have a little chat about 'special editions.' You're wasting some serious potential, especially with Minnova's first official drinking contest..."

We continued late into the evening. By the time we were done, Whistlemop left the run-down shack smiling, even under the blindfold.

CHAPTER SIXTY-SEVEN
UNDER PRESSURE

Today was the big day. My first time seeing a completed brew in my new life. I'd spent the past week coaching and making preparations with Whistlemop, but today would determine if those plans moved forward or if they were all for naught.

"Attention everyone!" Jeremiah said in a commanding tone that echoed around the brew floor. We were all assembled there: John, Johnsson, Richter, Aqua, Annie, Balin, and another blue-haired dwarf that I realised with a start must be Aqua's father, Tom.

"You've all worked hard! And that hard work has been rewarded!" He swept his arm around the shining room. "Not a single batch was lost this time. We achieved a *perfect brew*! Congratulations!!"

There was a raucous cheer. I was really curious about the next step. Usually I would use a beer hydrometer to check for completed fermentation, but that didn't exist here. I had to add it to my list of necessary items. It was likely that Jeremiah simply went off bubbles in the Kräusen – no new bubbles meant the fermentation was complete and the beer was ready.

"As is tradition, the first drink will go to Penelope! Long may she live!"

Aqua brought forward Penelope alongside a wide and shallow mug with a goat motif.

"Long may she live!" Everyone intoned reverentially.

"Wait, are we really giving the first drink to *Penelope*?" I blurted it out before I could stop myself. Gods, the place was called the Thirsty Goat and Penelope had a hankering for beer. The dots were all there, Pete!

"Yes, indeed. It has been a secret tradition for Thirsty Goat Brewing to give the first sip of each new batch to Penelope. That's why our Penelope is the Five-Hundred-and-Fourth. As long as this brewery stands, there will always be a Penelope." He scratched at Penelope's floofy head.

maaaaah [Translated from Prima Donna Goat] "Why are you all standing around? Where is my libation, peasants?"

"I think Pete is worried that –," Balin began with a giant grin.

"If this is another Goat-lover crack, I will *END* you, brother."

"Never mind."

The ceremony continued unhindered. A spigot slightly above the floor of the first fermentation tank was opened and a trickle of amber liquid poured into the mug. Penelope greedily drank it up and gave a happy *maaaah.* Everyone but Balin and I gave a small sigh of relief, and then they broke into a joyful, cheering song.

> Another batch is done at last,
> And so the dice of life are cast!
>
> A perfect brew is much to ask,
> When all we want is one full cask!
>
> We'll pop the cork to test the taste,
> Then drink it down, with none to waste!

The ritual was repeated at the other dozen-odd tanks, and Balin and I were even able to join in on the song by the last few.

"Indeed, a perfect brew." Jeremiah said, with a slightly sad smile. Both elation and the weight of age played across his face. "Richter and Johnsson, start filling barrels. Balin, thanks for your hard work on those, stay and make sure there aren't any leaks. Aqua, contact our distributors and tell them the beer is back on. Pete, take Penelope back to her pen, then come back and get Annie. Tom, you and John can take the evening off, you've earned it. Annie... come and see me." He gave me a solemn look as Annie followed him curiously.

I guessed that meant our time had come. Annie and I were going to have free rein for the next batch. No big changes, Jeremiah had said, but if we could make a clearer and slightly fizzier beer without any explosions, we had his blessing.

Bing!

Quest Complete: Middle Management!
Congratulations and welcome to middle management hell!

Gained 0.2 charisma! Your new charisma is 12.2!

Bing!

New Quest: Proud Owner
Why be satisfied with management when there's a company to own? Become a partner or full owner of the Thirsty Goat Brewpub.
Rewards: [Mental Maths]

Do you accept?
Yes / No

Excellent. It was time to move forward with my plan. But first, I had a little science experiment that needed doing!

"Whoof." I gently placed the heavy crate down next to a fermenting tank in the Thirsty Goat and stretched my back. I levered it open with a crowbar and chortled. "Science rules!"

Then I jumped as Annie peeked around the tank. "Ahh! Annie, don't *do* that!"

She ignored me and peered into the crate, pointing at the squat objects sitting within. "What are those? They look like really big potion bottles or really small milk jugs."

"Uh, they sort of are. They're how I plan to get better fermentation."

"How do they work?" She picked one up. It was slightly taller than it was wide and made of a thick transparent glass that tapered up to a fluted neck with a bump in it. Any serious drinker from Earth would recognize it immediately as a Belgian ale bottle. "And what's this thing at the top?" She fingered a wire contraption nestled around the neck of the bottle.

"It's a lightning stopper." I flipped it open and shut to show how it worked. The thick wire contraption placed a metal and cork cap over the mouth of the bottle, and then levered down to create a strong seal. It was a style often used for kombucha back on Earth.

Designing a good stopper for my bottles had taken a few days. Cork was abundant in Greentree, but corks weren't ideal for what I wanted to do here, and bottlecaps required large-scale industrialization. Thankfully, any tinker with half a brain could make a lightning stopper.

"Why is it called a lightning stopper?" Annie asked, popping it open and closed. "Hey, this is kind of fun!"

"You know what? I'm not sure. The original inventor of it was a man by the name of Karl Hutter. At least I think he invented it? He popularised it at a cork competition, and it became a standard form of bottle stopper for hundreds of years. Maybe he called it that because it could be opened as 'fast as lightning' or some such nonsense."

"Well, we aren't on Earth. You can call it what you want." Annie resumed poring over my glass bottles. There were a dozen, and each would hold nearly a litre of beer.

"That's a good point... I think I'll call them bucks."

"Why?"

"Because the buck stops beer." I waggled my eyebrows.

"What?"

"Gods, I feel old. I'll think of a good name for them later." Or not, because I couldn't be bothered. We'd probably end up calling them Whistlestops for branding purposes.

"You're the youngest person in this brewery!"

"Age is a state of mind. Give me a hand filling these bottles. You'll need to fill them nearly to the brim." I demonstrated.

Annie took a bottle and placed it on the spigot at the bottom of the fermenter. I was using the newly completed batch for this. We were out of barrels, and two tanks were sitting full until Balin finished making new ones.

I labelled my bottle '1' with a grease pen. Then I pulled a small box out from under my jacket and opened it. It contained a series of tiny vials filled with clear liquid. I grabbed a vial labelled '1' and poured it into the bottle, then levered the lightning stopper shut. Annie passed me the next bottle and we repeated this eleven times before placing the bottles back into the wooden crate. The lid was nailed back into place, and 'Bottle Test Number One' was ready to go.

"What was in the vials?" Annie asked as we looked down at my little science experiment. "And are you planning to sell beer in those bottles? That's actually kind of neat! It will make the beer more expensive though." She pulled out her notebook.

"It's complex, but I'll be happy to explain while we walk. Your dad said no explosions, so I need to move these."

"WHAT!?"

"Shhhh!!!!" I looked around. I didn't want to get caught by Jeremiah doing this, since it was maybe a little bit technically against the spirit of our agreement. Not the letter though.

"No walking! Explain first!" Annie hissed, her hands flexing murderously. "I just got put in charge here and you want more boom!?"

"Alright. Alright." I waved my hand at the box. "These bottles are the solution to your carbonation dilemma. At least in the short term."

"You have my attention." She crossed her arms. "How?"

"Getting fermentation just right with open-top brewing is hard. Pressurised fermentation is a lot better – that's what you tried to do by the way – but it can be really, really dangerous. These bottles are a specific design that's good at containing high pressure. Same with the lightning stopper. We'll get to pressurised fermentation eventually, but it's going to take a lot of time that we don't particularly have."

Well, time we didn't *used* to have, but I was keeping my deal with Whistlemop secret for now. The extra *pressure* of impending bankruptcy was my ticket to making changes in the brewery and I didn't want to lose that. I felt a bit guilty, but people could get weird about a sudden influx of cash. Like how you were never supposed to tell anyone when you won the lottery. I'd tell everyone after the first new brew was complete.

"Since we can't do any pressurised brewing, and I'm not allowed to add much of anything to the beer, our best bet in the short term is *bottle conditioning*," I continued.

"I'm going to guess it involves putting beer in those bottles and waiting? Hey... we could do something like the Whistlemugs with those, couldn't we?!" Annie grew excited.

"Sort of. It would actually be better if they didn't turn into collector's items. We want to incentivize people to return these. To answer your question, you're correct. Bottle conditioning is a form of secondary fermentation. Secondary fermentation is when you *rack* – that means pour – your completed beer into a barrel and let it sit for a few weeks or months longer."

Annie nodded. "That's how Light Brew works. I don't know the specifics since we don't make it, but I've heard chatter amongst other brewers."

"Right, lagers need to secondary ferment in a cold environment for an extended period of time. Any time you do that, no matter the circumstances, it's secondary fermentation. It does change the taste of the beer though."

"We don't want to change the flavour of the beer." Annie shook her head. "Especially not for my first solo batch since –"

"Right," I interrupted. "That's not what we're aiming for. What we want is very little change of taste with a little more carbonation. That's where bottle conditioning, priming sugars, and my Milestone come into play." I pulled an empty vial and showed it to Annie. She took it in her hand and sniffed.

"It smells... sweet?"

"That's right." I nodded. "It's sugar vine."

Annie rolled her eyes. "You and your sugar."

"Yes, yes, well in this case it's *priming sugar*. When the fermentation in these big babies is done," I patted one of the giant fermenting tanks, "there are no simple sugars left for the yeast to break down.

During secondary fermentation, the yeast begins to attack more complex sugars and esters in the barrel. We don't want that, so we add a little bit of priming sugar to the bottle. Wait a week or so while the yeasts concentrate on that sugar instead, and we get more carbonation and alcohol! Tadah! Fizzy beer!"

"That sounds great! But... beer goes bad quickly when we pour it. Most kegs need to be drunk within a week or two." Annie pointed out.

"That's where my Abilities come into it! When we pour the beer out of the fermenters, it adds oxygen to the beer, which oxidises and gives an awful taste. I have an Ability that should prevent that, and Richter is working on something that might help too!" I actually had Richter investigating *several* pieces of magic for me, and I was excited to do my first enchanted brewing! His acquisition of Archie's Blessing had been lucky timing! I winced as I realised luck probably had nothing to do with it.

Annie tapped her foot nervously. "We usually try to avoid using Abilities during the brewing process. It makes a brewery too dependent on a single individual."

"Do I hear the voice of 'tradition' speaking?" I teased.

Annie snorted. "It's a good reason and you know it."

"Maybe. I personally think it's a waste of literal God-given gifts. It doesn't really apply in this case though. The Milestone is just a stopgap until I can get the technology working. If you lose me, you lose it all *anyway* so there's no real difference." Although I was one to talk. I had [Carbonate] coming down the pipeline with zero intention of using it outside of carbonating my own drinks. I guess I subconsciously agreed with her.

Annie's face fell. "Please don't talk like you're going to suddenly die on us Pete. That's bad luck!"

"We can reduce that chance by getting these bottles to the cart outside."

Annie grimaced as she helped me carry the box out to an awaiting goat-cart pulled by Penelope. "Just, be careful. If something happens to you, Balin will never forgive me."

Well, *that* wasn't ominous at all.

"Are these really that dangerous?" Whistlemop asked as he looked over the twelve bottles. Each of them was contained within a separate solid steel container inset with heavy glass panels.

"Yeah. I don't actually know the correct ratio to use for the sugar vine, so I tried twelve different amounts. Each of those bottles has an increasing amount of sugar added, and some of them are *absolutely* going to turn into *bottle-bombs*. The carbon dioxide will –" I paused and glanced at Whistlemop, who was decidedly *not* taking notes.

"Never mind."

Whistlemop tsked. "I'd be willing to pay you a good amount for the secret to dwarven brewing techniques."

"Not happening."

"For an extra 10 percent on the Whistlemugs?"

"Not for one hundred. Even this feels like I'm giving away a bit too much."

"Yes, well, since I have you, I wanted to show you the special edition we were talking about the other day."

Whislemop brought me over to a small table in the warehouse we'd bought. A cloth was placed to artfully hide an object on top. Whistlemop whisked it off with panache.

"Tadah!"

The glass on top of the table was instantly recognizable as a Whistlemug – with a few changes. The usual image of a winking gnome was still there, but the other side now had the crest of Minnova on it. There were some tiny etchings of drinking paraphernalia and fancy lettering that said 'Minnova's First Octa-millennial Drinking Competition.'

I looked it over, admiring the workmanship; the Ralphs were *great* at their job. "Are you really allowed to use the city crest in your work?"

Whistlemop took the mug back. "I have to pay a tax to do so, but yes. Are you sure I can really charge double for these? I haven't raised prices because I was afraid of pushing customers away."

"Oh, absolutely. Maybe even more." I waved the worry off. "You aren't increasing the price of your Whistlemugs, you're releasing a 'special limited edition.' With a personal recommendation from one of the top ten drinkers in Minnova."

"And I can keep doing that?" Whistlemop stared at his reflection in the depths of the glass and I could practically see the greed in his eyes.

"Then it wouldn't be a *limited* edition."

"Ah, then we can only do it once." Whistlemop sighed. "Though… why limit it to just the drinking contest? I could do one for every holiday! For every local event! I could partner with the adventurer's guild, or the church!"

"Now you're getting it! Remember, when this goes on sale, I want that poster of me put up on your wagon." The poster was my first attempt at advertising. Putting stuff up around the *city* was illegal, but there was nothing stopping merchants from putting up signs on their *own* wagons or stores. The poster featured a picture of me holding a Whistlemug and the slogan, "I use Whistlemugs to speed drink all my favourite Thirsty Goat beers."

It was a work of art.

Whistlemop frowned. "Will it really help sales?"

I sighed. He still had so much to learn. "I need to talk to you about celebrity endorsement."

I looked over my experiment and added the final step, though I wouldn't know if it was successful for at least a week or two. "[Stabilise Mixture]!"

"You don't need to say that aloud, you know."

"Spoilsport."

CHAPTER SIXTY-EIGHT
HOPBACK

Knock, knock, knock

"Balin, do you want to get that? Ugh, what *time* is it?" I rolled over in my bed.

The two of us were sharing a tenement room a little ways away from the brewery. We finally had enough money to live independently, and I refused to allow my brother to live under the same roof as the woman he was courting.

groaaaan

Not that it mattered. He still snuck out to make out with her every night.

KNOCK KNOCK KNOCK

"Argh, fine, I'll do it. ONE MINUTE! Wake up, Balin. We're installing the hopback today."

GROOAAANNN was my only answer.

I put on a tunic and leather pants and made my way to the door. I tried to pat my beard down, but I always had the *worst* morning beard, and it poofed up practically to my eyes. The knocking grew louder. "Don't get Lunara's Lace in a knot!! I'm comin'!!"

I swung the door open.

A red false-mustachioed gnome in a wide brimmed cowboy hat and cloak stood at my door. He looked panicked.

"Whistlemop? Do you have any idea what time it is!? Why are you in that dumb disguise?"

"Pete, it worked too well!"
"What?"
Bing!

Quest Complete: Dwarven Influencer Part 6/10!

Keep up the great work!

*Gained [**Carbonate**]!*

Bing!

New Quest: Dwarven Influencer Part 7/10!

The dwarves need your help. Influence 1,000,000 dwarves with your otherworldly alcohol knowledge.
Dwarves influenced: 345/1,000,000

*Rewards: [**Pete's Poor Manasight**]*

Do you accept?

Yes / No

[**Carbonate**] – *Add a small amount of aether to any other kind of aether. You can only create aethers you are very familiar with. This Ability can be used once per second.*

My eyes bugged out, and I barely registered the fact I'd gotten a new Ability and could now properly Specialise. Barck said I'd like what I got for Dwarven Influencer Part 7, but this was something else! "Is that what I think it is!?"

Whistlemop whirled around, "What! Did they follow me!?"

"Ergh, never mind. Get in here." I pulled him in and slammed the door, my mind whirling with the thought of *magic*.

"Careful... Careful... A little to the left, Richter. A little right. Ok, stop there. Johnsson, start putting in the fasteners."

Richter heaved the large contraption into place and Johnsson began hammering nails. I clutched my head as the ringing echoed in my ears and moaned. Annie stood at my side and nodded.

"It fits almost exactly. Great work on the trusses, Balin." She gave him a thump on the back and he groaned and nearly fell over.

"Bad morning, you two?" she asked. Then she winked. "Or a busy night?"

"We were awoken by a rather annoying acquaintance," I grumbled, my eyes black-rimmed. We hadn't really gotten a chance to eat breakfast; Whistlemop had been way too energetic. He was currently hiding in our tenement room. On the bright side, we likely had a *lot* of gold coming in. On the downside...

"There's a riot in the Grand Market!" Aqua burst in through the door, and Balin and I moaned in unison. She looked confused. "What's wrong?"

"Don't mind tham." Richter put in as he stepped away from the tall wooden structure. "Balin and tha miss were keepin' tha rest o' us awake till tha wee hours. Pete's jast not a mornin' person."

Annie turned scarlet and Aqua wolf-whistled, then looked around guiltily to see if Jeremiah had heard. Luckily for Balin's good health, he wasn't in. Actually, he hadn't been in the brewery all that much recently.

"A riot?" Johnsson asked, as he finished hammering.

"Aye!" Aqua said excitedly. "It started in the central square and spread to the main stores! Nobody knows what caused it yet, but the city guard are out! It's the most exciting thing I've seen in decades! Anyone want to go?"

There was a chorus of "No," and Aqua's face fell.

"Awww, not even you, Pete?"

"I *just* got off the city's shit list. Why would I risk it?"

"Oh, good point. Aww, biscuits. That would have been fun."

I walked over and patted her shoulder. "I'll take you to Raspi's next concert to make it up to you."

She brightened up immediately. "Your treat?"

"Sure."

Johnsson looked at us suspiciously. "Are you two datin'?"

Aqua and I looked at each other then burst out laughing.

"Sooo... what is that?" Aqua asked a while later, after all the laughter died down. Johnsson had left to ensure our daily shipment of erdroot was still arriving, and Balin was double-checking the contraption that now stood nestled between the boiling kettle and the mash tun.

It was a large metal bowl, roughly the size of the kettle. We'd attached it to the existing scaffolding so that it made a neat triangle with the mash tun and boil kettle. A funnel attached to the side of the bowl was placed to accept the trough that usually went from the boil kettle to the fermentation tanks. Arcane sigils marked its surface, which made it look *quite* different from the copper boiling kettle and wooden mash tun.

"Do you want to explain?" I asked Annie.

"Love to." She gave a grand gesture to the bowl. "I present to you, Erd's first hopback."

"Hopback?" Aqua repeated, her mouth feeling the word. "Does it actually hop?"

I chuckled, though Annie ignored it. "No. It's a way to improve the clarity of our beer. Come see. Richter, can you start a mash going? I want to check if this all works like Pete says it will. Charge the sigils first, though."

"Aye, miss." He gave a small salute.

"Oh, you of little faith," I muttered.

Annie elbowed me in the ribs. "You've never used enchanting before, so this is new to you too. There's no guarantee it will work."

"Eh, the general thermodynamic principles are the same; it's just a heat-sink. The only difference is that I'm using magic to do it instead of... other stuff. Which is *awesome*, but most of the actual magic got done by the family of hyperactive gnomes with fancy crystal tools that we hired to make all the enchantments. *I* want to do the magic."

AN ADVENTURE BREWING

Aqua and Annie both nodded. They, like all beings, could understand the awesomeness that was magic.

"Well, maybe we'll get lucky with a Milestone from using magic in our beer production." Annie pointed out as we climbed the stairs to the upper catwalk.

"I still can't believe that the methods for getting Milestones aren't documented," I whined. "Considering how hidebound our society is, I'm surprised more stuff like that isn't bound in hide."

"What?" The two chorused.

I mimed opening and closing a book. "Books. Why aren't there books on how to get Milestones?"

"Oh, lots of reasons!" Aqua said cheerfully. "Most of the time people don't figure out the exact method, they just get lucky. Other times it's because the Titled folk just don't really care to research it, they're too busy doing what they love."

"The methods can change, too," Annie put in. "But the main reason is that it's controlled information. It's actually a major point of contention right now. The nobility hoard that knowledge and don't allow the greybeards to share it." She shook her head.

We arrived next to the bowl. Up close, there was a slight hum, and Aqua shivered as the temperature dropped a few degrees. "It's cold?"

"That's right." Annie nodded. "The bowl is actually a chiller."

"Why?" Aqua's teeth chattered. "It's freezing!!"

I added a note to my notebook about ambient magic leakage. We'll need to be careful of that in the future. "I thought about building an immersion chiller originally. That's a lot of copper tubing with cold water running through it. But magic is cooler, in every meaning of the word."

"It's not that cold," Annie chided. "Let me start from the beginning. Do you see that funnel? The hot wort gets poured into it from the boil kettle. The funnel is filled with some branches used in our bittering agent in a heavy burlap bag. We'll need to change the branches out every day or so, but it isn't a major expense."

"What branches?" I asked, my pen at the ready. Annie had refused to tell, only providing a full burlap bag in exchange for a promise not to peek.

"Good try." She smirked. "The hot wort passing through the

branches pulls out some of the oils and adds aroma, but not much flavour. The burlap acts as a filter, to remove any of the mash or bittering agents that got into the wort. It'll make for a stronger-scented and cleaner beer with less chance of yeast contamination." She looked at me for confirmation.

I nodded. "Good so far."

"Wait, how do you know all this?" Aqua interrupted.

"Pete told me." Annie shrugged.

"How does *Pete* know?"

"I learned of it a long time ago in a galaxy far, far away."

Aqua's eyes narrowed. "Ok, how is that *true*? Are you pulling my beard?"

"You're distracted, Aqua! Pete's weirdness is *not* the topic!"

"Hey!"

Annie continued, pointing at the metal bowl. "After it passes through the filter, the hot wort flows into this enchanted bowl. The sigils on the side cause it to be chilled rapidly. See those vertical prongs in it? They help maximise the amount of liquid that gets affected by the enchantment."

"Why chill it?" Aqua leaned in to look at the runes. "Who designed these?"

"Richter." I pointed at the sigils. "His new Title allows him to see mana structures, and he used it to help me get everything just right. I had some plans for the engineering side, but the magic side is all him. It's a good thing – a local family of [Enchanters] did all the engraving and they were going to charge a *lot* more if they had to design it too."

"Speaking of which," Annie said as she looked askew at me, "how *did* you afford this."

"I made some money," I prevaricated.

"Nothing illegal, I hope?" she pushed.

"I am *not* planning on going back to that mine."

"See!?" Aqua threw up her hands. "Weasel words!!"

"I can promise that the money was deserved." I poked Aqua in the side and she squeaked.

"Hmmm. Good enough I suppose. Where was I? Right, the chilling. Quickly chilling the wort causes the proteins and tannins to drop out of the wort as a crud called *cold-break*. Those are usually what make the beer cloudy and astringent, though Pete says *tannins* aren't a concern with our beer." She looked at me for confirmation. I nodded. "After that, the cooled wort gets run through that trough to the tanks like usual and we clean the cold-break out of the bowl."

"Tannins?" Aqua chattered, as she began to visibly shiver. I added another note to my book and she glowered at me. "Are you using me as a test subject?"

"I'll tell you all about it, Aqua. Let's go back down." Annie put a hand on Aqua's shoulder and guided her away.

I stayed behind and stared down at the hack-job magitech abomination I'd created with the Erdian magical equivalent of duct tape. It was beautiful.

"Are you coming, Pete?" Annie asked as they headed down the stairs.

"Later. I need to talk to you and Balin sometime this afternoon. Can you set aside some time?"

"Sure, is it important?"

"To me."

"Alright. Do this first test with Richter while I get Aqua warmed up, and we'll chat after."

"Works for me."

"Mebbe you can come and help turn tha wheel, Pete?" Richter called from below.

I ignored him and stared at my beautiful, *magical*, invention. Soon Pete, only... a million dwarves to go.

"Any taim now."

"Fiiine."

CHAPTER SIXTY-NINE
SPECIALISED

"Alright, Pete. What was so important it couldn't wait?"

Annie and Balin sat across from me in Annie's office. It was a new office attached to the brew room floor that Balin built for her. A picture window looked out over the brewery, and the only furnishings so far were a simple wooden desk and a trio of plain stools.

"I need to make an important decision. The last time I did this I kind of rushed it, and this time I want to seriously talk it over with someone first."

"Alright…" Annie said with trepidation. "*What is it?*"

"You can tell us whatever you need, brother." Balin patted me on the knee.

"Thanks, Balin. Okay, here it is. I have my first Specialisation. Tadah!" I gave a 'surprise' gesture, though they were both *actually* surprised enough that they didn't react for a few moments.

"Really? Congratulations Pete!" Balin thumped his chest and then pumped his fist.

"That was obscenely fast," Annie said, frowning. "You weren't even Blessed a year ago. I don't think I've ever heard of anyone getting their Specialisation so quickly. Come to think of it… Bran, Richter, Balin, you, me. There have been a *lot* of Blessings going around."

I ignored that last part, no need to freak them out. "I get Milestones quickly because of my quests."

"What quests?" Annie and Balin said together.

"I get rewards for completing certain tasks. It's part of my [Otherworlder] Milestone and helps me grow faster."

Annie gasped. "That's practically cheating!"

"Yeah, and it gives me stats too."

"Now, isn't that somethin'! Yer goin' to be a right powerhouse someday, Pete!"

"I asked you to stay because I wanted yer thoughts on the Specialisation options. You may have some insights I lack." I put out my hands, pleadingly. "Can you help?"

They looked at each other and nodded.

"Aye!"

"No question! What are your options?"

"Let's find out!" I pulled up the Specialisation menu and chose five Milestones.

Specialisation Possible!

Please select 5 Milestones to combine into a Specialisation!
*You have selected [**Otherworlder**], [**Stabilise Mixture**], [**Carbonate**], [**Ingredient Scan**], and [**Bottomless Barrel**].*

Merge Milestones?

Yes/No

I hit "Yes" and a new notification popped up.

Specialisation Gained

You have decided to Specialise! Specialisation is an important decision that will guide your future growth. Your selected Milestones will combine to give you powerful new Blessings that will help you down your chosen path. Choose wisely, for what you choose will come to define you.

The following four Specialisations are available to you.

Dimensional Drinker
Otherworldly Brewer
Aether Alchemist
Chosen Alchemist

"I've got four different options."

Annie nodded. "You should be able to focus on them to learn more. Start with the first one and we'll discuss it."

"Aye." I focused on [Dimensional Drinker] and began to read aloud.

Possible Specialisation: [Dimensional Drinker]
*Combine [**Bottomless Barrel**] and [**Otherworlder**] into the Blessing [**Dimensional Barrel**].*
*Combine [**Stabilise Mixture**] and [**Ingredient Scan**] into the Blessing [**Preservation Field**].*
*The Milestone [**Carbonate**] is not affected.*

*As an [**Alchemist**] you have always pushed for greater flavour, and your desire for alcohol pushes you towards the path of a [**Drinker**]. As an Otherworlder, you have tasted drinks that no other mortal in this realm can comprehend, and as a [**Dimensional Drinker**], you will be able to share that experience.*
Increases the chance of developing drinking Milestones and the chance of finding hidden alcohols.

Go forth, young dwarf, and drink!

[Dimensional Barrel] – *Your spirit has found a new spark! Your mental statistics remain replaced with their previous values and you gain a greater memory of what once was. You can touch an empty container and for the next one minute, a non-magical drink of your choice can be poured out of it. If the liquid is not poured into an appropriate container or imbibed within the next twenty-four minutes, it disappears.*

This Ability can be used once per hour.

[Preservation Field] – *You can stabilise all food and drink within a 12-metre radius of where you use this Ability. Reduce any toxicity or instability and increase shelf life by one day per use.*
This Ability can be used once per hour.

"I want it!" By Barck's Beautiful Beard, this was the greatest thing I'd ever seen!

"Take it!" Annie nearly jumped out of her chair.

"Could ya make liquid mithril with that?" Balin mused. We both looked askance at him.

"That's a good question –" I began, but Annie interrupted.

"It doesn't matter! Dad has an Ability that can tell him the components of a drink! If you pour alcohol from your world, he'll be able to recreate the recipe!"

"You know? I don't actually know what Mr. Goldstone's Title is." I mused.

"You don't? He's an [Ancestral Brewer]."

"That... is the most dwarvish thing I've ever heard of."

"It is, and it's annoying," Annie sighed. "The Milestones for it are a secret of the Honourable Guild of Brewers, and you have to take an oath to be given the process for getting them. I don't really need it, but Dad was barely driven enough as a brewer to get his Title, let alone his Specialisation."

"So, you think it's the best bet?"

"Yes. Take it now. Everything you've told me about your world's alcohol makes me incredibly curious. It's possibly invaluable if we sell tastings."

"Maybe... though I can *make* a lot of, if not most of, those drinks with enough time anyway."

On the other hand, there was a good chance that creating an alcohol with [Dimensional Barrel] would mean Barck could create it too. A possible deific reward there? Or maybe not, given what he told me about his punishment. [Preservation Field] was a dud, though it would be helpful around our new kitchen. Overall it looked perfect, but for one small problem...

I read it again, carefully. "[Dimensional Barrel] removed the wording for 'easier Blessings and Milestones' from my [Outworlder] Ability. I think I'll lose my quests."

"Ouf..."

"That's a pretty tough trade."

"It does put a damper on things. Higher Specialisations are a lot more powerful, right? I'd be tradin' unlimited delicious drinks for faster progression. I'll... need to think about it."

"A dwarf usually needs decades or even centuries to get their *first* specialisation." Annie mused. "That is actually a really tough choice."

"Well, let's look at the next option then." I opened it up.

Possible Specialisation: [Otherworldly Brewer]

*Combine [**Carbonate**] and [**Stabilise Mixture**] into the Blessing [**Refine Brew**].*

*Combine [**Otherworlder**] and [**Ingredient Scan**] into the Blessing [**Minimap**].*
*The Milestone [**Bottomless Barrel**] is not affected.*

*As an [**Alchemist**], your endeavours pushed you towards the humble art of brewing alcohol. While a regular [**Brewer**] constantly seeks out new ingredients and opportunities to further their craft, an [**Otherworldly Brewer**] transcends worlds to do so.*
Increases the chance of developing brewing Milestones and the chance of brews being successful.
May your brew be you and to yourself be true.

[Refine Brew] – *You are able to refine and stabilise a container of alchemical liquid with a touch. If the brew contains any unstable magical aethers they will be forced into equilibrium. The brew will become more nutritious and have a longer shelf life.*
This Ability can be used once per second.

[Minimap] – *Your spirit has found a new spark! Your mental statistics remain replaced with their previous values, and you are more likely to gain Blessings and Milestones! You also gain a minimap to help find your way around this new world. People and monsters as well as major landmarks will be marked on your minimap. You can also mark crafting ingredients or quests and quest items.*
This Ability is always available.

I liked it. I liked it a lot. But...

"[Dimensional Drinker is better]." Annie said firmly and I hesitantly agreed.

"I dunno, Annie," Balin put in. "This feels a lot more like Pete. He *likes* drinkin' but he seems ta *love* brewin'."

They both looked at me, and I slowly nodded. I did love beer. And wine. And whiskey, and rum, and a dozen other drinks, but they were just what I loved to drink. What I *was* brewing a brewer, and this Specialisation practically defined me. It didn't have anything fancy like [Dimensional Barrel], but [Refine Brew] sounded helpful, and the reference to 'magical aethers' appealed to me. Especially with [Pete's Poor Manasight] coming down the pipeline.

I'd lose [Carbonate], but I'd given it a try and it was a little disappointing. Shooting tiny spurts of flames from my hand had been cool for all of five minutes. It wasn't anything close to the magic I'd seen Diamond use. Honestly, of all my Abilities, it was the smallest loss, even if it would make carbonating my drinks easier.

[Minimap] was just straight up cool, and a staple of any good fantasy adventure. Being able to spot monsters and quest items could be lifesaving. Imagine if I'd had that back in the mine!? It also mentioned crafting ingredients – would I be able to set the filter to 'hops' or 'bitters' and see them on the minimap? That would make shopping so much easier than wandering around pinging [Ingredient Scan].

I read it again. "It's nothing special, but it's solid. It also keeps my quests, as far as I can tell."

"Another thing to keep in mind, Pete, is that further Specialisations build on your first one. There's also a focus on brewing Milestones, which means you'll be more likely to unlock more brewing-specific Specialisations." Annie pointed out.

"Hmmm... good point. I'll put it *just* below [Dimensional Drinker] for now. Let's see what's next."

Possible Specialisation: [Aether Alchemist]
*Combine **[Otherworlder]** and **[Carbonate]** into the Blessing **[Aether Form]**.*

*Combine [**Bottomless Barrel**] and [**Stabilise Mixture**] into the Blessing [**Form Aether**].*
*The Milestone [**Ingredient Scan**] is not affected.*

*As an [**Alchemist**], you focused on the study of aether; yours was the path of fire and water. As an [**Aether Alchemist**] you gain greater control over your craft, and as an Otherworlder, can even pass through to the realm of Aaron himself.*
Increases the chance of developing Aether Milestones and increases Aether affinity.
Take to the sky and become one with your new element!

[Aether Form] – *Your mental statistics remain replaced with your previous values, and you are more likely to gain Blessings and Milestones. You have decided to eschew your new spark, but can now convert your body fully into an aether of your choice. Your physical statistics change based on the type of aether chosen for twenty-four minutes.*
This Ability can be used once per hour.

[Form Aether] – *You can touch a container that contains no more than twenty-four litres of non-magical liquid and gain total control of it. For the next twenty-four minutes, the aether within the container will expand, and can be shaped and moulded by your will alone. Additionally, you can command the aether to become more or less solid.*
This Ability can be used once per hour.

"That's a powerful set of Blessins' rig't there," Balin said.

"I don't see the power in [Form Aether]," Annie frowned. "Though turning your body into aether is a coveted Blessing. Most don't see it until their third or fourth Specialisation. Your [Otherworlder] Milestone seems to grant very powerful effects. That's likely why you are being forced to combine it at your first Specialisation; it would be far too powerful combined at a higher Specialisation."

"Does [Aether Form] mean I could fly? Or turn into fire? Or invisible? That's amazing!" I said excitedly.

"Aye." Annie nodded. "All of those. The utility is what makes it so powerful. You'd also be nearly immune to physical damage."

"I don't really know if it's 'you' though, Pete." Balin said.

I had to agree. It was super cool, and if I wanted to move towards being an adventurer, it would be an amazing Specialisation. Then my mind wandered towards enormous ants wreathed in flame. I shivered; no adventuring for this young dwarf, no siree!

"I agree with Balin," I said, and cut off Annie's protest. "It's just not me."

"I can see that. It's a shame though." She sighed. "What's the last option?"

I choked as I scanned the next Specialisation, and looked askance at Balin and Annie. They smiled back expectantly, their eyes full of happy curiosity. They always did right by me, and they were my new family. A family couldn't be built on lies, and between the Whistlemugs and the amnesia thing, I was getting a bit too comfortable doing just that. I took a deep breath and began to read aloud.

Possible Specialisation: [Chosen Alchemist]
Combine [**Otherworlder**] and [**Stabilise Mixture**] into the Blessing [**Stable Otherworlder**].
*Combine [**Bottomless Barrel**] and [**Ingredient Scan**] into the Blessing [**Barck's Box**].*
*The Milestone [**Carbonate**] is not affected.*

*You did not choose to become an [**Alchemist**]; you were chosen. While some struggle to find their way in life, you have already lived fully and been God-given the chance to do it again. As a [**Chosen Alchemist**] you bear Barck's Blessing and a path paved with power.*
Increases the chance of developing spark Milestones and the chance to find rare alchemical ingredients.
Stride boldly, Chosen, and change the world!

[**Stable Otherworlder**] – *Your spirit has found a new spark but denies its influence with the blessing of Barck. Your mental statistics remain replaced with their previous values, and you are more likely to gain Blessings and Milestones. Any influence your body has had on your mind is reversed, and any future influence is greatly reduced. Grants greater resistance to mental*

and bodily manipulation as well as increased resistance to all elements and damage. Long may you live!
This Ability is always active.

[Barck's Box] – *An alchemist often needs to forage for their own ingredients, but you are able to make your own. You can touch a container that contains no less than twenty-four grams of non-magical biological matter and grant it a touch of infinity. For the next one minute, anything you remove from the container and use in your alchemy does not reduce the amount of material in the container. If the material is not used in some form of alchemy within the next sixteen minutes, it disappears.*
This Ability can be used once per hour.

When I finished reading, Annie's eyes were glazed over and Balin's mouth was practically below his collar bone. Annie yelled first.

"BY ALL THE BITS OF THE GODS! WHAT!?"

I was totally stealing that.

CHAPTER SEVENTY
CHOSEN PATH

"I WANT BARCK'S BOX!" Annie almost screamed and then clamped her hand over her mouth. She flushed crimson.

"Phrasing?" I muttered. "Also, keep the volume down."

"That's... a crazy Specialisation, Pete." Balin said, slightly shell shocked. "I know ya said you 'worked things out' with Barck, but all of that's a bit more than 'worked things out.' A lot of 'chosen' and 'yer God' bein' bandied about..."

"Who cares!" Annie hissed, her face still a bright red. "It's insane! For your first Specialisation!? Take it!"

"I dunno... I still prefer [Dimensional Drinker]." [Chosen Alchemist] *was* pretty amazing. But... "There's a lot of really big problems with [Chosen Alchemist], Annie."

"What possible problems? No, never mind. Let me write the exact text down in my notebook first."

"Uh...." I began.

"I'll burn it in the furnace after." She rolled her eyes. "Geeze, Pete, I'm a brewer. If there's one thing we do well, it's privacy."

"Smart. Balin, you write it in my notebook too."

"Aye." I passed him my notebook and he grabbed a pencil. "Go."

I read the Specialisation again, this time out loud. Annie scribbled in her notebook as I read and looked up after I finished.

"Nope. I still don't see any downside. Do you realise how much money that could save us? Some of the ingredients in the bittering agent are pretty expensive. Brewing counts as basic alchemy, so [Barck's Box] would make it free!" Annie became more and more animated as she continued, and her eyes glittered with excitement. "We could experiment with new, rare ingredients or sell usage of the Ability to other [Alchemists] in the city. This is the kind of Ability that could impact *all of Minnova*. Maybe even all of Crack!"

Balin and I drew in our breaths and looked at each other.

"Annie..." Balin began.

"That may not necessarily be a *good* thing," I finished.

"What? Why not? Everyone would want it! Oh..." Her face fell.

Balin and I nodded. An Ability that powerful could become a curse. It was the kind of thing that people might kidnap or even kill me for. Imagine if I could replicate some non-magical dungeon material that was restricted. I wouldn't even blame City Hall if they decided to arrest me on the *off-chance* that I might mass produce it.

"It's powerful." Balin said. "If we could make it work, it would be amazin'. Plus, it says ya were 'chosen' as an [Alchemist] by Barck, Pete. I don't know if ya realise, not bein' from here, but that's a pretty big deal."

Ugh. There was that 'chosen' again. "Obviously being chosen by a *literal God* is a big deal, Balin. But... what if I don't *want* being 'chosen' to define my life? Annie, you said Specialisation would set me on a path. This path practically guarantees a life dedicated in part to Barck." I hesitated for a moment. "I-I don't really want to do that." It actually made me *very* uncomfortable, especially since he owned my soul. That felt like a pretty vast power differential. And a Specialisation that tied me to him even further? Nuh-uh!

"By Barck's Beard," Balin chuckled. "A dwarf might think ya were worried Barck would eat ya! Having a life dedicated to one of tha Gods is an *honour*, Pete!"

"Balin's right, Pete," Annie added. "A Specialisation that references the Gods is always *very* powerful, *very* prestigious, and *highly* coveted. At least we can be sure that you're not cursed by Barck now. Unfortunately."

"Unfortunately? I thought you were worried about that," I said as she reached into her pocket and passed a few silver to Balin. "Wait, were you *bettin'* on it!?"

Balin raised his fist in a salute. "I believed in ya, brother."

"You really *do* have little faith in me!" I pointed accusingly at Annie. She shrugged in reply.

"Just hedging my bets."

I crossed my arms. "At least Barck understands my genius."

"That's literally his job, Pete," Balin put in.

"Whatever, the Barck issue isn't one I expect you two devout souls to understand, and it doesn't matter anyway. There's actually a bigger problem. Look at [Stable Otherworlder]," I said, reading it carefully once more. Annie and Balin did too.

"It looks like quests may still be there... I see the line about 'easier Milestones.'" Annie said. "I don't see the problem. Actually, I think this last line means the Specialisation comes with an enhanced lifespan, which is amazing. It looks like an all-around boost to everything."

"Ooh! Less damage, too!" Balin said appreciatively.

"The problem is the bit that says 'Any influence your body has had on your mind is reversed, and any future influence is greatly reduced,'" I pointed out. "That could be really bad."

"What does it mean?" Balin asked, raising an eyebrow that hadn't been singed off in weeks.

"It means... that I wouldn't be 'me' anymore." I huffed out a breath. Balin and Annie looked at each other in confusion. Then back at me.

"What?" Annie asked.

I explained; it took a while. How to explain all the little things they took for granted as life-long dwarves? That I suddenly felt beards were attractive. That I dropped the occasional 'g' at the end of words and didn't even notice. That I was just a bit more boisterous and outgoing. That I loved the taste of mushrooms now. That I had a hard-headed streak that was just a bit harder. It was like getting comfortable in a set of new jeans, and it felt... *good*.

I don't think Peter Phillips would have fit into the Thirsty Goat as well as Peter Roughtuff. By the Gods, I wouldn't have even *dreamed* of 'adopting' a new family so quickly as a human. By the Gods, I used 'By the Gods' when I swore now! The mind-whammy from Tim had left me wary of mental manipulation in this world, but this didn't feel like that. This felt more like the last stage of grief – acceptance.

And [Stable Otherworlder] might take that away.

Annie wiped away a tear when I was done. "I take back my vote. You should choose [Dimensional Drinker], Pete. It's not worth the risk."

We both looked at Balin, who drummed his fingers on his thigh, lost in thought. After several seconds of silence, I nodded at Annie.

"I agree. [Dimensional Drinker] is amazing. It might cost my quests, but it's my favourite by far, especially since I'd finally get a decent drink around here."

"Hey!" She protested.

"No offence meant."

"Lots taken!"

"On the other hand, [Otherworldly Brewer] has no downsides." I finished. "I also like the idea of getting more brewing Milestones. [Refine Brew] may be necessary for my current plan to work too, though I could always cheat with [Carbonate] instead; [Dimensional Drinker] does let me keep it." I rubbed my head, then pulled at my beard. "Arggghhh! It's such a hard choice!"

Balin broke in.

"May yer brew be ya and to yerself be true."

"What?"

"It's what [Otherworldly Brewer] says. I think we're too focused on tha' power or money these Specialisations could bring us – tasty treats and gold and fancy tricks. Specialisations are gifts from tha' Gods to help us on a path to greatness. Pete, who do ya want to *be*?"

Annie and I stared at Balin and then turned to stare at each other. A pair of identical smiles slowly spread across our lips.

AN ADVENTURE BREWING

"Bran!"

Bran looked up from where he was arranging his knives in their new cupboard.

The door from the brewroom banged open as Annie and Balin came running in.

"Aye Annie, what is —" he began.

Maaaah! [Translated from Prima Donna Goat] "I seek more carrots, servant. Fetch them for me at once."

Bran sighed and tossed her one of his carrot muffins. She took it with a greedy *Meeeeeh!* and went to a corner to eat.

"Bran, can you make something? Quick?" Annie pleaded.

"Maybe." Bran wiped his counter with a cloth. "What do ya want?"

"Just a cake or somethin'," Balin said. "It's fer a good cause."

Bran smiled. "Well, if it's for a good cause, I'd be happy to. Where's Pete?"

"We asked him to run a quick errand," Annie answered.

"Tha treat's fer him! It's cause he —"

Annie clamped a hand on Balin's mouth and gave a strained smile.

"It's a surprise," Balin's muffled voice finished.

"Hrrrmm...." Bran bit his upper lip. "Pete, huh? Pete owes me one. Dunno if I *want* to make him a cake."

"Argh, Pete!" Annie groaned.

"Pleaaase, Bran?" Balin begged.

"Of course, *he* could always make the treat for *us*." Bran pointed over at Penelope.

Balin and Annie turned to look. Penelope stood in a dark corner of the room munching down on her late-night snack. A nondescript shadow was crouched behind her.

"Pete... are you hiding behind Penelope?" Annie asked with trepidation.

"Meeeeh?" A masculine and completely totally goat-like voice replied.

"He's learnin' goat so's he can ask Penelope on a date," Balin stated wryly.

I stood up in outrage. "Slander!"

Balin grumbled as I walked over to join them. "I can't believe ya found us so quick."

"Behold the power of [Minimap]!" I gave a wide grin, and Annie sighed.

"That Ability is going to make him even *more* insufferable."

CHAPTER SEVENTY-ONE
FISHY SITUATIONS

"Alright Bran, what am I supposed to teach you?" I grumbled. "And how do I owe you?"

"You promised to teach me a recipe." Bran pointed at the large steel contraption bolted to the floor in the corner. It was a deep fryer, though one with a small furnace beneath it. I'd been surprised to learn that deep fryers didn't exist on Erd, so I had designed one with Bran's help. The final product made some mean fries and was likely to start a revolution in Dwarven cooking. Vive la Rév-oil-ution! Whistlemop would take it to market after his little legal problems blew over. I had zero interest on that side of the business, and I was happy to let him handle it. I even upped his percent share.

"Are you bored of chips and fries already?"

"A little, but I need ta know *how* to make 'Fish and Chips.' 'Specially since it's *on the menu*," he emphasised, and I flinched.

"Ugh, those names!" Annie moaned. "It's 'Fish and *Fries*'!"

"We've been over that Annie. You won. Give it a rest already!" I smacked her on the shoulder and she punched back harder.

Ow.

I rubbed my shoulder and turned back to Bran. "Fine, I do owe you that. I guess I'll make *my own* congratulatory feast. You can all enjoy some fine West Coast cooking." I cracked my fingers and strutted into the kitchen.

"West Coast?" Bran said, confused. "Just so long as it's better than pruno..."

"Hey! We don't talk about pruno!"

"And I thought this was supposed to be a surprise. Congratulations fer what?"

"Uhh...."

Annie, Balin, and I all looked at each other in concern. To tell or not to tell?

Well, we'd already invited him to the brewery, and he could probably *ruin* us with a well-timed radler.

"We should tell him." I said firmly.

"Are ya sure?" Balin asked.

"I agree with Pete," Annie said.

"Tell me *what*?"

"I got my Specialisation. I'm a [Brewer] now."

Bran's jaw dropped past his collar-bone. "WHAT!?"

"Alrighty, Bran." I grabbed a bowl and then opened the cupboard to grab erdroot flour. Bran watched me with suspicious eyes.

"How do ya know where everythin' is in my kitchen? I just moved it all around this morning."

"Neat trick, isn't it! It's my new Blessin'!"

"Still can't believe ya got that so quick..." He muttered.

My new Specialisation still felt a bit uncomfortable – kind of like new shoes. It may have been the unearthly tingle of power that had come with it, but it was more likely the fancy new [Minimap] sitting in my head.

It was... well, it was a minimap. It popped up just like my quest windows did, and I could enlarge it or stuff it into the back of my awareness. There were a dozen different filters, but it wasn't a series of drop-down menus or anything like that. Instead, I simply had to focus on the minimap and I'd get a vague idea of what I could ask it to reveal.

As far as revealing 'crafting ingredients' went, I was limited to ingredients I'd used in alchemy before. That included beer brewing *and* cooking, which made a pretty massive list of ingredients. Most of them were Earth-related, like 'hops' or 'honey' or 'maple syrup.' The last one was interesting, because I couldn't search for 'pancakes' or 'Canadian bacon.' Crafting ingredients only, and if it had other uses that was just a lucky coincidence. I'd need to spend some time over the next few days playing around with it.

All in all, it was super neat. Especially in a kitchen, where I could set it to 'Fish' and BAM! there it was. I also grabbed lemons from the cold-storage fridge and filled a tankard with beer.

"Bran, do you want to whip up the fries while I prep?"

"Aye, I blanched 'em this morning." Bran ducked into the fridge and returned with a bowl of fries. Blanching was something that I considered a must for good fries. The process was easy; all Bran needed to do was deep fry the fries half-way and then stick them in the fridge. When he pulled them out during the dinner rush, they would fry a lot faster, and get that perfect crispy outside.

I was making a special fish and chips recipe passed down through generations of my family – nah, it was just a bog-standard beer-batter fish and chips recipe.

Pete's Lemon Zest Fish and Chips Ingredients
Skinless Cavetrout Filet
Erdroot Blanched Flour
Salt & Pepper
Baking Powder
Radler
Pickles

I made the radler in secret. No need to start a panic.

In a shallow dish I mixed the flour, salt and pepper, and the baking powder – or 'floof' powder, as Caroline used to call it. When it was well blended, I slowly poured in the radler. It bubbled happily as the lemon reacted with the powder. I hoped the awful beer wouldn't ruin the taste TOO much.

"Why tha beer?" Bran interrupted, his eyes drinking in my every move. "Other than taste?"

"Cold beer makes the batter go crispy in the fryer, and the carbonation causes it to puff out. There're more reasons, but I don't remember them."

When the batter had a smooth-but-not-runny consistency I set it aside and grabbed a piece of fish. The trout needed to be dry, so I picked up a small clean dishcloth and patted it. We did *not* want to use the same dirty towel over the course of a dinner rush, so Bran would need a steady supply of clean towels beside the fish table.

"Annie! Can you add a note to buy a towel station for the kitchen?" I called.

"Ergh. More gold! My wallet weeps!" she complained, but wrote it down anyway.

Bran finally popped the fries out of the fryer and set them on a plate. They were thin-cut and golden brown – perfect specimens of the ideal French fry. A light dusting of salt and they were ready for plating.

I carefully dipped four fish sticks into the batter and made sure they were thoroughly coated in goop. Then I placed them in the frying basket and gently lowered it into the deep fryer. The oil roiled excitedly and I shook the basket a few times to make sure the fish didn't stick to the bottom.

Four minutes later, I pulled out stunningly golden beer-battered trout. I laid it on a plate alongside some fries and garnished it with pickles. No tartar sauce this time, unfortunately.

Soon, all four of us were beard-deep in delicious fish. The moist centre of each piece had a lemony aftertaste that spread from the crunchy batter of the exterior. The beer only made everything a *tad* sour, which isn't that bad for fish and chips. The fries were *perfect*, and I added a dash of rock salt to mine. I missed ketchup and didn't know how to make it.

"It's great, Pete."

"Delicious."

"Yumm!"

"MmmmmmmMm"

Meeeeeh! [Translated from Prima Donna Goat] "What a delicious smell. Thank you for the meal!"

"Argh, no Penelope! That's mine!"

MEEEEHHHH!!!!

I sat contentedly back in my chair as Balin wrestled Penelope for his last piece of fish. The dish was a huge success, and my new Specialisation was even more so. With [Minimap] I *never* needed to worry about getting caught off-guard again.

Somewhere else.

In a dark space stood a white stone gazebo, and mist rose from several incense bowls surrounding it. A black mountain rose up in the darkness, seeming to touch the sky. A circular marble table sat in the centre of the gazebo, and a group of cloaked figures sat around it in ornate wooden chairs.

Master Brewer Browning sat before the assembly, his face slightly swollen. He held a pack of ice to one eye. "My fellow Master Brewers! I have called this emergency meeting to deal with dire news."

One cloaked figure put up a hand, interrupting him. He sighed melodramatically. "Yes, what is it?"

"What happened to your –"

"MY FACE IS FINE! No more questions! I've called you because of –"

"He got his stuffing knocked out trying to get at one of the *Limited Edition* Whistlemugs," Master Brewer Malt said in his quavery voice.

"HAR!"

"SHUT IT, DRUM!" Browning crowed.

"MAKE ME, ya idjit! What were ya even doin' there? You could have made an apprentice do it!"

"I wanted to experience it..." Browning grumbled. "Imagine my horror to learn it was a celebration of that thrice-damned drinking contest! I smashed it as soon as I received it. How was I to know that would set the crowd off!"

"I think it was you calling the crowd a 'degenerate rabble' –" Malt added, "then usin' yer Blessin' to pop half of Whistlemop's stock."

There was a general gasp.

"Preposterous!"

"Uncalled for!"

"Shameful behaviour that I'd expect from a human!"

"You'd better pay for those!"

"QUIET!!" Browning roared. "I didn't call this meeting to be lambasted for an error made in anger. I'll pay Whistlemop for the damages – if he ever shows his face again." He smirked.

"Would ya hurry it up then, Browning?" The voice of Jeremiah Goldstone rang out in the sudden silence. All the eyes in the room snapped to him. He looked tired, and bored. He hadn't been at many of the meetings recently.

"Well, Jeremiah, I'm happy you asked." Browning said sweetly, holding up a sheet of paper and laying it down on the table. Malt reached out a hand to look at it and pass it around. There was a brief bark of laughter when it reached Drum, but Jeremiah barely glanced at it. A smiling image of Pete was depicted with a catchy slogan.

"What *is* this?" a feminine voice asked.

"Where did you get it from?" a deep voice added. "Was it up on the Thirsty Goat? I don't see a problem with it. A bit gaudy, but young folk are like that."

"It was up at Whistlemop's," Browning said, then his voice rose as he continued, "because apparently, he has joined hands with one Peter Roughtuff from Thirsty Goat Brewing. The *same* Peter Roughtuff that I have recently learned was responsible for the *radler* abomination we've been suppressing!" He slammed an axe into the poster, pinning it to the table.

There was a series of gasps and 'oh mys.' One dwarf fainted dead away. Jeremiah merely twitched.

"Were you aware, Jeremiah, of what kind of dwarf you hired?" Browning hissed.

Jeremiah shrugged. "He's a good lad. A hard worker and loves brewing."

"But does he love the Sacred Brew?" Browning and Jeremiah shared a cold stare. After a few embarrassed coughs from the crowd, Browning sat back in his chair.

"Did you really call an emergency meeting over a damnable poster, Browning?" Drum asked.

"No. I called an emergency meeting because I've been hearing troubling rumours from the Thirsty Goat. I understand that Jeremiah Goldstone has handed over the next batch to Annie Goldstone, and several large shipping boxes were recently moved into the brewery. I suspect she is attempting to change the brewing process again, and you all remember how that went *last* time."

Jeremiah leaned forward, and his fingers grew white as he clenched his fists on the table. "Are you spyin' on my family, Browning?"

Browning spat. "I'm looking out for the community by keeping an eye on a known dangerous variable."

"That's not a no..." Jeremiah cracked his neck and glared daggers.

"Ah, stop with the melodramatics you two." Malt interrupted. "I want to get to my nap. Get on with it, Browning. What do you want to do about it?"

"These youngsters need to learn not to play around with millennia of tradition. The Sacred Brew is *sacred*, you all know that. Or *used* to know it." He pulled a small bottle out of his pocket and laid it down on the table. "I hold you, Jeremiah Goldstone, to your oath. You will ensure this bastard batch ends in failure. The magic in this vial of unrefined lily-leopard liver oil will ensure the fermentation process fails. You are to continue using it until your foolhardy daughter returns to *proper* brewing practices!"

"Browning, I'm not sure –" Drum said haltingly.

"You can't –" a dwarfess began hotly.

"I'll not budge on this!" Browning roared, dropping the ice pack and revealing a massive black eye and torn lip. "You all swore to the ancestors and the Gods to uphold your oaths! Will you disgrace your ancestors and stand forsworn before the Gods, Jeremiah!?"

Jeremiah glared back with hate-filled eyes, his voice dripping with venom. "You would have me taint the Sacred Brew?"

"Their brew is already tainted. We are simply ensuring only pure brews succeed."

There was a dull silence in the room as every eye stared at the inky bottle.

"If you need more, I have another flask." Browning said, a smug and callous look on his face. "The will of the ancestors."

The refrain was repeated uncertainly by all assembled.

"THE WILL OF THE ANCESTORS."

The assembly filed out of the room in silence until the only dwarf left in the room was a small, hunched Jeremiah Goldstone.

CHAPTER SEVENTY-TWO
GRAND OPENING

"Steady," I muttered.

"I don't think I can do this, Pete!"

"Steady, Aqua!"

"Bran, are you ready?"

"Aye, Annie!"

"Steaaadddyyy!"

"Annie, I don't *want* to be a waitress!"

"It's just until we can hire someone, Aqua!"

"STEAAADDYY!"

"Alright, open the door!" Annie shouted.

The doors swung open, and the storm descended.

"Welcome to the official grand opening of the Thirsty Goat Brewpub! Come on in!" I said with a beaming smile.

The massive crowd bustled up to a stand that said "Please wait here to be seated," and Aqua and I were soon busy taking dwarves to their tables. That, and dodging a barrage of questions.

"Do you know Whistlemop!?"

"Will there be limited edition Whistlemugs for sale here?"

"Congratulations on placing in the top ten!"

"Is Rumbob here?"

"What did it feel like when ya fed Raspi yer butter?"

I deftly dodged and redirected most conversations towards how delicious our food was.

"Why yes, I do know him. He finds our food delicious."

"No special editions here, you'll need to wait for next time. Try some nuts while you wait!"

"Thank you!"

"Rumbob is right over there! Eating our yummy food."

"No comment on my butter."

The room was soon full of bustling chatty dwarves. Every once in a while, a booming "Ho, ho, ho," came from a corner where Tania and Rumbob were set up. They had a private booth to write autographs on people's Whistlemugs and provide that celebrity *je ne sais quoi*.

We were worried about repercussions from our relationship with the pro-drinking crowd, but it looked like we were free and clear. That, or Balin acting as a bouncer at the front door in his golden armour was keeping any troublemakers away.

All in all, the grand opening was going swimmingly.

The final menu that I designed with Bran was the epitome of pub fare.

THIRSTY GOAT MENU

Snacks

Pretzel *– A length of dough twisted into an iconic shape and lightly dusted with salt crystals.*
Doughy, crusty, fresh-baked goodness. Comes with house mustard.

Crisps *– Round, thinly sliced erdroot, deep-fried in oil and seasoned with our secret spices.*
Crispy, crunchy delights that go great with beer.

Truffle-Fries *– Thick strips of erdroot deep-fried in oil and dusted with salt and truffles.*
Greasy goodness. Comes with house tomato sauce. Added cheese is extra.

Honey-Roasted Nuts *– Greentree nuts roasted with honey and hot pepper.*

A sweet and spicy spin on a Minnova classic.

Stuffed Mushrooms – *Minnova mushrooms roasted and filled with melted goat cheese.*
A deliciously gooey new take on your favourite fungus.

Meals

Beer-Battered Fish and Fries – *Cave-trout fried in our special beer batter with a plate of fries.*
A crispy twist on a flaky favourite. Comes with vinegar for the fries.

Beer-Braised Roast Goat – *32-hour Beer-Braised Goat with a creamy mushroom sauce.*
A savory feast for the refined palate. Comes with roasted veggies and whipped Erdroot.

Goatherd Pie – *Steamed goat and vegetables with a baked layer of whipped Erdroot.*
Moist and nutritious, filling and delicious. Comes with a helping of butter.

Goat-crisps and Cheese – *A heap of crisps baked with goat, mushrooms, and melted cheese.*
A crowd pleaser that's crispy, cheesy, and meaty. Comes with a side of diced tomatoes.

Chicken Wings – *A tub of honeyed chicken wings breaded and baked. Pick lemon or garlic.*
Fall-off-the-bone goodness with a sweet taste. Comes with a side of cream sauce.

Beer

True Brew – *A dwarven tradition made on site. Beer never tastes better than when it's fresh.*

I grumbled a bit as I read over the menu. Annie had forced me to change a lot of the names, declaring the earth names to be 'daft nonsense.' Namely...

"Why *chips* if they aren't chippy? If they're supposed to be crispy, call them crisps!"

"I like fries. Simple and to the point; how refreshing."

"Pretzel is an odd, twisty name for an odd, twisty snack. Fine, you can keep it."

"Why are the chips in 'Fish and Chips' actually fries? Chips should be crisps and fries should be fries!"

"I've never heard of a nacho, and I swear to the Gods if you sing that you're 'notch-my man' one more time I will ask Balin to *murder* you." And so on and so forth.

Annie and I also discussed adding radler and ginger pop to the menu. I... thought about Tim and advised dropping the radler idea. We also didn't have enough workers to pull off mass produced ginger pop yet. Baby steps, baby steps.

After the initial rush, I moved into the kitchen with Bran while Annie went to help Johnsson do the dishes. Bran was pure poetry in motion, dashing between stove and fryer and oven. He sliced erdroot with wild abandon and was a master at that fast-chop thing.

There were a few complaints about our use of beer in the food, but they were quickly drowned out by exclamations of delight and pure joy. It looked like our gamble on using True Brew in all of our pub fare had paid off in spades!

Bran put me on deep-fryer duty since that was pretty hard to get wrong. Heck, I'd taught him how to do it! He went absolutely wild over the deep fryer when I showed him how it worked. I was surprised to learn deep frying was new to Minnova, and I was pretty sure truffle-fries and chips were going to take the salt-and-mushroom-loving dwarves by *storm*.

At one point, Bran and I both turned at the same time and bumped into each other. Two dishes flew into the air, and we somehow grabbed them before they fell to the floor, the food completely intact. We nervously laughed and thanked Bran's [Artisan Luck] before moving on.

Things progressed quite well as the evening wore on. The pretzels were a massive hit, and people seemed to prefer the chi – *sigh* – *crisps* to the fries. That was fine, since we made the crisps ahead of time and plating them was a lot easier. We might eventually set a plate of them for free at every table – some finger food to get people talking and thirsty for more beer.

Annie had banned me from using the term finger-food.

I was humming MJ's *Beat It* while I chopped carrots when I saw a familiar face walk through the door with two hooded figures behind him.

Prophet Barnes... we meet again. I moved to intercept Aqua before she brought their menus. My chief weapon would be *surprise*!

"This place is certainly interesting." One of the cloaked dwarves removed his hood to look around the bustling brewpub. His long white beard was practically a mane, as it met with his head in a near perfect circle of long, straight white hair. His moustache-less face was etched with time and stress. He had a bearing that spoke of one used to command, as he loomed over the other dwarves in the room in both height and presence. "The decor is rather unique."

"It certainly is, Joshua." Prophet Barnes said with a wide grin. "But that isn't what's special about it."

"Ge-he-he!" the maned dwarf guffawed. "Leave it to my brother to present me with a fascinating little puzzle the day before we leave! Is it the menu that makes this place special? I gave it a read out front, and I really want to try that truffle-fries thing! There was another one on there that caught my attention too. Chicken-wings?"

"Chicken-things." Barnes said. "And that's still not the right reason."

"Was it that gaudily armoured bouncer?"

"Terrible guesses, as usual. You'll see soon enough. Can you guess, my dear?"

The remaining cloaked figure looked around the pub before speaking in a feminine tone. "I may, but I'd rather not. Did you really need to choose this place, uncle?"

"Oh, yes. I heard about it when I was grabbing your Whistlemug, dear brother."

"That Whistlemug is a *fabulous* bit of workmanship! Just the kind of innovation that helps our proud country thrive! I'm going to see about passing it on to... *you know*." Joshua gave a not-so-subtle wink.

"Well, how fortuitous for Whistlemop," Barnes drawled.

"Yes, I suspect –" Joshua broke off. "What *are* you looking for, Mal?"

"Just... a friend," the cloaked figure said nervously.

"Oh, really?" Joshua leaned forward on the table. "And who might this friend be? Someone I know? We may be here incognito, but I could always throw some weight around and demand to speak with the owner."

"No! Don't you dare, grandfather! Besides, I don't see them." Tourmaline said.

Joshua waved her away. "Fine, fine. Can you give me a hint, brother?"

"Not even a little one. You'll need to figure it out on your own." Barnes smirked.

"Bah. Well, here comes the waiter. You there! Menus!"

I made my way stealthily towards the table, but the massive dwarf with a pretty impressive coiffure managed to spot me.

"You there! Menus!"

I straightened up and approached the table. It wasn't like I planned to *actually* bonk the [Prophet] or anything, but a stealthy 'Can I help you' that made everyone jump would have been nice payback.

AN ADVENTURE BREWING

"Hello, and welcome to the Thirsty Goat Brewpub! I'm Pete and I'll be your waiter for today."

I handed out some menus and looked around the table. There was Prophet Barnes, the regal-looking guy, and one cloaked figure who hadn't gotten the message that indoor hoods were so last millennium.

"My goodness!" I continued, sweetly. "Is that you, Prophet Barnes? I didn't recognize you without your robes of office!"

Barnes chuckled. "I have a forgettable face."

"I do have to apologise, the last time we met I simply *dropped off the face of Erd* before we got a chance to really say goodbye."

"Oh, not a problem. No need to make a *mountain* out of a molehill."

"Oh, but I must insist! Let me cover your meal tonight. It would be the *pinnacle* of rudeness if I didn't *pay you back* somehow."

"No need, no need." Barnes waved a quavering hand. "Though the braised goat looks interesting, and I can't wait to *just try it.*"

We both smiled, with our teeth. The dwarf beside him looked back and forth between the two of us in confusion.

"Barnes, do you know this lad?"

"Indeed, Joshua. We had a *fascinating* encounter just the other day. I can't help but think we'll keep running into each other. It must be fate, coming to his restaurant."

I paused at that. I had a recent interest in the concept of fate, and Barnes was likely a wellspring of information. I wanted to keep a low profile, but Barnes *had* to have an inkling of my status. I didn't want him to know I was a 'Chosen' or anything like that, but I was obviously involved with the Gods. I might be able to turn this encounter my way if I played my cards right. Besides, I wasn't going to hold an actual *grudge* over a good prank.

I pitched my voice a little more cordial. "Yes, I'm quite happy we bumped into each other, [Prophet]. I was in need of some spiritual guidance, and you may be able to help me."

"Oh?" With the ease of long habit, Barnes switched gears into an officious persona. "I'd be pleased to offer you my aid in the ways of the Gods, my child. If your spirit requires guidance, you need but ask." He put up that wonky hand sign, and I did my best to copy him.

The cloaked figure coughed, or choked, and I refocused my attention.

"I'll have to leave the pleasantries for later. Would you like a drink while you read the menu?"

"Yes! Bring me three tankards!" The dwarf named Joshua pounded his fist on the table, which bounced. His strength must be massive! Up close he was nearly as big as Jeremiah!

"I'll just have one," Barnes said.

"I'll have one too," the cloaked figure said with a slightly muffled voice.

"I'll be right back to take your orders." I went to fetch their drinks.

I returned to find them in a heated debate.

"It's the kitchen!"

"No."

"Grr... the location!"

"Wrong again."

I walked up with the drinks. "Here are your –"

Joshua pointed vehemently at me. "It's him!"

Barnes chuckled. "I'm not going to tell you, brother, so stop trying to get the answer out of me. Now stop that. It's rude to point."

"You're the only dwarf that dares to correct me." Joshua growled.

"Excepting her Grace."

Joshua coughed. "Well, of course."

I raised an eyebrow, wondering what they were about. "Here are your drinks."

There was a series of gruff thank-yous as I passed the drinks around the table.

"So... Prophet Barnes, are you going to introduce your companions?" I asked.

The big guy nodded at me. "I'm Du – *cough* Joshua, Barnes's brother. It's nice to meet you, Pete. The oddly nervous one over there is my granddaughter, Tourmaline. Honestly, Mal, why are you still wearing that silly cloak!?"

My eyes swivelled over like turrets as the cloaked figure lowered her hood. A river of white-gold ringlets spilled out and I met a pair of umber eyes. She had soft features and a pair of sweeping silver eyebrows. Her voice was oddly familiar as she spoke.

"Hello, I'm Tourmaline. Nice to meet you, Peter."

CHAPTER SEVENTY-THREE

TOURMALINE

I kept bouncing back to have quick chats with Barnes's table until his brother Joshua invited me to join them. Since the main rush was done, and I was a bit peckish anyway, I obliged.

Joshua and Tourmaline were originally from the Capital, Kinshasa. Joshua was cagey about his profession, and only willing to say that he was a very successful businessman. Apparently, he was incognito in Minnova on business, and he asked me to keep quiet about it. I had no problem agreeing to that, though I made a mental note to check the wanted papers at the Adventurer's Guild later.

Tourmaline was a [Toxicologist], which was a Specialisation of the [Researcher] Title – a combination of Barck and Archis's Blessings. She was the first I'd met, and I wasn't going to lose a chance to pick her brain. Especially since I was pretty sure she was the one Barck had mentioned in our meeting. Our heads bent together as we made notes and diagrams in my notebook. It reminded me of talking to Annie, and I suspected the two of them would get along great.

I stopped her in the middle of a dissertation on the difference between a [Toxicologist] and a [Poisoner]. "Why is [Toxicologist] based on [Researcher]? I would have guessed it to be a Specialisation of [Alchemist]."

"It's not well known, but the same Specialisation can come from different Titles. In my case, I studied magic and alchemy and how it relates to the dwarven body. That gave me the [Researcher] Title. I then focused on potions, toxins, and poisons, and also how to improve them."

"'Mal is a quick study, and has a knack for obtaining Milestones." Joshua said around a mouth full of fish.

"Don't talk with your mouth full, brother," Barnes tutted.

"Yes, *Mother*."

Tourmaline looked up at the pair of them. "Rude."

I had an odd feeling of deja vu from the byplay, but ignored it. Easy Milestones marked Tourmaline as a possible Chosen, though that seemed unlikely. "What got you so interested in potions and poisons?"

"My mother." Tourmaline replied, then took a bite out of her braised goat.

I waited a moment to see if she would explain further. To broach or not to broach? Curiosity won out. "Your... mother?"

"Yes, my mother was poisoned when I was younger. She still suffers some residual effects. I studied magic and alchemy on the off chance that I could learn something to help her. I have been able to replicate the toxin in question but have not been able to reverse its effects. It has a non-standard attack vector and I have been unable to isolate its exact path through the body."

"I'm sorry to hear that." Quick Pete, change the subject! "Your research sounds interesting. Do you get funding from any universities?"

"No."

Our conversations were a fairly solid mix of this. She could talk forever about alchemy or chemistry but seemed reluctant to discuss anything else. I didn't know if it was me or what, but whenever I got close to any personal questions, she seemed to deftly sidestep.

I tried a slightly different tack.

"How long have you been in Minnova?"

"A while."

"Are you doing any interesting research here?"

"Just digging around."

"Oh? Are you looking for specific alchemical ingredients?"

"Yes. I need a few ingredients for my next potion that are best found in Greentree. There are some equivalents in Kinshasa but they will have a lower efficacy."

I thought about it for a moment. Helping her could get me in with Prophet Barnes, and she might be able to help me with alchemy. I even had a useful new tool for it. "Do you need help looking? I might be able to give you a hand."

"We're leaving tonight."

"Oh, that's unfortunate."

"Thank you for offering."

"Of course! Any time!"

"This beer is quite good!" Joshua interrupted. "Some of the best I've had! It's smoOOoooth!" He swayed a bit.

Tourmaline frowned. "You're such a lightweight, Grandfather. A dwarf should be made of stronger stuff."

There it was again. A strange feeling of deja vu. Barck said he placed Tourmaline 'near' me, but I'd never seen her in my life. Or last life. Yet, she felt familiar, and I couldn't place exactly where or how. I tried the direct approach.

"Have we met before? Tourmaline?"

Barnes choked on his beer and we looked at him with concern until he stopped choking. He waved at us to continue and took a bite out of his goatherd pie.

"It's always possible. Minnova isn't that big of a city," she replied.

Huh.... she was using a lot of weasel words. It took a weasel to recognize a weasel, and she sounded *exactly* like I did when I side-stepped Midna's [Truespeech]. Oh well, it wasn't like I was here to interrogate her. I was a guest at their table, so I dropped it and moved on to a more agreeable subject matter.

"Do you know much about alcohol?" Ah, the old standby.

She gave me her full attention. "I do. I assume that you do as well?"

"I do! I'm a brewer myself. We're actually right in the middle of making some changes to our brewing method."

Joshua and Barnes looked up with interest, and Joshua piped up.

"Is that why this beer tastes so good?"

I nodded. "To a degree. Our first few changes involved improving sanitation in the brewery, and the resulting beer came out with a consistent taste and very little contamination."

Tourmaline frowned. "Sanitisation is a vital step in any alchemical process."

"I can't discuss it, but not all brewrooms would necessarily agree with you." I frowned with displeasure.

Tourmaline nodded. "While brewing is counted among the alchemical professions, very few brewers have any actual training in alchemy. All their methods and techniques are traditional and, as far as I know, have not been updated in millennia."

"That's about right." I concurred.

"It's a shame. Brewing is amongst the many pillars in our society that could do with a bit of a shake-up."

Barnes moaned. "Not *this* again."

"Mal, I would have hoped that your... *recent misadventure* might have taught you something." Joshua said haltingly.

"Bah! You said so yourself, Grandfather. This beer is the smoothest you've ever tasted."

He sighed and took another swig. "There is that."

I laughed. "Hah! You'd fit right in around here, that's for sure! It's like talking to an old friend!"

She actually *blushed* and muttered something under her breath.

A quick glance around told me that the pub was starting to get busy again. That and Aqua was making stabby motions in my direction. With a knife. One of *Bran's* knives! He was going to *kill* her.

"If you're interested in seeing how things turn out, keep an eye on our next few batches. We're going to have something really special for the citizens of Minnova. Now, I really need to get going, but I hope you enjoy the rest of your meal." I stood up to go.

"It's absolutely delicious. The crunch on this fish is *incredible!* You need to give me the recipe!" Joshua replied.

"It's a secret recipe for now, but keep an eye on Whistlemop's Wonders! Oh, before I go, can I set up a meeting with you for later, Prophet Barnes? I really need your advice."

"Hrm. Set up an appointment through the Cathedral like everyone else. Unless you have something that would make you special?" He leered.

"My good looks and winning personality?"

"Hmm... not that good, and I'd say a runner-up at best. Talk to the acolytes."

"Oof. It was a pleasure to meet you, Tourmaline. I hope to see you again! Joshua, Prophet Barnes." I tipped an imaginary hat and ran off to get scolded.

"He's a nice lad," Joshua remarked as they watched Pete run off.

"Aye, that he is," Barnes remarked, taking a swig from his glass.

"You seemed to know him..." Joshua's eyes narrowed, then widened. "Ge-he-he! *He* was what's so interesting about this place! You side-tracked me!"

"Ugh. NO! Uncle Barnes brought us here because nearly all the staff are from the Minnova Reform Mine." Tourmaline rolled her eyes. "There, are you happy?"

Joshua started. "You mean the—"

"Yes! Now stop embarrassing me and eat your food!"

Joshua ignored her and focused on where Pete was being harangued by a blue-haired dwarfess and her golden-locked companion. "How interesting. Are they friends of yours?"

"Yes... maybe... I felt so." Tourmaline mumbled, her eyes never leaving the trio in the corner.

"Hmmm..." Joshua regarded his granddaughter as she fidgeted in her chair. She was always so sure of herself, and it was surprising to see her so affected. On one hand, she needed some real friends, not just servants or hangers-on. On the other hand, they would soon be returning to Kinshasa, and it was likely that the dwarfess known as Wreck would never return to Minnova again. He looked down at the amber dregs in his mug and had a thought. He leaned over and whispered into Barnes's ear.

"You know, brother... Mal may be right."

"Hrmmm?" Barnes said around a mouthful of whipped erdroot

AN ADVENTURE BREWING

and goat. "This goatherd pie is amazin'. I'm comin' here to eat whenever I can."

"Never mind that. Listen! Perhaps we *do* need to shake things up a bit. Now is a good time, since the King's drinking contest has the High Council up in arms. How about something that would appease them, but only on the surface?"

Gulp "Go on."

"I'll petition His Majesty to open a brewing contest alongside the drinking competition. We'll invite the greatest brewers in all of Crack to come to Kinshasa and present their brews to the King! But – we'll design the competition so the guilds are *forced* to innovate!"

"Interesting. I like it!" Barnes grinned wolfishly.

Joshua leaned back in his chair and nodded to himself. Yes, that would do the trick. It would take some time, but he was certain that His Majesty would listen. He'd be able to grease the wheels a bit as Duke, but the rest would be up to these hopeful young dwarves. Perhaps Tourmaline would get to see her friends sooner than she could have hoped.

***

It was only a short while until I was back to working in the kitchen. Bran was taking a quick breather out back, and I was busy stirring mashed erdoot and chopping vegetables. Aqua stood beside me and kept watch on the deep fryer. It was boiling hot in the kitchen, and I decided that the next big purchase was going to be some kind of air conditioning. If it didn't exist, I would design a magical one with Richter and then retire as a gazillionaire.

"Oh, is Bran not here?"

We looked over to the entrance of the kitchen in astonishment – nobody else was supposed to be in here.

"Excuse me –" Aqua began.

"Doc Opal!" I shouted with joy.

"Pete?" she replied.

"Opal?" Aqua asked.

"Opal!" Annie cried as she ran over.

"Annie!" Opal reached out to give her an embrace.

"Opal?!" Bran shouted as he ran in, led by Balin.

"Bran!" she cried, her face lighting up.

"Doc Opal!" Balin's muffled voice was barely audible through his golden helmet.

"Balin!?" Opal said in astonishment.

Meeeeeh!!!! [Translated from Prima Donna Goat] "Hello!"

"PENELOPE!!!" we all shouted.

"Owff!" said Opal.

"It is a *beautiful* dress," Bran said, as he handed Doc Opal a handkerchief.

"It *was* a beautiful dress." Balin muttered. Annie stomped on his foot.

She was dressed in a stunning rhinestone dress that accentuated her curves. Or maybe those were real diamonds – who could tell?

Dwarves. Dwarves could probably tell.

"Honestly, the tomato sauce should come right out with a little lemon juice," I put in, trying to be helpful. Aqua had removed a protesting Penelope to her pen, and Balin had followed with his tool kit. It looked like someone was going to be in time out.

Opal barked a laugh. "Same old Pete! Still on about his lemon juice." She took the handkerchief and daubed at her dress, which was coated in red goop. She'd fallen head-first into a bowl of tomato sauce after Penelope's boisterous greeting. "Ugh, maybe I will try that lemon trick."

"I'm sooo sorry, Opal." Annie rubbed her hands grievously.

"It's quite alright, Annie. I'm just glad I was able to be here on Bran's special – I mean, *your* special day."

"Thank you." Annie blushed at the older dwarf's praise.

Cough We were interrupted by another presence at the door to

AN ADVENTURE BREWING

the kitchen. Joshua stood there alongside Tourmaline, looking in. Barnes was nowhere to be seen. "It seems you're busy?"

"Joshua! Just a moment!" I called.

"Your Gr –!" Opal started in a shocked voice, then bit her tongue. She turned around and began wildly daubing at her dress with the handkerchief. Bran and Annie watched her with concern while I ran up to Joshua.

"Thank you for coming. I hope you enjoyed your food!"

"It was delicious! We just wanted to say goodbye." Joshua patted Tourmaline on the shoulder. She fidgeted a bit and then leaned through the doorway to address everyone.

"Goodbye."

We stared back in confusion, except for Opal, who stared at her dress.

Annie waved first. "Uh, bye? Thanks for coming to our grand opening?"

"Aye, glad you liked it!" Bran echoed.

"You're welcome any time!" I gave a fist pump.

Tourmaline swiftly turned around. "I'm leaving, Grandfather. I'll meet you outside."

"Aye, I'll come with you. Thank you again, Pete. I look forward to trying your next batch."

I gave a cheery wave. "Thanks! So long! I hope we meet again!"

"I look forward to it." Joshua said, completely not ominously.

CHAPTER SEVENTY-FOUR

THE NEW BREW

"Alright everyone, listen up!"

Annie waved to catch our attention. Just like last time, the entire brewery was in attendance; Aqua and her dad, Richter, John, Johnsson, and Balin. The only difference was that this time Jeremiah was standing to the side, his face dour. I guess he was feeling a bit melancholic watching the next generation preparing to take over. That, or he had indigestion; he'd been out drinking with his guard buddies all night.

Speaking of last night, Bran was out at the Grand Market with Opal purchasing new supplies after our *immensely* successful opening night! We didn't have the staff to stay full-day hours, so the pub wouldn't reopen until mid-evening.

Balin and I had actually gotten a decent rest last night. We'd gone to bed full of fish and chips, and dreamt odd dreams. At least I did. There'd been a gorgeous dwarf woman with a curly blonde beard and a horned helmet. She'd spent the evening singing "Call Me Maybe," and I was still on the fence whether it had been a sweet dream or a nightmare.

I flicked the filter on [Minimap] to "Animals" while Annie launched into a speech about the importance of working hard. Penelope was... in the kitchen, rooting through the cold storage. Either Bran left the door open, or she learned how to turn the handle. I was going with the second. We needed to find a way to keep her out, or she'd keep helping herself to the veggies. Then again, maybe I could start a betting pool on how long it took Bran to figure it out. I gave him a week, minimum. There were some very small dots scurrying around outside which I figured had to be rats. With all our new food we were going to need some traps set up soon. A dozen bigger dots descended on the rats and there was some yowling from outside. Maybe not on the traps, then.

I planned to run through the Grand Market searching for hops with [Minimap] during my break this afternoon. I hadn't found any yet, but I wasn't giving up 'hop-e'! I'd quickly learned to toggle "People" off as it turned the map into a useless sea of dots. While "Enemies" wasn't a setting, "Monsters" was. Apparently, a map can't really tell if someone wants to kill me, but it can tell if they want to eat me.

Whistlemop was still hiding in our tenement room. He was dealing with a lot of Titled [Lawyers], and Balin and I were getting a bit tired of all the extra company. There were multiple rumours surrounding the riot, but everyone agreed on one thing – it had started at Whistlemop's cart.

Whistlemop swore up and down that some dwarf had blown up half his stock. Unfortunately, the ledger of purchasers had been lost during the riot, so he didn't know who. He had some good ideas, though, and had some adventurers investigating. Whistlemop's [Lawyers] were sure that he wasn't going to be held responsible, but he was still in legal limbo for now. For their part, City Hall had hired a [Psychometer] who could talk to objects and he had the broken Whistlemugs under arrest. Which was only the fourth most ridiculous thing I'd heard this week.

" – big thanks to Pete for all his hard work!" I looked up at my name as everyone began clapping. I bowed and waved back. Thank you, thank you, yes, yes. Annie resumed her speech, and I switched my [Minimap] to "Quest Items." I didn't have any quests where specific items were relevant, so nothing showed up. "Monsters" was the same. Good thing, that.

Then there was a lot more clapping, and I joined in. My attention snapped up as Richter and Johnsson moved forward. It looked like it was time to start! I ran to my station next to the boil-kettle and stood at the ready.

"And now, we will begin the first batch of our new brew!" Annie announced proudly. That wasn't entirely true – we'd tested it yesterday – but close enough.

John went over and grabbed a big bag of the roasted erdroot that served as our malt. He brought it over to Johnsson, who began turning the crank to grind it into grist. I spat on my hands, rubbed them, and began to operate a hand-pump next to the brew-kettle. There were some gurgles, then some spurts, and soon clean water was roaring into the large copper pot.

There was some excited chatter as the process began, but I ignored it to focus on pumping. I'd cleaned and washed every single surface last night and again this morning, and even checked the roasted erdroot for disease or rot. I'd asked Balin to do a maintenance check on all the equipment, and Richter triple-checked all the sigils on the hopback chiller. This was the realisation of my ambitions, and I wasn't going to chance anything going wrong.

John's reedy voice rose in song, and he was soon joined by Johnsson. The rest of us began to stomp our feet to the upbeat jig. It was clearly a mining song, but it seemed appropriate for the occasion.

> Strike your pick, move it quick,
> In the length of a candlestick!
> In the black, watch your back,
> Crack the stone with a mighty whack!

> Heave! Ho!
> Heave! Ho!
> Heave! Ho!
> Heave! Ho!

> Dwarf be bold, search for gold,
> Comb through the rock and moss and mould!
> Specks of light, fight or flight,
> Steel yourself for a bloody night!

> Heave! Ho!
> Heave! Ho!

Mortal coil, work and toil.
Dwarven life is a raging roil!
Swing and dig, lazy pig,
Back at home, dance a merry jig!

Heave! Ho!
Heave! Ho!

Johnsson swore once when the crank smacked his shoulder, but the grind went off without a hitch. John lugged the grist up the steps of the catwalk connecting the hopback, mash tun, and boil kettle. He tossed the grist into the mash tun and Richter connected the water trough from the kettle, sending boiling hot water pouring over the yellow vegetable matter.

Now it was Richter's turn for some hard manual labour as he began stirring the enormous wooden spoon, turning the mix of hot water and grist into mash. While he worked, Johnsson and I took a short break as Aqua brought us some water to drink. Even dwarves needed to stay hydrated!

Annie went up the catwalk to observe and soon called down. "All good so far! Dad, do you want to do the honours for the bittering agent? Johnsson, Pete, get off your butts and raise the mash tun!"

Johnsson and I groaned and went to turn a crank that drove a screw underneath the mash tun. The tun was raised above the boil kettle and Annie reattached the trough to a spout at the bottom of the tun. Richter turned the spigot and soon hot, steaming wort rushed down into the copper boil kettle. Small flecks of erdroot travelled with it, and I tsked. I'd been so focused on the hopback I hadn't thought about setting up a lauter tun! I pulled out my notebook and added 'lauter tun,' along with a note about exploring temperature regulation during the mash. Oh well, it didn't *really* matter for this run, but it was something to improve for next time.

"How does the wort look, Annie?" Aqua called up.

"Looks normal! But we haven't really done anything new yet. Hurry up, Dad! What are you doing?"

Jeremiah was standing at the foot of the stairs, holding several burlap bags full of his 'secret bittering ingredients' and staring at the brew kettle. He seemed practically in a trance. I shuffled until I was close by.

"You okay, Jeremiah?" I muttered. "Yer daughter is going to worry about you. You can have an existential crisis later – I'll even buy the beers! Just get those sacks up there!"

Jeremiah shook himself and looked over at me. A series of conflicted emotions crossed his face until it settled on 'resigned.'

"Yer a smart lad, Pete. M'Annie seems to think you can do anythin' when it comes to brewin'. She *says* yer tha greatest brewer that ever lived."

"That's about right, Mr. Goldstone." I gave a smile that I hoped didn't come across as cocky.

"I pray to tha Gods that's true. Sometimes a dwarf has got ta trust in the strength of tha castle he's built. I want yer oath that you'll make this brew a perfect batch no matter what." He stared at me with intense eyes.

"I'll try." He stared harder. "I swear."

He nodded and ascended the stairs one at a time, each foot causing the steps to creak under his weight. There was a gravitas to the moment that brought silence to the brewery, broken only by the sound of boiling wort.

"Here ya are, Annie," Jeremiah croaked. He held out the sacks, and I had to give him credit, his hands only shook a little. Annie didn't notice though, only having eyes for her father's etched face.

"Thanks! Do you want me to throw them in?" She made to take a sack and Jeremiah clutched them tight.

"No. No, I'll do it. No need ta get yer own hands dirty." He gave a sick smile and Annie laughed. He walked over and pitched the sacks into the wort, where they were quickly pulled under by the convection currents. Annie stood beside him, taking one of his muscled fingers into her own smaller hand, and the two stared down into the roiling umber liquid for a while.

A moment passed as we all watched them from below. Two dwarves, a father and daughter, preparing to pass on the torch. John sniffled, and Tom put his arm around Aqua's shoulder. I thought back on a life that was, and buried a gasping sob. I had a chance to go back to that now, even if it was a bit of a pipe dream. But no, unless Barck showed up and said, "you're in the top three," I was doubling down on my decision not to fall for the bait of the Gods. This was my new family now, and they were all wonderful too.

"I'm proud of ya, Annie," Jeremiah said. "Yer mum would be proud, and yer... yer ancestors would be proud of ya too. Yer twice tha brewer I ever was."

"Did you know your accent changes when you get emotional?" Annie said, a tear streaming down her face. "It sounds ridiculous."

Jeremiah scooped her up in a big hug. "I'll always love ya, Annie Goldstone, no matter... no matter what."

"I'll always love you too, Dad."

There wasn't a dry eye in the place. Jeremiah was the worst, with giant tears streaming down his sloppy face.

It was always hard to see your child grow up.

The rest of the procedure went as well as we could have hoped. When the wort had boiled long enough, the burlap bags were pulled out with a (fully washed) hook, and the transfer trough was manoeuvred to the hopback. Hot, steamy, cloudy wort flowed into the hopback, complete with some trub made of sticks and leaves and gooey mash. Steam immediately rose from the branch and burlap filter as the wort passed through. As it dripped through into the chiller, the change was immediately apparent; nearly all the trub had been removed. Annie and I shared a triumphant grin; the filter had worked! Since it was made with bitter branches, I decided we could call it our *bitta' filter*. Nyuck.

The sigils on the chiller lit up as Richter channelled mana into them. We could also use a monster core, but those were expensive. Richter and I discussed the problem at length, and the final design was capable of using personal mana *or* monster cores as an energy source. It was a small piece of future-proofing that only cost a few extra gold. Annie stirred the wort in the chiller into a frothing whirlpool that rapidly grew more and more clear as the proteins separated out and fell to the bottom. In a few minutes, all that was left was crystal-clear wort. It had the placid stillness of glacier water and had a heavy, musty, aroma.

Annie stared into the sparkling depths, her eyes reflecting a rainbow sheen on the surface of the wort that only she could see. She whispered reverentially. "Let's get this into the first tank."

Johnsson switched the trough over and the clear liquid flowed into the fermentation tank. A gooey film of trub was left at the bottom of the chiller. I ran up the stairs to clean it up with a mop and bucket. The gunky trub was easy to clean now, but it would become a nightmare if we left it caked on for any real period of time. A few deft twists of the mop and a splash of hot water would do for now, but I really needed that sanitiser! I had Whistlemop working on it, so I had nothing to do but wait.

Annie went down from the catwalk towing Jeremiah behind her. Her face was stuck on 'joyous' and she exclaimed with a wild tone. "It's done! Now we wait two weeks and the first new brew in millennia will be ready for the next stage!"

I looked around with pride. I was one step closer to saving beer from it's awful Erdian fate. Was this how Superman felt?

The crowd cheered, and Jeremiah wept for joy. I patted the big lug on his back. He'd get over it eventually. Maybe we could buy him a fancy magic wagon or something.

CHAPTER SEVENTY-FIVE
WAITING A WEEK AWAY

Waiting for beer to ferment can drive a dwarf crazy. Thirty-two-hour days didn't help.

It's like putting on a pot of water to boil. You can't help but stare at it, desperately willing it to boil faster. Fermentation is like that, but with a lot more crusty Kräusen.

So we waited, and kept ourselves busy during the time the pub wasn't open. Every morning, Balin and I woke up and had a simple breakfast of goat sausage, eggs, and oats. Balin would run to schmooze with Annie while I schmoozed a cup of coffee at Joejam's café.

I would arrive mid-morning to help Bran do prep work in the kitchen while Johnsson, Richter, and John cleaned. Annie did paperwork, Aqua ran errands with Tom (whom I *still* hadn't been introduced to), and Balin did preventative maintenance.

Then we all met for lunch in the pub while Bran served us a delicious new meal every day.

Today was Beet and Goat stew with Garlic bread.

Yesterday was Fried Chicken with Fries and Gravy.

Tomorrow was Beans on Toast with Braised Goat.

After that we had the early afternoon to do whatever we wanted. It didn't really equate to a break though, since there was just so much to do.

A week thus passed.

"No, no, no!"

My voice echoed through the room, bouncing off the myriad glass surfaces in an odd fragmented reverb.

"Look, the neck of the bottle here *needs* to be reinforced, or the Whistlestop will break it when the pressure gets high enough!"

Whistlemop and I had decided that *Whistlestop* was a good name for the Lightning-stopper bottle-topper. I didn't care enough to tell him 'no,' and the name had a certain poetry to it. In return, I got a concession that we would *not* be naming everything in the brand *Whistle-whatevers*.

Ralph took the bottle back and turned it around. "Hrm. Ma son designed this one. Looks like he was cuttin' tha thickness of the glass to improve the flow. If you make the opening too small it'll be damn hard to drink."

"It's fine, trust me! Drinking from a bottle works fine, even if the neck is really small. As long as you can fit a finger in, that's good enough."

Ralph brought the bottle to his lips and stuck his tongue in it. "You're sure?"

"Yes, absolutely."

"Yer funeral."

"My *gold* too."

Ralph grumbled as he moved along. Whistlemop replaced him, walking over to poke me in the side.

"*Our* gold, thank you very much."

"Our gold. How is the investigation goin'?"

Whistlemop gave a simultaneous sigh of long suffering and relief. "Oh, swimmingly. The [Psychometer] was able to get witness testimony from the mugs that an Ability was used on them. Combined with testimony from other witnesses and some vetting by Statustician Diamond, I am off the hook and can reopen my shop."

I frowned. "That may not be a good idea if whoever did it is still out there."

AN ADVENTURE BREWING

"I'm not too concerned. The city promised me a full-time [Guard], and I hired a [Wizard] to flesh out my personal security."

We shared a fist bump, which was the dwarven societal equivalent of a high-five. "May I recommend a new limited-edition Whistlemug to commemorate the Grand Market Riot?"

Whistlemop gave a high-pitched laugh. "Hah! That's a little too mercantile even for me! I don't think City Hall would appreciate it."

"Ah well, it was worth a try. Any word on my experiments?"

"Yessss...?" Whistlemop tasted the word, his anxiety obviously spiking.

"That bad, huh?"

"One of the protective cases cracked when the bottle inside exploded. It *cracked* Pete. That glass was capable of holding a *mushfolk*."

I shrugged. "Now you see why I wanted it to be that strong. Do you have anything more to inspect here, or can we move to the warehouse?"

"I didn't believe you! It sounded ridiculous!"

"Uh huh." I gave Whistlemop the barest sliver of my attention as we made our way through the shiny new glassworks. Rows upon rows of translucent glass bottles were stacked along the walls, awaiting the completed batch.

Soon. But first, it was time to see which priming sugar ratio won my little science experiment.

"Beer's not allowed in tha Library, Pete," Richter hissed at me.

"Pshaw, the librarians don't care so long as you don't spill it." I wave a hand in dismissal. "I've seen a half-dozen other dwarves drinkin' in the last week alone."

"Oh. I nevah noticed."

"Of course not. Your eyes are always stuck deep into whatever book you're reading. Sometimes you need to look up and appreciate the world around you, Richter."

"I cahm to tha library ta *study*, not look around!"

"We are all students of life, Richter. No dwarf is an island."

"Tha's a stupid sayin' and ya should be embarrassed ya evah came up wit it."

I sputtered. "I didn't – you can't – whatever..." I held out a beer bottle filled with amber liquid. "Drink this."

He took it from me and turned it this way and that, observing it. "What is it?"

"Beer."

"Aye can see *dat*. What's it *in*?"

"It's a beer bottle."

"A what, now?"

"A bottle is a piece of glassware with a wide bottom and a fluted top, it is commonly—"

"Ah *get* that, Petar!"

I chuckled. "It's something Annie and I have been workin' on. More importantly I want someone that actually likes beer to drink these two bottles and tell me how they taste."

"Who doesn't like beer?" Richter muttered as he grabbed the bottle. "Why naht ask Balin or Annie?"

"We were already scheduled to meet today for our study session on magical diagrams, and I wanted to thank you for your time! I can promise that you're in for a treat!"

"Yer more than welcome Petar. I got ma Blessin' tha last time, so I got no issue tutorin' ya whenevah." He fumbled with the Whistlestop while he talked, but quickly figured out how to operate it. "Huh, neat."

I jerked as I realised my mistake; Richter had never opened a bottle before! "Richter, WAIT!" I dove on top of the books on the table, blocking them with my body.

POP

PSSSHHHHHHH!!!!

"Argghhh!!!"

"SHHHHHHHHHHHHH!!!!"

"SORRY!" Richter and I chorused. He glared at me, his face and chest sopping wet. I had the good sense to be bashful; that was totally my fault.

AN ADVENTURE BREWING

"Let me... go get a towel for you." I stood up and handed him my cloak to catch any drippage.

"Ya do dat." Richter grumped, then sniffed the open beer bottle with curiosity.

"Okay, I'm dry. You're dry. The table's dry. That beer is probably *extra* dry. Let's do this."

"If tha librarians complain, I'm leavin' *you* out ta dry."

"Fair."

I popped open my own bottle of beer with a practised hand, releasing the pressure slowly to avoid another 'a-pop-alypse.' The familiar 'psshhh' of escaping carbonation was music to my ears.

"Yer pretty good at dat," Richter noted.

"Thanks. Cheers!" I held my bottle out and he clinked it with his own.

"Cheeahs!"

I pulled my head back and drank.

I'd chosen the bottle with the highest ratio of priming sugar – ratio number six – which was the highest after the other ones had all exploded. Three total had gone *KA-BREWIE!!* and another two had exploded when I'd shaken them in their protective shells. I tossed ratio seven just to be safe.

The higher ratio meant it would be slightly sweeter and have a higher alcohol content than regular beer, but I wanted that anyway. Richter had ratio number four, which would be closer to that 'authentic True Brew taste.'

The beer foamed up as I tipped the glass, exploding onto my palette like electric fuzz. It sparkled between my tongue and teeth, foaming as it went down my gullet. It was my first time drinking a heavily carbonated drink in over a year and I almost choked on it. Beside me, Richter actually *did* sputter, foam freckling his orange beard.

The beer was just as sour and gritty as I remembered. I swished it around in my mouth to appreciate the mouthfeel. It was a little over-carbonated, and the higher alcohol content had affected the taste rather severely. It still wasn't *good*, but it was certainly better. The bittering agents was my biggest complaint, but I had no control over that.

All in all, an excellent attempt. I was a little sad that my quest to make a New Brew didn't complete; I probably needed to brew it from start to finish. First, though...

"How is it?"

Richter had a stunned expression on his face and was staring at the bottle.

"Pete... this is just beer."

"Yeaaahhh?"

"It's just... REALLY GOOD BEER!"

"Oh?"

"It actually explodes in mah mouth! Ah can feel it cracklin' in ma mouth and fillin' ma stomach."

"That's right! It –"

"The fizz comin' out o' tha' bottle brang wit it tha scent of tha Brew and draws me closer, daring me to taste tha Pinnacle o' delights within!"

"Yeah, you can –"

"Then tha flavour of it! It's got tha' cleanest taste of any brew I've ever had! There's no metallic aftertaste from tha copper in tha mug, or a slight taste of wet wood. Each sip tastes just like the last! It flows from tha glass like tha Great Waterfall roars from tha Pinnacle!"

"You know, I'd really like to –"

Richter stood on his chair and held his bottle up into the air.

"Tha clear crystal o' the bottle gives me a full view o' the wonders I will soon drink, their precious flavours beggin' ta be imbibed. No dwarf has evah drank it's like, and I dare any dwarf to claim themselves its equal!"

I looked around nervously. We were gathering a crowd. "That was really poetic, but you should probably –"

"I declare this the GREATEST BEER IN ALL O' MINNOVA! NAY, ALL O' CRACK!"

Ahem

… AN ADVENTURE BREWING

"Ah can't believe ya got us thrown outta da library."

"ME!? It was *your* Gods-bedamned soliloquy!"

Richter sighed and collapsed onto the stairs. "Aye, it was. That was an incredible bottle o' beer, Pete."

I pulled out my notebook. "You had ratio number four. Would you say it tasted similar to a regular brew?"

Richter looked at me like I was a crazy person. "Did ya not hear me?"

"There were a lot of adjectives that don't play nicely with my nice, neat, scientific process."

"It tasted… Like normal, but better."

"Go on."

"Do ya… have more?"

"Hey Aqua. Drink this."

"Wow, hello to you too, Pete." Aqua looked at the already opened bottle in her hand. "What is this?"

"Just drink it. It's beer."

"Is there something wrong with it?"

"No…?" I hedged.

"Just because you *believe* it's true, doesn't mean it's *actually* true."

I bit my lip. "Richter said he would kill everyone in the brewery for another taste of it."

Aqua's eyes widened to the size of saucers. "*Richter* said that?"

"I'm still on the fence about whether that's a good thing."

"Richter is mellower than a cat in a sunbeam. It must be good." Aqua peeked in through the opening. "Is that… sparks?"

"It's carbonation fizzing out through the bottleneck. You have sugar ratio number three. Are you going to drink it or not?"

"Fine, don't rush me!" She took a sip. Then a gulp. Then a chug.

Wow, Aqua could drink! She must have been taking lessons from Tania during opening hours!

She finished and wiped her lips with her arm, splattering fizzy beer all over her well-groomed blue beard.

"How was it?"

"MORE!" She grabbed my shirt.

"AHHHH!!!"

"AAGGHHHHHHH!!!!!!!!"

I burst into the tenement room, my shirt torn and filthy. The armour, it did nothing!

"Pete?" Balin asked. He was sweeping up the space Whistlemop had occupied until this morning. The little bugger took up a surprising amount of room. Though a gnome wasn't *that* much smaller than a dwarf. I still had a nagging mental image of gnomes as knee high, instead of the chest high they actually were.

"You need to hide me, Balin! They're coming!"

"Who's comin'?"

KNOCK KNOCK KNOCK

"No! Don't —" I hissed, but it was too late.

"Who is it?" Balin asked, walking up to the door.

"It's Aqua and Richter, is Pete there?"

Balin looked at me with questioning eyes and I made a slicing motion across my neck.

"Erm... No. I haven' seen 'im." Balin said, robotically. I rolled my eyes. There was a brief pause.

KNOCK KNOCK KNOCK

"We know you're in there Pete! We just want to talk!!!"

I whimpered and started piling chairs against the door.

Balin tried to stop me. "Hey! Don't break those! I spent a long time makin' them!"

"It won't matter if we die today! Hurry and help me!" I continued tossing furniture against the door, which was making increasingly loud banging noises. Unnoticed behind me, a brown bottle rolled out of my hastily dropped rucksack and rolled across the floor. Balin picked it up.

"What's this? Hey, it's tha bottled beer ya were talkin' about!" He levered it open with a *pop* and the banging on the door grew more frenzied. "Smells real good! Can I try?" He took a sip.

"Balin!!! NOOOOOOO!!!!"

Bran looked at me with concern as I despondently peeled erdroot beside him.

"What happened to *you*?"

"I don't want to talk about it."

"You ok?"

"I think... I'm a doomed genius."

"Uh huh. Well, yer holdin' the peeler upside down, 'genius'"

"Ugh."

There was a patter of feet on the floor as Annie burst into the kitchen. I moaned and dropped into a curled-up fetal position. "Not you too! I'm out of bottled beers!"

"Are you still moping about Aqua's prank!? Get over it, I need you!"

She grabbed me by the arm and pulled.

I pulled back. "What! PRANK!? That *dirty little MINX!*"

"There's something wrong with the brew!!!"

I was up and running in an instant.

CHAPTER SEVENTY-SIX
CAULDRON BUBBLE

We looked down into the bubbling vat of the open-top fermenter. The Kräusen was foaming and bubbling merrily, a clear sign of a healthy yeast culture. The problem was…

"It's fermenting too fast." I said, giving it a stir with the ladle.

"It started this morning. The Ancestral Seed shouldn't be so thick already, and the bubbling is far too vigorous." Annie said, wringing her hands. "What's happening?!"

I was worried enough that I didn't even care about the awful name.

"We didn't do anything that should be causing this. Even if it was a yeast infection, it should be causing the fermentation to *fail, not speed up.*"

"So what *is* it!?" Annie asked again, beginning to hyperventilate. I looked at her sharply, and realised her face was turning white; she was going into shock.

"Bran!" I called. "I need you! Get in here!"

Bran peeked his head in through the door from the pub. "I thought I wasn't allowed in here yet. Somethin' wrong?"

"Yes. I need you to go get a bag. Make Annie breathe into it. Annie, go with Bran. I'll see if I can figure out what's going wrong."

"Oh Gods. I can't have it all go wrong again." Tears leaked from the corners of her eyes as Bran led her away.

I turned back to the tank and gave it another spin with the ladle.

Over my lifetime, I had hundreds of failed brews. I suspected the average dwarven brewer saw even more. There were dozens of reasons a brew could fail, but they all had certain tell-tale signs.

I gave the brew another stir, watching the colour and texture of the Kräusen. It had the thick white-cheese-like consistency of a healthy batch, and none of the signs of a yeast infection. That was a good sign, since it indicated our sanitization efforts were doing their job.

The next step would be to check the pH and specific gravity, which would give me the rate of fermentation. Unfortunately, I couldn't measure pH or specific gravity without the proper tools. For the umpteenth time I cursed the stagnation of the brewing profession. Even if they didn't want to change their precious brew, they could have at least improved *how* they made it!

Bran came back in. "I've got her propped up in one of my booths. She's huffin' into a burlap sack. Dunno what that's supposed to do, though."

"Maybe nothing, but it gets her out of here. Keep an eye on her. Is anyone else in the brewery right now?"

"No. Everyone went out after lunch and hasn't come back yet."

"Where's Jeremiah?"

"I haven't seen him all day."

"John?"

"Left with Johnsson for some family bondin' time."

I grit my teeth; I knew where everyone *else* was. They were probably yucking it up in my tenement room after they'd yanked my chain. I took a deep breath. It had been a good prank, and they couldn't have known an emergency like this would pop up. It was fine, I could deal with it.

"Keep an eye on Annie. When she's well enough to leave unattended I want you to run to my place. Do you know where it is?"

"No, but I can ask Annie."

"Alright, go."

He went. I looked around the brewery and began to methodically check every tank. They all showed the exact same symptoms: overly thick Kräusen, far too much bubbling, and a slightly vinegary scent. I decided to go through my own personal 'Help! Help! My batch is bad!' checklist.

Heavy Kräusen could mean too much sugar in the wort, a chemical imbalance, or a high temperature. The usual solutions were to add more water, use softer or harder water, or buy fancy, useless, chemicals from the craft-brew store. As for temperature...

I ran into the kitchen, grabbed a finely crafted meat thermometer, and gave it a thorough wash. I dunked it into the brew and waited a few seconds. It read... hot. Fermenting beer had a temperature of 20-22°C and this was fermenting at closer to the dwarven equivalent of 25°C. That was hotter than the room, which meant something was wrong with the *brew* and not the surroundings.

I looked around the room. Every tank in the building was doing this. All fourteen of them. That eliminated any kind of contamination caused by dropping something into one of them.

Chilling the wort wouldn't cause this, and removing the cold break proteins that fell out shouldn't be a problem either. Same with the rest of the hopback processes. A bad sanitizer could cause it, but we only used boiling water! I growled with frustration and moved on.

Next on the checklist was the smell. A vinegary scent like that was caused by excess acetic acid in the beer. Acetic acid is a completely normal part of regular beer, and usually doesn't cause any problems. Heck, most lambic beers were notable for their high acetic acid levels. It didn't mean the beer was ruined, just that something was *wrong*. If it smelled like throw-up or mouthwash it meant the beer was bad, but most 'food' smells like vinegar, apples, butter, or bananas just meant an imbalance of some kind. Some ales or lagers even aimed for those smells; True Brew had a smell closer to cheese. The cause for the vinegar smell was most likely the higher temperature.

The last symptom was the bubbles, a sign of rapid breakdown of the sugars into alcohol and carbon dioxide. That was – again – contamination, too much sugar, or high temperature. I couldn't do anything about contamination right now, so I focused on temperature.

A high temperature was most often caused by a poor pitch rate. Pitch rate was determined by the amount of yeast added to the wort. A low pitch rate could cause the fermentation stage to fail completely,

AN ADVENTURE BREWING

while a high pitch rate could result in higher temperatures and a faster fermentation.

This looked like a high pitch rate. Which made no *sense*. A high pitch rate in all fourteen tanks was unlikely, but we *had* changed the brewing process enough that the old pitch rate might be wrong.

I almost laughed at my own desperation. This was the first 'bad batch' I'd fretted over in decades. A failed brew was just one of those things, and I couldn't remember the last time I'd been so invested in a single brewing.

"Pete." Annie came back through the door. "I sent Bran to go fetch everyone. Talk to me, what's happening?"

I looked at her with concern. Her face was still a bit white but was regaining colour quickly. "Are you feelin' a bit better? If you get faint, I'm going to need you to sit back down."

"No, I'm fine. I just... had a bit of a flash-back. This is my brewery, and I need to know what's going on." Her voice grew firm.

I nodded, happy to oblige. "It's a high-speed, high-temperature fermentation."

She came up alongside me and took the ladle, stirring a tank for herself. "Any idea what might have caused it?"

"Either we added too much... Ancestral Seed. Or there was some kind of contamination. Those are the only things that make sense."

Annie brought some of the Kräusen to her mouth and gave it a smell and a lick.

"It tastes fine, and the colour is right, but the smell is wrong."

She hopped down and walked around the brew-room, examining every surface and peeking into the tanks. I followed after.

"I used the regular amount of Ancestral Seed. Could the hopback have changed the amount required?"

"Honestly? Maaaaybe? I really, really, doubt it though. Contamination makes the most sense."

"Why? Are there any contaminants that would result in a good, but too quick, fermentation? I've never seen anything like this."

I sighed. "Honestly Annie, you haven't seen anythin' like this because you haven't been experimenting with your brewing enough. I've seen so *much* stuff like this that there are almost too many possibilities."

"Give me some."

I began counting on my fingers. "Contaminated wort. I know there have been difficulties with the erdroot supply chain, and that seems the most likely.

Next is the water. We're underground so some kind of mineral contamination is always a possibility. That would help explain the vinegar smell. Some kind of mineral oil would explain the bubbles since oil increases fermentation rate. A high pH or hardness water could cause issues, but they would present differently.

Then there is contamination of the cleaning supplies. All things considered, that seems unlikely.

The last possibility would be contamination of the bittering agent, but I don't know enough about those to comment on them."

Annie waved her hand dismissively. "Dad gets a lot of the ingredients for the bittering agent from local [Alchemists]. I would make that the least likely."

"Okay, that leaves the water and the erdroot."

Annie grabbed an erdroot from a nearby sack and gave it a bite. I swore.

"By all the Bits of the Gods, Annie! We're discussing if those are *contaminated!* Don't EAT them!"

"It tastes fine," she said flatly.

"It could be a kind of bacteria that you can't taste, or a wild yeast, or a chemical it absorbed while it sprouted! No, stop that, no more!" I grabbed her hand before she could take another bite out of it.

"Fine. Let's get an [Alchemist] to test the water."

"Okay. If that's the problem, there are chemicals we could add to offset that. They would change the taste of the beer though, and we wanted to avoid that."

There was a *bang* as the door to the brew-room from the foyer flew open. Aqua, Balin, and Richter tumbled in.

"What's happenin'?"

"Annie, are ya alright!?"

"Pete! Can I halp!?"

"Balin!" Annie ran over and embraced her beau. He stroked her hair as she gasped into his chest. Then he hollered as she grabbed both ends of his handlebar moustache and stared into his eyes.

"Not the moustache again!"

She twisted a bit and his shriek fell to a whimper. "Balin, I need you to take a bucket of our water to the nearest [Alchemist] and ask them to test it for hardness and contamination. Take some gold and do it, *now*."

"No, wait." I blocked him as he went to grab a bucket. "We don't want people to think there's something wrong with our beer. Go to an [Alchemist] on the other end of town. No, wait. Drum! Go ask for Drum at the Rusty Battleaxe."

"That bastard?" Annie scoffed.

"He's a friend through Sam," I explained. "I trust him, sort of." Well, he'd helped me with a kinda-maybe-kidnapping, so I was already kind of screwed if he chose to stab me in the back. Not that Annie needed to know that.

"Ugh, fine. Go to Drum, Balin."

"Aye, I'm gone."

While the three of us conferred, Richter moved around the tanks and Aqua clambered up into the rafters. She methodically poked around the dark, but clean, corners of the ceiling.

"Hey!" She called down; a blue fairy hanging above the brew-room.

We ignored her, busy with our own conversation.

"Hey, listen!"

We all looked up.

"Pete, Annie, you need to see this!"

"What *is* that?" Annie muttered.

I frowned. The angle of the light up here caused the tanks below to take on a slightly rainbow sheen. It wasn't visible from the ground, but from up here we could see an odd shimmer over all the tanks.

"It looks like pellicle, or oil contamination? But... weirder?"

"What's pellicle?" Aqua asked.

"It's like cold-break. Except while cold-break is a clump of proteins that falls out during chilling, pellicle forms a biofilm on the surface of fermenting beer. It's a sign of spoilage. But that isn't what this looks like – *this* looks more like a weird kind of oil contamination."

"Would that cause what we're seeing?" Annie asked, hope in her voice.

"Like I said earlier, oil acts as a catalyst that increases the rate of fermentation. It helps the yeast consume sugar faster and it would absolutely cause all the different symptoms we're seeing. It's just abnormally fast, and it's making so much Ancestral Seed that it's just... like... magic..." I petered off as I considered a terrible possibility.

I leaned down and shouted at Richter. "Yo! Can you use yer fancy new magic eyes?"

Richter called back, "Aye – Hey! Ah'm sensin' weird mana comin' from dis one! I don't tink that's supposed to be happenin'?"

"WHAT!?" We all chorused and rushed back down. –

"Da strange mana is in all fourteen tanks." Richter stated, coming down from the catwalk.

"Is that normal, Annie?" I asked. I wasn't an expert on this by any means.

"I doubt it. Aqua, were there any magical ingredients in our supplies? Or anything we purchased from someone that might have accidentally got in?"

"No." Aqua shook her head. "No, absolutely not."

"Damnit!" Annie slammed her fist against the side of a tank. "I can't *believe* this! Is it really the ancestors cursing my brew!?" There was a hushed silence as we all fell deep into thought.

There were a lot of things I could help with, but this was outside my purview. Richter would be far more helpful, and even he didn't know what to do. His primary fields of study were magical constructs and mana diagrams. If only I had [Pete's Poor Manasight]... I did a quick [Flash of Insight] as a habit, just in case it –

"[REFINE BREW]!!!" I shouted, startling everyone. "My new Ability consumes magical ingredients in alchemical concoctions!"

"That's right!" Annie gasped. "What does it say, *exactly*?"

I pulled it up and read aloud.

[Refine Brew] – *You are able to refine and stabilise a container of*

alchemical liquid with a touch. If the brew contains any unstable magical aethers they will be forced into equilibrium. The brew will become more nutritious and have a longer shelf life.
You can use this Ability once per second.

"Will it work?" Aqua asked.

"Who knows!?" Annie moaned. "Nobody's ever done anything like this with beer before! Normally we'd just scrap it! I just don't want to lose my first batch!"

"It may be betta to jast let it go?" Richter said hesitantly.

"Not without trying this first. Pete, do it," Annie said with conviction.

I pressed my hand up against the side of the tank. "Okay, here goes. [Refine Brew]!"

Nothing happened.

"It's completely unnecessary to say Abilities aloud," Aqua muttered.

Then I got the prompt.

Bing!

Milestone Used
*Combine [**Unrefined Lily-Leopard Liver Oil**] with [**Beer**]?*

Do you accept?
Yes/No

I hit "Yes" and my hand glowed with an inner light.

CHAPTER SEVENTY-SEVEN
LILY-LIVERED

Bing!

Milestone Used!
*[**Unrefined Lily Leopard Liver Oil**] has been successfully combined with [Beer].*

My hand stopped glowing, and I waved the notification away. And... that was it. There was no flash of light, the tank didn't glow or change colour or anything like that. It was a bit anticlimactic, actually.

Annie's desperate face popped in front of me.

"What happened? Did it work?"

"I think it did? There was a notification on it. But..." I looked around the room at everyone. "What the heck is unrefined lily-leopard liver oil?"

It took almost an hour, but the tank I'd refined began to slow down its rate of fermentation. Soon, it was obviously different from the rest of the tanks, and the vinegar scent became less pronounced – [Refine

Brew] had worked. There was a lot of cheering and back-slapping, followed by a serious debate on whether I should do it again. We weren't sure what "combining" a magical ingredient with beer meant, or what it would do. Was it even safe to drink?

After some discussion, Annie made the executive decision to use [Refine Brew] on all of the tanks before they spoiled. Hopefully it wouldn't be poisonous or mess with the bottle racking step. It took less than a minute for me to walk between the tanks, activating the Ability on each in turn.

When I finished refining everything, I walked into Annie's office. She and Aqua were busy pouring over paperwork. Aqua was checking out supply lists, and Annie was running numbers to see if we could afford to scrap the entire batch if necessary. In the meantime, Richter was combing the bags of Erdroot with his [Manasight] while Balin was still out delivering our water to Drum.

I grabbed a chair and scooted next to Aqua, reading over her shoulder. "What's our first suspect?"

"Our supplier for the bittering agents is Alchemist Black. The Black family has been our primary supplier for over three thousand years. He also supplies over half the brewers in the city. Something like this could ruin him." Aqua muttered. "A mistake is possible, but I just don't see it happening. It *has* to be the water. It's the only thing that makes sense."

"Where else could it have come from?"

"It could have been in the erdroot we used?" Annie said, standing up and walking over.

"Maybe." I shrugged. "But how would a magical ingredient even get into the erdroot? A contaminated water-source or contaminated supplies from the Alchemist make the most sense."

"Annie, would your dad have any ideas?" Aqua asked.

"He might, if he's home. Pete, can you check with your map?"

The Goldstone clan home was right next door to the brewery. It was the windowless fortress-style building I'd originally assumed was empty.

"It's too far away. My [Minimap] only has a range of twenty metres or so."

Aqua whistled. "That's still pretty amazing. Can you tell me your secret for easy Milestones?"

"I could tell you, but then I'd have to kill you." I gave a vicious smile.

Aqua laughed, then grew pale. "Wait, that was true? You –"

"Hold on, let me check something." I interrupted, and then searched the filters in my map. "It is! Since I just did some brewing with it, the leopard-oil can be toggled on my [Minimap]!"

I flicked it on, but no dots appeared. "*Nuts*, that would have been too easy."

"What?" Annie asked.

"There's good news and bad news. The good news is that our water and erdroot are probably fine. I don't see any sources of lily-leopard oil in the brewery. The *bad* news is that we already threw away the bags of used bittering agents a week ago, so there's no way to check them."

"Ugh. Okay, I want to get Dad. I'll see if he's home, give me a moment." She ran off.

"Do you really think he'll be able to help?" I asked Aqua.

"Maybe. He has an Ability that tells him the ingredients of a finished brew, and another that's kind of like your [Refine Brew]. Oh, and [Check Quality]! It tells him if something is safe to drink."

"Great. We're *really* going to need that. Can he tell us what's in the tanks?"

"No, it only works on *finished* brews."

"*Double* nuts."

After a few short minutes, Annie came running back, her face stormy.

Aqua jumped out of her seat. "What is it?"

"Dad's on his way, but he's... drunk," Annie hissed. "It's the middle of the afternoon! I didn't take over all of this so he could drink all morning! Argh! I can't believe him!!!"

"Oh." Aqua patted Annie gingerly on the back.

"It can be really hard to step away from something you've done for hundreds of years," I pointed out. I really felt for Jeremiah. Not only was his daughter moving on, but she'd immediately pulled his little beer empire in a completely different direction, forsaking generations of Goldstone tradition. He had to be wondering if any of what he'd built meant anything. Or worse, whether he was even necessary anymore. Back on Earth, people would up and die a year or two after retirement as their body and brain essentially went 'why bother?'

"We need to get him active," I said firmly.

"What do you mean?" Aqua asked.

"Jeremiah's going to be in the middle of his midlife crisis. We need to get him a magic horseless carriage or something, and focus his energy towards new hobbies. Maybe a girlfriend? Sorry, Annie."

"Anything would be better than what I just saw. Even an evil stepmother," Annie grumbled. "But his only hobbies are beer-*making* and beer-*drinking* with his buddies."

"See? That's the problem. Now that he isn't working as much, he only has one hobby left. What else does he do?"

Annie began hesitantly, "Before... before mom died, Dad used to take me fishing. He also liked to do weightlifting and wrestling."

I whistled. "That explains quite a few things." Jeremiah was built like a bodybuilder because he *was* a bodybuilder.

"Afterwards, he spent so much time taking care of me, and focusing on the business, that he just... stopped. We couldn't really afford people to watch and take care of me, so he kept me in the brewery and taught me the ropes while he worked. He... he was a great dad. I never meant for this to happen! And our first brew almost failed! Maybe it already did!" Annie looked like she was about to cry and then smashed a fist down on her small side table, denting it. "By Lunara's Lace, I swear that I'm going to get to the bottom of this!" She circled the room, clearly winding herself up.

Aqua and I looked at each other with worry and then back to Annie. I tried using a soothing tone to calm her down.

"I'll see about taking him out fishing with Balin. Maybe we can catch enough to reduce our costs for the pub. In the meantime, do you want to reach out to any of his old friends and see if they'd be willin' to take him to the gym?"

Annie visibly calmed. "Yeah, I can do that."

We sat around and waited a few more minutes, but Jeremiah didn't show. Annie was considering running back to the house when Richter popped his head in.

"Dere's no magic anywhere but Bran's kitchen and tha hopback. Unless you tink it could be *him*, I'm stumped."

"Okay." I stood up from my seat. "I think there's better things for me to be doing right now. Richter, can you come with? I might need your help."

"Where are you going?" Aqua asked, standing up as well.

"I'm heading to the library to look up this leopard-oil junk. That may offer some clues. Since it's magical, Richter might be necessary."

"Aye, good plan." Richter nodded.

"You need to make sure you're back in time to open the pub." Annie warned. "This little event isn't going to stop us."

"Obviously not." I smiled. "We're all stubborn as goats."

For the first time this evening, Annie smiled. "Good luck. I hope you find something."

"Me too. Let's go Richter." As we stepped out the door, I looked up to the sky and frowned at the entire situation. Come on Barck, aren't I your Golden Brewer? Throw me a bone here!

Bing!

New Quest: The Malted Mystery!

Your first brew was mysteriously contaminated with a magical alchemical ingredient.
Who or what caused it?
Culprits Found: 0/2

Rewards: +0.2 Wisdom, [White Lie]

Do you accept?
Yes / No

Ask and ye shall receive! But... culprits, plural? That didn't bode well. I would need to talk about it with Annie when I got back. I accepted the quest for now and ran after Richter.

AN ADVENTURE BREWING

"I found it." Richter pointed to a spot in his book.

I leaned over to see. "Wow, you read that fast."

"I got an Ability fer it last week! A Milestone fer readin' over eight hundred books!"

"Nice!

We were both seated across from each other in the alchemy shop. Librarian Uric hadn't let us back in the library, though we'd been able to talk him down to a one-week ban.

Rather than run across town to the next library we headed to the nearest alchemy shop, a quaint little place called *Primrose's Philters*. The purple dots indicating lily-liver oil were all over the place, so we were clearly on the right track.

I considered just *asking* the [Alchemist] for help, but I think Annie still wanted a modicum of secrecy so people wouldn't start wondering why the staff of the Thirsty Goat was suddenly curious about a possible poison.

Instead, I bought all the books on basic alchemical ingredients in Crack and Minnova. It was only three books, but they cost ten gold each!! The alchemy store had a place for people to study, so we sat and started reading.

I wished someone like Tourmaline was around to help with this. I wasn't a real [Alchemist], and this was a terrible crash course.

Richter's book was titled *Bestiary of Greentree: Common Monsters and Their Componen*ts while I was reading *Alchemical Ingredients: A Primer*.

The passage he found read:

"Lily-Leopard: This vicious half-plant beast is commonly found at the edge of inner Greentree. It stalks the area where the internal light of the dungeon has not yet illuminated the forest, and the light from Minnova's crystal does not quite reach. The *Darkwood* is often the first hurdle that truly challenges new adventuring parties, and the Lily-Leopard is one of the main culprits.

Lily-Leopards have a sinuous, catlike body with a slightly yellow tint and brown spots and a tapered green tail-root.

Instead of fur, their skin is made of a tuberous material, and their head ends in a lily-like flower that peels back to reveal rows of teeth that are used for ripping flesh from bone.

Lily-Leopards are carnivorous and obtain most of their nutrients from blood, but can also plunge their tail-roots into the ground in order to ingest valuable minerals. They often sleep in this form, their buttocks firmly 'planted' and their mouths open, appearing to be no more than a common giant tiger-lily. Adventurers should exercise caution around giant lilies in the Darkwood.

Lily-Leopards are prized for their livers, which filter the magical energies they absorb, and their teeth, which can be used for certain weapons. Once refined, their liver oil was a common ingredient in some basic potions."

"That's it!" I gave Richter a fist-bump. "This stuff is used in potions, so go read *Basic Potions: A Cookbook*."

While Richter searched through the next book I found a section in mine on Lily-Leopard Liver Oil. It was a rather boring blurb that simply repeated what we'd found in *Bestiary of Greentree*.

"Here, Lily-Leopard Oil." Richter said. "Ah found it. It say dat it's a common potion ingredient, and lists a few different ones it's used in. It say – 'Da unrefined oil can cause an upset stomac,' but da refined version enhances gut health and stamina. A propa' catalyst and infusion o' mana can enhance da stamina-recovery aspect to create a basic stamina potion.'

It reminded me of cod-liver oil. I shuddered at the memory of that foul liquid drawn from the guts of hell itself.

"Okay, great work. Let's go back to the brewery and tell everyone. Hopefully Jeremiah can tell us more."

We left the alchemy shop and ran back to the brewery as fast as our short little legs could carry us.

CHAPTER SEVENTY-EIGHT
YOU CAN LEAD A GOAT TO BEER

Richter and I arrived at the Brewery to find everyone already preparing to open the pub.

"Pete!" Annie waved me over as I walked through the door to the brew-room. "What did you find?"

"Lily-liver oil seems to be a pretty standard ingredient in potions. It's fairly safe." I passed her the books we'd bought, complete with strips of paper marking the relevant sections. "But it's from the dungeon, so I think our water is out as a contamination source."

Annie nodded. "I agree. Balin said the [Alchemist] he went to gave it the all-clear too."

"That leaves Alchemist Black's bittering agent as the most likely suspect."

"I agree. I don't know if we'll ever be able to prove it though." She said bitterly.

I looked around but didn't see Jeremiah. "Where's your dad?"

Annie frowned. "He came and went."

"What did he say?"

"He used [Check Quality] on the tanks and gave me the all-clear – the drink isn't poisonous. He actually found it funny for some reason; started laughing really hard."

"That's... a bit weird. Maybe he thought it was hilarious that your first brew had such a crazy mishap?" It sounded dumb even to my ears. Midna's Mullet, Jeremiah was taking this *bad*.

"Who knows. Did you find out anything else?"

"Aye. I went through my [Minimap] filters on the way here, and both 'unrefined' and 'refined' lily-leopard liver oil are available options. I think that means when I used [Refine Brew], the oil was 'refined' before it was subsumed into the brew." I shrugged. "The refined stuff is actually good for you and counts as a healthy magical ingredient. I may be able to use that in our advertising. How did the math turn out on your end?"

Annie sighed and massaged her temples. "The pub is bringing in enough that we can afford to lose this batch if necessary, but I still want to try. At least I'm not going to be up all night worrying about it. Just *most* of the night."

I considered her haggard appearance. She was distraught, stressed, and losing sleep, and most of it was over a monetary problem I had secretly solved. As her future brother-in-law, and as a good dwarf, I couldn't keep ignoring it. There was always a chance that she'd simply toss the brew if she knew money wasn't really an object, but I was fairly confident she wouldn't. She was just as curious and hard-headed about brewing as me, and she would want to see this brew to the end. Plus, I needed her approval to move forward with my bottling scheme.

"Speaking of tonight, can I talk to you after closing? It's really important."

"Again? I hope you haven't gotten your next Specialisation already. I'd need to shave your beard off out of sheer jealousy." She gave a pained laugh.

I crossed my arms protectively over my beautiful bristles. "No, it's good news."

"I could use some. Anyone else need to be there?"

"I think... just you and Balin for now. Aqua may ask some questions I'm not ready to answer yet. Speaking of which, where is she?"

"I sent her to go and ask Alchemist Black some leading questions with [Truespeech]. I... really hope this was all an accident, but we need to make sure." She nodded at Richter, who had entered the building behind me. "Richter, could you make some deliveries tonight? A new drinking competition is being held at one of the nearby beer gardens and they want some kegs of our beer."

AN ADVENTURE BREWING

"Aye, Miss. That's excitin'!"

"Isn't it! Things are coming together. Other than..." she gestured expansively at the tanks, "all of this."

"Can I take da Princess ta 'elp pull tha cart?"

"Sure. Probably for the best. Bran found out she's been getting into his cold storage, and he threatened to use her for tonight's braised goat." She passed me a few silvers, her lips a thin line.

"It took him longer than a week, eh? You're terrible at betting." I remarked with a grin.

"Shove it."

"I'll shove it right into my wallet." I tossed the silver in my coin-pouch. "If there's nothing else, I need to go help Bran. Crisis averted, contamination vector narrowed down, mission accomplished."

While I cut vegetables with a halfway-apoplectic Bran, a certain quest sat uncomfortably in the back of my mind. We'd narrowed down the [Alchemist] as our most likely source of contamination.

Except, my quest hadn't been updated. We probably had to find proof first – but how?

A week passed in relative boredom. There were no other emergencies with the fermentation, and the pub was thriving. We had two small brawls, but those were standard in dwarven establishments. Between Balin and Tania – who was becoming a regular while Greentree was still off-limits – any fights were quickly stomped out.

Aqua gave Alchemist Black the all-clear. He either didn't know there was contamination in our bittering agent or had an Ability that could bypass [Truespeech]. Aqua seemed to think an Ability like that was highly unlikely for an [Alchemist], which left 'freak accident' as our most likely scenario.

Normally we would have moved on at that point and counted ourselves lucky that the worst had been avoided. But I had a little quest that said we were off base. I confided it to Annie, and she asked me to keep an eye out but not to tell the others for now. We'd just be *extra* careful for the next batch.

I considered making some new advertising posters for Whistlemop's cart, but decided to wait until we knew the quality of the brew. Even if it was safe to drink, it could still turn out awful.

And then, it was the big day.

The crowd in the brew-room was a bit smaller than usual; Tom and Jeremiah were notably absent. John and Johnsson were in attendance and talking up a storm with Richter. Johnsson had changed his haircut again – this time he'd frosted the tips and put dozens of fine braids in. It looked good on him.

There was a fairly obvious undercurrent of nervous expectation. Everyone was worried the brew was going to taste awful or be completely undrinkable. We'd know as soon as Penelope took her traditional first drink. If she drank the whole bowl, the batch was a success. If she spurned it, we'd need to throw it all away.

"Is Mr. Goldstone seriously not coming!?" I whispered up to Annie, who was standing on the catwalk preparing for her usual speech. "I haven't seen him all week!"

"No! He gave me some lame excuses and disappeared." Annie's face was a bit drawn. It was clear that Jeremiah's absence was a big emotional blow. I was seething too. Regardless of how Jeremiah felt right now, he shouldn't have missed this. It was like skipping his child's graduation ceremony because he had empty-nest syndrome. I was going to give him a piece of my mind later.

"Any luck getting in contact with his old fishing buddies?"

"Sort of. I asked Drum and Captain Morris and they agreed to help. Drum was strangely agreeable, and Captain Morris is more than happy to take him fishing."

"Sounds good. I like Drum, and Captain Morris seemed like a good guy when I met him in the mine. Heck, I may want to go fishing with them!" I briefly thought of Wreck's little barb about strength. "Maybe I'll go to the gym too; I need to increase my strength."

"Couldn't hurt. All of Bran's fine cooking is going straight to that paunch."

"Oof!" I doubled over in mock agony.

Annie waved her hand in a clearing gesture. "Setting aside my father's *issues*, is everything ready?"

I rubbed my own hands with glee. Annie had been angry at my deception at first, but eventually agreed it had been a good idea. Especially when I gave her my last bottle to drink; then she'd *enthusiastically* agreed. With her approval, I'd set Balin to crafting the final piece we needed, and he finished it just in time.

"Balin did a great job. It works perfectly. We hid it behind the tanks this morning and Whistlemop's men arrived with the bottles a few minutes ago. They're waiting out back with Balin."

"Ok... let's do this." Annie slapped her cheeks then raised her arm. "EVERYONE! I want to thank you for coming to the very first racking of the Thirsty Goat Brewpub!"

There was a general cheer. I felt tears welling in my own eyes, a mix of pride and nostalgia. It reminded me a bit of our first batch at Beavermoose Brewery back on Earth. That had been one of the greatest moments in my life, besides my marriage to Caroline and Sammy's birth. I habitually reached out beside me for a warmth that wasn't there, and a single tear broke free to trickle down my cheek and wet my beard.

I looked around at all the happy and excited faces. Aqua was jumping up and down, Johnsson was hooting, John was clapping calmly, and Richter was pumping his fist and hollering. I felt something in my heart shift, and a bit of the ever-present ache disappeared. Time would heal these wounds, and I had a lot of that, along with the best new family a dwarf could ever ask for. I raised my arms and joined in with a ragged cheer.

Annie waited until the noise died down, then continued. "It's been a hard couple of years. Between accidents, mass quitting, and money troubles, you are the dwarves that stuck with us through thick and thin! As a Goldstone, I want to thank you for your hard work and dedication." She gave a close-fisted salute at chest height. Everyone repeated the gesture back, and I copied it a beat behind.

"This marks a new page in the history of the Thirsty Goat. All of you are aware of the incident last week and are probably just as anxious as I am to see Penelope's reaction. Before that, though, I want Pete to come up and tell everyone the exciting news!"

I walked up the catwalk to curious murmuring. We were close-knit enough that everyone had a pretty good idea of what this was about. However, very few of them had the full picture. It was time to present that picture in 4k.

"Hi! As many of you know, I've been working on a method to improve the carbonation of our beer using bottle conditioning. Some of you even tasted it already and went to *great lengths* to tell me how good it was." I pointedly glowered at Aqua, who blinked back in mock innocence. I raised my voice to a shout. "So, here's the news! Bring them in, Balin!" The doors to the back alley burst open as Balin pushed in a cart piled high with wooden boxes. Each box was just big enough to contain sixteen bottles and was stamped with the Whistlemop logo. A string of carts stretched behind him in the alley.

"I'm proud to announce our partnership with Whistlemop's Fineries as we release Crack's first bottled brew!"

There was stunned silence. Then the shouting started.

The shouting eventually turned into a Q&A session. Aqua was first, and wanted to know how we were going to afford it. I told her how much money we had at our disposal and she kicked me in the shins.

Johnsson wanted to know if the bottles were going to be sold as collectibles like the Whistlemugs. It was a great question, and one I'd spent a lot of time considering. I had an answer at the ready.

"No, I actually want people to return these. The plan is to sell them at an inflated price with a small refund for people that bring back the bottle. That way we can reuse them and not waste the glass.

AN ADVENTURE BREWING

These are actually a bit of a stop-gap measure until we can get pressure kegs and fermenters up and running."

"Couldn't we 'limited edition' this first run though?" John asked, putting his hand up. "It worked really well for Whistlemop. Everyone's still talkin' about it."

I looked at Annie, who shrugged. "Why not? It's a bit late to etch each of them, though."

"That's fine," I said. "We just need a tube of paper, some sticky-sap, and a starving artist. What do we call it though? 'The New Brew' is a bit on the nose."

"Ah 'tink y'all are gettin' ahead o' yerselves," Richter interrupted. "We don't know if da brew is tastee." He pointed down at Penelope, who was growing increasingly irritated at being forced to wait. She pawed at her fancy goat-bowl and glared at us.

Meeeeeeeehhh!!! [Translated from Prima Donna Goat] "Where is my libation, peasants!? I've been waiting for *minutes! MINUTES!*"

Ah, yes. The moment of truth.

"As is tradition, the first drink will go to Penelope! Long may she live!" Annie intoned.

"Long may she live!" We all repeated, a bit nervously this time.

Annie opened the tap of the first tank, and the beer fountained into Penelope's dish. It had the same colour as usual but was crystal clear with a creamy finish. The usual mishmash of cloudy proteins and leftover trub was nowhere to be seen. The hopback had done its job *perfectly*. Everyone *ooooh*-ed at the sight.

Then Annie placed the dish in front of Penelope, who stepped forward and sniffed it. She took a hesitant lick and swished it around in her mouth. We all leaned in, our breaths caught in our throats and our eyes wide. If she spat it out, the batch would be considered a failure. But if she drank it...

She shoved her muzzle into the amber liquid and greedily chugged the rest of the bowl.

The room erupted into cheers and celebration. We clapped, hugged, and jumped for joy in the sheer relief of the moment.

Unnoticed amongst the shouting, there was a low bass *rumble.*

CHAPTER SEVENTY-NINE
LET'S GET READY TO RUMBLE

What followed was a lot of back slapping and congratulations.

"Pete! It worked!" Annie ran up and pulled me into a hug. We were soon joined by Balin, then Aqua, then everyone else.

"We did it!"

"Huzzah!"

"Congratulations!"

"Did anyone else hear that sound?"

"It looks amazin', I can't wait to try it!"

Meeeeeeh!!!! *Burp*

We broke apart and considered Penelope, who had finished the bowl and was pushing it towards us with a stamping foot.

"Do ya want more, princess?" Richter chuckled. "Yer a greedy goat, aintcha?"

"We have to give her *thirteen* more, technically," Annie said, looking around at all the tanks.

"Can I have some first?" Johnsson pleaded. "I never got to try any of the bottled beer, and Aqua and Richter keep teasin' me about it."

"It's technically not done yet. It needs to be bottle conditioned." I pointed out.

"EXCUSE ME!" Aqua shouted, capturing everyone's attention.

"Yes, Aqua?" Annie asked, sweetly.

"Did nobody else hear that?"

We all tipped our ears attentively.

AN ADVENTURE BREWING

That was when it happened.

BRAP

Every head turned to regard Penelope, whose beady eyes slowly crossed in consternation.

Meeeeeeh??? [Translated from Prima Donna Goat] "Surely that wasn't my most elegant self???"

BRAAAAAAAPPP!!

Penelope let out a fart so massive that it actually shook her tail. She jumped nearly a metre into the air and bucked behind her. She waved her single horn wildly, as though attacking some unseen enemy.

MEEEEEHHH!?! [Translated from Prima Donna Goat] "Treachery! Mine own royal body betrays me!?!"

We all stared in shock as Penelope let loose a few more musical *toots* from her behind. She furiously pranced from foot to foot with each eruption.

"Penelope?" Aqua said with trepidation. "Are you ok?"

MEHEHEHHEEE!!! [Translated from Prima Donna Goat] "What foul manner of magic is this!? Have at thee, blackguards!!"

She then began angrily butting her head against Balin's shins. He summoned his golden armour, and his legs rang like a bell after every strike.

"What... what was that?" John asked.

"Penelope farted?" I said. John rolled his eyes.

"Is tha princess well?" Richter asked with concern.

Annie bent over the goat to examine her, but besides the initial shock, Penelope seemed fine. After a short while, she calmed down, went back to her bowl, and began pawing at it.

Meeeeehhh!!!! Meeheehee! [Translated from Prima Donna Goat] "Please excuse my impropriety. I apologize and let nobody speak of it ever again. Now fill my bowl, peasants!"

"Are we... letting her drink from the next tank?" Annie asked, uncertainly.

"Jeremiah checked it. He said this stuff is safe to drink. Maybe she just had indigestion?" I said. Everyone nodded, but nobody looked convinced.

Annie brought Penelope's bowl to the next tank and poured from the spigot. She placed it on the floor and Penelope immediately buried her nose in the bowl, greedily chugging it down. When it was empty, she raised her head and licked at her lips before pushing her dish to the next tank. She stood next to the spigot and waited expectantly.

We all regarded her for a minute.

Then there was a *rumble.*

Meeh? *Burp*

BRAAP

Penelope went ballistic, kicking and bucking and running around the room. Her voice went up an octave until she was angry-screaming. Every once in a while she'd smash into Balin's shins, just for good measure.

"Okaaay?" I deferred to Annie. "You're in charge."

"Great, thanks." She grimaced. "What do you think is happening?"

I used [Flash of Insight] to help jog my memory. "The unrefined liver oil is supposed to cause indigestion, and when it's refined it promotes gut health and stamina recovery." I thought back to certain medicines on Earth. "Maybe it's acting like a fast-acting probiotic, or a gas-relief agent?"

BRAAAAAP!!

*MMMMMM*MMAAAAAAHHH*HHHHH!!!!!*

GONG "Och, that one actually 'urt!"

I did my level best to ignore the chaos and concentrate on the problem at hand. A difficult proposition when a crazed caprid is trying to put their horn through your brother's kneecaps. "A digestive of some kind seems the most likely, but I don't know magic." I looked at Richter.

He shook his head. "Don't look at me. I've not studied anytin' like dis." His eyes shimmered for a moment. "But I can say dat tha' beer ain't magic anymore."

"I guess an accidental potion beer was too much to ask," I grumbled under my breath. "Maybe it has long-term health benefits."

Aqua and Balin eventually managed to soothe Penelope with some gentle pats and she went to shiver angrily beside her bowl. Either she hadn't realised the beer was causing her outbursts, or she was just a greedy guts. Maybe both.

"Do we keep letting her drink?" I asked.

Annie shook her head. "I don't think that would be fair to her. Let's see about –"

Rumble

We all turned to look back at the first tank. Johnsson was standing next to it with a mug in his hand. He only looked *slightly* guilty.

"What? *Burp* I wanted to try it too. It's delicious! Tastes just like tha True Brew, but it's smoother and feels more lively on me tongue! It's tha best beer I've ever drunk, and it makes me feel all warm'n fuzzy! And Pete, you said it isn't even –"

BRAAP

"Och!" He held his stomach. "By Aaron's Arse, that's an odd feelin'."

BRAAAAAAAAPPP!!

We all stared at Johnsson as his butt let loose an entire musical number, complete with dance routine. He dropped his mug and grabbed one cheek in each hand, his face turning bright red.

"HA!"

Everyone but Johnsson (who was busy) turned to look at John, who had begun belly laughing so hard he was crying.

"HA, HA, HA! You should see yer face, son! You look more confused than Penelope did! HAW, HAW, HAW!!

Aqua tittered next. Then Balin began to guffaw. Then the entire grumble fell over laughing.

We all took a turn at drinking the brew and ripping one out, even John. Aqua practically rattled the walls on her turn, and she fled the brewery in shrieking shame. The beer seemed to give an almost imperceptible increase to stamina, then cause tummy rumbling and a burp followed by one or two *massive* toots. There were no discernable side effects, and we didn't get any [Conditions] from drinking it. That meant it was safe to drink.

Annie still wanted to wait a while before we bottled it. She needed to talk to Jeremiah and take some time to consider our options.

In the meantime, we had a pub to run. The world wouldn't wait while our bosses contemplated the ethics of beer that could cut cheese. The regulars arrived first, headed by Tania and Beatbox – no Rumbob tonight. Prophet Barnes even made an appearance; now there was a dwarf that *loved* his goatherd pie.

I looked up from my musings to welcome the next set of guests. My nose itched as it was assaulted by the smell of onions and I resisted the urge to sneeze. I was *not* made to be a waiter, and Aqua and I were desperate for Annie to hire someone to do this full time. In the meantime, we switched back and forth over the course of the evening.

"Hello, welcome to the Thirsty Goat Brew –"

I petered off as I recognized the party that had entered the pub. It was Master Brewer Browning and his posse. I gritted my teeth and prepared for the worst. These guys were *Grade A* assholes, and if they were visiting a place they'd deemed disgraceful, they were only here for one reason – to make trouble.

I immediately turned management mode on to 100 percent.

"Master Brewer Browning, how wonderful to see you! Welcome to our humble brewpub! I greet you on this most auspicious day! We're so happy you could take time out of your busy schedule to come and see us!" I sketched a humble bow.

Browning looked me up and down, his eyes practically screaming contempt.

"Hmph. We were made aware of your so-called 'Grand Opening' by some of our apprentices. It would have been customary for you to invite the Honourable Guild of Brewers to a tasting on your first night. Not," he sneered, "that I would have expected an outsider like *you* to understand that. I did expect *better* from Annie Goldstone, though."

My eyebrow twitched, but I kept my tone level. "Oh, I'm *so* sorry. I don't know how we could have missed sending out your invitations! It's just been so busy around here with the renovations. Please, let me take you to your seats, and the first round will be on us as an apology."

An elderly dwarf behind Browning grunted. "He's got a tongue sweeter than yer wife's tarts, Browning. Take me to my seat lad. My legs aren't gettin' any younger."

"Of course, Master Brewer...?"

"Malt."

"It's a pleasure to make your acquaintance, Master Brewer Malt. If you'd please come this way." I gestured towards a table in the back. Master Browning stepped in front of me and walked towards it while I led the rest of the group.

"Our special today is a glazed rack of goat with roasted rosemary erdroot and sauteed carrots."

"Tiara's Teats that sounds delicious!" Malt said, his eyes glittering. "Who's yer chef, and how much do you want for 'em?"

"I'm afraid Bran isn't for sale, sir. But you're welcome to come and eat at the pub as often as you please! We have a new special every week, and they're all unique to our restaurant." I liked this guy. He was one of those old people that reached a certain age and decided, "I've lived a long life, so watch out – I'm comin' through, y'all!" People like that were always a delight, except on the highway and in public changing rooms.

"Stop fraternising and take a seat, Malt," Browning harrumphed.

Malt shrugged apologetically at me and sat down beside Browning. The rest of the grumble were a twin pair of ginger dwarves with ducktail-beards, a fairly stunning green-haired dwarfess in heavy makeup, and a distinguished dwarf with grey muttonchops. They were all dressed in the same severe black armour.

I passed each of them a menu in turn and was rewarded with a combination of angry glowers and stark silence.

"Can I get everyone a beer?" I asked sweetly.

"Yes. How *is* the beer?" Browning asked, with an odd inflection. "When it isn't shamefully being used in the *food*."

"It's Thirsty Goat's finest True Brew," I replied.

"I'll be the judge of that. I'd heard you children were *experimenting* with new brewing techniques." Browning said, with a tone that sent shivers down my spine and set off alarm bells. "I can't help but feel that any such attempt would summon the wrath of the ancestors. Especially given the unfortunate events that transpired here the *last time*."

What in tha Nether was this? Was this guy playing silly buggers or what? I put a blank smile on my face and began to formulate an answer when I noticed it.

A tiny purple dot sat on my [Minimap]. A single, solitary icon that indicated the presence of unrefined lily-leopard liver oil. Right on top of Master Brewer Browning.

Quest: The Malted Mystery!

Your first brew was mysteriously contaminated with a magical alchemical ingredient.
Who or what caused it?

Culprits Found: 1/2

That-SON-OF-A-NETHER-SPAWNED-BILLY-GOAT-BRED-CHUCKLEHEADED-SCUM-SUCKING-SCIVEY-SAMSQUANCH!

I burst into Annie's office.

"What —pl" she began.

"It was *BROWNING*!"

"Ugh, is that jerk here? What does he want?"

"He *wants* to screw us over! Just like he already did!"

"What? Pete you aren't —"

"HE'S CARRYING LILY-LEOPARD LIVER OIL!" I shouted, my body vibrating with rage.

"What?" Annie asked again, her brows drawing together.

"He's carrying lily-leopard liver oil, and my quest to find the source of our contamination ticked up when I saw it. It wasn't an accident, it was *sabotage*. That absolute *bastard* of a brewer spiked our brew!"

Annie's face went from shock, to bewilderment, through anger, and ended up on rage. "How dare he? *How DARE he!?* How dare he contaminate the Sacred Brew!? He calls himself a Master Brewer!?" She stood up to storm out of the room and I grabbed her by the shoulders.

"No! We can't. As much as I want to slug him in the face, we have no proof, and he's got way too much clout for us to accuse him."

"City Hall –"

"I know! I know the Ordinances Annie. But this isn't about laws, it's about tradition and image and respect. If we go out there and accuse him of sabotage it will *destroy* the Thirsty Goat. We're too vulnerable!"

"But, but..." Annie sputtered, then sat down in her chair with a *whomf.* "Ugh, you're right."

We sat in angry silence for a moment, each of us flexing our hands as we wrung an imaginary neck.

"I'm... not an expert in dwarven society, Annie. What can we do in this situation?" I asked, haltingly. "He's the Guild Master for the Brewers Guild! Can you even sell beer if he decides to blacklist you? As far as I can recall, the Ordinances barely even mention guilds."

Annie drummed her fingers on the table. "We can, but it would be an uphill battle. None of the local restaurants would carry our beer out of fear of retaliation, and our name would be mud with the grocers. The cost to buy erdroot would go through the roof and it would be hard to make big sales."

"So, it would be possible."

Annie nodded. "Just expensive."

I made a fist. "But we have an alternate revenue stream they can't touch. That's good. Anything else?"

She grimaced. "We could declare a Feud."

"That's the thing where we Challenge them to a Contest, right? Could we win?"

sigh "No... They would get to choose the form of Contest, and you're right; we're too weak. If we declare a Feud we'd just be crushed. Feuds favour the challenged party by design."

"Hmmm... but only if *we* declare one. If *he* declares it, we have a chance at winning."

"I don't know what you're thinking Pete, but even *if* you can get Browning to declare a Feud, I'm not sure we have any way to beat an entire guild."

"Oh, I think we do." I leaned in with a feral grin and explained my plan. Annie's eyes widened and then her smile grew to match my own.

CHAPTER EIGHTY
FEUD

"Do you want to do the talking, Annie?" I asked, as I adjusted the carry platter. The moment would be ruined if I spilled the drinks.

"Yes. You can come across as insincere. Sorry, Pete." Annie shifted from foot to foot, pumping herself up.

"No, no. I absolutely *am* insincere when it comes to crap like this. It's a habit from dealing with a world where the customer is always right."

"Sounds awful. Is Balin ready?"

"He and Tania both gave me the signal a moment ago." Aqua called from the door to the kitchen.

"Let's do this." Annie moved forward and I followed behind.

There was no fanfare, nothing that would mark the next events as out of the ordinary. This was simply the owner walking over to greet some distinguished guests.

"Master Brewer Browning!" Annie said, making a small bow. "You made it! I greet you on this most auspicious day!"

Malt waved. "Hallo little Goldstone!" Annie gave him a strained smile.

Browning looked up from his menu. "Annie Goldstone. I see you've made a lot of changes in the scant few weeks you've been in charge."

"Yes, I –" Annie began.

"It's a shame so much of it is a slight against your ancestors," Browning interrupted. "Do you really think all those Goldstones hanging in your foyer would be proud of this circus?" He gestured around the busy brewpub.

Annie grunted as though punched in the gut but continued to smile. "I think my ancestors would be proud that we've made the brewery a place where dwarves can come and partake in our heritage. We actually took some pointers from Master Drum, one of the *senior members* of the Guild. I wasn't aware that brewpubs were frowned upon."

"They're not," Malt butted in. "Browning's just wound up tighter than Lunara's Lace 'cause he's never eaten half the things on this menu. He's just jealous."

Browning glared at Malt. "I was *saying* that a little more decorum could be in order. I noticed those *pro-drinkers* seem to have their own booth!" He pointed to where Beatbox and Tania were signing autographs. Tania looked up at the motion and fixed Browning with a steely glare. He wilted immediately, then turned back on Annie.

"Your... *labourer* promised my table a round of drinks 'on the house,' to apologise for your lack of etiquette," he said with a derogatory emphasis on 'labourer.' Jerkwad. "In case you were not aware, it is customary to invite the Honourable Guild of Brewers to the opening of a new brewery."

"Of course, Master Brewer Browning," Annie replied with false innocence. "However, we weren't opening a new brewery, simply *re-opening* after a renovation. If I'd been aware that you wanted an invitation, I would have been happy to extend one. Unfortunately, the Guild has not been communicating with us recently. Either way, I am happy to make good on *Brewer* Pete's offer. He received his Specialisation last week."

"She's got you there, Browning," Malt interjected. "Congratulations, lad!"

"Not now, Malt!" Browning ground out.

"Aw – go suck on Solen's Socks, Browning, and get off yer tall goat. Are those our drinks? Bring them here!"

I swept in and deposited a mug in front of each of the brewers. The twins barely gave me a second glance, same with the green-bearded beauty. At least the gentle-dwarf with the muttonchops gave me an acknowledging nod. I passed the last mug to Annie and she raised it in a toast.

"To the future of Beer in Minnova! Long may our brews prosper. FOR THE ANCESTORS!"

The six dwarves each raised their mugs and echoed, "FOR THE ANCESTORS!" Malt paused and sniffed the air for a moment, confused. Then everyone brought their mugs back and chugged.

As one, five dwarves spat their beer across the table, instantly showering the party with sticky brown liquid. All except Annie, who finished her sip with a stately gesture, and Malt, who swished with interest.

"This, this...!" Browning sputtered. His lips puckered, and his eyes dilated until they were nearly all iris. The other brewers cried out in distress or rage. One of the twins actually fainted in his chair. The dwarfess shrieked so loud my ears rang for a moment. All around us in the pub, activity ceased as everyone turned to see what had happened. There was a hush in the rest of the room, like the calm before a storm.

"Do you like it?" Annie asked in the silence. "It's the newest product that we're considering releasing. We call it 'radler.' Isn't it *scrumptious*?"

"LIKE IT!?" Browning jumped to his feet. "This is an affront to beer! An abomination from the deepest pits of the nether! Your ancestors would be ashamed of you!" He slammed his fist down on the table and one of the mugs tipped over, spilling lemon-fresh beer all over the table. It spread in all directions and began to drip onto the ground. Muttonchops pushed away from the dribbling liquid as though it would bite or infect him with radical new ideas.

"Ashamed of ME?" Annie slammed her own mug down on the table, spraying radler all over the fainted brewer. He woke up, cried out in horror, then passed out again. "I pour everything into my brewing! It is what I love and what I am. *Everything* I do is to the betterment of my brew and my craft. Can you truly say the same? Or are you *lily-livered*, Master Brewer?"

The assembled brewers paled slightly at Annie's words. Browning went white, then purple.

"HOW DARE YOU!?" Spittle and flecks of radler flew from his

beard. "I am the Guild Master of the Honourable Guild of Brewers! You will treat me with the RESPECT owed to a Greybeard!"

"A Greybeard?" Annie scoffed. "The only grey in your beard is from fear. From quaking in your boots at the thought of a future where beer is more than an institution. From the idea that *any dwarf* could take part in the glorious *dwarven* tradition of brewing!"

"I'll... I'll throw you out of the Guild of Brewers! Your ancestors would be spinning in their graves! Where is your father? Does *he* know what his horrible spawn is doing to the Goldstone legacy?"

Annie's face turned a shade of puce. "You leave my *father* out of it! I've been wondering what was wrong with him, and now I think I know. If I had to deal with a bunch of mudslime like you all the time, I'd be falling apart too! You want to throw us out of the Guild? Who cares! We'll continue selling whatever we want! Our radler will be in every restaurant in Minnova within the year!"

"We won't let you!"

"There's. Nothing. You. Can. Do. About. It." Annie grated out each syllable with gritted teeth. She and Browning were practically standing nose to nose. Beside them Malt had shrunk back, cradling his radler. He took a small sip and nodded appreciatively.

"Browning, maybe we should –"

"A FEUD!" Browning roared, and the entire pub jumped. "I DECLARE A FEUD! THE HONOURABLE GUILD OF BREWERS CALLS OUT THE GOLDSTONE CLAN!"

Annie looked ready to pop him in the nose, so I decided that was my time to step in. Losing her cool was *not* part of the plan. Besides, her part was technically done. She managed to step back but continued to glare daggers at Browning.

"You declared a Feud. What is the Challenge?" I said smoothly.

"You! You are the instrument of all this!" Browning rounded on me, and Balin moved forward.

Tania grabbed him by the collar of his golden armour and held him back. She shook her head. "No, not yet."

"I think you'll find that I am merely the instrument of a greater power." I puffed out my chest with a bravado I barely felt. Then again, it *was* completely true. Over by the kitchen, Aqua choked.

Browning barked a laugh. "The Nether? I can believe it."

"You declared a Feud, *Brewer*." I left off the 'master' and added an insulting inflection. A vein in Browning's forehead practically burst. "Annie Goldstone has given me full authority to speak on her behalf. What – is – your – Challenge?

"You! You will never be allowed to brew in Minnova ever again. You will cease any more *desecration* of our Sacred Brew. In fact, I extend that to the entire Goldstone Clan! That is our Challenge!" There was an audible *gasp* around the pub. A few dwarves stood up menacingly, but Balin and Tania moved to keep everyone in their seats.

I gave a savage grin. So far everything was going to plan. "Do you speak for the entire Guild of Brewers, or the Browning Brewery?"

"I speak for *all* Brewers when I declare you an affront to our most dearly held traditions!" Browning snapped. The twins and the dwarfess nodded with savage satisfaction, though Muttonchops looked a little unsure. Malt jumped up with a look of horror.

"Now hold on a minute, Browning! If we lost, the entire Guild would be unable to brew!!"

"AM I NOT THE MASTER OF THIS GUILD, MALT!?" Browning rounded on the elderly dwarf, shoving him down into his seat. "These upstarts are a threat to the very institution of brewing! I hold you to your OATH, to protect brewing in Minnova!"

"You've been layin' a bit hard on that Oath recently, Browning." Malt snapped. "This isn't what it's for!"

"If you have a problem with it, then vote me out." Browning hissed. "But I suspect the majority of the Guild will agree with me." Malt's expression grew dark and cloudy, but he sat quietly back in his seat. For a few seconds the only sound in the pub was the *drip* *drip* of spilled radler. Everyone in the pub waited to hear our answer.

"By the Nation of Crack Ordinances Ver. 1130, Chapter 1, Section 4, Subsection 21, the Goldstone Clan accepts your Feud. By our own grace, we offer the Honourable Guild of Brewers clemency. Should we win, the Challenge will only apply to the Browning Brewery." My voice sat heavy in the silence. This step was important, because it set the Browning clan as our real enemy. It would help us look good in the eyes of the dwarven population, who might otherwise be furious at

AN ADVENTURE BREWING

the possibility of losing the entire Guild of Brewers. Browning tsk'd, but Malt's face relaxed with relief.

"As if you have a chance. As the Challenge is accepted, you may declare the Contest." Browning crossed his arms in impatience.

"The Contest will be in the field of brewing!" I pronounced with gusto.

The brewers laughed, their mocking jeers echoing in the pub, and even Malt looked amused. Browning was practically beside himself with mirth.

"Ha! You think that you can compete with the entire Honourable Guild of Brewers in *brewing*!? Annie Goldstone, does this fool truly speak for you?"

"This is the Contest!" I pitched my voice to carry in the entire room. "The octa-millennial fast approaches! Now is the time to reinvigorate our traditions! To celebrate the meeting of the new and the old! To spread the word of the Sacred Brew! For our Challenge, we will make Minnova talk about beer!"

That shut them up. The brewers looked at each other in confusion, and there was a low murmur in the rest of the pub.

"Talk about beer?" Malt asked.

"Yes. In two weeks the Goldstone Clan and the Honourable Guild of Brewers will each release a beer they think the dwarves of Minnova will appreciate. Sixteen days later, the beer that is most discussed by the populace will be the winner!"

"What, do you think your *radler* will be capable of sparking anything other than horrified whispers?" Browning said with a barking laugh. "At least your Contest is one worthy of the Sacred Brew! We accept! But..." Browning frowned, "how do you plan to judge it?"

It was still going according to plan. Browning was such a pompous ass he never even considered the dangers hidden in that Contest. I hid glee in my heart and began, "We'll start with a random sample of dwarves –"

"I think I can be of help," a voice interrupted from behind me.

The crowd parted to reveal Prophet Barnes. I'd completely forgotten he was here! Argh, this was no longer going to plan! The elderly dwarf padded forward and everyone made the usual holy sign.

"Prophet Barnes," Browning said respectfully. "Are you here to judge these forsaken souls in Barck's name?"

"You presume much, Master Brewer Browning, to use Barck's name. Shut yer trap," The [Prophet] snapped. "Only one of us speaks for the Gods here, and it certainly isn't you!"

I mean, *I* probably could in this one particular instance. I was pretty sure Barck would be on my side for this one.

Browning shrunk back and bowed in obeisance.

"Now," Barnes continued, "this Feud has a wide enough impact that it interests the Gods."

There was a gasp around the room, and even Annie looked horrified. Knowing Barnes and the Gods in question I... withheld judgement. Seven of those Gods weren't really on my side.

Barnes waited a moment to build suspense and then dropped a bomb. "Midna, Goddess of Communication herself, will provide the result of this Feud."

Bing!

New Quest: Beer Feud!

You have been challenged to a Feud that will decide the course of Brewing in Crack forever! Will you win?
Midna will be the judge of that! Don't you dare lose.

Feuds Won: 0/1

Rewards: +0.2 Charisma, [Blessed] condition

Do you accept?
Yes / No

Yep. Barck was *definitely* on my side in this. Honestly, a little deific reminder that I was doing the right thing was nice every once in a while.

After a moment of stunned silence, the pub rocked on its foundations.

CHAPTER EIGHTY-ONE
RACK'EM AND STACK'EM

"Oh Gods, oh Gods, oh Gods."

"Lever goes there, Balin."

"Got it." *Clank*

"Oh Gods, oh Gods, oh Gods."

"Is the spigot in place, Richter?"

meeeeeh!!!

"Aye."

"Let it go, Balin!"

CRUNCH

"Oh Gods, oh Gods, oh Gods."

"Was it supposed to make that sound?!"

"Uhh... let me check."

"Oh Gods, oh Gods, oh Gods."

"Aqua!" I grabbed the pacing dwarfess as she walked past me and shook her shoulders. "It'll be fine! Calm down!"

"Calm down!?" Aqua was nearly in tears. "How am I supposed to calm down?! We started a Feud with the entire Brewers' Guild last night! The *GODS THEMSELVES* are judging it, and the whole city is going to have their eyes on us! Do you know how many Feuds the Gods have judged in the history of Minnova!?"

"Erm, no. I'm surprised the number is higher than one, actually. How many?"

"A couple thousand," Richter grunted, as he tightened a rope.

I looked at him in surprise. "What, really?"

"We 'ave a long history, and tha Gods are nosy," Richter chuckled.

I patted Aqua on the shoulder. "See? It isn't even that uncommon."

She rounded on Annie. "Arrgh! Annie! I can't believe you agreed to this! Even if those rat bastards poisoned our brew!"

Annie sighed. "I've explained this to you Aqua. They didn't *poison* it, they *contaminated* it."

"Same difference! How can you beat an entire Guild? We're barely a tenth their size!"

"Size doesn't matter, Aqua," I muttered slyly. She looked me dead in the eye and stomped on my foot. "Ow!"

"It'll be fine, Aqua." Annie came down and held her friend's hand. "We have a really good chance. The Brewers actually have an uphill battle! Do you want to explain, Pete?"

"Yep. The trick is that the Challenge is 'who can make the most dwarves talk about their beer.' It isn't 'who sells the most' or 'who makes the best,' just 'who gets the most talking.'"

"Oh." Aqua stood still and thought for a moment. "OOOHHH!!!!"

"Right? They think we're going to try and do it with the radler. But that stuff is so radioactive it'd be dead in the water. It's too different, which means a significant swath of the population would ignore it completely. Especially if news about Midna's involvement spreads."

"Radler would be a terrible idea," Annie agreed.

"But Browning doesn't know," I gestured around the fourteen full tanks, "about this."

John laughed. "This stuff will certainly get Minnova talking."

"Do you really think so? Won't people still think it's too different?" Aqua whined.

John made a 'perish the thought' gesture. "It tastes just like True Brew, it's just... different. You and Richter drank the completed product Aqua, how was it?"

"Amazin'," Richter said. "Best beer I've eva had. Da fizz, da flavour, da colour. I can't put it inta words, John. Dis lot's a pale imitation right now. Wait and see what it's like after tha' bottle conditionin'!"

Aqua nodded reluctantly. "It really was good. It won't *actually* drive everyone crazy, but I still can't wait to try it with this cleaner, clearer, batch."

"Aw, thanks, guys." I clasped my hands over my heart. "That means a lot to me!"

"Yer welcome, Pete. But if we lose tha' brewery ova this, I'm gonna make you pay." He flexed his biceps in a fake threat. At least, I hoped it was fake.

"Okay. I feel a little better," Aqua huffed. "What is this thing you're setting up?"

"That depends on if it just broke. How is it, Balin!?"

"All good! Just a crack in one of the smaller pipes. I've blocked it off, but we won't be able to use it."

"Just one?"

"Aye."

"That's fine." I pointed to the long bamboo pipe with a series of small wooden spokes that Richter and Balin had attached to the spigot on tank number one. "I present to you the amazing, incredible, 'Udderly Fantastic, Bottle Stick'!"

Everyone gave me a blank look. "The what!?"

"It's a giant udder! See?" I made a grand gesture.

There was some uncomfortable silence.

meeeeeeeeeh. [Translated from Prima Donna Goat] "Pervert."

"It's not a *bad* name, Pete." Balin patted my shoulder. "Just a bit odd."

"The name is *fine*." Johnsson said. "I don't see what's wrong with it."

"See? Johnsson thinks it's okay!" I whined. "There's nothing wrong with udders! They're perfectly natural. The name even kinda rhymes!"

"Ehh, my boy may not be tha best judge of that, Pete." John remarked. "Some dwarves can get weird around udders."

"Dad!" Johnsson cried indignantly. "Your own flesh and blood!"

"Enough!" Annie shouted from her perch on-top the catwalk. "We have an immense amount of work to do today, and I don't want to waste any more time. Pete, show everyone how your –" She put a hand over her face. "No, never mind. I can't do this. Balin! Give me a name!"

"It's an industrial bottle stick." Balin shrugged. "Made it out o' bamboo and corks."

"Perfect! Pete, can you show everyone how to use your *industrial bottle stick*?"

"Fine," I grumped, and walked up to the contraption. It consisted of a thick five-metre-long bamboo pipe running parallel to the ground. Ten smaller pipes, each just wide enough to fit inside a bottle, hung off the bottom. At the end of each small pipe was a cork with a stick poking out of it. The main pipe was attached to the spigot at the bottom of the fermentation tank and was supported by some wooden sawhorses.

"This is a bottle stick. It's really easy to use, but this job is still goin' to take a long time." I pointed at the boxes of bottles lining the walls. "Those are going to all need filling, and it'll take a couple thousand bottles to empty a single tank."

"Ugh!" Johnsson shouted in shock. "We can't use the kegs!?"

"Not this time." I shook my head. "Until we get some steel casks, I don't want to chance it. We're going one hundred percent keg-free this time. They'll be useful for a demonstration though, pass me one."

Richter tossed me a small keg and I took it over to tank number two. I crouched down next to the spigot and began my demonstration. "When racking – that means filling – a keg, or any other kind of container, the most important thing is to minimise the amount of air that comes in contact with the alcohol. In the case of a keg, we do that by inserting the spigot into the bunghole – that's the hole right here."

Johnsson raised his hand. "We know what a bunghole is, Pete."

"Aw, go put a cork in *yer* bunghole." I waited for any other interruptions, then continued. "It's important to fill the barrel *all the way*. You don't want any excess air at all. If you have to, let a bit spill out of the bunghole when you push in the cork. Can anyone tell me why?"

Annie put up her hand and I pointed at her. "The beer still comes into contact with the air in the barrel, which is why our beers have a shelf life. As soon as it enters the barrel, there's a chance the beer will go bad in under a week."

"That's right, thanks Annie." I nodded.

"So that's why we don't store any of our beer? And why we try to make sure it all sells within a week or two?" Aqua asked, leaning over to look at the barrel.

"Correct, but my [Refine Brew] changes that!" I stated proudly. I opened the spigot and allowed the beer to fill the barrel. When it reached the lip, I stamped a cork into the bunghole, spilling a small amount of beer on the floor. I gestured to Richter, who grabbed a mop and cleaned it up.

"This beer is now on a timer, but with the Blessings of the Gods the oxidation reaction is stopped before it even begins! [Refine Brew]!" My hand glowed briefly and then flickered out.

Balin put up his hand.

"Yes, Balin?"

"Ya don't need ta' call out tha Blessin's, Pete."

I slit my eyes. "Penelope, go say 'Hello' to Balin."

Meeeeeh!

"[Golden Armour]!"

"Hypocrite!"

After we got Penelope off of Balin, I passed everyone a large box filled with small packets. Aqua looked at one suspiciously and gave it a sniff.

"Is this... sugar?"

"It's priming sugar. I already explained it to Annie, but the long and short of it is that this sugar made the fizz you liked so much, Aqua."

"What do we do with it?"

"Let me demonstrate." I grabbed a bottle from a case and walked over to the *sigh* industrial bottle stick. "Did you turn the spigot already, Balin?"

"Aye, it should be full."

"Okay. Observe." I opened a packet of sugar and poured it into the bottle. "The bottle *and* the bottle stick have been sanitised. We want to keep it that way, so please make sure you don't touch the sugar when you pour it in. After that, you slip the bottle around it like this." I slid one of the pipes into my bottle. "Notice the stick on the end of the cork? When that stick gets pushed against the bottom of the bottle, the cork is shoved into the pipe and the beer can flow out."

I pushed the bottom of the bottle against the stick and the clear glass began to fill with bubbling brown liquid. The entire brewery leaned forward to watch the momentous occasion: The first bottle rack in the history of Erd! It took a while to fill – dwarves were big drinkers, so we'd made each bottle big enough to contain one litre of beer.

When the beer reached the lip of the bottle, I pulled the stick out.

"Next you lever this stopper attached to the bottleneck into place." I demonstrated. "And swirl the bottle to mix the sugar in. Put the bottle back in the case and you're done! Oh, and please remember to give the bottle stick a rinse with boiling water every once in a while to reduce contamination. Any questions?"

A couple hands went up and I went down the line answering them. This crew was pretty sharp, and soon everyone was racking bottles one at a time. Assuming.... twenty seconds per bottle and six people working at once... I looked at the enormous tank. We'd be able to empty maybe one tank per day. We really needed more workers.

Four hours later, the first tank was empty and everyone was dead on their feet. Annie was forced to call a break to rest before we opened the pub. Thankfully, Beatbox had offered his daughter Lemontwist to help Bran prep in the kitchen. I don't think we would have been able to keep the pub open otherwise.

Annie had me on full-time Feud duty, so I set to work using [Refine Brew]. Thank the Gods, I was able to activate it on an entire box of bottles at once! I'd been dreading using it on every bottle.

I looked up at the stacks and stacks of boxes and sighed in satisfaction. I had some ideas for names, but considering the circumstances... I'd go run them past Annie first. Time to design some ads, and find a starving artist to make bottle labels. Minnova wasn't going to know what hit it, and after he lost Browning would never brew in this town again! Muhahahahahaha!

Master Brewer Browning glanced possessively at his journeymen as they ran to and fro beneath him. They had just completed another perfect brew, and he stared deep into the murky wort. A stick bobbed to the surface like a salute, the universe itself telling him 'good job!'

Did those upstarts really think they could take on the best brewers in the history of Minnova with something as simple as lemon juice mixed with beer?

That's right, he knew the recipe for this dreaded *radler*. He'd obtained it from a miner who'd been in the City of Minnova Reform Mine with Peter Roughtuff. The layabout had been over*joyed* to tell him the recipe in exchange for a paltry dozen gold.

Browning chuckled darkly. The Thirsty Goat would need a massive number of lemons to make enough radler to even stand a chance. The Contest might be in *brewing*, but he could still throw around the weight of the Guild. His apprentices were out there right now, purchasing every lemon they could find in the city. He'd also contacted his primary suppliers and told them they might want to be 'out' of lemons for the next couple weeks if they wanted his continued patronage.

This Feud was going to revitalise the brewing industry in Minnova. Browning looked forward to the droves of thirsty dwarves that would soon descend upon his brewery, desperate for the nostalgic taste of True Brew. Those pathetic wannabe 'Brewers' at the Thirsty Goat weren't going to know what hit them.

CHAPTER EIGHTY-TWO
RELEASE DAY

I awoke to banging, and the familiar sound of Whistlemop screaming at my door.

I sighed and pulled myself out of bed. I was exhausted. We barely managed to get the conditioned bottles properly labelled and stacked last night, and today was probably going to be a zoo. At least the hard work was worth it!

Bing!

Quest Complete: The New Brew 2/10!

For the third time in dwarven history, a new brew has graced the world!
All the Firmament shall rejoice!

Gained one karmic reversal.

Bing!

New Quest: More Brews Part 1/5!

You've completed your first new beer. More! MORE!
Invent eight new drinks. Mixes don't count.
Drinks Invented: 3/8

Rewards: +0.2 Strength.

Do you accept?
Yes / No

Bing!

Stat Increased: [Agility]!
Your agility has increased by 1! Your new agility is 12!

I still didn't really know what a Karmic Reversal did. The description wasn't overly useful either. I really needed those theology lessons from Prophet Barnes.

Karmic Reversal [One Use Remaining] – *You can call upon a karmic reversal to reverse the flow of fate. After one hour passes, the weight of destiny shall descend again. However, only Gods are truly bound by fate and it is the right of mortals to fight against its current.*

At least the agility was nice and clear. I flexed in the mirror as I grabbed some clothes and admired my toned and hairy pecs. Looking good, Pete!

"Balin, wake up!"

Moan

I threw a pillow at him, and it bounced back onto the floor. He rolled over and blindly grabbed under his bed. "Where's me socks! Not leavin' without me socks!"

I pulled on a tunic and pants and made my way to the door. "It's release day. We have lots to do. I'll go grab us coffee, so get my dress armour ready."

That's right, today was Feud day!

Our bottle-conditioned brew had turned out *perfectly!* It was clear as topaz, with a generous fizz that bubbled inside the bottle. Just the bottle itself was amazing to look at, let alone the experience of opening it up to a satisfying *pop*! The beer was smooth and consistent, with zero acrid aftertastes or bloody *sticks* floating in it. The clarity still wasn't *perfect*, but we could always add fining agents next time.

The crew at the Thirsty Goat went *wild* when they got to taste it last night. It still tasted awful to me, though. At this point, I was willing to murder something for some hops to use as a bittering agent. Anything other than that Godsawful alchemical bundle of sticks.

Then there was the gimmick and, oh, what a gimmick. I was usually against gimmicky beer, since it pigeonholed you and was usually a cover for bad flavour. But our gimmick was just the juicy wet cherry on top, the fabulous flatulent fruit.

It was why we'd decided on the name *Ass-Blaster Ale*.

I stumbled to the door and threw it open.

"What is it this time, Whistlemop?"

Whistlemop was wearing his horrid rainbow coloured suit again. In combination with his shining bald pate, it made him almost painful to look at. "Pete! Pete! You won't believe this! You need to get to the Grand Market! RIGHT NOW!"

I moaned. "*Now* what?"

We knew we were approaching the Grand Market because of the line. It started several blocks away and it was noisy, surly, and *loud*.

We tried to push through first. "Excuse me!"

"Get in line, bub!"

"No skippin'!"

"I've been waitin' since yesterday! Get to tha' back!"

Whistlemop, Balin, and I scurried off to an alleyway, but simply found *another* line snaking through the backstreets.

"What *is* this?" I groaned. "We don't need another riot, today of all days!"

"I've not seen a city so worked up withou' a monster stampede," Balin huffed.

"The Honourable Guild of Brewers decided to release their brews at the Grand Market too. These lines stretch between my cart and their garden," Whistlemop hissed. He peeked outside the alleyway and then looked back at me. "It looks like they aim to piggyback off the success of your advertising."

I rolled my eyes. "Oh, *now* they're okay with the way we do things?"

"Do you see those lines!? They'd need to be *idiots* not to!"

I grumbled. "I thought they were! Browning is at least. This feels like Drum's doing, or Malt."

I hadn't been idle for the past two weeks. My first task had been scouring Minnova for a good artist. I found one through Lillyweather: a gnomish [Artisan] named Littlefoot. He was an incredible artist, his every stroke capturing both the essence and energy of his subject. He was also the first gnome I'd ever met without a moustache. Apparently, he regularly sold it to local beard parlours in order to afford paint.

He'd been overjoyed to take part in such an interesting new project. I gave him enough gold to hire a small army of art students to stamp bottle-labels while he did the big stuff.

I was originally worried the central square merchants wouldn't want to help me. In fact, they'd been more than willing – they'd been downright accommodating. Because of the auction underlying the Grand Market, those that lost were always happy to find some way to give the Main stores a black eye. Our Feud was the perfect opportunity to nail one of the big Guilds to the wall, and the little guys all wanted to see it happen.

The result? A fancy poster declaring the 'Great Minnova Beer Feud' could be found attached to nearly every stall in the central square of the Grand Market. The poster starred Penelope holding a bottled beer and rocketing into the sky, propelled by – well, let's just say that if Penelope was capable of understanding that poster, I was a dead dwarf walking. A label featuring the same image was affixed to every bottle of Ass-Blaster.

We also sold a few talking coasters that made goat screams followed by a fart, just because.

The next thing I'd done was put together a jingle riffing on *Stacey's Mom* that I'd titled *Thirsty Goat*. It contained glorious lines like, "Thirsty Goat has got me eatin' oat," and "I'm in love with Thirsty Goat."

It wasn't my best work. What mattered was that the Ordinances allowed bards with an entertainment licence to sing in establishments and squares at specific times. There were very few limitations on *what* they were allowed to sing, so the local taverns and gathering places had been overrun with various renditions of *Thirsty Goat* for the last two weeks. Curiously, most of the local bards seemed to be sporting pink hair of late.

"We *need* to get back to my cart!" Whistlemop hissed. "Aqua and Annie are selling beer as fast as they can, while Johnsson and Richter help my guards keep order. It's not enough. We need Balin's glorious [Golden Armour] to direct the crowd."

"Wait, then what do you need *me* for?" I asked.

"This situation is entirely your fault," Whistlemop snapped. "Take responsibility and be helpful."

I harrumphed. "What about yer fancy new [Wizard]?"

Whistlemop flushed pink and turned his face away. "His pay was too high, considering he just sat around all day."

"You *fired* him!?"

"I know, I know! I should have waited until next week. But he cost *sooo* mu-hu-huch!" Whistlemop whined.

Balin pointed at the crowd. "Want me ta use me armour ta push through tha line?"

"No. We don't want to set everyone off..." I drummed my fingers on my thigh and considered. I looked up to the top of the single-storey house we were standing beside.

"Is there any reason we can't run on top of the buildings?" I pointed.

Balin and Whistlemop looked up.

"Are you crazy!?" Whistlemop shouted.

"It would technically be trespassin'," Balin began, then paused. "Even then, so long as ya' leave when yer asked it shouldn't even be a fine. Lotta drunk dwarves wanderin' into the wrong house in a big city like Minnova."

"So we could do it, if we're fast enough?"

"Aye, but we might end up in a fight, or real trouble if someone inside gets mad at us fer runnin' on their roof."

"That just means we need to avoid stepping over occupied rooms." I began searching for a barrel to stand on.

"How are we gonna do that?"

AN ADVENTURE BREWING

From up on the rooftops we could see the lines stretching off into the distance. Everywhere we looked, there were dwarves, gnomes, and the occasional human waiting patiently in the queue. Impromptu games of hitball had started up in various locations, and it looked like entire clans were out. I even spotted a gnomish picnic.

After a few minutes of careful running and jumping, we dropped down into the Grand Market. A couple people pointed at us, but we were soon lost in the milling crowd.

"That's an incredible Ability, Pete!" Whistlemop applauded.

"Seems a waste to use it like that," Balin grumbled.

"Actually, that's exactly how a minimap is supposed to be used."

As we made our way through the crowd, I began to see dwarves holding bottles of our beer. There was also the occasional *BRAAAPPP* followed by uproarious laughter. The mood in the market was practically *festive*.

Mostly. Some of the other merchants were understandably irritated by all the commotion.

[Translated from angry toothless gnome] "My Cabbages!"

Everywhere we walked, the name *Thirsty Goat* could be heard. Balin and I looked at each other and smiled ecstatically. It looked like things were going poorly for the Honourable Guild of Brewers.

Ahead of us, Whistlemop's cart stood out from the rest of the square. An enormous billboard with a picture of Penelope blasting off proudly pronounced: "Come try our new bottled beer. It's so fresh and fizzy that your vitality can't possibly contain it. The Thirsty Goat proudly presents: Ass-Blaster Ale!"

With so much fanfare, and so much evident impact... maybe getting that wish from the God's game wasn't impossible? Maybe...?

"Pete!"

"Comin' Balin!"

Master Brewer Browning's eye twitched as he looked down on the busy beer garden from the Master's Booth. He should be overjoyed! At this very moment, the spotlight should be moving away from those perverted pro-drinkers and back onto his Guild where it properly belonged! This was *his* moment!

"Ooooh, look at 'em!" Malt crooned beside him. "We're gonna be swimmin' in gold by tha' time this is done! Maybe I'll be able to afford ta get the missus one o' those sigil-inscribed footbaths!

Browning's hands clenched so hard his nails drew blood. He couldn't believe it! They never planned to release the radler at all! Now he was stuck with hundreds of gold worth of rapidly spoiling lemons with nothing to show for it. Worse, that awful goat song was stuck in his head, and he'd been hearing it in his *nightmares*.

"This isn't a good thing, Malt!" Browning ground out. "Look at them! They're buying our beer, but then they're leaving! They're not *talking* about it!!!"

"Yes, I can see that, Browning," Malt chuckled. "I have to wonder where this *Ass-Blaster* came from. They must have had a batch already brewed. The bottles can't have been something they came up with on the fly either. They baited you into this Feud, you know. You got played, Browning!"

"Damnit!!" Browning smashed his fist against the railing, and some of the dwarves in the beer garden looked their way. One waved a hand holding a beer bottle at him. He gritted his teeth and turned away. A faint *braaap* echoed out behind him, followed by laughter.

"I can't believe this! Beer that makes you... you –"

"Gassy?" Malt looked aside as an apprentice ran up and passed him a package.

"It's disrespectful!" Browning raged. "As if the radler wasn't bad enough! This turns our Sacred Brew into an object of mockery! How will any dwarf take us seriously ever again!?"

Malt carefully unwrapped the package. "We change our name to the Honourable Guild of Tooters?"

AN ADVENTURE BREWING

"THIS ISN'T FUNNY, MALT!"

"Oh? I'm having a lovely time. This is one of the biggest beer festivals I can remember, and I'm a good deal older than you, Browning. A fact you keep forgetting."

Browning turned to look back down at the crowd in the beer garden. He counted at least a dozen of those bottles, and everywhere he saw one, dwarven heads were bent together in discussion. "What are we going to *do!* We might *lose!*"

"Mhm. Sounds like a *you* problem."

"This could alter the image of beer forever!"

"Actually, these bottles seem very well suited for beer. The stopper on top is rather ingenious too. I wonder if those youngsters came up with it?" *pop*

"Why aren't you more worried about this!? Those upstarts are going to destroy the image that we've spent millennia creating! The image that you personally spent *centuries* building!" Browning pointed down to where a trio of dwarves were competing for the loudest fart. "Look at these fools!"

Malt chuckled. "The label is fairly amusing. I can imagine my family crest on one of these. Maybe on a brown bottle, instead of clear? I wonder how it tastes?" *glug*

"Who cares how it tastes! This is a catastrophe!"

rumble Browning wheeled back to look at Malt, who had a bottle to his lips. Browning's mouth dropped open in indignation as Malt shrugged.

"It's quite *burp* tasty. Almost exactly like a good batch of True Brew, but with a bit more fizz."

"MALT!" Browning roared, his face twisting up with rage.

BRAAAAAAAPPP!!

"Hoh! 'Scuse me!"

Everyone in the garden looked up as a primal scream erupted from the raised wooden structure that contained the Master's booth. The scream was followed by a brief scuffle, and then someone in the booth shouted "[Shatter]!" One second later, every glass bottle in the vicinity exploded, showering everyone with glass and fizzy beer.

Accusations were levelled, fists began to fly, and the garden was soon overrun with sticky, swearing, dwarves.

A patrol of guards arrived moments later and quickly dispersed the crowd. They were intrigued to learn of the exploding glass. After all, a similar event had set off a riot in the Grand Market just a few weeks ago. The culprit was still at large, and City Hall was *very* interested in finding them.

CHAPTER EIGHTY-THREE
WINNERS AND LOSERS

I underestimated the power of advertising in this new world.

I already saw how successful it could be with my little speech in the arena. I *should* have been ready for the absolute shitshow that descended upon the Grand Market. But even I couldn't have expected the massive event that struck the city like a wave. It was a zoo, a deafening explosion of exuberant dwarves and demanding gnomes desperate to try a new take on an old cultural favourite. The fact that Midna was going to judge the words of every person in the city was icing on the hype cake. Things settled down after the second day, but there was still a near constant line.

The verdict was in. Our beer was smoother, clearer, *fizzier*, and more fun to drink. Since dwarves mostly drank as a social exercise, the fun factor pushed it over the edge.

We sold out in four days.

After the first day, Whistlemop hired some additional hands to sell beer while the brew-crew bottled a fresh batch of Ass-Blaster in the brewery. The new batch didn't get to bottle-condition properly, which really needed a whole week – but it was good enough.

We started the feud with over one hundred thousand bottles. By the end of the first week we'd sold over one hundred fifty thousand litres of beer.

Our profit was insane.

Annie was walking around in a fugue state, her body unable to determine if it was overjoyed or over-stressed.

Whistlemop began randomly cackling whenever he thought no one was watching.

Balin developed a nervous twitch trying to keep thousands of dwarves from overrunning Whistlemop's cart every hour of the day.

Johnsson and Richter were complaining that one more hour of racking bottles and they would file a worker safety claim with City Hall. Even John was rubbing his wrist and complaining about aches from non-existent weather.

Bran delivered an ultimatum regarding staffing and hired Lemontwist full-time.

Aqua was… cheerfully Aqua.

As for me?

I felt *glorious*! I was on top of the world, like *The Carpenters*, or a stalker God!

This was so different from the radler. Did *some* dwarves give us the old death-stare when they passed by? Sure, but there were always going to be luddites. This time there were no fights, no angry declarations of war, no *shaved beards*. The general consensus was that Ass-Blaster was just *better* than True Brew. We even got a few requests to release a non-flatulent variety for the more… discerning dwarf.

A request we were desperately happy to answer. Unrefined lily-leopard liver oil was *expensive*!

The bottle return scheme was working well, and even had an unanticipated bonus – nearly half the times a dwarf brought a bottle back, they bought another beer!

All told, the Thirsty Goat was on the lips of nearly every denizen in Minnova.

"Ok, Annie, I think that's the last of the boxes!" I called.

"Good! We need to hurry back!"

I set the box of bottles down in Whistlemop's cart and stepped out. It was still early morning, which meant the crowd was *only* a few dozen dwarves deep. I recognized some of them as regulars, but most were new. In the back of my mind the 'influence' quest was buzzing up like a slot machine. It was slower now, but at this rate I was still likely to hit one million dwarves by the end of the year.

I looked up at Whistlemop, who was standing on his usual podium next to the cart. He was still selling his Whistlemugs, and even had a 10 percent special on for dwarves that bought an Ass-Blaster with a mug. "How's it going, Whistlemop?"

His face practically *glittered*. "It's going well, Pete!"

"That's good to hear! I wanted to chat later about a new idea."

"I'd love to, but I'm going to be busy making preparations." Whistlemop gave a savage smile. "I'm bidding on a Main Store in the Grand Market."

Bing!

New Quest: Grand Market!

Your business needs to expand!
Why own a cart when you can own a store?
Obtain a Main Store in the Grand Market!

Rewards: +0.4 Charisma.

Do you accept?

Yes / No

I whistled and hit "Yes."

"Can we really afford that?"

Whistlemop laughed. Then he cackled. "Do you know what our profit margin is on your beer and my mugs? Let alone the value of the Whistlestops or the possibilities afforded by my glass business? We're severely limited by the size and location of my cart. We need to *expand*."

"Sounds like a plan." I nodded. "Do you need me for it?"

Whistlemug waved me away. "It's just maths and finances. I can handle it." His gaze grew stormy and he pointed off to the right. "But I won't handle whatever that is. Annie!"

Everyone's attention snapped in the direction Whistlemop pointed. A contingent of dwarves in brown and black armour was heading towards us. Their beards were done up in ornate knotwork, and the smell of onion preceded them.

It was the Honourable Guild of Brewers. They marched with Malt at the head, and stopped a bare stone's throw away from the cart.

"What do you want, Malt?" Annie demanded.

She stood atop Whistlemop's little riser, having taken it over when the brewers arrived. She stared down at the assembled brewers in contempt. There were over two dozen, and I only recognized a few of them. There was Malt, Drum, Muttonchops, Greenbeard, the ginger twins, and even... Jeremiah Goldstone!? Annie's gaze swept over her father, and he gave a weak wave. She brushed him off and nailed Malt with another glare.

"Did you come to try and mess with our operation? I'll have you know that we're prepared to fight if necessary!"

"Calm down, calm down, young Goldstone," Malt chuckled. "So fiery. She got that from her mother, didn't she Jeremiah?" He glanced back at Jeremiah, who nodded, a smile flickering briefly across his face. Malt frowned and looked back at Annie. "We aren't here to fight you."

"No? What then? If you want more time, we refuse to give it to you." Annie crossed her arms.

At this point we were gathering a crowd. The two dozen dwarves in our line had ballooned to nearly a hundred, and more were collecting as fast as their stubby legs could carry them. The brewers clustered together, clearly uncomfortable with all the attention.

Malt gave a wide smile. "On the contrary, actually. We're here to surrender."

There was shocked silence as everyone considered his words.

Annie sputtered. "Y-you-wh-what-why-you can't do that! We agreed on two weeks and Midna's judgement!"

Malt waved his pointer finger from side to side and tutted. "We don't need a *Goddess* to show us the obvious. That would be a disrespectful waste of her holy time. It is clear to everyone that you have won this Feud. Ach, give me that flag, Drum!"

Drum solemnly passed forward a long stick with a white flag atop it and Malt waved it back and forth.

AN ADVENTURE BREWING

"For the dwarves in the back! WE! SURRENDER!" *cough* Malt yelled hard enough to hack up a lung at the end.

Bing!

Quest Complete: Beer Feud!
You won! Was there ever any doubt? This stuff is delicious by the way. Lunara hates the side effects, which makes it even better. Gained 0.2 charisma! Your new charisma is 12.4!

*Gained [**Blessed**] Condition!*

Bing!

Condition Gained: [Blessed]!
*You have gained the [**Blessed**] Condition! Your vitality is increased by 4 for the next year.*

I pumped my fist. Score! As I glanced over the notifications, my vision was arrested by a blinking dot on my [Minimap]. I felt my heart quicken and my mind go numb. The next few moments passed in a blur, like a video-game simulating shock.

Everyone began cheering. It started with Aqua, moved on to the guards around the cart, and then spread through the Market. There was a lot of back slapping and fist bumping and general cheerful violence. Then Annie had to ruin it. She gesticulated wildly until the crowd grew silent, and nailed Malt with a steely glare.

"Why are you the one to tell me this, Malt? I want to hear it from Guildmaster Browning. I want to hear him admit that he'll *never* brew in Minnova again! I want to hear him admit that our brew is *not* an abomination!"

A couple of the brewers coughed, and Malt gave an ironic smile.

"I'm afraid that will be difficult, Annie. You see, Browning was voted out as Guildmaster last night. *I* am the current master of the Honourable Guild of Brewers."

"What!?" Annie's sentiment was echoed by the crowd.

"Oh, yes. He was becoming absolutely *intolerable* to live with," a hooded brewer muttered.

Malt hushed him. "Aside from that, Browning is... *indisposed*."

Annie was shell-shocked. "What do you mean?"

Malt's eyes glittered.

"I understand that he was arrested this morning. He will likely be headed to a certain City of Minnova Reform Mine by the end of the week." He winked. "So, do you accept our surrender? I can't stand around here all day, my knees will give out!"

Annie barely managed a tiny nod.

Beside me, Aqua burst into tears, and that was enough to get the crowd cheering again. For their part, the brewers just looked uncomfortable.

Aqua buried her head in my beard and soaked it with tears, then wrapped me in a hug. "Pete! Can you believe it!? We won!" She paused and looked up at me with confusion. "Pete?"

I barely registered her presence.

My attention hadn't wavered from my [Minimap]. A knot roiled in my stomach, and my heart was pounding like a drum. My fists were clenched so tight the knuckles were white and my arms shook. A solitary purple dot indicated the presence of unrefined lily-leopard liver oil. Right on top... of Jeremiah Goldstone.

"Pete?"

Bing!

Quest Complete: The Malted Mystery!

You have found the culprits that contaminated your beer!

Gained 0.2 wisdom! Your new wisdom is 14.4!
*Gained [**White Lie**]!*

[**White Lie**] – *You gain a bonus 4 charisma when you tell a lie that is not intended to harm someone. The lie will read as 'true' to abilities that can discern truth and lies.*

This Ability can be used once per minute.

Aqua was shaking me, and I glanced down at her. Her eyes were filled with concern. "Are you okay, Pete?"

AN ADVENTURE BREWING

I smiled with my lips and told a little [White Lie]. "I'm fine. Just shocked we won already."

She smiled back at the truth in my words, and I brought my hands behind my back to hide my bleeding palms.

Jeremiah Goldstone awoke in his chair as water splashed against his face. His eyes rolled and he sputtered. "Wha-who?" He tried to stand, but stumbled, still half-drunk. He looked wildly around the environs of Drum's pub, the *Rusty Battleaxe*. *The building was empty of patrons, and Drum was nowhere to be seen.*

"Drum!" He roared, water dripping from his beard. "What in tha Nether is this?"

I chose that moment to step into his vision, and Jeremiah gasped as though struck in the heart.

"Pete?"

"Hello, Jeremiah. I think we need to have a talk, dwarfo-a-dwarfo."

"What are you doing here? Drum! DRUM!?" Jeremiah tried to stand, his eyes wide with panic, but his legs weren't listening to him. His mighty frame heaved with exertion and a vein popped up on his nearly bald head. He managed a single tottering step, but then the world spun, and he fell to the ground in a heap. I watched impassively, making no move to help; crawling on the ground suited him right now.

"DRUM!" He screamed.

"Drum's finishing up with some stuff out back. Just you and me, *Mr.* Goldstone." I grabbed a barstool and pulled it in front of Jeremiah, taking a seat. My voice grew sarcastic. "Or should I call you *Master Brewer* Goldstone?"

"I-I-don't know what yer talkin' about," Jeremiah moaned. "I need to-to go home, Pete. I can't talk right now."

"You *do* have poor communication skills recently. Can I get you a glass of water to help you sober up? When *was* the last time you were sober, if you don't mind me asking?"

"I can't remember..." Jeremiah licked suddenly dry lips.

"Does this jog yer memory?" I tossed a small black vial up into the air with one hand. Jeremiah's eyes followed it, watching with a hypnotised gaze as it spun and sparkled. I caught it in my palm with a *smack* and Jeremiah flinched away as though struck.

"I've been wondering why you did it," I said. "Drum tried to explain, but I need to hear it from you."

Jeremiah continued to look around the pub, anywhere but at my stony face. "H-how do ya know Drum?"

"He's a friend of a friend," I drawled. "Yer avoidin' the question, Master Brewer."

There was a moment's awkward silence, broken only by Jeremiah's ragged breathing.

"I... I swore an oath. To the Gods and upon my ancestors," he began, nearly whispering. "I kept that oath fer four hundred years. Even after ma wife died and I only had Annie, I still kept ma oath. To protect tha Sacred Brew that my parents and my ancestors crafted with love and devotion. To uphold the tenets of the Guild in the face of all opposition." His voice cracked. "I swore an *oath*."

"THAT'S *IT*!?" I bellowed, and smashed the bottle on the floor. "You betrayed our *trust*, your daughter's *future*, for some stupid OATH?"

"I HAD NO CHOICE!" Jeremiah's voice cracked in anguish. "What more do ya *want* of me!? I've given ya me brewery! Me daughter! My life's work! Would ya see me be forsworn before tha Gods too? To sully tha' unbroken honour o' my ancestors? Just... just leave me be." He began to weep. "*Damn ya!*"

My face slowly changed from disgust to concern as Jeremiah fell apart before me. The straightforward Mr. Goldstone, the backbone of Thirsty Goat brewery, reduced to a blubbering mess.

"Was it *really* worth all this?"

"Aye, it was," Drum interrupted, coming in from the back door. "Jeremiah Goldstone was always an honourable dwarf. No better dwarf around. Better than me, that's fer sure." He pointed his silver hand at me, and it morphed into a shining short blade. "Better than you too, eh!?"

"I *never* would've chosen my job over my daughter, and don't think you're off the hook in all this Drum," I hissed.

Drum grunted a laugh, his hand changing back to a silver fist. "See, that's where yer wrong, Pete! Brewin' ain't just a job, or even a way of life fer dwarves like us. It defines our family goin' back thousands of years, an unbroken line o' duty and trust. It seeps into us from tha moment we're born and never leaves us till tha day we die. Browning made Jeremiah choose between his family or what makes him a *dwarf*." He nodded at Jeremiah, who lay weeping. "A choice like that would break a stronger dwarf than Jeremiah Goldstone."

I glowered, but didn't gainsay him.

Drum walked over to Jeremiah and lifted him up. "Aye, and Browning was wrong, to force that choice. He should have asked one o' us ta sneak the oil in. To test yer loyalty like that was a step too far. I speak fer all the Honourable Guild o' Brewers when I say we're ashamed, Jeremiah." He pulled Jeremiah into an embrace, then sat him back down in a chair and turned back to me. "I'm not a [Counsellor], Pete. I don't know how to make this better."

I groaned and walked over to the fireplace. I rubbed my head in my hands for a few minutes as the two reprobates waited in agonizing silence. Occasionally I paced around and swore while pulling at my beard. Finally, I let out a resigned sigh and spoke. "I don't see why this is my responsibility. Jeremiah, it's going to be painful, but you need to tell Annie."

Jeremiah looked up with terror and I patted his back. "Broken trust is hard to regain, but honesty can patch the cracks. Annie needs the support of her father. If Drum can understand, then I *know* Annie will too." I chuckled darkly. "She may want to beat you around the head for a while, but I think deep down you probably want that. Throw yourself on your daughter's mercy, Jeremiah. She's a strong dwarfess. She doesn't need you to destroy yourself to protect her from the truth. If you keep walking away, one day you're going to look back and she'll be gone."

Jeremiah looked deep into my eyes. The eyes of a father that had forever lost his only child. Jeremiah took a deep breath, steadied himself, and nodded.

"Oh, and one last thing. [Basic Slash]!" I pulled back an arm and punched Jeremiah in the nose. He toppled off his chair with an *Arrghh!* Drum stepped forward in shock, then gave me a wry look.

I nursed my slightly bruised knuckles. "Wow, that *is* cathartic!"

"Are ya sure I shouldn't be in there, Pete?" Balin grumped. "I can hold him down while she kicks."

Balin and I sat camped in the alleyway behind the Goldstone compound. The sound of screaming and smashing bottles came from within.

"No, they're long overdue for some father-daughter bonding time. He's just lucky everything turned out alright. I think everyone would be a lot more angry if the brew had actually failed." I took a long deep drink from a bottle, then gagged. "Ugh, this stuff *still* tastes like shit."

CHAPTER EIGHTY-FOUR
SHAREHOLDER

I sat in Annie's office and spun a pencil around my index finger. It was a favourite trick of mine, and it had taken a while to get my thick dwarf paws to do it properly. Beside me, Aqua was trying to copy the motion, and I snickered as her pencil flipped up and smacked her in the nose. She scowled and shoved me, then got back to her paperwork.

I sighed and looked down at my own messy desk. If there was one thing I hadn't missed from Earth, it was paperwork. Now that I was a shareholder of the Thirsty Goat, I had to do paperwork. At least, that's what Annie told me while she went gallivanting off with my brother.

We weren't back in the Honourable Guild of Brewers yet — there were too many hard feelings. At least Guildmaster Malt wasn't sanctioning us for our actions, and he had confided behind closed doors that we'd be allowed back in "eventually." I didn't trust the dwarven definition of eventually — it probably wouldn't happen in my lifetime.

"[Mental Maths]. Aqua, why is there fifty gold earmarked for 'clothes shopping'?" I pointed at the offending column.

Aqua leaned over to look. "Because we still need proper shoes. Johnsson slipped again last week, and Annie thought it would be nice if we got some Thirsty Goat branded clothes. Oh, and work outfits. Especially since Ass-Blaster paraphernalia sells so well."

"Ah, good! Good! The student becomes the master!" I signed off on the expense and added it to my *out* pile. Only fifty gajillion more sheets of paper to go. I shooed Penelope as she nibbled at the pile. " No, Penelope, you can't eat that."

Maaaaaah! [Translated from Prima Donna Goat] "Mine!"

"No!! Bad Goat! That took me an hour to write!!!"

MEEEEEHHH!!! [Translated from Prima Donna Goat] "This is vengeance for that poster!"

"NUUUOOOHHH!!!"

I was saved as a muscled arm reached down and plucked Penelope off the ground with an offended bleat. I looked up at the jolly face of Jeremiah Goldstone. He wore a set of brown slacks and a white undershirt. A simple half-chest cuirass satisfied the need for armour and a tacklebox lay on the ground behind him. He flashed a toothy smile. He was looking a lot better now, though his face seemed to have aged fifty years in the past month.

"You need to behave, Penelope! Just because I'm not around doesn't mean you have the run of the place. You know the rules!"

Penelope spun miserably in the air, held aloft by Jeremiah's hand gripping her mane.

Meeeeeehh... [Translated from Prima Donna Goat] "The indignity..."

Jeremiah dropped Penelope and she pranced off with a pompous flick of her tail. We watched her go, and he chuckled. "I can see why Richter calls her Princess."

"You have to admit, she's the best cute animal sidekick a dwarf could ask for."

"What?"

I pointed at the tacklebox. "Are you headed out?"

"Aye, I'm meeting Captain Morris at the east gate. We're going to try and catch some fresh cave trout. Bran said he wants to make something you called sashimi."

My mouth watered and I wiped it with my sleeve. "I wish you all the luck of Barck in your endeavours."

As Jeremiah turned to go, he stopped and spun back around. "Pete."

"Aye?"

"I wanted to say thank you. For everything. I didn't trust you at first, yet you saved my brewery, my home, and my family. I am forever in your debt. I owe you a life debt."

"You don't need to do that!" I protested. Especially because I had no idea what a life debt was, and it sounded annoying. Plus... I was still miffed at Jeremiah. He was trying, but he was still persona non grata around the Goat. Partly forgiven, but not forgotten.

"You deserve it, Pete. Annie still isn't really talkin' to me, but at least she says 'hello' now and again. I may have lost most of her trust, but I didn't lose my daughter. Thanks to you, I have enough spark left in me to make it up to her. Cheers!" Jeremiah saluted and left me with one last bombshell as he walked out the door. "Also, your brother finally asked me if he could court Annie! I said yes!"

I bumped my desk and dozens of papers fell to the ground. "Dammit! Wait!! WHAT!?"

A short while later I stood in the front entrance of a Grand Market Main Store. It was a rare two-storey affair, with a stairwell leading up to a second floor that overlooked the front entrance. The shop on the main floor had a beer-tasting and sales counter, and upstairs was converted into a glass emporium.

Whistlemop descended the stairs and gestured around with pride. "How is it?"

"I think you looked better with that stupid red moustache."

Whistlemop scowled. "I mean the store."

"It looks amazing! I especially like the *enormous picture of your face* hanging over the mezzanine!" I pointed at the garish logo.

"Isn't it amazing?" Whistlemop sighed with pleasure.

"It's fine." I pulled at my beard. "And everyone in the city knows your face by now, so it's an effective brand."

"First Minnova, soon the world!" Whisltemop laughed maniacally.

"That's a pretty big ambition for such a tiny gnome."

"Bah! Not like you're much taller. Come in, I'll show you around."

Whistlemop led me on a tour of our new store, *Whistlemop's Emporium of Fine Goods and Beer*. It had the solid feeling of dwarven stone construction with some subtle nods to gnomish tastes, like the wooden panelling and fine detail work. There was glass in the windows, and the interior was lit with a mix of purple light from outside and yellow solstone chandeliers. Sigil-inscribed glass coolers lined the walls of the bottom floor. They contained a mix of Thirsty Goat and Guild brews.

A chalkboard above the counter listed special beers of the week. Ginger Pop, Ass-Blaster, and a non-flatulent variant we'd named *New Brew* were the only things listed at the moment. I had high hopes for that chalkboard. I expected it to be filled with new craft beers as Minnova underwent a beer renaissance. Led by yours truly, of course.

The second floor was filled with Whistlemop's old wares – a collection of vines, runestones, and other dungeon paraphernalia. I noticed a small collection of glassworks tucked against a corner and chuckled. It was a display case of uniquely shaped vases, marked down as *clearance*.

Surprisingly enough, our biggest moneymaker wasn't the beer or the Whistlemugs, but the bottles. Every brewery in the city was buying bottles from us as fast as we could make them. Most breweries were still selling True Brew, but they loved the versatility and potential of bottles. Malt's brewery even had a sticker with a brand-new logo of an erdroot on each bottle!

"It looks great!" I said after the tour ended.

"Doesn't it? I can't wait for opening day!" Whistlemop rubbed his hands together with glee then held up a finger in realisation. "I have some more of your share if you want it." He reached into empty air and pulled out a sack of coins.

I took the sack and similarly reached out into the air. "[Big Money]!" The bag vanished.

"You know, you don't need to say the Milestone to activate it." Whistlemop chortled. I briefly considered pushing him down the stairs.

[Big Money] was a Milestone both Whistlemop and I earned last week. We got it after our profits exceeded eighty thousand silver in a single month. It gave us a small subspace pocket to store gold and other forms of cash. It wasn't a complete substitute for a bank, but it beat a wallet. The other three options had sucked, and I was seeing a theme for Milestone options. One option was always great, and the other three usually weren't as good.

I made out like a bandit in the last month, and not just in gold. I'd managed to increase my intelligence by one after several more lessons with Richter and Barnes, and all the pen twirling had nabbed me an additional dexterity. When combined with the bonuses from completing the "Grand Market" and "Proud Owner" quests, I had a pretty sweet Status Sheet.

Status: Provided by the Firmament
Name: Peter Roughtuff
Age: 49
Conditions: [Blessed]
Race: Dwarf
Blessings: [Flesh of Stone], [Flash of Insight], [Strength of All: Held], [Regeneration], [Minimap], [Refine Brew]
Title: [Otherworldly Brewer]
Milestones: [Power Pick], [Basic Slash], [White Lie], [Mental Maths], [Big Money], [Bottomless Barrel]
Strength: 15.4
Vitality: 19 [23]
Agility: 12
Dexterity: 12
Wisdom: 14.4
Intelligence: 13
Perception: 17.4
Charisma: 12.8

I could get my second Specialisation if I wanted it, but with zero brewing Milestones that wasn't going to happen.

After a little bit of shop talk, I gave Whistlemop polite excuses and headed out. The Thirsty Goat family had a special dinner planned for tonight, but first came the dinner rush...

Later that night, we all sat around one of the longer tables in the pub. Bran stood at the head of the table, expertly cutting slices of raw trout into sashimi. The pub had closed an hour before and the dishes were all done. We would have normally gone home, but the fish were fresh caught by Jeremiah and it seemed a shame to waste them. Trout usually wasn't safe for sushi, but Bran had a new Ability called [Purify Food] to take care of that.

We just started eating when Annie and Balin arrived back at the brewery, arm in arm. Annie's eyes were sparkling, and Balin had a goofy look on his face.

Aqua twigged to it first.

"YOU ASKED!" she screeched.

Annie blushed and nodded while Balin curled his beard with pride.

"SHE SAID YES!" Johnsson jumped up and tipped over his bench, knocking Richter to the floor as he did so. Richter swept Johnsson's legs out from under him and the pair began to wrestle on the floor while the rest of us caught on.

The room broke into cheerful congratulations interspersed with outraged shouting. I made sure to get some friendly beats in on my bro, while Jeremiah scooped his daughter into a big hug. He gave Balin a friendly clasp on the shoulder and the two of them shared a nod. We made room at the table for the lovebirds, and Bran set up two new plates of sashimi.

"How did he ask?" Aqua demanded.

"He put on his Golden Armour and sang me a ballad while standing atop a pile of gemstones," Annie sighed with pleasure at the memory. "He was *wonderful*."

Aqua shrieked, "He was probably *terrible*."

"It wasn't that bad..." Balin grumbled.

"I dunno, I've heard you sing in the shower!" I shot back.

"Balin has a *lovely* singing voice. Don't listen to them dear," Annie sniffed.

"Since we're sharin' happy news, I got some," Bran interrupted, then blushed. "Opal is goin' to be finished with her stint at the mines next year. City Hall says she'll be back in Minnova by spring."

"Are ya goin' to ask her too?" Balin asked, his hand clasping Annie's.

Bran choked.

"I have something to announce as well." Jeremiah stood up, and raised his glass. "It's been a long time coming, but I think now is as good a time as any. Annie, I'm proud of you. You've grown into something that I never could've imagined. Between the Pub and the Feud, you've proven that you're more than capable of running this old place. Your mother would be overjoyed by the wonderful, incredible, dwarf you've become. So, I'm releasing my ownership of the Thirsty Goat to you. You're in charge now, and nothing can change that. May Aaron Bless your endeavours and Barck grant you luck."

There was a shocked silence, and then Annie launched herself from her seat and clung onto Jeremiah in a massive bear hug. The rest of us erupted into applause.

I hopped up on the table and raised my glass. "It's been a long half-year! What started as a small Thirsty Goat is now one of the most successful breweries in Minnova! We have new family, new friends, and new futures! We few stood against the powers that be and survived. Though the mighty sought to strike us down, we succeeded against all odds and brewed the first new brew in millennia! That doesn't mean it's time to rest on our laurels; now that everyone knows beer has potential beyond True Brew and Light Brew, we will bring forth a new age in brewing! May our beers and our beards be Blessed! Cheers!!" "CHEERS!!" *Meeeeh!!*

I choked up a bit. After all that hard work, my dreams were finally coming true; the first shackle had come off, and beer was taking a single tottering step to freedom. I had so many more brews to introduce to everyone, and I couldn't wait to get started.

In the back of my mind, thoughts of winning a certain Great Game and the faint possibility of going back home slipped a little further away.

Outside, the purple light of the great crystal shone down on the sleepless city of Minnova. Some dwarves cooked, others smithed, a few danced, and even fewer brewed. In darkness, a keg was placed down, and some malt boiled. In basements around Minnova, the first craft brewers in eight thousand years took a chance, for better or for worts.

tink
 plink
 plank
 thunk

"Argh, my toe!!!" The angry voice of Magelos Browning rang out in the darkness. He threw his pickaxe aside and nursed the foot he'd struck. He raged in his heart. This wasn't *fair*! He was an upstanding member of dwarven society, a pillar of the community! How *dare* those ungrateful bastards in the Guild toss him out! He'd been more than willing to pay that Whistlefop, so what right did the City have to throw him in this-this-den of *criminals*?

"Watch where yer tossin' that, eh?" A red-haired dwarf with an incredibly bushy beard complained. "I don't need ta lose more o' my head than I already have bein' stuck in here with a daft bugger."

Browning began to hotly retort but held it back. A few tussles with Sam had revealed the futility of that endeavour.

Sam walked up the tunnel and smacked him on the shoulder. "Now hurry up, we've only got another hour before they set tha' next charges. Did I tell you ma' boy Pete invented them?" He chuckled with fatherly pride.

Oh yes... Browning knew that name. He cursed it every day and every hour that he was stuck in this Godsforsaken place. They even served that Netherborne monster's radler with every damn meal in here! It was an outrage!!! It would only take a decade or two, but he would be out, and he would have his revenge!

"You've got such a dour look, Browning! Liven up! I can't imagine six months in here with ya if yer goin' to be such a sourpuss. Come on, sing with me!"

Sam broke into a merry ditty, his slightly off-tune voice a grating throb in Browning's ears. The plink of axes, the thunder of minecarts, and the cheerful voices of dwarves echoed through the mine.

Brothers in the dive rejoice!
Swing, swing, swing with me.
Raise your pick and raise your voice!
Sing, sing, sing with me.

Down and down into the deep,
Will we find Tiara's Keep?
Diamonds, mithril, gold and more,
Hidden in the mountain store!

I am a dwarf and I'm digging a hole.
Diggy diggy hole, diggy diggy hole!
I am a dwarf and I'm digging a hole.
Diggy diggy hole, digging a hole!

EPILOGUE

Somewhere else.

On the side of a cliff stood a white stone gazebo. Mist fell from a great waterfall that stretched beneath it, vanishing into the clouds below. A black mountain rose up behind it, seeming to touch the sky. A circular marble table sat in the centre of the gazebo, and a group of cloaked figures sat around it in ornate wooden chairs.

A board lay on the centre of the table, eight ornate pieces atop it. The pieces moved about in an ancient game that no mortal could ever hope to comprehend.

The players of the game were currently arguing.

"This is ridiculous! How is he beating my Chosen!? He isn't even pretty!" Midna whined.

Lunara scoffed. "How is *pretty* supposed to mean anything when you chose a *writer*, Midna!?"

"Stop teasing her, Lunara. I'm more surprised that he's beating Solen's Chosen." Tiara opined.

"Hmph. I doubt that will continue for long." The bronze dragon Solen opened a maw filled with fire.

"I'm not sure I like the sound of that." Archis muttered.

A young gnome girl's voice squealed from under the table. "Your pretty pop-princess is losing, Archie!"

"It's *ARCHIS*, Yearn!"

AN ADVENTURE BREWING

BRAAAAPPPPP!!

Seven eyes turned to look up the mountain. Barck sat on his bluff and looked down upon the world. He held a bottle of beer that depicted a rather rude image of a goat and was devouring a pretzel the size of a football stadium. Every once in a while, the mountain rocked as he roared with laughter.

"Ugh, he's going to be insufferable if he wins this," Lunara muttered.

The lanky Aaron stood from his chair. "I'm going to get some fries and see what's going on."

There was a general mutter of agreement as the Gods went to watch their favourite streams.

On the board in the now unattended gazebo, an ivory dwarf carrying a bottle moved into opposition with another dwarf wielding a shepherd's crook. Far below, mortals whirled through the intricate dance of life, blissfully unaware of a Great Game that was slowly building into a storm.

Balin passed through the stone archway to the Adventurer's Guild and looked around. The Guild was located near the gate closest to Greentree and served as a hub for merchants and adventurers alike. A stream of monster hunters, porters, and middlemen poured through the grand stone entrance alongside him.

The Adventurer's Guild was made entirely of thick stone blocks, and the double-wide door held a portcullis that could easily accommodate wagons of supplies. Its basement stretched deep below the city, and it was connected to several different water sources. In the case of a monster stampede, it was meant to act as a last line of defence for beleaguered citizens.

The general feeling around him was of eagerness and repressed bloodthirst. Adventuring parties sharpened their weapons and prepared to enter the outskirts of Greentree for the first time in nearly two months. The city had announced the reopening of the dungeon just one day prior as the various displaced monsters had finished settling into their new territories. Balin spotted multiple six-man parties and even a couple of twelve-person raids. Then there were the singleton stragglers – either newcomers like him, or powerful named adventurers. Speaking of named adventurers, Balin spotted the one he had come to meet and waved.

"Tania!"

The dwarfess spotted Balin and waved back. "Balin, over here!"

Balin picked his way through the crowd and trotted up next to her. She was dressed for battle, her thick plate-metal armour covered every inch of her body, and her heavy two-handed meteor-hammer was polished to a mirror finish.

"Everyone, this is Balin." She gestured to a group of dwarves arrayed around her. They were all rough-and-tumble veterans of Greentree dungeon. "Balin here wants ta become an adventurer. Balin, this is my party, *Bloody Beard*."

There was a murmur of welcome, though no great cheer. These grizzled warriors were all too aware of the dangers to cheer for anyone mad or desperate enough to become an adventurer.

"Wait, I think I recognize that name," the brawniest of them piped up. He wore little more than hide armour, his legs bare and covered with tattoos. His face bore an enormous scar that stretched from his left cheek down to his chest. "Yer tha one the [Guards] were discussin'! I'm Drake, tha party [Berzerker]!"

Balin blushed but stuck his chest out proudly. "Aye, I've heard that. Nice to meet you."

"The one that fought the warrior stoneants? Och, you'll fit right in here, then! I'm Drack, Bloody Beard's one and only [Wizard]," a dwarf in the robes chuckled.

"We don't have space fer a newbie," a dwarf wearing spotless chainmail grouched. "I'm busy enough just doctoring you lot!"

"Aw shove off! I just wanted to introduce 'im. He's going to join one of the new teams." Tania smacked the [Doctor] on the shoulder.

Balin nodded. "Captain Morris wanted ta' pair me up with his daughter's team."

"*Brightstar*?" the [Berzerker] mumbled. "Aye, they were lookin' fer a meat-shield. If what I've heard is true, you'd fit the bill. [Knight],

AN ADVENTURE BREWING

right? That'll match perfectly with those uptight – *ahem* – What made ya decide to become an adventurer anyway?"

Balin frowned. "Aye, I'm a [Knight]. As fer why I'm here, it's 'cause someone recently tried ta mess with ma' family. Between that and the false alarm with tha' monster stampede, I'm sick o' my kin bein' threatened. I'm goin' to get strong enough, and famous enough, that nobody will come near 'em again!" His voice pitched lower as he spoke, his voice and demeanour shifting to a simmering rage.

The truth was, with the amount of money they were making, the Thirsty Goat could now afford to hire carpenters. His skills with a saw weren't *necessary* any longer. Yet each day he sat with a hammer in hand, ignoring the power within his Title and [Golden Armour]. It was a waste of a mighty gift, and he'd finally had enough. He spoke with Annie, and the two of them agreed: The likelihood that the Guild of Brewers, or some other ne'er-do-well, would try to sabotage their work in the future was high. However, if he became a named adventurer? Nobody Feuded with a clan that had one of those.

So here he was, joining a party of dwarves he'd never met. To stand at the front as they pushed into the deadly dangers of the dungeon.

"Yer in the right place. If you can survive long enough to make it count!" The [Wizard] chuckled and took a swig from a bottle. Balin jolted as he realised it was a bottle of Thirsty Goat's *New Brew*. Not Ass-Blaster though. "You can see what yer' future holds on tha board over there! Grab a job or two! Don't ferget to read tha notices. They'll save yer life!" He pointed at a wall-spanning cork board. It was covered with posters, leaflets, parchments, and various odds and ends. A crowd milled in front of it, and every so often someone would reach up to rip a piece of paper off the wall and take it to the front desk.

"You'd better not be drunk when we hit the dungeon..." Tania scowled.

"Relax, it'll be at least an hour before we get there." The [Wizard] made a shooing motion. "Go get the newbie signed in."

"You lot keep an eye on him." She pointed at the [Wizard]. "Balin, come with me, we need to go get you registered."

She led Balin to the enormous front desk. A dozen connected

booths stretched floor-to-ceiling, each containing a uniform clad clerk. The adventuring guild uniform was a black-and-red-chequered studded leather affair, notable for the enormous feather each clerk wore in their bascinet helmet.

Upon notifying the clerk of his intention to join the Adventuring Guild, Balin was required to provide ID, fill several forms out in triplicate, and then provide a bit of his blood for an adventurer's tag. He performed all the tasks with his usual quiet enthusiasm, and was partway through reading a waiver that absolved the Adventuring Guild of all fault if he died in the dungeon, when there was a commotion at the front door.

A panting dwarf ran into the hall and made his way to the board. He wore a uniform that marked him as a page from City Hall, and a commotion sprang up as adventurers noticed his presence. A request from City Hall usually paid very well, and fighting over who could complete it first wasn't uncommon. Then there was the possibility that it was a notification or warning.

The page nailed his notification to the board and then left posthaste, leaving a rapidly increasing circle of curious onlookers.

"What is it?" a burly dwarf in chainmail shouted.

"It's a notification from Kinshasa!" a gnome shouted. The hubbub grew in intensity at that.

"What's this got to do with us?" a half-naked dwarf wielding a broadsword grumbled.

A gnomish [Wizard] in a pointy hat scoffed. "It's probably going up at every message board in the city. There's nothing special about *you*, idjit."

Balin walked forward and began reading the notice as a fight broke out. As he read, his eyes grew wide.

Attention Citizens of Crack!

The King seeks his greatest Brewers to take part in a competition that will shake the foundations of Crack!

Few are the Guilds of Brewers within our borders, but fewer are those that have risen to the top. Which Guild has the greatest brewer within the dwarven kingdoms?

The octa-millennial is the perfect opportunity to reveal how well we have kept the traditions of our ancestors. Or perhaps, how much we have advanced with the gifts they gave us!

Given eight thousand years, which brewery has truly perfected the art of Brewing?

Starting in four months, each city shall hold a contest whereby all the brewers will compete for the title of best brewery. Each Guild will select up to eight breweries to compete from among their members, and the City Lord will judge them.

The top Brewery in each city will be invited to Kinshasa, where a brewery and pub will be provided to them. In return, they will be expected to provide the citizens of the Capital with their top-quality brews. The final contest will take place over four months in a series of Feuds leading up to the final contest. The winning Brewery will become the official Royal Brewer of Crack!

Brewers, make your country proud!"

"Huh. Think yer' buddies might want to take a crack at that?" Tania muttered beside him, "Can they, with you not being members o' tha guild anymore?"

"I think..." Balin grinned. "Pete can probably figure something out."

Beers and Beards will continue in Book Two, A Brewtiful Life!

THANK YOU FOR READING AN ADVENTURE BEGINS

We hope you enjoyed it as much as we enjoyed bringing it to you. We just wanted to take a moment to encourage you to review the book. Follow this link: **An Adventure Brewing** to be directed to the book's Amazon product page to leave your review.

Every review helps further the author's reach and, ultimately, helps them continue writing fantastic books for us all to enjoy.

Also in Series:
An Adventure Brewing
A Brewtiful Life

Check out the series here:

Want to discuss our books with other readers and even the authors? Join our Discord server today and be a part of the Aethon community.

Facebook | Instagram | Twitter | Website

You can also join our non-spam mailing list by visiting www.subscribepage.com/AethonReadersGroup and never miss out on future releases. You'll also receive three full books completely Free as our thanks to you.

Looking for more great books?

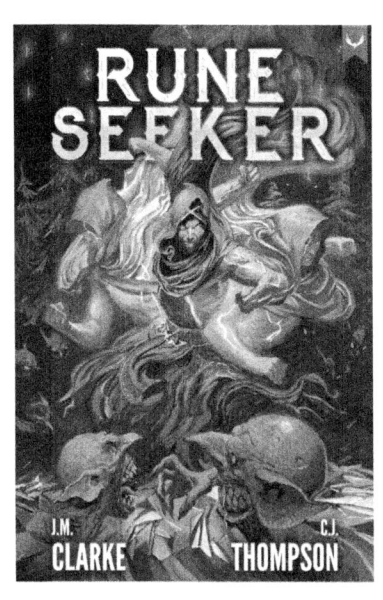

The Everfail will rise. His enemies will fall. *Hiral is the Everfail, the weakest person on the flying island of Fallen Reach. He trains harder than any warrior. Studies longer than any scholar. But all his people are born with magic powered by the sun, flowing through tattoos on their bodies. Despite having enormous energy within, Hiral is the only one who can't channel it; his hard work is worth nothing. Until it isn't. In a moment of danger, Hiral unlocks an achievement with a special instruction: Access a Dungeon to receive a Class-Specific Reward. It's his first—and maybe last—chance for real power. Just one problem: all dungeons lay in the wilderness below the flying islands that humanity lives on, and there lay secrets and dangers that no one has survived. New powers await, but so do new challenges. If he survives? He could forge his own path to power. If he fails? Death will be the least of his problems.* **Don't miss the next progression fantasy series from J.M Clarke, bestselling author of Mark of the Fool, along with C.J. Thompson. Unlock a weak-to-strong progression into power and a detailed litRPG system with unique classes, skills, dungeons, achievements, survival and evolution. Explore a mysterious world of fallen civilizations, strange monsters and deadly secrets.**

Get Rune Seeker Now!

JOLLY JUPITER

AN ADVENTURE BREWING

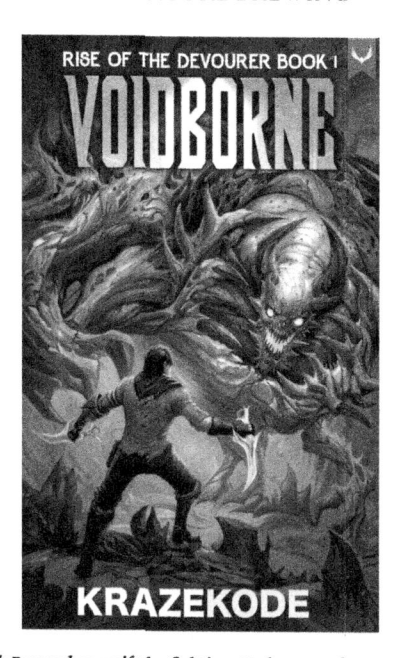

RISE OF THE DEVOURER BOOK 1
VOIDBORNE
KRAZEKODE

Noah Brown has a gift for fighting. Unfortunately, punching things doesn't pay the Bills... *At least, that was the case until Noah died and an Eldritch god found his soul. The strange encounter brings him to a new world, summoned by bloody cultists. Even worse, he's got nothing but the shirt on his back and a strange item in his System menu described as: [???] : A source of infinite potential. If he wants to survive, maybe even thrive, perhaps it's time he finally put his gift to good use. Don't miss the start of an action-packed, crunchy, isekai LitRPG series from KrazeKode, author of The First Law of Cultivation. Loaded with stats, skills, combat, and power progression, it's perfect for fans of Iron Prince, Road to Mastery, and He Who Fights with Monsters!*

Get Voidborne Now!

JOLLY JUPITER

AN ADVENTURE BREWING

There is no weapon more powerful than the [Psychokinetic] mind. Astrid, a mischievous noble teen, long dreamed of exploring the ancient cities preserved beneath the waves, left behind from a time before the ocean swallowed the world. She's been training all her life to become a magic swordsman capable of doing just that. But when an ancient monster long thought dead assaults humanity's last bastion—a floating ship-city—she awakens her System early. Only, she's not a warrior as expected. She's forced to walk the path of a [Psychokinetic] Mage. With Spawn-infested oceans, pirates looking to plunder, and mysterious monsters that lurk within Bubbled-Cites at the bottom of the ocean, Safety is anything but guaranteed. She'll learn levitation, ovject throwing, eyeball pulling, and more, all the way to the apex of psychic powers. But, what happens when she discovers that her world was a lot larger than she—and the rest of humanity, once thought?
Don't miss the start of this action-packed and often hilarious LitRPG Apocalypse series about a young survivor with a craving for adventure and fighting. Perfect for fans of Azarinth Healer and Eight.

Get Psychokinetic Eyeball Pulling Now!

For all our LitRPG books, visit our website.

Printed in Great Britain
by Amazon